GONE TRILOGY

Stacy Claflin

Contents

GONE

Gone – Book One

Stacy Claflin

http://www.stacyclaflin.com

Watching

SITTING IN HIS warm truck across from the park, Chester Woodran watched her walk across the open field. An overhead light turned on as she passed under it in the dusk. Her long, dark hair swished back and forth behind her. She wandered around the playground, walking between the climbers and slides until she stopped in front of the swings.

He had spent hours watching her. Studying her. He knew her almost better than she knew herself.

The moment of truth would arrive soon. She'd come a few minutes early, but he wouldn't deviate from the schedule. He would act exactly on time. He'd laid the groundwork. He wasn't going to let her change a thing.

Chester pulled out his phone and scrolled through the pictures, stopping at his favorite. It was the girl in the park for sure, although he couldn't see the details of her face up close yet. He would have to wait a few minutes.

From the phone, her light brown eyes shone at him. Her shy, almost insecure face smiled sweetly.

His heart sped up at the thought of many weeks of work coming together at long last. The waiting was about to end.

Clenching the steering wheel with all his might, he took several deep breaths to calm himself. Every precaution had been taken. Prepared with painstaking care. There was no chance of anything going wrong so long as he stayed with the plan.

The alarm on his digital wristwatch beeped. He turned it off and then leaned back into the seat, adjusting his over-sized glasses.

It was time.

Taken

MACY MERCER SAT on the swing, clutching the cold, metal chain. Soon she'd meet Jared, the sweet and adorable boy she met online. She pushed the dirt with her foot, swinging back and forth, listening to the leaves rustle nearby as a breeze picked up. The temperature felt like it had dropped ten degrees, so she zipped up her hoodie as far as it would go. She should have worn a coat, but it was too late to go back home.

A crow cawed in the distance, giving her the chills.

To distract herself, she grabbed the new smart phone she'd received for her fifteenth birthday. She checked the time. Jared still had another five minutes. Macy had been so eager to meet him that she'd sneaked out of her house a little early, eager for her first real date. Her parents had a stupid, outdated rule that she couldn't date until she turned sixteen. There was no way she would wait an entire year. Not when her friends all went out every weekend.

She looked around the empty park once more, the swing chains groaning as they carried her back and forth listlessly. Jared was supposed to meet her after his baseball practice. He was the star of the team, and sometimes had to stay a little late because the coach expected more from him than anyone else. She scrolled through their latest texting conversation, her excitement building.

The phone buzzed, startling her. Hoping that it was Jared, she scrolled to the bottom of the screen and smiled.

Sorry, coach is keeping me late

Macy sighed, shivering in the cold Washington breeze. *How long?*

Abt a half hr

The last thing Macy wanted was to put the date off, but it was really cold. *U sure 2day still works?*

You want my dad to get u?

Macy ran her hands through her freshly-styled hair. Going with a grown man hadn't been part of the plan. She was just supposed to meet Jared and go the mall, or maybe a movie or to the arcade. They were going to play it by ear.

Is it ok? Or u wanna wait?

It was getting colder, and no way she wanted to sit here that long. The mall was too far to walk to, but with his dad she'd be warmer and see Jared sooner.

They'd talked for so long over computers and texts. Macy didn't want to wait more. She'd show everyone she wasn't afraid to go out with a boy, no matter what her parents said.

She texted him back. *He's ok driving me?*

He offered

U can't come now?

No. I have to help

Ok. Your dad can pick me up

K c u soon

Sliding the phone back into her pocket, she looked around again. Something didn't feel right, but she pushed it aside. She and Jared had known each other for a whole month, and he was sweet and funny. If he thought it was okay for her to go with his dad, it was fine. She wasn't a little girl anymore. Macy held her chin a little higher.

A green pickup truck with a black canopy pulled into the empty parking lot. Macy squinted, trying to see if the driver looked like an old version Jared's profile pictures. She couldn't tell.

The lights flashed the high beams, and she took that as her cue to go. She held her handbag close, stood tall, and walked to the truck trying to look mature and sophisticated.

As she neared the truck, the passenger door opened. The man sitting in the driver's seat looked nice enough. He had dark, straight hair with a receding hairline and big, geeky glasses. He kind of reminded her of her biology teacher, who always cracked science jokes that only he laughed at.

"Macy?" He readjusted his glasses and ran his hands through his hair.

"Yeah." She leaned all of her weight on her left foot, biting the right side of her lower lip.

He gave her an awkward smile. "I'm Jared's dad. He said you needed a ride to his practice?"

She nodded. The car radio played classic rock, like what her dad listened to. She relaxed a little.

He patted the bench seat. "Come on in. He's almost done with practice."

"Okay." Macy climbed in and closed the door. The warm air felt good after being out in the cold. She buckled in. "Thanks for the ride."

"No problem. Jared didn't want you sitting outside in the cold. Did you have a good day?"

"Sure." She shrugged. "Just school and stuff."

He pulled out of the parking lot and turned right. His phone made robot noises, and he pulled it up to his ear. "Jared. What's going on?…Yeah, she's here with me…Oh, okay. I'll let her know." He put the phone away. "Jared has to stay a little longer. Hey, I have a quick errand. Mind if I run to the hardware store before dropping you off at his school?"

"Well, how much longer is he going to be?" Macy spun a ring around her finger, nervous. "Maybe I should go back home. I can always meet him a different day. It's okay."

"I get it. I'll take you to the school. I don't want you to feel uncomfortable. You don't even know me."

"Or back to the park. I can just walk back home." Her heart pounded. Something wasn't right.

"Jared will be so disappointed. Let me take you to the school. I didn't mean to creep you out." He turned and smiled at her. "I wasn't thinking."

She sighed. "Okay." At least she would be able to get out of the truck. She could take a bus back home, or if worse came to worse she could always call her parents. She'd be grounded for sneaking out, but that might not be so bad. Just so long as she could get out of the truck.

Macy's stomach twisted in a knot, growing tighter the farther they went. Her mouth grew increasingly dry. She watched as street sign after street sign passed by.

"Maybe I should go back. I think I might have forgotten something at home."

"Oh? Are you sure?"

"Yeah. I need to go back home."

"Well, if you really think so. I'll break the news to Jared. I'm sure he'll understand." He pulled out his phone and activated the voice command. "Call Jared."

"Wait."

"Yes?"

"Well, uh…." Since he was being so nice, maybe she was overreacting. "You don't have to call him."

"If you're sure." He pushed a button on his phone and put it back in his pocket.

Macy took a deep breath. She needed to pull herself together or he might think she was immature. What if he didn't want Jared to see her? She sat taller and flipped her hair back.

He turned left down a road where he should have gone right.

"Wait," Macy said. "Jared's school is the other way."

"I know."

Her blood ran cold. "What…do you mean?"

The door locked beside her. "We're not going to a school."

"Where are we going?" She clutched her purse tightly against her.

"We're going for a drive, Macy."

"I don't want to. Take me home."

"You're not going back home."

Her heart beat so loud, it sounded like it was in her ears. She pulled on the door handle, but it wouldn't budge.

"Child locks. You can't open it from the inside."

She felt light-headed. "What about Jared?"

"There is no Jared, sweetie."

Her breath caught. "Did you kill him?"

He laughed. "That's hilarious. No, *I'm* Jared."

The blood drained from her face. "You...mean...?"

"I'm the one you've been talking to all this time."

Macy's stomach turned. She was sure she would throw up. "You're lying."

"No. It was me that you shared all your secrets with. All I had to do was throw on a picture of some random kid I found online. Everything else was me."

"You better take me back home. Once my parents figure out I'm missing, they can have the cops go through my laptop. They'll be able to track your IP address. I know that much."

"That's the thing. Before I picked you up, I was in your room and I reset your computer to factory settings. No one is going to find a thing."

Macy's head swam. "No you didn't. My parents are home. You're totally lying. Just let me go, and I swear I won't ever tell anyone about this."

He turned the music down. "I got in using your code to the garage right after you left. You mom was reading her Kindle in your parents' bedroom, like you told me she always does. Your dad was in his office on his computer. They didn't hear a thing. I went into your room and took care of your computer."

"Liar. You'd have to know my password."

"Ducky256."

She gasped. "How did you know that? I never told you."

"You didn't have to. You told me enough. Ducky is the pet ferret you got not too long ago. After your cat died, right? Snowflake, right? And 256 is your student number at school. You gave me everything I needed without even knowing it. From there, it was easy to figure out your various passwords. I had to ask innocent enough questions, and it all came together." He looked at her again, raising his bushy eyebrows.

"I don't believe you went into my house. You're just saying that."

He tossed a small, framed picture at her. She picked it up and stared at it. It was a picture of her family. She had looked at that very picture before she sneaked out. He *had* been there. Had he seen her looking at it?

"But, why? Why me?" And then, the question too terrifying to ask: what did he plan to do with her?

"That's a long story. I'm going to save that for later. Now really isn't the time."

Macy took several deep breaths, trying to calm herself down. If she was going to get away, she had to think clearly. She knew that much. Maybe he was lying about the child locks. She would try to unlock it again when they stopped. If it opened, she would run before he knew what had happened.

"Can you tell me something? You must have a good reason. I mean, really. You spent hours and hours chatting and texting with me. Did you choose me for a reason, or was I the only girl who would talk to you?"

"It was you. I actually tried a few different personas until I found one you paid any attention to. For whatever reason, you liked Jared."

"But why? What's so special about me?" Macy asked.

"You look exactly like her. It took me a long time to find you. I spent weeks online looking for someone close to her age who looks exactly like her. I almost gave up, thinking it was impossible, but then I found your profile picture. I actually couldn't believe it. You look so much like her, you could be her."

"Her? Who her?"

"My Heather."

"What happened to Heather? Where is she?"

"You ask too many questions. You need to stop."

"But you—"

"See this?" He held up a flashlight as long as his arm.

"Yeah. Why?"

"I told you no more questions." He swung it and hit Macy on the side of her head.

Everything went black.

Gone

ALYSSA MERCER FINISHED putting on the final touches of mascara, and then stood back to look at herself before nodding in approval. She looked good, and she knew it. She was going to make everyone at the gym jealous again. No one ever thought she could be the mom of two teenagers, and that's the way she liked it. When she was out with them, she was often taken for their sister.

She picked up her curling iron and perfected a couple of curls before returning to the bedroom. Her eyes fell on the clock. She'd still have time to stop for a skinny latte before working out. Pulling her workout shoes from under her bed, she slipped them on and went into the hall.

The house was quiet. The kids were probably still sleeping. They would sleep into the afternoon if she or her husband didn't wake them. As she passed Macy's room, she could smell the ferret cage. Why had she let Macy talk her into getting the thing? It was cute, but if they didn't keep the cage clean it got smelly fast. Alyssa was going to have to tell her—again—that they would get rid of Ducky if Macy didn't keep it up.

Going down the stairs, she tripped over a pair of pants and grumbled under her breath. She had followed the books since they were little, teaching them the value of chores as toddlers. It never stuck. As they got older, it even seemed to backfire. Alyssa picked up the pants and threw them to the top of the stairs.

She readjusted her black and purple velour pants and went to the kitchen. Smoothie bags filled the fridge, and Alyssa emptied one into the blender, with some fat-free milk and fresh bananas. As it blended, she went over everything she needed to do that day.

When it was ready she poured it into a glass, leaned against the counter, and drank her breakfast. She set the empty glass in the sink, turned around, and nearly bumped into her thirteen-year-old.

"Alex, what are you doing?"

He looked disoriented. Probably because he was awake before noon. His brown, wavy hair stuck out in twenty directions and for some reason, he looked pale. Alex looked up at her, and looking into his eyes Alyssa knew something was wrong.

"What's going on?"

He blinked a few times. "Have you seen Macy's wall?"

"No. Why? Did I miss a personality quiz?" The joke sounded weak, even to her.

He pulled his tablet from his bathrobe pocket and held the screen up to her face. She took it from him and looked at his news feed, not seeing anything important. "Tell Charlie he needs to watch his language."

Alex took the tablet and looked at it. He looked like he was going to be sick. "No, Mom, it got pushed down." He scrolled down and pointed to his sister's latest status update.

Alyssa's heart sped up as she read it. "Is that some kind of joke?"

"She's not in her room." He stared at her so intently, it felt like he was looking right through her.

Without a word, Alyssa ran past Alex and back upstairs, bursting through Macy's door. It looked like her daughter was in bed. She ran to the bed and pulled away the blankets. Several large stuffed animals lay strategically to look like Macy was there. How long had she been gone?

Her heart and mind were both racing. She looked around the room for any clues. Macy's laptop was on her desk. Alyssa sat down, feeling light-headed. She opened the laptop and turned it on.

It didn't start up like it should. It took too long. Then it prompted her to set up the computer. Had Macy erased everything? She couldn't have. She wasn't technologically inclined. She was always asking Alyssa for help with it.

"It's true?"

Alyssa turned around to see Alex standing in the doorway, looking ill. "She couldn't have gone far," Alyssa said. "She's probably just mad because we won't let her date."

She cursed her husband under her breath. She and Chad had argued over that point countless times. Alyssa had never even convinced him to let Macy go on group dates. He didn't want boys anywhere near her. She had told him that Macy would rebel.

She had told him. Alyssa buried her face into her hands, feeling dizzy.

"I'm going to get Dad."

Alyssa nodded, not even looking up. She had to do something. She pulled her cell phone from her pocket and called Macy's number. She would tell Macy that the age restriction was lifted. Who cared what Chad wanted? She had to get her baby back.

The call went straight to voice mail. She listened to the entire message, feeling a small sense of relief at hearing her daughter's voice. She ended the call, doubtful that Macy would get the message if she had turned her phone off. Alyssa found Zoey's number and called. Zoey was Macy's best friend. She would know what was going on.

"Hello?" Zoey sounded half-asleep.

"Zoey, this is Macy's Mom."

"Mrs. Mercer? What's up?"

"Have you talked with Macy?"

"Uh…no. Why?"

Alyssa took a deep breath. "Did she say anything to you about running away?"

"What? No. Oh, crap. This is bad."

"Yes, this is very bad. Anything you know will help. Don't worry about getting her into trouble. We need to find her. That's the only thing that matters."

"I'm guessing you didn't know about her date last night."

"Her what?"

Zoey sighed. "She was getting together with a guy she met online."

The room shrank around Alyssa. "What…?"

"Yeah. Jared something. Wait. Hold on. He messaged me on

online, asking some questions about her. Let me look."

Alyssa took several deep breaths as she listened to the rustling sounds of Zoey on the other end of the line. Things were going from bad to worse.

"I can't find his message, Mrs. Mercer. Wait a minute. Oh, I see the problem. He deactivated his account. I can still see the messages, but his name's gone, and there's no picture. I wish I could remember his last name. Is Macy going to be okay?"

"I hope so. Listen, Zoey, if you hear anything else, or think of anything, call me back. Okay?"

"Yeah, sure. I'll see if I can find anything else."

"Thanks. Bye."

"Bye, Mrs. Mercer. I'll do anything to help find her."

Alyssa nodded, knowing, and not caring, that Zoey couldn't see her. She opened the app on her phone and went to her daughter's profile, searching for clues.

Awake

THE GROUND BENEATH Macy bumped up and down, waking her. She looked around, her head pounding, and reached for the side of her head. A tender bump stuck out near her forehead. The last thing she remembered was going into the truck with the madman who had pretended to be Jared.

She rolled to the side of the truck, slamming her already-sore head as they took a sharp turn. On all fours, she crawled to the back of the truck to see if she could unlock it. Everything was sealed tight. Not that she was surprised, given how much effort the guy had gone to with everything else.

The two of them had spent hours and hours messaging and texting. "Jared" had always seemed so interested in her, like she was special. But all he really wanted was to figure out her passwords. She wanted to kick herself; her parents had told her countless times not to give out personal information online. She had thought Jared was safe, but she had obviously been wrong.

Macy went to the sides of the truck, feeling around for anything she could open. She searched every single inch of the truck bed and canopy. It was no use; he had made sure everything was locked. All she found was a blanket, folded up and tucked into a corner.

Where was he taking her? And who was Heather? That name seemed important to him. Maybe if Macy could figure out why, she could figure out a way to escape.

The truck stopped, and the engine cut. Her stomach rumbled, and Macy realized how hungry she was. She hadn't eaten anything since lunch, and who knew how long ago that had been? She'd been planning to eat with Jared, who didn't even exist. She leaned against the corner of the walls.

Minutes ticked by as she waited. She shivered and grabbed the blanket, wrapping it around herself. It had the light scent of a girl's perfume.

As she started to doze, a loud click snapped her back to reality. The door of the canopy opened and the madman looked in. "Good. You're awake. I got some food. You'd better eat it because we're not stopping again for a while." He threw a wrapped hamburger at her. "I know you're vegan, but that's what you're getting. Eat it or go hungry."

He lowered the canopy door.

"Wait! Where are we going?"

"You'll find out soon enough." The door slammed, and Macy heard the lock slide into place.

She stared at the hamburger, sitting on the blanket. She hadn't eaten meat in more than six months, but her stomach roared, begging her to eat the greasy, dead animal.

The irony didn't escape her. Macy had gone vegan to lose weight, tired of everyone calling her "Muffin-top Macy." She'd lost the weight, but the name had stuck. That's what had led her to seek a boyfriend online. Now, here she was.

She wouldn't let the psycho win. She wasn't going to eat his burger. He might have poisoned it, anyway, or slipped something in to make her more agreeable.

She'd show him. If he saw she couldn't be controlled that easily, maybe he would give up and let her go. She had skipped meals plenty of times. When she first went vegan, her parents hadn't taken her seriously and continued to serve meat-filled meals.

Once they figured out that she would starve herself if that's what it took, they changed their minds—and Macy's diet.

She threw the burger across the truck. She wasn't going to eat it. If nothing else, it would take off a little more weight.

She leaned her head against the wall of the truck bed, tired and scared. There was no getting away yet, she knew that. So she let herself fall asleep again, thinking that at least she might be rested when the time came to escape.

The truck went over a large bump, waking her. How long had she been asleep this time? She could smell the cold hamburger. It permeated the entire truck bed. Her stomach rumbled again, but it twisted at the same time. As hungry as she was, the burger was the last thing she wanted to eat.

Pulling the perfumed blanket up close to her chin, she wanted to go back to sleep. No, what she wanted was to go back in time and never talk to "Jared" in the first place. Why had she been so stupid? Why hadn't she changed her passwords more often? She'd always heard how important that was.

Before long, boredom struck. It felt strange to be bored when she could be killed any moment, but the waiting was the worst part. Waiting wasn't her strong suit—but really, was it anyone's?

Of course, she knew that once the truck stopped she would probably give anything to be bored again.

How was she going to fight him? She should know something about self-defense given how many hours she'd been forced to watch her brother's karate tournaments and practices. There was something to do with pressure points, but she couldn't remember what. She had never paid any attention, usually playing a game, texting, or reading.

Why hadn't she agreed to take the lessons with him? The sound of her dad's voice telling her that it would be good for her bounced around her head. Why hadn't she listened? There were so many things Macy would have done differently, if only she'd known. So many things.

The truck hit another bump, and as Macy went into the air she realized she had to go to the bathroom. Bad. What was she supposed to do? Peeing in his truck would have made her happy, but she didn't want to have to smell it, or worse, land in it at some point.

They went over another bump, and she knew that she had to do something before she lost control of her bladder. The last thing she wanted was to soak her clothes. Macy squeezed her pelvic muscles and looked around in desperation. She noticed something behind one of the tires. Was that some kind of container? Why hadn't she noticed that before? Her stomach sank as she realized it was there for her to pee in.

Holding her breath to keep control of her bladder, she crawled over to it. It was an empty juice jug. That was going to have to do the job. They hit another bump, and she dropped the container as she leaked a few drops of urine. "Crap!" She scrambled for the jug and, feeling like an idiot, dropped her pants.

When she was done, a feeling of relief washing over her entire body, Macy grabbed the lid and twisted as tight as she could get it. If she knew she was getting out soon, she would relieve herself in a corner to spite him.

She pulled her pants back up and returned to the blanket. It was so cold, and she was starting to shiver. Lowering her pants hadn't helped. Even with the blanket, she hadn't been warm enough. As she settled down with the blanket, the pee jug caught her eye.

Oh, that was gross. How could she even think that?

But it *was* warm, she couldn't deny that.

No. She would wait. She wasn't going to warm up with a pitcher of her pee. Macy looked at the ceiling, but before long, she was shivering.

Shoving the blanket aside, she crawled over to the container and brought it back to the blanket. Sticking it in her lap, she pulled the blanket over her again. The warmth from the pee felt good, as disgusting as that was. Macy imagined it was one of those heat packets she put in her pockets when they went skiing.

Macy must have fallen asleep again, because the jerk of the truck stopping woke her up. She blinked her eyes, trying to get her bearings. She felt groggy, and that had to mean she had been asleep for a while. Were they out of state? When she had been in the cab of the truck, they were heading east, more than likely leaving Washington. But where?

The canopy opened again. Her abductor looked around, and then smiled when he saw her.

"Don't get any funny ideas. If you try to escape, I'll go back and kill your entire family."

"What?"

"I got in once. I can do it again. If you get away, I'll go after them instead of you. Well, I will go after you too, don't get me wrong." He laughed. What a freaking psycho.

Macy shuddered.

"You still haven't eaten the burger I was nice enough to get you? Get one thing straight: you're not getting anything else to eat until you finish that first."

"But it's old and gross."

"Maybe you should have thought of that when I gave it to you. Don't test me, girl. I will wait as long as it takes for you to eat it before I give you anything else. It saves me money."

"But you know I don't eat meat."

"Looks like you're going to have to. It's going to be even less enjoyable as cold as it is. I wouldn't let it get any older, because it's sure not going to get better."

"Where are you taking me?"

"You'll find out soon enough. Eat the burger."

"What'll you do if I don't?"

"Don't you listen? I won't give you anything else to eat. I need some rest, so we're going to stop for a bit. Eat that damn burger, if you know what's good for you."

He slammed the canopy door shut, and locked it. Tears filled Macy's eyes. Was he serious about killing her family? He was crazy enough to kidnap her, so he was probably serious about killing them.

They hadn't done anything wrong. This whole situation was on Macy, and she knew it. She had been the one stupid enough to get herself into the truck in the first place. She would have to figure something out.

Her stomach rumbled again. Macy looked at the burger, disgusted. Would he really make her eat it? Why did he care what she ate? There had to be a way she could hide it, so he would think she ate it. Where? There weren't exactly hiding places in the truck bed.

She tried to focus on calming her stomach. Once it relaxed, she stared at the burger, imagining she was having a staring contest with it.

"I'm losing my mind," she muttered. If she was going to eat it, it needed to be soon. The burger wouldn't get any fresher. Which was the more appealing choice? To starve, or to eat the cold, greasy burger? She would have chosen to go hungry, except that she didn't want to be forced to eat it a day or two later. At least it was somewhat edible right now.

The minutes ticked by as Macy stared at the burger. But the more she thought about it, the more she thought about having to eat it days down the road. That convinced her. She crawled across the cab and carried the burger back to the blanket.

"I'm sorry," she said to the cow she was about to eat. She unwrapped the waxy paper, and looked at the wilted bun, shaking her head. Her stomach growled, begging her to give it the nourishment.

Closing her eyes, she bit down. The cold grease shocked her taste buds, and she had to force herself not to spit it out. The way it felt as she chewed it up only made it worse. It stank too. She plugged her nose, and took another bite, relieved to discover she almost couldn't taste it.

She shoveled it in, eating as fast as she could without choking. Macy tried to pretend she was eating a veggie burger, but it didn't work. It was an old, disgusting slab of meat cooked in grease, no matter what she told herself.

After finally finishing it, she threw the wrapper and tried to ignore how disgusting she felt. Her skin felt oily from the grease, and her stomach didn't feel right. Hopefully once it settled she would have more energy for getting away—if she could.

Interrupted

CHAD MERCER WAS typing at his typical 120 words per minute when there was a knock on the door. He ignored it. His family knew to leave him alone when the door was closed.

The knocking continued, distracting him. Why couldn't they let him get his work done? Well, it wasn't actually work. Not yet, anyway. He had a popular sports blog, where he posted his opinions. People loved his sense of humor, and he always had good statistics.

With his monthly page views and low bounce rate, he was able to get a lot of really good advertising on his site that actually paid some of the bills.

He was popular online. People loved him. Unlike at home, where no one appreciated him.

The knocking wouldn't stop, and Chad lost the funny quip he'd been searching for. He sighed. "What is it?"

"Dad! Let me in!" Alex pounded on the door again.

Chad shook his head. "You know I'm busy." When would they ever start appreciating what he was trying to do for the family? His wife already didn't have to work, but no one seemed to care.

"Dad! Macy's gone!"

Gone? He got up and unlocked the door, and then opened it. "What do you mean, she's gone?"

"She's not here. She posted something online about running away."

Shaking his head, Chad went back to his desk. He minimized his blog and opened up a new window. Nothing from Macy showed up on his news feed. He typed in her name to pull up her profile. Sure enough, her latest update was one big, public tongue-sticking at him.

The house phone rang next to him. He looked over, seeing the caller ID. It was his in-laws. His mother-in-law must have stopped playing Sugar Saga for three minutes and seen Macy's update. He shook his head. Alyssa was going to chew him out. They had argued nonstop about Macy and what age she should be allowed to date.

Alyssa had told him countless times that he needed to give Macy room to grow up or she would rebel. Macy had been giving him attitude for a while, and now she had taken it public. This was just a publicity stunt. His daughter wanted to rally support.

Chad's cell phone rang. He picked it up from his desk. It was Valerie Carter, Zoey's mom. He clicked ignore and put it back down.

"What are you going to do?"

He had forgotten Alex was still there. His son looked like he was going to be sick. Macy would never believe how worried her brother was about her. With all his teasing and picking on her, he still adored his sister.

Chad took a deep breath. "I'm going to look online and see where her phone is. You guys have those Child Protect phones where the GPS tracking can't be turned off." He turned to his computer screen, went to the site that tracked the kids' phones and logged in. He could only see Alex's phone, which of course was at their address.

He scrolled the site for contact information and called them. When someone answered, he interrupted them before they could say two words.

"I have one of your Child Protect phones, and my daughter's phone isn't showing up. Mind telling me what's going on? I was told that this couldn't happen."

"Sir, if the battery has been removed, we can't track the GPS. It has to have the battery."

"What good are you? Do you know how much we pay for these? I want a refund!"

"If you calm down and give me your information, we can—"

"My kid is missing. You guys are supposed to be a technology company. Use it to figure out who I am and then send me a refund check." He ended the call. "Dipsticks."

The house phone rang again. This time it was Sandra McMillan from the homeowners' association.

When he found Macy, he was going to give her the punishment of a lifetime.

"How are we going to find Macy?"

Chad looked back up at Alex. His lips trembled.

Did Macy think of no one besides herself? First with the whole vegetarian—no, "vegan" thing, and now this. Did she find joy in making him miserable? He could see her sitting somewhere, laughing at the stress she was putting everyone through. All because he wouldn't let her to go on a date. After this stunt, she wouldn't be going on any dates until she graduated.

The home phone rang again, and this time he took the batteries out. That girl had close to a thousand friends on social media, and now every single one of them knew she had run away. Chad took a deep breath and then turned to his son again. "Do you know anything else? Anything besides what's in her update?"

Alex shook his head.

"Well, I guess she'll come home when she's hungry. Why don't you go check on your mother?"

Alex nodded, and Chad was struck by how much his usually tough son looked like a little boy. It was easy to forget how young thirteen really was. The look on his face reminded Chad of when Alex was a preschooler, chasing after his big sister and wanting to do everything she did.

For a moment Chad thought he should give his son a hug, but he stiffened. There was no need for that. "Don't worry about her. She's trying to scare us. I'll bet you she's at Zoey's house hiding out. She's going to lose her phone for a long time for this one. Don't you ever try it."

Alex didn't look convinced. He turned around and left the room.

Chad ran his hands through his hair. If only his parents were still alive. There was nothing better than talking with his dad when he had a problem. He had always had a level head and could point Chad in the right direction. They had been killed in a car accident when the kids were really young, so he hadn't had their advice for any of his parenting questions.

Sick

MACY'S HEAD SLAMMED into the truck's side and she woke up, realizing she'd fallen asleep again. She rubbed the new bump, hoping they would stop soon. Her stomach felt worse than it had after eating the burger. The movement of the truck hadn't helped, she was sure. The motion and the bumps wreaked havoc on her.

Her stomach lurched, and she turned her head in time to throw up without getting anything on the blanket.

She wiped her mouth and put her forehead against her knees, crying so hard she shook. What had she done to deserve this?

What if it got worse? What did that psycho have in store for her? Would he really kill her family? Or was that something kidnappers said to keep their victims in line?

Some kid in the news had recently escaped after being grabbed at the mall. Hadn't Macy heard that that kidnapper had made the same threats? He never killed the kid's family. But he was also in jail.

Macy closed her eyes, still breathing through her mouth to avoid the smell of her own puke. She figured she might try to get more sleep, because who knew what would happen once they stopped? All she knew was she would need to think and act fast.

As she drifted off, she breathed in through her nose. Immediately she gagged at the smell of her own vomit. Being trapped in the enclosed bed of the truck made the stench even more unbearable.

The truck slowed to a stop. She could hear the engine cut and the driver's side door slam shut. Footsteps on gravel came closer. Macy's heart pounded, and when she heard the key turning close, her heart nearly leapt out of her throat.

She breathed in fresh air as the back opened up. Macy covered her eyes in the bright sun. When her eyes adjusted, her eyes focused on her captor.

His mouth formed into a cruel twist. "What is that smell?"

"My stomach couldn't handle your burger."

"You're going to have to clean that up, you know." His bushy eyebrows came together.

Macy scooted back. "With what? It's not even my fault."

"Shut up. I was kind enough to get you food and even a blanket, and this is how you repay me? Close your trap and clean my truck. That's disgusting." His scary glare bore into Macy's eyes.

"You were kind enough—?"

"I said shut up!" He put his face less than an inch from Macy's. "Find a way to clean it up. You made the mess, you clean it. Got it?"

Macy blinked, but she kept quiet.

"Got it?" he yelled. His coffee-scented spit splattered on her face. The smell made her stomach turn again.

She wiped her face. "Don't yell at me."

"I'll yell at you if I want to. You destroyed my property. The acid in that will eat my paint. Get it cleaned up! Do you understand?"

"Okay."

"Good." The door slammed and locked again.

Her lips shook, and her eyes filled with tears. He had done this to her, and now he expected her to clean the mess? With what? Did he actually think he had done anything kind to her? He was a monster.

The hot tears spilled onto her face. She wiped them with her sleeve. Her nose dripped, so she wiped that too.

The smell of the vomit made its way back to her nose. Her stomach lurched again, but she was determined to keep it down this time. She had to have some kind of control over something.

The door unlocked, opened slightly, and something soft bounced toward her. Then something hard and loud landed a few feet away. The door slammed and locked again. Wiping her tears away, she picked up the object next to her. It was a roll of paper towels. She reached for the other thing. It was some kind of spray bottle.

"Get cleaning!" the guy shouted from the outside of the truck.

Her adrenaline pumped. Macy wanted to choke him the next time he opened the door. Wrap her hands around his neck and squeeze as hard as she could. Her hands clenched, breaking the skin.

Macy pulled off a paper towel and wiped her face, then blew her nose. She threw the towels in a corner, held her breath, and grabbed the spray bottle.

Crawling to the mess, she began to whisper, "I hate you. I hate you. I hate you." She ripped off several paper towels and wiped at the mess. She had to breathe through her mouth, and with every breath in and out she kept cursing him under her breath. She threw the towels to the side and grabbed more, soaking up the mess until it was gone. Then she grabbed the spray bottle.

Whatever was in there reeked of chemicals. It made her nose burn and gave her a headache. She wiped the floor where she had sprayed, hoping the headache wouldn't last. When she thought she had the whole mess cleaned up—it was hard to tell with such little light—she threw the paper towels with the others and went back to the blanket.

She sat in the corner and wiped away sweat. The air was cold and soon she was shivering, even with a hoodie. She played with a nail as she waited. He was taking forever and the chemical smell was making her head spin.

After a while, the driver's side door slammed again, and the engine started. Her head throbbed. How much further did they have to go?

Macy had seen enough TV to know this could get ugly.

Rubbing her temples, she tried to push those thoughts out of her mind. But as soon as she pushed one away, another would replace it.

She knew enough to know that by forcing her to eat the meat, he was trying to show her he was in control. She also knew that anyone who needed to control others was actually scared and weak, despite their actions.

She'd heard a quote somewhere, probably at school, that said something along the lines of abusers and bullies being scared little boys and girls deep down. People who were happy and confident didn't treat people bad. Maybe Macy could find his weakness and use it to her advantage.

Head pounding, she leaned against the wall again. The road had grown bumpier, and somehow it helped to lull her to sleep despite the jostling. She didn't wake up until the truck stopped.

Her head still hurt as she came awake, but it wasn't as bad as it had been. Before she knew it the lock turned again, and both the door to the canopy and the truck bed opened.

Bright light shone in Macy's eyes, and she had to cover them with her arm. Her headache made the rays of light slice like razor blades.

The man grabbed her shirt, and yanked her out of the truck. Outside the light was even worse, but at least she could breathe easier. Her head even felt a little relief until he slammed her against the side of the truck with both hands.

He stared her down, less than an inch away from her face, and he narrowed his eyes. She had never seen anyone so angry before. He tightened his grip on her shoulders and pushed her against the truck again. "Don't you ever—*ever*—talk back to me again. Do you understand? When I tell you to do something, you do it! Don't question me." He dug his fingers into her shoulder, and she could feel her skin bruise. "Do you understand?" he shouted.

She nodded, afraid to speak.

"Good. Now come with me." He grabbed her arm and yanked so hard that she thought he might have pulled it out of the socket.

Macy walked behind him, trying to keep up. He never stopped squeezing; she could feel his fingers squeezing down to the bone. She looked around, trying to figure out where they were. To their left, she saw fields of corn close by. Straight ahead, she could see a farmhouse and a dilapidated red barn. They appeared to be heading for the barn.

"What are we doing?"

"I told you not to talk back!" He stopped, turned and stared her down, squeezing her arm even harder. "Don't speak unless spoken to. Ever again."

She looked away, and he yanked her along again. Macy couldn't help rolling her eyes. *Ever again*? Seriously? For a scared little boy, he was sure full of himself. She had to hold onto the image of him as a frightened child if she was going to keep her sanity. She wouldn't let herself develop Stockholm syndrome and feel sorry for the creep. She was going to get away. She was.

They went through the barn door and Macy looked around, trying to figure out what he had in mind. She half-expected to see the barn converted into a torture chamber, but it was just a barn. A couple of horses stood to the left, some cows off to the right, and she could hear sheep somewhere. The smell of manure was all around, but after being trapped with the smell of her own vomit, it was a welcome scent.

Rays of light shone through some of the rafters above, and dust danced through them. The fact that the sun could get through the walls encouraged her. She probably could too if she tried hard enough. They walked through the length of the barn, and stopped near some empty stalls.

He bent over, forcing her to join him as he clutched her arm. He brushed aside some hay from the floor and lifted up a round piece of metal. A trap door opened up.

Macy held her breath. She'd been wrong. He'd built the torture chamber beneath the barn, not inside it.

Frantic

ALYSSA STOOD FROM Macy's bed, clutching one of Macy's teddy bears. Trying to figure out a status update wasn't doing any good. Her daughter was gone…gone. It wasn't the time to play detective. Alyssa needed to get out there and find her daughter. She set the bear on a pillow.

She ran down to the front door, throwing it open without even taking the time to put on her shoes. She ran down the driveway, frost crunching under her socks. They started to get wet, but she didn't care.

Willis from across the street was out in his front yard, doing some yard work. Alyssa ran to him.

He looked up, appearing shocked. "Alyssa. Are you okay?"

"Have you seen Macy?"

"Not this morning. Is everything—?"

"No! No, it's not." She felt like her throat was closing up. "If you see her, bring her home."

"What's going on? Can I help?" Willis asked.

"She's missing!" Tears spilled out onto her face. Admitting it to someone she barely knew felt like defeat. "She's gone," Alyssa whispered. "I have to find her." She burst into a run, heading down the street.

As she ran in her socks, she stepped on a number of little sharp rocks. Failing to put on shoes now seemed like a stupid decision. She was only slowing herself down more when what she needed was speed. She had to talk to as many people as possible.

She saw another neighbor loading her kids into the car. Alyssa ran to them. "Jane, have you seen Macy?"

Jane shook her head and Alyssa ran off. She didn't have time to explain anything to anyone. What she needed was to find someone who had seen Macy.

Alyssa ran as fast as she could through the neighborhood, only stopping to ask anyone she saw if they had seen her daughter. It was a pretty tight-knit community, so at least everyone knew their family. She didn't have to deal with explaining what Macy looked like.

Finally, she circled back around to her house. No one had seen her. Of course they hadn't. Not if Macy had been gone since the night before. She ran back to her house and once inside, she pulled off her bloody socks and slid on some flip flops. Her feet burned and throbbed, but she didn't care. She had to get back out there.

"Where have you been?"

She turned around to see Chad at the top of the stairs. "I've been out looking for Macy. What have you been doing?"

"I've been on the phone, talking to everyone under the sun who's seen Macy's status update." Chad's eyebrows came together.

Alyssa ran her hands through her sweaty hair. "Okay. You keep talking to them. I'm going to talk to more neighbors. Someone has to know something."

He folded his arms. "We need to call the cops."

She leaned against the wall. "You're right. They can get more done than we can. You do that while I keep looking for her."

The corners of Chad's lips turned downward. "She's not out there. She's with some kid she met online, giving us a very public middle finger. This is her way of trying to let us—"

"Stop! I don't care what she did, Chad. I need to find our daughter. Call the cops—please."

"And have them take her downtown," he muttered. "That'll teach her."

Alyssa stared at him, unable to find words. Had she really heard him correctly? She didn't have time to argue with him. He'd been such a jerk lately, and this wasn't the time to try to change that. "Just call them."

She ran out the door again. Her feet ached more as the drying blood stuck to the flip flops. "Macy!" She looked around. Maybe if Macy was around hiding and saw how upset Alyssa was, she might come out of hiding. "Macy!"

This time, she ran to the park. Families were already gathering there. She screamed for Macy the entire way. Who cared if anyone thought she was crazy? She needed to get as many people looking for Macy as possible. She couldn't do this on her own.

Dungeon

H ER CAPTOR SHOVED Macy toward the hole in the barn's floor. She pushed against him, trying to stop him. She didn't want to go down there. She didn't even want to know what could be there.

"Are you testing me?" he growled. "Climb the ladder before I have to throw you down. You'll break a bone—I guarantee it."

"What's down there?"

"It's only a storm shelter. Get in!" He shoved her with more force.

She gulped and let go of him. He still squeezed her arm, but she lowered herself to the ground and stuck her feet down the hole. She had to feel around before finding the ladder. It was made of rope, and swung as she tried to steady herself. As soon as she was on her way down, he let go of her. Once her head was all the way below, he slammed the door shut over her. She could hear him moving the hay around over the door. Something clicked. A lock?

Macy stared up at the closed door above her until she felt a crick in her neck. Her eyes started to adjust to the light. She looked down and saw a few bales of hay. Sunlight shone in through walls of packed dirt.

Unsure of how long the ladder would hold her weight, she climbed down and put her feet on the dirt floor. She looked around. Everything was dirt. She walked around the square little storm cellar. It was a relief to see that it wasn't a torture chamber like she had feared. It was only a dirt cell with hay.

The hay actually helped it to smell a little better. It was musty, but the almost-sweet scent of the hay made it bearable. She sat on a stack of two bales and looked up at the light, watching the dust dance around for a little while.

She had to think of a way out.

But even if she were to stack all of the bales on top of each other, she wouldn't be able to reach the boards by the ceiling.

At least she was away from that psycho. Being alone was much better than being around him.

Her stomach rumbled. It was finally steady enough to be hungry again, but she had no desire to eat. Whatever he would give her, if he was going to give her anything else at all, would probably only give her more problems. She kicked her feet against the hay several times and looked around the room.

The wood at the top, near the ceiling, was old and cracking. Maybe she could pull the boards off piece by piece, if only she could reach them.

The dirt walls were dry, but not crumbling. Maybe she could find a way to make a ladder or steps in them if she could find something to dig the holes. It wasn't likely, but at least it was an idea.

Something squeaked. A rodent. How did it stay alive? Was there something to eat? Not that she wanted to eat mouse food, but it might come to that. She shuddered at the thought.

How much worse was this going to get? Macy didn't want to know. She jumped off the hay and climbed up the ladder as fast as she could. It swung every time she moved.

Holding on as tight as she could, she managed to get to the top without losing her footing. She pushed her foot into a corner of the walls, steadying herself once the ladder held still. Letting go of one hand, she pushed on the trap door. It didn't budge, so she pushed a few more times. She may as well have tried to rip off the whole ceiling.

Macy wrapped her leg in the ladder and braced with her other foot. Letting go of the rope, she pushed with both hands and all of her might. She ignored the rope as it swung again, but on her third push she lost her balance. As she fell upside down, her foot caught in the rope and anchored her in place.

Macy breathed a sigh of relief, glad to have not broken her neck. She grabbed onto the rope, grateful no one could see her as she hung upside down, feeling ridiculous. She was probably stupid for thinking she could get the door open.

Holding on, still upside down, she tried to pull her foot loose. It was stuck. Making sure not to let go, she pulled herself up little by little until she could reach her foot. With one hand, she pulled her foot free. It slid loose, and she maneuvered herself back into an upright position before climbing down.

Once on the ground, she looked around the room again. The rodents stayed out of sight. All she had left were the boards near the ceiling. They were well out of reach, but she had to try. She had to do something.

She went to one of the bales of hay, bent down, and pushed. It moved, but not much. It was a lot heavier than it looked. But what else was she going to do? Watch TV?

Sweat beaded on her skin as she pushed the bale again and again. Finally, it reached the wall, and she sat down on the hay to rest. It felt good to get a little exercise. Her muscles burned a little.

She was thirsty. When was the last time she had anything to drink? Not wanting to stop for long, she picked another bale, and pushed it toward the first one.

By the time she had the two bales against each other, she was wiping sweat from her eyes. How was she going to lift the second one on top of the first? She would have to wait; she didn't have the energy to try yet. She lay down on top of the two bales, imagining she was on a bed.

Something poked into her back. Macy sat up and saw something shiny in the bale. She pulled out what appeared to be a tube of lipstick. She pulled the top off to find exactly that.

Why was there makeup in the hay? She tossed it on the floor and lay down again.

Macy shivered, starting to get cold. As she readjusted her position, she noticed that the hay below her had grown warm. Maybe she could use it to hold heat. She sat up and dug her fingers into the hay, pulling out as much as she could, earning several scratches. That didn't matter. When she had a nice pile, she lay back down, and pulled as much of it over herself as possible, using it like a blanket.

It didn't take long to warm up. She closed her eyes, allowing herself to rest. She could hear hooves moving around above her. She hoped the ceiling was strong. The last thing she wanted to deal with was a cow or horse falling on top of her.

Guilt

Z OEY CARTER CLOSED her laptop in frustration. She had spent the last two hours searching for anything she could find on that Jared guy. It was as if he had ceased to exist. That wasn't possible—she had chatted with him. She could still remember his photo: an adorable selfie taken at one of his baseball games.

He was so sweet and had wanted to know what Macy liked. Jared had been so excited about their upcoming date, and had had a million questions. He didn't want to mess anything up, and Zoey had been more than happy to help him out. Macy had never had a boyfriend or gone on a date or anything. Her dad was so over-protective; he wouldn't let her do anything.

He wouldn't even let her watch PG-13 movies until she turned thirteen. Zoey always made sure they watched the good ones at her house so Macy could see what everyone else was seeing. Kids were always making fun of her, and Zoey didn't want to give them another reason.

The door opened, and her mom came in. "Has anyone heard from Macy yet?"

"No." Zoey frowned, fighting tears. "She's going to be okay, isn't she?"

Her mom walked over and wrapped her in a hug. "I sure hope so."

"But she would have called me. Why hasn't she texted or anything?"

"Well, her wall post sounds pretty upset. If she really wants to get to her parents, she would stay away from contacting you because she'd know they would call you first."

"Still, she should let me know if she's okay. She should know I can keep a secret."

"You know in a case like this, it's more important to break secrets, right?" Her mom raised an eyebrow.

Zoey rolled her eyes. "Of course. But she should tell me, you know?"

The landline rang.

Her mom gave her another hug. "I'd better get that. Maybe it's news about Macy."

Twirling a strand of jet-black hair, Zoey looked around her room. There had to be something she was forgetting. Something that would give an important clue. There was no way Macy had run away. If anyone would have seen it coming, it would have been Zoey. They told each other everything. Well, almost everything. There was that one thing she hadn't told Macy.

Macy had been looking forward to that date so bad. It was all she had talked about for the last week. She spent more time planning what to wear than she did on anything else. She was as excited about sneaking out as she was about going on a date with Jared. She had been tired of being a goody two-shoes, and couldn't wait to prove she wasn't anymore.

She spun around in her chair, looking at all the things that reminded her of Macy. *Would* Macy have run away with Jared? To spite her parents?

Had the thrill of sneaking out with Jared been enough to unlock her wild, crazy side? Was that why she took off with him? A smile tugged at Zoey's mouth. Maybe that was it. This could have been a loud, defining moment for Macy. Think of the fun times they could have when she came back, assuming her parents got the message and finally gave her some permission to have fun. They were probably going crazy right now not knowing where Macy was.

Zoey's mom came back into the room. "I'm sorry to do this to you, but we have to go down to the police station."

"What? Why?" Zoey felt like she had been punched in the gut.

"The police want to question anyone who could know anything

about Macy's disappearance."

Zoey ran her hands through the length of her hair. "Isn't there a twenty-four hour wait or something? She ran away, didn't she?"

"The police aren't assuming anything. She met with someone online that nobody can even locate. They want to eliminate all possibilities."

"Wait. You mean they think she might have been kidnapped?"

"Nobody knows. There are a lot of child predators out there. That's why I'm always telling you not to give out any personal information."

Zoey took a deep breath. "But I talked with Jared. He was nice. I saw his picture."

"Did you ever meet him?"

She shook her head.

"If you want to help Macy, we need to go downtown."

"Can I have a few minutes to get ready?"

"Sure, sweetie." Her mom squeezed her shoulder and left the room.

Zoey closed her door, then put her ear to it to make sure her mom really had walked away. She grabbed her jacket and slipped it on, opened her window, and climbed out onto the ledge. She looked at the woods that faced her back yard. Could Macy actually have been taken by some pedophile?

Zoey stuck her hand into her pocket, grabbed a box and pulled out a cigarette. She lit it and took a puff, holding it in for a moment. Letting her breath out slowly, she tried to relax.

She'd started smoking to look cool around the new kids she'd been hanging out with, but now she actually felt like she needed one. If her mom knew she was smoking, she would have a fit.

The last thing Zoey wanted was go to the police station. What if she said something that could get Macy into trouble? What if she got herself into trouble? Could they charge her with something because she knew her friend was going to sneak out? By law, she was only a kid.

Her heart sped up as she thought about different kinds of worst-case scenarios. What if they sent her to juvie? What if everyone hated her for keeping Jared a secret? She didn't let her mind go to the absolute worst case—something actually happening to Macy.

As much as she didn't want to admit it, deep down she thought that might be the most realistic option. If Macy had planned to run away with Jared, she'd tell Zoey and not post it for everyone.

Zoey took another drag.

Guilt punched her in the gut again as she thought about the other secret she was keeping from Macy—the one far worse than smoking.

What if Macy had found out about that? Would that have been enough to send her over the edge to run away?

Zoey took one last drag, then smashed the cigarette into the roof tile next to her. She needed another one, maybe the whole pack, but there wasn't time for that. She climbed back into her room and sprayed some air freshener. Then she opened her door and listened for her mom. She could hear her downstairs, talking on the phone.

Zoey grabbed some clothes and ran to the bathroom for a quick shower. What should she tell the cops? She should probably stick to Jared and what little she knew about him. She kicked herself for not downloading his picture.

Maybe one of Macy's other friends had talked with Jared and had been smart enough to save the picture.

Zoey got out of the shower and brushed her teeth to get rid of the last evidence of her new habit. She looked in the mirror, examining her teeth, and then she brushed her long, black hair. She promised herself that the next time she saw Macy, she would come clean. She would tell her everything. The thought that she'd caused Macy to run away ate at her.

There was a knock on the door. "Are you ready yet, Zoey? They're expecting us at the station."

"Hold on!" Zoey grabbed her black eyeliner. She gave her eyes a smoky look before putting on some mascara. She loved her exotic eyes. They were so dark and mysterious, thanks to her dad's Japanese roots.

Her mom drove her to the station in near-silence. Zoey really didn't want to talk about anything, and her mom usually respected that.

When they pulled into a parking spot, her mom turned to her. "Just tell them everything you know. Don't be nervous, okay? You're not in trouble. Everyone just wants to find Macy. You're her best friend, and you might know something that no one else does."

Zoey nodded. "Sure, Mom." She got out of the car, not wanting to talk about it any more.

They walked into the station together. Her mom told the officer at the front desk why they were there, and he filled out some paperwork. Then he looked up at Zoey's mom and then back to Zoey.

"Are you adopted?"

Zoey rolled her eyes. If she had a dollar for every time some ignorant bonehead asked that, she would be rich. Because she looked so much like her dad, everyone assumed she couldn't be related to her fair-skinned, auburn-haired mom. "My dad is Japanese."

The buffoon looked around. "Where is he?"

Zoey narrowed her eyes. "Isn't that the million-dollar question? Probably Japan, but who knows? If you figure it out, let me know."

He raised his eyebrows. "Okay. Unknown." He scribbled more on his paper. "You two can have a seat over there." He indicated toward the waiting area.

Zoey followed her mom to the chairs. Her heart raced as she looked around at the plain, white walls and numerous windows. Yelling came from somewhere down a hall.

Just as she was getting ready to jump from her seat and run back to the car, she heard familiar voices. She looked up to see Macy's parents and brother walking out from behind the main desk. They must have been questioned. Her mom and dad stopped at the desk and talked with the loser filling out paperwork.

Zoey's mom went up and gave Macy's mom a hug. Alyssa burst into tears, and the women held each other. "Oh, Valerie. I can't believe this is happening."

Zoey looked away, afraid of crying herself.

Alex sat down next her. His eyes were red and puffy.

"You okay?" Zoey asked, feeling stupid. Of course he wasn't.

"They have, like, a million questions. They're acting like Macy's dead." He shook his head and took a deep breath.

"She's fine. You know how tough she is. I'm sure it's like her update said. She wanted to get away from everything."

Alex shrugged. He looked into her eyes but said nothing.

Zoey looked over at their parents. They were talking with each other, paying no attention to the two kids. She put her hand on top of Alex's. He flipped his hand over and laced his fingers through hers.

"I don't know what I'll do if anything happened to her." He cleared his throat. "I couldn't—I mean, what would I do?" His eyes shone with tears.

"She's going to be okay." She squeezed his hand. "She is. You know what? She's probably off having the time of her life with Jared, with no clue what she's putting us through."

He nodded. "I hope. When she gets back, I'm gonna beat the crap out of her."

"Alex. We're leaving," Chad called.

He squeezed her hand before standing. They held their eye contact, their fingers lingering also. Before Alex reached his parents, he mouthed, "Call me."

Zoey nodded.

Identity

A THUD WOKE Macy up. She opened her eyes, confused.

"I see you've made yourself comfortable."

The trap door was open, and she could see her captor staring down at her.

"Do you want something to eat?"

She sat up, nodding. "And something to drink."

He laughed. "I'll bet you're thirsty after moving those bales around. I'll get you something, but you have to do one thing for me, Heather."

Heather?

"What?"

"Call me Dad."

Dad? Had he lost his mind? Then she remembered in the truck, he said something about her looking like his Heather. "Why?"

"Because, Heather. I'm your dad. I need to hear you call me Dad."

"Tell me your real name and I'll think about it."

He glared at her. "You know my name, Heather. It's Chester Woodran."

Chester? His name was *Chester*? No wonder he was such a jerk. With a name like that, he'd have to be mean to get any respect.

"Well?" He narrowed his eyes.

"You're not my dad! And I'm not Heather."

He shook his head. "See. That's exactly why I need you to call me Dad. As soon as you do, you'll get your food and water. One more chance."

"Never."

"I'll come back and see how agreeable you are later." The trap door slammed shut, and she heard the same click as before.

Was that why Chester had taken her? Had something happened to Heather, and he was trying to use Macy to replace the girl? If he thought she was going to call him Dad, he had another think coming.

Tears poked at her eyes as she thought about her family. Did they know she was missing? She wasn't sure how long she'd been gone, but since she had sneaked out of the house, they wouldn't have found out until the morning. Maybe not even late morning, if it was one of those days when her parents let her sleep in.

Even if they did know she was gone, would they know where to look for her? She had to be several states away, if not more. Would her friends have figured out that something was wrong? She had told her closest friends she was meeting Jared. Would they be worried that she hadn't texted them about it?

Burying herself further into the bed of hay, she gave in to the tears until she was sobbing and shaking. Where were her parents? What were they doing? What about her annoying brother? What she wouldn't give to even see him and put up with his relentless teasing.

Without realizing it, she cried herself back to sleep. She woke up when something tickled her hand, which was hanging out of the hay. She opened her eyes to find a black beetle crawling on her hand.

"Augh! Get off. Off of me!"

She shook her hand, but it didn't come loose. She used her other hand to flick it away. She wiped the back of her hand on the hay furiously, as though that would get rid of whatever remnants of the bug were left on her skin.

Was she going to die in this room? Was this going to be the last place she was ever going to see? Sleeping in hay with bugs crawling on her, surrounded by rats and who knew what else?

A loud crack made her jump. Macy buried herself deeper into the bale of hay, even though she knew it couldn't protect her. Rain slammed against the barn with such force that it practically shook above her. Thunder clapped again, and with it rainwater came dripping down the wall next to her. It pooled noisily on the ground.

Did it flood down there? The rats weren't running for cover, so maybe—hopefully—that was a good sign. She could hear animals stomping around up above. They whinnied, mooed, and bahhed, making the storm even more eerie than it already was.

Macy lay there in her hay nest, listening to the sounds of the storm and of the animals. It was the distraction she needed, and finally she relaxed for the first time since the ordeal had begun. Storms had always been somewhat comforting, in a strange sort of way. At home, she used to love watching the rainfall from her house. It was almost magical, even though she was too old to believe in that stuff anymore.

The storm gave her hope, almost like a sign she was going to be okay.

Her stomach rumbled along with the thunder and the hunger ate at her, making her feel weak and light-headed. She had been hungry before and knew this phase would pass. There was no way she was going to let him win. If nothing else, she would walk away from this skinny at last.

Focusing on the storm, she ignored the hunger pangs. She thought of her poor old cat Snowflake. Imagining him beside her helped Macy relax further. He had always been able to sense when she was upset, and would show up to comfort her.

As suddenly as it had begun, the storm stopped. The quiet rang in her ears, and all she could hear was the water dripping down the wall from the spaces above. Macy closed her eyes. She wanted sleep to take her away again, but it wouldn't.

Her stomach growled again, rumbling over and over, making her light-headedness even worse. Her mouth watered for food that didn't exist.

At home, she could walk into the kitchen and grab anything—well, anything without meat or animal by-products. Alex always waved cheese slices in her face after she declared herself a vegan. Cheese had been her favorite, and was probably the sole cause of her muffin top.

A noise caught Macy's attention, and she looked toward the trap door as it opened.

"Did you enjoy the storm? I was watching it by the fire, listening to music while lunch cooked in the oven. How did you like it from in here, Heather?"

"My name isn't Heather."

"The sooner you come to terms with the fact that you're Heather, the sooner you'll be able to get out of here. For now, are you ready for some food?"

"I'm not calling you *dad*."

"That's a shame. I've got some food here for you. Can you smell it?" Chester waved his hands around, like that would send the smell her way.

"Nope."

"Are you sure you won't change your mind?"

"I'm not Heather, and you're not my dad. I want you to take me back to my parents. Everyone's looking for me, you know. They've figured out by now that I'm missing. They'll find you."

"Don't count on that, Heather."

"They know something's wrong."

He shook his head. "You posted a note online, telling everyone of your intention to run away."

"What?" She sat up.

"You didn't think I could figure out those passwords, either?" He laughed. "Snowflake415. Your precious kitty and the date you decided to become vegan."

Macy gasped. "They'll still look for me. Even if I said I was running away." She clenched her fists. Would they, really? They had to. Her parents wouldn't shrug their shoulders and carry on with life if she ran away.

"Your note said not to look for you, that you would come back when you were ready."

She tightened her grip, digging her nails into her own flesh. "They won't believe it."

"I think they will. I know all your typical typos, your lingo, and all the chat-speak. They'll have no reason to doubt you wrote it from your own account."

He'd thought of everything. Even so, there was no way everyone would sit around, was there? She was a kid. The police would be forced to look for her, wouldn't they? Or did they not bother with runaways? Not that they would know to look for her below a barn in the middle of nowhere, probably states away.

"So, Heather, are you ready for lunch? I made you some vegetable soup—vegan approved."

Macy's stomach growled again, and her mouth filled with water. She couldn't let him know how much she wanted the soup.

"I'm not calling you dad. You're not my dad."

"Eventually, you'll be hungry enough to be agreeable. I thought you'd be now, but it looks like you'll need some more time. I'll leave the bowl up here and you can think about it while I go to the store. I might make some other stops too. Come to think of it, I might be gone for quite a while. Are you sure you don't want to eat now?"

She wanted to eat it more than anything, but there was no way she was letting him know that. "I'm fine. If you know me so well, you know how I lost my weight. I can go a long time without eating."

"Suit yourself. You're only human. Oh, that reminds me." He held a bottle of water. "You'll at least need something to drink if you're going to survive. You may be able to go a long time without food, but you can't go long without this. Drink it." Chester dropped it, and as it bounced on the dirt floor, he slammed the trap door shut and locked it.

Her mouth watered at the thought of the soup, reminding her how parched she was. He was right, and she knew it. She needed water. Macy climbed out of her little nest and ran to the bottle of water, picked it up, and stared at it. It was still factory sealed. There weren't any punctures in it anywhere.

Why had he given that to her? She told him she would never call him dad. Was he not planning on killing her? Did he want her to live? If that was the case, what was his plan? Did he actually want her to become his daughter? Like that would ever happen.

She twisted the cap off and guzzled the entire bottle. She put the lid back on and threw it into a corner.

In the distance, she heard an engine start, followed by tires driving on gravel.

Sneaking

ALEX SPRAWLED OUT across his messy bed, playing games on his cell phone and trying to distract himself from how stressed and worried he was. It didn't fix anything, but at least he could get his mind off Macy for a little while.

As if it wasn't bad enough that Macy had taken off—or been killed, by the sounds of what the police thought—he and his parents had been questioned. Zoey, too. She had to be as worried as he was. She'd been besties with Macy for as long has he could remember.

He moved up a level in Factoryville, and then chucked his phone across the room. He didn't care about any of the games. Not now. The police had said they were going to go through Macy's room if she didn't turn up soon, and told them not to leave town. Where would they go? Jerks.

Rolling over onto his back, he stared at a poster of his favorite band on the ceiling. When would Zoey call? It felt like forever since he saw her at the station. He hoped she was okay. She seemed about as well as could be expected, but that was before talking with the cops.

Alex's parents had been in the room when he was questioned, since he was a minor. The same should hold true for Zoey. He would feel a lot better being able to talk with her.

If they could talk, maybe they could figure out what really happened. What two people were closer to Macy, really? Sure, Macy and Alex didn't spill their secrets to each other, but they were pretty close. That was why she put up with his teasing. It was their thing. Always had been.

The doorbell rang, and Alex groaned. Let it be Zoey, and not the cops. He could tell by the way they looked at him that they didn't like him. His hair was past his ears, and he liked it scraggly. The older cop seemed to have him pegged as a thug. Did he seriously suspect that Alex had anything to do with it? That was ridiculous.

Opening his door, Alex could hear muffled conversation down-stairs. At least it was a break from his parents arguing. They didn't get along anymore since Dad had started that blog. People online started thinking his dad was all that, so his head got big and he walked around upset that he didn't get the same respect at home.

Alex thought about closing his door to continue hiding, but he wanted to find out what was going on. Maybe the police had found something. Macy's picture was all over the TV. Every discussion on social media was about her, too. That's why Alex had been playing games—he didn't want to read any more crazy theories. His friends had come up with everything from alien abduction to witness protection.

If Alex didn't stay away, he would end up beating the crap out of half the student body on Monday. Let them talk, but he wasn't going to have anything to do with it. He made his way downstairs and saw his parents talking with three cops. One officer he hadn't seen at the station tipped his hat. Alex nodded back and stood a distance away, not wanting to be dragged into the conversation.

It didn't sound as though they had anything new to share.

"We need to search the house and we need you to step outside while we do," said the one who had given Alex the evil eye back at the station.

"What?" Alex exclaimed. He looked at his parents, begging them to say no. "Why do we have to leave? We didn't do anything wrong."

Hat-tipper looked at him. "Then you have nothing to worry about, son. We should be in and out of here in no time. If there are any clues to your sister's disappearance, then we need to find them sooner rather than later. The first twenty-four hours are critical."

Alex frowned. "Can I go back and get my cell phone?"

Jerkwad shook his head. "No can do. You can have it back when we're done. Now, please step out of the house."

"Fine." Alex walked past his parents and the cops, out the door.

Alyssa looked at him. "You can put your shoes on."

He glared at the jerk cop. "Wouldn't want to interfere with the investigation."

Chad narrowed his eyes. "Alex, it's the middle of November. Put some shoes on. Why are you being like this?"

"Why? Because my sister is missing and we're being treated like criminals."

"That's how he expresses sorrow." Chad picked up a pair of flip-flops and flung them at Alex.

He caught them. "Awesome." After putting them on, Alex walked down their walkway. "Am I allowed to walk down the street?" He didn't wait for a response before making his way to the sidewalk. He looked down the street and saw Zoey's mom's car parked in front of their house, two doors down.

Before he even made it to their driveway, Zoey ran outside. "Sorry I didn't call you. My mom wouldn't stop talking to me. I swear, she needs to get married and leave me alone."

"That won't solve anything. Trust me."

"True. Your parents haven't been getting along lately."

"Want to go to the park? The cops are going through my house."

"That bites. We're probably next, though. Yeah, let's go there."

Alex grabbed her hand, and they walked the three blocks to the park in silence. They went to their typical hiding spot underneath a tree with many swooping branches and sat down against the trunk, hidden from the world. Zoey leaned her head against his chest.

"Where do you think she is?" asked Alex.

"I hope she's having a good time with Jared, but the fact that he's gotten rid of everything identifying worries me. Why would he do that? I went through the messages he sent me, and there's nothing in there about him. All he did was ask me about Macy and say how much he wanted to make her happy. The police even said that sounds really suspicious."

"They should try to get into his account."

Zoey looked at him. "They did. They called customer support and everything. He covered his tracks by hiding his IP address or whatever.

I don't know all that lingo."

"So, basically, they have no idea where or who Jared is."

"Nope." She pulled out a cigarette. "Want one?"

"I'll share with you. Sorry I got you hooked."

"I'm not hooked. I can stop anytime. I think it'll take the edge off." She lit it, took a drag, and then handed it to him.

Alex took the longest, slowest drag he could manage. He wanted to make it last since they were sharing. He didn't want to admit how good it felt. He knew if his sister was there, she would be mad at both of them, especially for encouraging each other.

They sat in silence until the cigarette was gone. Alex shoved it into the ground, twisting it back and forth.

Zoey leaned back against him. "What do you think is going to happen?"

He shrugged. "At home, I keep expecting her to walk around the corner. I know she's not there, but I keep thinking she's going to. It's stupid."

"No, it's not. I keep waiting for her to text me or something. I keep wanting to call her, but then I remember I can't."

"Do you think Jared was real? Or some old creeper?"

"I don't think it was the kid in the picture. He looked too sweet and innocent to do anything wrong. You know, the kind of guy who would insist on opening her door, not talk her into running away."

"What if we never see her again?"

"It's too soon to think like that."

"But you said—"

"Remember all those positive thinking CDs your parents used to make us all listen to when we were kids? If there's any truth to them, what Macy needs is for us to thinking she's going to come back. She needs our positive thoughts. They'll reach her and help her."

"You really believe that crap?"

"I don't know. It seemed to work."

"Did you actually try?"

"Yeah. Maybe."

"It didn't help my family. My parents fight all the time and they pushed Macy away."

"But they don't listen to those anymore, do they?"

Alex shook his head.

Zoey took his hand and slid her fingers through his. "See? They got along when they did. Remember?"

"I guess."

"They did. I was jealous. Trust me."

He wrapped his arm around her and sighed. "This whole thing sucks balls."

"It's an effing nightmare. When she comes back, I'm going to give her a hug, then I'm gonna slap her across the face."

"You and me both."

"When she comes back, we really should tell her about us."

Alex looked at her in surprise. "You think so?"

"Well, yeah. I always feel bad about keeping it from her. I was afraid she'd hate me. But if she cares about us, she'll be happy for us. Then we could all hang out together. We won't have to hide from her."

"Your parents would never let you spend the night again. We wouldn't get easy make out sessions anymore."

"Who said anything about telling them?"

They sat for a while, watching the feet of people go by and listening to kids squeal and shout at each other. Alex thought back to when they were all kids. Zoey had practically grown up with him and Macy.

She had been like a sister to him his whole life until last summer. Somehow she'd started to seem different to him. Then one night, Macy fell asleep while they'd all been watching a scary movie. A frightening scene came on, and both Alex and Zoey screamed. They looked at each other and laughed, but when they made eye contact, something changed.

When the movie ended, they sat there on the couch, talking for hours. They stayed up until about four, discussing everything from what the scariest movie was to which Pokémon was the strongest. They laughed over old memories and talked about jerks at school. Then, heart pounding, Alex made the riskiest move of all. He leaned over and kissed her on the lips, not knowing if she would push him away or kiss back.

Zoey had kissed him back, surprising him with her passion. He had expected her to shove him on the floor and tell on him. They decided not to tell Macy—or anyone.

For some stupid reason, it was okay for guys to go out with girls two years younger, but girls couldn't. They had always planned on eventually coming clean to Macy. She deserved to know, and if anyone was going to figure them out it would have been her, but as far as they could tell, she was clueless. She definitely didn't know that when Alex snuck out, he was meeting with Zoey.

Zoey had been afraid to tell Macy and lose her best friend. Even though Alex and Macy bickered, she was quite protective of her little brother. She always had been. One time, a girl from school had been teasing Macy and she said some remark about Alex becoming sexy. That was the one time they had seen Macy get really pissed. She went off on that girl like nothing Alex had ever seen. He had thought for sure that Macy was going to deck the girl, but she had stormed off instead.

Macy wouldn't stand up for herself when it came to kids at school, but when someone said something about Alex, the inner monster had been released. Alex didn't want to have that turned on Zoey, and Zoey didn't want her lifelong best friend hating her.

Zoey sat up straight. "I can feel my phone vibrating. I'm sure Mom wants me back home."

"I should probably get back too. My parents are going to freak out and not let me go anywhere now that Macy's gone. My days of sneaking out are about to end. What are you going to say about smelling like smoke?"

She flipped her hair back. "The usual. I ran into kids smoking at the park."

He nodded and then kissed her, hoping she wouldn't get mad at him for kissing her while Macy was gone. Instead, she kissed him back, holding him tighter than usual. Her phone vibrated again, and he could feel it.

Zoey stood. "I should go before my mom has a nervous break-down."

"Yeah. Me too."

She gave him a quick kiss and then walked away. He watched her until she disappeared from sight.

Anxiety

MACY LEANED AGAINST the bale of hay she had been pushing and wiped the sweat from her forehead. She was determined to pile them up so she could reach the wood near the ceiling. She had been staring it at it long enough. She knew that if she could reach it, she could pull the boards loose and squeeze through.

Sure, she didn't really have a plan beyond that. She didn't know how to get off the farm, or where to go once she reached a main road. She had to take everything one step at a time and the first thing was to get the bales piled on top of each other.

She looked around, searching for a way up to the boards before the madman came back. She didn't know how long he had been gone, but it felt like forever. He was bound to be back soon.

What did he have planned for her? Would he let her starve if she never caved and called him Dad? She didn't have the best relationship with her own dad, but she wasn't going to give in and disown him.

Too exhausted to even attempt pushing one of the heavy bales on top of another, she paced the room. As she thought about how she was going to get out, her mind wandered back home. Was anyone worried about her?

If that jerk was smart enough to remove her cell phone battery, there was no way anyone would ever find her. She remembered when her dad had gotten those phones. How could she forget? He had gone on for nearly an hour explaining how they would always know where she and Alex were with those. Macy and her brother had rolled their eyes at each other, both knowing they could leave their phones somewhere if they were going to sneak anywhere.

Not that Macy was one to sneak around. Her brother was the master of sneaking in and out. She knew he was seeing friends who smoked with him, but she wasn't about to tattle. He assured her that he wasn't doing any other drugs. She had told him that as long as he wasn't doing anything dangerous, she would keep their parents out of it.

Macy was sure if she ever got back home, she wouldn't sneak out again. At least not to meet someone she had never met before.

"Focus!" She shook her head. Thinking about all that wasn't going to help her get back home. Or even out of the barn.

She continued to pace in circles, staring at the bales of hay and the wood she was determined to peel away. As she walked, the room felt like it got smaller. She felt it might close in on her if she didn't do something soon.

With a sudden burst of determination, she ran at the nearest bale of hay and pushed on it as hard as she could from the bottom. It moved up into the air a couple of inches before dropping. Macy moved her fingers out of the way in time.

She balled up her fists and went to the other side of the room, startling the rodents. She narrowed her eyes at the bale and crouched down as though in a race.

"Ready. Set. Go." She ran at the hay and used her momentum to push it up. It went up farther but soon dropped down again. Not to be deterred, she returned to the other end of the room and repeated the imaginary race. She got the bale a little higher, but again, it dropped.

She repeated the process about five more times until she was too tired to try again. She lay down on the bale she had made a bed of and kicked her feet in frustration. She pounded on the wall next to her, not caring that it hurt her hands. She felt blood dripping down. All she had to do was pile up the hay and she could get out, but she couldn't even do that.

Light shone through the boards, mocking her. She pounded on the wall harder, so much so that little specks of dirt fell onto her, getting on her face. She wiped them away, and leaned against the wall. Hot, angry tears fell to her face, and she did nothing to stop them.

She let herself sob. Feeling the pain deep down in her gut, she let out a scream. She heard the animals move around above. She didn't care. She screamed again, that time louder.

"Why did I get into that truck? Why was I so stupid?" She got up, tears still pouring down her face, and kicked the hay. "And why won't you help me, you stupid bales?"

Macy reached down and pulled out pieces of hay, throwing them around herself. She grabbed more and threw them too. They came out easier where she had been kicking. She pulled out as many as would come and chucked them around the suffocating, little room. She let out another scream for good measure.

"Why? Why? Why?" She leaned against a wall and slid down until she was sitting on the ground. How had she been stupid enough to get herself into this situation? No one else she knew had been kidnapped. Only her. She had to be a special kind of stupid. It was no wonder no one at school ever wanted anything to do with her. In fact, the only guy who ever had any kind of an interest in her was a fake. He was a stalker. Some old dude, determined to turn her into his probably-dead daughter.

She put her head onto her knees and sobbed again. What was she going to do? Was there any possibility of her getting out? Even if she managed to get one bale on top of another, would she be able to get enough piled up to reach those boards?

And did it even matter? Her family would think she ran away. Maybe they would think she was happier without them. If Chester came back and killed her, it might be the best thing for everyone.

Face still on her knees, she continued to wail. What was the point of trying to get away? So she could go back to school and have everyone laugh at her and call her fat?

What was she fighting for, really? Was going back really so important? She could imagine the comments her "friends" were probably leaving on that post about her running away. They were probably telling her to stay away, saying good riddance. It was probably her most-liked post of all time.

Memories

ALYSSA STOOD BY the window in her bedroom, staring into the woods behind their house. She had run out of tears, but not grief. The longer Macy was missing, the more it ate away at her. She thought of the last thing she had said to her daughter the night before. It had been an irritated list of things for her to do over the weekend.

Why hadn't she given Macy a hug? Told her how much she loved her? A fresh lump formed in her throat. Sure, her kids annoyed her with their selfishness and lack of responsibility, but they were teenagers. Being moody and messy was practically in their job description. Alyssa hadn't forgotten being a teenager. Why couldn't she be more understanding? She had always promised herself that she wouldn't turn into her mom.

She was like her own kids in many ways, now that she thought about it. She was focused on her appearance, going to the gym daily. She was also busy distracting herself from the pain of the recent direction of her marriage.

Alyssa looked around her room. She missed the days when she and Chad would spend hours in there, talking and dreaming. If only he was there to hold her. Alyssa wanted to pour her heart out to him, but she couldn't even bring herself to leave the room and find him.

He had been in his study, avoiding her since they found out about Macy. He probably felt guilty—as he should. He was the one who had driven Macy to run away, if in fact that was what had happened.

Macy had to have snapped and run off, not wanting to be controlled any longer. Alyssa could remember hating control when she was a teenager. She had wanted so badly to be seen as an adult.

Her eyes landed on her old scrapbooks, sitting under a pile of other books. She hadn't looked at those in years. She walked over and picked them up, sliding the other books onto the shelf. She took the scrapbooks to the bed and opened the one that had Macy's baby pictures.

Alyssa couldn't help smiling at the memories in front of her. She needed to look at these more often to remind herself how much her kids meant to her. It was easy to forget when they threw their snarky attitudes at her, but seeing the old pictures made her heart swell with love. They were the same as they always had been, only bigger now, and rightfully wanting some independence.

She flipped through the pages until she couldn't keep her eyes open any longer. She gave into their heaviness and rested her head on top of one of the pages, giving into sleep.

Fear

MACY WATCHED THE rain drip down the wall next to her. She hadn't heard the truck return, and had no idea when Chester would be back. She was no longer hungry. She had spent so much time skipping meals that it got to the point where being hungry felt good.

Her stomach stopped rumbling while she was crying earlier, and she was grateful for some kind of pleasure. She wasn't sure how long the good feeling would last. Usually it went away when she saw or smelled food. The soup above was probably disgusting from sitting there so long, and knowing that helped her stomach to continue feeling good.

With every passing minute, she became less and less convinced she'd be able to get out. No matter how hard she tried, she couldn't get even one bale on top of another.

She thought about her brother. What did Alex think of her disappearance? He was so hard to read these days. They still got along, but they weren't close. It was as though something had come between them. His teasing bothered her more because of that, but she never said anything, not wanting to give him another reason to make fun of her.

He would be worried, though. It gave her comfort realizing that. Sure, he could be the most annoying kid on the planet, but he cared about her. He had been the first one to notice when she started starving herself. He had practically begged her to stop. Deep down, he was still the sweet kid he had always been.

She pulled more hay over herself and turned away from the wall. She could still hear water streaming down. It made her have to pee again, but she didn't want to get up. She'd wait until she couldn't hold it.

Was her best bet to pretend to be Heather? She really had no chance at escaping, unless the psycho moved her somewhere else. Why would he? He probably knew she wouldn't be able to get out.

Thunder cracked, and she jumped. She pulled more hay over herself, trying to hide from it.

If she pretended to be Heather, would he give her more freedom? An actual bed, maybe? Would he let her stay in the farmhouse with him? Obviously she wouldn't get her cell phone back, but lying in a bed sounded so nice. Maybe she would even get some fresh clothes.

Maybe if she pretended to be his daughter, he would be nice to her. What if he continued to be a jerk? What had happened to the real Heather, anyway? She could try to find out if he let her out of the basement. It was worse than being in jail. Prisoners at least had rights and meals. She had nothing.

Why was she even considering giving into him? That was what he wanted. She was down there so he could turn her into an obedient captive. Macy had taken psychology. That was exactly his plan. But maybe if she knew that, she would be able to keep herself from getting Stockholm's syndrome and becoming sympathetic to him.

He wouldn't really go back and kill her family. He was only playing her.

Macy needed a new plan, and unfortunately, that meant she was going to have to pretend to be his daughter. She would have to think of herself as a performer. The farm was her stage, that jerk was her audience. On the outside, she would be Heather, but on the inside, she would remain Macy.

She had to. It was her only real hope of escape.

Was the time passing slowly, or was that jerk staying away for a long time to mess with her? She rolled back over and looked up at the boards.

She had probably been dreaming, thinking she could actually get out on her own. Chester would have taken every measure to make sure she couldn't get out. He might have even put something in the bales to make them heavier.

Now that she wanted out, she wasn't sure what was worse: being alone in the horrid dungeon or pretending to be Heather and acting like Chester was her dad. She didn't even want to look at him, much less act like his kid, but it was her only hope of escape.

A noise outside caught her attention. At first, she thought it was the rumbling thunder again. Soon it sounded like wheels on gravel. Her heart picked up speed. Was he coming to check on her? Would she soon be climbing the rope ladder to never see the awful room again?

Macy held her breath, listening to the sound of crunching gravel. She sat up when she heard a slight squeal of brakes. She couldn't hear anything over the pounding of her heart.

"Please come in the barn," she whispered.

She took several deep breaths, trying to calm her racing heart. She heard a car door slam, followed by what sounded like footsteps over wet gravel. Soon, all she could hear was the rain. She held her breath, trying to hear more.

Something moved above her. She heard shuffling noises. Something clicked, and then creaked. Macy stared at the trap door, squeezing the hay in her hands.

The door opened, and after what seemed like forever, he put his face down where she could see it. "Looks like you've been busy. Did you throw a party while I was gone?" He laughed. "Did you have enough time to think about what we discussed?"

What they *discussed*? She stared at him, refusing to answer. She wanted to choose her words carefully. If she said the wrong thing, he might lock her up again.

"Not feeling talkative? I've got some things for you, if you're ready for them, Heather. We'll start with a vegan lemon and asparagus pasta. You can have a shower and put on your new clothes. It's the same outfit you wanted before we went on our trip. Do you remember? Try to forget about what happened to your mother. There's no sense in replaying that in your mind over and over."

What was he talking about?

"Do you remember what you have to say in order to get out of here, Heather?"

Macy clenched her fists. "Yes, Dad."

His eyes widened, and then he smiled. "Good. Good. I'm so glad to hear it, Heather. You get this place cleaned up, and I'll get everything ready." He slammed the door shut, and then Macy could hear the click of the lock.

She stared at the door in disbelief. He hadn't let her out? How much longer was she going to be down there? Tears filled her eyes, and she wiped them away before they could fall to her face.

What exactly did he mean by clean up? Did he only want her to pick up the hay she had thrown around? Or did he want her to put the bales back where they had been? Unable to bear the thought of spending any more time down there, she got up and started the process of moving the heavy bales back to their original positions. At one point, she slipped on the tube of lipstick.

Macy picked it up and examined it. It was an expensive brand. She recognized it as one that Zoey's mom liked to wear. It was strange that pricey makeup would be in a bale of hay in an underground cellar in the middle of nowhere. She didn't have the time or energy to figure out what it was doing there. She shoved it into the hay and continued to push the bale.

Angry tears filled her eyes as she pushed the hay around the room. What was it going to take to finally get out of the horrible, little room?

Her muscles burned from pushing the hay around. They weren't used to being used, and they protested. She had no other choice except to ignore them, right along with her stomach. The labor made her hungry again, and it didn't feel good in the slightest. Macy was getting dizzy, and beads of sweat broke out around her face.

Too tired to keep going, she stopped and leaned against the bale, breathing heavily. She tried listening for noises, hoping Chester would be back soon, but she couldn't hear anything over the sounds of her own heartbeat and her heavy breathing.

She noticed the individual pieces of hay she had thrown around the room. Sighing, she stood and picked up one after the other, stuffing them into the bale that had a dent from where she'd taken them, until there were no more left lying around on the floor. She looked around the room again, frustrated at how much more work she had to do to get the bales put back where they were originally.

Her legs and arms ached, as did her shoulders, back, and stomach. The last thing she wanted to do was push them around anymore. Did she dare risk leaving them as they were? He would probably know most of them still weren't where they belonged.

Macy kicked the nearest bale, hurting her toe inside the shoe. It felt like everything hurt, and her stomach growled. Her throat was parched, with her tongue practically sticking to the roof of her mouth. She knew she couldn't move another bale, at least not until she either had some food or rest.

Perhaps she could beg him to let her eat before moving the rest of them. She needed something. Her aching muscles couldn't be denied any longer, so she threw herself on the hay, unable to take her body's pleas any longer. Her eyes closed on their own, and she didn't fight them. She half-listened to the mice.

The now-familiar sounds of the door in the ceiling caught Macy's attention. She looked up to the door and saw Chester.

"It looks much better down here. You're finally ready to come to the house with me."

Clean

MACY STUMBLED AS she walked through the field between the barn and the farmhouse. It felt good to stretch her legs, and she hadn't realized how stale the air in the cell had been until she got out into the fresh, country air. She gulped it, even though her lungs burned.

They walked in silence. Macy had so many questions, but didn't want to risk getting thrown back into the hay room. At least until she had some food, and maybe even a shower. Both sounded like luxuries.

When they reached the house, Chester opened the door without unlocking it. He indicated for her to go in first. She walked in without looking at him. Smells of cooking food assaulted her, making her feel hungrier and yet a little nauseated.

"Doesn't it feel good to be back at your grandparents' house?" He closed the door. "Some things never change, do they? I swear, this place is the same as when I grew up here." He looked her over. "They certainly wouldn't approve of how filthy you are. Let's get to your room and you can clean yourself up. I need to put the blackberry pie in the oven, anyway. Do you remember where your room is?"

Was he crazy? Macy shook her head, still not looking at him.

"I thought you might have forgotten. They're right. We need to visit more often. They miss their only grandchild. They're due back soon, so I'm glad you finally came around. I don't know how I would have explained you being in that barn." He shook his head. "Follow me."

He went past her, down the hall, and stopped in front of one of the last doors. "Does this ring any bells?"

Macy shook her head again, keeping her gaze off him.

"We're going to have to work on your memory. I'll have to pull out our old family albums. It might hurt to see pictures of your mom, especially after what happened. I know your grandparents are going to ask about her. We're going to tell them she decided to stay in Paris. Can you do that?"

She nodded.

"Say it."

Macy took a deep breath. "Mom stayed in Paris."

"Good." He opened the door, showing what was obviously the room of a teenage girl.

Macy's eyes lit up despite herself. It was gorgeous, and most importantly, the bed was huge and looked really comfortable.

"Find yourself some clothes, and I'll show you to the bathroom. You probably don't remember where that is, either." He sounded irritated, as though it was a huge inconvenience to give her the tour of a house she had never seen before.

She walked past him into the room. As her gaze passed over the two windows, she noted that they were bolted down. Had he turned the house into a prison, too?

Opening a drawer, she picked out a shirt. She went through the rest of them, until she had a complete outfit. She looked down at what she was wearing. The dirty clothes would probably have to be burned.

"You done yet?" He tapped his toes.

Macy nodded, still facing away from him. She turned around and left the room, following him to the bathroom. It had a large tub, without a shower. She was going to have to take a bath. She couldn't even remember the last time she had taken one.

"Towels and everything you need are in there. Try not to take too long, because the food will get cold soon. I know how much you hate cold food, Heather."

She cringed at being called Heather, but figured she would have to get used to it for the time being.

He closed the door, and she turned around and locked it. She looked at everything in the cozy little country bathroom. It was all exactly what she would expect from a farmhouse bathroom. She turned the water on, got it to a comfortable temperature and jammed the plug into the drain at the bottom.

Macy looked down at her clothes again. She would have to get rid of them, not only because they were dirty beyond cleaning, but also because the psycho certainly wouldn't let her hang onto anything from her real life. She had to peel everything off, as it was all sticking to her skin.

Macy threw everything into the garbage. She stepped into the tub, but immediately jumped out. The water burned her frigid skin. She checked it with her fingers, finding it to be fine. She would have to climb in and let her exhausted body adapt to the temperature.

Once she acclimated to the water, she scrubbed herself clean. She didn't want to waste any time. Chester was sure to become angry if she took her time.

When she put on the clean clothes, she found them to be exactly her size. He had really done his homework, finding someone who even wore the same size as Heather. If Macy hadn't lost all that weight, she'd be too big to replace Heather. Then she might not even be in this mess. In a way, this mess was the fault of those jerks at school.

Macy shook her head. It didn't matter now. For now, she needed to eat and then explore the house to see if there was a way out.

Once dressed, she dug through the drawers to find a brush. All she could find was a comb, and it didn't want to go through her hair. But after everything else she had been through, that was a minor inconvenience.

Looking in the mirror, she barely recognized herself. Her skin looked horrible, and she had dark circles under her eyes. Her stomach rumbled as she combed her hair into place as best as she could.

She rummaged through the drawers for makeup, but found none. Seriously? Nothing? Macy sighed. It probably didn't matter. Who was she trying to impress?

Macy hung the towel on a hook and took a deep breath. Now was the moment of truth. She was going to have to walk into the kitchen and face her abductor. Hopefully he would feed her without making her jump through any more hoops. Her stomach growled again. She could smell the cooking food, and it made her mouth water.

Turning the doorknob, she took another deep breath as she prepared herself for what would come. As she walked down the hall, she could hear a TV. It sounded like the evening news. They were talking about politics. Boring.

When she entered the kitchen, she saw two places set at the table. Her fake dad had his back to her, cooking something over the stove. She stood still, not wanting to alert him to her presence. She looked around the room, hoping to find a way of escape. Not that she expected to get away just yet—all she wanted was to eat, anyway. She would attempt to get away later, perhaps while he slept.

Finally, unable to take the smell of the food, she cleared her throat. He turned around. "Oh, good. You're all cleaned up. You must be starving. Sit down and eat. Tomorrow's a big day."

Macy raised an eyebrow. What did that mean? She didn't intend to stick around and find out. She would go along with him for the time being, but at night she could find a way to escape. Then she would never have to know what else was up his sleeve.

He laughed. "Don't seem so surprised, Heather. We need to get you ready to see your grandparents again. Sit and eat. I know you're hungry." He turned back to the stove.

She stared at the food on the table, the smells tempting her. Finally she walked to the table. As she pulled the chair out, her mouth watered enough that she had to swallow it to keep it from escaping.

Sitting, she stared at the pasta, the fruit salad, and the cornbread. She was so hungry that she wasn't even going to question what was in it. She'd already broken her vegan diet, who cared if the bread had milk or butter in it?

Piling the food on her plate, her hands shook from hunger. She stared at the full plate for a moment before picking up the fork.

Then she dug in, barely stopping to breathe as she emptied the plate. When she was done, she was surprised to see him sitting at the table, also eating.

He smiled at her. "So good to see you eating again, Heather. Have some more. I made it for you."

She held her face still. Would she get used to being called Heather? Now that she finally had some food, she wasn't going to complain.

"Tomorrow's a big day since you haven't seen your grandparents in so long. It's getting dark, so we'll get ready for bed soon."

Macy's heart skipped a beat. What did he mean by getting ready for bed? This nightmare wasn't going to get even worse, was it?

He set his glass down, and smiled again. "In case you forgot, my room is next to yours. So if you need anything tonight, that's where I'll be."

She let out a sigh of relief. It was bad enough that he was trying to convince her that she was his daughter, but at least that was all it was. At least he wasn't trying to make her into a wife.

"I'm not used to you being so quiet. Hopefully after a good night's sleep, we'll be able to pick up where we left off." He went back to eating.

Pick up from where? What had happened to the real Heather? Macy took the glass in front of her and drank it down. She looked at the food sitting on the table, but didn't dare take more, even though she could have eaten it all. Her stomach had been empty, so she had to take it easy or she would throw up, and he would make her clean it up again.

"Are you full?"

She nodded.

"You want dessert? I can save it for tomorrow. I know how much you like cold pie for breakfast."

Cold pie for breakfast? That sounded weird, but also good. She shrugged her shoulders. Then she went back to the bathroom, with her mind racing. As she brushed her teeth, ignoring the fact that the toothbrush was obviously not new, she decided to stay awake as long as possible. She would make her escape after he went to bed.

Communication

C HAD ENTERED THE bedroom, relieved to see Alyssa sleeping. He hadn't wanted to deal with her any more than he had to. The looks she shot him while they spoke with the cops told him that she blamed him for all of this. It wasn't his fault Macy had run off with that kid. He didn't tell her to do that. In fact, he had set up the rules to avoid exactly this.

He didn't buy the story the cops were trying to sell them. He'd been studying her online profiles, and Macy's latest status update was nothing more than her flipping the bird at him in front of the whole world, especially since the post was public. She was saying loud and clear that she wouldn't be controlled. At least that's what he hoped. He couldn't bring himself to think about the alternative.

Reading through the comments on her post, it looked like a lot of her friends agreed with him. They were begging her to come back, and some kids were even apologizing for making fun of her at school. Everyone but the police and his family thought she was off having fun, and probably checking her account to see everyone's reactions.

Chad sat down next to Alyssa and picked up one of the photo albums. It opened to a page full of pictures of a camping trip they'd taken when the kids were younger. They all looked so happy roasting marshmallows. There was even a picture of him kissing Alyssa. A smile crept across his face as he remembered Macy snatching the camera and taking the picture, giggling and teasing them.

He set the scrapbook down and ran his fingers over Alyssa's hair. What had happened to them? They had been high school sweethearts, and each other's first love. Neither one had ever even gone on a date with anyone else. Maybe that was the problem. They knew each other too well. There was no more mystery or magic.

Only laundry and errands.

Chad had thought that would improve once Alyssa stopped working. Instead, the house was no cleaner, and they argued more. Apparently, not working only magnified the fact that he was so busy. It gave her more time to fret and fuss about them not spending as much time together as they used to.

Didn't she understand that it wouldn't last forever? Once he made enough with his blog to support the family, he would be able to quit his job. He could work on his blog at night and they could have the days to spend together. Or he could work during the day, and they could have long romantic evenings like they used to.

Alyssa stirred in her sleep. He brushed some hair away from her face. Her eyes opened and a look of surprise covered her face—but he saw none of her usual disdain.

"Shh." He moved some of her hair behind her ear. Looking at her ear, he remembered how much he used to love nibbling on it and making her giggle. He ran a finger along it. He looked back to her face, surprised to see her looking directly into his eyes.

"What are we going to do, Chad?" Tears shone in her eyes.

His heart nearly leapt out of his chest. He felt like he was young again, when he would have done anything to keep her from hurting. He pulled her up and held her in his arms. She shook and he rubbed her back, whispering that everything would be okay. He expected her to snap at him that he didn't know that, but she didn't.

Chad knew he should say something. If only his parents were alive. Oh how he missed being able to talk to them. His dad always knew the right thing to say.

Finally, she leaned back and looked at him again. "I don't know what I'll do if—"

Chad put a finger to her lips. "We can't think like that. We can't let ourselves go there. She just ran away, like her status update says, and then she'll be back."

"We don't know that. Don't we need to prepare ourselves in

case…?"

"Remember those CDs you used to make us listen to? We have to think positive."

Alyssa frowned.

"If the cops are right and Macy is in trouble—which I don't think is the case—then we need to do what we can to help her."

"Do you really believe that?" Alyssa asked.

"You don't?"

"Haven't you noticed I threw those CDs out?"

"Of course. You still know what was on them. We all do."

Alyssa's cell phone rang, and she glanced at it. "It looks like Sherry from down the street. I'm so tired of talking on the phone. I only want to leave it on in case Macy tries to call." She pushed ignore.

Chad nodded. "Between my phone and the land line, I'm ready to smash them all."

"If it weren't for the chance of Macy calling, I would join you."

He smiled. "Could you imagine that? Us running around, destroying the phones?"

One corner of Alyssa's mouth curled up. "That would be quite a sight."

Chad's phone rang. "We could always start now. I've been wanting to upgrade anyway."

She shook her head. "Who's calling now?"

He looked at his phone. "Sherry again."

"Maybe we should answer. What if it's important?"

Chad handed her his phone.

Alyssa rolled her eyes, but took it anyway. "Sherry?"

"Hi, Alyssa. I'm sorry to bother you, and I won't keep you. I want to let you know that a bunch of the kids from the high school put together a candlelight service at the park near your house. It's supposed to start around seven. Then in the morning, there's going to be a rally. Missing posters have been printing all day and people are going to hand them out."

Alyssa stared into space, trying to take it all in. "I'm a terrible mother."

Chad gave her a questioning look.

"What do you mean?" Sherry asked. "Of course you're a wonderful mom."

"I should have been the one to put all that stuff together. I've been sitting around feeling sorry for myself."

"You're doing everything you can. You've been talking with the police and everything, dear. The community wants to rally around you. The news keeps talking about the worst, but the good news is that everyone is banding together. Everyone wants to help Macy return safely."

"Thanks, Sherry. Where's the rally?"

"Everyone is meeting at the high school around eight in the morning. You guys don't need to show up, but I think the support would really help."

"Of course we'll help. We'll be at the front of the line."

"We'll see you tonight. Just to let you know, the news media will probably be there."

"Good. The more coverage, the better. Thanks, Sherry." Alyssa ended the call and looked at Chad.

"What's going on?"

She repeated everything Sherry had told her, barely getting through without tears.

Chad held her again. "We'll get through all of this—and of course you're not a bad mom. How could you say that? You're the best mom around."

Alyssa couldn't hold the tears in any longer. She buried her face in his chest and sobbed.

The broken look on her face made him want to make everything right again. He kissed the top of her head and held her until she calmed down. "We've done what we could. Dealing with the police has been time consuming and stressful. They're being nice enough, but still treating us like we could be criminals. Family is always the first suspect."

"They need to get out there and find *Macy*."

"Between the fliers and the news coverage, everyone is going to know what Macy looks like, and hopefully someone will see her. When they do, they'll recognize her immediately."

"I hope she didn't get kidnapped. Do you think that's what happened?"

"I've been staring at that status update, and it sounded exactly like her. They say a predator could have forced her to log in and write that, but I don't know what to think. I've been so sure she was flipping us a giant bird for all to see, but with each passing hour, I start to doubt a bit more. She wouldn't be gone this long on purpose, would she?"

Alyssa shook again, more tears falling down her face. "It's not like her. She always threatens us before she does something. Even before going vegan, remember? She told us several times if we didn't start making healthier meals, she was going to follow the Hollywood trend and get skinny like the actors."

"I don't want to think about her being abducted. I can't." Chad blinked away tears of his own. "Teenagers are impulsive. They don't think anything through. She's been complaining that I let Alex get away with murder. She may have decided to stick it to me, and now she's afraid to come back, knowing I'll ground her."

"We need to give her more freedom. We have to. She's right. Her younger brother can do more than her."

Chad took a deep breath. "I don't want to have this argument now. We need to stick together. I don't know about you, but I can't make it through this, living at odds like we have been."

Alyssa looked like she was going to say something, but nodded instead. Chad moved the scrapbooks out of the way. "Let's get some rest before the rally." He grabbed his phone. "What time should I set the alarm?"

"Six."

He got comfortable and extended his arm. She crawled next to him and for the first time in a long while, they fell asleep in each other's arms.

Thwarted

MACY SAT IN the bed, listening for sounds of her fake dad going to bed. She could hear a sitcom, and every once in a while, his laughter. She didn't want to lie down—if her head felt the pillow, she knew she would be asleep right away.

It had already been two hours. When was he going to go to bed? She yawned, unable to deny how tired she was. Sleeping in a bale of hay had been almost as bad as not sleeping at all. Sleeping in the truck had been even worse.

She could hear music, and it sounded like a new show starting. Maybe he was staying up on purpose—to keep her inside. His laughter drifted in through the door along with canned laughter from the sitcom, as though in response to her thoughts.

Perhaps sleep was her best option, at least for the time being. Maybe it would take a couple of days for him to trust her enough for her to get away.

Giving into her heavy eyes, she set the alarm for eight, figuring that would be enough time. She wouldn't need a shower, and the cold pie would already be ready.

She dug through the drawers for some pajamas. At least Heather had comfortable ones.

Who was Heather, anyway? Aside from being his daughter, of course. Being in her room, Macy had a feel for the kinds of things she liked, but still knew nothing about her. Most importantly, where was she?

It sounded like her mom had been killed, but she didn't know for sure. She was supposed to say the mother was staying in Paris. Macy shook her head. Whatever had happened to Heather, it couldn't have been good.

Unless she and her mom really had stayed in Paris. It stood to reason that they would have wanted to get away from Chester. Maybe they were living it up under the Eiffel Tower—eating cold pie for breakfast—while Macy was forced to be the fill-in daughter.

She climbed into bed and pulled the covers up. She looked around the room before lying down. If she wasn't able to make her escape soon, she would go through the room to figure out what she could. She turned off the light on the nightstand.

As her head hit the pillow, she fell right to sleep. She dreamed of her family and Zoey. In her dreams, she was back home and everything was back to normal, except for everyone asking her where she had gone.

Macy sat up in bed, clutching the blankets. She didn't know what had woken her. She couldn't remember any bad dreams, nor did she think she heard any sounds. The house was quiet, so much so that she could hear some of the animals from the barn. Maybe that was what had woken her.

She certainly wasn't used to those noises when she slept in a bed.

The sun was starting to come up.

Could this be her chance? She climbed out of bed, holding her breath, fearful to make even a small noise. She tip-toed to the door, cringing each time her foot found a squeaky board.

Macy took a slow, quiet, deep breath before grabbing the doorknob. Should she get dressed first? In case she was able to make a run for it? She shook her head, holding her breath. She needed to check everything out first.

Turning the knob as slow as possible, she was relieved to find that it made no noise. She pulled the door open, silent except the noise of it sliding over the carpet. She stepped out of the room and gasped, covering her mouth.

Leaning against the wall, on the floor in front of her was the picture he had stolen from her house. Her parents, her brother and herself all smiled from the frame. She stared at it for a moment before closing the door as quietly as she could, her heart pounding nearly out of her chest.

She leaned against the closed door, trying to catch her breath.

He was reminding her of his threat to kill her family if she tried to get away. He was letting her know that he had gotten into her house once, and he could do it again.

Her heart sank. She couldn't risk the lives of her family.

What if she ran away, and then he went straight to her home and killed them?

She looked around the room. What if Chester had killed Heather and her mother? Someone crazy enough to kidnap would be nuts enough to kill.

Shaking, she climbed back into the warm bed. Even with the covers pulled up, she couldn't stop shivering.

What was she going to do? She couldn't live here, pretending to be Heather. Someone would have to figure it out, wouldn't they? He had said something about grandparents. Surely they would know Macy wasn't their granddaughter. They would have to. Even if Macy looked exactly like her, there was no way she spoke and acted like her.

Heather had to have gone to school and had friends. *They* would know she wasn't Heather. Zoey would know right away if someone posed as Macy.

Pulling her knees to her chest, Macy held her legs close, and took deep breaths. She couldn't stop shaking, nor would her heart slow down.

Even though she had called Chester "dad," he didn't trust her yet. How long would that take? When would she have enough trust to be able to sneak away?

She sighed and looked around the room, which was slowly getting lighter. If she stayed up a little longer, she'd have enough light to go through the room and see if she could find anything out about the girl who had lived there.

Hopefully, Heather was in Paris with her mom, but what were the chances of that? Who was Macy kidding? She couldn't imagine Chester leaving without them. He would have insisted they come with him, even if he had to threaten them. Either they had run away, like Macy wanted to, or Chester had done something to them, like he had threatened to do to her family.

She had finally stopped shaking. Even though she knew she would have to get up soon, she still felt sleepy. With a little more rest, she would have the energy to get away if given the chance.

Sometime later a loud, obnoxious beeping woke her up. She sat up, looking for the alarm, not remembering where it was. When she saw it, she hit every button until it turned off.

She would have to fix that before she set it again. Macy was a light sleeper. She didn't need an alarm loud enough to wake the dead.

Pulling the covers up, she wanted to stay in bed. She remembered the horrible room under the barn. At least this was better than that. She had an actual bed, and even food. She could even pee in a toilet. Who would have thought that would be a blessing?

Macy got up and went to the drawers, finding something to wear. The clothes were dull compared to what she normally wore, but at least they were clean.

She found a couple pieces of makeup in a box on top of the dresser—mascara and pale lip-gloss. She was going to have to get used to seeing herself without eyeliner, unless she was allowed to go to the store and get some—which she figured was out of the question.

Using the mirror on top of the dresser, she put the makeup on, refusing to think of how gross it was to wear someone else's products. Her mom had always lectured her on how unhygienic that was. But what else was she supposed to do? She was even wearing Heather's underwear, which she didn't want to think about.

When Macy was done, she looked in vain for a brush. She would have to go to the bathroom.

Macy took a deep breath. She didn't want to face the picture again. But when she opened the door, she was surprised to see it was gone.

Was he messing with her? She almost laughed at herself. Of course he was messing with her. That's what all of this was about.

She found a brush in the bathroom. Her hair had gone wild, sticking out in every direction. Brushing only made it worse. She dug through the drawers, hoping to find something. There were no gels or anything. Didn't the girl even have a cheap, drugstore brand flat iron?

Something?

All she found was a small container full of hair bands. She pulled out a black one and pulled her hair back into a ponytail. Yuck. She hated how she looked in those. She saw some clips and pulled her bangs back too. There was no way she would be able to style her side bangs without a flat iron or hairspray.

Macy looked in the mirror. She looked like someone else with her hair pulled back and barely any makeup. Was that the point? So she would forget who she really was?

Her stomach rumbled, so she went to the kitchen. Chester sat at the table, reading a newspaper. Some music played in the background. *Music? That's classy*, Macy thought sarcastically.

He looked up. "Oh, good. You have barely enough time to eat. I left the pie in the fridge, so it will be as cold as possible—just how you like it, Heather. Grab some and sit down. I've already eaten."

She nodded, not wanting to engage him in conversation. As she walked to the fridge, she could feel his eyes on her. She remembered him shoving her into the side of the truck, threatening her. Chills ran down her back, but she got the pie out, doing her best to act normal—whatever "normal" meant.

Macy opened a couple of cupboards, looking for a plate.

"Don't tell me you forgot where those are too, Heather. Over the microwave." He sighed with heavy dramatic flair. What a tool.

She grabbed a plate and put a piece of pie on it. She found the utensils on her first try. Then she sat down across from him, as far away as she could get. She ate the pie, which was too sweet for breakfast, trying to ignore him.

"You're not talkative, are you?"

Shoving pie into her mouth, she shrugged, not looking up at him.

"Well, I'm sure that will change in time. You have to get used to being here. So how did you sleep?"

She shrugged again.

"That's not an answer. How did you sleep?"

"Fine."

"Do you want to know what we're doing today?"

"Sure." Macy kept eating, not taking her eyes off the food.

"First, we're going to get your hair done."

She looked up at him in surprise. What did that mean?

"You look too different from how you did before our trip to France. We'll need to lighten your hair. Your mom always insisted on getting your hair colored. Obviously all that's grown out. Then you'll look exactly like your old self. When we're done with that, your grandparents should be back. Won't that be fun? They've really missed you."

Macy's heart raced, and tears sprung to her eyes. She blinked them away.

"Don't look so crestfallen, Heather. Change is good. I think we'll cut your hair as well. We'll say you decided to do that while we were away. It was the style over there."

Her stomach twisted in knots. She didn't want to cut her hair—or color it. She liked it long and dark brown. Was he going to strip away everything about her identity? She remembered the pictures of Heather. She had long hair in every one of them. "But H—my hair was never short. Look at all the pictures over there."

"Like I said, change is good."

"Are you afraid I'm going to look too much like the pictures in the news with my hair long?" Macy hadn't meant to say that. She backed up, afraid of the look on his face.

"What did you say?"

"Um, that I'd like to talk about this?"

He leapt up and came at her, grabbing her arms and squeezing hard before forcing her out of her chair. "Don't ever talk back to me. Do you understand? Ever. Unless you want to find yourself back in the barn. Is that what you want?" He pushed her, shoving her against the fridge.

Macy shook her head.

"Good. Because your grandparents are coming soon, and you need to be on your best behavior. Not acting like this." He pulled her back and threw her against a cabinet, a handle jamming into her side.

Macy let out a cry.

He glared at her, his nostrils flaring. "Don't you forget it." He stormed out of the room.

Desperate

C HAD CHECKED HIS blog for comments, holding on to hope that someone would have seen Macy. Per the norm for the last few days, he hadn't been able to sleep. Even when he did manage to drift off, a nightmare would wake him up.

He always went to where he was loved—his blog. After the candle-light vigil in the park, he had written a heart-wrenching post about Macy's disappearance. He knew the news was national, and he was already getting some comments on his other posts asking about the situation, so a post about her was exactly what was needed.

It had helped him to feel better. Not only was he able to get his feelings, his own story, out there, but it might help to get her back too. His daughter could be anywhere, and his readers were from all over the world. He had hits from nearly every country on the globe.

Chad had uploaded all kinds of pictures of Macy onto the post. First, he had put their latest family photo. That was already on his "About Me" page. It was a perfect picture. Then he grabbed some from his phone and also Macy's social media accounts. Did all teenagers post so many pictures of themselves?

She had pictures of herself doing everything under the sun. He had griped about it before, but now, with her being gone, he couldn't have been more grateful. Not only could he use them on his blog, but they had become special to him in a way they never were before. He couldn't stop looking at them.

His heart broke, wishing he had taken more time for her. He had spent entirely too much time harping on her. He had told her to wear more colors, smile more, study more, eat some meat once in a while, and stop posting silly stuff all the time.

Why hadn't he taken some time to get to know her, instead of always trying to change her? Looking through the pictures now, he noticed how beautiful she was. She also looked a little sad, even through all the goofiness.

Hadn't he learned anything when he lost his parents in that car accident? He knew how suddenly someone he loved could be snatched from him.

Scrolling through the pictures on his post, he sighed. What if she had run away with that dipstick kid she met online? Would she come back, or had he pushed her so far away that she never wanted to return? Or what if the police were right and that kid wasn't a kid at all, but a child abductor?

Chad needed a new post. He needed to keep getting the word out about Macy. He went into his dashboard to schedule a new post for the next day when he noticed his stats. His blog had more than tripled its usual page views. In fact, it was close to quadruple.

People really *were* paying attention to his story about Macy. He needed to post about her often. The more he posted, the more likely it was that someone would recognize his daughter from somewhere. Maybe his blog would be what saved her.

He opened a new tab and went to Macy's profile again. There were hundreds of new messages posted from her friends. Chad saw that some of the kids had even put pictures of Macy along with their posts. He needed to put some of those in his upcoming blog posts.

After uploading about a dozen new pictures to the post, he realized he was out of words. What was there to say? There were no new developments in the case. She was still missing, and he wanted someone to find her. Chad couldn't handle her being gone any longer. Someone somewhere knew something, and his blog was the best way to reach that person.

Sure, the news was reaching a lot of people, but they weren't saying what he wanted them to say. Both times his family had been interviewed, what they said was edited down to practically nothing. At least on his blog, which ten thousand people were looking at every day now, he could say what he wanted.

People were so curious, and he was sure that the names of his entire family were being searched at unprecedented numbers. That was obviously why his blog was getting so many more hits than normal. He had to take advantage of that. He began typing again.

Thank you all for your concern about my daughter, Macy Mercer. This is obviously a sports blog, but you surely understand the posts about the horrors my family is enduring.

Writing about sports with my typical humor isn't in my heart, and I appreciate your understanding. To my fans, I'll get back into it as soon as I can—when Macy is back home, safe and sound. For those of you who are here to learn more about Macy, please see my last post. You'll find pictures not shown on the news sites, and you'll hear about everything from my own perspective, minus the media edits and BS.

Not that I don't appreciate the media getting the word out there, but if you know me, and I know many of you don't, I get tired of the media's crap on a regular basis. They only tell people what they want to hear. It's not real reporting.

My previous post, that's the real story. That's what's going on with my daughter. She snuck out to meet some boy online and now she's gone. All you girls reading this—learn from Macy's mistake. Don't meet a boy you don't know by yourself. If you feel the need to sneak out because you think your parents are too strict, then set up a group date. Please. Just stay safe.

Practically nothing is known about the guy that my daughter met online. His name was supposedly Jared, but all of his social profiles have been removed. The police think he might have actually been a man posing as a boy. It would have been easy for him to snatch a picture of some random kid and pretend to be a friendly teenager.

I hope to God that's not the case. I would much rather Macy be off with some harmless kid, sticking her tongue out at me for being over-protective. But with each passing hour, that scenario becomes less and less believable.

Seeing the worry in Macy's best friend's eyes tells me that my daughter hasn't contacted her either. If this were about Macy sneak-ing out or even running away to get our attention, she would have contacted her best friend. What fifteen-year-old girl could go that long without instant messaging, or whatever it is kids are up to this month?

Please, please pay attention to the pictures in this post and my last one. There are pictures of her with her hair pulled back, down straight, curled, and wearing hats. Who knows what she could look like when she walks down the street next to you?

Macy didn't take any extra clothes or makeup. She wasn't planning on being gone for more than the evening. Someone has my baby girl, and one of you could be the one to help find her. Thank you again.

Chad pushed the schedule button and then sat back in his chair. So much for not having any words. He took a deep breath, ignoring the lump in his throat. What else could he do? His work had given him the week off with pay, so he had nothing to do except worry about Macy.

He looked at his scheduled post, scanning for errors. He couldn't see any mistakes, but that didn't mean anything. He wasn't thinking straight.

Going back to Macy's Facebook profile, he saw even more comments from friends. Or at least he assumed they were her friends. Maybe she had opened her page up for anyone to see. It had obviously been too long since he had given her a lecture about Internet safety. He was online all the time, he should have been more aware of what his kids were doing.

Reading all the messages, his eyes became heavy. He looked out the window and saw that it was still dark. He knew he wouldn't sleep long anyway, so he turned off his screen and went to the couch at the far end of his office. He pulled an afghan over himself and fell right to sleep.

Changes

MACY STOOD BY the window in Heather's room, looking outside. Absentmindedly, she ran her fingers along the tops of the nails that kept her inside. Leaves lay all over the ground, and the ones in the shade still had frost on them.

She heard a noise behind her and turned around. Chester held a gray plastic bag in one hand. "We have something to take care of."

"What?" Macy eyed the bag, unable to tell what was inside.

"No questions. Follow me."

Her shoulders slumped, and she followed him into the bathroom.

"Ladies first." He moved aside.

Macy's heart pounded as she stepped inside. He grabbed a dark green towel and wrapped it around her shoulders. Then he pulled a white box from the plastic bag and set it on the counter. It was a box of hair dye.

"What's that?" Macy exclaimed. He was actually going to change her hair color, wasn't he?

"I said no questions." He opened the box, looked at the instructions, poured one bottle of stuff into another, and then shook it. The liquid turned a bright, orange color. He turned to her, and Macy held her breath. He had to be joking.

Chester squeezed the cold liquid onto her hair and rubbed it in. He piled the hair in a messy heap on her head and told her not to move. Then he pulled out his phone and appeared to play a game.

Macy looked into the mirror in horror. What was he doing to her hair? After what felt like an eternity, he forced her head into the sink and rinsed out the dye. She gasped in shock at the sight of her newly colored hair.

"Use the towel to dry it." He shoved another towel at her.

She stared at him in disbelief.

"Was I speaking in a foreign language? Dry your hair!"

Macy flipped her head down in front of her stomach and dried it as best she could with only a towel.

Chester pointed to the toilet. "Sit."

Blood drained from Macy's head. "You want me to go to the bathroom?"

His eyebrows came together. "No. I'm cutting your hair. Now sit!"

She sat.

Chester pulled out a large pair of scissors.

"Have you cut hair before?"

"I watched a video online. Now shut up."

Macy's stomach twisted in knots. She closed her eyes, unable to watch. The slicing, snipping sounds of the scissors sounded all around her head.

"Done," Chester said. "Now, we need to get ready for your grandparents' return. They're eager to see you. Do you remember what to say when they ask about your mom?"

Macy clenched her fists. "She's still in Paris."

"Perfect. After lunch, it'll be time to clean."

Macy nodded and stood up. She glanced at the mirror, almost unable to recognize herself. It was still her face, but she looked so different with lighter, shorter hair. To her surprise, the haircut actually looked almost professional.

Chester directed her to the kitchen to make sandwiches. He turned on the TV and flipped through the channels, landing on the news. The newscasters were discussing a missing person. Then her latest school photo flashed on the screen.

Macy's heart skipped a beat, and then it raced.

He changed the station to some western movie. He turned to her as though nothing had happened. "Put plenty of meat on my sandwich."

She nodded, and went to the fridge to see what she could put on the sandwiches. Shaking, she pulled out all vegetables for hers. Once those were on the counter, she found stuff he wanted: lunch meats, mayo, and cheese. She didn't see any vegan mayo, so she'd have to use the one made with egg.

If she could even eat. She was still shaking from the shock of seeing her face—and old hairstyle—on the news. Did that mean her family knew she hadn't really run away? Or were they treating her case as a missing runaway? She'd barely heard anything before Chester changed the station.

Macy took a deep breath, trying to calm herself. She was going to spill something if she didn't. She spread the four pieces of bread on the counter and organized everything else. Once her hands were steady, she made his sandwich. Then she cut the cucumbers and everything else she needed for hers.

She put the food away, and then put the sandwiches on plates. She took them to the table before grabbing some grapes and chips, setting those in the middle of the table. Hopefully that would meet his expectations.

She sat down, hoping he wouldn't notice. But he did. He got up and sat next to her. "This looks great. You always make a great lunch, Heather."

Macy shrugged, not looking up. She bit into her sandwich, trying to ignore the strong taste of non-vegan mayo. It assaulted her taste buds, but she knew that was the least of her problems.

Her family was actually looking for her, but they had no idea where she was. *She* didn't even know.

Chester stood up. "When you're done, it'll be time to clean up. You can clean the kitchen and living room. I'm going to go back and clean the bathroom and your grandparents' room."

Was he actually going to leave her alone?

Macy waited, expecting him to return or something else to happen. There was no way that he would leave her in the big, open front part of the house…was there? Unless it was some kind of test to see if she would listen. She looked around for a hidden camera, but couldn't see anything.

Her heart started racing. Was this her chance to get away, or would she end up back in the barn? He wouldn't do that, though. He was too eager for her to meet his parents.

She tip-toed into the hallway leading to the front door. He was down the other hall, near the bedrooms.

"Did you need something?" he asked.

"No. I was looking for something, but I…don't see it." She hurried back into the living room. Going through the front door wasn't going to work. If she went that way again and he was still there testing her, he would definitely know something was up.

Macy wandered around the living room, looking at the pictures again. His parents looked like nice, happy people, but they had raised him, so who knew? They could be monsters, too. She looked at another picture of Heather. It was unnerving, because the picture could have been Macy—especially with the new haircut and color.

The house was still quiet. She looked around at the big windows. If she was able to open one and get outside, she should be able to get enough of a head start to get away. It didn't matter that she had no idea where she was. She could figure it out when she found a road.

Holding her breath, she looked around. She couldn't see anything stopping her. The windows weren't locked down. This was her chance, and she had to take it right then. Who knew when she would be able to try to get away again?

She walked over to one of the windows. Her pulse was on fire as she looked for a way to unlock the window. It was unlike any window she had ever seen. There were ropes at the top, which were obviously used for opening and closing it somehow. She would have to open it and hope for the best. The window only needed to be opened enough for her to squeeze out.

Macy saw a knob and twisted it around. Something clicked. She turned around to make sure that he hadn't returned. She was still alone. She put her fingers in two grooves at the bottom and pulled up. The window opened!

She pulled it further, but not much because it was surprisingly heavy. That's when a loud, high-pitched screaming sound surrounded her.

The alarm.

He came around the hallway, glaring at her. The look on his face was scarier than it had been at any other point. Macy backed up and looked at the window, which still wasn't open wide enough for her to squeeze through.

"I…I was just—"

Eyes narrowed, he grabbed her elbow, squeezing painfully. He dragged her to the front door where a coat rack stood. He pushed it aside and punched buttons on a white box. The alarm finally stopped.

"The alarm is set. If any of the doors or windows are opened, that horrible alarm you hate so much will go off. It looks like you figured that out already, didn't you?" He squeezed harder, his eyebrows coming together.

He grabbed her other arm and shook her so that her head hit one of the hooks on the coat rack. He shoved her back, digging her back into the wooden rack. Jackets pushed around her face. "I thought we had an understanding. You were going to obey. We need to get the house cleaned before your grandparents get here, Heather." He yanked her back and threw her against the opposite wall.

She hit her head again. "I thought we could use some fresh air. Look at the window. It's only opened a crack."

He grabbed her shoulders and pushed her further against the wall and lifted her so that she wasn't able to touch the floor. "No fresh air! We're already out in the country. We couldn't ask for better quality air. Don't do anything to change the house—ever again! Do you understand me?" Spit flew onto her face. Macy couldn't wipe it away.

She nodded.

His angry eyes came closer to hers. "It looks as though I'm going to have to do the cleaning myself. You're going to spend some time in your room and think about what you've done. When your grandparents get here, you need to be on your best behavior. Do you understand?"

"Yes." She squirmed, hoping he would let go of her.

"When they get here, you're not to try anything funny. Nothing! The only reason I'm not sending you back to the barn is because they're so close to arriving. Keep that in mind." He shoved her and then let go.

Macy fell to the ground and then stood up. At least she had tried to get away. It hadn't worked, but she had tried.

Discovery

THE BEDROOM DOOR closed behind Macy. She could hear something slide against it, keeping her inside. She sighed, looking around the room.

She needed to calm down. Obviously, there was no texting or online games, but maybe Heather had some books. Then Macy could at least escape into her mind for a little while.

She couldn't see any books, but there had to be something. Macy would even take classic literature at that point, as much as she would have preferred to read about some hot vampires or werewolves.

Where would books be? Maybe near the stuffed animals. Macy had all but ignored that part of the room. There was a small shelf underneath the little hammock holding the toys. She sat down and looked at it. The top row was full of DVDs, which she wouldn't be able to watch.

Macy scanned the books on the next shelf. Most of them *were* literary—things teachers forced kids to read. One had an interesting title that she had never heard of. She grabbed it and noticed that it felt odd.

What was that? She narrowed her eyes and looked inside the book. It didn't open as easily as a book should. When she had it open, she saw that it had been hollowed out and another book rested in it. It looked like a diary.

Her heart stopped. Was that Heather's journal?

This might be her opportunity to find out more about what happened.

Her pulse pounded so loud in her ears that she was afraid Chester would hear it. She took a couple of deep, long breaths. She had to focus. Once she calmed down, she turned to the first entry. Her hands shook.

The first entries were pretty basic stuff.

Heather liked some boy at school, she hated homework, one girl in the neighborhood wouldn't stop bothering her...wait. Neighborhood? Where had they been living? Definitely not on the farm. There was nothing even close to neighbors. Not once had Macy been able to see anything other than farmland.

She wanted to read every word in the journal, but knew she didn't have much time left. She flipped through the pages, skimming the first few lines of each entry.

One caught her attention about a third of the way through. *My mom is still not back.* Macy stopped. She had never bought the story about Heather's mom running off with some guy in France—not that Macy would blame her for running from Chester.

Macy went back to the previous entry and read it word for word. More about the boy that Heather adored. Heather wasn't sure if the boy even knew she was alive, but she couldn't stop thinking about him. It was getting in the way of her schoolwork, and her dad could tell something was up. She wasn't going to admit to him that she was distracted by a boy. He would freak out.

No kidding.

She read on. Heather went on about the boy's eyes and some answer he gave in a class. Then Macy held her breath. His name was Jared. Heather had been in love with a boy named Jared. Chills ran down her spine. That couldn't be a coincidence. Obviously, that was why Chester had chosen that name. She looked back at the paper.

This morning when I got up, Dad was eating breakfast alone. That was really strange, because Mom and Dad pretty much—like always—eat together. Then I joined them for a few minutes since they make me have breakfast every day. I'm like the only kid in school who eats breakfast. Everyone else sleeps in as long as possible and then eats cold pastries or something. Anyway, I have no idea why I'm going on about that. Guess this is my place to ramble.

So I asked Dad where she was, and he wouldn't look me in the eyes. That was weird, but I was worried that she was sick or something, so I didn't really think much about it. He just said she wasn't there. Obviously, I could see that. So I kept asking questions, and he finally looked at me.

The look in his eyes was scary. I'd never seen anything like it. I wanted to run out of the house. He said she had some stuff to take care of. Of course I wanted to know what kind of stuff, but he wouldn't say. I wanted to know when she'd be back, but he wouldn't tell me that either. He said don't worry about it. Don't worry? How was I supposed to do that?

He told me to sit down and eat. I didn't feel like eating at all, but you know how he gets. I made a small bowl of oatmeal. I didn't think I could keep any more down. I knew I'd probably piss him off, but I kept asking questions about Mom. He wouldn't tell me anything. Finally, he slammed a fist on the table and told me to go to school.

Since I knew I wouldn't get anything else out of him, I got up and left. I hope she's okay. It's so weird that she hasn't gotten a hold of me. I mean, she could text me or send me an email. Usually, she sends me goofy texts in the middle of the day. She says she wanted to make sure I smiled at least once at school.

There hasn't been anything new on her profile either. She always posts articles that she finds interesting. By always, I mean lots every day. The last was last night. Almost a full day ago. Her friends are even posting, asking if she's okay. Wish I could answer for her and say something, but Dad won't get off his laptop and give me any answers.

Guess that means I gotta get my homework done now or I'm going to have more late assignments. I'm close to a few teachers contacting my parents about that. I keep hoping Mom will come through the door. Doesn't she know I would worry? Why would she leave without saying anything?

Macy read on, skimming over the next few entries. Mostly, it was

Heather pouring out her worries about her mom. She wanted to know if Heather ever found out. Macy wanted to know if Chester had killed her mom.

A few pages later, an entry started with *My mom is back.* Macy held her breath and continued reading.

When I got home from school today, Mom was sitting on our couch. She didn't even look up when I came into the room. I stood right in front of her, but she was staring off to the side. She was holding on to the blanket so tight her hands were turning white.

I kept saying 'Mom' over and over, but it was like she couldn't hear me. I started crying and begged her to look at me. Finally, she turned, but it felt like she was looking through me. I finally sat down and leaned my head against her. I was crying, but she didn't even notice. She never ignores me when I'm upset. Never!

What had happened to her? Where had she been?

We sat there not talking for so long, I finally stopped crying. There was nothing left in me. I started asking her questions about where she had been and stuff, but she kept acting like she wasn't even there. She wouldn't say a thing! Not one thing. I asked the same questions over and over. I hoped that maybe she would finally answer one of them.

I know I sound like a baby, but I want my Mommy back. I missed her so much when she was gone. It was so hard not talking with her. Some kids hate talking with their parents, but not me. My mom is my best friend. I can tell her anything—anything at all. She doesn't judge me about anything, no matter what it is. Boys, kids doing drugs, you name it. Nothing's off limits with her. She doesn't go crazy like some of my friends' parents.

Even when I wanted a pink streak in my hair, she was behind me. Dad said no way, but Mom let me get one underneath so I could pull my hair up at school and all the kids could see it there, then I could take it down before Dad got back from work. She gets me. Not even my friends get me like she does. I can't even explain it.

Macy sat back, taking it in. It must have been nice for Heather to be able to talk to her mom about anything. The pink streak reminded Macy of Zoey—not that Zoey would ever want to wear anything pink, but Zoey always wanted to do things to stand out.

What had happened to Heather's mom? Macy had been certain that she had disappeared forever. It wouldn't have surprised her if she was dead. Would this diary tell her what happened to them?

She listened, not hearing anything. The last thing she wanted was to be caught reading the diary. Chester would take it away.

My mom wouldn't get up for dinner. She just sat on that couch staring at nothing. I didn't even know if she knew she was home. Why wouldn't she acknowledge me? Not even a nod of the head or something? Something!

I couldn't even look at Dad. I knew he had something to do with this. Who knows what? But something, and he wasn't talking. The stupid jerk was acting like everything was fine. He thought I should be happy that she was back. Of course I'm glad she's back, but I'm not even close to happy about how she's acting. How can he not be concerned?

After dinner, I got my homework and did it on the couch. I talked to Mom like everything was normal, even though it's totally not. It couldn't be more not-normal. I'm pissed off, but trying to put on a smile. I told her about my friends and the latest drama with the stupid cheerleaders who have been playing pranks on us. Then I talked about Jared and how I still couldn't bring myself to talk to him, and about Parker who likes me, but I really don't like him like that.

Dad overheard me talking about the boys and he got upset. He lives in the dark ages and thinks I shouldn't have any interest in boys. Never mind the fact that he had girlfriends when he was younger than me. For some reason, I'm supposed to be above that. Hypocrite. Sometimes I think Mom and I need to move across the country to get away from him.

I don't know if she'll ever get over what's going on though. I mean, I hate to think this, but what if she has brain damage?

What if she's never going to be herself again? I can't think of any-
thing else that would make her like this.

Macy read on. There were several more days' worth of entries where
Heather essentially said the same things. Her mom wouldn't respond to
anything. She wasn't sure if her mom was even eating, but she had to be
getting up to go to the bathroom at some points, so Heather thought
maybe she was eating, only not in front of her.

Then about four days later, something changed.

I slept in really late today. Usually, I sleep in on the weekends, but
not like this. It was afternoon when I woke up. I guess I needed it
after all the stress of worrying about Mom. Even with having her
back, my stress is still through the roof. Maybe worse. Before, I
could at least tell myself that it was possible she was on a personal
vacation. I don't have that now.

Anyway, I got up and Mom was standing by the window.
Standing! I didn't know if I should say anything or not. I was
almost afraid that if I said something, she'd like go back to the
couch and never leave again. So I went and stood by her. She
didn't seem to notice.

I whispered to her and she looked at me. She actually looked at
me! Not through me. I had a million questions running through
my head, but I asked her what she was looking at. It seemed like a
safe question. I didn't want to send her back to hiding inside herself
again. I decided not to ask where she had been, at least not yet.

She pointed to a kid riding a bike across the street. Then she
started talking about when I was little and learning to ride a bike.
I didn't know what that had to do with anything, but I let her
keep talking. She was actually talking. Would she keep talking
until she told me where she had been and what caused her to act
like this?

Mom talked about my childhood for a little while and then
stopped. She looked outside for a while, even after the kid went
inside. I asked her if she wanted to eat something, but she shook her
head. At least that was a response. I wanted to ask her about where

she went, but I was so scared that she wouldn't keep talking.

I didn't know what to do. I've never been so scared in my life. What if I said the wrong thing? I just wanted her back, the way she had been before. Finally, I took her hand. She actually smiled! Then she moved a little closer to me, but she still didn't say anything. I stood there with her until she wanted to take a nap. She went back to the couch. It's pretty much her new bed now.

Should I dare ask about where she went? I don't know what to do.

Macy continued reading about Heather's fears. She wrote them out over and over, most likely because she had been trying to figure out how she felt about what was going on. She hadn't told any of her friends, because she didn't want anyone thinking her mom was weird. So the diary had been her only confidant.

Heather didn't mention it, but Macy couldn't help wondering if she was also afraid of her dad. He would undoubtedly lose it if she told anyone at school what was going on with her mom.

The next day's entry showed that Heather had made a decision.

After getting all my worries out in here, I decided to ask Mom my questions when I woke up. I was so anxious about it, I woke up early. Dad was still sleeping, so I had that to my advantage.

Mom was back at the window again. That had to be a good sign, right? I walked right up to her, took her hand, and said good morning. She squeezed my hand and talked about the squirrels and birds playing in the yard. I waited for her to pause and then I prepared myself to ask my questions.

I was so nervous that I was holding my breath without even realizing it. So, I had to take a deep breath before saying anything. Then I asked her where she went. I told her that I had missed her a lot.

She squeezed my hand again and then looked into my eyes. My eyes! She asked if I wanted to sit. I would have agreed to anything at that point. So we sat on the couch and she covered both of us, not herself, with the afghan. She looked around. She was obviously nervous about something—probably Dad. I told her that he was sleeping. I waited a minute and then asked her again where she had been.

She looked at me and said, "The barn."

What barn? I asked her if she meant the one at Grandma and Grandpa's. She nodded yes.

Macy turned the page. It was the last one and nothing else was written.

"That can't be all," Macy whispered. "There has to be more." She carried the diary back to the shelf and looked behind all the books. There were no more diaries. She slid it back into place where she'd found it.

Macy lifted the mattress and dug through Heather's stuffed animals, not finding anything. She looked through the clothes in the dresser. There was no diary there either.

The doorknob jiggled and Macy went to the bed and sat, pretending to act natural.

Deeper

CHESTER WALKED INTO the bedroom. "Get out to the living room. Your grandparents are here."

Macy followed him out there and looked out the window. The old car pulled up the long driveway at a snail's pace. What were Chester's parents like? And how was she ever going to convince them she was their granddaughter? They were bound to figure it out. And what would Chester do?

The rocks in the driveway crunched as the car came closer to the house. Macy put the picture back into place and looked out the window again. The car doors opened, and two people about her own grandparents' age got out of the car. The lady had big glasses and short, curly hair. It was probably supposed to be black, but it shone blue in the sun. The guy was mostly bald, except for a thin line of grayish-white hair along the back of his head.

A wave of fear ran through her, and her heart started racing. When was she going to get away? This couldn't actually be her new life. It couldn't be. She turned to look inside. The room felt as though it was going to swallow her up. Was it actually shrinking?

"Wipe that sour look off your face, Heather," Chester said. "You need to greet your grandparents with a smile." His gaze bore into her soul. Macy could almost feel the evil emanating from him. He narrowed his eyes. "I need to see you smile. Smile, dammit!"

Her throat closed up, while at the same time tears filled her eyes.

His lips turned white as they formed a straight line. Anger covered his face. "Don't make this difficult, Heather. You don't want to go back into the barn, do you?"

The blood drained from her face. She shook her head. "No, please. Don't."

"Then smile." The lines around his eyes deepened as he furrowed his eyebrows. "If you like that bed more than you like bales of hay, you better get over yourself and show your grandparents how happy you are to see them. Do I make myself clear?"

Out of the corner of her eye, she could see them walking toward the house. She swallowed, and then nodded. She forced a smile.

He stepped closer to her. "That's pathetic. You couldn't convince a blind person you were happy."

A tear spilled onto her face and then forced her smile even wider.

He frowned, shaking his head. Stepping closer, he grabbed her shirt. Macy gasped, stepping back. He tightened his grip and pulled her forward. She could smell him, he was so close. "You need to stop being a spoiled brat and get over yourself. Do I make myself clear? Do I?" Spit sprayed onto her face.

Macy nodded, blinking back tears.

"Stop being selfish and make your grandparents feel welcome. They haven't seen you in a long time. Pull yourself together." He shoved her backwards. The window sill jabbed her in the back.

Without thinking, she reached back to rub the spot.

"You're not going to make this difficult on me, are you?"

She shook her head.

"Good. Because if you do, I guarantee you'll regret it." The look on his face told Macy that he meant it.

"Okay." She already regretted ever getting into the truck with him. The last thing she needed was to regret anything else. She took a deep breath. All she needed to was to get through this, and then she would find a way out. Even if she had to run out the front door, sounding the alarm in the middle of the night. That would give her enough of a head start that she could get away.

She had already had some meals and her strength had gotten a lot better. She wasn't back to normal, but she wasn't as weak as she had been earlier, in that dungeon—and there was no way she was going back there.

He got in her face, so close that he bumped her nose with his. "Remember, if you keep acting like an ungrateful brat, you're going to wish you had never been born. Make your grandparents feel like the most important people alive." He stood back, adjusted his shirt, and then walked toward the front door. He reached for the alarm system. Macy could hear him pushing the buttons. He turned back to her. "I'm going to reset it so that if any door or window is opened, everyone in the house will be alerted, so don't get any ideas."

Staring at him, she refused to acknowledge his words. She was going to hang onto whatever shreds of dignity she could, even if it was something as small as that.

As she heard the alarm disengage, a key sounded in the front door.

Chester turned around and glared at her. The look in his eyes told Macy that he would hurt her if he had to. Maybe even kill her. She had never had someone look at her like that before. Cold fear shot through her.

Still giving her that look, he pointed to the ground near him, the intensity of the anger and hate burning deeper on his face. "Get over here. Now."

Macy ran over to him. She would rather do what he said than find out what he would do if she didn't.

The door opened. He turned his attention to his parents. "Mom, Dad. It's so good to see you." He smiled as though he hadn't just threatened Macy. "Let me help you with your bags." He stepped forward, taking both of their suitcases. "Did you have a nice trip?"

Macy stared, unable to pay attention to what they were saying. Before she knew it, she was wrapped in an embrace. Her *grandma* was giving her a hug. Macy knew she had to play the part well if she wanted to keep Chester happy. She put her arms around the old lady, hugging her tight.

"It's so good to see you, Heather." The woman stepped back, looking Macy over. "You're so beautiful—and you haven't changed a bit. Except that you're taller. My, how you've grown. Look at her, George."

The elderly man turned to her and smiled. "She looks exactly like you when we met, Ingrid."

Ingrid looked back at Macy. "You know, you're right. We could have been twins had we been the same age. There's no doubt we're related, is there?" She gave Macy a warm smile.

Macy nodded, not sure how to respond to that.

George looked at her. "Where's your mom, Heather?"

"I…." Macy's eyes widened. What was the story? Had she been told what she was supposed to say about her fake mom? If she had been, she couldn't remember. Everything was a blur, and really, she didn't care about some fake story.

Her captor glared at her again. He then turned to his parents, giving them a fake-genuine look of sadness. Macy knew better. "I didn't want to tell you over the phone, but she decided to stay in Paris."

"What? Why?" Concern washed over Ingrid's face.

"Let's sit down and talk about this over lunch," said George.

Ingrid shook her head. "I need to hear this first."

"We can hear it while we get lunch ready." He shook his head, and then walked around them to the kitchen.

Everyone followed him into the kitchen, where he was already pulling everything out of the fridge. Ingrid joined him, throwing things into a large pot. Was she going to make soup from scratch? Macy watched her in awe, forgetting that she was being held against her will. She had always wanted to learn to cook, to really cook—from scratch, but her mom never wanted to make anything. Why make it when you could buy it?

Ingrid looked at Macy. "Come help me, Heather."

"Okay." Despite everything, Macy actually smiled. At least she was going to get *something* out of this nightmare. Maybe she could cook her family some real food from scratch when she got back. Ingrid handed her an apron, and then pointed to some potatoes.

"Peel those."

Macy nodded, slipping the apron over her head. She wanted to kick herself for feeling excitement, but it wasn't as though the sweet, old lady had anything to do with her kidnapping. Macy grabbed the peeler and rubbed it against the potato. Not even a thin slice of skin came off.

"Oh! Has it been that long?" Ingrid exclaimed. She grabbed the potato from Macy, glaring back at her captor. "Haven't you had her make any food all this time? Don't tell me you've been buying her packaged food, Chester."

He glared at his mom. "You know I go by Chet."

She shook her head. "Not around here, you don't, Chester."

A smile spread across Macy's face. Chester shot her a menacing look, but it didn't have the same effect with his parents between them.

Ingrid brought the potato out from the sink. "First things first, Heather. Now that it's washed, you hold it at an angle like this. Watch." She slid the peeler down, and as she did, a perfect slice of potato skin fell onto the cutting board. "Now you do it."

Macy gave it a try, and before long, she had a perfectly peeled potato. She was actually proud of herself. She managed to chop it into small pieces without cutting herself in the process, though there were a few close calls.

Soon, she and Ingrid had put together a full pot of soup. Ingrid winked at her. "That will be ready in time for dinner. Shall we eat the sandwiches your grandpa made?"

Macy was disappointed she would have to wait so long for the soup, but at the same time, she wasn't really all that hungry. Sandwiches would be perfect. They all sat at the table. As Macy stared at the couldn't-be-less-vegan sandwich, she decided that given everything she had been through, she was going to stop thinking about her veganism. She needed strength, and that could only come from eating. She could go back to being a vegan once she was back home.

Maybe after this whole ordeal, her parents would even support her food lifestyle. That was another benefit to the nightmare. She bit into the roast beef sandwich with five layers of cheese, unsuccessfully pretending it was avocados and cucumbers with sesame seeds. It definitely wasn't that.

Ingrid finished hers before Macy got through her first half. She looked at her son. "All right, Chester. What happened with Karla? Why is she still in France?"

He glared at his mom. "Chet, Mom. Call me, Chet."

"Where's Karla?"

"In France, Mother." He slammed down his sandwich.

George glared at him. "Don't treat our table that way, son. What's going on with your wife?"

Chester made a face. "She doesn't want to be part of our family anymore. I didn't want to talk about it in front of Heather. You know how close they were."

Ingrid dropped her fork. "She doesn't want…? I don't understand. You and Heather are her life. I've never seen a more doting mother."

"Until she met Jacques, Mom."

Ingrid's mouth dropped open. "Chester, you don't mean to tell me she met someone else?"

"Chet! My name is Chet." He glared at Macy, who was again, trying not to smile.

"Fine." Ingrid stared at him. "What did Jacques have that you don't?"

"Do we need to talk about this? Heather doesn't need to hear about it."

George looked at him. "It does no good to hide the truth from anyone, son. Tell us what happened."

He sighed. "Karla fell in love with the city. She wanted to move there, but I didn't. We fought a lot, and she started going out for day trips on her own. That's when she met him. He promised her the world. She came back one day, demanding that we move there or she would leave us for him. I told her no, it was time to come home. But she said she was staying there. I tried to reason with her, but she wouldn't listen. You can't use logic with crazy. So she gave up her family for the lights of the city. Are you happy now? She ruined our lives, and now you know everything."

"That's awful. My poor baby." Ingrid got up, walked around the table, and wrapped her son in a hug.

Macy watched his face. He looked as though he really, truly believed his lies. She was almost convinced herself.

Room

A S MUCH AS Macy hated her new bedroom, it was better than spending any time with Chester.

Never before had she hated someone so much. He was such a horrible person. Even his own parents got irritated with him. He argued with them, often even ordering them around. They weren't rude to him, but she wouldn't have blamed them if they had been. If she ever had a kid who talked to her like that, she wouldn't take it.

Their early morning conversation drifted into the bedroom, and she could smell coffee brewing. They were probably getting breakfast ready. At least they didn't appear to expect her. She went to the bathroom, trying to be as quiet as possible.

When she finished she almost flushed out of habit, but then decided against it. If she did that, she may as well have rang a bell and shouted that she was awake.

Not wanting to wash her hands for the same reasons, she squirted some sanitizer onto her hands.

Macy tip-toed back to the room, praying she wouldn't be caught. Even just a few more minutes of solitude would be appreciated. She made it back to the bedroom and closed the door. What a relief.

Before she could even crawl back into bed, she heard the doorknob turn behind her. She jumped up and ran to the dresser.

The door opened. "So you're up." Was his tone harsh, or was it her imagination?

She nodded, flipping through clothes.

"Look at me."

Her blood ran cold. She hadn't imagined the tone. What had she done to upset him this time? She swallowed and turned to face him.

"Were you up already?"

She stared at him. No matter what she said, it would probably be the wrong answer. What did he want to hear?

"I asked you a question." He narrowed his eyes and stepped closer.

Macy dropped the pants back into the drawer. It was probably better to tell him the truth. For whatever reason, he probably knew. She nodded.

He moved closer, looking angrier with each step.

Macy swallowed, looking around. Even if there was an exit, she would be stupid to try and avoid him. She would upset him further, and then probably end up in the barn again. Was he mad that she had gone back to the bedroom?

Chester stopped. He was only about an inch from her face. She could smell coffee and eggs. He grabbed her arms. "Don't ever walk away from the bathroom without flushing. Do you understand? That's gross. Gross! Do you know what kind of germs live in there?"

"I—I didn't know. At home, we don't flush if someone is sleeping. If it—"

He stepped even closer, bumping into her forehead with his. "*This* is your home. I don't care what happens in other houses, but here, we flush. Every time. I don't care if you're sick and barely conscious. You flush. Do you understand me?"

She nodded. "I didn't want to disturb any—"

"No excuses. Don't do it again. You've been warned." He narrowed his eyes further, deep creases around his eyes showed.

Macy's eyes widened. "Okay."

He continued to stare, still touching her face. How long was he going to stand there?

"I won't forget."

Mistake

MACY SIGHED AS the third rerun of *Night Court* began. It was actually a funny show, but she really wanted to get out of the living room. She needed to find a way to get out of the house.

Weren't old people supposed to go to bed early? She looked at the clock for the five-hundredth time. It was nine, and she had been watching reruns with Chester and her fake grandparents for hours. Their only break had been for dinner. The soup had been delicious, and Ingrid promised to teach her to make other kinds.

She looked around the room as canned laughter roared in the background. Chester was fidgeting. Obviously, he wasn't all that excited about the show either. Ingrid and George appeared to be having the time of their lives, laughing along with the TV every time someone said something funny.

Usually when Macy watched TV, she was busy texting or playing a game. Her family never just sat in front of the TV. Her dad usually had his laptop. He didn't want to take too long to respond to a comment on his blog. Her mom and brother texted as much as she did.

Her legs ached from sitting so long. She stood up.

Chester looked at her. "What are you doing?"

"Stretching my legs. I have to go to the bathroom."

He glared at her. "We're spending time with your grandparents."

"Let the girl use the bathroom," George said, without taking his attention off the show.

Macy went to the bathroom, finding it hard to believe that she was going into a bathroom because it was more exciting than the alternative. She needed a change of scenery and couldn't take anymore 80s fashion or hairstyles, much less the corny jokes.

She went to the bathroom and washed her hands three times. The last thing she wanted to do was to go out there and watch more TV. What she wouldn't give to be able to text. She stopped. Her phone couldn't be far. In fact, it was probably in Chester's room. He had said he used it to post on her profile, right?

Again, everything was a blur. It was hard to keep anything straight, but at any rate he had to have it. She opened the door as slow as possible and looked up and down the hall. No one was in there. She could hear a beer commercial coming from the living room.

Her heart pounded so loud she was sure the others could hear it. She knew they couldn't, so she did her best to ignore it. She went across the hall, holding her breath. She was listening for anyone coming, but couldn't hear much over her heart and the TV blaring. George spoke pretty loud; Macy thought he might be hard of hearing. Maybe that would be to her advantage, since no one would be able to hear her sneaking into Chester's room.

Even so, she would need to hurry. He would probably check on her if she took too long. Macy opened his door. It squeaked a little, but not loud enough for anyone else to hear.

The room was dark and chilly. He had to have kept the heat off completely to get it that cold. She got the chills as she stood, looking for where her phone might be. She scanned the room, letting her eyes adjust.

Macy was about to give up when she spotted her clothes in a corner, near a dresser and a chair. Hadn't she thrown them away? Why was he keeping them? They were disgusting. She looked back down the hall. Seeing no one, she walked toward the clothes she would never wear again. She rifled through them, not finding her phone.

There was a stack of papers on the dresser next to her clothes. She picked up the papers and saw her phone behind them. She picked it up, knowing it was too easy. The power button did nothing, which meant the battery was either dead or had been removed. She tried turning it on again, but of course it didn't work. It felt lighter than usual, so she was sure the battery had been taken out.

She opened a drawer full of socks and searched it, hoping to find her battery. It wasn't there. She closed the drawer, and then heard something. She froze. It was footsteps.

Someone was coming her way, and she had left the bedroom door open. Why hadn't she closed it? She looked around for a hiding spot, but Chester appeared in the doorway before Macy could move.

He looked around. At first, she thought he didn't see her, but then she realized his eyes were adjusting. She was about to duck to the ground when he stared in her direction. His eyes narrowed. "What are you doing in here?"

"I…uh, went into the wrong room." It sounded more like a question than a statement, and definitely sounded like a lie. Hopefully, he wouldn't notice.

Taking a few steps toward her, he kept staring at her. "Then why didn't you walk out once you realized your error?" He stared at the phone in her hand.

"I was bored. I wanted to play a game."

Anger flashed over his face. "Bored? You're worried about being bored?"

"I was just—"

"How could you even think that?" He took a few more steps closer. He was close enough to grab her if he wanted. "After spending all that time in the barn, I would think watching some funny shows with your grandparents, after a couple nice meals, might I add, would be a treat. But it's not enough for you?" He took another step.

She swallowed, taking a step back. "I usually play games or text when I watch TV. It's just—"

He grabbed her arm, squeezing hard. Macy tried to push him away, but he only added more pressure. "We're here to spend some time with your grandparents. They haven't seen you in over a year. Forget about games and texting. The only thing you need to worry about is spending time with them. Didn't you see how excited they were to see you?"

Macy didn't respond.

Chester twisted her arm, causing sharp pains.

She let out a cry of pain. "That hurts."

He furrowed his eyebrows. "Answer my question."

"What?" Her arm hurt so bad she couldn't even remember what he had asked.

"Your grandparents. Didn't you see how excited they were to see you?" He twisted her arm even further.

Macy winced. "Yes. Will you stop?"

He shoved her back, jamming her side into the dresser. "Stay out of my room. Got it? Don't ever come in here again."

She nodded, again trying to push his hand off her arm. He shoved her again. The dresser dug into her side. It hurt as much as his fingers digging into her arm. She dropped the phone, and it landed on the stack of papers.

Chester pushed her hand away, digging his fingers deeper into the skin. "Since you don't want to watch the show with your grandparents, go clean the kitchen. I'm sure they would appreciate that. Then if you're still bored, let me know and I'll find plenty more for you to do. Understand?"

Macy nodded, wincing from the pain.

"Answer me." He squeezed harder, this time, digging his nails into her flesh. She could feel it break the skin. Warm blood ran down her arm. She watched as several drops fell onto the pile of her clothes. "I said answer me!" He pulled her closer, grabbing her other arm. "Do you understand? Boredom will not be tolerated, you selfish, spoiled little brat."

Swallowing she nodded. "I understand."

"Don't be ungrateful for everything I've done for you."

She nodded, hating him even more than before. He had done nothing for her—nothing. Ripped her away from her family, forced her to eat meat, locked her in the back of his truck and then in the barn's dungeon, and then he had completely taken away her identity. She wasn't going to let him brainwash her. She would pretend if she had to, but deep down, she was going to hang onto every ounce of her dignity until she could get away from him.

He stepped back and shoved her toward the door, finally letting go of her arms. She rubbed them, glaring at him. How dare he? What made him think that he had the right to do all of this to her?

"Get out there and clean the kitchen for your grandparents. They're tired from their traveling."

She stared at him, wanting to give him a piece of her mind. Rubbing her arms, and thinking back over everything she'd been through in the last several days, she didn't think it was worth it. What if he put her back in the barn? She couldn't deal with that again.

"What are you waiting for?"

"Nothing."

He stepped toward her and grabbed her arm again. "You look like you have something to say. Say it."

"No. It's nothing."

A terrifying look covered his face. "Tell me."

"I don't want to."

"Too bad. You have to do what I say now, and I'm ordering you to tell me."

She stared at him, fear running through her. "Let me go. I want you to let me go."

He shoved her arm into her side. "I wasn't touching you when I first asked. That's not what you were going to say."

A lump formed in her throat as tears threatened. "Please stop."

"Please stop," he mocked her. He shoved her against the bed, her head hitting the post. "What were you going to say? Tell me."

Her heart raced. It didn't matter what she said, he would keep hurting her. If she lied, he would know. If she told him the truth, he would make her pay. "Let me go."

"Not until you tell me what you were going to say."

Tears filled her eyes. Macy stared at him with defiance. If she was going to tell him the truth, then he may as well know how much she meant it. "I want to go home."

"Home? You are home. At least for now, this is your home."

Macy's eyes widened. What did that mean?

He grabbed her shirt, bringing her close enough that she could smell him again. She gagged as she tried to pull herself from his grip.

He tightened his hold on her collar. "This is home, and this is your only family. Those other people don't appreciate you the way we do. They're not your family. I brought you here to keep you safe. You need my protection. Only I can keep you safe. Those idiots couldn't find their own shadow in the middle of the summer."

"Don't talk about them like—"

He threw her into the bedpost. "Don't talk back to me ever again."

She turned around in time to see his fist headed right for her face. She raised her arms in defense, but didn't have enough time to block him. She heard a cracking noise as he made contact. Pain shot through her nose and then hot, thick liquid drained from it. She brought her hands to her nose, feeling the blood pool in her palms.

Chester shook his head. "Stupid girl. Look what you did."

What she had done?

He turned around and grabbed her gross clothes he had taken from the garbage. He shoved them into her arms. "May as well use these. You didn't want them anyway, did you?"

Macy grabbed them, wiping her nose. It burned on the inside, where the blood gushed from. It ran down into her throat, burning that as well. The awful, metallic taste made her gag as some of the blood made its way into her mouth.

By the time her nose stopped bleeding, the clothes were covered in blood. He snatched them out of her hands and threw them back on the floor. "Are you ready to start being grateful?"

She nodded, too angry to say anything.

"Good. Go in the bathroom and clean your face off."

"You broke my nose."

"Stop being dramatic." He felt her nose. "It's not broken. Bruised, sure, but I assure you it's not broken."

Macy rubbed it, glaring at him. Why did she have the feeling that he had enough practice with hitting people that he knew what he was talking about?

"Get in the bathroom. Your grandparents are going to wonder where we've gone."

Without thinking, she glared at him. "They're not my grandparents!"

A look of fury covered his face. His fist came at her face again. She tried to move out of the way, but was too late. She felt his knuckles make contact before everything went black.

Clothes

A LYSSA LOOKED AROUND her dark room, unsure what had woken her. She couldn't hear anything now. Rolling over, she saw that Chad wasn't in bed with her—of course. They were getting along, but he wouldn't leave his computer, afraid he would miss a comment on his blog saying they had found Macy.

Pain seared through her broken heart at the thought of her daughter. Where could Macy be? If she listened to what people had to say on the various shows, the likelihood of Macy still being alive was low. She looked at the time; it was after one in the morning. It had now been seven days since Macy had gone missing.

An entire week. Alyssa didn't know how she had survived those days. Everything was a horrible, heart-wrenching blur. Nothing was worse than not knowing where her child was. More than anything, all she wanted was to find Macy and hold her in her arms and never let go again.

Tears filled her eyes. Would she ever see Macy alive? Had she run away, or had something far more sinister happened? There was no evidence either way.

Her phone rang. Was that what had woken her up? She found it under her pillow and saw that she did have a missed call. She didn't recognize the number, but she didn't care. It could be someone with information about Macy.

"Hello? Who is this?"

"Mrs. Mercer, this is Officer Anderson. We have information about your daughter."

"What? Did you find her? Where is she? Where can I—?"

"Ma'am, please calm down."

Calm down? How dare he tell her to calm down? The only way she was going to calm down would be if Macy was back home, safe and sound. She grabbed a blanket and squeezed. "Go on."

"Some clothes have been found, and we need you and your husband to come down to the station and identify them."

Alyssa froze. Why did they think the clothes were Macy's? Where would she be without her clothes? It had to be a mistake—a horrible, horrible mistake.

"Mrs. Mercer, are you there?"

She gasped for air. "Yes. Where did they find them?"

"Near the mall."

"She could be close?"

"We can answer your questions at the station. Will you two be able to come down?"

"Of course. You want us to leave now?"

"The sooner the better, Ma'am. If they're identified as hers, we'll need to proceed as quickly as possible."

"What do they look like?"

"It would be better if you came here to see them."

The tone of his voice was enough to send chills through her. Something was wrong. "What aren't you telling me?"

"Really, it would—"

"What aren't you telling me?"

He sighed. "There is some blood on them."

Alyssa's throat closed up, and as it did an awful sound escaped. Blood on Macy's clothes? She shook her head as tears filled her eyes. "No."

"Ma'am? Do you need us to send someone to pick you up?"

She didn't want to be at their mercy, waiting to go back home until someone could drive them back. "We'll be there." She ended the call, taking deep breaths. She felt as though she was going to pass out. Bloody clothes? No. That wasn't right. It couldn't be. Macy had run off with a little punk from the Internet. A young, stupid teenager who didn't know the difference between a knife and a gun.

Her body felt like a lead weight. She couldn't move from the bed. She didn't *want* to get up. Seeing those clothes could be the end of her hope. What if they were Macy's? And worse, what if they really *were* bloody?

Alyssa had never been particularly religious, but she had found herself praying a lot over the last week. Her stomach twisted in knots at the thought of it being that long. Alyssa put the phone on the headboard and grabbed an armful of blankets, clutching them tight. "God, please, *please* let Macy be alive and safe. Whatever happens with the blood, bring her back to us, alive."

Hot tears fell to her cheeks. She had to find a way to pull herself out of bed. She didn't want to face the fact that the clothes could be Macy's. What would that mean if they were? If it was bad, she didn't want to know. She would rather get back outside, searching for her.

Was that how the clothes had been found in the first place? The search team? Where had they been found? How? Alyssa felt a renewed sense of purpose. Even if the clothes were bloody, it could be a clue to finding Macy. What if she wasn't far from where the clothes had been found? What if Alyssa herself was the one to find and save her?

She jumped out of bed, nearly tripping over the blankets she had been hanging onto. "Macy, we're coming, baby. Hang on."

After she threw on some clothes, she ran downstairs to Chad's office. He was sleeping with his head on the desk again.

"Chad, wake up. We have to get to the police station. They might have a lead."

He sat up, making a snoring noise. He looked at Alyssa, obviously trying to process what she had said. "What? What kind of clue?"

"They found some clothes. They might be hers."

He rose from his chair, grabbing several things from the desk. "What makes them think that?"

"I don't know, but they want us to look at them. After we do, we need to go to wherever they found them and search with a fine-toothed comb. We're getting close. We can find her."

Panic covered his face. "But something has to be wrong. Why do they want us at this hour?"

"Because they don't want to waste any time, and neither do I. Let's go." She knew she should tell him about the blood, but she couldn't bring herself to say it. It would be like admitting defeat. They had to find their daughter.

Chad shook his head. "It's been a week. This can't be good. Did they say anything else?"

She twisted some of her hair around her fingers. "There was a little blood."

"On the clothes?" His eyes widened, and his face lost color.

Alyssa nodded. "We need to go. We don't even know if they're hers."

He sat in his chair, or possibly fell. Alyssa couldn't tell.

"Let's go. We need to go."

"Blood?"

"Chad, we have to look at the clothes. Whether they're hers or not, we need to find out."

He slammed his fist on the desk. "I'll hunt down the stupid bastard myself and beat him to a pulp. He'll wish he had never messed with our family." He stood again, grabbing his coat from the back of his chair.

They got into Chad's car, and as it roared to life the radio blared. "The case of missing Macy Mercer has grabbed our town by the heart. She's become everyone's daughter, even for those of us who never met her. I was talking to one of the people leading up the search party, and he—"

Alyssa turned it off. "I can't listen to that."

"Me neither." Chad pulled into the road and they drove in silence.

As they pulled into the parking lot, Alyssa asked, "Do you think the clothes are hers?"

"I have no idea. They could be anyone's. They could've fallen out of someone's gym bag."

"Someone's bloody gym bag?" Alyssa asked.

"It could happen."

After Chad set the alarm, he grabbed Alyssa's hand. "We're on the same team."

She nodded, feeling like a teenager herself, holding his hand as they walked through the lot. He had been holding her hand more since Macy disappeared, but it still felt unnatural.

When they got inside, they were whisked into a room with a dark plastic bag sitting in the middle of a table. The officer inside introduced himself as Anderson, the same one Alyssa had spoken to on the phone.

Alyssa stood, staring. "Are the clothes in there?"

The officer nodded. "Have a seat. We have some questions first, and then we'll have a look at the clothes."

She complied, but couldn't take her eyes off the bag. What were the clothes in there? Were they really Macy's?

"Ma'am?"

"What?" Alyssa turned to the cop.

"I have a few questions for you."

She nodded, and then answered some routine questions that she had already answered about fifty times since Macy disappeared. What was the point of asking the same questions over and over? Did that really do anything to help find Macy?

"Do you remember what she was wearing that night?" Anderson asked.

"Last I saw her, she was in her pajamas," Alyssa snapped. "She was tired from school—or so she said. Obviously, Zoey knows a lot more than I do. Didn't she describe what Macy was planning on wearing? We were out of the loop on that one. She didn't tell us she was sneaking out to meet someone she met on the Internet."

"I understand, Ma'am. We have to ask the questions to verify that the answers haven't changed."

She narrowed her eyes. "And why would they be different?"

"It's routine. Please, don't take it personally."

Alyssa heard Chad chuckle next her. She ignored him, keeping her attention on the officer. "Nothing has changed. We want to find our daughter. You brought us down here in the middle of the night, the least you can do is to show us the clothes."

Officer Anderson looked over his notes. "We've gone over every-thing we need to up to this point." He got up, walked over to the door, and opened it, poking his head out. He said something that sounded like gibberish to Alyssa. He came back in with not one, but two more policemen.

Did it really take five adults to look at a bag of clothes?

Chad stood. "Where were these found? And by who?"

Anderson put a hand up. "First things first, sir. This is Officer Reynolds and Detective Fleshman."

They all shook hands. Alyssa was certain that she would forget everyone's names, although she did recognize the two new men. "Can we see the clothes, please?"

Detective Fleshman walked to the bag, opening it slowly. Was he doing that on purpose? Alyssa thought she might explode. Dump everything out! What was he waiting for?

He held up a light blue camisole covered in blood.

Alyssa gasped. Chad wrapped an arm around her. "Is that Macy's?"

"I think so. But look at all that blood. Oh, dear God."

Reynolds looked at her. "You think it's hers? Or it *is* hers?"

"Macy wears those under her shirts all the time, but then again so do her friends. She's always liked that powder blue color. How would I know if it's hers? It could be anyone's." Tears filled her eyes. It was the right size. What would have happened to her baby to make her bleed like that?

Fleshman placed the camisole flat on the table, and then pulled out a black hoodie with little, red flowers all over it.

"Macy has one like that, but it has purple flowers," Alyssa said. Then it hit her: the flowers were covered in blood—that was why they were red. Her stomach lurched, and had she eaten anything the day before, it would have come up. "That's blood. It's covered!"

Chad held her tighter. She buried her face into his chest, sobbing.

"Where did you find the clothes?" Chad demanded.

"Near the mall," Anderson said. "By the jogging trail."

"What does this mean? Are you any closer to finding her? Will this help?"

"The next step will be to find out the blood is hers."

Alyssa sat up. "What do we do now?"

Fleshman gave her a sympathetic look. "Go home and get some sleep."

Dread

ZOEY PEELED SOME midnight-blue nail polish off her pinky nail. It had chipped badly, but she didn't care. Usually she kept her nails perfect, but with Macy gone, nothing seemed to matter anymore.

Her mom yawned next to her. "They call us down here at this ungodly hour, and then they make us wait. Not everyone works the graveyard shift." She glared at the officer sitting at the front desk.

He looked at them. "The girl's parents are looking at the clothes now. I'm sure it won't be much longer." He looked back at the computer screen in front of him.

"I'll bet he's playing games," muttered Zoey's mom.

"Do you want to go home, and I'll have one of them bring me back?"

Her face softened. "No, Zoey. Honey, I'm sorry. I'm so tired. I know this has been a hellish week for everyone. I'm here for you, and I'm not going to leave your side. If I have to miss work again tomorrow, then I will."

"Tomorrow's Saturday, Mom."

"Work hours don't make themselves up. It's going to take me a few weekends and evenings to make up the time I've already missed, and I'm sure to miss more. Don't worry about it."

Zoey rolled her eyes. Why would she worry about her mom's work schedule? She went back to picking at her nails, and her mom pulled out her tablet. Zoey ignored her, pretending that her nails were most interesting thing around. She wasn't even fooling herself, the one person she wanted to.

Her stomach churned acid. All this time she had told herself she was mad at Macy for running off with Jared, but deep down she knew that wasn't like her best friend. Her shy, vegan friend who often hid behind Zoey wouldn't run off with a guy she had just met. As nice as that would be to believe, it didn't make sense.

What did make sense was what they were waiting to see: clothes with blood on them. It couldn't be—not Macy. The last week had to have been one long sick and twisted nightmare. But if that was the case, why couldn't Zoey wake up?

Conversation caught her attention. Zoey sat up, forgetting about her nails. It sounded like Macy's parents. The voices got closer, until she could see them talking with a cop. They rounded a corner, entering the waiting area.

Zoey stood up. Where was Alex? Did they leave him home? In a way, she was jealous. She wished she could get sleep instead of waking from nightmares constantly. Her dreams wouldn't leave her alone, always reminding her of what she was truly afraid of. She had woken up from almost every scenario possible: Macy being shot, stabbed, poisoned, strangled, hanged, drugged, and more.

Alyssa turned their way. Mascara streaked down her face, and her eyes were red and puffy. She had obviously been crying—a lot. Zoey's heart sank. Why were they even there? The clothes had probably already been identified as Macy's from the looks of it.

Her mom got up and gave Macy's parents both a hug. Nobody spoke about the clothes or Macy.

When Alyssa made eye contact with Zoey, she nodded. "Thanks for coming down here, Zo. You've always been such a good friend to...." Tears fell down her face, further smearing the mascara.

Zoey looked away, afraid that she would cry too.

Chad caught her attention. "We do appreciate you, Zoey. Both of you." He looked at her mom. "If you guys ever need anything, let us know."

"I'm the one who should be offering you something, Chad."

"Where's Alex?" Zoey blurted out.

Her mom glared at her. They both knew she couldn't help it, though. When she was uncomfortable, her mouth did its own thing.

"Oh, Alex!" Alyssa's eyes widened, and her lips wobbled. "I'm the worst mother ever. Macy is gone and we left without Alex."

Zoey's mom shot her a dirty look and turned to Alyssa. Zoey sighed. How was she supposed to know Alyssa would get even more upset?

"Alyssa, I'm sure he's better off at home, sleeping. You guys have been through enough."

"But we didn't even think to check on him! I forgot all about him when I got that phone call. I'm not—"

"He probably won't even know you're gone."

Alyssa looked at her. "But, Valerie, I forgot about my son. I forgot about him!" More tears fell, and she wiped at them, spreading the mascara sideways. Zoey wished she had something she could give her to wipe it all off.

The officer behind the desk called Zoey and her mom back. They said their goodbyes to the Mercers and followed him to a room with nothing except a table, chairs, and a black bag.

Three policemen came in, introducing themselves as Anderson, Reynolds, and Fleshman. Zoey let her mom do all the talking. She enjoyed being in charge and quickly dominated the conversation.

Zoey stared at the black bag, curious and disgusted at the same time. She wasn't sure if she wanted to run away or look at the clothes.

Before she knew it, one of the cops grabbed the bag. Zoey jumped, startled. She'd been so lost in her own thoughts she hadn't been paying attention to anything being said.

"Why are we here? Didn't Macy's parents just see the clothes?"

Her mom sighed. "Didn't you listen to anything they said?"

Fleshman said, "It's okay. We know it's a stressful time." He turned to Zoey. "With you being her best friend, you might be able to offer additional insight that her parents couldn't."

Zoey shrugged. How could she help? She didn't know anything.

The detective pulled out Macy's pants. Zoey recognized them right away. They had spent hours at the mall looking for pants. Macy didn't like any of the ones she had, saying they were too out of style. Zoey thought her pants were fine, but she knew how cruel some of the popular girls had been to Macy.

"Do you recognize these?"

Holding her breath, Zoey nodded. She took a slow, deep breath, trying to control herself. "She bought those for her date." Zoey slunk down into a chair. She covered her face with her hands, not wanting anyone to see her cry. She had held herself together up to that point, but seeing the pants was too much.

Her mom was talking with the cops. She didn't want to hear any more. She was done. She sat up. "Can I go now? I told you those are her pants."

Fleshman walked around the table and put his hand on her shoulder. "We really need you to look at the rest of them. Can you do that much for us? For Macy?"

She sighed. "Fine." She took a deep breath, determined to keep herself together. The pants hadn't had any blood on them. Maybe the police had only mentioned blood to get them down there at two in the morning.

One of the other cops pulled out Macy's favorite hoodie. Why were the flowers red? The blood drained from her face. "Is that blood?" Without thinking, she grabbed the hoodie. It crunched in her grasp. "Is that Macy's blood?"

"We don't know yet. It's going to take some time to process. We wanted to have the clothes identified first because we have to send them to a larger department that has those capabilities."

Zoey dropped the hoodie onto the table. "It's hers, like the pants. Can I go now?" The room spun around her. She wanted to get out.

Anderson pulled out Macy's new camisole, which was covered in blood.

A foreign sound escaped from Zoey's throat. "I gave that to her for her birthday. Her old one was too big after she lost weight." She sat back down in the chair. How much more of this would she have to endure? They showed her socks, but Zoey didn't know if they were Macy's.

Zoey waited for them to bring out underwear and a bra, but they didn't. Was that a good thing?

"Where did you find these?" Valerie asked.

"A jogger found them near the mall."

"That's where she was supposed to meet him." Zoey felt lightheaded. "They were just supposed to go to the mall."

One of the cops looked at her. "But that area had been gone over. The clothes weren't there a couple days ago."

"Does that mean she's close?" Zoey sat up, hopeful. "We've got to find her."

Fleshman shook his head. "The clothes appeared to have been placed there. There wasn't a sign of struggle or anything else suspicious. We had some dogs brought in, and they couldn't detect a thing."

What could it all mean? Zoey looked at each of the cops. None of them appeared to know more than she did.

"When will you know whose blood that is?" Valerie asked.

"It could be as long as a week. We're going to request they make it a priority, but it's not our department. We can only hope they'll comply since it's a missing child case."

Zoey ran her hands through her hair, not caring how much she messed it up. She had to get out of there. The walls were closing in on her. Her eyes were also getting heavy. She needed to get some sleep, even if it was riddled with nightmares. Her eyes closed, giving into their weight.

She drifted off to sleep right away. Images of bloody clothes filled her dreams. Somewhere, Macy was calling for help.

"Zoey, we're leaving now."

Not wanting to move, she pretended not to hear her mom. She didn't care that she was sleeping in a chair down at the station. At least she was sleeping.

"Come on, Zoey. You can sleep in the car."

She mumbled something that not even she understood.

"A little help, please?"

Zoey felt hands slide under her legs and around her back. She had the vague awareness of being carried. Good. She didn't feel like opening her eyes or walking.

Bound

MACY OPENED HER eyes, but it was just as dark as when they were closed. She looked around, trying to see anything. Was she back in Heather's room? Something covered her mouth. Macy moved her mouth back and forth. It felt like duct tape.

She went to sit up, but couldn't move. What was going on? She moved her arms, but they wouldn't budge. She tried her legs next, and they were stuck, too. She wiggled around, feeling pressure around her wrists, ankles, and knees. Was she tied up?

Her hair rested on her cheek, making it itch. She moved her head to scratch the itch with her shoulder. Instead, she scratched her face on something hard, breaking the skin. She moved her head around, feeling a poking sensation along her face.

No.

She was back in the barn. She was lying on hay. She looked around again, hoping to see something as her eyes adjusted to the dark. She couldn't make anything out. Not a single shape. It had to be really late, unless her eyes had been covered too.

Squirming, she managed to get her shoulder up to her face. Something was wrapped around her eyes. It could be the middle of the day for all she knew.

She could hear hooves up above. If she'd doubted she was back in the dungeon, those doubts were gone. She could hear the rodents moving around in the room somewhere.

What could she do? George and Ingrid were on the farm. If she screamed, they would hear her if they were near the barn. If they found her, she could tell them everything. They could call the police and get her home.

On the other hand, Chester could hear her screaming and make things even worse for her.

She didn't care. It was worth the risk. She had to take it.

Macy took a deep breath, preparing herself to yell louder than she ever had before. She let out the loudest, bone-curdling scream she could muster. It barely made a sound because of the duct tape.

Her stomach growled. How long had she been back in the dungeon? More importantly, how much longer would she be there? She had to find a way out this time. Although it would clearly be more challenging now that she was bound up.

The last thing she was going to do was to wallow in her misery. She needed to find a way to get herself free. She couldn't tell for sure, but it felt like zip ties were wrapped around her wrists and ankles. They were skinny and tight, painfully digging into her flesh. He probably made them too tight on purpose. He wanted her to pay for talking back to him.

Did he seriously believe that he was doing her a favor? That she was lucky? He might have hoped that tying her up and sticking her back in the barn would make her need him more, but it had backfired. She was pissed off, and after she freed herself she would attack him when he came back for her.

He would regret ever taking her. Strike that. He would regret ever having seen her online in the first place. She had seen enough of Alex's karate to put some of it to use. She wished she had paid more attention, or even taken lessons herself, instead of texting and playing games, but it wasn't like she could have predicted that she would end up kidnapped.

Stupid jerk. He was going to pay. She wiggled and squirmed. No matter what it took, she was going to get up, and then she would find a way to free herself. As she fought to sit upright, she pictured the dungeon. In her mind's eye, she looked around for anything she could use to free herself.

Nothing came to mind, but she would have to find something. A sharp piece of wood sticking out from a wall, maybe. There had to be something.

As she continued to wiggle around, the hay scratched up her arms and face. She wasn't even sure if she had moved at all. When she had watched shows with someone tied up, she thought it had been over-dramatized. Now it seemed under-done. She wasn't getting anywhere, and she was starting to break out into a sweat.

The cloth over her eyes was collecting moisture and feeling heavier. Macy continued to fight, but no matter how much she struggled, she didn't get anywhere.

Her throat was dry, and she had to go to the bathroom. She had to find a way out of the restraints, if for no other reason than to relieve herself. With more fight than before, she struggled to get off the bale. Maybe she could at least try to stand up. Then she could find some-thing—anything—to break the zip ties.

Her bladder burned, especially as she moved around. With each movement, it protested. She finally made some progress and rolled onto her stomach.

Tears of joy escaped. If she managed to roll over once, she could do it again. She moved her head to the side, getting her face out of the bale.

The pressure on her bladder was too much. She wasn't going to be able to hold it until she could get the ties off and her pants down.

No. Please.

Her burning bladder was all she could focus on. She had to go so bad. New tears ran down out of her eyes, soaking the blindfold.

She was about to pee herself, she knew it was only a matter of minutes, if that. She squeezed her muscles together to keep it in, squirming and rolling with as much force as she could. She rolled again, feeling a strange sensation. She was falling. It felt further than one bale. How far was she going to fall?

Thud. She landed flat on her back. She let out a cry, and then her bladder released its contents. Warm liquid ran through her pants, puddling around her.

Macy stayed in place, crying again. More than before, she wanted to get home. Back to her family. *If I ever get back, I swear I will appreciate them. I'll do what I'm supposed to.*

She stayed there, making promises into the duct tape until the puddle around her went cold. Her stomach growled again, but the smell of her urine made her gag.

Shivers ran through her. It was getting cold, and being in a puddle wasn't helping anything. Having learned a little bit about rolling over while restrained, she was able to roll over onto her side easier than she had before.

It felt like hours had passed since she woke up. How long was he going to leave her down there? Her blood ran cold as the most horrible thought struck: what if he had left her down there to die? Was he looking for a new Heather even now?

Macy knew his name and his parents' names. She could easily describe the barn and the farmhouse. She was a risk for him to let go if he had decided she was too much trouble.

Fresh determination ran through her. She had to get out of the barn—alive. She didn't care what it took; she was going to find a way out and then get home. She didn't care if she was clear across the country. She would do it somehow.

The first thing she had to do was to roll until she hit something, preferably a wall. Then she would find a board to rub against the zip tie holding her arms together. She ignored her drenched, cold pants and rolled herself over again.

She was getting tired and she was still hungry and thirsty. She knew she could go about three days without water, but she didn't even know how long it had been already.

No matter what it would take, she *would* get out and back to her family.

Reminders

C HAD PULLED HIS arm away from Alyssa. She had finally fallen asleep after insisting that he hold her. She had been so upset with herself for forgetting about Alex when they left for the station.

Alex would have figured they left him to sleep. The poor kid hadn't had much rest himself the last week, and the last thing Chad had wanted was for his son to have to deal with seeing Macy's clothes. Alex was already upset enough about her disappearance.

Alex was just like Chad, keeping his feelings to himself, but Chad could read him like a book. He could see that Macy's disappearance was eating Alex up.

Sitting up, he fixed the blankets around Alyssa. Even though it was late and he was exhausted, he couldn't sleep. How could he after seeing his daughter's bloody clothes?

Chad knew enough about blood loss to know that the amount on the clothes wasn't enough to kill her. It was more like a cut. A bad one, but not enough to be fatal.

A sick feeling settled into his stomach. How could anyone do that to his daughter? He would personally hunt down the one responsible and beat him within an inch of his life. He would find out what he did to Macy, and then he would do exactly the same thing to the sick bastard.

Maybe someone had posted something on his blog. Since her clothes had been found, maybe more evidence would pop up, too. The traffic to his blog had more than quadrupled over the last week. In fact, it had received so much traffic that it had shut down for a while. He had to pay for more hosting because his plan couldn't handle it.

He couldn't afford to let it be down. What if someone had news about Macy?

Knowing that his family would probably think he was a jerk, he got up out of bed and went down to his office. It was for Macy, no matter what they thought about him being on his blog. It was to help her.

At least with the blog, he could give his side of the story. He was able to let everyone know what his family was really like. He posted pictures that the news wanted nothing to do with. Ironically, those were the ones that the blog visitors loved the most.

His broken heart hurt even more knowing he couldn't call his dad. When he had been alive, Chad had been able to call him any time he needed to talk. What would Dad tell him? Probably to fight for Macy. That was what he had to do.

Chad climbed out of bed, careful not to wake Alyssa. He grabbed her phone from the headboard and took it with him downstairs. People called around the clock these days, and he didn't want anyone waking her.

He went to his office and went straight to his laptop. In another situation, he would have been thrilled looking at the numbers. He had more comments than he had time to read. The page views were unlike anything he had ever seen, even the day before. All those people cared about Macy.

He pulled the chair up and went to his comments. He read through them, answering each one. When he looked up to check the time, he saw that three and a half hours had already passed. It was getting light out. The house was still silent, which meant that Alex and Alyssa were both getting the sleep they needed.

His eyes were getting heavy. As much as he wanted to write a post, he knew he didn't have it in him to write a good enough one. Macy deserved better, and so did the people reading the posts.

There also wasn't much to report, since he wasn't supposed to say anything about the clothes. If people were really interested in what he had to say, they would read his replies to all the comments.

People would stop visiting if he didn't get a new post up soon. His vision was blurry, and his body ached. Surely they would understand

and could wait a few hours. His neck and shoulders were sore from so many hours spent sleeping against his desk or on the couch.

He got up and went up to his room, sliding in bed next to Alyssa. She didn't even stir. The moment his head hit the pillow, he was asleep.

When he woke up, Alyssa was gone. He looked around, listening. The sun was bright, slipping in through the blinds. He felt rested. How long had he slept? It had to be after noon. He climbed out of bed and went to the bathroom, noting Alyssa's makeup spread around her side of the counter.

She hadn't put on makeup since she found out about Macy. However much sleep she had gotten must have helped to get her in a better frame of mind. He checked on Alex and found his bed empty too. He searched the house, but they weren't anywhere. They had probably gone to search for Macy.

He should probably join them, but first he needed to check his blog. His stomach rumbled as he passed the kitchen. He looked inside, knowing it would be bare. Shopping hadn't been on anyone's priority list. Alex was the only one eating regularly.

Chad grabbed the last frozen burrito and stuck it in the microwave. He had always wanted to try to order groceries online. Maybe he could try that while he checked his blog. Then at least there would be food in the house for his family. The microwave beeped, and he took his food out. He found a clean fork and headed for his office.

The computer was ready for him. Two hundred and fifteen new comments. How long had he been asleep? That was an unheard of amount of comments in that amount of time. He should order the groceries first. By the time he was done with the comments, they would be delivered.

Once at their grocery store's site, he created a login and filled a virtual shopping cart with items he was pretty sure they usually had on hand. He threw in a few things that he thought Alex and Alyssa would like that they rarely had, and then he checked out. It would be at their door in two hours. He wanted to join the search party before that, but it might take that long to get through all those comments.

Up until this point, he had replied to every comment ever left on his blog—excluding the spam comments which he removed as soon as he saw them. He didn't need their links ruining his ranking. He wouldn't have been able to get the advertisers he had if he allowed crap like that on his site.

He readjusted himself in the chair, making himself as comfortable as possible. The first comment was someone expressing their heartfelt sympathy for their loss. It sounded like they thought Macy was dead.

Most of them were similar, saying something along the lines of being sorry for Macy being gone. Many said they were praying for her safe return. No one had mentioned anything about the clothes. He really had expected someone to leak the information and for the news to eat it up. Surely they would once they found out.

Before he knew it, the groceries had arrived. He put them away as best as he could. He didn't know where anything went, but at least they had food and the perishables were in the fridge and freezer. Nothing was going to spoil.

There were some more comments left unanswered, but he would have to get to them later. He found a baseball cap and put it on, not wanting to deal with a shower. He needed to get out there and join his family. The headquarters for the search parties had been at the park down the street over the past week, so he would walk.

As soon as he got to the sidewalk, he could see the temporary tents that had been set up. It looked like as much effort had been put into this search as the ones last weekend. He moved the bill of his hat to get all of the sun off his face. It was warm out, especially given that it was almost winter.

A few people milled around the park. They were handing out fliers. Chad saw a couple of women standing near a table full of supplies. One of them saw him and waved as he entered the park. He waved back and made his way to the table.

One lady he recognized from the homeowners' association smiled. "Chad, it's so good to see you. We all appreciate you updating your blog so often. We were talking about that a little while ago."

Another one nodded. "We love the pictures. They make us feel like we know you guys better, you know?"

He nodded. "Thanks. Did Alyssa and Alex come by? They left while I was sleeping."

The first woman nodded. "They went out with a search team near the mall. She said you hadn't been sleeping much, so they wanted you to get some rest. I can't even imagine what it's been like for you."

Chad cleared his throat. "Thanks. So, am I too late?"

She shook her head. "No. Parties have been coming and going all day. It shouldn't be long before another group arrives. We've got people canvassing with fliers and others out searching. We're going to do everything we can until she's found."

The second lady looked behind him. "Here comes a group now."

Chad spun around. He saw five people walking toward them. They came to the table. Each one recognized him and gave their condolences. He hated it. Macy was missing, not dead. Three of the group had to leave, and another to rest. That left someone he knew all too well.

Lydia.

She gave him a hug. "So many people have been working hard all day. Someone will find Macy. I can feel it."

He nodded, trying not to make direct eye contact. "Thanks."

One of the ladies from the table handed him a stack of fliers. "Why don't you two go hand out more of these? It's going to be dark soon."

Chad looked at Lydia. "I'm not sure—"

She grabbed the pile of papers. "Let's go." She took two water bottles from the table and handed him one. "We can't let these fliers go to waste."

He couldn't argue with that. They left the park in the opposite direction of his house.

"What are you doing, Lydia?" Chad asked.

"Helping to find Macy. What else?"

"Look. We're out of everyone's earshot. What are you really do-ing?"

She gave him a wounded look. "Helping to find your daughter."

"Lydia, we can't continue…what we had going."

"Haven't you noticed me giving you space? I haven't even tried to contact you in the last week. Although, I hope you know that if you do need to get away, I'm here for you day or night."

"Alyssa and I have been trying to work things out."

She kept her face straight, but he could see the hurt in her eyes. She flipped her hair behind her shoulder. "Of course. You two need to work together now. Alex needs you two strong more than ever."

"Yes. I know." He looked forward, not wanting to look at her. Now that he and Alyssa were getting along, and especially with Macy being gone, he regretted ever hooking up with Lydia. It was a mistake, and guilt ate at him. He had nearly forgotten all about her as soon as he found out about Macy being gone.

It was obvious Lydia wasn't going to go away. Why else would she be so active in the search efforts? She was obviously trying to show him that she was still there for him…and would be waiting.

"I can't imagine your pain. I've been reading your blog. It's beautiful. You have such a way with words. You're going to be a full-time writer soon. Then you're dream—"

"Lydia." Chad raked his fingers through his hair. "I'm trying to turn my marriage around."

"Chad, I'm not going to put any pressure on you. Honestly, I can't even fathom the hell you're going through. You know Dean and I never could have kids. I—"

"Where is Dean? Why aren't you out with him?"

"He's working. What else? It's a day that ends in 'y,' you know."

Chad nodded. They had both been lonely in their marriages, and that was what got them talking in the first place. One conversation had led to another, until one day they found themselves fulfilling each other's needs in other ways.

"I'm sorry he still has his head up his rear. You don't deserve that, but I can't replace him any more."

Her eyes shone with tears and she cleared her throat and adjusted her shirt which could have been buttoned higher. "I know you need this time with your family. I'm not going to bother you, but when you're ready to come back—and you will—I'll be waiting."

Chad looked around and seeing no one, he took her hand. "Lydia, you deserve better than Dean. You should find someone who can treat you well."

"That's why I'm going to wait for you as long as I need to."

"Please don't. It's over." He let go of her hand. "Let's hand these fliers out."

They rounded a corner and came face to face with Alyssa and Alex.

Spiral

Zoey STOOD BY herself at the park only a few feet away from the others. They had just arrived after handing out the last flier. She kept her focus on Lydia. Something was off about her, but Zoey couldn't tell what. She looked perfectly normal, holding the stack of fliers and a water bottle, but she looked a little too comfortable standing next to Chad. Her shirt was also too low-cut for a search party.

Alyssa smiled at Lydia. "We appreciate you putting together the search parties. Really, we couldn't have asked for anything more. The fliers are perfect, and I think every inch of our neighborhood has been looked through."

Lydia smiled. "Glad to help. In the last HOA meeting, we were talking about other ways we can help your family. We want to do more." She stepped a little closer to Chad.

Zoey narrowed her eyes. She knew Macy wouldn't like it. She looked at Alyssa, who seemed oblivious to Lydia's behavior. Granted, Lydia was being subtle, but *something* was going on.

"If you guys need anything else, say the word." Lydia smiled again. Why was she smiling so much? She was talking to two parents who couldn't find their child.

Alyssa nodded. "Thanks. I'm going back home. You'll be home soon?" She looked at Chad.

"Sure. I need to get out and look for her myself."

"I'd join you, but I'm exhausted. Someone told me how we can try to recover the information from Macy's computer. It might still be there. Maybe we'll find something useful."

Chad put his hand on Alyssa's arm. "I'll help you when I get home.

I shouldn't be too much longer."

Alyssa threw herself into his arms. "Thank you. I don't know much about computers. I don't want to mess it up and accidentally delete anything."

"Just go home and rest. I'll come back when we've handed out all these." He indicated to the stack of fliers in Lydia's hand.

Zoey didn't like the look on Lydia's face. She was tired from all the walking and drained from Macy's disappearance, but she wasn't going to let Lydia spend time alone with Macy's dad. Macy wouldn't have wanted that. Lydia had her eyes on Chad; there was no denying that.

Zoey grabbed Alex's hand. "We'll join you, Mr. Mercer. That way you guys can hand those out faster."

He looked relieved. Maybe he could tell something was up with Lydia, too.

Valerie looked at Zoey. "Are you sure? I know you're really tired."

"Yeah. It won't take long."

"Okay." Valerie turned to Alyssa. "I'll tell you what. While you're working on the computer, I'll make dinner for you guys. You probably haven't had a decent meal all week, have you?"

"Nope," Alex said.

Valerie turned to Lydia. "That's what the homeowners' association should do to help. These guys need to eat. Someone should make them meals. Dinners, at least."

Lydia grinned, grating further on Zoey's nerves. "That's a great idea. I'll take tomorrow."

Chad's eyes widened. Zoey wondered if maybe there wasn't something more going on other than just Lydia having the hots for Mr. Mercer. After all, Macy's parents hadn't been getting along for a while.

Zoey's mom and Macy's mom waved and then headed for the park, which they had to go through to get to their street. Zoey talked about everything they had done all day while canvassing, not letting Lydia get a word in edgewise.

Every once in a while, Alex would give her a strange look, but she didn't want to tell him what she was thinking. What if she was wrong? Her mom always said she had an overactive imagination. With everything else going on in Alex's life, she didn't want to give him something else to worry about.

She knew he was tired from walking all day, and neither of them had been sleeping well. Their frequent middle of the night texts proved that. They never really texted about Macy, but that was why they were both awake. Sometimes, it was nice to pretend that wasn't why they were awake.

They made their way around, handing out papers to everyone they came across. The further they went, the more Zoey's legs ached. Not only her legs, but her entire body. Maybe she would actually get some sleep tonight—if the dreams didn't disturb her.

Even though she was tired, she kept her eyes on Chad and Lydia. Zoey really wanted to be wrong about Lydia. This would have been the worst time for someone to go after either of Macy's parents.

When they got back to the park after handing out all of the fliers, Zoey was ready to drop. She could tell that Alex was, too. He looked about ready to pass out.

Lydia and Chad were talking with the people at the main table. Alex looked at Zoey. "Want to go back? It's getting dark."

She looked over at Alex's dad. He was standing a good two feet away from Lydia. "All right. You look like you need to sleep. I'm sure my mom has dinner ready by now."

He nodded, and then turned to his dad. "Hey, Dad. We're going back to the house now."

"I'll go with you two." He turned to the adults and waved a good-bye. They started the short trek back to the Mercer house. Normally it was a short walk, but after the day's searching it felt much longer.

No one spoke. Zoey wanted to know what Chad was thinking, but given the look of relief on his face when Zoey said she would go with him and Lydia, he was probably innocent. Lydia was probably going after him because he was weak. Or maybe she saw some kind of opportunity.

Or maybe Zoey was so desperate for something other than Macy to think about that she was making something out of nothing.

When they got to the front yard, Zoey felt like collapsing on the lawn, but forced her feet to keep going. Within the front door, a delicious smell greeted her. She guessed dinner was ready. She kicked her shoes off out of habit, feeling at home, and went to use the bathroom. She hadn't realized how bad she had to go until then.

By the time she got to the table, everyone else had already sat. Zoey took the seat next to Alex. Dinner smelled like herbs and chicken; her mouth watered. It had been Macy's favorite whenever she spent the night, at least before she went vegan. There were so many nights that they had eaten that meal and then ran up the stairs, giggling and whispering secrets.

Zoey's chest tightened as she thought about her best friend. What would she do without her? Tears filled her eyes as she filled her plate, not looking at anyone.

The discussion was light, mostly the Mercer's thanking Valerie for making the meal. The three of them scarfed down their food. Had they eaten since Macy disappeared?

After everyone had eaten, Zoey's mom made eye contact with her. "Will you help me with the dishes?"

"Sure."

Valerie looked at everyone else. "You guys get some rest. We'll take care of the kitchen."

They all said their thanks and went off in various directions. Zoey felt a little more energized after having eaten. She picked up the plates, stacking them on top of one another.

"I hate to do this to you, Zo, but my work needs me to travel to China for a few days. I feel bad about leaving you, and I wish I could be here for Macy's family, but this way I can catch up on my lost work hours. I can't afford to lose my job, honey. We don't want to lose the house."

Zoey put the plates on the counter. "What does that mean for me?"

"I know you could probably stay home and be fine, but I would feel better if you didn't. Would you be willing to stay here? Alyssa already said you were more than welcome. But if you don't want to stay in Macy's house, I understand. We can ask another of your friends' parents."

Her mom was offering for her to spend the night at Alex's house for a few days? "Here is fine."

"There's more." Her mom sighed. "You're not going to want to hear it, but I want you to."

"What?"

"I want you to go back to school on Monday."

"What? Mom—"

"Zoey, hear me out, I said. I don't want you falling behind, and you've already missed a week of school. They also have counselors there who are already talking with students, helping them deal with Macy's disappearance. I was told that you can go and talk with one at any time. They have extras on hand because so many kids want to talk about it. You would have priority, being her best friend."

"Kids are talking to counselors about her? Most of the kids made fun of her, and didn't stop even after she lost her weight."

Her mom's face became sad. "Those kids might be the ones who need to talk to someone the most. They might have a lot of guilt."

"They should! They're the ones who forced her into finding a boyfriend online. I hope those snarky bi—"

"Language, Zoey."

"Ugh." She rolled her eyes. "I'm not going to sugarcoat the truth. They're complete and total b—"

"Enough. Do you want to stay here? And are you willing to go to school? At least try it on Monday. If it's too much, we can have the teachers send work home."

"Sounds like you've really thought about this."

Valerie nodded. "Alyssa and I have been talking. She wants Alex to go back to school, too."

"I can't imagine he wants to go back any more than I do, but if Alex goes, I'll go."

"You might be the one to lead the way for him, Zo. I know he's Macy's kid brother and he probably annoys you, but I see the way he looks at you. He looks up to you. You have an opportunity here to make a difference in his life. His parents are overwhelmed with grief, so they're limited in what they can give him."

"Okay, I'll go to school for Alex."

"And you'll stay here?"

"For Alex."

Valerie hugged her. "Thank you, honey. I know it's really hard on you too."

Despite the grief, Zoey couldn't stop a smile tugging at her mouth. She was going to spend the night at Alex's house.

Stranger

Zoey tossed and turned in Macy's bed. As tired as she was, it was too weird being in her best friend's room. Sure, Zoey had been in the room countless times, and it had always felt like her second home. But with Macy being gone, she didn't feel right being there.

She sat up, looking around the room. Macy loved night-lights, and there were enough of them around the room that Zoey could see everything. The desk looked bare with the computer gone.

Would Macy really know how to return it to factory settings? She always called Zoey when she had to do something on her computer. Macy knew nothing about computers aside from turning them on and starting up the Internet and a couple of programs she needed for school. Zoey was no computer whiz, but she often felt like one compared to Macy.

Sure, it was possible that Macy had Googled directions, but she wouldn't have been able to follow them. It didn't make any sense that she would have wiped the computer clean before leaving.

What if Jared had done that? He had removed his social media profiles, so it would stand to reason that if he had done something with Macy that he could have reset her computer. How would they have gotten into the house? It had been Macy's first time sneaking out. She wouldn't have sneaked back in with him, would she?

There were too many things that didn't add up, and again, she came back to the fact that Macy wouldn't ignore her. If Macy ran off with Jared, Zoey would have been the first to know. Even if it was only a quick text. She would have let Zoey know something.

She needed a cigarette. There was no way to sneak out onto the roof from Macy's room. It was a steep drop, and she wasn't stupid enough to risk it. If Chad and Alyssa were sleeping, she could go into the back yard. If they were awake, she would have to get creative. She really needed one.

Zoey got out of bed as quiet as possible, threw on a hoodie and then slid a pack and a lighter into the pocket. She opened the bedroom door and jumped when she saw Chad standing next to her, just outside the room, looking to the side. "Mr. Mercer, you startled me."

Wait. Why was he wearing a baseball cap and sunglasses, with his hoodie pulled on top of his head?

He turned and looked at her. Chad didn't have over-sized glasses, bushy eyebrows or a beard. A nine o'clock shadow, sure, but nothing like what this guy had.

Zoey's heart dropped. "You're not Mr. Mercer."

"And you shouldn't be in Heather's room."

"What? Who's Hea—?"

The man grabbed her, covering her mouth before she could scream. Zoey hit and kicked him, fighting even harder as he tightened his grip. He pinned her arms to her body. She kicked even harder, trying to bruise his shins. She couldn't scream, so she tried to bite him, but she couldn't even get her mouth open.

He moved his finger to block her nose. He was trying to kill her. Struggling to breathe, she continued to kick. She tried elbowing him, but she couldn't move her arms. Her fingers were free, so she pinched his legs on both sides. He let out a gasp and swore at her, shoving his finger further against her nose.

Zoey felt dizzy. She kept kicking his shins and squirmed with all her might. If she could squirm enough, maybe she could loosen his hold and get away. It was her only hope. She couldn't breathe, and she was getting dizzier by the second. It made it harder to fight him.

His grip on her tightened. She kept kicking and squirming, but suddenly she couldn't keep it up. She couldn't think straight, and her vision went dark.

When Zoey woke up, she was cold. Where was she? She blinked several times, but it was too dark to see anything. She got the shivers.

She was on a cold floor. She stood up, banging her head against something metal. The floor was especially cold on her feet. Where were her socks? Hadn't she gone to bed with socks on?

She stopped. She had gone to bed in Macy's room. What happened after that? Everything flooded back into her memory. That man hadn't killed her after all.

Where was she?

Desperation filled her, and she forgot about how cold she was. She felt around, walking as quietly as she could.

If he was nearby, the last thing she wanted to do was let him know she was awake. Zoey's hand touched what she was sure was a car. She kept her hand on it, walking alongside it. When she got to the other end, she felt around for something else she could use to guide her.

There was nothing in her reach, so she continued along, following the car. Why was it so dark? Was it still night? Were there no windows in this…whatever the place was? A garage, maybe. Hopefully that meant she wasn't being watched. Chills ran down her back as she pictured that guy watching her with night vision goggles. Again with her overactive imagination.

She picked up speed, eager to get out of the garage. She felt around the air as she walked, and eventually found a table or some kind of bench. It might have been Chad's tool bench. It was right where it should be if she was in their garage and she was walking alongside Alyssa's car. If she followed the bench to the other side, she should get to the door leading to the house.

More than anything, she needed to get inside to the Mercers. What if he had done something to them? She picked up her speed, praying that she wouldn't find them all in pools of their own blood.

Zoey felt along the bench until she reached the end. She walked to where the door should have been and found the handle. Holding her breath, she turned it. The door opened with a low squeak. The inside of the house was lighter than the garage, and as her eyes adjusted she could see she was in the Mercers' downstairs.

Before running up the stairs, she listened for any sounds. Everything was silent. It was too quiet, in fact. All kinds of bloody images flooded her mind. She had to get up to Alex's room to make sure he was okay. She ran up the stairs, unable to get images of an ax jammed in his head out of her mind. All she could imagine was his dead body lying in his blood-soaked bed.

By the time she reached the hall leading to the bedrooms, she had herself convinced that Alex was dead. Tears ran down her face. He was dead, she knew it. Two of the most important people in her life were gone.

She threw open his door and turned the light on. She didn't see any blood—she couldn't see anything for a moment. The light was blinding until her eyes adjusted. The first thing she noticed was Alex covering his head with a pillow.

"Turn it off. It's too bright." His voice was muffled.

Zoey let out a sigh of relief. He was alive. She turned the light off and leaned against the wall, gasping for air. She hadn't realized she had been holding her breath until she released it.

"What's going on?"

She ran to his bed, throwing herself against him, into his arms. "I'm so glad you're alive."

"Why wouldn't I be? What's going on?"

Snuggling closer, she found his face and gave him a prolonged kiss.

He returned the kiss for a moment, but then pulled away. "Why are you so upset?"

"I'm so glad you're alive," she repeated.

"Why?" He sounded out of breath. Alex pulled his head back and looked at her. They could barely see each other from what little light was coming through the window.

"I don't want to talk about it."

"You have to. Why are you so freaked out?"

She frowned, sighing. He was right. Even though she didn't want to talk about it, she needed to. She was still shaking. "I was going to go out for a smoke, but then I ran into someone in the hall."

"My parents?"

"No."

"What do you mean? Who?" Color drained from his face.

She leaned her head against his shoulder and then told him the entire story, shaking. Zoey left out the part about him calling Macy Heather. It was too weird, and it was a stupid detail, wasn't it?

Alex wrapped his arms around her, holding her tight. "Are you okay?"

"I am now. I was so afraid he had gotten to you. I was way more worried about you than anything else."

He looked her in the eyes. "We need to get my parents."

She shook her head. "No. I don't want to talk about it again."

"You have to tell them everything you told me. Some guy broke in here, Zoey. He could have hurt you worse than he did. What if he's still in here? Or if he took something? What if he comes back?"

Fear washed over her. "Just hold me."

He pulled her closer. "We still need to tell them. It's for all of our safety. Somehow he got in even though we have a security system. That's not good. You said you're worried about me, right?"

She nodded. "I was so scared I lost you. I can't lose you. I can't." She clung to him.

"Then you have to tell them. He could come back after you go back home. What then?"

Zoey shook again, tears running down her face.

Alex rubbed her hair. "Come on. We need to get my parents."

"Okay."

He wiped her tears with the back of his hand, and then kissed both of her cheeks. "I'll be with you when you tell them."

She nodded again.

"It'll be okay. I'm sure he's gone by now."

"Let's get this over with."

He grabbed her hand and led the way to his parents' room.

Telling

ALEX WAS SURPRISED to see his mom and dad in the bed together. They were even snuggled against each other. He almost hated to disturb them, but the thought of an intruder in the house drove fear straight into his core, especially after what the man had done to Zoey. They needed to get the d-bag and throw him in jail.

"Mom! Dad! Wake up."

They both sat up, mumbling.

"Someone was in the house."

His dad stared at him. "What?"

"Zoey saw him."

"What? Are you okay?" his mom asked, looking at Zoey.

Alex squeezed her hand, and she went over the story again.

His dad jumped out of bed. "We need to call the cops. How did he even get in? I set the alarm before I went to bed. Did one of you turn it off?"

They both shook their heads.

Zoey started crying. "Do I have to tell the cops? I don't want to relive it again."

Alex's mom climbed out of bed and gave her a hug. "I'm so sorry that happened to you, Zoey. We promised your mom we'd keep you safe, and then this happened. We need to tell the police so they can catch him."

"Then we're changing all of our locks and codes. Lyss, you call them while I check everything out. You guys all stay in here." He put on a robe, grabbed a baseball bat, and left.

"I'm going to call the police. You two sit down. This might take a few minutes," said his mom.

They sat on the bed, Alex not letting go of Zoey's hand. His parents hadn't noticed their hand-holding, but then again, it was still dark. He could see his mom scrolling through numbers on her phone. "Officer Anderson? This is Alyssa Mercer. Our house was broken in-to…yes…no…okay. Thanks. Goodbye." She put the phone down, and looked over at Alex and Zoey. "They're going to come over and check things out. Probably the same ones who talked with us down at the station last night, since they've already been working with us."

"Should we go downstairs?" Alex asked. He squeezed Zoey's hand again. He could hear her sniffling, but he didn't dare wrap his arms around her like he wanted. Then again, maybe his mom wouldn't think anything of it under the circumstances.

"Let's wait for your dad to get back. We don't even know if the intruder is still here." She looked at Zoey. "How long ago did you see him?"

"I don't know. I was pretty cold when I woke up in the garage, so I had probably been there a while."

She gave Zoey another hug. "I'm so sorry. I feel horrible."

"It's not your fault."

Alex scooted closer to Zoey, and the three of them sat in silence until his dad returned. "No one's here now. I checked everywhere."

"What about the alarm? Was that still set? Is anything gone?"

"The alarm is set, and no, I didn't notice anything missing. Who knows what might have been taken? But running into Zoey could have distracted him enough to leave." He turned to Zoey. "You could be a hero in all of this."

"I might have given him some bruises, but I'm no hero."

"We're all safe, and you're the only one who saw him. I'd say you're a hero."

One thing Alex appreciated about his dad was that he was good at making people feel better when they were upset. He always found some angle that no one else would ever think of, and then cheered the person up. Alex let go of her hand and wrapped his arm around her. "I agree. You're braver than you think."

The doorbell rang. His parents ran out of the room. Alex helped Zoey up and gave her a kiss he'd been wanting to since they entered his parents' room. "It's going to be okay. Are you?"

She sighed and leaned her head against his. "I hope so. I don't know how much more I can take. Everything with Macy and now this."

He rubbed her back. "I know. How much are we supposed to put up with? Maybe after this, our parents won't make us go back to school."

Alex grabbed Zoey's hand, and they went downstairs. Zoey dropped his hand once the grown-ups were in sight. His parents were sitting in the living room with the same three cops from the night before.

The only two places left to sit were at the opposite ends of the room. He let Zoey pick one, and then he sat in the other. He kept his eyes on her, hoping that would express his support as she went over her story for the third time.

When she was done, Detective Fleshman turned to Alex. "Did you see or hear anything?"

He shook his head. "I was sleeping. I didn't hear anything until Zoey came and got me."

"What did she say?"

"Um, she said something about being glad I was okay."

"Then what?"

"Then I asked her what happened, and she told me exactly what she told you. Then I said we needed to tell my parents, so we did."

Officer Reynolds looked at Zoey. "Can you think of anything you left out? Anything, no matter how insignificant can help."

Zoey hesitated, but then shook her head.

"What is it?" asked Detective Fleshman.

"It's stupid." Zoey bit her lower lip.

"Let us be the judge."

Zoey looked at Alex and then back to the detective. "Well, he said I shouldn't be in Heather's room. But I was in Macy's room. Maybe he had the wrong house."

"Could be," said Anderson. "Or it could be important. Thank you for telling us." He scribbled on his notepad.

"Is there anything else, Zoey?" asked Reynolds.

Zoey shook her head.

The policemen were done asking questions and said they wanted to look around. When the room cleared out, Alex sat next to Zoey, wrapping his arm around her. "What's the deal with Heather?"

"I have no idea. I feel dumb even bringing it up."

"Maybe it'll be a major clue. You never know."

Tears filled her eyes. "Maybe. I just want to forget about it."

"I know. Me too."

Alyssa came back into the room. She started to say something, but then saw how upset Zoey was. She sat down next to her, wrapping her arm around her. "I can't apologize enough for what happened. Are you going to be okay?"

Zoey nodded. "I don't want to talk about it."

She kissed the top of Zoey's head. "We need to tell your mom about what happened."

"No." The tears spilled onto her face.

Alex felt helpless. He wanted to move his mom out of the way and comfort his girlfriend. "I can tell her what happened, Mom. Don't make Zoey go over it again. She's been through enough."

"You're so sweet, Alex. You've always been such a good friend to Zoey. Don't worry, I'll call Valerie in the morning and let her know what happened. Our house will be safer now. The police are going to have someone watch our house. That, and we're getting all the locks changed as soon as the stores open in the morning."

Alex glared at his mom. "She looks tired. Can we go to sleep now?"

"That's a good idea. Get some rest, you two."

The three of them went upstairs, Alyssa staying close to Zoey. She said goodnight to Alex in the hall and then followed Zoey into Macy's room. Alex watched as they went into the room, wanting to stay with Zoey, but knowing that would have to wait.

He went into his room, intending to wait until his mom went to bed so he could talk with Zoey, but as soon as he saw his bed he realized how tired he was. He climbed in, falling asleep almost immediately—the only benefit to all the crap in his life.

As he was dreaming of a reunion with Macy, something woke him. He felt a hand on his arm, but he knew that if he woke up, he would lose Macy. He fought to stay in his dream and be with his sister.

The hand shook him, and a voice whispered his name. In his dream, he hugged Macy, clinging to her. He begged her to stay, but knew the dream would vanish in a poof soon. With tears in his eyes, he begged to her come back home. "I need my big sister, Macy. I love you."

She vanished before his eyes and it took him a moment to realize that Zoey was sitting next to him.

Her eyes were wide. "I can't sleep. Not after running into that guy. I don't want to be alone. Can I sleep in here?"

Alex's heart raced. "Sure."

"Thanks." She climbed in while he scooted over.

A strange mixture of emotions ran through him. The desperation from wanting Macy back lingered, along with a lump in his throat, but at the same time nervousness and excitement ran through him having Zoey in there with him. "Are you okay?"

"Not really. I was so scared. I didn't know if that guy was going to kill me or what. I didn't want to end up missing too, so I fought harder than I thought I could. He still over-powered me, though." Her voice sounded unsteady.

Alex reached his arms around her. "You're safe now."

"I don't feel like it."

He felt a tear land on his arm. He scooted even closer to her, holding her tighter. "You are. I'm here and there are cops sitting out front. That dude would be stupid to come back."

Zoey rolled onto her back, rubbing her eyes. "Why did he leave me in the garage? I don't get it."

"I don't know, but I'm glad he did. I couldn't take it if something happened to you too."

"Do you think someone took Macy like that?" asked Zoey.

"She went willingly, right?" At least that's what Zoey kept telling him. "She's off with Jared, having the time of her life."

Zoey sighed, but didn't reply. She probably didn't believe it any more than he did. He had a feeling that she kept talking about Macy being with Jared so she didn't have to deal with the pain. She turned, looking at him. "Do you think she's okay?"

"She has to be. She's the most stubborn person I've ever met. If anyone can survive…something bad happening, it's her."

"I worry about her, you know?" Zoey said. "She never really stood up for herself against the bullies at school. She just hid inside herself. There were times she wouldn't even talk to me after those stupid jerks went off on her. She built such a high wall, keeping everyone out."

Alex played with a strand of her hair. "I know. Why do you think I kept teasing her? When we were kids, making her laugh always worked. She'd come right out of her shell. But it's more than a shell; she built a fortress around herself. If she wasn't letting either of us in, what was really going on?"

"Only Jared knows. I knew she told him more than she told me, but I never pushed it. I guess because I felt bad about keeping us a secret. I wish I had been there for her more. Maybe she would still be here." Zoey sniffled.

He sat up, forcing her to also. "Are you kidding me? I've never seen a better best friend. All of my life, you've been there for her."

"We drifted apart, Alex, and I did nothing about it. I went out practically every night instead of spending the night with her since she couldn't go anywhere."

"Don't blame yourself. She was shutting everyone out, like you said."

"I shouldn't have given up so easily! Don't you see that? If I would have come over more, maybe she would have opened up." Zoey wiped at her eyes again.

"There's plenty everyone could have done to change things. I could have stopped teasing her. Dad could have stopped being so critical. Both my parents could have given her more freedom. Neither one of them noticed that she was practically starving herself while she lost her weight. Dad was just mad about her refusing to eat meat. Those kids at school—don't even get me started. They're the ones to blame."

Zoey shook, not saying anything.

Alex pulled her close, listening to her breathe and took in her scent. He wanted to know what she was thinking, but figured it was best to give her space to think. She leaned her head against his, both of them silent.

Finally, she spoke. "I'm so scared, Alex. I don't want anything to happen to Macy and I don't ever want to see another intruder again. I want everything to go back to the way it was."

He held her tighter, hoping that showed his agreement. He wasn't used to seeing this side of her and wasn't sure how to react. Usually she was so tough, but that guy had really shaken her up—not that Alex blamed her.

She rolled over so that she was in his lap, and stared into his eyes. He moved some hair out of her face and kissed her lightly on the lips. She pushed herself against him, kissing him harder.

Alex was surprised, but he pulled her closer, returning the kiss. Unable to breathe, he ran his hands through her hair. After a moment, he sat back and looked at her. "Are you okay? Are we moving too fast?"

"No." She forced her lips on his again, this time opening his mouth with her lips.

His eyes opened wide with surprise. Was this really the time for this? His heart raced. Of course he would have loved to take things to another level, but were they really ready? She already had so many regrets with Macy's disappearance. He didn't want her to have more regrets—especially when it came to him.

She brought her tongue into his mouth and he jumped. They bumped noses.

"Ow." Zoey sat back, rubbing her nose. "I don't think that's sup-posed to happen."

He couldn't help smiling, and they both laughed.

She leaned back against the pillow. "Maybe now isn't the time for that. I think going to sleep in your arms would be nice enough."

"Me too." He put his arms around her again.

She ran her fingers along his arm, and he couldn't help flexing. She kept rubbing his arm, and then after a minute her arm fell to the bed. He could hear her breathing heavily.

"Sweet dreams." He kissed her hair and closed his own eyes.

Light

MACY FELT SOMETHING move along her hand. She didn't even bother trying to roll away. What was the point?

Part of her wanted to cry, but she couldn't. She had already cried and screamed more than she could bear. Her shoulders were in constant pain from having her wrists tied behind her back. Her legs were wet and cold from not being able to remove her pants to relieve herself. Even worse than that, the back of her legs burned with a relentless intensity. She could feel the sores back there from the dried excrement.

She had passed being hungry. Earlier, she had been so hungry she would have eaten rodents if she could have. Now she felt nothing in her stomach.

She was sure she had been down there for a few days, though she had no way of knowing for sure with cloth over her eyes. And even if it weren't for the blindfold, her thoughts were all over the place, and she was pretty sure she was going crazy.

Although the fact that she questioned her sanity gave her hope that she still held onto a shred of it.

Her throat was parched.

Chester had left her water before, but even if he had this time she had no way of getting it. She had rolled around the floor at one point, hoping to find some. It had been futile, and she had only made herself thirstier in the process.

Sounds of the trap door moving caught her attention. Was she actually hearing it? Or was this further proof of her slipping sanity?

Thud. That sounded like something landing on the floor above. *Squeak, squeak.* That sounded like the ladder. *Thump.* Two feet landing on the dirt floor. Was he going to rescue her?

"Are you ready to follow directions now, Heather?"

The voice sounded real, but so had the others.

"You have to be thirsty." She felt fingers tugging on the duct tape. In one solid, painful motion, the tape was ripped from her face. Then she felt tugging on the blindfold. Bright light blinded her. Macy closed her eyes as tight as she could and shoved her face into the dirt floor, trying to get away. After so long in the dark, it was too much. "You didn't answer my question. Are you ready to be good?"

She kept rolling around, trying to escape the light. Even though she closed her eyes, they refused to adjust.

"Your grandparents are going to be gone for a couple of hours, so now is the time to go back to the house and get cleaned up. Or I can leave you here longer. It's up to you."

"I'll go. Take me with you."

"Are you going to be good now? I need to know we won't have a repeat of the other night."

"Yes. Anything."

"Looks like we'll have to throw these clothes away. Or should I save them as a reminder in case you act up again?"

"No."

"Good. Let's get you up there so you'll be cleaned up when Grandma and Grandpa get back. I told them we took a road trip. You'll be able to go along with that story, right?"

Macy nodded.

"What? I can't hear you."

"Yes."

"And do you remember falling down the stairs?"

"What?"

"That's how you got all those bruises. Do you remember?"

"I remember."

A shadow blocked the sun as he moved behind her. There was a snip, followed by another. Her arms fell free to her sides and then her ankles spread apart from each other. Pain shot through her arms, and tears stung her eyes.

"Look at those marks. You'll need to wear long sleeves until they heal. Understand?"

Macy nodded, focused on how much she hurt everywhere.

"Stand up." Chester kicked her in the side.

Keeping her eyes closed, she pushed against the ground. Sharp pains ran through her arms. Her butt and legs stung where sores had formed. "I can't."

"There is no can't. Should I leave you here?"

"No!" She ignored the pain and forced herself to stand up.

"Open your eyes."

Macy's legs wobbled underneath her. What would he do to her if she fell? She swallowed and forced her eyes open. The light was even worse, but she couldn't risk him leaving her down there again. She blinked fast, trying to get her eyes to adjust.

"Are you thirsty?"

She nodded. The pain in her shoulders was too much. She pushed her arms behind her back, relieving some of it.

"There's some water in the house. Let's go."

Macy groaned. Could she even make it that far?

Chester went to the rope ladder and climbed up. He looked down at her. "Come on up."

She forced one foot in front of the other, stumbling with each step. Pins and needles ran through her legs, feeling the most painful at the bottom of her feet. The sores hurt even worse as she moved her legs.

The ladder was about six feet away. How was she going to make it there, much less to the farmhouse?

"Can you hurry up? We need to get you cleaned up before your grandparents get back."

She stumbled forward, forcing herself to go faster despite the various pains screaming out at her. Tears stung her eyes again, making her vision blurry. She managed to get to the ladder, but as soon as she brought her arms forward the pain became so intense that she jumped. She couldn't even bring them to her sides without it hurting. How was she supposed to pull herself up the ladder?

"What are you waiting for?"

"I can't."

"What is it with you? Are you an Ameri-can or an Ameri-can't?"

She stared at him, ignoring the pains in her neck. What kind of a stupid question was that?

"Get up here or I'll leave you down there until they leave again. I can't guarantee when that will be." He moved the door.

"No. I'll do it."

Macy held her breath, anticipating the pain. She moved her hands in front of her as fast as she could, hoping that would eliminate some of it. It didn't help. She would have to push through it.

Her grip was weak, but she managed to grab onto the ladder. She closed her eyes as the tears began to fall. Soon she would be getting out of the dirty clothes and getting cleaned up. That's what she had to focus on; otherwise the pain would be too much. Beads of sweat formed around her face.

She cried the whole way up, but she made it, thinking of the bath-tub and new clothes. Maybe she could put some ointment on the sores on her legs. They were probably infected since she hadn't been able to clean them. Each sore felt hot, and it got even worse every time her pants rubbed against her legs.

When she reached the top, she wasn't able to pull herself up onto the floor. Everything hurt, and she didn't have the strength. She had barely made it to the top of the ladder. What if she fell to the ground below?

"Help me. I ca…I need help."

He stared at her.

"Please," she begged.

"Oh, all right. Since you asked nice." He reached down and grabbed her arm, roughly, and yanked her up.

She fell to the floor, rubbing her arm where he had grabbed her.

"Get up. They're going to be back soon. You need to get cleaned up, and I have to get rid of this beard. I've gone too long without shaving."

Groaning, she forced herself back up again. He slammed the trap door shut and kicked some hay over it.

"Let's get to the house." He walked on ahead of her. Did he expect her to keep up?

She forced herself to walk. Her muscles ached, and the sores burned, but at least the pins and needles had gone away. That was something at least. Her arms naturally went behind her back, relieving the pain. She would have to hold them forward once George and Ingrid came back, but for now, she was going to nurse her wounds.

He turned around and waited once he got to the barn door. "Hurry up."

"I'm going as fast as I can."

"You can do better than that. Oh, by the way, I saw your old family."

Macy stopped. She stared at him, her many questions not reaching her mouth.

"They were all sleeping when I got there, so I let myself in. Your best friend was in your room. She wasn't sleeping, and that threw me off. I had to shut her up."

The blood drained from her body. "What did you do?"

"Oh, she's fine. She woke up cold, but otherwise unharmed. I couldn't let her wake anyone else. Pick up your pace, and I'll tell you more."

Her heart raced. What had he done? Was Zoey okay? What about her parents and Alex? She walked faster, ignoring the searing pain. "What did you do?" she asked again.

He walked through the door, waited for her to exit, and then he closed the barn door. "First, I got rid of your bloody clothes. Your old family was pretty upset about seeing them." He turned to look at her. "They probably already think you're dead. That's the plan. They're going to move on, so you don't need to worry about those ties anymore. You're Heather, and I'm your dad. Don't forget that."

She nodded. Her family wouldn't move on. They wouldn't. Or would they?

"Oh, and keep in mind that I got back in again. I didn't hurt anyone…this time. Don't get mouthy with me again, or I won't be so nice next time."

Her sores burned as she walked. He thought this was nice? Why had he gone into her house again? Just to threaten her? Had he actually done anything to her family? He admitted to doing something to Zoey, but supposedly she was okay. What exactly did he consider "okay?" He probably thought Macy was okay, but she needed to have a doctor look at the sores. She knew that would never happen.

When they finally got to the house, he opened the door for her. "Why don't you go to your room and grab some clean clothes? Then you can get a bath. I'll shave in my room—don't worry about me."

As if she would. She nodded and walked past him.

"Wait."

She stopped.

"Give your ol' dad a hug."

Was he serious?

He opened his arms. Apparently he was. "Come on, Heather. I've missed your hugs. Throw your dad a bone."

Macy caught a glance of the barn through a window. She didn't ever want to go back there again. She stifled a gag and walked to him. He wrapped his arms around her.

"That's not a hug, Heather. Give me a real hug."

Gritting her teeth, she wrapped her arms around him, ignoring the pain, and gave a little squeeze. Even more pain shot through her arms.

He hugged her tighter. "That's my girl. Now go get cleaned up. We're going to have a great time with your grandparents when they get back."

Macy walked back to the room that was supposed to be hers. It was Heather's, and always would be. When she walked through the door she froze, her heart skipping a beat. Her favorite teddy bear from her real bedroom was sitting on the bed.

He really had been back to her house. Chills ran down her back. Even so, she ran to the bed and scooped up the bear, hugging it tight, not caring about how much her arms hurt. It was something familiar, something loved.

The smell of her home, her *real* home, brought instant comfort. She squeezed the stuffed animal all the tighter, pretending that she was back home and that she had never sneaked out to meet Jared.

She threw herself onto the bed, careful not to hurt her sores, imagining that she was back on her own bed. Macy buried her face into the bear's stomach and breathed in the smells even harder. She could see her room in her mind—every detail.

Would the bear hold the scent forever? Could she go back home in her mind whenever she wanted now?

A pounding on the door brought her back to reality. "Are you going to get in the bathroom? Your grandparents are going to be back soon," called Chester.

"Coming!" She squeezed the stuffed animal, never wanting to let go.

Hardware

CHAD FELT DIZZY looking at all the choices for door locks. Wasn't a lock just a lock? The aisle was full of different types. Not wanting to read another box, he grabbed five boxes of the most expensive lock on the shelf. It had to be the best or it wouldn't cost so much.

Just as he set the last one in the basket, his phone rang. It was Alyssa.

"Is everything okay?"

"Just wanted to let you know that someone from the home security will be here in a couple hours. They're going to look at everything and make sure nothing is faulty. If it is, they'll upgrade us for free."

"They're going to upgrade us, period. I'll be there before they arrive. I've got the locks. Do you need me to get anything else?"

"No. There's a police car out front, so if there's any trouble, they're here."

"Good. I told them not to leave while I was gone. I'll be home soon."

"Okay. Chad?"

"Yeah?"

"I love you."

His heart swelled up. "I love you too, Lyss. Stay safe."

"Okay."

The call ended and he stuffed the phone back in his pocket. It was so nice to be getting along again, and he had been surprised at how quickly his old feelings had returned. He found himself eager to get back home to her. He picked up the basket and headed for the registers.

He had to turn down another aisle to get there. As he did, he saw

Lydia. What was she doing in the hardware store? Had she been following him?

Chad turned around, but it was too late.

She ran to him. "What are you doing here?" she asked.

"I was about to ask you the same thing. You're not following me, are you?"

Lydia's face fell. "I thought we were close."

"Look, Lydia, you're a really sweet person—"

"Oh, geez. I can tell where this is going."

"I appreciate you being there for me when I was going through a tough time, but I need to focus on my family now."

"Right. That's why I've been giving you space."

"Space? You're making my family dinner tonight."

"Do you want to explain to Alyssa why you don't want me over?"

Chad narrowed his eyes. "You know the answer to that."

"Then let me come over and cook you guys a meal. Everyone wants to help out. I called all the members of the homeowners' association, and each one signed up for a night to cook or bring you takeout. Everyone. Besides, I know how much you love my lasagna. I'll make it and leave. I don't have any ulterior motives. Well, maybe one."

"What?"

"Just to let you know that I'll be waiting. I'm not going anywhere, Chad. When you're ready, which I know you will be eventually, you can find me. I'll drop anything to spend time with you. I appreciate everything you do. Your blog is amazing. I know you'll be able to quit your day job any day now. And even though I doubt you've worked out lately, you still look hot as—"

"Okay, Lydia. Point taken. Why don't you try to rekindle things with Dean?"

She gave him an exasperated look. "The man who comes home three nights a month? No. You know why I stay with him: so I don't have to work. He works so much, I don't have to. Sure, I may have to fix a sprinkler head once in a while"—she held one up—"but other than that, I have the perfect life. Well, when you come over to play, I do."

Chad ran his free hand through his hair. "I need to get back home."

Lydia looked in his basket. "New locks? What's going on?"

"Why don't you ask Alyssa about it tonight? It'll give you something to talk about. Either that, or watch the news. Everything we do seems to end up there. I can't wait for the media to find someone else to stalk."

She raised an eyebrow. "I hope everything is okay. I'll see you tonight."

He nodded and turned to walk away. Why was she everywhere? He needed to get her out of his life so he could focus on Alyssa. She was the one he loved. Lydia had been nothing more than a distraction when Alyssa wouldn't give him the time of day. Lydia was a mistake, and one that he intended to forget about.

When he got to the register, the girl behind the counter stared at him.

"Are you all right?" he asked.

"You're...you're the guy from the news."

He nodded. "I need to buy these."

"Oh, right. Sorry." She grabbed the basket and scanned the first box. "I'm so sorry about your daughter. She's beautiful, by the way. I hope she's okay."

Chad squirmed. This was why he hated going anywhere any more. It had been this way since Macy disappeared.

"Are you changing your locks?"

"Um, yeah."

"Aren't you afraid that if she tries to get in, she won't be able to? Won't she feel like you're trying to lock her out?"

Anger burned inside of him. "Not that it's any of your business, but our house is a target. If Macy comes back, she has the smarts to knock or use the doorbell."

A manager walked up to them. "Is everything all right here?"

Chad turned to him. "I'm trying to buy some locks to keep my family safe, and your cashier is trying to give me a guilt trip about my daughter."

The manager stared at him for a moment. Then recognition covered his face. "Oh, Mr. Mercer. We're honored to have your patronage. Please accept my apologies. This is my daughter, Sarah, and her mouth gets out of control when she's nervous. Let me give you those locks at a discount. Does fifty percent sound good?"

"I'm not looking for a discount. I want to get home and get these locks in without having to explain myself to anyone." He was aware of people staring, but he really didn't care.

"Seventy-five percent off. Now that's a deal, and those are our best locks. Houdini himself couldn't get through a door with those."

Chad shook his head. He pulled out his wallet, counted out the cash, and put them on the counter. "Keep the change." He stormed out of the store, never more eager to get back home. He was going to have to find a new hardware store.

He was glad to have the job of replacing all the door locks when he got home. He needed the distraction. But it didn't work; he kept hearing the voice of the cashier saying he was locking Macy out. By the third door, he couldn't take it anymore. He threw his tools down, swearing.

Chad needed his dad. He would know what to do. In fact, his parents would have flown in the moment they heard Macy was gone. He tried to picture his dad standing next to him. It was useless. His imagination wouldn't bring his parents back any more than it was going to bring back his daughter.

He leaned against the door and slid to the ground, staring into the back yard. Tears filled his eyes, blurring his vision. What was he supposed to do? He wanted to keep the locks that Macy could use, but at the same time he *had* to protect his family. Someone had gotten into their house while they all slept. He had no other choice. Macy would understand.

She loved them all and wanted them safe. Just as he loved her and wanted her safe.

But there was nothing he could do to protect her. He hated feeling helpless, and this was the worst kind of helpless.

Sure, he was the kind of dad who would tell his kids to toughen up when they got a scrape, but it wasn't that he didn't care. He just wanted them to be able to handle life.

He sighed, more tears welling up in his eyes, threatening to spill out.

Did Macy need him as much as he needed his parents right now? He rested his head on his knees, shaking with sobs.

This was the worst part: not being able to do anything. At least with the doors, he could do something useful. He was protecting his family. But that cashier had planted doubts in his head about even that.

Screw her. He stood up and grabbed his tools. Screw that cashier. What did she know, anyway? Did she have a missing kid? Was her family in danger? Screw her. She was probably one of those snot-nosed employees who ran to her dad whenever she had a problem.

He worked on getting the doorknob off so he could remove the lock. His vision was still blurry and now his hands were shaking. Why had he gone to that hardware store in the first place? He wouldn't make that mistake again, and he had every intention of writing all about it in his blog.

But Chad knew better than to write while he was upset. He didn't want to say anything that would hurt his reputation. If he came off as a jerk, that could potentially ruin how well his blog was going, or even worse, piss people off who were looking for Macy. He needed to keep the public's sympathy.

"Are you okay?" came Alyssa's voice from the other side of the door.

"Yeah," he lied.

"Can I come out?"

Chad wiped his face dry. "Sure."

She opened the knobless door and froze when she saw him. "What's the matter?"

"What do you think?"

"You don't need to snap at me."

"You're right. I'm sorry." He told her what had happened with the cashier, breaking down halfway through.

Alyssa's face softened. "Oh, Chad." She gave him a hug, and they stood in the back yard holding each other. "You know, you don't have to hide when you're hurting. I know you always want to talk with your dad, but I'm here. You can talk to me. This is something we're going through together."

"Do you think she'll understand?"

"Macy? Yes. She would want you doing exactly this. She would want us to be safe and to keep Alex protected."

"Why are we talking like she's dead? She *would* say this or that."

"Not because we think she's dead." Tears filled Alyssa's eyes. "Only because she's not here and we can't ask her."

He shook his head. "We're talking like she's dead."

News

C HAD STARED AT the computer screen, unable to focus. Lydia was in the kitchen, preparing the lasagna—because she knew how much he liked it. Why was she even in their house? Why hadn't he been able to stand up and tell her no?

Because that would have looked suspicious, and the last thing he needed was for Alyssa to figure out what he had done. It didn't matter now, because it was over. He wasn't going to see Lydia anymore. He was going to repair his marriage and find a way to get his daughter back.

The screen saver popped up, startling him. He leaned back in the chair, rubbing his hands over his stubble. He had to find a way to get Lydia out of his life. At least she lived at the other end of the neighborhood. It wasn't as though she was next door. He could avoid her easily enough. She would find another guy to keep her distracted from thinking about her own husband.

He got up and paced around the office, picking up stray items. The office was a mess. He hated how he let it get so messy in there, but when he was in there, he was focused on the computer. After what seemed like only a few minutes, his office was organized. Alyssa had always complained about the mess, but she hadn't said a word about it since Macy had been missing.

Where *was* Macy? He picked up a stack of business cards and threw it across the office, sending cards everywhere. What would he do if she never returned? There he went again, allowing himself to think about her being dead. That was the last thing he wanted, but he couldn't seem to keep his mind from going there. The more time that went by, the harder it became to keep his hope alive. It had only been a week. What would he be like in another week if Macy was still gone? How would he survive another week? He needed her back.

Chad picked up a pen from his desk and chucked it at a bookshelf. Distress rising in him, he picked up the coffee mug holding all of his pens and pencils. He squeezed it and then threw it at the wall above the couch. It burst into tiny pieces all over the cushions and floor.

It felt good to break something. He went over to the bookshelf and grabbed a handful of paperbacks, throwing them one by one across the room. Once he had thrown them all, he picked up all his knick-knacks and threw them at the couch, knowing that if they broke he would later regret it.

With the shelf empty, he went over to the couch and grabbed a throw pillow, shaking the broken mug pieces onto the floor. He put his face into the pillow and screamed as loud as he could until his throat hurt. No need for his family or Lydia to hear him.

The cell phone rang. He stared at it on his desk. A feeling of dread ran through him. What if it was bad news? He picked it up and recognized the police station number. How sad that he recognized that number now.

"Chad here."

"Mr. Mercer, this is Officer Anderson. We need you and your wife to come down to the station."

"Again? Why?" Chad demanded.

"We need you two to come alone."

His blood ran cold. Had they found Macy? "Tell me what this is about."

"Sir, we received the results from the clothes."

"What? You said it could be a week or more."

"With this being such a high profile case, they rushed it to the front."

"Why do you need us to go back downtown? Can't you tell me over the phone? My family has been through enough, wouldn't you agree?"

"I can't deny that, but it's policy."

"You think I care about policies? If you have something important to tell us, either tell us over the phone or drive over here yourselves."

"Mr. Mercer, please. We—"

"I'm not dragging my wife back down there. After what happened last night, I'm sure as hell not leaving the house without my son. He's only thirteen. After everything we've gone through, he'll be lucky if we ever leave him alone again."

There was a sigh on the other end of the line. "If you really want us to come to your house, I'll talk with my supervisor. I'll see if we can make an exception."

"I think you probably can." Chad hung up before he said something he would regret. He stuck the phone in his pocket and went upstairs to find Alyssa. When he passed the kitchen, he saw her talking with Lydia.

His stomach twisted in knots. Lydia wouldn't tell Alyssa anything, would she? No. She wouldn't want word to get back to Dean.

Chad looked at Alyssa. "I need to talk to you for a moment."

A look of fear washed over her face. "What's going on? I don't like your tone."

"I got a call from the station."

She got up and grabbed his arm, dragging him up the stairs toward their bedroom. "What do they want? What's going on?"

"They got the results on the blood."

Alyssa stopped. She stared at Chad expectantly.

"I don't know, though I'm assuming it's Macy's. They wouldn't tell me over the phone. Anderson wanted us to go down to the station, but I told him that wasn't going to happen, so they're going to come here."

She leaned against the wall. "Do you really think it's her blood?"

"Who else would it belong to? Those were her clothes, right? If it was someone else's they would have told me over the phone, don't you think?"

"What are we going to do?"

"Keep looking. Keep hoping. It's like I said before: sure it was a lot of blood, but it wasn't enough to k…to do any real damage. I've bled more than that when I've been punched in the nose. Obviously, the clothes were removed because they needed to be replaced. The cops found them by the mall, so she probably bought some new clothes, put them on, and dropped those. This is actually good news."

Alyssa looked at him as though he had lost his mind.

"I'm serious. It means she's probably alive, and not too far away. The clothes weren't found right after she disappeared. It was about a week later. So she has to be nearby." Maybe if he kept talking, he would start to believe the crap coming out of his mouth. "It means we have to canvas the neighborhood even more. Maybe we should even accept an invitation to speak to the press again. We need all the public sympathy we can get. If people hear from us directly, you know, the ones who haven't visited my blog to hear from us there, maybe they'll help us look harder."

She looked a little bit more convinced than she had before.

"You know I'm right, Lyss. Once word gets out about this, people are going to want to hear more. It's the perfect time for us to get in front of the cameras and beg for people to help us find Macy."

"I think you're right."

Chad gave her a double-take. "What?"

"I know. You think you'll never hear that again, but you're right. This is probably good news. It gives us hope. She's probably not too far away. Maybe she'll even see the news. If she's hiding somewhere, mad at us for something, maybe seeing us on TV will be enough to bring our baby home."

He nodded, trying not to seem surprised that she had bought his load of horse manure.

"This is actually a good thing. My parents are still planning on coming Monday, so they'll be able to help us out. This is perfect. Everything is coming together."

"All we need is Macy."

Alyssa sighed. "That's all we need. Maybe if us speaking to the cameras isn't enough to bring her home, maybe my parents would do it."

"That's good. Should we tell Alex what's going on? He should know."

Alyssa nodded. "He should."

Chad rubbed his eyes. He wasn't used to Alyssa agreeing with him so much. He went to Alex's door and knocked. He could hear a noise behind the door. It sounded like something heavy falling onto the ground, followed by some rustling noises. "You in there, Alex?"

"Yeah. Come in."

He opened the door. Alex was sitting up in his bed, not wearing a shirt. "Where's your shirt and why are you sweaty?"

"I'm tired. I haven't slept in, like, a week. This is how I sleep now. What's with all the questions?"

There was a rustling noise at the other end of the bedroom.

"What was that?" Chad asked.

"Uh…um, I was playing with Macy's ferret. Yeah, that's it. He looked lonely."

Chad raised an eyebrow. "Don't let that thing get lost. Anyway, the police are on their way over with news about Macy's clothes. Did you want to be there to hear it? They didn't think you should be, but Mom and I wanted to ask you what you want. She's your sister, and if you want to hear the news when we do, you can."

The color drained from his face. "Is it going to be bad?"

"We don't know. But Mom and I think even if it is Macy's blood, it's good news." He repeated his stupid theory to Alex, who also seemed to buy it. "So, we'll see you downstairs?"

Alex nodded.

Alyssa moved next to Chad. "Well, we'd better tell Zoey. She'll probably want to be there, too."

"No!" Color drained from Alex's face. "I mean, I'll tell her. You guys do…whatever it is you have to do. I'll get her and then we'll meet you guys downstairs."

Chad raised an eyebrow. "All right. We'll see you guys down there. Don't forget to put the ferret back in the cage."

Alex sighed. "Yeah, okay."

Chad closed the door and walked downstairs with Alyssa.

Despite everything, the smell of the lasagna made his mouth water. He wasn't sure what Lydia put into it, but hers was the best there was.

"Do you think Alex was acting strange?" Alyssa asked.

"He's thirteen. I'd be more worried if he wasn't acting weird."

"I suppose. Well, I'll let Lydia know what's going on. I'm not sure how much time is left until the food's ready, but it smells so good, it must be close."

Chad nodded. He went into the living room and saw the police cruiser pull up across the street. Now there were two cop cars sitting in front of their house. He stuffed his tools in a corner behind a chair and then opened the front door before they even had a chance to knock.

Chad exchanged greetings with the police, and they all sat down in the living room. Alyssa joined them, and Alex came down with Zoey a minute later.

The news had been what they all expected. The blood was Macy's, and even the cops agreed it wasn't a fatal amount. There was still plenty of reason to keep hope alive.

Even so, it felt like someone had punched Chad in the side of the head. He had known those would be the results, but hearing it out loud brought the truth to a whole new level. He looked over at Alyssa, who was staring out the window with tears shining in her eyes. He put his arm around her and pulled her close.

She started sobbing, shaking almost violently in his arms. "We'll find her," he whispered. "This is good news, remember?" He wasn't sure if he bought it any more than he had earlier, but he had to hold onto the hope that she was still alive. He had to.

Crushed

MACY BARELY HAD enough time to get ready before Chester's parents returned. They kept her busy walking around the farm, having her help with the chores. Every move she made hurt; she couldn't walk without the sores rubbing against her clothes.

She smiled through the pain so they wouldn't know anything was wrong. One wrong move, and she would go back into the dungeon. She might not get out if there was a next time.

The sores were so painful she had no chance of a getaway. Her joints still ached from being forced into one position for days. Even if she didn't have to worry about Chester running after her, it would hurt too much to get far.

After pouring some feed for the pigs, Macy sat down to rest. Tears stung at her eyes. She forced a smile. That's what Heather would do.

Ingrid walked by a minute later and stopped. "Heather, why does your dad insist on so many road trips? Three days this time. What did you two do for three days?" Ingrid patted Macy's shoulders. "And how did you manage to fall down two flights of stairs? Those bruises look so painful."

"Just clumsy, I guess."

Ingrid shook her head. "I'm sure you were distracted. I can't imagine how hard everything is for you. What with your mom being gone, he shouldn't drag you around, forcing you to stay in a car for days on end."

Macy looked into her eyes. She opened her mouth to say she wasn't Heather, but images of the cellar flooded her mind. She just shrugged.

George came over. "Tired? Poor girl. Does being around the animals help? It always did when you were little."

"Yeah, sure."

"We should tell Chester to take a road trip on his own," Ingrid said. "We can watch Heather. It would do her a world of good, especially since she has to deal with the divorce. It's too much."

"You know how he is," George said. "Remember that one kid picked on him every day?"

Macy looked up, suddenly interested.

"Juan, wasn't it?" Ingrid asked. "He was always envious of Chester."

"I don't know about that, but they were always fighting," George said. "Seems Chester came home beat up nearly every day for a while, but he just kept going back to school. When times are tough, he won't let anything stop him. Now he's forcing Heather to push through."

"He's a stubborn one. Seems those teachers should have done more for him." Ingrid shook her head. "They were old-school, even for that time. Boys will be boys, they told me every time I complained."

"The teachers practically encouraged the other kids to make fun of him. That's what Chester always said."

Ingrid patted Macy's arm. "We're upsetting Heather. Let's talk about something more cheery. Would you like your dad to take a vacation while you stay here?"

Macy's eyes lit up. "Yes, please."

George picked up a pitchfork that was lying on the ground and leaned against the wall. "I should convince him to go back to Paris. He needs to try harder to get Karla back. Heather is her life. Why would she throw everything away? And why wouldn't Chester fight for her?"

Ingrid cleared her throat. "We ought to let Heather get some rest."

When Macy finally made it to her bedroom, she was so tired that she climbed into bed without putting on pajamas.

Aside from being physically wiped out, she was mentally tired from pretending to be someone else. But the last thing she wanted was to go back to the horrible room under the barn again, so she kept up the facade. Spending time with the animals in the barn was a painful reminder of where she would go again if she didn't do exactly what Chester wanted.

Her mom was off in Paris, sowing her wild oats. Her dad was the deranged lunatic who had nearly left her to die just to prove a point. The kind elderly couple were her grandparents. The farm was her home, and she had no friends aside from the animals. This was her life.

When she looked into the eyes of the animals, they almost seemed to know that she was unhappy. She could plaster on a smile for George and Ingrid, but there was no fooling the large, brown eyes of the cows and horses. When she was near them, they stared at her as though staring into the depths of her soul. Macy had felt understood each time she made eye contact with them. They knew her secret somehow, and they were going to keep it safe.

She moved aside the pillow to pick up her teddy, but it wasn't where she had left it. Dread washed over her. Even though she was fifteen, she needed that bear. She had slept the previous night with it in her face the whole time.

Macy picked up the pillow, lifting it over her head. Nothing. She put it back and looked around on the floor. It could have fallen off, even though she had been careful to leave it right next to the pillow that morning. She wanted to keep it safe, comfortable even. Obviously, it was a toy, but it was more than that.

Not caring about her sores, she crawled around on the floor, looking for where the bear could have gone. It wasn't under the bed or the dresser. It was nowhere.

She had to get it. She picked up the covers from the perfectly made bed. Chester made her keep the room pristine, so she would have seen a lump if it was there, but she had to look anyway. She moved to the closet, searching for it in there.

After she had looked everywhere three times, she threw herself onto the bed and sobbed into the pillow. It was gone. Chester had to have taken it. Was it another cruel way for him to control her? Had he given it to her just to give her hope so that he could take it away, crushing her yet again? Trying to confuse her as to her own identity?

Could he be any worse? He wanted her to accept him as her dad, yet he acted like the world's biggest jerk. Hadn't he ever heard of winning people over by being nice?

Her stomach ached by the time she was done crying. She had nothing left in her. Macy felt like an empty shell of a person. Was that the point? Was that exactly what Chester wanted? If that was the case, he had won. Her heart felt as though it had been ripped to shreds.

She got up and turned the light off. She climbed into bed alone, with no stuffed animal to hold. Even though she was exhausted, she couldn't sleep.

The way he talked about himself, one would think he was a hero, saving her from her life with her real family.

She couldn't see an end in sight. Would he let her go to school? She had already missed however much time she had been gone. Why didn't his parents question it? If he sent her to school, she would at least get some time away from him and maybe make some friends. That was probably the exact thing he didn't want her to do.

She sniffed, needing to blow her nose. She couldn't recall seeing any tissues in the bedroom, so she would have to go to the bathroom to get some toilet paper. Maybe Chester had even put the bear in the hall as a mean reminder that she needed to stay in the room, just as he had done with the picture of her family. Macy hadn't seen that since the first night in the house.

She got out of bed and went to the door. She turned the knob, but her hand slid off. She tried again, but found it wouldn't move. He had locked her inside.

What if she had to use the bathroom? Hadn't he thought of that? She grabbed the knob and twisted it with all the force she could muster. It didn't move. She tried several more times before giving up.

Fresh tears poured down her face, and then she walked back over to the bed. Never before had she felt so dejected—and that was saying something after everything she had already been through.

She had no more fight left in her. She already knew the windows were bolted shut, so there was no way she was going to get out. Luckily she didn't have to go to the bathroom.

Pulling the covers up to her chin, she closed her eyes as the tears stopped. What was the point? What was crying going to get her? Macy found it too easy to push each and every thought out of her head. There was no point, was there? She couldn't get to her parents anyway. She didn't even know where she was, but Chester did. He had already gone back to her house, and the bear had been proof of that.

Had that been his real angle? To remind her that he could hurt them if he needed to? Would he really kill them all if she escaped? She wouldn't put it past him. He was cruel enough to put her through everything he had. It wouldn't take much more effort to finish someone off.

He didn't care about them. The people she loved the most meant nothing to him. He wouldn't even flinch at killing them. She was sure of it. If she were to get away, he would climb into his truck, drive back to her house, and kill them off before she could even figure out where she was, much less find a way to get back to them.

That was what the bear was all about. Just like with the picture, it was left for her to find it, and then it was gone. He wouldn't leave anything from her house long enough for her to hold onto.

But the memories were something he couldn't take from her. He could take everything else, and he pretty much already had, but he couldn't control her mind. She had every memory of her parents, friends, brother, house, and pets. He couldn't make her forget, even if he could make her call him dad. He would never *be* her dad.

Bar

ALYSSA SAT UP in bed, gasping for air. She was drenched in sweat, and her heart was racing. She had just had another nightmare about Macy. She had always had bad dreams about things happening to her kids, but since Macy had disappeared, waking up didn't help.

She wiped some wet strands of hair away from her face and looked over at Chad. He was sleeping, not snoring as usual, which meant he probably wasn't sleeping well either. When he was deep in sleep, he snored like a chainsaw.

Not wanting to have another bad dream, she got into the shower to get cleaned up. The images from her nightmare wouldn't leave. What made the nightmares worse was the fact that she had nothing good to focus on. When the kids were little, she would sneak into their rooms and watch them sleep peacefully. Even as they got older she did it on occasion, depending on how bad the dream was.

She couldn't do that now.

Physically, she was wiped out. Her legs ached and her neck and shoulders were sore. Had it not been for her racing mind, she could have crawled back into bed and slept for a day, if not more.

She couldn't stop thinking about the worst. Though she couldn't bring herself to say it out loud, she feared Macy's death. She knew that the longer she was gone, the higher the chances were of that happening. The thought of that made her want to vomit. No one had the right to take *her* child. No one. How dare they?

It just wasn't like Macy to take off like that. Even if she had planned on running away, she wouldn't have stayed away this long, causing all this mental anguish to her family. One time when she had been mad about not being allowed to go somewhere with her friends, Macy had staged her own personal hunger strike. That was her type of thing, not running away without a word.

Even if she had met someone online, she wouldn't have left like that. She just wouldn't have. As a mom, Alyssa knew these things. She wondered if her dreams were Macy calling out to her. Tears ran down her face, as they did so many times these days.

She cried until the water ran cold, and then she got dressed. There was no way she could stay in the house for another moment. After that last dream, too bloody to leave her mind, she couldn't sit still. Her home felt like it was closing in on her.

Chad stirred in the bed, startling her. He rolled over, letting out one short snore.

She sighed in relief. Normally, she would have hoped he would wake so she could talk about the dream. He was so good at calming her down, but she didn't want to be calmed down.

Hopefully getting out of the house would help. She grabbed her keys from the nightstand and headed for her car. It started up easily, despite the cold and its recent lack of use.

Alyssa didn't care where she went. She just needed a change of scenery. At least the roads were clear at this hour. She was able to just drive. Having something new to look at was nice, but it didn't change anything. Macy was still gone, and there was nothing she could do about it.

Her life was still spinning out of control. It would never stop until she had Macy back.

Before she knew it, she was at the other side of town. Chad always wanted to avoid the area, because it wasn't as safe as their neighborhood. Run-down apartment buildings lined the streets. There were far too many people on the sidewalks for that time of night. She was pretty sure she saw a drug deal go down at the trunk of a dilapidated old car.

Chills ran down her back. She hoped Macy wasn't here. She wouldn't come here on her own, would she? As Alyssa drove she scanned the people, hoping to see her daughter. Even though she couldn't stand the thought of Macy with the people she saw, she just wanted to see her baby, snatch her up and bring her home.

Not only would she have Macy back, but she would be a hero. She would be the one who found her daughter. Not that she really cared about fame, but after all the accusations, mostly in the media, it would be nice to shove it in everyone's face, letting them know she had absolutely nothing to do with whatever had happened to Macy.

After a few minutes, she was out of that part of town. In fact, she was out of their town and into the next one. It didn't look much different. There was still questionable activity on the streets, but she knew if she kept going she would hit the nicer part of the town. Eventually things became cleaner. There was a cute park, followed by some restaurants, and then a mall. Everything was closed.

A little beyond the mall sat a bar. Bright lights shone from inside, and the parking lot was nearly full. Her stomach rumbled. Maybe she could grab an appetizer and distract herself with whatever was going on inside. She flipped her blinker on and pulled into the parking lot, taking the first available spot she came across.

She checked her purse for cash, finding plenty. She could have a full meal and then some drinks, and still have money to spare. She didn't want to use the credit card and have to explain this to Chad later. She planned on getting back home before he woke up.

Even if he did wake up to find her gone, he wouldn't be able to blame her for needing to get out and see some new sights. It wouldn't fix anything, but maybe she could feel a little better for a short time. She grabbed a pink baseball cap and slid it on, hoping to avoid being recognized. Her family's images were all over the place.

She locked the car and headed inside. She could hear music and billiard balls clacking before she even reached the building.

When she stepped in, no one even glanced up at her. She saw an empty table near the back and took it. After she made herself comfortable, she watched everyone. A couple of rowdy games of pool went on at the far end of the bar. There were several TV's on the walls, all playing different channels. Music played from somewhere. It sounded like the music her kids listened to.

Her stomach rumbled, and she wondered if she was supposed to go up to the bar and order. She hadn't been to a bar in years, since before she was a parent.

Just as she was getting ready to get up, a waitress showed up in front of her. "What do you want?" She was chewing a big wad of gum. At least Alyssa hoped it was gum since she was serving food and drinks.

"Can I get something to eat?"

"Yeah." She pulled out a menu, handing it to Alyssa. "Anything to drink while you wait?"

"Do you have any specials?"

She nodded. "We have a good deal on a daiquiri in a fish bowl."

Alyssa looked around, noticing several others around the bar drinking from a fish bowl. She hoped there had never been fish in them. "I'll take one."

"Coming right up." She walked off, writing on her pad of paper.

It was nice to be treated like a normal human being for a change. For the last week, everyone had been treating her like a fragile doll—one wrong move and she would break.

She looked through the menu, her stomach growling hard. Why was she so hungry? She had eaten a lot of lasagna for dinner, despite being upset over the news about the blood. Maybe her body was trying to make up for lost meals. Didn't it know that the baby it had created was missing? Meals really didn't matter anymore.

The waitress came by, carrying a red fishbowl. She set it on the table in front of Alyssa. "What are you going to order?"

Alyssa ordered a plate of nachos and took a long drink from the straw, enjoying the warm sensations running through her as the liquid made its way to her empty stomach.

Her phone rang in her purse. Had Chad woken up? Grumbling, she pulled it out. It was Valerie. She was on the other end of the globe, and they had been playing phone tag since Zoey's encounter with the intruder. She was feeling more relaxed by the minute. She could handle the conversation now.

"Valerie. How are you?"

"Why is it so loud, Alyssa? Isn't it midnight over there?"

"Something like that. I couldn't sleep, so I put on a movie." Alyssa took another long sip. The fish bowl was half-empty, or was it half-full?

"Oh, okay. Well, what's going on? You sounded upset when you left the message yesterday. Although, you have every reason to be upset. I was just worried about Zoey. Is everything all right?"

"There was a little incident, but she's fine."

"What do you mean?"

It didn't feel like a big deal anymore. "Someone broke in our house, but we changed the locks and had the security system upgraded, so now everything is safer than ever. No one's getting back in." She took another drink.

"Is Zoey okay? Are all of you okay?"

"We're all fine. I didn't want to worry you, Valerie. She can tell you about it herself. She actually saw the guy—she was a hero. You should be proud. Because of her, they were able to draw a sketch of him. He looked like the unabomber, but they caught that guy, right?"

"Zoey saw him?"

"Yeah. She even tried to fight him off. Like I said, you should be proud of her. You raised a fine one, Valerie. Then she came and got us. She was upset, of course, but she didn't even want us to tell you what happened. We couldn't do that."

"She fought him off? Oh, dear lord. I've got to get back home."

"No. Don't do that. You've got all that work to catch up on. She's never been safer than she is now. At least at our house. No one is getting in or out without our knowledge. We got the most expensive of everything."

"Are you sure? I don't want to put any added pressure on you guys."

"No. Not at all. It's nice to have her with us. She and Alex are helping each other out. They've always been like siblings, and now they're really pulling together. It's cute actually."

"If you're sure."

"I can have her call you when I…when she wakes up." Alyssa took another drink, and the bowl was empty.

"Thank you, Alyssa. That would be wonderful. Oh, and get some sleep. You sound awful. If I didn't know you better, I'd think you were drinking."

She burst out laughing—a little too loud. "You know me. I won't touch the stuff." It was true; she hadn't touched it. She'd only drank it.

"Okay. Tell her I'm keeping my phone on me, and I'll answer her call no matter what time it is or what meeting I'm in."

"Will do."

"Bye, Alyssa."

"Talk to you later, Valerie." She put the phone away just as the waitress arrived with her nachos. She pushed the bowl aside. "Can I get a refill?"

Her eyes widened. "You already finished that? If you want more, I'll get you more."

"Can you make the next one a little stronger?"

"I…yeah. Okay." She gave Alyssa a concerned look and walked off.

Great. She was back to being a fragile doll. She picked up a chip covered in cheese. It was harder to get into her mouth than it should have been. Maybe she shouldn't have gone through the drink so fast. Who cared? At least she felt good, even if she still remembered why she had come here, and what she had been trying to forget.

She would keep drinking until she was able to forget for a little while. For now, she still knew her daughter was missing, even though it didn't feel as bad as it had earlier. She ate more nachos, focusing completely on that task since it was a bit of a challenge to get them into her mouth. She kept ending up with salsa on her face.

This was what she had come to.

Ride

ALYSSA LOOKED UP. A new fish bowl sat in front of her. When had that arrived? She grabbed the straw, drinking as much as she could. This batch was noticeably stronger. She drank until it was more than half-gone.

Alyssa blinked slowly, looking around. Her eyes wouldn't move fast at all. It was as though they had been put on a slow motion setting. Her arms didn't move as fast as she wanted, either. She looked at them as she moved around. They felt rubbery. It was a little bit fascinating.

She grabbed a chip, watching it in slow motion. It wouldn't go into her mouth, though. Somehow, she ended up with a sharp end of a chip up her nose, and it really hurt. Like, a lot. She put the chip down on the plate. It had red on it, but she didn't think that one had had any salsa on it. She rubbed her nose, and it felt squishy inside.

Something felt wet under her nose. It took a minute for her hand to get there, but she wiped it and saw red on her finger. That didn't look like salsa. She licked it. Ew. It definitely wasn't salsa. She had managed to give herself a bloody nose with a chip.

Someone sat next to her. She looked at him. He was tall and slim with curly hair and gorgeous eyes. He looked like he could have been on the cover of a magazine. "Who are you? What are you doing here?"

"Name's Rusty. I just want to make sure you're okay."

"Never better. I came here to forget something, and I can't remember what, so mission accomplished." She didn't like how slurred her words were. She reached for her straw, but the stranger moved the bowl away from her. "Hey." She glared at him.

"Maybe you should take a break from that for a minute."

"What's it to you?"

"You've had a lot already. You're a tiny thing. You can't be more than, what, a hundred and twenty pounds?"

"One twenty-five. What's it to you?"

"Just trying to look out for you."

"Why?"

"I'm a good citizen. Do you want me to get a napkin for your nose?"

She moved her rubber hand up to her nose, even though it took a long time. It was still wet. She shrugged, sure that she couldn't reach a napkin without knocking something over.

He handed her a couple napkins. How did he move so easily? It wasn't fair. Her body was made out of rubber and he moved like an Olympic athlete, in total control.

"What's your story?"

She raised an eyebrow, holding the napkin up to her nose.

"Why did you lie to your friend on the phone?"

"Did I lie? Was it that obvious?" She reached for the drink, but he pushed it further away. "Don't let that fall on the floor. I haven't even paid for that yet."

"I won't. You told your friend you were watching a movie."

Alyssa pointed to one of the TV's on the wall. "See? A movie. No lie."

"That's a replay of the NBA championship."

"Well, it's good enough to be a movie. Who did you say you were?"

"I'm Rusty. I've been trying to figure out what's going on with you."

"And I told you. I came here to forget something."

"You look familiar. Have we met?"

"I have one of those faces." There she was, lying again.

He nodded.

"Would you like a ride home?"

"I have my own car. I drove here."

"Do you think it would be such a good idea to drive it home? You can't even eat nachos without injuring yourself." He smiled. It was a beautiful smile. He probably had women lined up somewhere. What was he doing talking with her?

Alyssa glared at him. "I would hardly call it injuring myself. It's just a bloody nose."

"I wouldn't mind giving you a ride home. I couldn't live with myself if I let you get into your car in your state."

"Do I look like I'm ready to get back into my car? Hey—what's that?"

"What?" He turned around.

She grabbed the fish bowl and took another long sip.

He turned back and looked at her, shaking his head. Some curly locks fell into his eyes and he pushed them away. "Looks like you got me. Can I have some of that?"

"I don't know you. You could have all kinds of crazy germs."

He laughed. "Can I take that from you then? I'm afraid you're going to puke all that out."

"What's it to you? I'm not getting in your car."

"I think you should. I have a tow truck and I make a habit of offering free tows to those who shouldn't get on the road."

"Why? What's in it for you?"

"Plenty. I get to write off those tows on my taxes. More importantly, I save lives. Not only those poor souls who have had too much to drink, but also those they would have hurt or killed. That's why I hang out here in the wee hours."

"So you work all night doing that?"

"I work when I'm needed."

"Doesn't your family hate that?"

He shook his head, keeping her eye contact. "They were killed by a drunk driver years ago."

Alyssa dropped a chip she didn't even realize she was holding.

"I don't want anyone else to go through what I went through. I can't prevent them all, but I will prevent the ones I can."

She stared at him, at a loss for words. Finally, she pulled her cap off and ran her hands through her hair.

His eyes widened. "Wait. Are you that Mercer lady? Macy's mom?"

Alyssa put her hands in her face, fresh tears spilling. Even with all the alcohol she had consumed, she couldn't completely forget who she was or why she had gone to the bar. "Yes. I'm Alyssa Mercer. My daughter is missing, and we're all over the news. Looks like you figured out why I came here." She grabbed the drink and downed the rest of it before he could try to take it away. "And I can't forget it."

"You know, drinking isn't going to solve anything."

She stared at him through the tears. "Who asked you?"

"No one. I'm offering you unsolicited advice. Get counseling, but don't turn to alcohol. Please."

Alyssa sighed. "I don't even have closure. We don't know if she's dead or alive. They found her bloody clothes. Did you know that? The results just came back today. Someone broke into our house last night, too...or was it the night before?" She shook her head. "It doesn't matter. My life is falling apart, and if I want some alcohol, I'll have as much as I want. I'm sorry for everything you've been through. I'm sure it was as bad of a nightmare as my life, but you still don't get the privilege of telling me what to do."

He pulled a wallet out from his pocket and showed her a picture of his family. Alyssa held her breath as she stared at the photo of him with an equally gorgeous lady and two beautiful boys, no older than five.

Her breath caught. "They're gone?"

Rusty nodded, a look of sadness shadowing his face. "Have you ever been to a rehab facility?"

"What? No."

"Trust me, Alyssa. You don't want to. I turned to drugs, unable to cope with losing my family. I ended up almost losing my house, my job, and everything else. I didn't care. I couldn't get over the grief, and nothing else mattered."

"I don't want to hear this. This is the first drink I've touched in a long time. I think I deserve a drink after the week I've had."

"And I don't want to see you go down the path I did."

"Why do you care? You don't know me."

"I kind of do. I've been sitting here with you for a little bit."

The waitress came by and looked at Alyssa. "Do you need anything else?"

"Just another one of those fishb—"

"She needs some water."

"No, I don't. I want another bowl." She'd show him.

He shook his head. "I'm going to take her home. She's already had too much."

The waitress shrugged. "Water it is, Rusty."

Alyssa groaned. She couldn't even go to a bar and get drunk right. Her stomach didn't feel well. It wasn't exactly growling, but she couldn't ignore it, so she grabbed a few chips and managed to eat them without hurting herself. The waitress brought two waters and left without a word. At least the tow truck guy had stopped talking.

What if he went out and told everyone that he had found her drunk? Her stomach dropped. The media would eat them alive. "You're not going to tell the news that you found me drunk in a bar, are you? That's going to make my family look really bad. I don't—"

"No. I just want to help. I know what it's like to deal with grief that's too overwhelming."

She looked into his eyes, not able to focus on them. He seemed genuine enough. Hopefully he was. If he drove her anywhere other than her house, she wouldn't be able to fight him off. Not when her extremities were rubbery.

Her stomach continued to feel strange. She stuffed more nachos in her mouth, trying to appease it. Just before she finished off the plate, her stomach twisted in knots and heaved. She was going to throw up.

Alyssa covered her mouth and looked around, afraid she wouldn't find the bathroom in time.

"Over there to the right. Let me help you—"

She jumped out of her seat and ran to the restroom, barely making it in time. She threw up so much, she was sure it was everything she'd put in her stomach since arriving at the bar. That wasn't money well-spent.

By the time she got to the table, only the waters remained.

"Do you feel better now?"

She shook her head as she sat down.

"Whenever you're ready to go, just say the word."

"I guess I should get back home. I threw everything up. I can get myself home."

"No, you can't. All that alcohol is still in your blood."

She knew he was right, because she still felt dizzy and rubbery.

"Are you ready? The sooner I get you home, the sooner I can get home."

"May as well. I need to get back before anyone wakes up. I don't want to explain myself." She opened her purse to pay for her purchase.

"I already paid your bill."

She looked up at him. "You did? Why?"

"Consider it my good deed for the day."

A headache was coming on. "I could have paid it."

"I'm sure you could have. Find something good to put the money toward. Buy something for your son."

Alex. Hopefully, he would be sleeping when she got back. The last thing he needed was to see his mom coming home drunk, especially with some guy named Rusty dropping her off. "Let's go."

She took in the fresh night air as she watched him attach her car to the back of his truck. When he was done, he turned to her. "All set. You ready to go?"

"So, do I get in my car?"

He gave her a funny look. "Haven't you been towed before? You ride in my cab with me."

"Cab?" She looked around for a taxi.

Rusty pointed to the front of his truck. "Just climb in."

She nodded, feeling stupid. He opened the door, and she put her foot on the step. Her foot slipped, and she slammed her shin against the step. That would leave a mark. Possibly even blood.

He took her arm and helped her up. A couple of minutes later, they were driving back toward her house. She looked back several times to check on her car.

"It's fine. I know what I'm doing—really. I even have a license and everything."

"Sorry."

"No need to apologize. Do you want to give me your address to put in my GPS or do you just want to give me directions?"

If she gave him her address, he would have it permanently. Did she really want that? Or did it even matter? He would be able to figure it out once he got there. The headache was getting worse, and she didn't want to have to think. She told him the address, and closed her eyes. Hopefully, that would help. If not, at least it would keep the lights outside from making her feel dizzy as they drove past.

What had she been thinking? Why had she drunk so much?

Soon, the brakes hissed. She opened her eyes and saw her house. Had she fallen asleep? Is that how they had gotten back so fast?

He pulled the keys out of the ignition. "Let me help you get out. It's a big drop, and I don't want you getting hurt."

"You think I'm an idiot, don't you?" Oh, why had she said that?

"Not at all. I just don't want you injuring yourself. Just wait in here while I take care of your car."

She sighed and then waited. With any luck, no neighbors were awake to watch. There were several who loved to gossip, and they would eat this up—her arriving early in the morning in a tow truck. She looked at the windows she could see, but everything looked as it should: no nosy neighbors peeking from behind any curtains.

Her door opened, and Rusty put his hand out for her to take. With his help, she managed to get out onto the street without any more blood.

"Do you want me to leave your car here, by the sidewalk? I can put it up your driveway if you'd like."

Chad would know something wasn't right if her car was parked on the road. He wouldn't think anything of it being in the driveway, because half the time she didn't bother putting it in the garage anyway. She sighed and then handed him her keys.

When he was done parking the car, he returned the keys to her. He gave her a nod, his eyes full of kindness. "I hope you find your daughter soon. In the meantime, please don't turn to drinking."

She rubbed her head. "Not if it keeps feeling like this."

"Glad to hear it. Have a good night."

"Wait. Let me pay you something."

"No. Like I told you, it's a write-off. You're helping me out with tax time coming up."

"But you covered my food too."

"It's all a write-off. Just get in there and get some sleep. You're going to need it."

"Okay. Thanks."

"Goodnight."

Alyssa walked to her front door. When she got there, she turned around and saw that Rusty was sitting in his truck, watching her. Was he making sure she could get into her house? She must have been in pretty bad shape if he doubted her ability to do that. She pulled out her key and unlocked the door.

She turned around and waved, letting him know he was free to go. Then she opened the door and went in, resetting the alarm. She was half-surprised that she remembered the new codes, but at least she did.

The house was quiet and it was still dark. No one had any reason to get up early, so she was probably safe from having to explain herself.

When she got into her room, she let a sigh of relief seeing Chad in the same position he had been in when she left. She got in the shower to wash off the smells from the night.

She climbed into bed, her hair still wet, and she relaxed. Her stomach was still queasy, but the alcohol had done the job of calming her nerves. Things didn't look as bad as they had before. She could see that there was no evidence of foul play, so she had reason to cling to hope that she would see Macy again.

Alyssa closed her eyes and for the first time in a while, drifted off to sleep without any anxious thoughts haunting her.

Clue

THE SUN WAS shining into the room through the blinds. One ray of light made its way to Chad's eyes, waking him up. He rubbed his eyes and looked around. It was pretty bright, which meant that it had to be late morning. He looked over at Alyssa, sleeping soundly next to him.

How odd that she was still sleeping. She had never been one to sleep in to begin with, always off to work out or something. Now that Macy was missing, she usually got up even earlier. He knew she hadn't been sleeping well. She tended to talk in her sleep—she had as long as he had known her—but it had been much worse over the last week.

She had woken him up several times yelling out, though she hadn't managed to wake herself.

He got up, put on some track pants and an old college sweatshirt, and went into the hall. Both Alex's door and the door to Macy's room, where Zoey slept, were still closed. Not that that was a surprise. He remembered sleeping well past noon often as a teenager.

His stomach rumbled, so he went to the kitchen. He looked at the clock on the stove. It was almost eleven, which meant he may as well make lunch. He remembered the leftover lasagna. He would never be able to eat lasagna without guilt again. There was no way he was ever going to tell Alyssa about Lydia, but since he was never going to go back to her again, it didn't matter. The past was in the past.

Chad grabbed the tinfoil-covered dish from the fridge and piled a huge piece onto a plate. He stuck it in the microwave and waited. He looked through the fridge for something to drink. He was too awake for coffee, which was his usual morning fuel. Milk? No, it gave him gas. He didn't want to spend the whole day farting. Juice? Too sweet. Beer? Bingo.

He grabbed a bottle and opened it up just as the microwave beeped. He sat down with his lasagna and beer. The breakfast of champions. It was perfect, actually. Once he got to the middle of his food, it was cold, so he had to put it back in for another couple of minutes. He finished the beer while he waited.

Once the food was done, it was too hot. Stupid microwaves. He put the plate on a potholder and carried it to his office. He'd let it cool down while he checked the comments on his blog.

His latest post had over two hundred new comments. Not surprising since he hadn't checked in a while. Had he even checked the day before?

He read through the comments, answering each one. They were all typical as of late. Mostly condolences for what their family was going through. Those were easy enough to reply to. A simple thank you sufficed in most cases. Occasionally, someone had something special to say, and he needed to give it extra attention.

He went through the rest of the comments on the post and then checked for other new comments on other posts. There were about eighty other comments to answer. After he was done with that, he needed to write a new post. People would stop checking if he didn't update soon.

Once he had replied to the last comment, he checked all the local news blogs. They all mentioned the bloody clothes. Each one of them made it sound like there was a lot more blood than there actually was. He checked a couple of the national news sites, and they both said the same thing.

Oddly enough, none of his blog comments had mentioned it, so the news must have just been released.

He opened up a new post and let his fingers do the talking. He let the public know everything that he did. Yes, they found Macy's clothes covered in blood, but it wasn't nearly enough to be deadly. He suspected a cut, and would believe that until other evidence proved otherwise.

Before hitting publish, he went through pictures on his computer. Family pictures brought in a lot more visitors, and he wanted everyone to know the truth. He uploaded a dozen pictures, all including Macy, from the last ten years or so. People couldn't get enough of that.

Chad hit publish and then checked the live post. Even though he always previewed it first, he sometimes managed to catch errors that he'd missed. This one looked good.

Not only did he have high numbers, but he had a program showing how many times his content was shared, and his posts were getting shared thousands of times each week. That wasn't even counting all the re-blogs, which he didn't have time to track.

He refreshed the page and saw there were already comments. People had to have been sitting on his site, waiting for the latest bit of news. It was a good thing he had already upgraded his hosting to handle all the traffic.

Leaning back in his chair, he stretched. He would read the comments later. He needed to get his mind off everything. The worry and guilt ate away at his stomach. As much as he wanted to spend every waking minute focused on finding Macy, he needed breaks from it all.

It made him feel like a first-class jerk, but he knew that he was no good to anyone if he didn't take breaks. He went upstairs and found that he was still the only one awake. He ran a brush and some gel through his hair and headed outside for a walk.

He walked mindlessly through the neighborhood, purposefully avoiding the park. The last thing he wanted was to run into anyone, and as much as he appreciated everyone's efforts with the search parties, he couldn't do it right then. Maybe he could find a clue wandering through the neighborhood.

Eventually Chad's calves felt sore. He was going up an incline, and looked around to see where he was. He'd been so lost in his thoughts, he hadn't been paying any attention. The way the roads were set up, he was actually heading back home. It would take him longer to get there if he turned around.

"Is that you, Chad?"

Turning around, he prepared himself. He knew that voice anywhere. "Lydia."

She had dirt on her knees and held clippers. "What are you doing over here?"

"Just trying to clear my head."

"I like to get outside for that myself. Even though we have a landscaper, I like to come out and work on the rose bushes."

"They look great. I should get home, though. I'm sure my family will be waking up soon."

"You look thirsty. Want to come in for a drink?"

"I really shouldn't."

"Well, let me bring something out for you. You need to take care of yourself."

"Lydia, I—"

"Just let me grab something. I know what you like."

"Okay." He sighed.

She came back with two of his favorite diet sodas and handed him one.

"Thanks." Chad didn't realize how thirsty he was until he started drinking. He had finished the entire thing in a couple gulps.

Lydia smiled at him. "See? I knew you were thirsty."

He nodded. "I appreciate it. Really, though, I should get going."

She took his empty bottle and held his eye contact. "If you need anything, anything at all, don't be afraid to ask. I'll do anything for you."

"You've done plenty. We all enjoyed the lasagna, even though we were upset about the news."

She nodded, and then stepped closer. "Are your needs being met? I've always been able to—"

"I told you, I'm working things out with Alyssa."

"Of course. But after speaking with her, it's obvious that she's consumed with grief. It would help you to talk with someone neutral. Our heart-to-heart discussions are second to none." She stepped even closer.

Chad swallowed, still looking her in the eyes. He couldn't deny what she said, but that was the problem. If he opened himself to her he would put his relationship with Alyssa on the line. He would destroy his family.

"Chad?" Lydia put her hand on his.

Some of her hair fell into her face. Without thinking, Chad reached out to brush it behind her ear.

"What do you say?" Her voice was soft, and he could feel her breath on his face. She smelled sweet, even though she had been out doing yard work. "Come inside and tell me everything."

His breath caught, and for a moment he considered taking her up on the offer. Alyssa and the kids didn't deserve this. He needed to give Alex a good home life now more than ever. And Macy…he didn't want her coming back to a broken family, which is what would eventually happen if he didn't stay away from Lydia. He couldn't have both, and he knew it.

"Well?"

Chad stepped back. "Lydia, you're a sweet person. It kills me that Dean can't see that, but I need to be there for my family—all of them. Thanks again for the drink."

Disappointment washed over her face.

"I'm sorry. I never wanted to hurt you."

She nodded, and then waved. "You know where to find me."

Surprise

ALYSSA WOKE UP, unsure if the pounding came from her head or outside somewhere. The light was blinding and it hurt—a lot. She needed some powerful painkillers. With any luck, her stomach would be able to handle them. After throwing up the previous night, she was certain there was nothing left in her stomach to worry about vomiting.

Maybe she should eat something first. Aspirin on an empty stomach would cause more problems than she already had. She grabbed a bottle from the bathroom and headed down to the kitchen. She grabbed some frozen pancakes and put them in the microwave.

The house was quiet. Chad was probably working on his blog and the kids were probably still sleeping. Not that she could blame them, especially after getting up so late herself.

She had acted like an idiot the night before, running off and getting drunk. She hadn't done that since college, and even then it had been with friends. At this age, she was just pathetic. She needed to pull herself together. She'd already lost Macy—hopefully only for a time—and she needed to be there for Alex. He needed her more than ever, even though he acted tough.

The microwave beeped, indicating the food was ready. She took the steaming plate out and set it on the counter while she started a pot of coffee. That would help her headache. She usually tried not to drink too much of it, but she also didn't usually drink fish bowls full of alcohol, either. How many had she had?

Guilt hit her as she remembered the night before. What had she been thinking? What if Chad noticed her car was out of the garage? What would she tell him? The last thing she wanted to do was admit to the truth. He would understand drinking; he always kept beer in the fridge. But he didn't get drunk.

He was practically the perfect husband, and she hadn't let herself see that in a long time. He not only worked a high-paying job so their family never lacked anything, but he put nearly as many hours into the blog. Never once did he ask her to even get a part-time job so he could focus on it. Instead, he spent countless hours working while she complained about him not caring.

What had she been thinking?

The front door opened. Had he gone somewhere? She pushed the brew button on the coffee pot and went to see. Their eyes met, and he held her gaze.

"I needed some air, so I went for a walk."

Alyssa nodded. "I made some coffee. Do you want some?"

He wrapped his arms around her. "I love you. I'm sorry that I wasn't there for you when you needed me."

She hugged him back. "What do you mean?"

"Before. You know, when things were normal. I was so busy, I never made any time for you or the kids."

She leaned her head against his shoulder. "No. I'm sorry that I didn't appreciate all the work you were doing for our family. I haven't had to work in years, and yet you've worked so hard and asked for nothing in return."

"I wouldn't say 'nothing.' And you've given much more than I ever stopped to notice as well. You take such good care of the kids, always going to their school events. I should have been there with you."

"You were…sometimes."

"That's not good enough."

"I obviously didn't do that great of a job with the kids. Look what happened to Macy."

Chad stepped back, looking her directly in the eyes. He cupped her face and held on. "That isn't your fault. We don't know what happened. Sure, we could have been less strict, but you know what? We were trying to protect them. We were doing our job. She's out there somewhere, and we'll find her. Together."

Alyssa nodded. "Together."

Tired

MACY SAT UP in bed, gasping for air. She looked around the room, relieved to be there. She had dreamed of being back in the barn.

The teddy bear was still gone. She wanted to hold it and smell her house, her real house. Would she ever see it again? Would she see her family again? She missed them so much it hurt.

What she wouldn't have given to have Alex tease her, trying to rile her up. Who would have ever thought she would miss that? She would love nothing more than to walk into her dad's office and ask him about his blog. His face always lit up when he talked about page views and other stuff that Macy really didn't understand. She loved to see him excited. If she could, she would walk into her parents' room and for once, agree to go to the gym with her mom.

Macy had always been worried that someone from school might see her and make fun of her. She would never live down her nickname, and she had been afraid that going to the gym would be like admitting all those jerks had been right.

Now she might never have the chance to do that again. Any of it. Was her dad still working on his blog? Were they so worried about her that they weren't doing anything they loved? What did they think about the bloody clothes? Did they think she was dead? Would they really give up on her and move on? What if they moved away? How would she ever find them?

Tears filled her eyes. She wiped them away. Even if she had to wait a few years to get away, she would find her parents as soon as she could.

He couldn't have been more than fifty, if he was even that old. He looked older than her dad, but that didn't mean much. What if he was only forty-five? He could have a lot of years left in him. She didn't want to have to spend the next forty or fifty years with him.

What exactly was he planning? Whatever it was, she had to go along with it or she would end up in worse shape than before. He made things worse on her each time. She didn't want to find out what could be worse than being tied up for days.

If he wanted to her to become Heather, he had won. Just like a wild horse, she was broken. Whatever he said, she would do.

Macy decided to look for the bear again, even though she doubted she would find it. It was probably in his room, along with the picture of her family. He had made his point more than clear. She wasn't going anywhere near his room ever again. She rubbed her wrists, which were still sore from the ties. Chester made her wear shirts with sleeves so long they nearly reached her knuckles so his parents wouldn't see the marks.

Looking around the room, she tried to figure out where to look first. There was a pile of stuffed animals in a little toy hammock. That would be the obvious place to look, so it would be the last place. She continued to scan the room, and she stopped at the dresser. She had already gone through it, hoping to find better clothing options.

For some reason she couldn't explain, she wanted to look there again. The teddy probably wouldn't fit in any of the drawers with all the clothes in there, but she couldn't shake the feeling, so she walked over to it. Starting with the top drawer, she went through each one, not finding the bear.

Frowning, she closed the bottom drawer. Why had she been so sure she would find it? The drawer stuck halfway. She pushed harder, but it wouldn't budge. She stuck her hands in it, pushing all the clothes down. One of them was probably stuck and causing the problem.

She pushed again, but it still wouldn't move. Something was blocking it, but it wasn't coming from inside the drawer. Could it be something under the drawer?

Macy pulled the drawer out further and positioned herself so she could reach behind it. Something was back there. She felt it with her hand as best as she could. It almost felt like part of the dresser. She managed to wrap her fingers around it. Was it another diary? Had

Heather hidden one there, too?

Scratching her hand along the way, she managed to pull it out of the drawer. It did look like a diary! Would this one tell her more than the last one had? Heather's mom had spent some time in the cellar, but what had *happened* to them? Where were they now?

Macy leaned against the wall next to the dresser, so she would be hidden if Chester came in. She opened the book to the first entry.

Mom still hasn't come back. I still don't know exactly what she meant when she said she had been at Grandma and Grandpa's barn. She didn't say farm, she said barn. Why would she be in their barn all that time? They love her. Grandma always says Mom's the daughter she never had. Why would they make her stay out in the barn? Couldn't they see what it did to her?

I'll never know, because Dad won't let me call them. He took my cell phone away when he walked in on me calling them—he took it right out of my hand, ended the call, and removed the battery. Then he told me I'd never see it again. He said that would teach me to ask questions I had no business asking.

No business? He's insane. Of course I have business asking questions. He should be asking questions too! Mom's missing and he doesn't even care. How can he not be worried? I'm so scared I've been throwing up. Not that he cares. I know he can hear me, but he acts like nothing's wrong.

I even threw up a bunch of times at school and Sierra told Mr. Lee who took me to the school nurse. She called Dad and he told her I was fine. It was just a stomach bug. She told him I needed to go home, but Dad said he wouldn't authorize it. So the nurse had me stay in her office the rest of the day to keep an eye on me.

She was asking all kinds of questions about my home life and I was being as vague as possible. After Dad's threats to stay quiet, I wasn't going to say anything.

Macy put the diary in her lap. What had Chester threatened her with? Was there another diary that Macy hadn't read? The other one she had read didn't say anything about it other than the fact that he didn't want her talking about their family at school. She had also said that she was scared of the look on his face. That hadn't been a threat, though.

There was guilt stabbing at me right in my chest and stomach. What if Mom was in danger? Would it be better for me to say something so she could get help, even though Dad said he would lock me away and move me away from my friends? Would he really do that? I'm such a coward.

I couldn't get the look in Dad's eyes out of my mind. I wish I could explain it—the way just him looking at me made terror run through me. I never knew what the expression "frozen with fear" meant until he gave me that look. That's exactly how I felt, and even feel now thinking about it.

Before Mom disappeared again, she told me that if she disappeared again, I needed to take care of myself. She was speaking pretty cryptically, but it seemed like she didn't want me telling anyone about her being missing. I think she was worried about me.

If I'm frozen with fear, then Mom was paralyzed with it. Like I said in the other diaries, she never went back into her and Dad's room. Even though she talked with me, I don't think she ever talked to him. She definitely wouldn't look at him.

One day, she whispered something about a gun. What did that mean? I couldn't get her to tell me anything else, and I didn't know what she was talking about. Did Dad get one and that was why she was so scared?

Ugh. I'm rambling. Sierra and Jess keep saying I do that too much lately. Talking about one thing and then another, but not really getting anywhere. Either it's from spending all that time with Mom when she was back or I'm losing it too.

What am I supposed to do?! I mean, seriously. What? Mom's gone again—just when she was starting to return to her normal self. Dad has to be behind it. Otherwise he would at least pretend to give a crap. He won't even do that. What kind of a husband doesn't care that his wife is missing?

He's back to saying she's in Paris. That's a load bull crap and he knows it. I nearly said as much, but I thought he was going to hit me, so I stopped. I hate him. I really do. Mom always says I shouldn't hate anyone, that it'll make me sick and won't hurt the other person. What am I supposed to do, though?

I need to say something to someone. I have to. Whatever's going on with Mom is not right. People don't just disappear like she does. At least she doesn't do that. Maybe others do, but not her. Something is wrong, wrong, wrong. What if she comes back in worse shape than before? Like, what if she stops talking altogether? Or worse, what if she doesn't come back at all?

There's no way I could handle that. I just couldn't. There's no way I would survive. I'm barely holding it together now. I have tightness in my chest most of the time and my stomach hurts something awful. Jess says it's ulcers. She would know, her mom's a wreck. She says stress eats holes in your stomach. Maybe that's it. It doesn't matter, not when something is really wrong with my mom.

She needs me. I have to say something. Who do I talk to? Mr. Lee? The school nurse? The school psychiatrist? Dad already told me I better not ever talk to her. He says that our family doesn't need that kind of a reputation. Also, he said that his daughter doesn't need a shrink. Ha! Who else needs professional help than anyone with direct contact with him? I'll probably spend all of my adult life in counseling, trying to heal from everything I've been through lately.

There I go rambling again. I'm shaking too. I need to tell someone. I know it and I have to be willing to face the consequences. I can't sit around doing nothing while Mom needs something. I don't know where she is, but maybe someone could look in Gram's barn.

I wish I had my phone. I would call the cops. There's not even a landline here. Dad got rid of that when I was little. I never really thought about it, but now that I needed to make a call and don't have my phone, I'm stuck. Can I really wait until tomorrow at school? What if that's too late for Mom? I know she needs me.

Macy read four more pages of Heather's ramblings. Not that she minded, or even blamed her. If Macy had a diary of her own, it would probably be a lot worse than what she was reading. Heather actually seemed to be holding it together pretty well, considering everything.

When she got to the next entry, the handwriting was a lot messier. Something had to be seriously wrong.

Macy flipped the diary page, eager to find out why Heather's handwriting looked so distressed.

I really messed things up. Really bad this time. Dad's going to follow through on his threat for sure now. He's going to lock me away. He told me that I'm never going to see my friends again.

Today at school, I decided to talk to Mr. Lee. He could tell that something was wrong, so he called me to his desk during the quiz. He asked how I was, but I think it was pretty clear. I was shaking and I hadn't put on any makeup, so it was obvious, really obvious.

He took me into the hall and by then I was shaking so bad I could barely stand. He told me to sit down and then he sat next to me, asking questions. It reminded me of when I was on the couch with Mom when she wouldn't talk. Only I was on the other side. I couldn't find my voice, and even if I had been able to, I'm not sure I would've known what to say.

How would I explain everything that was going on? Where would I even start? Mr. Lee kept asking questions, and I just shook harder and harder. I needed to say something for Mom's sake. She needed me to. So, I finally found my voice and told him that Mom was missing again.

I can't remember what happened after that. Like, I literally can't remember a single thing. All I know is that somehow I ended up in the psychiatrist's office. She was asking questions about Mom. I was crying too hard to answer any questions.

At some point, the new principal came in. He said something about CPS. I asked if they were going to help find Mom. He said that they would help me. I stood up and screamed that I didn't need help. I threw my fists up and down, shouting that they needed to help Mom. I was fine—at least compared to her!

Both of them held me down in the chair, but I kept screaming all the more, so loud that my throat still hurts. Why wouldn't they listen to me? I wasn't the one who needs help. Well, I do. Not as much as Mom. They need to focus on getting her home safe.

I needed to make them listen to me. I kept kicking and trying to get my arms loose. They were holding me down so tightly that I still have marks. Anyway, I finally calmed down once I figured out that they wouldn't listen to me until I did. Yelling and thrashing around wasn't getting me anywhere so I had to try talking calmly.

So long story short, now I'm home in my room and Dad's talking to the CPS people. I'm supposed to be packing some clothes and anything soft I might need. I'm going somewhere for observation, apparently. I hope they have a search team looking for Mom. They need to forget about me and find her. Can't they see that? I'm here and she's not.

The look in Dad's eyes is even scarier than before. He's beyond furious. There's not even a word to describe how angry he is.

I just snuck out into the hall and listened to what they were saying. They're going to take me to the mental hospital! Holy crap! The loony bin. They think I'm nuts. No! He's the one who needs to go there. Why can't they see that? But on the bright side, at least I'll be safe from Dad. They'll figure out that I'm not the crazy one. I'll just have to stay calm and not scream and shout like I did at school. The truth will come out.

Well, I just listened again because I heard Dad yelling. One of the CPS guys said something to Dad about watching out or he'd lose custody. Does that mean that they would take me away from him?

Then Mom and I could move away and then…

Discussion

M ACY FLIPPED THE page, but the rest of the diary was blank. Why had Heather stopped in the middle of a sentence? Had she heard them coming for her and hidden the diary behind the drawer where Macy had found it?

Where *was* she? Was Heather in the mental facility? Did they take her there and leave her? Or had they taken away Chester's custody and put her up for adoption or foster care?

Had he tried to get her back, but couldn't? Was that why he went after Macy? Because he couldn't get to Heather?

She sighed, flipping through the entries again, looking for anything she might have missed before. There weren't any clues that she could find, tucked away out of plain sight.

Even though there were a lot of unanswered questions, Macy understood more about the entire situation. Something happened between Heather's parents to make Chester snap and put her mother in the barn, not just once but at least twice. There seemed to be a missing diary, so he may have taken her there more than once.

Had he tied her up like he had with Macy? He must have threatened her because why else would she have sat there, not talking to Heather? Either she really was that traumatized, or she had been trying to protect Heather. Being down there was horrible, but bad enough to stare at the wall for days on end?

Unless living with Chester all those years had done it to her. It could have been the final straw for her, and she snapped. Heather had snapped too, screaming at school. Had anyone at the mental hospital believed her about her mom? They must not have if Chester was wandering around free. Did he convince them about the Paris story, too?

Although they weren't staying at the family house—the one Heather had been dragged away from. Had Chester packed everything in a hurry, moving it back to his parents' house after losing custody? He had to have lost custody; otherwise he wouldn't have gone to the effort of taking Macy.

What if somehow Macy could find Heather? It was obviously a long shot, but if Heather had gotten away maybe Macy could too. Except that Chester would be even more careful in the future. He had already gone to great lengths to make sure Macy would do what he said.

She heard something in the hall, so she slid the diary back behind the dresser. It barely fit. She jumped up and pretended to be looking through the drawer that was still pulled out.

The door opened, but she pretended not to notice. Her heart raced again. She held up a pair of pants, pretending to decide whether or not to wear them.

Chester cleared his throat. Heart pounding, Macy turned and looked at him, forcing her face to look neutral.

He smiled. "Good morning, sunshine."

Macy's eyes widened. She couldn't find her voice.

"Mind if I sit?" His expression was relaxed.

She stared, afraid to speak. After everything she'd just read she had nothing to say. Where would she even begin?

He sat on the bed and then patted the quilt. Did he want her to sit next to him?

"Have a seat, Heather."

Macy put the pants back into the drawer and walked over to the bed. She looked at it, not wanting to sit.

Chester patted the bed again.

Afraid to anger him, Macy sat without a word.

"I know things have been rough, but we'll get through it. Everything is going to turn around, don't you agree?"

She looked at him, her eyes widening even further. The only way they would get better was if he would take her back home. She knew that wasn't what he had planned. Not if he was still calling her Heather.

"We can be a happy family now. You know your place, as everyone should. You're being more respectful, not like your mom was before she ran off to Paris. Maybe she'll even come to her senses and come back. Then we could be a complete family again. What do you think?"

Macy's breath caught, still unable to find her voice.

He gave her a sad smile and put his hand on her knee. "Yeah, I don't hold out much hope, either. That doesn't mean that we can't be happy. You and me, we're still together. Your grandparents are happy to have us here, and though we don't want to overstay our welcome, we can build a new sense of normal. Does that sound good?"

She bit her lip. How was she supposed to react to that? Did he really believe what he was saying, or was he only trying to get her to believe it?

Chester removed his hand from her knee. "I know. It's not perfect. As much as you've always loved being here, it isn't home. We just need this time away from everything to rebuild our family. After everything we've been through, we have to band together and get through it together. Things aren't going to be the same with your mom gone, and we can't pretend otherwise. She's gone, and there's nothing we can do about that."

He sighed and looked around the room, giving Macy a little space to breathe. Where was he going with all of this talk? Did it mean he was done locking her up? All she would have to do was pretend to be obedient, and she might get a little freedom? Would he be nice now that he deemed her changed?

Turning to her, he smiled again. It caught her off-guard. It would have been less worrisome if he was being mean. "What are you thinking, Heather?"

She held his eye contact, still not knowing what to say. What if she said the wrong thing and ended up back in the barn again? Would he leave her longer? She couldn't have taken any more. Would he leave her there permanently, trying to find yet another Heather, this time one who would be more agreeable?

"It's a lot to take in, I know. Especially with your mom gone now.

You two were close, but you know what? This gives us room to be closer. We've never been as close as I would have liked. It's a chance for us to turn over a new leaf. Isn't that exciting?"

Macy could see the eagerness in his eyes. She knew she had no choice except to respond. She nodded.

"Can't you say anything? I'm excited, and you can't even find one word?"

Certain she could hear irritation creeping into his tone, she knew she had to say something, even if it was a bold-faced lie. She couldn't go back into the cellar. "It'll be great. It's something we've never done before." At least the second part was true. Even with as horrible as he had been to her, she still hated lying.

He broke into a huge grin, his entire face changing. For that moment, he didn't look like the scary monster who had tortured her. He looked like a broken man finding a ray of hope. Macy almost felt sorry for him—almost.

Chester pulled her into a hug, squishing her face against his side. "This is a new beginning for us, kid. Things are really going to turn around. Even though things have been rough, we're going to be able to become a happy little family again. Life is going to be good again. Right, honey?"

Macy's eyes widened. Did he really expect her to agree with that?

He squeezed her tighter into the hug. "Right?"

"Yeah, Dad. It's going to be great." Macy rolled her eyes.

"I'm so glad to have you back, Heather."

Goodbye

C HESTER WALKED ALONG the overgrown path, his boots catching on loose pricker vines along the way. The trees overhead cast a dark shadow, giving him the chills. He should have grabbed a coat rather than just the flannel.

He looked at his watch. Forty-five minutes since he had left the farmhouse. Only another seven minutes before he arrived. She would wait as long as he took.

The forest was quiet, but that wasn't unusual for this time of year. The birds had flown south for the nearing winter, and the critters were all building their homes. A fat squirrel ran in front of Chester, chattering away. By springtime, they would all be skinny again.

It wouldn't be long now. Probably only three more minutes—no point in checking the time again. He took a deep breath, starting to feel winded. At least this trip was easier than the first one out there. Carrying all that added weight had made the trip more than twice as long.

Three rocks piled on top of each other, leaning against a hollowed out stump, reminded him to turn left. The pricker bushes were thick to keep the path hidden. Not that many people went this deep into the woods to begin with.

Chester leaned against the nearest tree, mentally preparing himself for the last leg of this relatively small journey. He kicked some frost on the ground as he thought about what he was going to say to her. It was going to be pivotal, as this would be goodbye.

He pulled some thorns from his boots before knocking over the pile of three rocks. He wouldn't need those again, and he certainly didn't need anyone else seeing them and figuring out that they pointed somewhere. The rocks sent dirt and frost flying in all directions.

He made his way to the hidden path, making sure there was no exposed skin between the thick, leather gloves and his flannel shirt.

A thick, curved stick sat at the base of one tree where he had left it last time. He picked it up and pushed aside the thorn bushes, allowing himself through. The branches snagged his back as they fell back into place behind him. His clothes would be snagged up, but that wasn't of any concern. He'd picked them just for this occasion.

Finally he made it to the small clearing. Frost covered the ground here more than anywhere else in the woods. Little footprints indicated small critters running through.

Four rocks piled on top of one another caught his attention. They sat off to the right of the field, looking sad and solitary. There she was, waiting for him. His heart picked up speed, and he walked over to her. He fell to his knees in front of the rocks. Tears shone in his eyes as he sat above her where she rested.

"Karla, my dear. How I've missed you. Have you missed me? I suppose you have, since you haven't had any other visitors." He pulled off his cap, raking his fingers through his hair, before replacing it. "It's been a while. I apologize for that, because I know you want answers. You wish Heather could be with you, but that isn't possible, my dear. I've gotten her back. Can you believe that?"

He paused, listening.

"She was mad at first, but who could blame her? I think she's missed you, but it's hard to say. She hasn't really asked about you. I wouldn't have told you—I know hearing that has to hurt—but it's the truth. She just hasn't asked. I had to put her in the barn a couple of times. I know how much you hate that. That was part of the problem, you know? You just had such a hard time accepting my decisions. I wish that hadn't been the case."

Chester removed his gloves and ran his hand along the frosty dirt, remembering how he used to enjoy running his hands along her back. "I don't know why you couldn't just accept my leadership. Why wouldn't you listen to me? Now you have no choice, and I wish you would have chosen your path when…before, my dear Karla. I would so much rather have you at my side, but you just wouldn't listen." He shook his head, feeling choked up.

"It's such a shame. Such a shame. Heather needs a mom, and she's looking for something. I can see it in her eyes. She knows I'm her dad. I love how it rolls off her tongue so naturally now. But my dear, we're not a family. Not without you. She knows it, even though she won't say anything. I wish she would ask about you, because then I wouldn't have to hurt you with the knowledge that she hasn't said anything. You two were so close, do you remember?"

He patted the ground as though patting her back. "Well, the truth is that life must move on. We don't have you with us, as much as I wish we did. Wishing doesn't make it so, just like that book you always used to read Heather when she was little. Do you remember that? Of course you do. It was about sinks, and you bought it before she was even born. I put the book aside, and I'll bring it back out and remind her when she's ready. For now, I think it's too painful for her to think about you."

His knees ached, so he readjusted. "I can't stay long, Karla. I'm not as young as I used to be. This is goodbye. Please don't cry—it has to be this way. Think of Heather. We need to move on, and we can't stay with my parents much longer. She's beginning to understand what you never would: the importance of following my leadership, and the fact that there are serious consequences for not doing so. Rebellion is not accepted. You know that now, don't you?"

Chester raised his hand to his face, kissed two fingers, and then placed them on the ground. "I can't say whether or not I'll ever be back. I hope so—I hate the thought of never seeing you again. You will always be my one true love. Please don't forget that. No matter what happens, I'll never be able to love another like I loved you. So rest sweetly, and don't get your hopes up. I wouldn't want you agonizing for me. Just expect that I won't return. It's for the best, as much as I know you wish I would stay."

He ran his fingers in a zig-zag pattern along the frosty dirt, thinking of all the times he had made the same pattern on her back. "We'll miss each other, but Heather needs us to move on. There are too many memories here. I haven't decided what to do with our house, either, Karla. What do you think? Should I keep renting it out, or should I sell it? The renters keep asking about buying it. Again, there are so many memories. I don't know if I dare bring Heather back there. What if she regresses? She's finally doing so well. She's really becoming obedient, you know? I'm raising her to be the way a woman should be. No stupid questions. Just sweet submission."

The sun had risen over the clearing, shining more light on it. It warmed Chester's back. "I ought to get going, my dear Karla. Everyone will be waking soon. Don't worry about us, because we'll be fine. I promise you that. I know it hurts you to hear that we're going to move on, but we must. Life has to go on. I'll come back and let you know how things turn out if I can. This is goodbye, but years down the road, I'll try to come back. I did knock down some of the markers, but I think I can find my way back without them if I had to."

Why was he being so wishy-washy? He had meant for this to be goodbye. No more returns. She would have to pay the price by never seeing him again. Why was it too much for him to bear? He couldn't think about his life without returning to her again. Karla had once been his whole life. But she wouldn't cooperate, despite how hard he worked to help her see the error of her ways. She just wouldn't listen.

Now it was time to move on and begin his new life with their daughter.

Chester rose and took his time getting back to the farmhouse. The sun beat down warming his back even as the frost crunched under his feet. By the time the farm was in sight, only frost in the shade remained.

He found Heather working in the barn with his parents.

"Heather, we need to talk. Come with me into the house."

She nodded and followed him without a word. Once inside he indicated for her to sit at the kitchen table. Chester sat next to her and didn't say anything for a minute.

Heather fidgeted without making eye contact.

Chester cleared his throat. "We're moving somewhere new. I can't tell you where, but it's quite a drive and we'll get a fresh start as a family. It's just what we need, don't you think?"

She stared at him, her skin looking pale.

"You're so excited you're speechless?" He smiled. "You'll love it and your new mom, too. She can't wait to meet you."

HELD

Gone – Book Two

Stacy Claflin

http://www.stacyclaflin.com

Moving

MACY MERCER WOKE up shivering. She rubbed her eyes and then looked around. Once again she was locked inside Chester Woodran's truck bed. Everything was quiet, meaning he was still in the hotel room where he had slept.

At least Chester had allowed her a sleeping bag and pillow, which was a far cry from the last time she had been in there. He had even let her use the bathroom and eat a meal before going to sleep for the night.

It was pretty full back there with everything they had packed for moving to their new home. As usual, she didn't know where they were, or even where they were headed. She actually didn't mind being in the truck bed this time. Not only because of the pillow and sleeping bag, but because she knew Chester wasn't going to kill her. If he had wanted her dead, he would have done it already.

No, he was serious about turning her into his daughter, Heather. Macy was already used to answering to Heather and calling Chester "dad." She felt traitorous to her real dad, but it kept her alive. He would understand.

Also, being in there gave her a break from Chester. He talked non-stop, giving her headaches.

She stretched and sat up. Though it was dark enough in there to not be able to tell whether it was day or night, she could see a little light trying to get inside. This was the day she would see their new home…and meet her new "mom."

What would she be like? Would Macy be given more freedom? The farmhouse had been locked up tight with no neighbors in sight. Would Chester continue to lock her in the new house, or would she have the chance to make friends? She wanted to talk to someone her age more than anything. Well, that wasn't true. What she really wanted was to get back home to her parents and brother, Alex. Then she wanted to run down the street to see her best friend, Zoey.

Macy ran her hands through her hair. It was getting greasy after so long on the road. What had it been? It felt like five days, not that she'd been marking anything on a calendar. It felt like they had been going in circles. She wouldn't put it past Chester to try to confuse her. He didn't want her knowing where they were going.

Not that it mattered since she didn't even know where they had started. She had never been able to figure out where the farm was located. Had they crossed one of the borders and moved into Canada or Mexico? She hadn't seen or heard any Spanish when outside of the truck, so they probably weren't in Mexico, but Canada was a possibility. The times she had been there, it had been pretty much like home.

Would Chester even attempt to cross the border? What if they wanted to search the truck? If they found her, he would be done for. No, he wouldn't do that. He had everything planned down to the last detail, and he wouldn't leave something like that up to chance. Not unless he knew someone who would let him pass, no questions asked.

She grabbed her travel bag and pulled out her last set of clean clothes. She got dressed as fast as she could and then ran a brush through her hair, sure that it didn't do any good. She felt gross and wanted a shower, but she knew better than to complain. She didn't want to find out if the new home had a place for him to lock her up again.

Macy put the brush back into the bag and rolled up her sleeping bag. She sat on it and leaned against some boxes, listening for sounds outside. She heard a car door in the distance, followed by muffled conversation. Chester wouldn't be much longer. He was eager to get to their new home.

Everything was quiet for a while, and then finally, she heard the familiar noise of the lock. She sat up straight, waiting. Was he bringing her breakfast? Most mornings he had. As long as she did what he said, he gave her regular meals and didn't tie her up or hit her.

Bright, morning light assaulted her eyes as he opened the back of the truck.

"You're already dressed? We're going to go into the hotel room so you can take a quick shower—and I do mean quick." He pulled his coat away from his side, letting her see a gun. "Don't try anything funny."

She nodded.

"Don't make eye contact with anyone, and whatever you do, don't talk to anyone."

"Okay."

"Breakfast is already up there. You can eat after you get cleaned up. Then we need to hit the road again. Like I said, today's the big day, Heather."

She climbed out of the truck, carrying the overnight bag. A light covering of snow crunched under her feet. That had to have been why she woke up cold. She looked up to the sky, seeing that it was clear and sunny. She saw pine trees in the distance, reminding her of home—her real home. Her heart ached. Would she ever get to see her family again?

"Come on." He glared at her. "We're not here for sightseeing." He closed and locked the back of the truck, and then led the way to the hotel room. It was a generic, cheap room. He pointed to the bathroom door and then patted his jacket where the gun was.

Going into the bathroom, she let out a sigh of relief at the thought of taking an actual shower. The farmhouse had only had a bathtub, and even though it was stupid to complain about, given everything she'd gone through, she didn't like taking baths. She put her clothes on the counter and stepped into the hot stream of water. The farmhouse water never got very warm, either.

This was like a dream. She knew she was supposed to hurry, but she couldn't help just standing there, enjoying the hot water running down. It almost felt like a massage. She closed her eyes and just enjoyed the experience until Chester pounded on the door and yelled for her to hurry up.

Macy opened her eyes and grabbed the hotel brand shampoo, lathering it through her greasy hair until it felt normal again. Then she spotted conditioner. Conditioner! She hadn't seen that since she had been kidnapped. She took a huge glob and ran it through her hair. She let it sit while she washed up.

Chester pounded on the door again.

"I'm almost done!" Even though she never wanted to get out, she rinsed off and got out. She grabbed the bottle of conditioner to take that with her, just in case. She ran her fingers through her hair, loving how it felt. Once she was dressed again, she put some lip gloss on and took a deep breath before joining Chester.

He was already eating at the little table. She sat down across from him, not making eye contact. A little paper bag sat in front of her. She poured the contents: a plastic fork, a napkin, something wrapped in wax paper and some toast wrapped in plastic fell out. She picked up the mystery item and saw that "vegan" was written on the side.

Was he pleased with her? He wasn't forcing her to eat any animal products? She opened it and saw some kind of breakfast burrito. The smell made her mouth water and she bit down.

"Are you excited, Heather? We get to move into our new home. It's in a nice gated community."

What did gated mean? Macy couldn't shake the feeling that it didn't mean what she envisioned. She nodded, her mouth still full.

"Did you sleep well?"

In the bed of a truck? Macy nodded again.

"Not too talkative, I see. Well, I suppose you're nervous. I would be too, if I didn't know where my new home was going to be. You'll like it. You'll have your own room again. Oh, and you'll finally meet your new mom. I know it's a little soon, but since your mom is off in Paris living the high life with Jacques, we need to move on too. I need a wife and you need a mom. It's not right for a girl your age to be without a mom."

Macy was sure that Heather's mom was nowhere near France, and from what she had read from Heather's diary, Heather hadn't thought her mom was there either. Macy swallowed and kept her eyes on her food.

"Your new mom is so excited to meet you. She's never been married and doesn't have any kids of her own, so she'll be able to devote herself to us fully. She might want to have kids of her own. I'm not sure, since the topic hasn't come up. But isn't this good news?"

Macy's stomach flipped and twisted more than an Olympic diver. "I guess."

Chester nodded. "You're nervous. I get it. Once you meet her, you two will hit it off. Then you'll see how wonderful everything is going to be."

Was the new wife marrying him because she actually *wanted* to be with him? Or was he forcing her to be part of the "family" too? She couldn't imagine anyone choosing to spend time with him, but maybe he had her fooled. He could have put on some hidden charm, pretending to be a great guy. He had probably even used the single dad card to gain her sympathy. Maybe she was one of those people who liked to fix broken people.

Hopefully, this meant things weren't going to get even worse than they already were. Although, her friend Marissa from school had a stepmom—not that Chester's wife would be Macy's stepmom—and she never stopped complaining about her. Every day in Algebra, Marissa had a new complaint about the horrible woman married to her dad.

"We don't have much farther to go today. Would you like to drive in the front with me?"

She looked up at him in surprise.

His light brown eyes peered through the ugly glasses and bore into hers. The corners of his mouth twitched. "I'll even let you pick the music. I can stream any kind you want—no commercials, even."

No commercials also meant no clues as to where they were. Although if she could see signs, that would help. Not that their location mattered all that much anymore. She had given up hope of escaping to get back home to her family. The new house would most likely be as secure as the farmhouse had been. Maybe even more, although she didn't see how. He had mentioned a gated community. Did that mean there was no way out?

"What do you say? We haven't had much time to talk recently, Heather. Dear old Dad has really missed that."

Macy gulped.

"Finish eating that and then give me a hug."

Her heart sank. The only thing worse than acting like his daughter was being locked up in the barn's cellar. Macy ate as slow as possible, wanting to put off the hug as long as she could. He didn't seem to notice. He rattled on about how much she was going to like the new house and her new mom.

He was excited, almost bubbly. Macy noticed that he was sipping coffee. She didn't remember ever seeing him drink it before. Maybe that was why he was in such a good mood.

Finally, she finished her breakfast. There was nothing else she could do to put off giving him a hug.

Chester smiled at her. "Come give your ol' dad a hug, Heather. This is going to be a great day."

Macy's stomach twisted, but she got up and shuffled around the table while he got up from his chair. He opened his arms wide and she pressed herself against him and wrapped her arms around him. He put his around her and squeezed tight, making it hard for her to breathe.

After what felt like an eternity, but was probably only about ten seconds, he let go.

"Let's hit the road. Your mom's waiting."

Exhausted

ZOEY HIT THE snooze button again. Why did her mom insist on her going to school? She could barely function anymore with Macy missing, and going to school did *not* help. The only thing that kept her going was time spent with Alex. They were able to talk, smoke, and…well, keep each other distracted.

If they felt like talking about Macy, they did. If they didn't, they sneaked away somewhere to light up or to one of their bedrooms to forget about everything else. So far, none of their parents suspected their relationship. They just thought the two of them were becoming closer because of Macy's disappearance. Her mom kept saying how Zoey had taken on Alex as her little brother.

The door opened and her mom appeared. "What are you doing still in bed? School's going to start soon."

"I'm too tired."

"You know, they're going to hold you back if you don't keep up."

"They don't hold kids back anymore, Mom. They don't want to hurt anyone's self-esteem. But you know what? At this point, I really don't care. Let them hold me back. I feel like I've been hit by a truck."

Valerie's eyebrows came together and she walked over to Zoey with a look of concern. She felt her forehead and then her cheeks. "You don't feel warm. Do you feel sick?"

Zoey shook her head. "I'm just exhausted, but really, that's not surprising. My life-long best friend has been missing for about a month. What else do you expect?"

She sat down on the bed next to Zoey. "I know, dear. You don't need to remind me. Have you spoken with the counselor at school yet?"

"Ugh. Not that again. I don't need a shrink."

"They're not psychiatrists, and they said a lot of kids have gone in to talk about Macy."

"Yeah, the jerks who feel guilty about bullying her. I have no reason to feel bad—I was always there for her. If I could be, I still would be. No guilt here."

"It's not about guilt. You need someone to talk to, and you sure aren't talking to me about it. Sleeping isn't going to solve anything. The counselor can give you strategies on how to deal with all of this."

Zoey glared at her mom. "I talk to Alex all the time."

"But you need to talk to someone neutral. I'm sure it's good to talk with him since you're both so close to her, but the counselors can offer a different perspective and they've been trained in how to deal with situations such as these."

"Yeah, well, you don't have to go to school and get judged for going to a shrink."

"Why don't I set up an appointment with an outside counselor, then? None of your friends would ever know, although I would question your friendship if they're going to judge you."

"Can't I just go back to sleep? Please. I'm so tired. You have no idea." Zoey yawned.

"What time have you been getting to bed?"

"I went to bed at nine, don't you remember?"

"And you went to sleep then?"

"Yes!"

"If you won't talk to a counselor or go to school today, I'm going to make you a doctor's appointment. Would that be socially acceptable?"

Zoey rolled her eyes. "Fine, whatever. If I can go back to sleep."

"I'll make you an appointment during my lunch break. Think you can be ready by noon?"

She nodded and then re-set her alarm. Zoey closed her eyes and was asleep the moment she hit the pillow.

Traveling

MACY CLIMBED INTO the front of the truck, not allowing herself to get too excited. It was a stupid thing to be excited about, but after having spent days riding around in the back with all of the stuff, she almost couldn't help it.

Chester was still almost giddy, rambling on about a multitude of topics. As she buckled up, he moved aside his jacket, exposing the gun again. Macy stopped breathing for a moment. It startled her to see that, she had almost forgotten about it with his new good mood. Obviously she wasn't supposed to forget it was there.

But he didn't miss a beat. He continued chatting about how great everything was going to be. He couldn't wait to be a complete family again. Once he pulled out onto the road, he asked what kind of music Macy wanted.

It had been so long since he had asked her opinion on anything— actually, he had probably never asked her what she thought about anything. Not since he was pretending to be Jared, anyway. That felt like a lifetime ago and was probably what he wanted. Chester wanted her to feel completely disconnected with her real family.

Macy hesitated. "Is there a top twenty station?"

"Of course. Like I said, I can stream anything." He scanned through the stations until he found one. A song was playing that Macy loved. She and Zoey often sung along to it, sometimes even dancing and using hair brushes or cell phones as microphones. She closed her eyes, welcoming the memories.

Another favorite came on, bringing another flood of memories. This one had been one of Alex's favorites, and there was nothing like watching Alex dance to a song. He was hilarious and would take up the entire family room, running around and dancing.

Her heart ached. Would they ever get to do that again? When the next song came on, she felt even worse. It was a song she had never heard, reminding her of everything she had missed over the last month.

Macy opened her eyes and saw that they were on a country road. There was nothing except open, grassy fields and livestock as far as the eye could see. She continued to ignore Chester's rambles. He hadn't stopped talking since breakfast.

After about twenty minutes, they drove through a small town. Macy's eyes lit up—she had been there before. She recognized the buildings and even the tiny, rundown park. Her heart beat so loudly she feared Chester would hear it.

A minute later, they were back to being surrounded by fields and farmland again, but her mind wouldn't stop racing. She *had* passed through that town before. It wasn't her imagination. She recognized it. That meant she had been along this road before too. But when?

Macy fought to keep her breathing steady. The last thing she wanted to do was to alert Chester to the fact that anything was amiss. She vaguely remembered being in the car with her family when she had gone through that small town before.

Did that mean they were near her home? Chester probably didn't know she knew where they were. She didn't actually know where they were. Not even the town name signs along the way helped. She had never heard of any of them.

They had to be back in Washington, but where? It could have been on the other side of the mountains or even in the southern part of the state. Or maybe they were in Oregon or Idaho. They had traveled other nearby states plenty of times for camping and sporting events.

Her pulse and breathing finally returned to normal. They went through another half an hour of open fields, only seeing a random grouping of cows or horses every so often.

Eventually, the scenery changed and they were in a forest. The green trees were a nice change of scenery. She was so immersed in their beauty that she forgot to keep paying attention to the road signs. She had always loved that part of the Northwest. Never once had she complained about driving for hours through the woods or mountains.

When they left the trees, they went through another small town. This one had a decent-sized high school and Macy held her breath. There was an actual stop light in this town, and when the stopped, she stared at the school.

She recognized it—and this time she knew why. They had driven there for one Alex's karate tournaments. He had competed in that gymnasium. Zoey had gone with her family, and while they waited for Alex's turn to compete, the three of them wandered around the school and had even chased each other through the parking lot. Alex had been threatening to dump his drink on them.

Where was this town? She really couldn't remember. It had been over a year since they had been there, and she hadn't been paying any attention to where they were back then, either. She thought it was two or three hours from home. The one thing she did know was that it was definitely in Washington.

Even though they were still far from home, they weren't *that* far. Assuming they didn't drive out of state, it was possible she could get away and find her way home. He wasn't taking her to the other end of the country or anything. She couldn't help smiling.

"You like this song, Heather?"

Macy looked over at him. She had almost forgotten he was there. "Yeah, this song is great."

He nodded. "I like it too. It has a good beat." He tapped his fingers on the steering wheel along with the song. Then he moved his left hand down and turned on the blinker.

Where were they going now? The scenery was nondescript; she didn't know how he could tell where he needed to turn. They went down a road to the left that Macy didn't see until they slowed down. It had a gate off to the side, making it look like they were entering private property. There were scrape marks on the pavement indicating that the gate had been opened and closed a lot. Was that what he meant by a gated community?

Her heart picked up speed, but she didn't know why. Wherever they were going couldn't be any worse than the hole in the farm that she had spent too much time in. They were going to a house with a mom...a stepmom. A fake stepmom. Macy twisted a strand of hair.

They drove along the road until it turned into a dirt road. It forked at one point and they went left. Chester finally stopped talking. Was that a good sign? Macy had too many questions, but she had a feeling the answers were coming soon enough.

There was still nothing as far as she could see. Just more grassy fields with the occasional tree.

Eventually, they passed a playground. It looked rusty, like no one had touched it for decades. Chills ran down her spine as she looked at it. She could almost feel the eyes of children's ghosts watching her.

Chester put his hand on her shoulder and she jumped. He didn't appear to notice. "We're almost home, Heather. Are you as excited as me?"

"I...." How was she supposed to answer without lying?

"Oh, I understand. You haven't seen it, so it's hard to be excited. We're almost there."

"Okay."

He picked up speed again. "Just wait until you see it. It'll be different from anywhere else we've ever lived."

That much was obvious. The road became even bumpier. They rode in silence for a few more minutes before he stopped in front of a tiny shack. If that was what it could even be called. It didn't look big enough for more than one room, and there was no way it had any running water or electricity.

"What's this?" Macy asked.

"We need to stop here before we get to the community."

It sound like Macy's blood was pumping right in her ears. She looked around, panicked.

"Is something the matter, Heather?"

She turned to him. "I don't want to go in there." She begged him with her eyes. Maybe if he really did love Heather, he would listen to Macy this one time. "Please."

"Don't worry, Heather. I'll be there with you. I know this building is a little rundown, but it's not our home. It's where we're going to meet some of the residents."

The way he said *residents* didn't sit right with her.

Chester's eyes crinkled as he smiled. "Everything's going to be just fine. You'll see. Let's get out and meet the most important people of the community."

She looked out the windows. What were her chances of getting away?

He patted her shoulder again. "You worry too much. You always have. Just relax."

Relax?

Three men and one woman came out of the building. How had they even managed to fit inside? They were dressed in all white and were headed for the truck. If it was dark, it would have been the perfect setup for a scary movie.

The woman was fairly tall and had her almost-black hair pulled tightly behind her. A man about her height walked with her slightly in front of the other two men. The men all had short hair and the one in front had thick, bushy eyebrows and a beard that looked more like a nine o'clock shadow. The two men in back were taller and thinner, both with dark hair and piercing eyes. They all appeared to be full of confidence, almost like they were on a mission.

Macy clenched her fists.

"It's time to get out." Chester unlocked the child locks and opened his own door. "Come on."

Heart racing faster than ever, she opened her door and got out as slow as possible. She closed the door, but refused to walk toward the people dressed in white.

As they walked her way, their eyes seemed to look into her soul. Their faces showed no emotion, not helping to ease Macy's fear. She wanted to run away, but her feet wouldn't move. These people were probably going to tie her up and leave her somewhere, just as Chester had done when he first took her. She wanted to run—but her body wouldn't cooperate. Fear paralyzed her.

Chester took her hand. Where had he come from? Macy hadn't

even noticed him walk around the truck. He pulled on her hand. "We need to meet them, Heather."

Her feet still wouldn't budge.

"Come on. Don't be rude." He pulled on her harder, forcing her to walk or fall down.

Luckily, her feet cooperated. Though she stumbled, she walked with Chester as he held her hand. They stopped when they were only a couple feet from the four creepy strangers.

The shortest man, the one in front, nodded at them. "You must be Heather. Your dad has told us so much about you."

She stared at him, her mouth too dry to reply.

"I'm Jonah and these are my assistants. You'll get to know us quite well. Has your dad told us anything about us?"

Macy shook her head no, hoping that was the right answer.

He smiled, his dark brown eyes squinting as he did. "Good, good. He's followed our directions. Our community is private and we don't discuss it out in the world. Is that something you can agree to also?"

Macy nodded, swallowing. She would be happy never mentioning anything that she had been through, if it meant she had the chance to get away.

"Let's go inside and get acquainted. The sooner we get the rules out of the way, the sooner you two can settle into your home. Your new mom has been busy getting the house ready. She's so excited to meet you."

Community

T HE SHACK WAS nicer on the inside than on the outside. It had a clean, beige carpet that covered the room. Furniture was minimal, but nice. It was all the same color as the carpet. The walls were white and a table with eight chairs sat off to the side.

Jonah pointed to the floor. "Let's sit."

Macy looked at the couch and back to him. Was he serious? All the adults sat down. Apparently he was. She sat next to Chester. It bothered her that she felt more comfortable next to him. But then again, she at least knew that he wasn't going to kill her. The other four—who knew?

No one said anything for a full five minutes. Macy looked around, her pulse still pounding in her ears.

Finally, Jonah looked at her. "Before you two you enter our community, you must go through the purification process to wash the world off. You can't have even a trace."

Macy's eyes widened.

As if answering her thoughts, Jonah continued. "The world is full of evil and we all must become clean before leaving it. Anytime we are forced to go back out there, we must purify ourselves before entering."

Macy nodded even though she had no idea what he was talking about.

"Once you're clean, I will explain everything. Your dad is the head of your household, so he will go first." Jonah rose and so did Chester. They walked to a door that Macy hadn't noticed. Jonah opened it and Chester walked in, closing it behind him.

The lady looked at Macy. "My name is Eve, Heather. I'm looking forward to having you join our community."

"Thanks." Macy couldn't take her eyes off the door the Chester went through.

"Your dad is cleaning the world off."

Just then the sounds of a shower were heard.

Eve continued, "When he has scrubbed its evil away, he will put on clean, white clothes and join us. Then it will be your turn. You'll find the cleaning supplies in the bathroom and it's important that you scrub every inch of yourself. We can't have any remnants entering our land. Will you be able to do that or do you need help?"

"I can scrub myself."

"You'll have to work hard. Your skin should burn."

"Okay. So hard it burns. Got it."

"Good. We'll give you a proper welcome after you've gone through the purification. You understand we can't touch you while the vile world is still on you."

Macy nodded, but had no clue what Eve meant. She had a feeling that she would understand all too well soon enough.

"We'll sit in silence while we wait. Meanwhile, reflect on good and evil."

What did that mean? Macy looked down at her hands, pretending to think about it. It felt like forever before she finally heard the water stop. Did that mean Chester had purified himself? And did that mean she was about to take another shower? Why had he had her take a shower before they left? Did he think she needed to be extra clean?

The door opened and he came out, wearing white pants and a white shirt that resembled a pillowcase with arms and his hair was wet. Beads of sweat broke out around her hairline.

Eve looked at her. She had a serene look on her face. "It's your turn, Heather. Don't touch your dad since he's pure and you still carry the evils of the world."

She had no problem avoiding Chester. Macy got up, never so nervous about a shower. Chester nodded to her, walking far away from her. There was no way a shower had cured him. If they were so worried about keeping evil away, they were bringing it in with welcome arms by accepting him.

She went into the bathroom. It was a tiny room with barely enough room to move around, which was no surprise given the size of the building. Everything was so clean it sparkled. The shower was nothing more than a stall and she saw a pile of white clothes on the counter. Those were her new clothes.

Was she going to have to wear them all the time now? Did everyone in the community wear all white?

Macy noticed a trash can in the corner. She walked to it, seeing Chester's clothes piled inside.

There was a knock on the door. "Do you need help starting the shower?" asked Jonah.

"No. I was just about to start it," she called. There was no lock on the door, so she would have to hurry. The last thing Macy wanted was to have someone walk in on her. She pulled off her clothes and threw them on top of Chester's. The tile was cold on her feet as she walked to the shower stall.

There was only one knob for the shower, and it was market with a "C." She took a deep breath before turning it on. Hopefully it was mismarked and she could still adjust the temperature. Macy turned the knob and gasped as icy-cold water rained down on her. She turned the knob further, finding that it didn't help.

The water was so frigid that it had to come directly from outside, where snow still remained in the shady spots. She had to get out as quickly as possible, but Jonah and Eve would probably check her skin to make sure it was red, showing that she'd scrubbed hard enough.

On the wall hung a scrub-brush and underneath it sat a jug of unmarked liquid that had to be soap. She grabbed the brush, not wanting to think about how many other people had used it before her. She poured some soap onto it and winced. It had a strong, unpleasant odor.

The scent was the least of her problems. The water was still freezing. She didn't have to press very hard for the brush to hurt. Her arm turned red as she washed without adding any extra pressure. She rubbed all over, hoping it would be enough and that they wouldn't send her back for a second shower.

Her teeth chattered in the cold and finally had herself clean for the second time that day. She rinsed herself off and then the brush. Was she supposed to use the soap for her hair? So much for the conditioner she had sneaked in from the hotel. If she used that, they'd know. It didn't smell anything like the soap. She finished the shower and finally turned off the icy water.

Shivering, she found a white towel sitting behind the clothes. She stood for a moment, wrapped in the towel just trying to warm up. What kind of sadists were these people?

A knock started her. "Are you almost done, Heather?" asked Eve.

"Just a minute," she called. Macy toweled off her hair and then put on the white clothes. They were stiff and uncomfortable, but at least they fit. She had been worried that she would have had to wear the same size as Chester.

What was she supposed to do about shoes? Macy looked around and noticed a pair of white shoes sitting against the wall next to the counter. A pair of white socks sat on top of them. At least she wouldn't have to go barefoot.

Macy went out to the main room, her hair soaking the back of the shirt. All five of the adults stood when they saw her. Eve took her hand and brought her to the group. "Now that you've been purified, it's time to go over the rules. Are you ready?"

Holding back a sigh, Macy nodded.

They all sat in a circle. Chester and Eve sat on either side of her. Jonah sat across from her and the other two men sat on either side of him.

Jonah looked Macy in the eyes. "You are indeed blessed, child. Most people never find the true way. It's hidden because of the evil in their hearts and minds. You've been given the gift many never know they want but cannot have."

She continued staring into his eyes. His hazel eyes bore into hers with an intensity she could feel.

"I'm Jonah, as you know, but what you don't know is that I'm the great High Prophet. I receive messages and visions to guide our community in the way of righteousness and pure living. It is my job to take care of my people, seeing to it that everyone makes it to the Holy Land beyond this world. It's my job, for lack of a better word, to find puritans such as yourself: the holy vessels of righteousness who will ascend with me on the great and magnificent day. Do you have any questions?"

Macy shook her head. She did have a bunch of questions, but Jonah wouldn't appreciate any of them.

"You've already met Eve. She's the High Prophetess as my first and primary wife. Eve receives visions also, but not at the volume that I do. Mine are daily, and each evening we gather as a community so I can share what has been bestowed upon me that day with the community."

Awesome.

Jonah indicated to the men next to him. "These are my primary assistant prophets, helping with the community. This is Abraham and Isaac. As you may have guessed from their names, they're father and son."

"Does everyone have Biblical names?" Macy asked. Would she be getting yet another name?

Jonah's eyes narrowed slightly. "Women do not speak to men unless spoken to. I did not ask you just now if you had any questions, but I will let it slide since we haven't yet gotten to the rules. Do you understand?"

Macy nodded, biting back a sarcastic reply.

"I asked you a question. Do you understand?" He sat taller, staring at her with an even deeper intensity.

Eve nudged Macy's knee with her own.

"Yes, I understand."

Jonah's face relaxed. "Good. Now, to answer your question, receiving a Biblical name is a high honor. Only those who have proven themselves get a new name. It's a day of celebration when that happens. We hold a Holy Festival in honor of the occasion. If you're blessed enough, you shall have a festival in your honor. But first, your father must have his own celebration as head of the household. Otherwise, you must wait until you reach maturity."

Macy's head spun. She wanted to put her hands on her head, but didn't dare.

"Now that you have a basic understanding—I wouldn't want to overwhelm you with everything in one day—we'll move onto the rules. You already know never to speak to a male puritan without being spoken to, although some may give you permission to speak freely. That is up to them. As mentioned, every night we gather to hear the message of the day. Never, ever miss that. It is of the utmost importance. Everyone must hear and apply it to remain pure so we can enter into the Holy Land. We are holy vessels of righteousness, remember."

Using those big religious words must make him feel important, Macy thought.

Jonah went on, explaining things such as proper foods to eat, what constituted as sins, and how the puritans were to cleanse themselves from all unholiness. Basically they had to go through a cleaning like she had just done, or endure a public shaming. Macy didn't ask what that meant.

"Will you be able to remember all of that?" he asked, looking back and forth between Macy and Chester.

Macy shook her head.

Jonah smiled, clasping his hands together. "No? Well, you're being honest. You're truly a chosen vessel, child. I can't express the joy that brings to my heart. Eve will stay in here and drill you on the rules until you have the basic ones memorized. While you two are doing that, I will take the men and we will cleanse, purify, and bless your truck and its contents. Then you may bring them into the community."

Eve took Macy's hand and led her to the couch while the men rose and went outside.

"Can I speak to you without being spoken to?"

"Of course, child. What is it?"

"What are they going to do to the truck?"

"First, Jonah will pray over it as he walks around it. Then the men will lay hands on it while praying and receiving visions. Once all that is complete, Jonah shall anoint it with a special blessing. Afterward, he will wait for a higher vision, and if he gets a positive one, you and your dad will be able to go home."

"That sounds like it could take a while."

Eve nodded. "It gives us enough time to drill you so you know the rules by heart. Are you ready?"

"I guess so."

"You are." Eve smiled. "Do you speak to a brother without being spoken to?"

"Do you mean a man?"

"Any male puritan. Even a child. We do not speak unless spoken to, child. It is the holy way of righteousness. The world looks down on such things, but truly, it is an honor. We are the blessed ones, learning to live in pure submission."

Macy took a deep breath. It was no wonder Chester liked this place.

"When do we go to our daily meetings to learn from the holy visions?" asked Eve.

"Every night."

"Correct."

"Now list for me as many sins as you can recall."

This was going to be one long afternoon.

Unexpecting

Z OEY SAT IN a nondescript waiting room next to her mom. Her
mom had her laptop out, working from there. She never passed up
an opportunity to get in extra work. Zoey was still exhausted, even
though she had slept well over twelve hours.

A nurse opened the door next to the registration desk. "Zoey
Carter."

Valerie looked at her. "Want me to go with you?"

"No." Zoey stood up and followed the nurse. She refused to look at
the scale, not wanting to know what she weighed. When they got to the
exam room, she mindlessly answered basic questions as the nurse typed
the answers into a laptop.

The nurse stood and went to the door. "The doctor will be right in.
Do you have any questions?"

"Nope." Zoey leaned her head against the wall next to her. She
looked at the paper-covered table, wanting to crawl on it and fall asleep.
Maybe she would if the doctor took a long time.

Zoey's eyes grew heavier as she waited. Five minutes turned into
ten, which turned into fifteen. Finally she couldn't take it any longer,
and she closed her eyes. The door opened and Zoey fought her eyes,
struggling to open them.

"Zoey Carter?" asked a young, pretty lady in a doctor's coat.

"Yeah."

"I'm Doctor Hernandez. It's nice to meet you. So, you're here for a
checkup?"

"I guess."

The doctor sat down and read from the laptop. "You've been over-tired lately? Has there been any stress in your life?"

Zoey laughed bitterly.

Dr. Hernandez raised an eyebrow. "I take that as a yes?"

"You've heard of Macy Mercer, right?"

"The missing girl. Why?"

"My best friend."

A look of sudden understanding washed over her face. "That would certainly explain fatigue. Have you spoken with anyone about how you're feeling?"

"Just my boyfriend."

"No counselors?"

She shook her head. "Just my boyfriend," she repeated.

"You should really consider it."

"That's what my mom says."

"Well, you should listen to her. Anyway, I'll give you a full checkup and make sure that nothing else is going on. Sound good?"

Zoey nodded and then went through another tiring round of questions. Then the doctor looked in her eyes, ears, nose, and mouth, followed by listening to her heart and lungs.

"Everything looks good. One question I have to ask, given your age. I have here that your last menstrual cycle was six weeks ago. Is there any chance you're pregnant?"

Zoey's heart nearly stopped. She stared at the doctor, unable to speak. Was that why she was so tired? Did being pregnant make people tired? Didn't they only throw up in the beginning? It wasn't possible—she couldn't be pregnant.

"Did you hear me, Zoey? Is there a chance you could be pregnant? You mentioned that you have a boyfriend."

She twisted her hands together, unable to find her voice. They hadn't used protection the first few times. The first time had just happened so unexpectedly, and then the next times following were all over the same weekend when she had been staying at the Mercer's house.

"Zoey?"

"Maybe," she whispered. She couldn't be. She just couldn't.

Dr. Hernandez didn't even flinch. She just nodded as though they were talking about the weather. "We have two options. You can either take a blood test and wait for the results or you can urinate in a cup, and then we'll know in several minutes."

"I…I don't know."

She opened a cupboard and pulled out a little cup and then pointed to one of the two doors. "That door leads to a bathroom. Fill this about halfway and then bring back here. A nurse will run the test real quick." She handed Zoey the cup.

"Doesn't the test have to be first thing in the morning or something?" Zoey looked back and forth between the cup and the doctor.

"No. Tests today are sensitive, so it can be any time of the day."

"You're not going to tell my mom, are you?"

"Not unless you want me to."

"No." Zoey grabbed the cup.

She went into the bathroom. Everything felt unreal, but on the bright side, she wasn't tired anymore. The fear got rid of that. How could she be taking a pregnancy test? She was only fifteen—and Alex, he was only thirteen. Sure, he would be fourteen soon, but still.

Her pulse was on fire as she stared at the cup. She barely managed to fill the cup without making a mess. She nearly dropped it into the toilet bowl twice. If she couldn't even pee into a cup, how would she handle a baby?

By the time she made it back to the exam room, her stomach was twisted so tight she could barely breathe. A nurse stood in the room, and she held out a little tray. "Set the cup here, please. Then have a seat."

Zoey placed the cup on the tray, and then sat down. She shook and her mind spun out of control. How could this be happening? Why had they been so stupid? If she would have known they were going to do it, she would have bought protection earlier. She thought for sure they were okay. It was only that one weekend they didn't use any.

Where was that nurse? Or the doctor? Were they trying to teach her a lesson?

Unable to sit still another moment, Zoey got up and paced the small room. What was taking them so long? How long did it take to run a simple test? Didn't they just dip in a stick and get the answer? Were they sitting back there gossiping about her?

Gossip. That's what would happen at school if anyone found out. She wrung her hands together. No. That wasn't going to happen. The test was going to be negative, so she wouldn't have to worry about what people would say.

The door opened behind her. Zoey turned around and tried to read the doctor's face. She couldn't tell either way. Dr. Hernandez had the perfect poker face.

"Why don't we have a seat, Zoey." It wasn't a question.

Zoey sat down, still trying to read her face.

She made eye contact with Zoey. With no emotion she said, "The results were positive."

"What on earth does that mean?" Zoey demanded.

Dr. Hernandez reached over and put her hand on Zoey's. "You're pregnant. The line was quite dark, indicating the probability of a strong early pregnancy."

Everything disappeared around Zoey as she stared into the doctor's dark brown eyes. Her mouth wouldn't budge.

"Do you know what you want to do?" asked the doctor.

Zoey shook her head as tears filled her eyes, blurring her vision.

"There are two options. You can terminate or proceed with the pregnancy. It's your choice, and of course we don't have to tell your parents."

"You'd have to find my dad to tell him—which you're more than welcome to." Anger burned in the pit of her stomach. "That's exactly what he deserves. He's never been here for me and look what happened."

The doctor patted her hand. "Let's focus. You don't have to make a decision today, but if you're undecided, I'll need to send you with some prenatal vitamins. They should help you to feel better, too. The baby is going to continue to take a lot from your body and you really need the vitamins."

"I'll take them."

Dr. Hernandez turned to the laptop and typed for a few moments before she turned back to Zoey. "I'll also send you with some contraceptives."

"It's not like I'm going to get pregnant."

She cracked a smile. "No, but you don't want to get any diseases."

"We're each other's firsts."

"That's what they all say, dear."

Zoey narrowed her eyes. "I've known him forever. He's telling the truth."

"Still, I'm going to give you some. Use them."

Whatever. If she was already pregnant, what was the point? "Fine."

"I'll also get some pamphlets to answer your questions. You'll have some later even if you can't think of any now. There are also some websites listed, you can find more answers there. When you have questions, go to those websites. Don't search online or ask your friends."

"Okay."

"Also, you can call our office anytime, but I'll have the front desk schedule you to come back in four weeks. In the meantime, I'd like you to speak with a counselor. They wouldn't tell your parents anything, either. I can get you a pamphlet for that too. Do you need anything else?"

Zoey's head spun...or was that room? "No."

The doctor typed more into the laptop and then told her a nurse would be in shortly.

Zoey nodded. She couldn't make sense of anything, much less the fact that she was pregnant. The weight of its reality was hitting hard. "How come I haven't thrown up?"

"Not everyone does," said a different voice.

She looked up to see a nurse. Dr. Hernandez was nowhere to be seen. When had they switched places? "Where's the doctor?"

"Oh, she's just talking with your parents."

"Just my mom. My mom!" Zoey stood up. "What's she telling her? I thought she wasn't—"

"She's telling her what she can. Everything except the pregnancy, since you don't want her mentioning that."

"What's there to tell?"

"That you're taking new vitamins and she would like you to see a counselor."

Zoey swore. "I don't want to see a counselor."

The nurse handed her some sample vitamins packs. "These should get you through until your next appointment. You really should decide what to do as soon as possible though. A counselor can help you with that."

She put the vitamins in her backpack. Then she was handed a stack of papers that she probably wouldn't even look at. The nurse spoke, but Zoey couldn't focus.

Home

CHESTER CAME INSIDE with the prophets after what Macy guessed to be an hour and a half of Eve drilling the rules into her head.

Jonah looked at Eve. "The truck and its contents have been purified."

"And the child has a full understanding of the community rules."

"We're all set. Let's show our newest vessels to their home."

Eve rose and Macy followed. They all walked outside and Eve pointed to the truck. "You may travel with your dad."

Macy went into the truck with Chester, and the others climbed into a van—white, of course. Chester started the truck and they followed the van for several miles until they reached a paved parking lot in the middle of nowhere.

After parking, Jonah and company got out of the van and opened the back doors. They pulled out a cart and dragged it to the truck.

Chester looked at her. "You stay in here until we have everything loaded."

"Okay." At least she didn't have to do any heavy lifting. Chester had packed most of their two rooms into the back of the truck.

He got out and Macy could hear the back of the truck open. She bounced up and down in the seat as they removed things from the back. Before long, the back of the truck slammed shut. Chester opened her door and moved aside so she could get out. She slid out without a word.

Jonah looked at her. "We men will pull the cart while you and Eve push from the back. Once we're inside the community, we will have a horse pull it the rest of the way to your home."

Since Jonah hadn't given her permission to speak, Macy went to the back of the cart without replying. The wood was rough and full of splinters. She tried to find a place to push that wouldn't tear her hands apart, but there were no smooth spots. The cart was heavy, and with all of them moving it, Macy still broke out into a sweat before they had even made it a few feet.

It felt like hours, but she really had no idea how long it took to get it to the gate. She wiped her brow when they were done, gasping for air. Her muscles burned.

Eve turned to her. "Before we go in, you and your dad are going to have to wear head coverings."

"Head coverings?"

"You'll need to wear them until tonight's meeting. We'll have your unveiling ceremony to welcome you into the community. Then you will become official members. After that will be the wedding, followed by a time of celebration."

"They're getting married today?" Macy's eyes widened. She didn't even know her future fake stepmom's name.

"Tonight, yes. We can't have you all living in the same house otherwise. She is in another home, getting ready for the ceremonies so that you and your dad can settle in."

The men came around the cart. Isaac carried a pile of white cloth, which he handed to Macy and Chester. Macy held hers up, trying to figure out how she was supposed to wear it. Eve helped her put it over her head. There was only one slit on the head peace, allowing her to see. How was she supposed to breathe?

She looked down and noticed that it hung down away from her shirt, allowing air in.

"One more good push," Jonah called. "We've got the gate open."

Macy groaned. She was already sweating. Wearing the head piece would make it worse.

Eve looked at her. "Hard work is a privilege. It teaches us many things and we should always appreciate it."

"Okay." Macy nodded, unsure if Eve could even tell. They pushed the cart several yards, passing through a thick, wooden gate. Once inside, Jonah and Abraham closed and locked the gate behind them.

The gate was part of a larger fence with no space between the slats. It was about ten feet tall and had metal spikes on the top. No one was getting in or out. The fence went on beyond what Macy could see. As far as she could tell, it wrapped around the entire town—or community, as they called it.

She saw various buildings, some looked like homes and others looked they had other purposes. Macy turned to Eve. "How big is this place?"

"It goes on for miles, Heather. We're entirely self-sustaining with everything we would ever need here inside the walls. It helps to keep the world out. It's unusual for anyone to leave, because there's rarely need. What does the world have that we want?"

Macy could think of several things off the top of her head, but knew better than to say any of them. One of the rules of the community was not to speak of *the world.*

"The horse is attached," Isaac said, walking around the cart. "I'll lead it to the house."

Chester, also covered with head garb, walked with Jonah to the front.

Eve took Macy's hand. "The men will lead the horse and we'll follow behind the cart."

Macy nodded, making sure Eve could tell through the cloth covering Macy's head. Eve let go of her hand and they walked in silence for what felt like more than a mile. The people that they passed, dressed in all white of course, paused to watch them. No one else had anything over their heads.

They were like fish in a tank with everyone staring at them from outside. Macy was glad for the covering, because she didn't want everyone staring at her. She'd never been so embarrassed in all of her life, though she didn't know why. All of the other people were all dressed in the same white clothes as she was, living with the same ridiculous rules she had just learned.

One girl who looked about Macy's age had a large "G" pinned on the front of her shirt.

Eve walked closer to Macy. "That's part of the shaming we discussed. The G is for greed and everyone who sees her knows she committed an act of supreme selfishness. She was already purified, but now must pay the price of her sin."

Chills ran through Macy. What had she done that was so bad? She didn't dare ask, remembering they weren't even to speak of sins committed. They could, however, speak of preventing them before they happened. But they had to be careful, so as not to become tainted.

As they continued to walk, more people came out of homes and buildings to watch the newcomers. What were they hoping to see? The only thing they could see was how tall they were and maybe their eyes, but no one came close enough to get a good look.

Macy tried to tell what she could of the people, but they were mostly nondescript, all wearing the same white clothes. The girls and women had their hair pulled back in tight buns, some of them wearing odd, white hats. The guys all had super short hair, and again, some wore hats, while others didn't.

Finally, they stopped. The horse and cart stopped first, and then Macy and Eve stopped also. She looked around, seeing a few small homes on either side of the dirt road. They all looked the same. Which one was going to be their new home? Not that it mattered. Wherever they moved wasn't going to be her *home*.

Jonah walked to the house closest to their left. He opened the door, not appearing to have unlocked it. Were there no locks?

Seemingly out of nowhere, about a dozen men showed up. They removed items from the cart and carried them into the house.

Eve took Macy's hand again and tugged. They stepped back several feet.

"We'll let the men do the heavy lifting. Once everything is inside, you two can settle in. Remember to keep the covering on until it's removed in the ceremony. Then and only then can it come off."

Chills ran down her spine. "Why doesn't anyone have a coat?"

"We don't wear coats. Suffering and trials lead us on the path to purity."

"What about when it snows?"

"No coats. Some go out in it specifically to become more pure. Sometimes it can turn into a fun competition." She smiled, her eyes shining.

Yeah, that sounds like a great time, Macy thought sarcastically.

Before she knew it, she and Chester were inside the chilly, little house, unpacking. She got the shivers again. "Is there no heat?"

"You're not to speak until spoken to, Heather."

Macy's stomach dropped. She stepped back. Was he going to hit her? Lock her up? Make her wear a letter?

"You're free to speak—don't worry." It sounded like he was smiling behind his curtain of white. He actually sounded joyful. "Just don't forget it when other males from the community are around. About the heat: electricity is believed to be one of the evils of the world. See that wood stove?"

"Yeah." She looked at the small, black stove in the corner.

"I'm told those keep the homes nice and toasty. Would you like me to start a fire?"

"Yes, please. I'm freezing."

"Have a seat and make yourself comfortable."

Macy stared at him. Was he serious? He wasn't going to put her to work? She sat on the couch, pulling a heavy afghan over herself.

"Your new mom made that. She made a lot of things in here."

"Have you even met her?" Macy asked.

Chester picked up a log from next to the stove and shoved it in. "Yes, although not in person yet. We've been corresponding through letters. She's excited to meet us."

Macy looked around the room, feeling like she'd stepped back in time. Everything looked like the *Little House on the Prairie.* A few years before, she and her mom watched all the seasons. Macy never would have guessed the show would become her life one day.

Chester looked at her through his head dress. "It might take a bit for this to warm the place up. Why don't you unpack your room and get settled in? That way you don't have to worry about it after the wedding."

"Uh, sure." She rose, keeping the blanket around her.

"I'll get the rest of our stuff ready."

She found her bedroom. It was a tiny room with just a bed, a shelf, a desk, and small dresser. Obviously, they didn't have a wide variety of clothes, so a large dresser or a closet was unnecessary.

Macy set a box on the bed and opened it. She gasped. Her teddy bear was on top. It was the one that she had had at home—her real home—that Chester had stolen and teased her with. How long would she have it back? Picking it up, she smelled it. It mostly smelled like the farmhouse, but when she breathed deeply, she could smell her home.

Images of her room filled her mind. She heard a noise outside the room and stuffed the bear next to the pillow. Could she find a place to hide it so that Chester couldn't take it away again?

Disagree

AS SOON AS school was out, Alex texted Zoey again. She hadn't texted him all day, and he needed to know what was wrong or if everything was okay. He had texted and called a bunch of times during lunch, but her phone had to have been off because it kept going to voice mail.

He found an empty seat on the bus and sat by himself, hoping everyone would leave him alone. He was tired of all the questions about Macy. As if it wasn't bad enough that he had to deal with his sister's disappearance, he also had to put up with everyone's stupid questions and comments.

He sent another text, and just as he hit send, someone sat next to him. He groaned, not caring if he hurt anyone's feelings.

One of the jocks looked at Alex. "Hey, dude. Any news on your sister?"

Alex jumped up. "You really think if there was, I'd just be sitting on the bus?"

"Whatever." The jock shrugged and went to the back.

Alex looked out the window, ignoring everyone else until he reached his stop. The house was empty. His dad had had to go back to work not long after Macy disappeared, and his mom often went out look for Macy or passing out fliers.

After eating a banana, he threw his bag into his room and headed back outside. If Zoey wouldn't answer his texts, he'd go to her house.

When he got to her house, only two houses away, Valerie answered.

"Sorry to bother you, Ms. Carter. I didn't know you were home." Maybe that was why Zoey was ignoring him.

"You're never a bother, Alex. I'm just working from home today. Zoey hasn't been feeling well and I wanted to keep an eye on her."

"Is she okay?" He regretted the urgency in his voice, but he couldn't help it.

"I think all the stress of the last month has finally caught up with her. You should take care of yourself too. The doctor gave her some vitamins to help with her energy. You might want to look into getting some if you're tired."

He was already on anti-depressants, but he wasn't going to tell her that. He hadn't even mentioned it to Zoey. She probably wouldn't care, but it was still embarrassing. "I'll keep that in mind, thanks. Can I talk to her?"

"I think so. She's locked herself in her room. Want me to check on her?"

Zoey appeared around the corner behind her mom. "I'm up. Can I walk around the neighborhood with Alex? I bet some exercise and fresh air will do me some good. Right, Mom?"

Valerie looked relieved. "I'm so glad you want to get out of the house." She gave Zoey a hug and then tousled Alex's hair. "I love that you two are still close, even with Macy missing. How are your parents, Alex?"

He shrugged. "Still getting along, but upset about Macy. Sometimes I hear them crying when they think I'm not listening. It sucks."

"I wish I could do something to make this better. I'm worried sick about Macy. If anything ever happened to my Zo, I don't—"

"Mom, please don't." Zoey pushed her way around Valerie and stood next to Alex. "We won't go far, okay?"

Valerie nodded, still giving him a look of pity. "Do you guys have someone making you dinner? I haven't heard from homeowners' association. They were the ones putting that list together.

Zoey grabbed Alex's arm. "Mom, if they need you to make dinner, they'll ask."

Alex nodded. "After everyone from the HOA made our meals, some church took over. I think there are even some other churches that want to help too. We're covered for a while, but thanks."

Valerie leaned against the door frame. "Oh, good. Okay, you two have a good walk. Be home by dinner, Zo."

"Okay." Zoey managed to give that one word three syllables. She yanked Alex down the driveway. "Can you believe her? I swear, she never knows when to stop talking."

He shrugged, pushing some of his bangs out of his eyes. "She's not so bad. Did you turn your phone off? I texted you, like, a million times."

"I slept all morning and then I forgot my phone at home on the charger."

"You should at least check it, you know. I was worried something had happened."

"Sorry." She looked like she meant it. "I just haven't been feeling myself lately. I need more sleep or something."

"Is that what the doctor said?"

"Something like that." She looked up at the dark clouds. "It's going to snow again. I hope Macy's somewhere warm."

Alex's heart sunk. "I hope so too. But she's smart. She can take care of herself."

"Not smart enough to come home."

Alex scowled. "It's okay to admit it hurts. You don't have to say crap like that."

Zoey rolled her eyes. "Did your shrink tell you that?"

He pulled his arm from her hold. "What's with you?"

Her eyebrows came together. "I'm. Tired."

"No, it's something more than that. What's going on? Tell me."

"Nothing," she said, way too fast.

"Whatever. Don't tell me. I'm only your boyfriend who loves you." He walked faster, forcing her to speed up if she wanted to catch him.

"Alex, come on."

He stopped and turned around, letting her catch up. He grabbed her arm, forcing her to stop too. "You're keeping something from me. Why? Just tell me something so I'm not completely in the dark."

She yanked her arm away. "I'm just under a lot of stress. I'd think you'd understand that."

"Don't give me that. If you don't want to tell me what's bothering you, just say so."

"Fine. I don't want to talk about it." She crossed her arms and stared at him.

"At least you're finally admitting it. Let's go smoke. I really need one after today."

A strange look came over her face. "I'm going to skip that today."

"Really? Why?"

"Because. Got a problem with that?" Her eyes were shining. Was she about to cry?

Alex felt bad, but at the same time it irritated him that he didn't know what was going on. What was she keeping from him?

"I've been thinking about cutting back, Alex. Let's just keep walking."

They walked through the neighborhood, not saying anything. Alex tried to think of what he would have done to make her so mad.

Irritation continued to build in his chest until he couldn't take it any longer. "If you have something you don't want to tell me, that's fine. Just don't take it out on me. If I did do something to you, just tell me. I deserve that much."

Sounding bitter, she laughed. "It's not like that. Look, I have some things I need to figure out. Once I've got my thoughts organized, I'll let you know."

"Does it have anything to do with me?"

"You're not going to give up, are you?"

"Nope."

"Maybe I should just go back home."

"Maybe you should." He stared at her.

"Alex, please don't do this."

"Don't do what, exactly?"

"This."

"Congratulations. We're having our first fight. Call me when you're ready to make up." He spun around and headed back home, more frustrated than before. He would have been better off not even going to her house. Ever since Macy disappeared, they had stuck together, telling each other everything. Why was she pulling away now?

He walked fast, muttering to himself, not knowing if Zoey was following him or not. Part of him wanted her to be so they could talk about whatever was eating her, but part of him also hoped she had turned around and went home the other way. He didn't need her to take her crap out on him. He had the rest of the world for that.

Hopefully, whatever was going on with Zoey was temporary. But what if Macy's disappearance was too much for her now? Could she be ready to move on with her life? What if she wanted to get rid of every reminder of her best friend, including him? He stopped and leaned against a tree.

Zoey wouldn't want that, would she?

A minute later Zoey walked in front of him and stopped. "I didn't think you'd ever stop." She sounded out of breath.

Alex narrowed his eyes. "Are you going to break up with me? If so, just tell me."

"What?" She looked genuinely shocked. That was a good sign.

He frowned, not showing her his relief. "You heard me."

"Break up with you? Why would I do that?"

"How would I know? You won't tell me what's going on."

"So you jump right to me dumping you?" Her lips formed a straight line.

"No. It took forty minutes of walking and thinking to come to that. Best I can figure—since you won't tell me anything—is you don't want to hurt anymore, so you're moving on with your life. Getting rid of all the Mercers from your life."

"Why would I do that?"

"So you don't have to deal with the pain of Macy being gone. I'm just a reminder of her."

She looked at him like he was crazy.

"It sounded better in my head." He looked away.

"Oh, Alex." She wrapped her arms around him. "The last thing I want is you out of my life. I don't know what I'd do without you. Besides, I know Macy's coming back. Sure, it's been like a month, but she'll be back. If she doesn't, she knows I'll beat the crap out of her."

Alex breathed in the sweet smell of her silky, jet-black hair. It smelled fruity. "I'm glad to hear that. The part about not dumping me."

"You'd have to try a lot harder than that to get rid of me."

Dinner

MACY MOVED THE curtain a little and peeked outside. It was starting to get dark already, but that wasn't surprising, given that it was December. But what did surprise her was how many people were outside, wearing only their white garb. Did they wear any layers underneath?

At first, it appeared that no one was paying attention to their house, but as she looked closer, she noticed eyes turning their way, scanning the home. Were they as curious about her and Chester as she was about them? No one was staring hard enough to see her curtain barely moved out of the way.

She could hear Chester calling her from the other end of the house. Macy found him in the kitchen.

He looked her way, still wearing the head piece. "The ceremony will be soon, Heather. We should eat something."

Macy was glad they would remove the headpieces soon. It was challenging only looking through a slit. "Where's the fridge?"

"There's no electricity here, remember. See that? It's an icebox, and it holds the same purpose."

"How are we going to cook anything?" she asked.

"On the wood stove, of course. It looks like your mom made us some stew. Can you grab a pot from over there?"

She nodded and went to a metal rack that held pots and pans. She picked one that looked about the right size and then turned to Chester. He closed the icebox and held a ceramic bowl in his hand.

"Set that on top of the icebox and I'll pour in enough for us to eat. We shouldn't waste any, because I don't know yet what to do with leftover food. Clearly there's no garbage disposal around here."

Macy almost said something about not wanting to wear a "W" for wasteful, but thought better of it. He was in a good mood and she didn't want to do anything to disrupt that. She held the pot still while he poured the stew. Even though she had the fabric over her face, she could smell the meat.

As if reading her thoughts, Chester said, "I know it's not vegan, but at least it's organic. They don't use any kind of chemicals or hormones inside the community walls. Everything is exactly as nature intended."

Macy didn't care about the meat. She'd eaten enough since Chester took her that she wasn't a vegan anymore. Maybe someday, if she ever got away from him, she could be one again.

He pulled the bowl away and put the top back on. "Would you put that on the stove, and then come back to find a wooden spoon? I'm going to see what else we can eat."

She nodded, almost unsure how to respond to him being so nice. Why wasn't he barking orders? His politeness was unnerving, but the last thing she was going to do was to question it. She carried the pot to the wood stove. She hadn't realized how much room it had on top, but it had plenty of room for cooking meals.

Macy went back to the kitchen and explored the drawers until she found a wooden spoon. She went back to the living room and stirred the stew, which was already starting to bubble. Her mouth watered; whatever spices had been used smelled delicious.

When it was warm enough, she brought it back to the kitchen where the table was set for two. A fruit salad and a loaf of unsliced bread sat in the middle of the table. Chester's back was to her at the counter.

He turned around. "That was fast."

She sat down and then he joined her. Once her plate was full, she realized a problem. "How are we supposed to eat with these things covering our heads? We're not supposed to take them off, right?"

"We'll have to lift them. Just be careful not to get anything on it."

"Okay." She pulled it out and then up, but it covered her eyes. She was able to see down, but just barely enough to see her plate. "Can we just take them off to eat? It would be a lot easier, plus we wouldn't get them dirty."

"No. We have to follow the rules, Heather. Just be careful." He sounded the tiniest bit irritated.

"Okay. I was just asking." Macy held onto the covering with her left hand while feeding herself with the right. It took some maneuvering, but she managed.

When her plate was empty, she still wanted more, but she didn't want to deal with eating any more while holding the fabric. "What do we do with the dishes?"

"Wash them in the sink, of course."

"But there's no electricity."

"It's pumped in from a well outside. It's not warm, but it's clean. It's a lot better than the chemical-filled crap in the city."

"Don't you mean the *world*?" Macy covered her mouth, afraid he'd get mad at her for making fun of the community.

He laughed. "You're right. It's not like what they have out in the world. I think you've been paying more attention than me. We ought to hurry. The ceremony will start soon."

Macy took that as her cue to get up. Her mouth watered for more stew, but she ignored her hunger. She had to use both arms to pump the water into the sink. Chester had been right. The water looked clearer than she was used to.

She put her hand in and jumped back. It was ice cold—it was even worse than the shower she had taken earlier.

Chester laughed again. "We can warm it in a few of the pots. I'll help you in a minute, Heather."

Macy filled a pot with water, put it on the stove, and then went back for another. Before long, the water was the right temperature and she had a sink full of warm water. She mixed in some soap. It was had the same horrible smell that she had been forced to use in the shower earlier.

She heard Chester put something in the icebox and then he stood next to her, drying off the dishes she had just washed. He chatted about the house, telling her that they would warm their baths the same way, and then he explained the clothes would be washed in some kind of a basin.

He continued to talk until they had the kitchen clean. "Let's sit in front of the fire, shall we?"

"Okay." Macy followed him to the couch as he carried an oil lamp. It did an okay job of lighting up the rooms, but it didn't compare to a light bulb.

Chester sat down and Macy sat at the other end of the couch, as far away from him as she could get. He scooted closer until he was right next to her. Then he put an arm around her. "Aren't you excited about becoming a family again, Heather? We're going to have a mom, dad, and child. It's a beautiful thing. Who knows? We may even have more children. In fact, we probably will. I can't imagine they allow birth control here." He laughed again.

Macy squirmed. She didn't want to talk about birth control or him making babies with his new wife. Time to change the subject. "What's her name?"

"You'll call her Mom, but her name is Rebekah."

"Is that her real name?"

"It's her new name. Like us, she came from the world, but she ascended into her role in the community. That's why she's now allowed to get married."

"Even though you haven't ascended?"

"Correct. Jonah received a vision about me rising in the ranks quickly. I'm going to be the fastest person to become a prophet. I'll need to prove myself, but then our family will be one of the revered ones."

"How did you find the community if they never leave?"

There was a knock on the door.

Chester gave her a hug and then opened the door. A freezing cold gust blew in. Macy hadn't realized how well the little stove had warmed the house up.

Jonah and Eve stepped inside. Jonah looked at Macy. "Are you ready for your unveiling, Heather?"

"Yes," said Macy, since she had been spoken to directly.

"Good. Once we've completed that ceremony, we'll have the wedding. Then you get to come home as a family. This is a truly blessed day."

Eve walked over and took her hand, helping her off the couch. "Everyone is so excited to meet you two. Jonah has had so many visions and messages about your dad. I'm sure you already know what an amazing man he is, worthy of the reverence to be bestowed upon him."

All eyes were on her, so she nodded.

Eve let go of her hand and then took Jonah's.

Jonah raised his other hand. "Let us go. The time has arrived."

Ceremony

MACY TOOK IN the large room. She'd never seen so many people dressed in all white before. A hushed whisper ran through the room as people turned to look at them. There wasn't much to see. Their heads were still covered. They probably looked creepy—at least Macy thought so. Everyone else looked at them, appearing to be in awe.

They had another thing coming if they expected Chester to be a great prophet. He would only be able to keep his facade for so long before his true colors showed.

Jonah raised a hand and the crowd moved aside, creating a path. Jonah and Eve walked down first, hand in hand. Chester took Macy's hand and they followed. Macy was aware of all the eyes on her.

Once they reached the front of the room, Jonah let go of Eve's hand and raised both of his hands. All at once, everyone in the crowd sat on the floor. Jonah motioned for Chester and Macy to move to the left. Abraham, Isaac, and some lady stood at their right. Was that one of their wives, or was it Rebekah?

Stepping forward, Jonah looked at the crowd. "Tonight is a most special night. Not only do we have an unveiling and a wedding, but we are unveiling a future prophet. I've been sharing my visions of him since before his identity was revealed. He is the person who will rise to become a prophet faster than anyone besides myself. This is a most exciting night, is it not?"

"It is." The group spoke as one.

Jonah walked back and forth. The room so quiet the only sounds were of his shoes moving across the floor. The anticipation could be felt. Macy knew it wasn't just her nerves, but everyone before her was eager to see their future leader.

"I have received yet another vision this very afternoon." Jonah stopped and scanned the audience again. "It has been solidified and confirmed. The man here before you," he pointed to Chester, "is going to become a prophet even sooner than we believed. In three months, he shall be your newest prophet."

Gasps ran throughout the crowd.

"I know," Jonah replied, his eyes wide. "He is chosen specifically from above. There is a mission for him to complete, though what it is has yet to be revealed. I think he will help lead us into the great and mighty Promised Land, but that is purely conjecture on my part." He paced back and forth again.

Eve walked up to him. She carried two red flowers.

Jonah looked at her. "You may speak."

She faced the crowd. "The time has arrived for the unveiling." She handed Jonah the flowers. Together they walked over to Chester and Macy.

Macy swallowed, nervous. As she looked at all the people watching her, beads of sweat formed around her hairline.

Jonah handed Chester one of the flowers, and Macy the other. He turned around and touched Chester's arm.

Chester let go of Macy's hand, which she had forgotten he was holding. Her heart picked up speed.

Placing his hand on the top of Chester's head covering, Jonah looked back to the crowd. "And now I give you Chester Woodran." In one quick movement, he pulled the fabric off Chester's face.

Everyone rose and bowed. "Chester Woodran." It sounded more like a chant than actual speaking.

Jonah raised his hand and everyone sat.

"And now I give you his daughter—your new sister. Heather Woodran." Jonah walked around to the other side of her and yanked her head piece off. Macy could feel her hair pull up with the covering. Her hair had to have been sticking out in every direction.

The crowd stood again and gave a less dramatic bow. "Heather Woodran." Then they all sat.

Eve walked over to Macy and pulled her hair back into a tight bun. She then whispered in Macy's ear, "You must always wear your hair like this outside of your home."

Jonah paced again. He spoke of more visions and messages that he had received that day. Macy tried to pay attention. She didn't know if she would be quizzed. But she felt too self-conscious, standing in front of so many people.

Jonah turned to face Macy. It felt as though he was reading her thoughts. Somehow just having him look into her eyes made her feel exposed. Eve took her hand and led her to the middle of the stage, where Chester met them.

Waving his hands, Jonah came to stand with them. He spoke in words that Macy had never heard before. It sounded like another language, although it was nothing like one she had ever heard before. He raised his hands up high and Abraham and Isaac walked over.

Jonah placed a hand on top of Macy's head. She looked over to see he had his other hand on Chester. He was speaking faster and Macy still couldn't understand a word.

Her instincts were to run, but she knew better than that. Even if she could get out of the building, there was no way of escaping through the fence. Then what? Chester would be mad at her for ruining the ceremony. He would lock her up for sure.

Something wet fell on her head and dripped down the sides, running through her hair. She looked up to see Isaac pouring something from a small jar over her. Abraham had a similar bottle and poured yellow liquid on Chester, although he didn't have as much hair to catch it.

Once the bottles were put away, Jonah turned to the crowd again. "They have now been anointed with oil and are officially part of our great family. Now it's time for Rebekah to come up so we can have the wedding."

Macy looked through the audience, anxious to see the woman she would soon be calling "Mom." She couldn't see anyone at first, but then at the far end of the room, someone rose and walked over. She wore the same white clothing as everyone else. Didn't she want to have a special dress for her wedding day?

As she came closer, it was obvious that Rebekah was young—not all that much older than Macy—and beautiful. Even with her hair pulled back tight, no makeup, and wearing a nondescript white outfit, her beauty shone. If she lived outside the community walls, she could easily be a model or an actress.

She finally made it to them and she stood near Jonah and Chester.

Jonah looked over the crowd. "Now we are about to have a new family unit. Nothing is more prized than family. We are all truly blessed this day, but especially these three."

Macy couldn't take her eyes off Rebekah. She looked over and they made eye contact. Rebekah smiled, easing Macy's nerves.

Rebekah walked to the other side of Chester. Jonah still spoke about the importance of families. Macy couldn't concentrate.

It might not have been so unnerving had she been away from people for so long. For the last month, she had only been with Chester and his parents. She'd spent a lot of time alone, especially when he had her locked away under the barn.

Jonah raised his voice, startling her. He practically shouted about the beauty of marriage. He said it was an everlasting, eternal gift that would follow them into the beloved Promised Land. He lowered his voice and looked into the eyes of Rebekah and then Chester.

The silence made Macy's ears ring. Jonah knew how to make his voice take up the entire building, and when it stopped, deafening silence followed.

"And now," boomed Jonah, "I pronounce you husband and wife. Let the festivities begin."

Everyone stood, clapping.

Chester took Rebekah's hand and they both bowed.

No kiss? Even though Macy wasn't excited about the wedding, if it could even be called one, she felt gypped with no kiss.

Macy turned to Eve, who was still close. "No kiss?"

Eve shook her head. "Public displays of affection aren't appropriate. Are you excited? Now you have complete family unit."

Before Macy could respond, Jonah shouted again. "Time for a

grand celebration. Eat, be merry, and meet our newest brother and sister."

"I need to help bring out the food." Eve squeezed Macy's hand and walked off, followed by Abraham and Isaac.

Macy stood, watching the scene before her. People were lined up in front of Chester and Rebekah. Everyone was speaking, the noise making Macy dizzy. She wanted to run.

Jonah put his hand on her shoulder. "Stand by your parents and greet your new brothers and sisters. Everyone is excited to meet you."

Macy made her way to Chester, standing at his side. The lady speaking with him turned to her and clasped Macy's hands into hers. "It's so wonderful to have you two join the community. We've been looking forward to your arrival. Personally, I can't wait to see your dad grow into his role and become anointed as a prophet." Her eyes lit up and she squeezed Macy's hands. "We'll have to have you over for dinner soon. Oh, I'm so excited." She grinned and then walked away, allowing the next person to gush over Macy and Chester.

By the time the last people in line finally walked away, Macy was exhausted. Everyone was eating. Somehow while they had been meeting everyone, the room had been transformed into a banquet hall. Chester smiled, looking back and forth between her and Rebekah. "Shall we join them and get something to eat?"

Rebekah nodded. "Yes. I'd like to officially meet Heather first, if that's okay, Sir."

Sir?

Chester stood taller, obviously enjoying it. "Of course. I should have introduced you myself. Heather, this your new mom. Rebekah, this is Heather."

Rebekah smiled wide, showing perfectly straight teeth. She had to have come from *the world* also, because no one was born with teeth like that. She gave Macy a hug. "It's such an honor to meet you. You're so beautiful, Heather. You look just like your dad. Do you hear that all the time?"

Before Macy could respond, Isaac and Abraham walked up to them. Isaac looked at Chester. "You three will join us at our table tonight.

Follow us."

Chester took Rebekah's hand and then Macy's. Chester and Rebekah marched forward with smiles on their faces. Macy fell behind a little, and Chester tugged on her hand. Macy picked up her pace to walk in line with the two of them.

They made their way to the table, finding plates already waiting for them. Chester sat first, followed by Rebekah. Macy sat at the end, next to Rebekah.

Macy wasn't particularly hungry because of her nerves, but she ate anyway.

Decisions

ZOEY STARED AT her Geometry book, unable to concentrate. How did anyone expect her to get anything done? Was life just supposed to carry on like her best friend *hadn't* disappeared without a trace?

Was she supposed to go to counseling and that would solve everything? Right.

Zoey's eyes became heavy again. How long would she be so tired? Every time she sat down, she wanted to sleep. The last thing she cared about were isosceles triangles, so she climbed into bed. She would at least be only a year ahead of Alex if she was held back.

She closed her eyes, but instead of sleep all she could see was Alex's hurt expression when they were arguing. He knew she was hiding something.

Obviously she'd have to tell him about her doctor's appointment. More than that, about their baby growing inside of her, making her so tired. It didn't even feel real—how could she have a *baby* in her stomach?

Aside from being exhausted, she didn't feel any different. Did she look different? Zoey got up and stood in front of the mirror. She had bags under her dark brown eyes, but otherwise looked exactly the same.

She pulled off her shirt and examined her stomach. It was still flat…but for how long?

One thing she knew was that she wasn't getting an abortion. Over the summer, she had taken her friend Tara to get one and it almost killed her. Tara had begged Zoey to go with. She hadn't told anyone else, including the guy. They lied so Zoey could be in there during the operation and said that they were sisters, even though it was pretty obvious they weren't. Tara had bright red hair and Zoey was half-Japanese, thanks to her absent dad.

Everything had been going well with the procedure, as they kept calling it. Then Tara's face lost all of its color and her eyes looked cloudy. Zoey had been sure that Tara was going to die in front of her.

The nurses shoved Zoey out of the room. She was left to worry in the waiting for what felt like an eternity. She hadn't been able to get the look in Tara's eyes out of her mind. Every time someone came into the waiting room, she expected them to tell her that Tara hadn't made it.

Tara ended up being sent to the emergency room at the hospital. Zoey had to take the bus home alone, worried about Tara. She had to act normal when she got home, but it had taken months for the image of Tara to stop haunting her dreams. In fact, it was Macy's disappearance that distracted her.

She hadn't even been able to talk with Tara after the ordeal. Her family moved before school started and all of her social media accounts had been deactivated. Tara's parents had probably figured out what happened and freaked out, moving her away from all the bad influences. Like there wouldn't be other kids just like their group of friends wherever they moved.

Zoey's mom walked in, bringing her back to the present.

"What are you doing? Oh, Zoey, you've lost weight. You better take those vitamins the doctor gave you. I don't want to see you waste away, dear."

She almost laughed. Losing weight was the least of her concerns. "I'll be fine. I just haven't been hungry lately." She put her shirt back on.

"Are you hungry? The Mercers invited us over for dinner. Alyssa said they have enough to feed ten people."

Could she face Alex's family? Zoey could barely even look Alex in the eye, how would she face Chad and Alyssa? They would probably hate her when she had to come clean. The news people watched every little thing they did. Sometimes there was even a van out in front of their house, recording. She might destroy their reputation.

There had been a few times that Alex hadn't been able to sneak out to see her because of the stupid van. The last thing they needed was for his sneaking out to be broadcast to a popular online page.

"Zoey? Are you listening?"

"Sorry." Zoey shook her head, trying to clear it. "Yeah, let's eat at their house."

"Maybe that'll pull you out of your funk. Why don't you brush your hair?"

"Whatever."

Before long, they were over at the Mercer's eating from a huge spread. Dishes were piled high with food across the table and there was even more on the counters. A large pork roast sat in the middle of the table surrounded by mashed potatoes, a green bean casserole, fruit salad, a pasta dish, and even more.

"Is this supposed to last all week?" Zoey asked.

"You'd think," Chad said. "But it's just tonight's meal. I think that church is trying to fatten us up."

Alex wasn't saying much. Zoey could tell he wanted to know what she was keeping from him.

How would he react? He was only thirteen. He wouldn't want to become a dad. There was no way.

What if he got mad at her? Her stomach twisted in tight knots. She kept her eyes on her plate and forced herself to eat. As good as everything looked and smelled, she couldn't bring herself to eat much.

"Are you okay, Zoey?" Alyssa asked. She looked concerned.

"Just not too hungry today."

"I know what you mean. My appetite has fluctuated a lot over the last month."

She nodded, pretty sure that Alyssa's eating habits were due to Macy being gone, and not from being pregnant. Although she and Chad had been getting along lately. It was still doubtful.

Looking around, Zoey's appetite decreased even more. What would everyone around the table think of her when they knew? The Mercers had been her second family for as long as she could remember. Would they tell her she could never see Alex again? The sleepovers would definitely stop.

Her mom would find someone else for her to stay with when she went on business trips. Maybe she would even stop taking them altogether. Or maybe she would finally hunt down Zoey's dad and make him get involved in her life. That wouldn't be so bad. Zoey could think of some choice words to throw at him.

Somehow she made it through dinner, barely eating anything, yet pretending to eat more than she had. After she and her mom cleaned up the kitchen, she found Alex in his room.

He looked up in surprise. "Come on in." He patted the bed next to him.

She sat down, noticing that Alex didn't scoot closer.

"Do you want to sneak out later for smokes?" he asked.

She shook her head.

"You're serious about cutting back?"

"I've been having too many lately. I'm gonna get hooked if I'm not careful."

He raised an eyebrow. "I thought you already were."

"Whatever."

"Want to make out?"

"You could just kiss me instead of talking about it. It would be more romantic that way."

"Yeah, but you've been acting weird today. I don't want to do anything to upset you."

She sighed, too tired to argue.

"What's going on? You know can tell me anything."

"Not this." She shook her head.

"Why not?"

Tears filled her eyes, and Alex's face softened. He pulled her into a hug and held onto her, not saying anything. He really was a good person, she knew that. That was why she had hooked up with him in the first place. Most boys her age were jerks, or at the very least, idiots. He actually cared and he was smart and sweet.

Maybe she should just tell him. They'd been talking about everything for so long, and she hated keeping anything from him.

"Alex, I'm pregnant."

Silence.

She turned to look at him and he was staring straight ahead, his face pale. He dropped his arms from her sides.

"Alex?"

He looked at her. "You're… you're… p… pregnant?"

"That's what the doctor said."

His eyes grew increasingly wide. "Did they give you a test?"

She nodded. "It was a strong yes, apparently."

Alex jumped up and punched his dresser. He let out a string of profanities and then looked at Zoey. "What are we going to do?"

"You don't have to do anything. I—"

"Of course I do. I did this to you, Zoey." He picked up a book and chucked it across the room.

"Well, the thing is, I'm not getting rid of it." She explained what happened with Tara. When she got to the part about her nearly dying, Zoey cried so hard she shook. "I'd never been so scared of anything in my life. I never even got to talk with her after, because her parents wouldn't let her talk to any of her friends before moving her away."

Alex sat down next to her. "That doesn't usually happen. I mean, if it did, no one would get abortions. I heard about a girl getting one at my school last month. She's fine. She's on the tennis team and she didn't stop playing or anything."

Zoey shook her head. "After seeing Tara like that, I can't. I don't know if it's that post-traumatic stress thing or what, but there's no way. I'd rather get fat for a few months."

"But it's nine months. That's practically a year. Zoey, come on. You don't wanna do this to yourself."

"I don't care. It's better than dying."

"You won't die. I'll go with you and hold your hand the whole time. I swear I'll—"

"No." Zoey moved away from him.

Alex was quiet for a minute. "Are you gonna tell your mom?"

"I guess when I can't hide it any longer. She's gonna be pissed, but it's not like she can do anything about it."

"We should tell our parents together."

"No. I'm going to leave you out of it. Just let me take the fall. You're family's dealing with enough."

"I can't let you do that. It's not fair. You didn't do this to yourself. It was me."

"Look out front," Zoey said. "There's almost always a news truck out there. Everything you guys do is broadcast to the world. Do you want *this* all over the news?"

Alex balled up his fists. "Still, I couldn't live with myself if I let you deal with all alone."

"Just pretend to be a good friend, standing by my side. Besides, then we can keep our sleepovers."

"I'm not that kind of guy. I can't do that to you."

"No one needs to know who the dad is."

Alex looked like he was going to be sick. "I can't believe you just called me a dad."

"That's what you are. Sorry."

"You really won't consider an abortion?"

Zoey glared at him. "Didn't you hear a word I said?"

"Just checking. What about adoption? Then we won't be parents. Someone else will be."

"I'm going to keep it, Alex."

"You've really thought this over." Alex frowned.

"After seeing what happened to Tara, yeah. I've gone over this a million times, wondering what I would do if I got pregnant."

"But you don't have to *keep* it, keep it. We can pick out a nice family."

"No."

Alex took a deep breath. "Then we really need tell our parents."

Zoey shook her head. Maybe he really was too young to handle this, because telling their parents was not the answer. It wasn't like they spilled flour—she was pregnant. "Not yet. I need some time to figure this out."

"What's to figure out? You said you're keeping it." Alex narrowed his eyes.

"I don't know what I want to do! Okay? Are you happy?"

"Happy? Of course not."

They stared at each other.

"I never should've told you," Zoey said.

"What? Yes, you should have."

"Now we're fighting—again. This is going end up ripping us apart." Angry tears filled her eyes.

Alex's face softened. "Nothing's going to keep us apart." He kissed her cheek. "I'm not leaving your side, Zoey."

"Thanks." Zoey examined his face. He looked genuine, but could she really trust him? Would he really stick it out, or would he walk away like her dad had? Only time would tell.

They sat in silence before Alex finally spoke up. "We don't have to tell them today, but we have to soon. It's not going to take long for you to show since you're so skinny, you know?"

She leaned against him and sighed. "I know."

Family

MACY WAS RELIEVED to see her teddy bear still sat on the bed where she had left it. She took off the stiff, white clothes and put on her favorite pair of Heather's pajamas. They felt luxurious after the cardboard-like white clothes.

She took out the hair tie and shook her hair free before blowing out the candle. She made her way into the bed. It was stiff, just like the clothes. The blankets weren't particularly soft, either. Apparently, fabric softener wasn't something they used in the community.

Squeezing the bear tight, Macy closed her eyes. Even though the bed wasn't comfortable, it was better than being in a sleeping bag in the back of the truck.

Just as she was starting to drift off, a squeaking noise startled her. Her first thought was mice, especially after having been in the barn cellar. But it wasn't that kind of squeaking. It was a rhythmic, ongoing sound.

There was a thud, followed by silence. Whatever it was appeared to stop. Macy rolled over, closing her eyes again, relieved to finally be going to sleep.

After a few moments of quiet, the squeaking began again. Squeak, squeak, squeak. Squeak, squeak, thud. Squeak, squeak, squeak. Squeak, squeak, thud.

What *was* that?

She closed her eyes tighter, knowing that wouldn't help as the sounds continued. Was that something she was going to have to get used to sleeping through? Was it some kind of non-electrical machinery from somewhere in the community?

The rhythm was interrupted by another noise. What was that one? Macy sat up, clutching the bear. It sounded like a moan. A moan? What would…?

Oh, no.

Squeak, squeak, squeak. Thud, moan. Moan. Squeak, squeak, squeak.

No, no, no. It was Chester and Rebekah's wedding night.

Squeak, squeak, squeak.

"Gross, gross, gross." Macy threw herself down and covered her head with the pillow. She could still hear the noises despite having the pillow over her head.

She let go of the bear and pushed her hands over the top of the pillow. But she could still hear it and now that she knew what it was, it was even worse than before. That was the last thing she wanted to listen to, and it made her stomach sick.

"Make it stop," she begged to any force that might be listening. "Please."

Where were her earphones when she needed them? She would have to make her own music. Macy picked one of the songs she had heard on the radio on the way to the community and hummed the melody, focusing on it.

After she was done with the song, she listened for the noises.

Squeak, squeak—

Macy pulled the pillow back over her head. Were they ever going to stop? She hummed another song and managed to fall asleep.

When the early light of the morning shone on her face, she woke up. Macy rolled over, hoping to get more sleep. Instead, her mind raced.

Would they give her a job or would she be allowed to go to school? Macy couldn't imagine Chester letting her out of his sight, even within the impenetrable walls surrounding the community.

Would she be allowed to make friends? She had met some teens the night before. Maybe some of them were nice. What if one of them wanted to escape also? They could work together to find a way of escape. She'd have to feel everyone out, which meant acting like she was happy to be there.

She was becoming a first class actress, having learned how to pretend she was Heather, and that Chester was her dad. All she would have to do was to keep up that performance, adding in a fake belief in the prophets. Then if there was someone like her, Macy would be able to find them and get them to open up to her.

Acting like Heather had gotten Chester to be nice. It could probably gain even more benefits with a full community of people.

Though she hadn't spoken a word of her family in what felt like a lifetime, she made sure to keep them in the forefront of her mind. She often thought of her parents and Alex, constantly calling her parents Mom and Dad in her mind. There was no way she was going to let go and give into Chester.

Calling him Dad and *believing* he was her dad were two separate matters. She had to cling to her family, and so far, she had done a good job of it. They were alive and well in her mind.

There was a knock on the door.

Maybe they would leave her alone if she pretended to sleep. She stuffed her bear under the covers and closed her eyes.

Another knock. She held perfectly still, forcing herself to breathe naturally.

She heard the door open and footsteps head toward her.

"Heather?" It was Rebekah.

Her stomach turned. She didn't want to look at either one of them after last night.

"Wake up, Heather."

Macy held still.

"Heather, it's time for breakfast. I don't know what you like, and I want to make something you will."

Macy rolled over, rubbing her eyes. "Is it morning already?"

Rebekah smiled. She was wearing the white clothes everyone wore, but her hair was down and she was even prettier. Macy wondered what she would look like with a little makeup. Probably gorgeous.

"Do you like eggs?"

Obviously Chester hadn't told her about Macy being vegan. Her stomach rumbled.

"Is that a yes?" Rebekah smiled again, showing off her perfectly straight teeth.

"Sure."

"Oh good. Today we get to take it easy because your dad and I got married last night. We don't have to go to work or school."

Macy nodded. "Okay."

"Take a few minutes to wake up, and then come out for something to eat. I'm looking forward to getting to know you." Rebekah left the room, closing the door behind her.

She sat up and stretched, smelling food. Her stomach growled again.

Would it be okay for her to go into the rest of the house wearing the green pajamas? Rebekah hadn't put her hair up, so maybe it was okay to be lax.

She had to go to the bathroom, which was nothing more than an outhouse in the back yard. Macy would definitely have to wear white to go out there because the fences between houses were so low that if anyone was in their own yard, they would see her.

Smelling the breakfast, she decided to wait. She was hungrier than anything else. Besides, wearing her pajamas in the kitchen would be a good way to test what she could get away with inside the house.

A noise outside her room startled Macy. "Is she up?" asked Chester.

Rebekah said something, but it was too muffled for Macy to understand. "I'm up!" she called.

"Hurry up, Heather. It's time for breakfast."

Macy made her bed, knowing that having even the slightest mess in her room sent Chester over the edge. She held the bear from home, whispered *I love you* to her parents and brother, and then looked around for a good hiding spot. If she pissed him off, Macy didn't want him hiding the bear again.

There weren't many spots, but she had brought some of Heather's stuffed animals. Maybe if she put the bear with those, he wouldn't be able to tell the difference between that one and the others. She could hope. That was all she had.

She opened her door. Chester stood looking at her. He was wearing his white clothes.

He stared at her pajamas. "In the future, you're to get dressed in appropriate clothes before leaving your room. Technically, we shouldn't even let you sleep in those, but I suppose no one else will know. Just like how you have your hair down."

Macy looked at the pajamas. They had a high collar and covered her from ankles to neck. How were they inappropriate? Because they weren't white and uncomfortable?

She nodded.

Chester put his hand on her shoulder. "Let's see what Mom has made."

Macy held back a cringe. How was she going to get used to calling Rebekah *Mom?* Not only was she not her mom, but she was so young, barely older than Macy.

They went to the living room which was toasty warm from the fireplace. "I told Heather that she can wear these pajamas for now, but after today, she has to put on her white clothes before coming out here."

Rebekah turned around and smiled at Macy. "I don't mind her wearing those. They look comfortable." She looked at Chester. "But if you don't want her wearing them, it's your call."

Macy wanted to throw up. She was going along with his head of the household crap, too.

"Are you ready to eat?" Rebekah asked her.

"Yeah."

Chester squeezed her shoulder, but not too hard. "No informal speech in the community, Heather."

She looked at him, confused. What had she said wrong?

"No 'yeah' or other slang. A simple yes will do."

"Don't feel bad," Rebekah said. "It takes a while to get used to living here after being in the world. I still slip up once in a while, and I've received my true name. Grab a plate from the kitchen. It's almost done."

Arguing

ALYSSA PUT THE ferret back in its newly clean cage. She hated cleaning it, but she wanted it to be nice when Macy got back. Macy loved the little guy, and even Alyssa couldn't deny how cute he was. The irony was that she had been close to threatening to get rid of it because Macy hadn't been cleaning the cage. Now here Alyssa was cleaning it herself without complaint.

Ducky ran around, checking out every inch of the multi-level cage. Alyssa sat on the bed, watching. After a few minutes, she looked around the room and noticed that it was getting dusty. Macy couldn't come back to a room full of dust. Alyssa grabbed a clean rag from the pile of cleaning supplies on the floor and got to work.

When she was about halfway through the room, she heard the door creak open. She turned around to see Alex watching her. He looked pale and scared.

Alyssa's stomach tightened. "Is everything okay? Is there news about M—?"

"No, but I need to talk to you."

She had never seen him so worked up before. "Sure, honey." She set the rag down. "Have a seat."

"No, I mean with Dad too. He's in the living room."

"This doesn't sound good."

Alex didn't say anything.

"Let's go." They walked in silence downstairs, Alyssa's mind racing with possibilities. When they got to the living room, Chad was sitting on the couch, but he wasn't alone. Zoey and Valerie were sitting on the two recliners.

Her heart picked up speed. She looked at Chad. "What's going on?"

"That's what I'd like to know," Valerie said. "No one will tell me anything."

Alex and Zoey looked at each other, and then Alex sat on the love seat with her. Alyssa sat next to Chad.

"Why are we here?" Alyssa stared at Alex.

Zoey took a deep breath and sucked her lips inside of her mouth. A nervous habit Alyssa had seen since Zoey was little. Alex took Zoey's hand and Alyssa looked at Valerie.

Alex sat taller. "We have something to tell you guys. Please hear us out, and don't start yelling."

"I don't like the sound of this," Alyssa muttered.

Chad took her hand. "Just tell us what's going on."

"We want you to keep an open mind, Dad."

Alyssa could feel Chad tense up next to her. "It's getting less open the longer you stall."

"I'm pregnant," Zoey said.

"Oh, honey," Alyssa said. "I'm so sorry."

The look of shock on Valerie's face was crushing.

"Who's the fath…?" Alyssa's gaze wandered to Alex and Zoey's intertwined hands. "Alex?"

Alex nodded and then put his arm around Zoey. "We're in love."

"No." Alyssa covered her face. "No, you're not."

Chad sat up straight. "Is this true, Alex?"

He looked at the ground and nodded. "What were you thinking? Didn't you use protection?"

Alex narrowed his eyes. "You never even gave me the sex talk, Dad."

"Don't blame this on me!" Chad stood up. "Talk or no talk, you've had health classes. We signed the waivers for you to sit in on those discussions."

"How could you do this?" Alyssa asked, her eyes filling with tears. "Alex, you're just a baby yourself."

Alex's eyebrows came together. "Obviously I'm not, Mom."

Alyssa looked at Zoey. "And you!"

Zoey's eyes widened. She scooted closer to Alex.

"We invited you into our home and cared for you like a daughter—this is how you repay us? By taking advantage of our son? He's only thirteen. Thirteen!"

Valerie stood up. "She hardly took advantage of him. I'm pretty sure that he knew exactly what he was doing. Zoey didn't force him to ejaculate into her."

"Mom!"

Chad stood between Valerie and Alyssa. "Maybe we ought to sleep on this and discuss it when we're not all in shock."

Alyssa stood up. "I don't see what that'll accomplish. It's not going to change anything." She looked at Zoey. "I know you could have had an abortion without telling your mom. Are you planning on keeping the baby?"

"I'm not having the procedure."

"So, you're going to raise a baby at sixteen? I suppose you're going to want Alex to pay child support."

"What? No."

"Of course he will," Valerie said, stepping forward. "He did this to her."

"Okay, okay," Chad said. "What we all need is a break. We're too upset to discuss this right now."

Alyssa glared at him. "What does that have to do with anything? We don't need to be calm—it's not going to change anything."

Valerie moved around Chad and stared at both of them. "How could you two allow this to happen? I trusted you to take care of my daughter. Not only did she run into an intruder here at your house, but Alex and Zoey slept together right under your noses."

"Oh?" Alyssa narrowed her eyes. "Like it couldn't have happened at your house? If you were so worried about it, why did you even have her stay here in the first place?"

"I thought she was safe!"

Alyssa took a couple steps closer to Valerie. "She never once got hurt, not even when someone broke in."

"Hurt? What would you call this?"

"Look, Valerie, you've left her over here plenty of times over the years. She's been spending the night since preschool, and you've always known we have a boy here. It hasn't been a secret."

"Yeah, but I didn't think you would let *this* happen."

"Let it happen?" Alyssa clenched her fists. "What exactly were we supposed to do? Stay awake all night to make sure they both stayed in their own rooms?"

Chad stepped between them again. "Clearly, no one saw this coming—"

"Except your son!"

"And your daughter." Alyssa raised her fists. "Stop talking about Alex like he's some kind of monster. He's only thirteen. You think he would turn down the advances of a girl so much older than him? He's the—"

"Oh, would you stop with the 'he's only thirteen' crap, Alyssa? He knew exactly what he was doing to Zoey."

Alex stood up. "Stop! Would all of you just stop?"

Everyone stared at him.

"Zoey and I have been in love for a long time now. Like, way before Macy even disappeared. We didn't tell anyone, not even Macy. We saw each other right under all of your noses and no one thought anything of it, of us spending so much time together. I'm not sure why. I guess because nobody thought I was good enough for Zoey. But she thinks so, and you know what? I love her. She wanted to keep me out of this and not tell anyone it was me. But you know what? I told her I wouldn't do that to her. We love each other and you guys better get used to it."

Alyssa's mouth dropped open.

"You—" Valerie started.

"And that's not all," Alex continued. "Yeah, we made a mistake the first time we did it. We should have used protection, but it just happened. We were so stressed about Macy being gone and we weren't thinking."

Valerie glared at him. "I hope you enjoyed it, because you aren't going near her again."

Zoey got up from her chair and grabbed Alex's hand. "That's where you're wrong, Mom. We didn't tell you to get your permission to keep seeing each other. We told you to let you know what's going on. We could have dealt with this all by ourselves, but since I'm not having an abortion, we thought you needed to know."

Alyssa sat back down on the couch. "Where did I go wrong?"

Zoey looked at her. "I'm really sorry about this, Mr. and Mrs. Mercer. Really. You guys are already overwhelmed with everything about Macy. I know because it's killing me too. And Alex." She held up his hand. "I don't want you guys having to worry about the news finding out about this. I won't tell anyone else that he's the one."

"You think they won't figure it out, Zoey? They park across the street and have seen you come into our house countless times."

"But that doesn't mean they'll figure it out. I'm Macy's best friend; they'll probably think I have a boyfriend somewhere else."

Chad shook his head. "Alyssa's right. We appreciate you trying to protect us, but even if it was another boy, they would still speculate."

Valerie's eyebrows came together. "She's trying to protect you guys, but who's protecting her?"

"Mom, would you shut up?"

Fury covered Valerie's face and she slapped Zoey across the face.

Zoey's mouth dropped open. She put her hands on her face. "Mom!"

Alex jumped toward Valerie, but Chad blocked him. "Like I said, we all need to calm down before we discuss this. We're only going to say or do something we regret later."

"What's there to discuss?" Valerie yelled. "We're never speaking to any of you ever again. Come on, Zoey, we're leaving."

"I'm not going anywhere. You hit me!"

"That wasn't a hit. You're so dramatic. That's your problem: you think everything's worse than it is. It was a slap, and you're not injured. We're leaving."

"No."

"No?" Valerie asked.

"You heard me. I'm staying here. At least you don't have to worry about me getting pregnant."

Valerie gasped. "How dare you? I was never worried about that from the start—not here." She glared at Alex. "We need to go home and talk about getting that procedure done."

"I already told you: I'm not getting it done. I could have done it without you ever knowing, so you definitely can't force me. If you're worried about what everyone is going to think, you're going to have to get over it."

"We'll talk about it later. Come on."

"I'm not going anywhere."

Valerie looked at Chad and Alyssa. "If you let her stay here, I'm reporting you for kidnapping."

"Kidnapping?" Alyssa exclaimed. "Have you lost your mind?"

"If you do that, Mom, I'll report you for hitting me."

"You wouldn't."

Zoey narrowed her eyes. "Watch me."

Alex put his arms around Zoey. "Can't you guys just calm down? We need you guys to support us more than anything."

Valerie turned to him, raising her hand. "Support? You want support, you little—"

Chad stepped in front of her again. "Put your hand down, or you really will have problems, Valerie. You don't want to lay a hand on anyone else. Understand?"

"Don't tell me what to do, Chad. You have no idea what my life is like."

"I do know there are laws, and you have no right to lay a hand on anyone."

"Zoey isn't staying here. This is the last place I will ever leave her again."

Chad looked at Zoey. "If you ever feel unsafe for any reason, you can come here." He turned to Valerie. "We know you're a good mom and you don't want to hit anyone. We're all under stress now, and I have no idea what's going to happen tomorrow, but Alex is right about one thing. We need to pull together. We've always been friends. Heck, we've taken vacations together. Remember?"

Valerie took a few steps back, looking deflated.

Alyssa took Chad's hand and looked at Valerie. "He's right. We need to be here for both kids."

Valerie's lips formed a straight line and she sat down.

"Can we agree to sleep on this?" Chad asked. "There's really no way we're going to be able to have a reasonable conversation now. We need to calm down and process everything. All of us."

"Fine," Valerie said. "But I'm not allowing my daughter to spend the night in the same house as Alex. If Zoey wants to stay here, then Alex comes home with me."

Alyssa and Chad exchanged a look.

"What do you think?" Chad asked her.

It was a crazy idea, but she wasn't about to say anything to set Valerie off further. "I can live with that." Alyssa turned to Alex and Zoey. "Kids?"

Zoey folded her arms. "I'm not going anywhere after she hit me."

Valerie's eyes narrowed. "It was only a slap, Zoey."

"I'm not going anywhere."

Alex stood up. "I'll go over there."

Zoey jumped up and glared at Alex. "I can't let you do that. I'll go home."

"Aren't you afraid I'll hurt you?" Valerie asked, her voice dripping with sarcasm.

"Not with a police cruiser across the street."

Valerie shook her head.

"Let's get back together tomorrow," Chad said, "and we can talk with clear heads."

"All right." Valerie stood up. "I have evening meetings at work, but I can get away at lunch."

"Lunch it is," said Alyssa.

"I can't wait," Zoey mumbled.

Phone

ALYSSA FLIPPED THROUGH the channels, unable to sleep. She kept thinking about going back to that bar the next town over and drinking herself stupid again. It had been nice to escape from the pain and stress, even if it had only been for a short time and it was pathetic to get drunk alone.

What if Rusty, the tow truck driver, wasn't there again? If it hadn't been for him, Alyssa wouldn't have gotten home that night. That wasn't entirely true. She could've called a cab, but then she would have had to explain to Chad why her car was at a bar.

She needed a drink more now than she had before. How could Alex have gotten Zoey pregnant? Right under their noses, no less. Was it because she hadn't been paying enough attention to him? She and Chad had been so focused on Macy's disappearance that they hadn't been giving him the focus he deserved.

They hadn't even taken him to a single karate practice. He probably felt like he didn't matter; that all they cared about was Macy. The poor kid was lonely and desperate for attention and if he and Zoey were already developing feelings for each other, then Alyssa had given him the perfect setup.

Tears filled her eyes. This also was her fault. If she had kept a better eye on Macy, she wouldn't have been able to sneak out. And if she hadn't been so focused on Macy, then Alex wouldn't have thought he had to turn to Zoey. The hot, angry tears spilled down her cheeks. All of this was her fault. Her family was falling apart and she could have prevented it all.

Alyssa put the remote down, ignoring a dog food commercial. She looked around the family room, filled with so many memories. The kids had taken first steps in here. Macy pretended to be a rock star countless times, singing along with her favorite songs. Alex practiced for his karate tournaments in here. They'd had countless movie and game nights. They'd had friends over, birthday parties, family gatherings, and the list went on.

Alyssa swallowed a sob, not wanting to wake anyone. Chad and Alex had finally fallen asleep not that long ago. The three of them had spent hours talking, mostly listening to Alex. They had let him talk about anything and everything, wanting to make him feel like the most important person in their lives. They knew, too late, that they needed to give him more attention than ever before—not less, like they had been.

He told them how much he missed his sister and how he wanted to punch half of the kids at school for making stupid comments. Alyssa had started to tell him that violence wasn't the answer, but when Chad reminded her that they were there to listen, she stopped talking. Alex went on to talk about how much he adored Zoey. At first, he seemed to be testing the waters, to see how they would respond. When Alyssa and Chad listened without judging, he had really opened up.

It warmed her heart to see Alex opening up to them like that. She wished that it hadn't taken Zoey getting pregnant for that to happen. She wanted more closeness with him. Alyssa had always adored him, but had forgotten because of her grief over Macy.

Something caught her attention on the news and she turned to look. She thought she had heard Macy's name. Not that it should have come as a surprise. Despite there being no new clues, she was still a story each night locally. The national stations had moved on, at least somewhat. They still brought her up once in a while.

Alyssa had heard wrong. The news wasn't discussing her daughter, but instead showing a fire. The building looked familiar. It took her a moment to realize it was their dentist office. She realized everyone had missed their appointments a few weeks earlier.

One of Macy's pictures from one of her online accounts appeared on the screen. In the image, Macy was talking on her new phone. It looked like a candid; probably one that Zoey or another friend had taken.

Macy's picture shrunk and moved to the top right of the screen. A reporter held a microphone to some guy holding something. Alyssa squinted to see what it was. It looked like a broken phone.

Her heart dropped to her stomach when she made the connection. Had someone found Macy's phone—smashed? She tried to pay attention to what they were saying on the TV, but she couldn't process the words.

She pulled her own phone out of her pocket and scrolled, looking for the police department.

"Detective Fleshman."

"What's going on, Detective? Did someone find Macy's phone? The news, they—"

"Mrs. Mercer?"

"Yes, yes. What's going on with my daughter's phone? Is that what they're talking about? Is it true?"

"We just got word. Some idiot looking for his fifteen minutes of fame went to the news instead of us with evidence. Officers Anderson and Reynolds just left to take care of the situation. You might want to prepare to come down to the station, Ma'am. Once we have it in our possession, we'll likely need you or your husband to identify it."

Alyssa dug her nails into the coffee table. "So, it really could be hers?"

"We have no way of knowing until we have it. But at the same time, it could just be some attention seeker with a similar phone."

"Am I supposed to just wait until I hear from you guys?"

"That's about all you can do."

"I can't just sit around, waiting. Can we go down there and look at it when it arrives?"

"We have to process it first."

"Process it? What does that mean?"

"It means paperwork. I know our job looks glamorous—" Fleshman chuckled, "—but a lot of our time is spent filling out forms."

"Can you call me before you start the paperwork? That way we can at least get down there a little sooner."

"Will do, Ma'am."

The call ended and Alyssa threw her phone on the couch. If it really was Macy's phone, did it mean anything? When they found her bloody clothes, nothing had ever come from that. They were her clothes and the blood was hers, but it hadn't led to her.

It felt like an eternity had passed since then. The world was still moving along as though nothing was wrong. Alyssa's entire life was upside down, and now with Alex's news, even more so. How was she supposed to deal with her daughter being missing *and* her little boy becoming a father? It didn't even feel real. Alex was just a kid himself.

Not long ago, his voice had been cracking. He didn't even have braces yet! Alyssa put her face in her hands. What had she ever done to deserve all of this?

Sighing, she looked back up at the TV. They were still discussing the phone that appeared to be Macy's. How long until the police got the phone and called her?

She leaned back, watching and listening. It didn't sound as though they really knew anything useful. The phone was missing the battery— she and Chad knew that. They had gotten Alex and Macy the most expensive phones available to keep the kids safe. A lot of good that had done.

They would need to bring Alex's phone to the station. If the smashed up phone was in good enough shape, Alex's battery would bring it to life. They would know right away if it was her phone. She had a picture of herself with the ferret as the screen saver. Even if they couldn't get past her password, that alone would tell them it was her phone.

What if they couldn't get the battery in? How would they know it was her phone or not? The guy who found it could have been lying. What if he just wanted to get on the news?

Didn't she have the boxes the phones came in? The company had told them to hang onto those because they had serial numbers or something. She jumped up from the couch and ran to her room, straight for the closet. She dug around, looking for the boxes. She couldn't remember where she had put them.

Alyssa made a mess of their walk-in closet, but she didn't care. She had to find the boxes.

"What's going on?"

She jumped and turned around. Chad stood just outside the closet, rubbing his eyes.

"Someone found a phone that looks like Macy's. I'm trying to find the box, so we have the serial number."

"I put those in the garage."

"What? Why?" She stood up, bumping her head on a shelf.

"So they wouldn't get lost. I know right where they are. Did the police call? I didn't hear it ring."

Alyssa shook her head, picking up some of the things she had thrown on the floor. "I saw it on the news. Some guy found a phone that looks just like hers, but instead of taking it to the cops, went straight to the news."

Chad rolled his eyes. "Of course. Are we supposed to go down to the station?"

"Not yet. They don't have the phone, but as soon as they do, we can go."

"Why can't they ever find evidence at lunch time? Let me get some pants on and I'll get the phone boxes."

"Sure." Alyssa put the rest of the stuff away. She had nothing else to do while she waited for Fleshman's call anyway. His call—wait, her phone was in the family room. She dropped the slipper in her hand and ran to the other room. No new calls.

She heard the garage door slam shut downstairs. Chad must have found the box. Now it was a matter of waiting—again. They were always waiting for something.

Learning

"**H**EATHER?"

Macy mumbled something not even she understood. It couldn't be time to get up already—she was too tired. She'd had to hum herself to sleep again after spending the day learning from Rebekah how to run the household, which was now their job to share.

"It's time to get ready for school," Rebekah said.

"Why so early?" Macy stretched and opened her eyes. The room was dark, although she could see a little bit of light from behind the curtain.

Rebekah held a candle. "It starts soon and we need to get breakfast ready. You're going to help me."

"Can I have a shower—I mean a bath? I feel disgusting. Oh, sorry. That's not very...what was the word Ch—" Macy coughed to cover up her mistake. "—Dad used? Formal?"

"It's all right. I'm not going to get you in trouble for informal speech. I want to help you adjust to living here in the community. It's a lot to take in after living out there."

She reached over and brushed some hair out of Macy's face. Something on her arm caught her attention. "What's that?" Macy asked.

Rebekah pulled her sleeve down closer to her wrist. "It's a mark of shame from my old life."

"A mark of shame?"

"Let me speak plainly for a moment. I was in a pretty successful indie band. We lived the wild, dream life most kids in the world aspire to. Our songs had thousands of downloads, our videos had even more views, and our shows were always packed. My tattoo was a mark of pride, and is now my shame. I keep it hidden and now only your dad knows about it."

Macy's eyes grew wide. Rebekah was not only beautiful, but cool. "Can I see it?"

The corners of Rebekah's lips twitched as she obviously tried to hide a smile. "Promise not to tell anyone?"

"Yeah. I would pinky swear, but I'm sure you don't do that."

"This one time won't hurt anything." Rebekah held out her pinky. She smiled.

Macy couldn't believe it. Maybe she'd actually have a friend. In her house, even. Sure, Ingrid and George had been nice, but they were like grandparents, not a friend. Her eyes lit up and she slipped her pinky around Rebekah's.

Rebekah's eyes twinkled. "Remember, a pinky promise is for keeps."

"Of course. I can't wait to see it."

Rebekah pulled up her white sleeve, exposing a black and white sun with several symbols in the middle.

"What is it?"

"It was the logo for our band."

"That's awesome. I wonder why I've never seen it if you guys were so popular."

"We were mostly known on the east coast, where I'm from."

"Why did you quit?"

"To join the community."

Macy's mouth dropped. "For real? Why?"

"I was chosen."

"How? Why did you—?"

Rebekah pulled her sleeve back down. "I'll tell you everything, but later. We have to get ready for school. You'll need to get dressed and pull your hair back. I can help you with that if you need me to."

"No bath?"

"Sorry. We usually only bathe once a week unless we need to be cleansed."

"Feeling gross isn't enough?"

She put her hand on Macy's. "Your body will adjust and you'll stop feeling that way soon. All of the shampoos and soaps from the world strip away our body's oils, making us produce unnaturally high amounts. In a way, this is another way of purifying ourselves from our time out there."

Macy sighed. "I'll be out in a minute."

Rebekah squeezed her hand and then left without a word. Macy got up, excited about Rebekah. Not only was she nice, but she was cool too. A successful indie rock band and a tattoo. She was basically the best stepmom ever.

Fake stepmom. Macy rolled her eyes at herself. Now wasn't the time to start thinking about herself as part of this family. It was all a hoax and her goal was still to get back home.

She put on the stiff clothes and grabbed her—Heather's—brush. Her hair felt horrible after not washing it. At least it would be in a bun. She looked around for a mirror, not seeing one. There wasn't even a mirror in the bathroom, which was literally a bath-room. It only had a tub and a small sink.

Did the community think mirrors were evil too?

Macy brushed her hair back as best as she could, sure that it sucked. She could feel lumps on the top of her head. Maybe she would take Rebekah up on her offer to help.

Her stomach jumped around as she thought about starting a new school, even one that was full of kids dressed in white. Maybe that made it worse. Were they going to be nicer or worse than the kids at her real school? Maybe the fact that she was the "daughter" of the future prophet would give her an edge. Maybe she even stood a chance at popularity, whatever that meant in a place like this.

Macy tidied up the room and then went out to the living room, where Rebekah was cooking something on the stove.

"Do you mind if I help you with your hair?" Rebekah asked.

"Please."

Rebekah checked whatever she was cooking and then pulled Macy's bun out. "Where's your brush? Still in your room?" They went back to Macy's room and before long, her hair was done and they were eating breakfast.

Chester spoke excitedly about meeting with Jonah, Abraham, and Isaac that day. Macy couldn't stop thinking about what school would be like, so she could barely pay attention to him. She knew she needed to listen at least a little in case he asked her about it, which he often did, always wanting to make sure she was paying attention to his ramblings. She had learned to listen for key points when he talked without having to actually listen to every word.

"Are you excited about school?" He stared at her.

"I...I guess. I mean, I don't know what to expect."

He looked annoyed.

"I promise to use formal language there. I won't embarrass you."

"That's good to hear."

"You needn't worry too much about it," Rebekah said. "Don't use worldly slang and you should be fine. Everyone has leniency for new members. Also, I've heard your teacher is nice."

Chester and Rebekah exchanged a look.

What did that mean? Macy wasn't going to ask.

"One more thing," Chester said, "remember you don't speak to a male puritan unless spoken to."

Rebekah nodded. "That's one of the most important rules, and also one of the hardest to remember after leaving the world. There are many things that will receive leniency, but that is often not one of them."

"Even kids my own age?"

Chester set his fork down. "Even boys younger than you. Not even a toddler."

Macy's eyes widened, but she kept her thoughts to herself. Guys in the community must have huge heads. Where did they draw the line? Were moms allowed to speak to their sons before spoken to? If not, that was the most ridiculous thing ever.

"Do you understand?"

"Yes." She probably answered too fast, but she didn't want angry Chester to return.

He smiled. "Good. It really shouldn't be that hard. It's just a matter of respect and understanding where you are in the big scheme of things."

Rebekah gave her a reassuring look. "I'll do my best to help you."

Macy looked at her, confused.

"Rebekah is a teacher," Chester said.

"You are?"

"Yes. There are two of us and we sometimes split up the younger kids and the older. If we do that today, I'll be sure to go with your class. My ranking is higher than the other teacher, so it won't be a problem."

"How does the ranking work?"

"You'll learn all about it in school."

Why hadn't she figured that out herself? Had she really expected to study American History and Algebra?

"Are you ready?"

"I just have to go the bathroom—I mean the outhouse."

Chester gave her a serious look. "Hurry. You don't want to make your teacher late, Heather."

Macy got up and went out to the outhouse, hit by the cold. Why didn't they allow coats? There was a thick covering of frost on the ground and she could see her breath. Any sane person would want a thick, warm coat.

When she got back inside, Rebekah was cleaning the last dish. "Are you ready now?"

"I guess."

"You needn't worry. Everyone will like you, Heather."

Macy shrugged.

Rebekah wiped her hands on a towel and then squeezed Macy's shoulders. "You'll do great. No need to be nervous. Let's go."

When they got into the living room, Chester gave Rebekah a big hug and a kiss. Then he turned to Macy. "I wish I could go with you on your first day, Heather, but I need to spend the day with the high prophets. Give me a hug." He opened his arms wide.

Macy walked to him and wrapped her arms around him. He smelled of that awful soap, but then again, she probably did too. He put his arms around her and squeezed tight. "You have a good day, and don't worry. We'll all be back together tonight."

Don't worry? The only part of school she was looking forward to was being away from him.

Finally, he let go and they all went outside and he went the opposite direction as Macy and Rebekah. A lot of people were out, walking around.

"Don't make eye contact with males you don't know. It's considered rude, and if you look at the wrong one, you could end up with a letter on your first day. I'll insist on everyone at school having grace with you, but I have no control over anyone outside of school."

Macy gulped. "What's it like?"

"School, you mean?"

Macy nodded, keeping her eyes low. How was she ever going to remember all of the rules? Just avoid guys altogether?

"It's somewhat like school as you're used to. Desks and books, but instead of learning useless facts which have all been twisted by the world's government, we teach what is actually useful. You'll learn about the community rules, the prophecies, and the professions needed here inside the walls."

At least it was better than being stuck with Chester and his ranting all day. "So, do you celebrate holidays?"

Rebekah shook her head no. "All days are equal. Holidays were dreamed up by the world to meet their evil desires. True happiness comes from appreciating that every day is special. Finding joy in that is something the world will never understand."

"Are there days off? Don't a lot of religions have days to rest?"

"This isn't a religion. It's the truth. Jonah and the other prophets receive messages from up above, teaching us the truisms about this life and the one to come. As for the days off, we do take one day a week to listen to a special message from Jonah and the others, but as you know, we have meetings every evening. We're almost at the school."

Macy looked up, seeing what looked like an old fashioned school house. She held her breath.

School

"**G**OOD MORNING, EVERYONE," Rebekah said, closing the door behind her and Macy.

"Good morning, Teacher," all of the students replied.

Macy looked around, careful not to make eye contact with anyone.

"This is Heather," Rebekah continued. "You remember her from the unveiling ceremony the other night. Many of you know what it's like to be new here, so please be extra helpful. She is not used to our ways yet, although she's been doing very well at home. We are going to start with our copy work this morning, so find the appropriate book of prophecies and begin copying."

Rebekah led Macy to a desk with a cute guy who was busy reading. She told Macy that would be her permanent seat. As Macy sat, Rebekah gathered some books, which were really just stacks of paper held together by string weaved into a binding.

"Start with this one. It's the rules of the community. I'm sure Eve went over the basic ones with you, but to really learn them, you must copy them over and over again."

Macy took the book and ignored the boy next to her. Pretended to ignore him. He was really cute and found herself wanting to stare. He looked to be about her age, and she tried to imagine what he would look like in regular clothes. She couldn't tell which clique he would have been in, but he was adorable with his bright blue eyes and thoughtful expression. And that was saying something since it was hard for anyone to look good in the ugly, white clothes. Maybe that was the point.

"You'll get that copy work done a lot faster if you start," he said.

Macy jumped. She hadn't realized he had been paying any attention to her. "I—uh, yes. You're right." He had spoken to her, so it was okay for her to talk to him, right? But he hadn't given her *permission*. She picked up the large, awkward-shaped pencil sitting in front of her.

"Don't be nervous. It's not so bad here—once you get used to it." He smiled.

Macy could feel her cheeks warm up. "Are you...?"

"From the world? Yes. I've been here a few years, and I have to say that for the most part, the people are a lot nicer. They—uh oh, Teacher is looking our way. Better start writing."

Macy looked up to see Rebekah looking their way. She had a stern look on her face, but she didn't look angry.

Macy looked at the rules and copied them. Most of it she already knew from Eve quizzing her the other day.

After a while, she had to put the pencil down because her hand cramped up. She rubbed it as it protested by hurting even more.

The boy next to her looked up at her, his eyes twinkling. "Used to typing, aren't you?" he whispered.

She nodded.

"It's tough. Don't mention any kind of technology to the adults, but I get it."

"Right. We don't talk about the ways of the world."

He raised his hand.

Rebekah nodded at him.

"Teacher, Heather's hand is cramping. I don't think she's used to so much writing. May I take her outside to walk around and stretch her legs?"

"That's very thoughtful, Luke. Thank you."

"You're welcome, Teacher." He put his pencil down and stood, looking at Macy.

She got up and followed him outside. The sun shone brightly and was warm when she stood directly in it.

"Is it okay with you if we take a walk?" Luke asked.

"As long as it's not against the rules."

Luke laughed, but not in a rude way. "It's fine. We can't be alone in a home, and never near a bedroom, but walking out in plain view is perfectly acceptable."

"Okay."

"Make a fist and then relax your hand. Like this." He held up his hand and showed her, and then looked at her.

Her hand objected, but she made a fist and then let go.

"Good. Keep doing that while we walk around. How do you like the community?"

"Uh, I…well. I haven't really had time to get used to it."

"That's understandable. You were probably in your home all day yesterday for the family honeymoon, right?"

"Pretty much."

"Until you get used to things, you're better off staying quiet and just observing. You seem to be doing that already, so you're already doing well. Before you know it, you'll be used to it here and will have a hard time remembering what it was like before."

She squeezed her hand extra hard, digging her nails into her flesh. "I doubt that." She was going to hold onto every memory of her real family and never let go.

"I sense some animosity. Care to talk about it?"

Macy's heart raced. Did she dare tell him she had been kidnapped? Chester was practically revered by all.

"No pressure," Luke said. "You don't even know me, but if you want to talk with anyone, I'm here and I do know what it's like on the outside. Sure, I don't think about it often anymore, but the memories never leave."

She wanted to tell him, but what if he told Rebekah or Chester? Or someone who would tell them? No. She had to stick to her plan and feel everyone out. She could verbally vomit all over Luke just because he was cute and seemed nice. "Does anyone ever get out of here?"

"Only those who have been set free."

"Set free?" Macy asked, not sure she wanted to know the answer.

"Released from their earthly bodies."

"You mean the only way out of here is to die?"

Luke nodded, giving her an inquisitive look.

"Nobody has ever gotten thrown out?"

"Not that I've ever heard about. Usually, a few punishments is enough to whip anyone into shape."

"Have you ever been punished?"

"That's not usually an appropriate question, but—"

"Sorry."

"You'll find I'm pretty hard to offend. I don't mind answering, but don't go around asking other people. My first month here, I was rude to Jonah. I didn't mean to be, but what's considered rude here is not the same as what we grew up with out there. That night at the community meeting, he brought me up to the front and told everyone what I had said. The entire community called me rude over and over for what felt like hours. Then for the rest of the week, which was only two days, no one was allowed to look at me or talk to me, not even my parents. I had to read the rule books and do a lot of copy work. My hand cramped up really bad, but I wasn't allowed to stop. It took months for my hand to fully recover."

That explained why he was being so kind about her hand cramping. "That's awful."

"It was horrible. But you know what? It taught me what I needed to learn. I haven't gotten into any trouble since then. In the end, it was a blessing."

Macy's eyes widened. She would never let herself get to the point of agreeing that anything like that was good. Treating someone like that was inexcusable. Everyone here may believe the punishments were good things, but she never would. Somehow she would find a way out, but that wouldn't happen if she allowed herself to start thinking like them.

"What do you think of your dad being so close to Jonah? I've never seen Jonah take someone on so soon after their unveiling. No one has ever become a prophet so soon after joining."

"What's so special about that?" she asked.

"Your dad is going to be in the inner circle. No one has been welcomed in the whole time I've been here. It might mean we're moving even closer to entering the Promised Land."

"And that means...?"

"It's our primary goal. The Promised Land is a beautiful, magnificent place where we'll spend the rest of time."

"You really believe that?" Macy asked and then covered her mouth. "Sorry. Don't tell anyone I said that." Images of being shamed and then ignored filled her mind. If she publicly embarrassed Chester, who knew what he would to her? "Please. I didn't mean it."

Luke didn't look bothered. "I didn't believe it for a long time. I understand your hesitation, Heather. I was there. You'll need to get to a place where you believe for yourself."

"Why?"

He stopped and then turned to look at her. "When you're truly a part of the community, you'll receive your true name. You won't be able to enter the Promised Land if you don't have your name."

She stared into Luke's eyes, trying to see if there was a flicker of doubt. She wanted to see it, believing that he was someone she could open up to. If he knew she'd been kidnapped, maybe he could help her escape. If not, she could end up at the wrong end of Chester's fury again.

It was time to play it safe. No one was going anywhere—they were all trapped inside the high, fortressed walls. If she needed to spend weeks feeling people out, she would. She needed to find the right person to open up to. Someone who wouldn't turn her in for claiming that she had been kidnapped by a prophet.

Maybe Luke was that person, but maybe not. She would have to be a hundred percent certain. Chester was sure to have chosen a house with some kind of basement or cellar. He had planned everything out with such precision. There was no way he would leave out a detail like that.

"How does your hand feel?"

"Better."

"We should head back, but first let me see it." Luke took her hand and rubbed it, squeezing hard.

It took all of Macy's self-control not to cry out in pain.

"It's still sore. I'm going to tell Teacher that I think you should rest it for the remainder of the day. Maybe I can take you on field trip.

Have you seen the farms yet?"

Macy shook her head.

"Without the farms, we couldn't survive. I can't imagine Teacher disagreeing with a field trip there. What could be more educational than learning about what sustains our way of life?" He turned around and walked toward the school house, still holding onto her hand, rubbing it.

Two men were heading their way, so Macy looked down careful not to even give the impression of making eye contact. She pulled on her hand, sure that the men wouldn't approve of Luke holding it. He wouldn't let go, continuing to squeeze it.

When they crossed paths with the men, Luke stopped, forcing Macy to as well. He gave a slight bow and Macy kept her eyes on the ground, staring at a melting patch of frost.

"What is going on, Luke?"

"Her hand is hurt, so I'm helping. We're heading back to school."

"Carry on." The two men continued walking in the direction they were headed.

Luke tugged on her hand and they followed the path. It was strange that it was okay for him to walk with her, touching her hand. With all the weird, backward rules the community followed, she would have thought that boys and girls would have been expected to walk on different sides of the road, not even allowed to look at each other.

When they got back to the schoolhouse, Luke stopped and rubbed her hand again. "How does that feel?"

"It's still sore."

"Let me rub it a little more." He looked down at her hand and rubbed again. His hand slid and went to her wrist, his fingers resting under her sleeve.

Luke looked into her eyes. He appeared as surprised as she felt. Macy's heart leapt into her throat. Luke's fingers lingered on her wrist, and then he pulled his hand away and cleared his throat.

"We should head back inside." His cheeks were pink.

Macy nodded. What had that been about?

They went inside and Luke told her to go back to the desk while he spoke with the teacher about taking a field trip. Macy rubbed her hand, watching them from the corner of her eyes. She couldn't hear anything they said, but Rebekah kept looking back at her, nodding occasionally.

Macy could feel the stares of other kids, probably because she was the new kid. Or was she the freak again? Not because she was overweight this time, but because her hand hurt and she couldn't keep writing with the pencil. Surely the others like her, the kids who had come from *the world,* would have understood. Who spent hours writing anymore?

Luke sat down and nodded, but didn't say anything.

Rebekah walked to the front of the class and tapped on the chalk board with a ruler. "Excuse me, class. It's almost lunchtime. When we reconvene, some of you are going to take a field trip to a farm. It's been a while since we've had a field trip, and now that we have a new student, the timing is perfect. How many of you, ages twelve and older, are interested?"

About half a dozen hands went up.

"Quite a few of you. This is good. We still have some time, so I'm going to take a little walk and let the farmers know to expect you. In the meantime, keep doing your work. I want to see all of your copy work when I return. If you need to, go to the other class and speak with the teacher there."

"Yes, Teacher," said the entire class in unison, minus Macy.

"If the lunch bell rings before I return, you're dismissed to your homes."

Without a word, all the kids went back to their writing, and they didn't slow down when Rebekah left. That would have never happened at her old school. If a teacher ever had to step outside the classroom for even a minute, chaos ensued every time.

Macy made a fist and then extended her fingers. Her hand was still sore, but she decided she better try writing again. She didn't want to get the reputation of being able to get away with things just because she was the teacher's kid—fake kid.

News

THE LIVING ROOM was filled an awkward silence. Chad felt like he should lead the discussion, but he didn't know where to start. Valerie looked to be in a better state of mind than she had the night before.

"Who wants to start?" Chad asked.

Valerie put her face in her hands and then looked up. "I can't deal with this on my own. Times like this, I wish Zoey's dad was around. Maybe if he was, this wouldn't have happened. Honestly, you guys are more family to us than anyone else. I suppose that's why I never thought this would happen. I think of Alex as her brother. She's always been so protective of him, as if he wasn't only Macy's brother, but her own."

Chad looked at Alyssa. "And we should have seen it coming. We grew up best friends and then one day, it became something more. I don't know why we never thought it could happen to Alex."

Alyssa took a step closer to Valerie. "We can all pass the buck, blaming each other or ourselves, but that isn't going fix this. I don't know if anything in our lives can be fixed any more. But what I do know is that nothing needs to be decided now. Let's just be here for our kids—both of them."

Valerie nodded and then turned to Alex. "I'm sorry, Alex. I shouldn't have said those things. I was angry and I'm scared."

He looked down. "I'm sorry too, Ms. Carter. For this whole mess." He looked up and had tears shining in his eyes.

"Oh, Alex." Valerie gave him a hug and then pulled Zoey in. "I hope you guys know I love you, both of you."

"Me too." Alyssa got up and hugged them. "I'm sorry for getting mad, too."

Chad wrapped his arms around all of them. "We'll get through this together."

Valerie nodded. "I'm not okay with this, and I don't agree with keeping the baby, but we can figure that out later. For now we'll just focus on helping you two."

"I couldn't agree more," Alyssa said.

Valerie's phone beeped and she looked at the screen. "I'm glad we were able to have this little talk. I'm sorry to cut it short, but I have to get back to the office."

"I should get back to my blog as well," Chad said. He went to his office and stared at the blank screen. Before Valerie came over, he'd been unable to write anything for his new blog post.

He couldn't write under pressure on a good day, but this was even worse—and not even because of Alex and Zoey's announcement.

The previous afternoon, his boss had brought Chad into his office. Roger hadn't needed to say anything, because Chad knew exactly what was coming from the look on his face. His performance at work had tanked since Macy disappeared.

They had given him a couple weeks off with pay and his coworkers had donated vacation hours so Chad wouldn't have to use his own. But the time since he had returned, he was next to useless and he knew it.

An alert from his computer brought him back to the present. Twelve new friend requests. Why did everyone want to be his friend? Just because his daughter was missing didn't mean he wanted to be friends with everyone who hoped she would return.

He refused to accept the requests, even if it made him look like a jerk. He didn't know any of those people and if they were really interested in Macy, they would just follow his blog. That's where he put everything that he wanted people to know, not on social media. He went to the folder where he kept his copy and paste letters, copied the friend-denial message and pasted it to all twelve of them.

He checked his notifications, got caught up on what everyone was doing—not that he really cared at the moment, but it was a good distraction from what was bothering him. If he couldn't work, then what? His blog made enough to keep Alyssa home, but not him. If he worked at it full time, he would probably be able to pull in enough to keep them both home, but it would take some time.

Chad went back to his blank blog post. What was he supposed to write about? Detective Fleshman had told them not to talk about the phone because they were still processing it. What did it matter, though? It had already been all over the news.

What did the phone even mean? They already knew her clothes had been found covered in her blood. Could the phone tell them anything they didn't already know? If they could get some information out of it, they might be able to find out who she had been calling. Maybe they would even find fingerprints. Or would it have been wiped clean?

He wanted answers, but when it came to the police department, it would take longer than he wanted. They simply weren't able to process things any faster than they were.

Chad got up and went to the kitchen for some coffee. Yesterday's still sat in the pot. For a moment he considered warming some up, but ended up rinsing it out and making a fresh batch. Alyssa would probably want some too. He doubted she had gotten any sleep either.

While the pot brewed, he went upstairs to check on her. He found her in the bonus room, asleep on the couch with the news still going. Why did she do that to herself? He found a blanket and covered her up and then turned off the TV. She stirred and then gave him a confused look.

"What's going on?"

"Just turning the news off. Go back to sleep, Lyss."

"Nothing more about the phone?"

He shook his head.

She looked at the time. "You're not going to work?"

"I'm going to work from home today." He had through next week to use that excuse before he told her that he was out of a job.

"Okay." She closed her eyes again.

Chad went to Alex's room. He was sleeping soundly while his alarm beeped next to him.

"Are you going to get up, Alex?"

"Do I have to?" mumbled Alex.

"You've got school and your alarm is blaring."

"Ugh." Alex pulled his pillow from under his head and put it over his face.

Chad pulled the pillow away from him. "Get up. Want me to make you some coffee?"

Alex shot him a dirty look and then turned his alarm off. "Can't I just sleep in? Why do I have to keep going to school?"

"Does repeating the eighth grade sound like fun?"

Alex sat up and grabbed the pillow from Chad. "My sister is missing and I'm going to be a dad at fourteen. Does it matter if I learn about adverbs?"

Chad sat next to Alex. "We have a lot to figure out about the baby. In fact, it's so early in the game that we don't know if it will last. Do you know how many pregnancies end in miscarriage early on?"

"You're a jerk."

"I'll ignore that. I'm being realistic. Your mom practically lived in fear until she hit a certain point. And even if Zoey does end up having it, wouldn't you two give it up for adoption? Give the baby the best chance possible. There are lots of nice couples who can't have kids, Alex."

"That doesn't change anything. I'll still be a dad. The baby will still be mine even if someone else raises him."

Chad took a deep breath. "All I'm trying to say is that skipping school isn't going to help you. Getting an education is the best thing you can—"

"No, it's not. That's the lies your generation was told. Look at all the people out there with college debt flipping burgers. My generation doesn't want that. *I* don't want that."

"You're not going into debt in middle school. Where did you hear that, anyway?"

Alex rolled his eyes. "I don't want to have this conversation. Look, I'll go to school so you'll get off my back. Deal?"

"I'm not trying to irritate you. But it's important that you go to school."

"There's such a thing as summer school. Who better to do that than me? No one has a better excuse for missing school."

"You really want to spend your summer in school?"

"Forget it!" Alex got up and grabbed some clothes before storming out of his room.

Chad looked around the empty room and picked some of the mess off the floor, putting things on the chair for Alex to organize later. When he got into the hall, he could hear the shower.

Why was it so hard to get along with Alex these days? Chad thought things would improve after their talk the night they found out about the pregnancy, but it looked like it would take more than that.

Alex and Chad had gotten along so well when Alex was younger. In fact, Alex wouldn't leave him alone for a minute, always wanting his attention. It had been annoying at the time, but looking back, his heart ached. Was it possible to get close again? Or was all lost for the teen years?

The landline rang. Chad sighed. The only people that called that number anymore were solicitors and his in-laws. He went down to the kitchen and checked the caller ID. The police department?

"Hello?"

"Chad, this is Detective Fleshman again."

He hated that they talked with him so much they used his first name. "What is it? Why are you calling this line?"

"We called both of your cell numbers, but neither one was answered."

Chad felt his pocket, but it was empty. "What is it, Detective?"

"We need you and Alyssa to come down to the station."

"Again? I thought everything was squared away with the phone."

"This isn't about the cell phone. There's a possible new clue and we want to talk with you before the news gets a hold of this." The detective's voice was solemn.

Chad leaned against the nearest wall. "What do you mean?"

"Just get down here as soon as possible. The shift change is coming up and I want my team to tell you two."

"I'll wake Alyssa."

"Thank you, Chad."

He hung up and stared at the coffee. Why did the detective sound so serious? He took a deep breath. He needed to calm down before he talked to Alyssa, or he would freak her out. He poured some coffee and drank it black.

Maybe they just needed them go downtown for something routine. He could convince Alyssa of that, but he knew better.

Chad heard footsteps. Alex appeared and glared at him.

"Want me to make you some breakfast?" Chad asked.

"You're a jerk."

"Still?"

"Why'd you go through my stuff?" Alex's eyebrows came together.

"Go through…? I didn't go through anything. I cleared a path to the door."

Alex folded his arms. "Leave me alone." He turned around and ran out the front door.

Chad walked to where he could see outside, and watched Alex walk to the bus stop where a group of kids were already waiting. At least Alex would be at school while he and Alyssa were at the station. He drank the rest of his coffee and headed back to the bonus room. She was still sleeping on the couch. He hated to wake her, but what choice did he have?

Crushed

Alyssa and Chad sat holding hands in the police station waiting room.

"What's taking them so long?" Alyssa asked. She pushed the heel of her boot against the leg of her chair trying to squash the horrible thoughts forcing their way into her mind.

Chad squeezed her hand. "This might be good news."

Had he lost his mind? She gave him a look that told him how she felt.

"Think about it. When they found Macy's clothes they rushed us in, remember? If they're making us wait, it can't be that urgent. It could be good news."

What was wrong with him? Was he just talking to hear himself speak? She gave him an annoyed look.

"Well, so far they haven't found anything indicating that she's come to any harm."

"Yeah, but you know what they say about the first twenty-four hours," Alyssa said.

"I can think of several famous kidnapping cases where kids were found alive months and even years later."

"So you think she was kidnapped now? You don't think she just ran away?"

Chad gave her an exasperated look. "I was just giving you a worst case scenario that turned out well."

"This really isn't the time for worst case statistics. I know which ones you're referring to and they were forced to live as young wives for sick, old men. I can't let myself think about that happening to Macy."

"That didn't happen each time. I'm just—"

"Mr. and Mrs. Mercer."

Officer Reynolds stood by the front desk. He gave them a weak smile and tipped his cap. "We're ready for you two."

Even though Alyssa was still irritated with Chad, she held his hand as they followed Reynolds to a back room. Detective Fleshman and Officer Anderson came into the room as Chad and Alyssa were getting seated.

Chad looked at them. "What's going on? Is it the phone?"

Fleshman shook his head. "We don't know what to make of that, but that's now why we asked you to come down here."

Chad's face clouded over. "Why are we here then?"

Alyssa noticed that the three policemen's faces were solemn. "Is something wrong?"

Anderson nodded and then sat down next to Alyssa. "We needed to see you right away because it's going to be everywhere soon."

"What?" Alyssa demanded. "What is it?"

Looking back and forth at them, Anderson cleared his throat. "A body has been found."

Alyssa gasped. Tears filled her eyes and spilled out. She shook. He had to be lying or wrong, or both.

Reynolds knelt next to her. "No one knows if it's her. The body— we can't identify the face."

Chad stood up, letting go of Alyssa's hand. "What does *that* mean?" He was practically shouting.

Fleshman walked in front of him and spoke in a soothing tone. "The body was found in Clearview. We haven't seen it, but it's coming directly here to rule out it being Macy. Our team will check it against dental records and we'll move on from there."

"But what does that *mean*?" Chad repeated.

Alyssa felt cold, and she couldn't stop shaking. "Wh…when will we know?"

"That's our top priority, but at the same time, we're going to quadruple-check every step of the process. Another thing: just because the body can't be identified by the face that doesn't mean that we can't use other markers. Does she have any identifying marks that would help? Birth marks? Tattoos or piercings?"

Unable to deal with the thought of Macy's *body*, Alyssa put her face into her hands, sobbing. Someone put a hand on her shoulder and she was vaguely aware of Chad speaking.

They had to be wrong—they just had to be. It couldn't be Macy. No. She was safe somewhere, even though they didn't know where.

The air felt like it was crushing Alyssa from all sides. She struggled to breathe. What if it *was* Macy? Was that why they had found next to no clues up until now? She gulped for air, still shaking.

Something touched her back. It was probably Chad's hand, but instead of being a comfort, it felt like he was pushing her further into the suffocating nothingness around her.

Alyssa jumped up, looking around the room. She couldn't focus on anything, barely even aware that she was at the police station. Oxygen was lacking, and she felt light-headed.

The others surrounded her. They appeared to be talking, but she couldn't hear anything over the sounds of her fear. She threw her hands out in front of her.

Was someone screaming?

It was her.

Tears ran down her face, pouring like never before. They ran down her neck, drenching her shirt's collar. Chad's arms wrapped around her, and she fought him.

Alyssa may have still been screaming, but she couldn't tell. She had to get out of there and find Macy. Why hadn't they looked harder?

She wouldn't be able to go on if Macy was…she couldn't even think the word.

Officer Reynolds was inches from her. His mouth was moving, but she still couldn't hear anything. They were wrong—whatever body they found, it wasn't her child. It belonged to someone else.

Her stomach and chest felt like they were going to simultaneously explode and implode. She gave into the weakness overtaking her, and she went limp in Chad's arms.

She was vaguely aware of him readjusting himself, trying to keep hold of her. Soft, rich oxygen filled her lungs and the sounds of talking around her filled her ears. Chad held her tightly, running his hands over her hair.

The sounds of speaking slowly formed into words she could comprehend. Alyssa couldn't make enough sense of them to understand what they were saying.

She continued to suck in the air around her, filling her lungs, and starting to feel more normal. She still wasn't getting enough air.

Random thoughts ran through her mind. Everything from memories of Macy as a toddler to her last status update, saying that she'd run away. Images from news broadcasts, pondering every possibility—many of them had given her plenty of nightmares.

Someone said her name. Alyssa looked up, unsure of who was speaking to her. The room had stopped spinning and the sounds around her were natural. She still couldn't process what anyone was saying. Facts and images from Macy's disappearance ran through her mind, taking up most of her awareness.

Her mind felt like a computer, trying to make sense of what she knew. She was trying to find any clue that could prove her daughter was alive and well, even if they couldn't get to her.

Alyssa looked up, finally able to find her voice. "Wait. Our dentist's office burned down. It was on the news."

Fleshman raised an eyebrow, stepping closer. "That was your dentist?"

"I'll look into it," Anderson said. "I'll see if they stored their files online. You never know around here."

"You mean we might never know if it's Macy?" Chad asked, sounding agitated.

"There are other ways. DNA testing would be possible. But we always go for the simplest solution. Usually facial recognition is where we start, but since we can't do that…."

Alyssa put her hands back over her face, tuning them out. Was it possible the girl found in Clearview was Macy? That was pretty far away and she couldn't imagine her daughter going there—there was nothing there. Unless that was where the boy was from, if he even existed.

She heard something about Alex and looked up again. "What about Alex?"

Reynolds looked at her. "We can pick him up from school for you if you'd like."

"Why?"

"So you can tell him before he hears it from school. All the kids have the Internet on their phones. All it takes is one kid hearing the news and it'll spread to everyone."

"No." Alyssa stood. "He doesn't need to be picked up by the police. As much as we appreciate everything you've done, he doesn't need it. Kids are cruel. They'll jump to the worst conclusion and run with it. He's been through enough. We'll get him."

"Are you okay to drive?" Anderson asked. "You just found out startling news."

"I have to be there for Alex. We can't let him hear about this at school, by some little jerk who just wants to see him react." Alyssa stood tall, trying to prove that she was able to get her son from school.

Chad took her hand in his, still holding her close. "She's right. We'd better call Valerie too, so she can decide whether or not to pick up Zoey."

Still shaking, Alyssa squirmed out of Chad's hold and took out her cell phone. She tried to dial Valerie's number, but wasn't able to keep her finger steady.

Detective Fleshman gave her a concerned look. "If you can't even make a call, I don't want to send you anywhere in a car."

"I'll do it." Chad snatched the phone out of Alyssa's hands. He swiped around the screen. "Valerie? This is Chad." He explained the situation to her and then handed it back to Alyssa when he was done. "See? We're fine to pick up the kids. I'm fine to drive."

"How soon until the news finds out?" asked Alyssa.

Reynolds gave her an apologetic look. "Not long. They're vultures."

In the car, Alyssa asked if they were picking up Zoey too. "In there, you said we were picking up the kids."

He turned right. "Yeah. Valerie can't get away from work, so she said she would call the school and give permission for us to get her."

"I'm surprised she trusts us."

Chad put his hand on her knee. "You know she didn't mean the things she said the other day. We were all freaked out, and especially after everything we've gone through lately with Macy."

Alyssa's eyes filled with tears again. "And now this. Do you think it's her?"

"Honestly, I think it's a long shot. Clearview? Do you know how many kids go missing every day? A lot."

"But if she was taken against her will, she could have gone anywhere. By now she could be on the other side of the world." Alyssa's voice wavered so much she couldn't continue.

"That's just it. She could be anywhere—why Clearview?"

"Do they know what happened to the girl? I was too upset to listen to everything they said."

"Not until they do the autopsy. Some jogger found her." He pulled into the school and parked in the lot that adjoined the high school and middle school. "Do you want me to get both of them? Or should we split up?"

"I'll get Alex. I need to see my baby. I need to know at least one of my children is safe and sound."

"All right. I'll get Zoey." He gave her a kiss. "Don't worry. That body isn't Macy. She's safe—I can feel it. We'll get her back, alive and well."

Alyssa gave him a doubtful look. He didn't know any more than anyone else. She pulled down the sun visor to check the mirror. She hadn't put on any makeup so there was nothing smeared across her face from crying. Her hair was messed up, so she attempted to fix it before getting out of the car.

As she walked to the middle school campus, she went over what to say to Alex. He would know something was wrong since he was being picked up so early. He was probably only in his first or second class of the day.

How would they ever tell their son the news about the body? He was as upset as she was about Macy just being gone. She knew how he was feeling without him saying a word. It had been that way since he was a baby.

For some reason, Macy had always been harder to read. If Alex had been the one planning to run away, she would have figured it out. Why had it always been so difficult with Macy? It wasn't like they had a bad relationship, but it didn't come as naturally as with Alex.

Why hadn't she tried harder? If she would have put out more effort to figure Macy out, even though it was challenging at times, would Macy have disappeared? Could she have done something to prevent all of this heartache?

When she got to the office, the secretary told her that Alex was already on his way.

"Why? Is he okay?"

She nodded. "The detective called and said that you would be on your way. You know, my heart aches for everything you guys are going through. Our family prays for you guys every night. I don't know how you guys do it."

Tears stung at Alyssa's eyes. "Me neither."

Lunch

A BELL SOUNDED from somewhere outside. It reminded Macy of a church bell tower. The sounds of pencils being set on desks surrounded her, followed by the scuffle of chairs pushed under desks. A light murmur of conversation filled the room, surprising her. It was the first time she had heard most of them speak.

She put her pencil down and got up. She followed the kids outside and looked around for Rebekah. Where was she? Was she supposed to come back? Macy wasn't sure she remembered how to get back to their house. They had taken several turns and everything looked the same to her.

"Are you all right?" asked Luke. "You look lost."

"I don't see Re—Teacher. I thought she would walk home with me."

"You don't remember the way back?"

Macy shook her head.

"Do you want me to wait with you or show you the way?"

"You know where I live?"

"When you live within the confines of a fence, you learn where everything is. I could take you to any house or place of business."

"Do you think she's coming back here or going straight home after speaking with the farmers?"

"She didn't say."

Macy knew that. That's why she asked him. She bit back an irritated comment. If she made the wrong choice, she could piss off Chester and find herself locked up somewhere. "Do you think I should wait for her?"

315

"I'd hate for you to miss lunch. Why don't I take you to your house? We know she'll go there to eat if she comes back here to find it empty."

"Okay."

"How does your hand feel? I saw you were writing again."

"It's pretty sore, but I'll live."

Luke made friendly conversation as they walked along the streets. A lot of people walked around.

"Does everyone stop what they're doing to have lunch?" Macy asked.

"Yes. Everything stops while people eat and do light household chores. Some even take naps or relax. It depends on the family. We take a couple hours to rest in the middle of the day. It helps everyone to be more productive in the afternoon. Here's your street."

Macy looked around. "How can you tell the difference between the houses?"

He laughed. "Yours has that little patch of flowers by the porch. See?"

She squinted, looking at each of the porches until she found a small patch of flowers. "I see it."

"Have a nice lunch. I'd better hurry home. My mother will wonder where I've gone."

"Thanks for everything."

Luke smiled. "No problem, Heather. See you in a couple hours." He walked off with a little wave.

Macy went to the house with flowers, nervous that it was the wrong one. What if there was more than one house with purple flowers near the porch? When she opened the door, she recognized everything inside.

She heard some noise coming from the kitchen.

"Rebekah, is that you?" called Chester.

"It's Heather."

Chester came out of the kitchen, looking confused. "Where's your mom?"

"She had to do an, uh, errand for school."

His eyebrows furrowed. "So you had to walk home yourself?"

"No. Another student came with me."

"That wasn't very considerate of her. It's your first day and you don't know your way around here. She should have—"

"She was looking into something for me. My hand—"

"Don't interrupt, Heather." Chester's lips curved downward. "I'll need to talk with her. This is unacceptable."

Macy's heart sank. "She didn't do anything wrong. She was trying to help me."

"There's no reason for you to protect her. She's an adult, and she should have been watching out for you."

"But she was. She—"

"Stop. Not another word. Get lunch ready." He walked past her and opened the wood stove, poking at the embers.

"She was talking with—"

"I said not another word. Or did you not hear me?" He turned around, giving her a scary look.

Macy turned around and went into the kitchen, her heart pounding. She should have waited for Rebekah at the school. Why hadn't she thought it through? She should have known that Chester would get angry over not coming home with Rebekah.

He wouldn't turn his anger on Rebekah, would he? She was his new wife of only a couple days. Surely, he wouldn't. Except that she couldn't trust him in the slightest. Tears filled her eyes. Rebekah had been nothing but nice to Macy, and now Macy felt like she had betrayed Rebekah. She was so sweet. There was no way she would see his rage coming.

Macy pulled leftovers out of the icebox, almost without thinking. She had to find a way to protect Rebekah. It was all Macy's fault that Chester was angry. She should have just waited at school. It was so obvious now; why hadn't it been earlier?

She pulled out a pot and poured the contents into it. Then she wiped her eyes, removing the tears. When Chester saw weakness, he took advantage of it. She had to show him that she wasn't upset.

He turned around when she approached. His eyebrows came together. "I would have chosen the food from two nights ago so it won't go bad as fast, but I suppose this will do since it's already out." He stared into her eyes for a moment before snatching the pot from her. "I didn't hear the water run. I suppose you didn't wash your hands first, did you?"

Heart pounding in her ears, she shook her head.

"Figures." He slammed the pot onto the top of the wood stove. "Germs! They still exist out here. People still get sick from stupidity like that. Yes, everyone is a lot healthier here, but it's not because bacteria ceases to exist. You have to wash your hands when you prepare food. Always!"

Macy stepped back. "I forgot. I'll go wash them now."

"What's the point?"

She stared at him, knowing that whatever she said would be wrong.

"Just go to your room and wait for your mom to return."

"I have to go to the bathroom."

"I don't care. Just wash your hands after that. Do I need to spell everything out for you? Do I need to do your thinking for you?"

Macy shook her head.

"I should hope not. There are basic things in life that I shouldn't have to worry about. Things you should just do because they're common sense. If I have to think for you I will, but I have more important things to do."

A lump formed in her throat. She nodded, afraid that if she anything she would burst into tears.

"Just go!"

She ran out of the room, through the kitchen, and to the outhouse. The tears finally spilled out when she got outside. By the time she sat down, she was sobbing. She hadn't meant to upset him. If she would have known he would react like that, she would have just waited for Rebekah to return. Why was she so stupid?

Macy thought she heard the front door of the house. Or was it the door from another house? The wood walls of the outhouse were so thin, she could hear everything outside. That made her self-conscious, knowing people could probably hear her when she was in there.

When she got in the house, Chester was standing in front of the wood stove, his arms crossed. He didn't look her way, much to her relief. She also didn't see Rebekah. Was that good or bad? Surely that wouldn't have been enough time for him to hurt her.

She closed the door behind her as quiet as possible and then washed her hands in the ice-cold water in the sink. She wasn't going to go near him to warm it on the stove.

Just as she was walking through the living room, the front door opened. Was there any way for Macy to warn Rebekah about Chester's mood?

Rebekah smiled, looking back and forth between the two of them. Obviously, she wasn't yet aware of the tension filling the room. Rebekah held up a small box. "I brought fresh berries."

"Where were you?" Chester demanded.

She looked startled at his tone, but didn't react. "I needed to speak with the farmers because our class is taking a field trip this afternoon. It will help Heather to get acquainted with how the community is run. Farmer Daniel let me pick a box berries for us. Wasn't that nice?"

Chester knocked the box from her hands. It hit the wall and blueberries rolled in all directions.

Rebekah looked shocked. "What—?"

"Why didn't you walk back with Heather?"

She stood back, not stepping on any berries. "When I returned to the school, everyone was already gone. The other teacher told me that Luke had walked her home."

"A *boy* walked her home?" Chester stepped closer to Rebekah.

"It was perfectly appropriate. The streets are always full at the lunch bell."

"Heather is never to be alone with a boy, do you understand? Ever." She nodded. "I do now."

"Good. Now pick up those berries and wash them off. Lunch is almost ready."

Macy went over to the berries and scooped up a handful.

Chester glared at her. "I told your mom to pick those up. You go to your room."

"I just want to help."

"If *I* wanted you to help, I would have told you. I did no such thing. To your room."

Macy gave Rebekah an apologetic look and then went to her room. She was shaking as she closed the door. Why had she let her guard down? Why had she been dumb enough to think his good mood would last? His anger had probably been simmering underneath, just waiting for the opportunity—any excuse—to be released.

She heard him chewing out Rebekah. He wasn't yelling, but his voice was raised and he was being just as mean to her as he had been to Macy many times.

Pacing the room, she wiped tears from her face. Macy threw herself on the bed, crying into the pillow. Now Rebekah would probably hate her. Then her only friend would be Luke, if Chester didn't forbid Macy from ever speaking to him again.

Her door opened and Chester came in. "Lunch is ready. Get up and eat with us. If you haven't washed your hands yet, be sure to. Nobody needs to get sick and die because of you."

Macy sat up, using the bed covering to wipe her face. It was probably red and puffy, but she couldn't do anything about that. She wasn't about to splash ice-cold water on her face.

She took a deep breath and went to the kitchen, preparing herself for whatever might be in store. When she got there, both Rebekah and Chester were already eating, facing their plates.

She would have felt a lot better if Rebekah would have looked at her, but she didn't. Not that Macy could blame her. She had pretty much betrayed her.

Waiting

ZOEY CLUNG TO Alex's hand in the backseat. She knew by the look on his face that he was as worried as she was. Their parents had been so insistent that they get back to school, and now they were pulling them out before lunch? That didn't make any sense...unless something was wrong. Really wrong. And judging by Alyssa's red, puffy eyes, something was.

Neither Chad nor Alyssa said anything. It was obvious that they were waiting to tell them the news until they got home. The silence felt like a heavy weight. Zoey was sure that if she said anything, something would break. Probably Alyssa.

The only thing that made any sense was that there was bad news about Macy. That made Zoey sick to her stomach.

She squeezed Alex's hand. Her protective nature wanted to wrap her arms around him and tell him that everything would be all right. But would it?

A lump formed in her throat. Surely Chad and Alyssa wouldn't be driving them home so calmly if Macy was dead. They'd be freaking out. Whatever the news was, it wasn't that.

Zoey leaned her head against Alex's shoulder. He was shaking. She tried to scoot closer to him, but couldn't because of the seat belt.

Her head hurt horribly, and she wanted a cigarette. No, she needed one. That would fix her headache and calm her down. But she couldn't have one, even though she knew the withdrawals would get worse. She couldn't give the kid that kind of a start in life. If that was the only thing she could give him or her, that would be it.

They pulled into the Mercer's driveway. Zoey took her belt off and wrapped her arms around Alex, squeezing him tight. "Everything's going to be okay."

"Have you seen my mom? This can only mean one thing." Tears shone in his eyes.

"It can mean lots of things, Alex. More clothes found, maybe."

He shook his head.

"Come on, you two." The solemn tone of Chad's voice sent chills down Zoey's back.

She grabbed her bag and pulled Alex out of the car. Zoey noticed a police cruiser pulling in across the street. Had they followed them? Or were they just arriving to watch the house? It couldn't be a coincidence that they arrived at the same time.

Zoey's heart dropped. Maybe Chad and Alyssa did have the news that she and Alex were dreading.

Her stomach twisted in tight knots as she walked to the house. Zoey expected Macy to open the door, and she wanted to punch herself. She knew better than to expect to Macy.

The sinking feeling in her gut told her she was about to find out if she would she ever see her best friend again.

When they got inside, Alex threw his bag on the floor and glared at his parents. "What's going on? You brought us—"

"Let's sit." Chad walked to the living room.

Alex looked like he was going to have a nervous breakdown, so Zoey put her arm around him and helped him onto the couch. Alyssa sat at Alex's feet and put her hands on his knees. She wouldn't look either of them in the eyes.

Chad pulled another chair up, sitting about a foot in front of Zoey. He took a deep breath. "It's important we tell you two what's going on before you hear it anywhere else."

Zoey's heart picked up speed, almost feeling as though it had jumped into her throat.

"There's no reason to believe this has anything to do with Macy, but we have to prepare ourselves for gossip." He explained about body that had been found, again reminding them that there was no proof that it was Macy.

322

As Zoey tried to process what Chad was saying, she looked over at Alex. Large tears fell into his lap and his lips wavered. She held him closer, leaning her head against his. He was shaking even worse now.

Alyssa rested her forehead on his knees. She was crying too.

Chad was saying something about dental records, but Zoey couldn't focus. The lump in her throat was twice the size it had been, but the tears wouldn't come. She wanted to cry along with her boyfriend and her best friend's mom, but she couldn't.

She buried her face into Alex's side, not wanting anyone to see that she wasn't crying. It wasn't that she didn't care—she did, more than anything. In fact, she couldn't stop blaming herself. Why hadn't she gone with Macy to meet Jared? She could've left them alone after meeting and threatening him to be nice, but she hadn't been there for her best friend.

All she'd been able to think about at the time was that she couldn't go on a double date because she was in love with Alex. She had been afraid of Macy kicking her out of her life.

Zoey was a coward. *That* was why Macy was gone.

She shook, angry with herself and finally tears came. Someone put an arm around her. Zoey looked over to see Chad with his arms around both her and Alyssa. They were all in a huddle, sobbing together.

The house phone rang a few times and eventually Chad went to get it.

"It's not her, right?" Zoey asked, wiping her eyes. "The body, I mean." She knew she had makeup smeared all over her face because it got all over her hands. She looked at Alex's shirt and saw it smeared on there too.

"Let's hope not." Alyssa wiped at her eyes.

Alex sniffled. "When will we know?"

"I don't know, baby. They said something about checking dental records, but our dentist's office burned down. If she's...she's...." Alyssa's eyes shone with tears and she put her head back down, shaking.

Zoey and Alex shared a look of helplessness. What could they possibly say? It was obvious that Alex wanted to comfort his mom, but he couldn't even help himself, much less her.

"What would she be doing all the way in Clearview?" Zoey asked. "Think about it. She wouldn't go there. There's not even decent shopping." She had hoped the last comment would at least get someone to crack a smile, but it hadn't worked.

Alyssa looked up. "We can only hope."

Alex wiped his eyes. "But they have enough to think it might be her, right? Why else would they have told you?"

"They wanted us to hear it from them first and not the news. In fact, we probably want to avoid watching the news altogether." Alyssa sighed.

Chad came back and sat next to Alyssa.

"Who was that?" asked Alyssa.

He shook his head. "It's already hit the national news. Everyone wants to hear from us."

Alyssa's eyes filled with tears again. "Why do they need to? Can't they just leave us alone for once?"

Chad kissed the top of her head. "And that's why Anderson said he would give our statement as our family's representative."

She let out a sigh of relief.

"I told Anderson to direct people to my blog if they have any questions. Of course that means I'm going to have to write up something about this 'latest development' as they're calling it." He frowned.

"You shouldn't have to deal with that, Chad. They should just leave us alone—completely."

He looked away. "I do need the added traffic. I have to get more income from the blog now."

Alyssa gave him a confused look. "Are you not telling me something?"

Chad grimaced, looking directly at her. "I haven't been able to do my work at the levels of quality it needs to be…."

"What are you saying?"

"I'm being let go."

Alyssa's mouth dropped open. "When were you going to tell me?"

"There's been so much going on—more pressing matters."

She put her face into her hands. "What are we going to do? Are we going to lose the house?" She looked, staring at him. "We can't lose this house. This is the last place we saw Macy. This is where her stuff is— her room! Exactly how she left it." More tears spilled onto her cheeks. "I won't lose this house. Ever."

He put his hand on her arm, but she pushed it away.

"Listen to me, Lyss. They're giving me a generous severance package. I have time to work on the blog. Maybe we'll have to give up cable and movie streaming for a while, but we'll make it work." He paused. "We aren't going to lose the house."

Alyssa narrowed her eyes, but looked like she wanted to believe him.

"I promise," he said.

Alex sat up, causing Zoey to readjust herself. "Dad, I have an idea. What if I write an open letter to Macy? If you post it on your blog, do you think people would read it? Would it help with your click-throughs or whatever?"

Chad looked thoughtful. "That's a great idea, Alex. Not just for my stats, but just for you to write it."

Zoey cleared her throat. "I can write one too."

"That would be perfect, Zoey. Thank you. Not only would the world love to hear from you two, but like I said, I think it would be good for you guys. Maybe we could all do that. What do you think, Lyss?"

Her lips shook. "I don't know if I can."

"You don't?"

She shook her head. "I can't say goodbye. I won't."

"Mom," Alex said. "It's not that. I'm going to write mine hoping that Macy finds it and reads it. Maybe she'll decide to come back."

"Me too." Zoey nodded. "Macy would want to hear from you too. Maybe I can get some of her other friends to write letters too. Think of how she would feel if she was out there and read those? It could be a 'begging Macy to come back' campaign. We can let her know that no matter what the news says, we haven't stopped believing."

Alyssa nodded, taking a deep breath. "When you put it that way, how could I not?"

Locked

MACY HEARD SOMETHING shoved against the bedroom door. Chester was locking her in there for the rest of the day. Rebekah had been ordered to return to school not speaking about Macy's whereabouts. Chester didn't want anyone to have the impression that he couldn't control his family. Not when he was working so closely with Jonah and the other prophets.

Macy looked at the window, already knowing that it was nailed shut.

"Don't make a sound while I'm away. Do you hear me?" Chester called.

"Yes."

"Good. I'll be back when I get back. If your mom gets here before me, you're not to leave the room. Even if she opens the door. Am I understood?"

"Yes." Macy sat on her bed, listening to the sounds of his footsteps. First, he went up and down the hall and then he went into the living room. She heard the squeak of the fire stove door opening followed by a sizzling sound. Had he put the fire out with water? The house would freeze without that.

Of course he wouldn't want her comfortable while being punished. In fact, she was surprised that she was allowed in her room. He probably had something else in mind for when she really acted up.

This was just a warning.

Finally, she heard the front door close. She peeked through the curtain and watched as he walked away. It looked like he was talking to himself. Big surprise. He loved the sound of his own voice.

Even though she was locked in the room, it was a relief to be away from him. She actually would have preferred to go to the school with Rebekah. It had been so nice to talk with Luke, although it didn't look like that was going to happen again. After Chester's tantrum, Rebekah would be sure to keep Macy away from all boys.

Maybe Macy could find a way to speak with him when Rebekah wasn't looking. Surely there would have to be times that could happen. They shared a desk; they would have to speak sometimes.

It seemed like Luke had wanted to say more to her, and Macy intended to find out what. Would he be willing to find a way out of the community? It couldn't be sealed perfectly tight. If people could escape Alcatraz, then it had to be possible to get out of this place.

Or was she dreaming too big? Was she making too much out of her interaction with Luke? She sat on the bed, going over every detail of their interaction.

Even if she wasn't able to talk with Luke again, Chester couldn't stop her from making friends with the girls, could he?

The worst part was that she didn't know what would set him off. Even Rebekah, who was obviously a dedicated member of the community, hadn't expected him to be angry about Macy talking with a boy. If she knew the rules and he still caught her off guard, what would throw him into his next rage?

Macy would have to be extremely careful. Sometimes he blew up over such insignificant things that the only explanation was he wanted to explode, and took any excuse he could find.

That was it.

Maybe he wasn't mad about Luke at all. What if he'd had a frustrating morning with Jonah and the other prophets? If any of them had said or done anything to embarrass him, it would've been enough to send him into a fit. But being that he wanted to impress them, he wouldn't have taken it out on them.

He would have waited until he got home, looking for the first halfway reasonable excuse.

That would explain him blowing up about Luke.

Macy got up and walked around the room. How long was Chester going to leave her in there? Until dinner? Until the nightly meeting? He wouldn't leave her locked up through that. *Everyone* was expected to be at the meeting. Except maybe those who were being shamed. Macy wasn't sure about that.

Chester had sounded bent on keeping the "indiscretion" a secret, so maybe he was worried about what everyone thought of him that he would actually protect Macy from a shaming.

Something could be heard outside. It sounded like it was in their yard. Macy moved aside the curtain and saw someone walking toward their house. She narrowed her eyes, focusing. It was hard to tell with everyone wearing white. It was a woman, Macy could tell because of the bun.

Whoever it was walked right through the front door. Why not? There was no lock.

Did the lady even know that Macy was there? Or was she coming just to see her? Footsteps sounded like they were headed her way. Macy's heart raced. She backed away from the door, pushing herself against the dresser. Her breath caught as she heard something scrape against the hall.

Whoever it was, she was moving whatever Chester had pushed against her door. Macy looked around for something to grab if she needed to fight. She saw some scissors and took them, holding them behind her back.

The doorknob turned and Macy looked for a place to hide. There was no wasted space in the room giving her any place to slide under or behind. Her pulse beat in her ears, drowning out the sound of the door opening.

She shook as the door opened. It took her a moment to register that Eve stood in the doorway.

"What...what are you doing here?" Macy asked, nearly out of breath.

Eve smiled. "Good afternoon, Heather. I thought you could use some company."

Macy squeezed the scissors. "How did you know I was in here?"

"Your dad mentioned that you could use some guidance."

"He did?"

She smiled, not coming any closer. "He did. I'm sorry you had a rough morning. Can I see your hand?"

Her hand? Right, her sore hand. "Sure." Macy set the scissors down as quietly as possible, and walked toward Eve holding out her right hand.

Eve took her hand and looked it over. "It does look a bit swollen. I don't think it requires staying home from school, although it is your dad's call as head of the household." She stared into Macy's eyes.

Macy didn't say anything, but she held Eve's gaze, not wanting to appear guilty. She hadn't done anything wrong.

"I want to show you something. Is that all right with you?"

Macy's heart sank. Was this going to be worse than being locked up?

"You're not in trouble, dear Heather. It's going to help you find understanding."

That didn't help her to feel any better. But what other option did she have? She nodded.

"Good. Do you need to use the toilet before we leave? I don't imagine that you were able to use it before I got here."

"Yes."

"I'll wait for you in the living room." Eve turned and left the room.

Letting out a silent sigh of relief, Macy followed her, but then went through the kitchen when Eve went into the main room and stood in front of the wood stove, holding her hands in front of it. *Good luck warming up*, Macy thought.

When she got outside, Macy noticed that the temperature had dropped since she had been out last. She hurried into the outhouse, which wasn't much warmer, and went back inside. She was sure to wash her hands in the sink, aware of their obsession with cleanliness.

Eve smiled at her again when she came into the living room. "Are you ready?"

Macy paused, wishing she had a coat to take with her. Why did they insist on walking around in the cold winter without them? Didn't people get sick or worse, die? There was a reason that people wore coats, and it wasn't fashion. Not in the snow.

"Come on."

Macy hurried and went outside with Eve, shivering as soon as the frosty air hit her skin. She struggled to keep up with Eve who was walking fast—because of the cold? Or was it because she thought she was important, being married to the head prophet?

They went down several streets before they stopped in front of an odd-shaped building. It was almost round. Macy followed Eve around to the other side to a door.

Eve opened the door, but didn't go in. Macy gave her a questioning look.

"You need to go in on your own."

"Why?"

"Going in there, you'll find what you're looking for. If you're blessed, you'll see a vision into your future. Not everyone does their first time, but being Chester's daughter, I wouldn't be surprised in the least if you did. Go on."

Macy looked back and forth between Eve and the doorway. She couldn't see anything inside.

"Hurry, before it gets dark. And take this." Eve pulled out a candle, lighting it without even putting the candle down. She handed it to Macy.

Macy's throat felt dry as she took the candle.

"I'll be waiting out here for you. Take as long as you need."

Macy took a deep breath and walked toward the door, her pulse quickening.

When she entered the building, she gasped in horror.

Visions

MACY STARED AT the room, afraid to go inside. She held her breath and shook, this time it wasn't due to the chilly air.

Eve pushed her forward and then closed the door behind her.

The room was mostly dark, but the candle lit it better than she had expected because every inch of the walls and ceiling were covered in thousands of mirrors. She looked around, seeing herself and the candle flame everywhere she looked. The mirrors were of every size imaginable, each one reflecting off each other.

She didn't just see one image of her, she saw many. Why had Eve brought her there? Was this some kind of torture? The candle and her white garb made the room even creepier. It reminded her of a scary movie—which was probably where Jonah had gotten the idea for this place.

Had Eve been serious when she said that Macy might have visions in there? Was that supposed to be a joke, or did Eve really think people could see into the future with all the mirrors?

As she moved around in a little circle, the flame cast shadows all around. She could imagine going crazy in that room. That had to be how people saw visions. Was she supposed to stay in long enough to go insane and see visions? Of what—her future? A vision of how to escape would be nice, but that wasn't going to happen.

She stopped moving and stared at the reflections—which were a lot with the mirrors playing off each other. Even though she wasn't moving any longer, some of the images appeared to be. Was it because of the flickering flame or the reflections going on into infinity?

Or was she losing her mind already? Was it supposed to work that fast? No, it was probably because Chester had been working on her. She'd been locked in the barn cellar, dealt with Chester's threats and his locking her in Heather's room. Not to mention forcing her to cut and color her hair and everything else he had done.

She never knew what to expect because when he seemed to relax, a blowup wasn't far off.

Macy was almost jealous of Heather. She'd been able to get away from him. But where was she now? The last diary entry Macy had read, Heather was about to be taken away to a mental institute, removing Chester of his parental rights.

It was too bad they hadn't taken things a step farther and locked him up. They must not have found any proof of him killing his wife. Heather had been certain something horrible had happened to her mom, but no one would listen to her.

Chester knew how to get what he wanted, so it was no surprise that he had found a way to avoid being discovered having anything to do with whatever had happened to Karla.

As Macy stared into one mirror, she swore she saw the image of someone else join the hundreds of her in it. She jumped in surprise. She looked around the room, spinning in a circle. Her skin crawled. She was alone.

It had to have been her mind playing tricks on her. Maybe thinking about Chester wasn't the best thing to do while in the creepy room. She tried to stare at the floor, away from the trillions of images of her, but she couldn't. Her eyes pulled her to look up. Part of her was drawn to the images.

The reflections jumped as the flame flickered from her spinning around moments ago. She was adjusting to the many images, not finding them so creepy. She stared into her own eyes in one particularly large mirror. There seemed to be an infinite number of her.

It was actually kind of interesting. Looking at so many of her, trailing back like a slinky. A human slinky. But not just one. Due to all of the mirrors, there were countless reflections of her slinky-self from various angles.

She stared at the image directly in front of her. It narrowed its eyes as Macy did. It moved the candle up when she did. It scratched her nose when she did. Then it smiled.

Macy froze. She was sure she hadn't smiled. Not only that, but she felt like she was being watched. Of course she was being watched. She stared at the one that had smiled, waiting to see if it would do anything else.

Her mind had to be playing tricks on her. That was the only explanation. There was no way her reflection could smile on its own. Why hadn't she paid closer attention to the other images? Then she would know if any of them had smiled or if it had been just the one.

Of course it had only been the one she had been staring at. It only smiled because it was in her imagination. It was no wonder they had houses of mirrors at carnivals.

Did Jonah and Eve routinely send people there as a punishment? But Eve had acted as though it was an honor to go in. Macy would have to ask Luke about it later. Or what if she brought it up and no one knew about the mirrored room? They would think that she was crazy.

Her reflection winked at her. Macy stared, holding tighter to the candle, which shook. The wink had to have been from the flicker of the flame. Obviously her reflection hadn't winked at her any more than it had smiled.

Could she leave the house of horrors yet? Eve wouldn't send her back in, would she? Macy needed to get out before her mind *really* started playing tricks on her.

She took a deep breath and made her way back to the door. Macy turned the knob, but it wouldn't budge. Her stomach twisted in knots.

Macy twisted the knob again, this time making noise. If Eve was still out there, she would let Macy out. Wouldn't she? She would have to, right?

She looked around for a place to set the candle, but it didn't have a holder so it would roll to the ground, no matter what she did. She couldn't risk the flame going out.

Accidentally looking up, Macy saw the little flame in a mirror. As it moved back and forth, it became larger with each movement until it took up the entire mirror. None of the other mirrors showed the enlarged flame, but the one that had grown covered Macy completely. She blinked fast to get the image to return to normal, but it didn't.

She shook her head, finding that the blaze had grown even more. Macy saw herself, but not as she really was. The image of her walked out of the flame, looked around, and then ran. She looked terror stricken as she ran, the fire chasing after her.

Macy looked away and pulled on the knob, twisting at the same time. "I'm ready to get out!" She kept that up for a couple minutes, before giving up.

Had Eve gone back to Chester and the prophets? Were they all laughing at her? Maybe they were all standing outside the door, enjoying themselves.

"Let me out!" She banged on the door with her free hand. "I'm done!"

No response.

She tried the knob one last time and then leaned against the door, sliding to the floor. She looked around, still seeing too many images of herself. Soon she would see visions, but not because she was some kind of seer. Because she was going crazy.

Every time she thought things couldn't get any worse, they always found a way to do exactly that. She didn't even want to wonder what could top the mirror room. She looked at her feet, refusing to acknowledge the mirrors. They could force her to be in there, but they couldn't make her look at the reflections.

It was the one thing she could actually control, and she knew that focusing on that would be what would keep her going until she was finally presented with a way to escape—even if was years down the road.

She would let them think they could control her, but they would never control her thoughts. They couldn't get in there, and as far as Macy was concerned, they never would. Let them think she was stupid enough to believe their insanity. It was to her advantage. The moment she allowed them in, that was when she would lose.

As long as she held onto reality, she stood a chance at getting back home. It was a small chance at this point, but at least it was something.

It was more than just something—it was all she had.

Light from the candle shone on the floor, light also bouncing from the mirrors.

"Chester is not my dad. These people are not prophets." She repeated that until she grew tired of whispering. If anything, repeating it would reinforce reality so that they couldn't get in. She had to make sure that her defenses were stronger than their tactics to bring her down.

Sure, no one other than Chester knew the truth—that she wasn't Heather—but that didn't change the fact that they all wanted her to become an obedient member of the community. She couldn't put her finger on it, but for some reason, she couldn't help thinking that Luke wanted out too. Maybe it was the mirrors getting to her.

Even if she was wrong about him, there had to be others. Or at least *an* other. Surely, she wasn't the only one dragged into this place against her will, wanting to go back to texting and posting status updates. She missed taking selfies and even bickering with Alex.

While Macy sat surrounded by mirrors in the middle of a community of crazy people, was her family thinking about her too? Did they buy Chester's fake updates that she had run away? Were they mad at her? Did they have an inkling that she had been taken against her will?

Did Zoey know enough about "Jared" to figure it out? They were best friends and Macy told her everything. Zoey would know that something was wrong. She would know the status updates were fake. But would anyone listen to her?

Macy leaned her head against the door. The community would be the last place anyone would look for her.

The doorknob jingled above her. Macy jumped up before it would open and send her falling to the ground.

Surprise

ZOEY SAT IN front of her plate, pushing the food around. She had no appetite, and just looking at it made her sick. Was it because of being pregnant, the news of the body, or withdrawals from smoking?

"Aren't you going to eat?" her mom asked.

"How can you expect me to eat at a time like this?" Zoey snapped, and then glared at her.

"Don't look at me like that. You're the one supporting another life."

"I'm not hungry. If I really needed to eat, the food wouldn't turn my stomach."

"You can't think about only yourself anymore. That's what's going to happen if you decide to keep it. Nothing is going to be about you again. Every decision you make has to be in the baby's best interest."

Zoey bit her tongue, wanting to tell her mom that she'd already given up cigarettes, and the headaches were killing her. "You think I don't know that?"

"You need to eat."

"I'm not hungry!" Zoey slammed the fork down. "I'm going to puke if I eat. Why can't you have some understanding? Do you even know what it means that they found a body? It could belong to my best friend."

Valerie's face softened. "You know I'm worried about you."

"Do I?" Zoey's eyebrows came together.

"Of course I'm worried, Zo. I wish I could do something to fix the whole situation with Macy. I would love nothing more than to flip a switch and make it so that she never disappeared."

"I've hardly seen you shed a tear."

"I'm being strong for you. Not only that, but I have to take care of our family financially. You know that. I've cried over Macy's disappearance, but I don't have room to wallow. I have to take care of you. That's part of being a parent—a single parent, in particular. I can't rely on someone else to help out. It's all on me or we lose the house and other nice things we've gotten used to."

Zoey shook her head. "You could try showing a little empathy, you know. Just a little would be nice."

"Empathy? You think I haven't shown you any?"

"Not really, no."

"This is getting us nowhere. If you're not hungry, then go upstairs and get some rest. You need to take care of yourself."

"Whatever." Zoey threw her napkin onto the plate, stormed to her room and slammed the door.

Her headache roared in protest. When would that stop? The pain would go away as soon as her body figured out that she wasn't going to smoke anymore, right? She didn't bother turning on the light, enjoying the darkness of the room.

She got comfortable on her bed. She probably could have slept for a week if her mom would let her.

The cell phone's light was blinking. She grabbed it out of her bag and scrolled through a long list of texts. Tons of people were asking if she was okay and giving their condolences.

Macy wasn't dead! Couldn't they get that? *A body had been found. Why assume that it was Macy?*

She dropped her phone on the ground, not wanting to read any more texts. She wasn't going to shed another tear over that body until she found out it was Macy. No one who had known her had even seen the body—the cops wouldn't even let them look at it because it was in bad shape, whatever that meant.

Zoey's eyelids grew heavier by the second, and she gave into them, slinking down further under her covers. Sleep was most welcome, especially if it got her away from her headache and overall soreness.

Something woke her up, but she didn't know what. She sat up, looking around. A little light was coming through her blinds, but she didn't feel like she had gotten any sleep.

She heard a noise.

What was that? Is that what had woken her?

Heart pounding, she looked around the room, not seeing anything out of place. She pulled her hair back behind her shoulder. She had heard something; she was sure of that much.

Zoey grabbed the baseball bat she kept by her bed at her mom's insistence and crept out of bed. She tip-toed to her door, listening.

Everything was quiet. Zoey grabbed the door knob and turned it slowly, holding her breath.

The hallway was dark, having no windows to give any light. She looked down the hall, still not hearing anything. Standing still, she waited, clutching the bat. If she heard anything, she would swing. No questions asked.

There was the noise again down the hall to the right, near her mom's room. It sounded like a thump. She tip-toed in the direction, being as quiet as she could be, careful not to bump against the wall even though she stayed close to it.

Zoey stopped in front of her mom's door, listening. She heard the thump again. She couldn't tell what it was, but her mom could be in danger.

She heard something slide across the floor. The image of someone dragging her mom made her blood run cold. She threw open the door, ready to attack.

Her mom turned, looking frightened. "Zoey! What on earth?" She had a phone up to her ear. "I'm going to have to call you back." She closed the phone and set it on her dresser. "Are you all right, honey?"

Zoey lowered the bat. "What was all that noise? You scared the crap out of me."

"I'm sorry. I wasn't expecting you up this early. Are you okay?"

"Now I am, I guess. I thought I heard an intruder."

Sadness washed over Valerie's face. "We really need to get you into see a psychologist, dear. With everything you've been through, you're under a lot of stress. Do you remember I upgraded our security system after the Mercer's house was broken into? Not only that, there's always a cop across the street watching their house. If anything strange happened here, they would be right over."

"Who were you talking to?"

"Don't worry about it. Are you—?"

"Of course I'm going to worry about it. What time is it? Who would you be on the phone with this early? Grandma's not sick again, is she?"

"No, she's fine."

"What, then?"

"Zoey, there are some things that kids don't need to worry about."

"Kid? I'm no kid. I'm a teenager, Mom. I'm old enough to have a baby, because, oh, I *am* having one. After scaring the crap out of me, I think I deserve to know."

"I didn't mean to scare you. I'm sorry. I was just rearranging some of the furniture in here. It was bad timing, my nerves are shot these days too."

"Why don't you want to tell me who that was?"

A strange look came over her face, and then she patted her messy bed. "Have a seat, Zo."

Zoey sat, shaking her head in disbelief. "Let's hear it."

Her mom sat next to her, patting the top of Zoey's hand. "I don't want to put more on your plate, but you deserve the truth."

"What is it?" Zoey's stomach dropped to the floor and dread washed over her.

Her mom looked into her eyes. "That was your dad."

The room spun. "What? How did you…? I mean, what? How did you find him?"

"Ever since you told us about the pregnancy, I've been searching. It's obvious you're crying out for help. You need both of your parents, and that's one thing I can't give you by myself."

"I don't understand."

"I'm trying to get him to come back here. He needed the same speech I gave you about putting his child first."

Zoey clenched her fists. "I don't need him. He's never been here.

He has no right to tell me what to do. He took off without a word, never once doing anything to take care of me."

Valerie frowned. "I wouldn't say never."

"What do you mean?" Zoey stood up. "All he's done is provide DNA. That's it. Because he's Japanese, everyone thinks you adopted me. Just tell him to stay there. We don't need him."

"That's the problem. We do. You need your dad, Zo, and I should have had this talk with him long ago. Maybe you wouldn't be in this mess." She looked at Zoey's stomach.

"And you think bringing my dad into this is going to help? He doesn't know anything about me."

"I know. You two need to get to know each other."

"What's that going to help?"

"It's obvious that you need him in your life."

"Ugh! You keep saying that. We've done just fine without him."

"Just fine? You call this *just fine*?"

"Do you know how many girls get pregnant? It was probably different way back when you were in high school."

Valerie laughed. "It wasn't that long ago, Zo."

"Yeah, it was. Things were so different. Could girls get an abortion without their parents knowing?"

"I honestly wouldn't even know. I had a nurse try to talk me into the pill when I was a little older than you, but I wasn't interested. My focus was getting into college. All I wanted was to get the career that I now have."

"Well, whatever it used to be like, now some girls don't even bother with the pill. If the guy doesn't have his own protection, they just get the morning after pill or have an abortion. It pretty much happens all the time."

"Back to the topic. I want your dad to move over here."

"Don't bother. I'm sure he's happy with his own family."

"No, he doesn't have a family."

Zoey raised an eyebrow.

"He plays baseball over there. He always dreamed of playing, but couldn't even make the minors here, so he went back home to play."

"A sport is more important than me? What a tool."

"It's not like that." Valerie sighed.

"What's it like, then?"

"I didn't want to hold him back when I got pregnant. Neither of us were looking for a long-term relationship. We were just having a little fun. We met through some mutual friends one summer. I'm a strong woman and figured I could handle raising you on my own." She smiled. "I even thought it would be easier because then I wouldn't have to argue with him on how to raise you."

"That doesn't change the fact that he walked away."

"He hasn't forgotten about you. On a pretty regular basis, I receive 'anonymous' deposits in my account. He thinks it's important to support you. Since I don't need his money, I've been keeping it for you in a savings account. You have a nice amount built up for college."

"And you never once thought to mention this to me? Here I've been thinking that he doesn't care." Zoey crossed her arms. "You could have called him any time you wanted?"

Valerie shook her head. "It took me some time to find him. Like I said, he left anonymous deposits. I still don't have his address or anything. I managed to find an email address and then he agreed to talk with me on the phone. He was actually benched with an injury since last season. They're talking about letting him retire since it looks like he can't play this season either, so this might be the perfect time for him to return."

"I don't want him in my life!" Zoey ran out of the room before her mom could see the tears.

Discussion

T HE WALK TO school was an uncomfortable silence. Macy wanted to talk to Rebekah, but was afraid. Rebekah had barely made eye contact with Macy since Chester's outburst. Rebekah had been jumpy around both Macy and Chester.

Macy was still shaken from the whole vision room thing. She wasn't sure how she'd made it through the rest of the day. She hadn't been able to stop thinking about the mirrors—especially the images that appeared to change. Chills ran through her each time she thought about it. It had to have been her mind playing tricks on her. Or maybe it was the flickering light from the small candle.

It also didn't help that Eve had had a thousand questions about the experience, none that Macy had wanted to answer. She wasn't sure what Eve wanted to hear. Macy would have said anything—anything at all—to avoid ever having to go back in there again.

She had ended up admitting to having seen a couple things, and much to her relief, Eve hadn't pressed. Her smile had been wide; she had been thrilled that the daughter of the up and coming prophet had seen a vision. She told Macy that visions were private and needed to be kept to oneself until the right time.

"Are you okay?" Rebekah asked, bringing her back to the present.

"Yeah."

"No, I mean it, Heather. The way that your dad's been acting…I just want to make sure you're okay."

"I'm fine."

Rebekah came closer and spoke softer. "Does he act like that a lot, or he just stressed about training to become a prophet? You can talk to me."

If Macy said anything, would Rebekah tell Chester? Macy had to be careful with her wording. "He can be…a little moody. Don't tell him I said anything."

"Of course. I was shocked when he reacted like that. You looked more concerned than surprised, so I thought that wasn't the first time. Are there certain things that tend to set him off?"

Macy's heart raced. "I don't really know."

Rebekah gave her an inquisitive look.

Did she know that Macy was holding back?

"I don't want you to fear me, Heather. Yes, my first responsibility is to my husband, but as your new mother, I also have an enormous responsibility to take care of you."

That answered that. Chester came first, and if he ever pressed Rebekah to find out what Macy had told her in private, she'd talk. "Thanks," Macy said.

"I still want to tell you about my life before I joined the community. It sounded like you were interested, but that will have to wait. I do hope we can be friends." Rebekah smiled.

Macy nodded. "That would be nice."

"As far as today, please stay inside the schoolroom. I won't tell your dad if you talk to boys, but please—please—don't go anywhere with one. Luke is a trustworthy young man, and you would do well to become friends with him, but please also make friends with some of the girls. We don't want to upset your dad again."

"Okay."

They turned a corner and the school was in sight. Rebekah took Macy's hand and gave a squeeze. "Everything is going to be all right. If we work together, we'll figure out how your dad ticks and we'll learn to live in such a way as to not incite his anger again. Sound good?"

Macy had to stop herself from laughing. Good luck with that. "Sure." She hoped that Rebekah didn't pick up on her sarcasm.

"If your hand cramps up—and it might until you adjust—let me know. I'll have you do some reading or have one of the girls sit with you and go over some of what you need to learn."

They entered the schoolroom without a word. Everyone sat at their desks doing their work. Macy sat next to Luke.

He looked up at her. "I missed you yesterday afternoon."

"Something came up."

"I see." Luke held each her gaze for a moment and then went back to his papers.

She opened the book in front of her, getting ready to copy from it. She'd have to write slowly so that hopefully her hand wouldn't cramp. Why bother writing fast anyway? Was there a rush to learn this stuff? Of course not. What she needed was to find a way out of the community.

Even if she could get out, did they have the woods booby trapped? What about wild animals? How would she get home? Hitchhike? Then she would risk running into another Chester—or even someone worse. Macy shuddered.

"You all right?"

Macy looked over at Luke. "Yeah." She picked up the pencil and copied from where she had left off the day before. She wanted to talk to Luke, but how?

She sat in silence writing for what felt like hours. Maybe it was. It wasn't like there was a clock on the wall. They wouldn't want to use that evil electricity.

At least her hand felt okay. She was treating it like a wounded bird, careful not to let it cramp again.

A tapping noise in the front of the room grabbed Macy's attention. Rebekah stood in the front of the room, tapping on the chalk board. "It's time to stretch our legs and take a break. We'll reconvene in ten minutes."

Luke looked at Macy. "Want some fresh air?"

Her eyes widened. Could they, without her getting into trouble? She noticed some of the other kids going outside. If she talked to some of them she should be okay talking with Luke also. "Sure."

"It's all overwhelming, isn't it?" Luke gave her a reassuring smile.

"You have no idea." Why had she said that? Her mouth seemed to run on its own when talking to him.

His eyebrow arched, but didn't say anything. He held his hand out, indicating for her to go first and she headed for the door. When they got outside, the cold air felt good and the sun shining down felt even better. She stood off to the side, watching the kids talk.

Aside from the white clothes and the buns on the girls, they all seemed like normal teenagers. Except that they weren't goofing off or picking on each other. She wasn't sure if she missed the kids running around acting like caged animals.

She kind of liked the serenity of the community—not that she wanted to become one of them. Maybe she was just glad to be away from Chester. It had been torture spending so much time with him since he'd taken her from her family. At least here, she had school and Chester spent a lot of time with the prophets, but he made sure to drive Macy crazy when they were home.

"Care to share your thoughts?" Luke asked.

Macy shrugged. "Just taking everything in. It's a big change."

"It usually is. Some kids have a really hard time getting used to this way of life."

Something about the tone of his voice told her he wasn't referring to hand cramps. "What do you mean?"

"I've seen people have breakdowns or tantrums because it's too much of a change for them."

"Then what?"

"Sometimes they have to stay away from school for a while until they're able to come back and behave properly. Other times, they have to be shamed. It depends on what they do."

"What did you think when I didn't come back yesterday afternoon?"

"I hoped for the best since Teacher didn't say anything. You hadn't done anything wrong. Your hand just cramped up. I assumed that you were resting or studying at home."

"Something like that."

"Is your hand okay now?" Luke asked.

Macy held it up. "A little sore, but otherwise it's fine."

Luke reached for it and rubbed. Her heart raced. She loved the feel of his skin against hers, but what if word got back to Chester?

She closed her eyes. Whatever Chester did to her would be worth it. An adorable boy cared enough to hold and rub her tired hand. He couldn't take that away from her, even if she did get punished.

Luke's fingers slid down to her wrist under her sleeve again. Macy's eyes popped open. Luke smiled at her and then hid their hands behind his back. Macy stared into his eyes, feeling her face flush. He rubbed his fingers back and forth along her arm just above her wrist.

She opened her mouth to say something, but nothing came. Her skin tingled where his fingers touched her arm.

Luke slid his hand back down to hers, and then squeezed. He cleared his throat. "Perhaps I should introduce you to the others?" Luke asked.

"Yeah, sure." Macy shook her head, trying to clear it. "That's probably a good idea."

"Maybe." The skin around his eyes wrinkled a little as he grinned.

Macy's pulse quickened. He was adorable, and he wasn't repulsed by her.

"Come on," Luke said.

He walked to one of the groups and introduced them to her. She tried to remember their names, but they all had strange names. They all stared at her, not saying anything. Were they expecting her to say something? If so, what?

"It was nice to meet you all." She went back to where she had been standing with Luke, and the girls went back to their conversation.

Luke joined her.

"That went well," Macy joked.

"I think they're intimidated by you."

Macy laughed. He had to be kidding. "By me? Why?"

"You're the daughter of Jonah's new favorite. Everyone has been talking about your dad since before you guys arrived. Jonah isn't one to keep his visions to himself. He spends hours in the vision room and as I'm sure you've noticed in the nightly meetings, he loves sharing every single detail."

"Yeah. I've noticed."

Luke looked like was trying to cover a laugh. Macy thought it was cute the way he fought to keep his composure.

"Jonah received visions long before he met your dad. He left the community for a while, following clues from his visions until he found him. Did your dad tell you how excited he was to find out that he had been chosen?"

"He's mentioned it."

Luke raked his fingers through his hair. Macy watched each strand fall back into place. It looked so soft she wanted to touch it. His hair was a nice, sandy color. It had speckles of brown and blonde strands all throughout. She moved her gaze down to his eyes. Macy had never seen such kind eyes before. Or was it just because she was used to Chester and his frightening stares?

Either way, Luke held a genuine graciousness about him. His eyes lit up when he smiled, and his voice was soothing. That's when Macy realized that he'd been talking to her, but she hadn't heard a word of it.

"Don't you think?" Luke asked.

Macy's cheeks burned. "What?"

Luke gave her an amused look. Her stomach twisted in knots.

"How much did you miss? I said that Jonah wanted to return with your dad as soon as he found him, but your dad wasn't going to leave the world without you, so we had to wait."

Instead of replying, Macy looked up at the sky. A cloud reminded her of a sleeping cat. Macy and Zoey had spent countless afternoons finding shapes in clouds, and even going as far as creating elaborate stories to go with them.

A lump formed in her throat. Would she ever see Zoey again, or would she live out the rest of her days in the community? Worse, would she one day succumb to it?

Macy blinked away tears. Images of her being part of Jonah's inner circle flooded her mind. She would never let that happen. She was Macy Mercer, not Heather Woodran. Chester was not her dad. The community was not her home.

She looked over at Luke and saw him looking at her, his eyes full of concern.

"Are you upset, Heather? Do you want to talk?"

Her heart sunk at him calling her Heather. She looked deep into his light brown eyes. Could she trust him? She wanted to believe she could, but the truth was that she didn't know who she could trust.

"How did you end up here?" Macy asked. "In the community, I mean."

"We were down on our luck, and Jonah met my mom. My dad died and we were about to lose our house."

Macy gasped. "I'm so sorry. That's horrible."

"Thanks. It was a long time ago. Anyway, my mom's job was already on the line because she couldn't focus after losing my dad. Not only that, but she was dealing with me and my anger. She was waiting for an appointment to learn about state housing when Jonah approached her. The rest, as they say, is history."

"Is that what happens usually? Jonah goes out and finds people who are having a rough time?"

"Sometimes. He likes to find people who need hope. People like my mom. It's not the people living the high life who are looking for hope."

Macy studied his face again. "Are you glad to be here?" she asked.

"I'm grateful to be off the streets. Mom says that's where we were headed. She might have lost me otherwise. Who knows where I would be if we weren't here? And at least I'm still with her."

Macy felt like she could trust him—and she had to tell someone that she really wasn't Chester's daughter. Her heart pounded nearly out of her chest as she decided to open up to him.

She opened her mouth to say something, but Rebekah came out, announcing they needed to come back inside.

Revenge

ALEX ROLLED OVER, waking again. It was getting hard to tell the difference between dreams and reality. Was he really awake or was it just another dream? He pulled the blankets up over himself. He kept kicking them off despite being cold.

Weeks had passed since the body had been found. Alex wasn't sure how he had made it through them. He couldn't stop thinking about the body. Why did it take so long to get the results? They had sent it to Seattle because they were supposed to have more advanced equipment.

With three weeks, they should have been able to figure something out. What was wrong with them? Didn't they care? Or were they just stupid? The local cops had said that it might take months before they could get DNA results.

Why did it have to take so long? Three weeks was way too long to figure out if the body was his sister or not. How was he expected to wait even longer? Another month of this? He didn't want another hour of it.

Alex wanted answers, but on the other hand he wasn't sure. Did he really want to know if the body was Macy? What could be worse than losing his big sister? He hadn't even been able to say goodbye.

Alex pulled the pillow from under him and put it over his head trying to stop the tears that threatened.

Waiting sucked, and in this case, it really wasn't fair. Why couldn't they just have answers? They'd been waiting so long already.

It was enough to make him want to turn on the news or the computer, but he knew he would either end up depressed or angry. Some of the things he'd heard and read had really pissed him off. He knew he needed to avoid it now more than ever.

He rolled over again, keeping the pillow on top of him. What he needed was to think about something else. What else mattered, though? The things he used to enjoy only brought him more misery.

If he caught himself having fun, he was plagued with guilt, instantly remembering Macy. He shouldn't be having fun when she was probably out there somewhere not having any fun at all—or worse.

What would she think if she saw him? Would she think he was a jerk? Or would she be glad that he wasn't wallowing in pity?

A tear escaped, landing on his sheet. Why hadn't he been able to do anything to stop Macy? Had he pushed her away? She was always annoyed with his teasing. He knew that kids at school picked on her, even after losing her weight. Why had he been so insensitive?

Not that he was anywhere as mean as anyone at school, and he wasn't trying to be mean to her. He'd just been a normal brother. Brothers teased—even his dad told him that.

If he would have had any idea that she was going to disappear, whether running away or being kidnapped, he would have stopped. But there was nothing he could about that now.

Did she really know how he felt? She had to know how much he loved her. It wasn't like their entire relationship had been about him teasing her. They still talked and stuff, but obviously not enough.

This was getting him nowhere. Why couldn't he just sleep? Because his guilt wouldn't leave him alone even there. He should have been able to do something. What? He didn't know, but he could have done *something* to stop Macy from disappearing.

He closed his eyes tighter, trying to push the thoughts away. He focused on the black behind his eyes. He could feel more tears slipping out and all falling along the same path, pooling around his face.

He sat up. There was no way he could stay in bed. He couldn't stop thinking, and even if he could stop thinking about Macy, he would probably start thinking about Zoey and the baby, and he couldn't deal with that, either.

If Macy was dead, what would he do? How would he go on? Could he go on? Would he live with the guilt for the rest of his life? What would life be like? He didn't want to be an only child—he wasn't supposed to be. Macy was supposed to be there. They were *supposed* to bicker and bug each other. It was their job as siblings.

It was also his job to protect her. Even though he was younger, he was still her brother. He should have gone over to the high school and confronted those stupid jerks who were giving her a hard time.

He still could. It wasn't too late. *They* weren't missing. All of them were still at school, and Zoey knew them by name. He probably knew most of them too. *They* were the ones who had caused this. If they hadn't been so mean to her, Macy wouldn't have felt like she had to meet some guy online.

Alex had stopped working out after she disappeared, but it probably wouldn't take him long to get back into shape. He threw on a sweatshirt from the end of his bed and got up.

He went down to the garage to the punching bag and balled up his fists. He punched it. It felt good. He punched again. It felt even better. He imagined the faces of the jerks who had tormented his sister. He felt even better still.

Alex hit it until sweat poured down his face and back, and was breathing hard. He felt great. He would have to remember to use it daily. Taking deep breaths, he found that he had more energy. He went to his dad's weights and grabbed some dumbbells—the ones he was sure he had used last and did reps.

The muscles burned in a good way. He was doing what he needed and once he got himself back into shape, he was going to confront every person who had made fun of Macy. He didn't care that he wasn't supposed to hit girls—those ones had it coming.

He grabbed a different set of dumbbells and did some squats. He had to strengthen everything. It shouldn't take him long to get back to where he was. He'd only missed a month; it wasn't like he'd stopped for a year.

He grunted his way through the last set and put everything back in place. Not that his dad would notice anything had been moved out of place. He'd also stopped working out.

Alex went back to his room, allowing himself to enjoy the burn of his muscles. He felt powerful and he would face the ones responsible for pushing his sister away. Even if he didn't lay a hand on them—and how he wanted to rearrange their butt-ugly faces—he would at least know that he *could*.

Someone needed to stand up for Macy, and he was going to do it. Better late than never, as his dad always said. Those girls needed to pay, and they would. They probably thought they'd gotten away with it, but they were wrong.

In fact, he would find a way to make them pay in ways that would hurt worse than a good beating. They'd hurt Macy emotionally. Those horrible excuses for humans had nearly destroyed his sister.

He could still see the pain in Macy's eyes, which he'd pretty much ignored at the time. He felt bad, but instead of asking what he could do, he did what any twelve-year-old boy would do. He teased her. He thought if he could just get her mind off what the kids had been saying, she would forget about it.

Obviously, he hadn't understood just how much it had hurt her— or the lengths she would go to because of it. Going vegan was pretty extreme. Meeting a guy online, that wasn't so strange. But meeting him alone at night, that was pretty crazy. Even he knew that much.

He went to Macy's room. Hopefully she still hid her diaries in the same places she used to. He went to her bed and pulled back the mattress and felt for the loose fabric. When he did, he pulled it back and dug his hand around until he felt the diary. If Macy hadn't had such good hiding spots, the police would have found and taken them.

Alex pulled the diary and looked at it. He didn't recognize that one, so it had to have been new. At least newer. He hadn't read her diaries in a long time. He pulled it out and looked around for one of her hair clips. The clip was perfect for picking the lock—they always were.

He skimmed through the first pages; mostly she was griping about school. Then the whole tone changed when Snowflake, the family cat, died. Macy had loved him the most, always calling him a beautiful baby. Apparently, she had been so upset about it that her grades slipped.

Then the entries got even darker when she talked about the kids calling her "Muffin Top Macy," and she couldn't even eat lunch in the cafeteria without people mooing at her. Alex balled up his fist again, taking note of the names mentioned.

This was the type of crap that kids killed themselves over.

Those losers would pay—they would pay dearly. Alex would see to that.

He took the diary back to his room. Where had he put his phone? He dug around his messes until he finally found it.

Alex got the camera ready, he opened the diary to the pages about the girls at school and took pictures of the entries. Then uploaded them to his profile. He set them to public so the world could see.

Having the pictures was proof that Macy had written them. No one could argue.

Then he wrote a little intro to each picture, tagging as many of the girls as he could. He was "friends" with most of them, making it easy. Fury ran through him as he looked at the post button. With any luck, other kids would turn around and give them a taste of their own medicine. Those bitches were going to pay.

He pushed post.

Fretting

MACY'S MIND RACED as she did her copy work. She was all too aware of Luke sitting next to her. She kept sneaking peeks at him through the corner of her eyes. He was busy with his own work, appearing to be unaware of her.

The last three weeks she had tried to tell Luke the truth about her situation, but she had chickened out each time. In a way she was glad, because it gave her time to get to know him better—as well as she could only speak with him during their ten minute breaks twice a day.

Even though it wasn't a lot of time, it had been enough that she knew she could trust him. He wouldn't rat her out to Jonah or Chester. He wanted to help her, and even seemed to know that she wanted to tell him something.

Could things get worse if she told Luke that she'd been kidnapped? Maybe he would even help her.

But what if she was wrong about him? If Macy's desire to escape got into the wrong hands, she could get into trouble again. If she was publicly shamed, what letter would they pick? Would they give her B for blasphemy? Speaking out against Chester, who the almighty Jonah had received so many visions about? Or would it be an L for liar? They might just think she was making everything up about being kidnapped.

She sighed, louder than she had meant to.

Luke looked over at her, giving her a curious look. He was so cute Macy couldn't think of anything else when she looked at him.

Macy turned back to her papers and focused on her copy work, pretending he wasn't sitting there. The room felt like it was spinning out of control around her. Macy set her pencil down and took some deep breaths. White dots speckled her vision.

"Are you okay?" asked someone. Macy thought it might be Luke.

She tried to draw more deep breaths, but she couldn't get down far enough.

A hand rested on her shoulder. She looked up to see Rebekah. "Do you need air?"

Macy nodded.

"I'll go out with her," Luke said.

Alarm crossed over Rebekah's face. She pointed toward a girl and said something Macy couldn't understand.

Soon, she was standing outside with Luke and one of the girls he had introduced her to before.

Luke put his hand on Macy's shoulder and guided her to the side of the building. "Lean against the wall and put your head between your legs."

Macy looked at him like he was crazy.

"It'll help. Trust me."

Macy needed a sign. If she felt better after putting her head between her legs, then she would know she could tell Luke everything. Otherwise, if she didn't feel better, then it was a sign that he wasn't safe to talk to. She needed to stop being afraid of talking to him. He had done nothing other than be her friend for the last several weeks.

Macy positioned herself against the schoolhouse and bent over. She felt as ridiculous as could be, but hoped for an obvious sign.

"Stand up now. Slowly," Luke said.

Macy rose as slow as possible and looked around. The white dots were gone and her breathing came naturally. She had her answer. She would tell Luke everything as soon as possible.

"How do you feel?" he asked.

"Much better, actually."

"Do you want to stay out a bit longer?"

Macy nodded. She wanted to tell Luke about her being kidnapped right then, but didn't know anything about the girl. She looked her over at her. She had light brown hair and bright blue eyes. She looked nice enough, but then again so had Chester. Macy didn't know anything about the girl.

She gave Macy a look of concern. "Are you sure you're okay?"

"Yeah. I don't know what overcame me in there."

"I wouldn't worry about it. Everyone freaks out sometimes. It happens."

"What's your story?" Macy asked her.

"Like you, I was raised in the world. But then...well, life didn't exactly go the way I planned." She shrugged, looking away.

Luke looked at her. "Dorcas had a rough time transitioning to the lifestyle too."

"Dorcas? That must be rough." Where Macy was from, kids would have called her dork-us.

Dorcas smiled. "It's my Bible name."

"What's your real name?"

Dorcas and Luke exchanged a look. Luke turned to Macy. "We're not supposed to talk about our worldly names once we've received our new names."

"Of course. Sorry."

"What's your story?" Dorcas asked.

"Don't you know? Jonah found...my dad, and now here we are."

Dorcas looked around and stepped closer and lowered her voice. "Luke and I are trying to get out of here."

Macy's eyes widened. "What? Why are you telling me? I...I mean, I'm the daughter of Jonah's next prophet."

Luke stepped closer too. "There are a few of us who are working on it. I could tell by the look in your eyes at your unveiling that you didn't want to be here. I've been around long enough that it's easy to see who buys this stuff and who doesn't. After talking with you over the last few weeks, I know you want to leave also."

"But, you guys both have your new names. Doesn't that mean you've made your way through the ranks or something?" She turned to Luke. "The way you've been talking, it sounded like you believe everything they teach here."

"You're the daughter of Jonah's favorite. I had to feel you out even though I thought you wanted out too."

Dorcas nodded. "In case we can't find another way out, we're working our way up so that someday we'll be allowed to leave. You know, to look for new members. Only we won't come back."

Macy stared at them. Were they for real? "Wouldn't that take years?"

"More than likely," Dorcas said. "But at least it's better than nothing. I'd rather get out of here in ten years than never."

"I do want out too."

Luke and Dorcas exchanged a look.

"But I don't want to wait ten years," Macy said.

"Do you have a plan to get out sooner?" Luke asked.

"Well, no. But I want to come up with something. I need to get back to my family."

Dorcas tilted her head. "Chester isn't your family?"

"I…uh…well, it's complicated."

Luke stepped even closer. "Are you another kidnapped one?"

Macy's eyebrows came together. "How did you know? And what do you mean by another?"

"Are you really surprised that there are others like you?"

Macy shrugged.

"Trust me. You're far from the only one."

"Really?" Macy's stomach twisted in knots.

Dorcas nodded.

"Well, that gives us even more reason to break out of here. If there are others like me, we have to get them to their homes—their real homes."

Luke held up a hand. "Don't get anxious. One wrong move and we'll lose all chances of hope. We have to be meticulous and take everything at a snail's pace. It's fine to look for something else, but the best thing you can do is to try to move up the ranks, which means following the rules to a tee. Learn them, but don't internalize them."

"Isn't there a way to get out of the fence?" Macy asked.

"Have you looked at it?" Dorcas asked.

"What I mean," Macy said, "is that there has to be a weak spot. A loose board or something."

Dorcas shook her head. "There are people whose only job is to take care of the fence. They would spot something like that long before we did. And besides, it would be most suspicious if we were examining the fence."

"But it has to be worth a try. We could come up with a good reason for looking at the fence."

Luke gave me a sad look. "Shortly after my mom and I joined, someone did try to get out. A kid who was probably about our age."

"What happened?" Macy asked. She held her breath.

"I never saw him again."

Macy looked back and forth between them. "What does that mean?"

"He disappeared. No one ever mentioned him, either."

"You mean…you think he died?" Macy whispered.

"Do you have a better explanation?"

Macy felt sick. They were as bad as Chester. Maybe worse.

Dorcas looked at her. "We have to think long-term, and you actually have the best chance of getting out with your dad working so closely with Jonah, Abraham and Isaac. Your dad could take you with him sometime."

"But then, what? I couldn't just run and save myself. The rest of you, I would have to get you out too."

Dorcas shook her head. "For one thing—"

The door opened and Rebekah came out, looking at Macy. "How are you feeling?"

"Better now. The fresh air must have been what I needed."

"Good. Now come back inside. We have plenty more to do before we take our lunch break. We don't want to find too few pages done when Eve checks the work, now do we?"

"No, Teacher," Dorcas and Luke said in unison.

They went inside, but Macy couldn't focus. Luke and Dorcas actually wanted out, and not only that, but other kids in the same room as her had also been kidnapped.

The community was the perfect place for a criminal to go. Had the whole thing been masterminded by one? Was Jonah a mass murderer?

Or was he just power hungry, and it was only a coincidence that the community was the perfect getaway for someone who needed to hide?

Luke nudged her with his elbow. "At least *pretend* to do your work." He winked at her.

"Right." Macy picked up her pencil and looked at the book. She wrote a few sentences and then looked around the room. Who else in there was heartbroken because they'd been stolen from their families?

Macy felt something on her foot. She looked down and saw Luke's foot on top of hers. He moved it over so that it was next to hers with their ankles touching because the fabric of their pants had risen.

She looked over at him, eyes wide. There was no way that was allowed.

"What?" he whispered, his voice dripping with innocence. As if he didn't know.

Macy elbowed him, but hoped he wouldn't move his foot. He didn't.

She looked around the room and made eye contact with Rebekah. Rebekah nodded down, indicating for Macy to get to work.

Would Macy really have to pretend to work her way up the ranks in order to get out? Luke and Dorcas had probably been around long enough to know that there wasn't another way out.

Something bumped her knee and she looked over at Luke. He gave her a knowing look and she got back to work. She would have to wait until later to process everything.

Macy was lucky enough to have three people on her side. Now all she needed was a plan. But Luke would have to move his foot before she could concentrate enough to think of anything.

Undoing

C HAD GOT OUT of bed, careful not to wake Alyssa. She'd been awake half the night crying. So had he, actually. He hoped to God that the body didn't belong to Macy. If he thought about it, he knew that he would immediately start processing the emotions of it all, and he couldn't go there. Not unless he knew for sure.

Until he had proof of anything else, he was operating under the assumption that his daughter was safe somewhere. Where? Only she knew that, but he had to hold onto the hope. He wasn't giving up yet.

Since he couldn't sleep, he needed to get on his blog to publish the letters to Macy. In just the previous afternoon, the idea had exploded. Nearly everyone wanted to write their letter. He was going to end up with an entire series of posts rather than just one. Alyssa's parents wanted to write one, as did other relatives and some friends from school that Zoey had contacted.

Chad went to his office and sat down. He saw yesterday's coffee still sitting there. He looked at it, tempted. It was probably less than twelve hours old. He picked it up and drank. It tasted just as good as it had the day before, only cold. The caffeine gave him a jolt of energy and that was all he needed, anyway.

Taking another sip, he turned his laptop on. He opened the browser and it went to his profile, the last page he had opened. Chad almost typed in the address for his blog when he noticed an unusually high number of notifications. Fifty-six? He didn't even get that many when he took a weekend off.

His stomach twisted. Whatever it was, it couldn't be good. Had people been tagging him with more theories about the body? If that was the case, he would be unfriending and blocking each one of them, no matter who they were.

He scanned through the list of notifications, trying to make sense of them. There appeared to be some handwritten notes everyone was commenting on. He narrowed his eyes and nearly threw up all over his keyboard when he realized he was looking at Macy's handwriting.

Did someone find a note she left somewhere? Chad clicked on one of the images of the notes and noticed the date. It was nearly a year old.

He read it, feeling even worse. Had her friends actually said those things to her? Why hadn't she told him? He would have gone to the school and had it out with that wimp of a principal. Then he would have found the parents of those girls and given them a piece of his mind. No one talked about his daughter that way. No one.

He read through the comments left on the pictures of the notes, trying to catch up. Hundreds of people had left comments. Who had posted the pictures, anyway? He looked up and saw Alex's profile photo. He looked at the time of the post and read what Alex wrote.

Chad shook his head as he read through the rest of the comments. People were saying horrible things about the girls Macy had written about. People were arguing. Some were even using all-caps and swear words Chad had never heard before.

He clicked Alex's profile and saw several more pictures. Scrolling down, he saw there were even more. What had Alex done? Each one had over hundreds of comments each.

His head spun at the thought of trying to catch up. As he stared at the screen, new comments showed up faster than he could hope to keep up with.

What had Alex been thinking?

Posting those diary entries hadn't been the wisest of moves. Especially tagging the girls mentioned in them. The backlash could get ugly. From the looks of the comments, it already had.

Chad leaned back in his chair, scanning over the comments. Damage control. He had to think fast.

His head was spinning, so he got up and went to Alex's room. He opened the door to find Alex wrapped around his blankets. One bare leg was sticking out and Alex's head was hanging off the side of the bed. He was snoring.

Heart softening, Chad went over and moved Alex over to his pillow, fixing his blankets. How long had he been awake, reading Macy's diaries? How much time had he spent stewing over them?

Chad stood there, listening to Alex breathe. He hadn't done that since the kids were little. His heart ached, wishing he could run down the hall and check on his little girl. Blinking back tears, he leaned over and kissed Alex on the forehead.

He had mixed feelings about Alex posting the diary entries, especially since Chad was the one who would have to do damage control, but he couldn't be mad at Alex for standing up for his sister. When things calmed down, he would have to talk with him about discretion.

He couldn't blame Alex though. Those kids at school had been horrible. What else had Macy gone through? Those entries had to only be a snippet of the whole picture. Chad scanned the messy, darkened room for the diary, but couldn't find anything.

Chad sat in Alex's chair. Why hadn't he spent more time trying to figure out *why* Macy had done the things she had done? If he had asked her why she had wanted to go vegan, would she have opened up to him? Could he have helped her? Would she have avoided looking for love on the internet?

If he would have had any inkling of what she had been going through, things might have turned out differently. He knew it was useless looking back, thinking of what he could have done to change things. There was no going back.

He would have been a better dad—to both of them. And a better husband for that matter. But he couldn't do anything about that now. When Alex got up, he would ask him questions, and even more importantly, he would listen, really listen.

Looking over at Alex, he knew that would be a while. The kid had probably been up half the night, reading and posting. At least he was home, safe and sound. He was where they could take care of him.

Chad's heart swelled, watching his son sleep. At least he had a second chance. He hoped to God he would be given a second chance with

Macy, but either way, he was going to turn things around for Alex.

He would be a completely different dad from here on out.

Listening to the soft, rhythmic breathing, Chad felt himself getting sleepy. His eyelids grew heavy, and he didn't bother fighting them. He turned to the side in the over-sized chair and allowed himself to get some sleep too.

He felt hands on his shoulder, waking him. He blinked a few times, looking around. The room was bright like late morning. Alyssa stood in front of him, the light shining around her as if she was an angel.

"Is everything okay?" she asked. "Why are you sleeping here?"

Nothing would be okay until Macy came back, but at least he had the rest of his family and he had the chance to be a new man for them. He grabbed her and wrapped her in a tight hug.

She seemed surprised at first, but then put her arms around him too. "What's going on?"

Chad looked over at Alex, still sleeping. He put his finger over his mouth and pointed toward the door, indicating that they should talk somewhere else.

Alyssa nodded and then he stood and stretched. He took her hand and led her out of the room, closing the door behind them.

She looked at him, her eyes filled with worry. "Is Alex okay? Why were you sleeping in there?"

"Let's get some coffee and talk in the kitchen."

"Okay." It sounded more like a question, but she went toward the stairs.

He took her hand and then she gave him a look he couldn't quite read. It was filled with too many emotions, which he fully understood. When they got to the kitchen, he asked if she was hungry.

"No. Just coffee's fine."

He poured the ground beans into the coffee maker, he told her about Alex's posts. By the time he sat down with the two steaming cups of coffee, he was telling her about the comments.

She just stared at him. "I hate social media. I really do. What are we going to do?"

"The good thing is that Alex is doing this because he loves Macy."

"Have you already talked to him about this? Is that why you were in there?"

He shook his head. "He was already sleeping when I got in there."

"Everyone has already seen those posts?"

"If you judge by the number of comments left, yes. Hundreds. Probably a lot more by now."

Alyssa put her face into her hands. "I don't know how much more of this I can take."

"I'll take care of it; you can feel free to stay away from the internet. Let's just focus on writing our letters to Macy."

She looked up at him. "Kids are going to be furious with Alex for posting that stuff. What if those girls turn on Alex too?"

"I don't think they'd dare. There were so many people commenting about being pissed at what they did to Macy. They're going to be the ones who need to worry."

"But if those girls get bullied due to what Alex posted, he could get into trouble."

"It's a good thing he stayed home from school today."

Done

MACY HELD THE pillow over her head, trying to ignore the sounds from Chester and Rebekah's room. It was too gross to think about. She had been trying not to listen to them for weeks. She had lost count of the days.

She distracted herself by thinking about Luke. Her cheeks warmed just picturing his face. He was so cute and he actually liked her, at least as a friend. If she was going to be stuck in the community, at least she would enjoy spending more time with him.

Would he tell her more? Luke really hadn't wanted to talk about an escape plan that morning. His gorgeous face had been stressed telling her about the kid who had gone missing.

The more she thought about him, the more surprised she was that he had taken an interest in her. He probably just saw her as the key to getting out of there since he was working on that himself. She would gladly spend as much time as needed with him. But because of Chester, she would probably have to make sure that Dorcas was with them at all times.

Chester had questioned both her and Rebekah about who Macy had spent time with. Rebekah had told him that she was making friends with Dorcas, but didn't mention anything about Luke. Macy said the same things, and Chester didn't have a tantrum. He hadn't returned to the nice guy he had been, but at least he hadn't locked her up or yelled at Rebekah.

Macy was tired. The nightly meetings always ran so late, and then they had to get up early for school. She moved the pillow from her head, but then was greeted with the sounds of a squeaking bed.

"Ugh!" She pulled it back over her ears, closing her eyes. She just wanted some sleep. She was certain that Chester had to be sleep depriving her on purpose. It was one way to keep her tired and less likely fight back if all she wanted to do was sleep.

Whatever she did, she needed to start acting like she wanted to be a part of things. Luke had been pretty sure that she would be able to go out of the walls with Chester at some point. If that was true, she needed to do what she could to make that happen sooner rather than later.

On the other hand, she needed find out if there was another way out. Who knew how long it would be before she was allowed to go out with Chester? She would probably have to pass whatever test it was to get her biblical name first. Most everyone seemed to have those. She hadn't met anyone yet with a non-Biblical name.

Macy lifted the pillow from her ear and immediately heard the sounds again. How much longer could they go? It wasn't the Olympics. She covered her ears. She had discovered that thinking about her family and life back home made her too sad, so she tried to think about something else.

Her mind wandered to Heather. Was she still in the mental facility, wasting away? What if no one believed her about her mom? The fact that Chester was walking around free proved that no one had found a body at least.

When she got out, she would have to figure out where Heather was. She would find the hospital and tell them everything if it meant getting Heather free. Hopefully that would also be enough to get Chester into jail. Even though there might be no proof about his wife, he would have to go to jail for kidnapping.

He couldn't claim insanity. It was definitely premeditated, the way that he had stalked her and pretended to be a teenager to lure her out there. If he didn't go to jail, then maybe Heather was safer wherever she was.

As she thought about it, Macy finally drifted off to sleep.

She had dreams of climbing over the fence and getting cut on the wiring only to fall to the ground on the other side and end up attacked by wild animals with sharp teeth and ugly faces.

Macy sat up in a cold sweat, gasping for air. She looked around the room, taking a minute to figure out where she was. Her hair was a jumbled mess around her face and she clawed at it, getting it out of her way. Holding it between her fingers, she stared at the light color and shorter length Chester had forced her into.

The only good thing about her hair was that it was going to have dark roots soon, if she didn't already. There weren't mirrors available, she couldn't know for sure. Once Macy did have obvious roots, Chester would have to explain her hair to everyone. Or did it even matter? No one in the community knew what Heather looked like, so it probably didn't matter. And even if it did, he would have figured something out. He had everything planned out perfectly.

Anger and hate ran through her. Not only did he take her away from her family, but he had stripped her identity too. She moved her hand, looking at her hair in different angles, allowing the hate and rage to build.

She was *done*. Done being nice. Done pretending to be Heather. Done living in fear. It was over. She was going to find a way out if it killed her—and it very well might. She had spent enough time playing it safe. Where had it gotten her? Nowhere. She was still no closer to her family. In fact, she was probably farther away than ever.

They were probably worried sick. What if they thought she was dead? Chester would love nothing more. Then he wouldn't have to worry about them finding her, not that they would have any likelihood while in the community. No one in society even knew it existed.

A fresh wave of anger ran through her. She clutched her hair, ignoring the pain as she pulled against the roots. There were others like her—stolen from their families.

Macy pulled her hair tighter, almost enjoying the pain. She was so furious she wanted to scream. But she knew better. She would have to play nice for just a little bit longer, but she *was* going to find a way out. There was no way she was going to keep living like this.

She slid her fingers out of her hair and got out of bed. She looked outside, seeing no activity. The sun was barely coming up and the frost was especially thick. Macy shivered just looking at it. The room wasn't cold because somehow that wood stove always managed to keep the house warm. Probably because the walls were so thin, as evidenced by her knowing about Chester and Rebekah's nightly routine.

Sliding the curtain back into place, she paced the room. How was she going to get out? She couldn't do it without a plan. It was too bad she didn't have a bulldozer, then she could just bust through the fence. She paced faster, unable to think of anything realistic.

The last thing she wanted was to spend another week copying the crazy rules. If she had any say, she would find a way to have the community shut down. They had to know that kids had been kidnapped. That would be enough to have Eve and Jonah carted away, wouldn't it? Wasn't that aiding and abetting? With them and Chester gone, surely the community would dissolve.

Not only would she be a lost child returned home, but everyone would cheer for her for saving others just like her. She imagined the big welcome home. Confetti flying in the background. Her parents welcoming her with big smiles and bigger hugs. Alex would look at her adoringly and have nothing to tease her about—he would actually look up to her.

But first she had to get out. After she found a way out of the fence—there had to be a weak spot somewhere—she would run as fast as she could. She had never actually heard any animals outside the fence, so that had to be a myth told to keep people inside. Maybe she could find Chester's gun and take it with her.

She remembered back to when she went into his room at the farmhouse to get her cell phone. That hadn't gone well at all. She'd ended up locked up for nearly long enough to kill her since he hadn't given her any water that time. No. She would have to make her escape without his gun.

There was no way she would take a chance of him locking her up again. She needed a plan of escape that had nothing to do with him or any of his stuff.

The bedroom door opened, startling Macy. She turned around to see Rebekah.

"You're already up. Are you all right?"

Macy took a deep breath. She needed to calm down. "I just had a bad dream."

"Do you want to talk about it?"

"Not really. I suppose it's time to get up. Do we ever get a day off?"

"No. Sorry, Heather. We must work and learn every day. What would happen if the farmers took a day off? Or the prophets? Work is important. It keeps everything moving. Weekends are for the lazy."

Of course.

Rebekah tilted her head. "Are you sure you're okay?"

"I'm fine. I just need to shake off the nightmare."

"If you say so." It was obvious that Rebekah didn't believe her, but she closed the door behind her, giving Macy privacy to change.

Macy yanked off her pajama top and threw it across the room with full force. Being just a shirt, it didn't go far. She pulled off her pants and balled them up and threw them even harder. They bounced off the wall, half landing on the dresser. She slunk down to the ground and dissolved into tears. She pulled her knees up and wrapped her arms around her legs, sobbing as quietly as possible.

She wanted to scream. If she had her way, she would scream at Chester, right in his face. She would pull those big, ugly glasses off, and stomp on them until they were in a million little pieces. Then she would grab him and throw him against the wall, threatening him just like he'd done to her.

Then after beating him up, she would lock him up somewhere to rot until he couldn't go another hour without water. At that point, she would go in there with an ice-cold bottle and hold it just out of reach. Then she would gloat as he begged for it. Once he was in tears, she would drink it in front of him—the entire thing.

After that, he would stop breathing and not be able to hurt anyone ever again.

Anger

MACY SAT AT the table, not looking at Chester or Rebekah. She was too busy planning her escape. Chester yammered on about something, but Macy didn't care.

Anger burned inside of her. She had never hated anyone as much as she hated Chester that moment. She hated him not only for every single thing he had done to her, but also for what he had done to Heather and her mom. Someone so cruel didn't deserve to live, much less be revered by an entire community.

Macy's mom had once told her that people weren't evil, but rather that they only did bad things. Macy knew her mom was wrong about that. Chester was the embodiment of evil. If she believed in a devil, she would think he had come to the earth in the form of a human in Chester.

"Are you listening, Heather?" he asked.

She looked up at him, forgetting to hide her disdain.

"What's that look for? Did I do something to you?"

"She had a bad dream," Rebekah said, too fast.

"Don't cover for her. What's going on, Heather?"

Macy wanted to scream that she wasn't Heather, but she knew that wouldn't get her anywhere except locked up. She took a deep breath and forced her true feelings off her face. "Rebekah's right. I'm in a bad mood because of my dream. I can't shake it."

"Don't take your foul mood out on me. What do you say?"

"What?" Macy asked.

Chester stared at her through his thick, ugly glasses. "When you're rude to someone without cause, there's something you need to say.

What is it?"

Macy wanted to punch those glasses right into his skull. Even if her hand ended up bloody and needing stitches, it would be worth it.

"Say sorry," Rebekah whispered.

Not wanting to end up locked up, Macy muttered a barely audible *sorry.*

"What's that? I can't hear you." Chester furrowed his ugly, bushy eyebrows.

Macy pictured his glasses tearing his face apart as she punched him. "I'm sorry I was rude."

"Thank you. Now that wasn't so hard, was it?" He went back to eating his food.

She glared at him before going back to her breakfast. Somehow she made it through the meal without pissing him off or killing him with her bare hands.

On the walk to school, Rebekah was talking about proper behavior, but Macy couldn't pay attention.

She knew Rebekah was only trying to help, but Macy didn't want help. She wanted *out.*

When Macy sat at the desk, Luke gave her a strange look. "Are you okay, Heather?"

The anger built further at being called Heather again. Macy pursed her lips and shook her head.

"What's going on?" he whispered.

She clenched her fists. "I'm going to find a way out of here. Today."

"Whoa. Wait, Heather. You can't just do that." Luke turned and looked directly at her. "Remember what we talked about yesterday? Taking everything slowly and then—"

"You can do that if you want. I'm not waiting. I need to get back to my family, and I'm not waiting ten years. I'm not even waiting a week."

"Think about this first. You can get out with your dad soon. Have you been paying attention what Jonah has been saying about him in the nightly meetings? I know you're not used to the way things usually work, but I've never seen anyone move through the ranks so fast. You won't have to wait long."

A noise caught Macy's attention. Rebekah was standing in front of them, giving them a look of warning. "Is there a problem? You two should be working."

"No problem," Luke said. "I'm just helping Heather to understand the inner workings of the community. She was a little confused on a point."

Rebekah nodded. "Thank you, Luke. I think you're distracting some of the other students, so if you need to continue discussing this, grab Dorcas and you three can have a discussion group outside."

Luke nodded. "Yes, Teacher." He turned to Macy. "Do you need further explanation?"

Macy nodded, too angry to speak.

She went outside with Luke and Dorcas. Luke spoke, but Macy wasn't paying attention. She was looking into the distance to see if the fence was visible, but it was too far away to see anything.

"Do you have a plan?" Dorcas asked.

Macy looked at her. "There has to be a way out. There just has to. It isn't possible for them to have every inch of this place sealed tight."

Luke and Dorcas exchanged a worried look.

"Don't you remember what we told you about the one kid who tried to escape?" Luke asked. "No one knows what happened to him."

Macy clenched her fists. "Maybe because they're embarrassed that he escaped and they couldn't do anything about it."

Dorcas put a hand on Macy's arm. "No. That's not what happened. If you really want out, you've got to have patience."

"Patience? You want patience? You have no idea what I've been through the last few months or however long it's been." She shook her head. "It doesn't matter. I'm done playing by everyone else's rules."

Luke stood taller. "What's your plan?"

"Plan? I have none, except to find a way out of here. The sooner the better."

"I really don't want to see anything happen to you. We need more than that."

"And I don't want to spend another night here. Even if I have to do something extreme, I will."

"Like what?" Dorcas asked, looking worried. "You could get hurt."

"You guys don't have to join me if you don't want to. No need for you to risk yourselves."

"I just need more than what you're giving me," Dorcas said. "Luke and I have had our plan for a long time, and the one thing I like about it is that it's safe."

"And it's too slow. You guys probably have nice families to go home to here, or at least your actual families. I don't have that. All I have is—"

Luke stepped closer. "Shh. Don't talk about it too loud. You're getting worked up. There are lots of kids, even some adults, who have been brought in here that are kidnapped too. You're not alone, but the ones who survive, they take it slowly."

"Where has slow gotten them? They're still here. Some of them have probably either given up or worse, accepted this life. I'm not going to do that."

Luke stared into her eyes, giving her a look that made Macy's heart skip a beat. "You do have people who care about you, even if you don't feel it at home. People who don't want to see you hurt." He took her hand.

Macy swallowed, feeling her anger dissipate. She knew that by *people* he meant himself. Macy didn't want to do anything to put him in danger, either. But what was she supposed to do? There was no way she was going to wait years to escape.

He took another step closer. "I know you're frustrated. You have every right to be. Chester shouldn't have taken you away from your family or brought you here. Life gave you a really unfair hand of cards, but don't do something rash and throw it all away."

Macy stared into his eyes, unable to find her voice.

"Will you take a day to think about it? Maybe when you calm down, you'll be able to think of an actual plan."

"And by then I'll be ready to hide in a corner again, scared and helpless. Who's going to miss me if something does happen? I'll bet you my family already thinks I'm dead."

The look on Luke's face told her that he would be crushed if something happened to her. "Don't go on a suicide mission. Please, Heather."

"My name's—"

Dorcas cleared her throat.

Macy looked up, and Luke let go of her hand, stepping back.

The schoolhouse door opened and Rebekah came outside. She smiled. "How is everything going? Are you getting your questions answered, Heather?"

Macy took a small step back. "Yes. They're really helping me to understand how things work around here."

"Good. Why don't you three come on in? I wouldn't want anyone thinking that you're getting special treatment because of our family situation."

Luke gave Macy a look, almost begging her not to do anything stupid. Her heart fluttered and she looked away. They went inside and she started her copy work, not paying attention to what she was writing. At least her hand had finally adjusted to all the writing.

Her mind was on fire. She was all too aware of Luke sitting next to her, doing his own copying. She wanted to turn and watch him, and that very desire made her angry with herself.

She needed to focus on getting out of the stupid community, not thinking about him. How was that going to help her? And why couldn't she stop thinking about Luke?

Macy's stomach kept doing flip-flops. She didn't feel nervous. What was her problem? She needed to think about Chester and how much she hated him. That was the only way she was going to stay focused on what needed to be done. Thinking about Luke was only distracting her—big time.

The morning dragged on. She didn't care about the work in front of her and she kept wanting to sneak peeks at Luke, and each time she gave in and did, he caught her looking at him.

Macy missed Zoey more than ever. She wanted to talk to her best friend about Luke, the first boy who had ever paid her any real attention. Of course he didn't know that she used to be "Muffin Top

Macy." But after everything Chester had put her through, Macy was thinner than ever.

She remembered wanting to be skinny at any cost. How stupid she had been—wishing it at *any* cost. She'd gladly go back to her muffin top if it meant being back home, having never met Chester or his storm shelter where he had starved her until she agreed to take on Heather's identity.

When Rebekah finally announced the morning break, Macy decided she needed to make a run for it as soon as she got outside. Luke was only proving to be a distraction and she needed to get away. No more whining or wishing, it was time for action.

Once she made it outside, she looked around, making sure that no adults were anywhere in sight. The last thing she needed was to run, only to have prophets chase after her. Then she would end up like the one kid who mysteriously disappeared.

Everything was clear, so she burst into a run, heading left, where she was sure the fence was closest. She ducked between a couple of buildings and headed for a group of trees.

Footsteps could be heard from behind. Macy picked up her speed, not looking back. Why hadn't she listened to her parents and joined some kind of sports team? She breathed hard, gasping for air. She hadn't been used to running before Chester took her, and she was in even worse shape after a couple of months of his torture.

Macy looked down, seeing a root sticking up out of the ground, but it was too late. She stumbled over it and went down. It felt like slow motion, but she couldn't do anything to stop from falling. She landed with a hard thud, frost crunching under her.

A hand grasped her shoulder.

Impatience

M ACY ROLLED OVER, ready to fight. It was Luke who had her shoulder.

"What are you doing?" he asked.

"I'm finding a way out of here."

He shook his head. "Now?"

She sat up. "Yes, now."

"Can't you at least wait until it's dark?"

"No."

He looked around. "We'd better get back to the schoolhouse."

"I can't go back. I won't."

Luke grabbed her hand and helped her up to stand. "You need to. We'll meet tonight and figure something out."

Her heart raced. She noticed he hadn't let go of her hand. She shook her head. "I don't want to get you in trouble too if it doesn't work out."

"I'm already involved. Let's go."

"But, I can't—"

He walked, taking her along by default. "Your arrival has shown me that I need to step up my plan. I need to get the same fire as I see in your eyes."

"Like I said, I don't want to get you involved."

"And I'm already well past that point." He stopped and turned, looking into her eyes. He took her other hand. "What's your real name?"

"What?"

"I've noticed you flinch when you're called Heather. I want to know your real name."

Did she dare tell him? What if he accidentally called her Macy in front of Rebekah?

"I won't tell anyone. I just want to know who you really are."

She hesitated. "It's Macy Mercer."

"Macy. That's really pretty. It suits you." He squeezed her hands. "We'd better get back before we get into trouble. Then we wouldn't be able to follow our plan tonight, Macy."

Her heart skipped a beat. She liked the way her name rolled off his tongue.

"Okay."

He let go of her hands and they made their way back to the school house.

Rebekah ran up to them before they even crossed the dirt road. "Are you okay, Heather? What happened?"

Macy stared at her, not knowing what to say.

"She got spooked, Teacher. Do you hear the sounds of the farm slaughter?"

Rebekah looked around, appearing to listen. "No."

"Well, it was going on when we came outside," Luke said. "Heather had never heard it before and she thought something was wrong. She didn't even think, only reacted. Right, Heather?"

"Yeah. It scared me. I'm sorry."

Rebekah looked relieved. "Next time something like that happens, please ask someone rather than just taking off." She leaned close to Macy. "We don't need word of this getting back to your dad, you know what I mean?"

"I know. I'm sorry."

"Let's get back into the classroom." She led them back to the schoolhouse, telling the other kids that everything was fine.

Everyone looked at Macy and Luke, but said nothing. Dorcas gave her a knowing and sympathetic look.

When they sat down, Macy's heart still raced. Was it from running, the scare of being chased, or from Luke holding her hands again? Her heart fluttered.

He tapped her foot with his. She looked over at him and he raised an eyebrow and held up his pencil.

"Oh, right." She picked up her pencil and wrote where she'd left off. The rest of the morning dragged on until lunch finally arrived.

On the way back to the house, Rebekah warned Macy not to say anything about running off to Chester. It was obvious by the look on her face that she was still spooked about his tantrum a few weeks earlier.

When Rebekah and Macy sat down to eat lunch, Chester still hadn't arrived. That made her more nervous than if he would have actually been there. "Where is he?"

"He mentioned that Jonah and Abraham might take him out into the world soon to see if they could find anyone needing to join the community. Let me pray."

They bowed their heads and then ate after Rebekah was done with the prayer.

"How long will they be out?" Macy asked.

"Could be until the meeting tonight. It depends on whether or not they find anyone."

Macy tried to mask the excitement. If Chester and Jonah were gone, that might make it even easier to escape.

"Are you feeling better?"

Macy looked at Rebekah, confused.

"You were spooked from hearing the sounds of slaughter, remember?"

"Right. Yeah, I'm fine now." She couldn't tell by the look on Rebekah's face if she believed Luke's story or not. She didn't appear upset if she did doubt. It was also something she didn't want to discuss. "I want to hear more about your band. You told me a little that first morning, but nothing since then."

"I nearly forgot about that." She smiled, looking lost in thought for a moment. "We were really big on the indie scene on the east coast. We were performing in big clubs up and down the coast and had our sights set on Hollywood. But we figured we had a better chance starting out in Seattle. It's big, but not as big, you know?"

Macy nodded, her mouth full of food.

"The lead singer got busted for buying drugs and ratted us out. I was actually running from the cops when I ran into Jonah. They were going to arrest me and I already had a record, so the last thing I wanted was to get caught. He could see the desperation in my eyes. When he told me about the community, I thought it would be the perfect place to hide out for a while."

"But you're still here." Not that she could get out if she wanted to. "Did you ever want to leave?"

Rebekah set her glass down. "At first I was just glad to have somewhere to rest. I was pretty strung out. Eve took care of me for a couple weeks, telling me all about the community the entire time. By the time I had my unveiling and received this house, I was ready to stay. Eve and Jonah both said that I had a lot of potential. Since I had gone to school for teaching, they decided to put that to use."

"So you want to stay here forever? You never think about leaving?"

"This is much better than going to jail. I've been there, and there's nothing desirable. At least here I'm free. I can walk around without a care. Now I can even have a family."

Macy froze. The way that she said family didn't sit right with her. "Are you…expecting?"

Rebekah's face turned red. "It's too soon to tell for sure, but I think so. A woman knows these things. You can't say anything. Your dad wanted to tell you."

Why was Macy surprised? The way they went at it, she was probably carrying a litter. "Well, congratulations." Hopefully it was a little Rebekah, and not a little Chester.

She beamed. "I'm really excited. And I know you'll make a wonderful big sister. Your dad has told me how you've always wanted a sibling."

Macy fought a scowl. She *had* a sibling that she was very happy with, and she was quite eager to get back to him. "Yeah, that'll be great."

Rebekah talked about knitting baby clothes and teaching Macy how to so they could work on it together. Macy nodded, not saying anything. If she had her way, she'd be running through the woods that night looking for the highway.

"We'd better get lunch cleaned up." Rebekah stood up. "Are you all right? You're being quiet."

She forced a weak smile. "Just thinking about how great it's going to be having a baby around."

Rebekah's face lit up. "Oh, good."

They cleaned up and went back to the school. Macy made a beeline for Luke as soon as she saw him. "You haven't chickened out, have you?"

He laughed. The way the skin around his eyes crinkled made Macy melt.

Luke shook his head. "On the contrary." He tilted his head, indicating for her to follow him. Macy followed him to furthest corner of the schoolyard, where the younger kids were milling about.

Luke stood as close to Macy as possible without touching her. "Do you want to know my plan?"

"Tell me."

"We're going to burn down part of the fence and run."

Macy's eyes widened. It was brilliant. "How?"

"With matches of course. I've actually been saving them up. One here and there. I've got quite a collection."

"Why? Stamps aren't good enough for you?"

"I told you, I've been planning on escaping for a long time. I've had several ideas brewing."

"What about waiting twenty years before Jonah would take you outside?"

"That's my long-term plan. I'm not opposed to taking advantage of an opportunity arising, and in fact I've always wanted to be ready for such an event."

"When are we going to do this?"

"The way I see it, we have two options. We can try to sneak out during the meeting, when everyone is distracted or we can wait until everyone is asleep. You stay awake until I tap on your window."

Macy thought about it. "What do you think is better?"

"If Chester is in the spotlight with Jonah, then we shouldn't go then. It's possible they could call you to the front, and once it's discovered that you're missing, all hell is going to break loose. At least at night, everyone will be sleeping."

Butterflies danced in her stomach. They were really going to make a break for it that night.

"What do you think? Can you wait until everyone is sleeping?"

"I sure can."

Mall

"CAN WE GIVE Alex back his electronics?" Alyssa asked. "He's been punished long enough."

Chad looked up from his laptop. He hadn't even heard Alyssa come in.

"This can't go on forever. Especially since he was only trying to protect his sister."

He closed the laptop. "You know that was the agreement to keep him from being suspended."

"Who cares? He doesn't want to go back anyway. I can homeschool him or we can sign him up for that charter school and he can do everything online. I don't want to punish him any more, Chad."

"It's not like we've sent him into exile. Zoey comes over all the time and he's had several of his other friends come by. He's been watching movies with you. He's not without human contact."

Alyssa begged him with her eyes. "Come on. This isn't the time to lay down the law. Look what happened when we were too hard on Macy."

"You're going to bring that up?" Anger ran through him. "This has nothing to do with that, and for your information, if we would have taken away her laptop and phone, guess what? She wouldn't have been *able* to contact that child abductor. She'd still be here."

"Oh, so you don't think she could have borrowed someone's tablet at school and emailed him?"

Chad dug his nails into the desk, not wanting to take out his anger on Alyssa. He was angry enough to break something. He took a deep breath and counted to ten backwards. "Call the school and find out how much longer they want this punishment to last. If it's more than a few days, fine, look into charter schools or homeschooling or whatever you feel like."

"Really?"

"Yeah. While you do that, I need to call Detective Fleshman. You'd think they'd have called about the results from the body. Even if they hadn't found anything yet, they should at least keep us in the loop."

"No news is good news, right?" Alyssa asked. She turned around and left, closing the door behind her.

Chad picked up his phone and called Fleshman, who answered right away. "Chad, I wish I had answers for you. As I told you, your family's dental records were in the part of the office that was destroyed by the fire and they didn't keep those online."

"I know that!" Chad stood up, sending his wheeled chair into the wall. "Surely, you have something to tell me. I'm not waiting for takeout—this is my daughter's life."

"We're doing everything we can. It's out of our hands now that the body has been sent to Seattle. We're anxious to know the results too, but this isn't TV. DNA results don't come back in five minutes. There's a lot to consider. They're running the girl's fingerprints through the system, but again, everything takes time—weeks, usually."

"What else are you doing? Besides waiting on Seattle?"

"We're going through all the clues. Have you seen the room we have dedicated to Macy's case? Even with my entire team focused on it, nothing is moving as fast as any of us would like. I have a son, Chad. I can imagine what you're going through. If it was my boy missing, I'd be pulling my hair out. I'm working as diligently as if it was him."

Chad let out long, slow breath. "I do appreciate everything you guys are doing."

"And I answer your calls day or night, whether I'm at work or home."

"Am I bothering you at home?"

"You're not bothering me, Chad."

So he *was* calling him at home. "I don't want to keep you. Can you call me when you're on the clock?"

"I'd be glad to."

"Thanks." He hung up and looked around his office. It felt suffocating. In fact, the entire house did. He went upstairs and found Alyssa on the phone. "What's going on?" he asked.

"The school has me on hold."

"I'm going to the store. Need anything?"

She shook her head. "Did you hear anything?"

"Still waiting on Seattle, because tests take time and our dentist is an idiot."

"Yes, I'm still here," Alyssa said into the phone.

Chad waved and headed for the door. He knew he probably looked like a wreck, but he didn't even care enough to grab a baseball cap. Everyone knew who he was thanks to the news, so no one would give it a second thought if he looked tired and stressed.

He got into his car and drove to the grocery store. Once parked, he sat in the car for a few minutes. They didn't need anything. What was he doing there? Was he going to wander around, squeezing melons? Comparing prices? That was ridiculous. The mall wasn't so far away. He could at least wander and window shop.

Not only that, but that's where Macy's clothes and phone had been found. Maybe he could find a new clue.

Chad turned the ignition and drove to the mall. He parked as far away as possible and meandered through the parking lot, starting with the edge, looking for anything that could be a clue. There was nothing other than random litter, probably dropped from people leaving the movie theater.

He made his way to the entrance, looking for a valuable piece of evidence. He couldn't allow himself to miss anything. If there was anything he could do to help Macy, he had to do it.

Eyes still to the ground, he went inside. He hadn't seen anything other than trash, and given that they had a janitorial staff, anything useful would have been cleaned up and removed. He took his attention from the ground and looked around at the stores. Nothing interested him—how could it?

As he meandered, Chad noticed people whispering. Now he regretted not grabbing a baseball cap. He could've lowered it over his face to get attention away from him.

He would just have to ignore them, as uncomfortable as it was. Then a thought hit him: this must have been what Macy felt like at school. Only worse, being young and not understanding the nature of people who apparently didn't grow up just because they got older. Chad noticed ladies in their fifties whispering and pointing at him.

Way to outgrow high school, ladies, he thought sarcastically.

Maybe the mall hadn't been a good idea. Eyes burned his back, so he picked up his pace. His stomach was rumbling and he couldn't even remember the last time he ate. Chad headed for the courtyard. He ordered some burritos and sat down at a table in the corner.

People appeared to be more interested in their food than him at least. Just as he bit down, someone stopped next to the table. He groaned and looked up.

Lydia stood there, looking at him with a pitiful expression. "Mind if I sit?"

Chad swallowed his food. "I thought I made myself clear. We can't do this anymore."

"Can't we just have a seat at the same table? We're neighbors. No one is going to question anything. I've been so worried about you. The news—"

"Fine. Sit. I'm not going to be here long anyway."

She sat and ate from her own tray of food.

Chad noticed she had gotten a haircut, but he knew better than to say anything.

"You don't look so good, Chad. How are you holding up? The news—"

"I really don't want to talk about the news. It's a four letter word in our house these days." He tried to avoid her dark, beautiful eyes. He knew he was predisposed to pouring out his soul to her.

That had been what had gotten him into trouble in the first place. Alyssa was shutting him out, and Lydia was so eager to hear anything he had to say. Dean was almost never home and even when he was, he didn't pay attention to Lydia. It was a perfect setup.

"Do you need anything?" she asked.

"My daughter."

"You don't think that girl they found—?"

"No!" He bit into his burrito. Coming to the mall definitely had been a bad decision.

"I'm sorry. I've really missed you. We always had the best—"

"Lydia," Chad hissed. He looked around to make sure no one was paying any attention to them.

"I was going to say we have the best talks." She rolled her eyes. "I could always tell you anything, and you never judged me. It went both ways."

"I'm talking to Alyssa now. You should try opening up to Dean. Rekindle whatever it was that attracted you two in the first place."

She shook her head. "I've tried. I'm certain that he's seeing someone else."

"Then dump his sorry butt. He doesn't know what he's missing. You deserve better, but I can't be the one to give you what you do deserve. I'd be lying if I said otherwise. You're smart, you're fun, and you're talented. There are a lot of guys out there who would be more than happy to give you what Dean won't."

Lydia tugged on a strand of thick, dark hair. "I can't move on."

"Dean would have to give you spousal support since you've been a housewife all this time. You wouldn't be out of money."

"That's not what I mean. Sure, the money is why I stay, but I meant I can't move onto another man when I'm still in love." Lydia stared into his eyes.

Chad returned the stare, but with wide eyes. She was *in love* with him? They'd had a good thing before he cut her off—and it hadn't been easy. But he never would have guessed she was in love.

She continued to stare at him with eagerness in her eyes.

If he said one word, Lydia would bring him back to her large, empty house in a heartbeat. Chad cleared his throat. "I should probably get back home. I just came here to uh…um, look for clues."

"Are you Scooby Doo now?"

"Tell Dean I said hi."

Lydia frowned. "I guess you're not the mood to joke around."

Chad narrowed his eyes. "No, actually I'm not." He looked around and lowered his voice. "I'm a family man. I made a *mistake*."

She looked like she had been slapped.

"And I'm sorry I hurt you. Really I am. Like I said, you deserve a lot better—than both Dean and me. Alyssa deserves better too and given our history and the fact that we have a family together, I'm doing whatever I can to be that for her now."

"That's exactly why I'm having such a hard time moving on. I wish Dean was the kind of man that you are."

"Maybe if you show him the kind of attention you gave me, he'll come around." He finished off the burrito, eager to get through the next one. Lydia didn't look like she was planning to leave the table anytime soon.

As he unwrapped the last burrito, he saw Sandra McMillan, another neighbor. She was headed their way.

Chad's heart sank. Would she tell Alyssa that she'd seen Chad eating with Lydia?

Sandra waved and sat down. Her big, blonde hair nearly took up the entire table. "All we need is a few more neighbors and we would have an impromptu HOA meeting." She laughed loudly.

Lydia gave a fake smile—Chad could see right through it. "Good one," Lydia said. "How are you, Sandra?"

"Pretty good. Just trying to figure out how to get the new family in 1612 to remove those hideous flamingos. Can you believe them?"

"They're awful," Lydia said, though it was obvious that Lydia couldn't have cared less.

Sandra turned to Chad, her makeup-heavy eyes wide. "And how are you doing, sweetie?" She continued on, not giving him a chance to answer. "I've been talking with some of the other neighbors about forming another search party, but I wanted to find out what you guys want. What with everything the news has been saying lately." She shook her head. "The whole thing is awful, just awful."

Chad shoved as much burrito into as mouth as he could. At least Sandra was oblivious to the tension between Lydia and Chad.

Not even stopping to take a breath, Sandra turned back to Lydia. "And how is Dean? I haven't seen him at a meeting in so long. Does he still travel for work? Where is he now, dear?"

"He's in Siberia at the moment. Then he'll be off to India, and then Germany before he comes home to have some dinner and leave again."

Sandra patted Lydia's hand. "You poor, poor thing. You must get so lonely." She shook her head. "It's just too bad you two can't have any kids. They would be the perfect distraction for you."

Lydia and Chad exchanged a look. How could Sandra be so dense? That was a topic that ripped Lydia's heart out, and even if it wasn't, that was such an insensitive thing to say.

Chad swallowed the last of his food and stood up. "It was nice running into you ladies, but I need to get back home to my family."

Telling

Z OEY ROLLED OVER in bed. Her entire body ached and she just wanted to go back to sleep. Though she'd slept most of the day, she didn't feel like she had. Her mind raced, chasing sleep away.

Had they found anything out about that body? Her mom said that the chances weren't likely that it was Macy and not to worry about it. How would she know? No one knew anything.

Valerie was obviously worried about Zoey. She hadn't even made her go back to school since the body was found. She had also been on the phone with Zoey's dad every day. The night before, she'd wanted Zoey to talk with him, but Zoey refused. What was she supposed to say?

Her bedroom door opened and her mom came in. "Oh, good. You're awake. I just got off the phone with your dad, and he said as soon as he officially retires, he's coming here. He's been talking with the coach, explaining that he has a family crisis and that with his injury, he can't play anyway."

Zoey rolled her eyes. "So?"

"I want you to be prepared."

"He's the one who needs to be prepared," she muttered.

Valerie raised an eyebrow. "What does that mean?"

Zoey sat up. "That I'm going to give him a piece of my mind. Forget a piece—he's getting the whole thing. He's never been here for me, and I don't need him now."

"That's not entirely fair. It was an agreement that we had for him to stay there."

"So then you're equally at fault. But at least you've been here."

"He hasn't been completely absent. He's sent money all these years when he didn't have to."

"That's not being a father. He's a sperm donor and nothing more."

"Zoey! You'd better not talk to him like this when he gets here."

"Then you should tell him to stay in Japan, because I'm not holding back."

"He wants to be a part of your life."

"So all it took was me getting knocked up? Why didn't you tell me that sooner? I could have done that two and a half years ago."

Her mom sighed. "Obviously, he can't change the past, but he wants to make good on everything now."

"Sure. His career is over. If it was going strong, he wouldn't care about me, would he?"

"He's always cared. If he didn't—"

"Then he wouldn't have sent the money. Got it. It's too little, too late."

"Just give him a chance."

"Why?" Angry tears filled her eyes. "Why should I? Just because he supplied some DNA and sent some money? Now he feels guilty because I'm going to make him a grandparent. Except that he's not going to be a grandparent. You know why? Because he would have to be a dad first, and he's not! Unless he's gone and had kids with some other chick, guess what. He's not a dad. He's certainly not one to me."

Her mom sat on the bed. "I know you're having a hard time, and you have all those hormones making it worse, but please give him a chance. If you want to be mad at someone, be mad at me."

"If I *want* to be mad? I just want to be happy. Actually, no. You really want to know what I want?"

"What?"

"A cigarette."

Her mom's eyes widened, and her face turned pale. "What?" she whispered.

"That's right! I've been smoking, and that's the one thing I actually want. You wouldn't believe the havoc not having any has wrecked upon my body."

Her mom stared, not saying a word.

Zoey's eyebrows came together. *Good. Hit her where it really hurt.*

"You've really been smoking?"

"Yeah. Want to make something of it?" Zoey squeezed her covers.

"Even after your uncle died of cancer?"

"Yes. And I know how you feel about smoking, but I did it anyway. Turns out I'm pretty good at keeping secrets too. Wonder where I got it from?" Zoey narrowed her eyes.

Valerie got up without a word and left the room.

Zoey felt a little bad, but her mom had it had it coming.

She picked up her phone to check for texts. Alex hadn't sent her anything. She sent him a text asking if he was awake. Then she remembered that his parents had taken all of his stuff away after he'd posted Macy's diary entries.

When would he get those back? It was like living in the days before electricity. How did anyone survive before laptops and cell phones? Kids must have sneaked out way more back in those days. It was totally barbaric.

Her phone buzzed, startling her. She had a text from Alex: *He's still grounded, but hopefully will have his stuff back today. You're more than welcome to come over.*

Zoey smiled. *Thanks, Alyssa.* At least someone had a mom who got it.

She put her phone away. Going to the Mercer's house sounded like a good idea. It would be a lot better than hanging out with her mom. Especially after Zoey told her about the cigarettes.

She got into the shower and then went downstairs to find something to eat that wouldn't make her stomach turn. Wasn't pregnancy supposed to make people eat and eat? She had already lost ten pounds because everything sounded gross. Even her favorite foods had been making her gag at the thought of eating them.

As she looked through the pantry and the fridge, nothing looked good. She would probably lose more weight, because she wasn't going to eat anything that made her gag.

Zoey went to the door and put on a pair of shoes.

"Where do you think you're going?"

She looked up to see her mom standing at the end of the hall, hands on her hips.

"Over to the Mercers."

"No, you're not."

"Yes, I am." Zoey stared at her, daring Valerie to try to stop her.

"Not after the way you treated me up there."

"What? All I did was tell you the truth."

"How long?"

"How long what?"

"Don't give me that. How long have you been smoking?"

"I don't know. A while."

"You don't know? How could you not know?"

"Well, it's not like I wrote down the date of my first one. I'm not going to throw a party on the anniversary."

"Shut up, Zoey. Clearly I'm not looking for an exact date. *About* how long have you been smoking?"

"I really don't know. Okay? When Macy and I got scheduled for opposite lunch periods, I found some new kids to hang out with. They always went out to smoke. At first, I just went with them. Then one day I tried one and hated it. I didn't go near them for a while, but then at some point I tried again."

"What made the difference?"

Alex. Not that she was going to rat him out.

"Whatever, Zoey. Don't answer me. Where were you able to smoke at school? They have strict policies against drugs."

Zoey snorted. "The policies may be strict, but they don't enforce them. There's a big space in the blackberry bushes between the high school and junior high. That's where the smokers go. That and under the bleachers when it rains. Can I go now?"

"Why? Why would you start smoking? Especially after seeing everything your uncle went through?"

"Because sometimes I do things just because I want to, or because I want to make my friends happy." She stared at her mom, daring her to keep going with the conversation.

"Some things are no-brainers, and this is one of them. You saw what he went through."

"Doesn't mean I'll go through it myself."

Valerie took a deep breath, looking away. It looked like she was counting silently. "Do you promise not to go back to smoking?"

Zoey grabbed her aching head. "I'm not going to make a promise I can't keep."

"Zoey!"

"Can I go now?"

"Maybe you should tell Alex about your smoking. He could probably talk some sense into you. At least you would listen to him."

"Okay, I'll do that. Can I go?"

Valerie waved her toward the door, looking away again.

Zoey got out as fast as she could, before she could give her mom a chance to start talking again. She breathed in the crisp, cold air. As she walked down the sidewalk, she looked up at the sky and saw a cloud that looked like a pouncing cat. Zoey couldn't help remembering all the stories she and Macy had made up about cloud animals over the years.

Was Macy okay? Was it possible that she was happy? Maybe she was; she just couldn't get a hold of anyone since she didn't have her phone.

Blinking back tears, Zoey walked up to the Mercer's door. Zoey almost knocked, but suddenly felt overwhelmed with grief. She wanted Macy more than ever. They had always talked over everything in each other's lives. So much had happened in such a short time, and Zoey hadn't been able to tell her best friend any of it.

She sat on the steps and cried into her hands. She didn't need her dad—she'd gotten along just fine without him all this time. What she needed was Macy. It was great being able to talk with Alex, and Zoey couldn't have asked for a better boyfriend, but he still wasn't Macy.

He was also just as close to everything as Zoey was. His sister was missing and he was the baby's father. For all the new friends she had made over the last year or so, there wasn't one that she wanted to talk to about any of this.

Sniffling, she wiped her eyes and nose. She didn't want anyone to see her like this. She looked across the street, having forgotten to check for the media van. It wasn't there, but she thought she saw the back of a police car.

Her stomach twisted, making her feel nauseated. Zoey leaned against the nearest post, trying to imagine life a year from now if Macy was still gone. She'd have had a baby with Alex.

What if Macy was back by then? If so, would she be mad at Zoey for putting her baby brother in this situation?

New tears filled her eyes and she continued to look around the yard through her blurry vision. Images flooded her mind of climbing the tree with Macy. How many times had they pretended that Alex was the bad guy? They had thrown water balloons, balls, and so much more at him from those branches over the years, laughing and squealing the entire time.

Sure, those days were over because they were all teenagers—and other reasons she didn't want to think about.

More tears spilled onto her face and she sobbed into her hands again. "Macy, please come back. I need you."

Worried

Alex looked up, feeling guilty when the door to Macy's room opened. He knew that it wasn't Macy coming in as he read through her diary. It was his mom, and she looked more troubled than usual.

"I'm just looking for clues," Alex said, holding up the diary. "There might be something in one of these that—"

"You're fine, baby. I appreciate you going through those. I can't bring myself to read them right now. That's not why I'm in here. Have you heard from Zoey?"

Alex sat up, dropping the journal. "Is something wrong?"

"I hope not. Valerie just called looking for her. She left upset hours ago, and she was headed here."

He jumped off the bed. "She hasn't called or texted. I've had my phone since you gave it back."

"That's what I figured. I'll call Valerie back and let her know we haven't seen her."

Alex ran for the door. "I'm going to look for her."

"She could be anywhere. Don't get yourself lost too."

"I'm not. I can think of several places she might be if she's mad at her mom. I don't know why she wouldn't have come here first, though."

"Maybe she just wanted some alone time."

"I hope." Fear tore through Alex. What if something had happened to her too? He couldn't lose both his sister and his girlfriend.

Alex grabbed a coat from his room and then stopped by the front door to get his shoes on. As he ran out the door, he nearly tripped over

Zoey, who was sitting on the top step.

He stared at her with a mix of disbelief and relief. "What are you doing out here? It's way too cold." He sat down, wrapping his arms around her. Her skin was as cold as the air. "Let's go inside."

She shook her head.

"How long have you been here? Your mom said you left hours ago."

Zoey shrugged her shoulders.

Alex took his coat off and put it over her. "What's wrong?"

"What *isn't* wrong? That's what I want to know."

He shivered. "Now that you have my jacket, can we go inside?"

She gave him an exasperated look. "Fine."

Alex helped her up and into the house. "Mom! I found Zoey."

Alyssa ran down the stairs. "Oh, good. I'm so glad you're okay." She gave Zoey a hug. "I'd better call your mom."

Zoey made a face. "Please don't. I don't want her coming over here."

"But she's worried. I know what that feels like."

"Please, Alyssa. I really don't want to see her now. I really, really don't."

"Then I'll just call her and say that Alex went out and found you. Does that work?"

"Thank you."

After getting their shoes off, Alex helped her into the kitchen. "Let me make you some coffee, okay? You need to warm up."

"I'm not drinking coffee."

"Hot cocoa, then. Are you hungry? I can warm you up leftovers. We always have something." He filled a coffee cup with milk and stuck it in the microwave.

"No. Food just makes me sick."

"You should eat something. You can't starve."

"It's better than puking." She stared at a wall.

Alex thought he should change the subject. "I've been reading Macy's diaries. She might hate me for it when she comes back, but I'm hoping there might be something in there to help us find her."

"Are you going to post those entries online too?" Her voice sounded flat.

"Not after losing my electronics."

"Have you found anything?"

"Not yet, but I might not be looking close enough. I haven't even found her most recent one."

The microwave beeped and Alex took out the hot mug. He scooped in half a dozen spoonfuls of cocoa mix before stirring and then setting it in front of Zoey. He sat next to her, in Macy's chair. "There could still be clues in them. Given the circumstances, I think it's okay to read them. It's not like I'm going to use anything against her, you know."

She shrugged and then picked up the mug, taking a sip. "That's really rich."

"But it's good. You know it is." He gave her a playful grin, hoping to get a smile out of her. He could always make her smile.

Zoey stared at him for a moment before she finally cracked a small smile. She drank the rest of the hot chocolate in silence.

"Want to go up to my room? I can tell you what I read."

"Sure." She went to the sink and rinsed the cup out. They walked up to his room in silence, holding hands.

Sounds of a newscast could be heard coming from the bonus room.

Alex sighed. "Why does Mom do that to herself?"

Zoey gave him a confused look.

"She watches the news and then just gets upset about when they say anything about Macy. Though they haven't had much to say lately, barely giving her a mention these days. It seems like that upsets Mom just as much as when the news was nearly all about her."

"It could be her way of looking for clues."

"Maybe." He opened his door. "Sorry for the mess."

"Why? It's always messy."

Alex felt his cheeks heat up. "I'm too busy with other stuff to worry about cleaning. Do you think I should pick up?"

She sat on his bed, leaning against the headboard. "Do what you want."

He went around and sat next to her. "You're still so cold." He pulled his blankets over her and snuggled against her. "You know you can tell me anything, right?"

Zoey grunted, making it obvious that she didn't want to talk.

"Well, I've been reading Macy's diaries since I got up. Not that it's been all that long." He looked at his window, seeing that it was already starting to get dark. "I was tempted to post more pictures of entries about those jerks bullying her, but if I post anything else, my parents will probably sell my phone."

"Nothing about Jared or plans to move to Hollywood?"

"Hollywood? Did she ever say—?"

"No. Just throwing it out there."

"You don't have any ideas where she would go?" he asked.

"Definitely not Clearview."

"What if that's where Jared lives? Maybe she fell for a farm boy."

"Did you see that selfie on his profile? That was no farmer."

Alex shrugged. "Well, it's possible that kids in Hickville aren't wearing overalls with pieces of hay in their mouths."

Zoey leaned her head against his shoulder. "Do you really think she's still alive?"

"I have to."

"Me too. But I keep going back and forth. Sometimes I think she's off somewhere, living a good life. Then I get pissed. How dare she leave without saying goodbye? But then, what if, like, she saw something bad and the witness protection took her and said she had to make a clean break? Or what if something bad did happen to her? Then I'm a huge jerk for being pissed."

Alex took her hand and slid his fingers between hers. "I'm sure she'd understand. She'd be going through all the same stuff if one of us was missing instead of her."

"I hate not knowing. It's the worst."

He kissed the top of her head. "I know."

"What if we never know? How are we supposed to move on with our lives?"

"I have no idea. I hope we don't have to figure that out. I just keep thinking about the kids that were kidnapped and were found after a long time. There was that one girl who was gone almost a year. My parents keep talking about her. Then there was another one who was gone a really long time. More than ten years, I think. Even if Jared did kidnap her, she could turn up one day."

"But what are we supposed to do in the meantime?"

"The people who bring our food keep talking about praying. I'm starting to think maybe that's what we should do."

Zoey looked at him, raising an eyebrow. "You do?"

"It couldn't hurt, could it? What if there's a God and he's just waiting for us to ask him for help?"

Zoey looked uncomfortable. "What does your shrink say?"

"To think positive thoughts."

"Have you?"

He shrugged and looked away. "It's hard. She's gone, and it doesn't make any sense. How could any good have come from whatever happened to her? If she was okay, she'd have let us know somehow. Sure, she could be a brat at times, but she wouldn't do this to us. Not on purpose."

"So you think praying is thc answer then?"

"I don't know. It wouldn't hurt to try, I guess."

"Maybe. But if there was a God, why would he have let this happen in the first place?"

Alex thought about everything he'd heard from the people bringing meals to their house. "They said he doesn't interfere with free will, even if it brings heartache. But if we ask for help, he'll provide."

"That doesn't make any sense."

"It kind of does."

"Good luck with that. Let me know if you try." Zoey twisted her hair around and pulled an elastic band from her wrist, tying up her hair into a masterpiece.

Alex stared in amazement at her hair. How had she done that without a mirror? Even the way a few random strands hung loosely, it looked like a work of art, framing her ears and face.

She gave him a curious look. "What?"

"You're beautiful."

"Oh, stop."

"No, really. You are." He reached over and pulled a strand behind her ear. He let the back of his hand slide down her cheek, neck, and down to her stomach. Alex felt a slight bump on her stomach. His eyes lit up. "Is that…the baby?"

She nodded.

He slid her shirt up, exposing the bump. Holding his breath, he ran his hand over it. Finally, he breathed. "That's amazing."

"I guess."

"You don't think so?" He looked into her beautiful eyes, not moving his hands from her belly.

"It's hard when I feel so gross. I just feel bloated."

"Do you feel it moving around?"

"Nope. Doctor says it's too early."

Alex put his ear to the bump.

"I don't think you'll hear anything." Zoey laughed.

He kissed it and then sat up. "You never know."

"It's weird to think we'll be parents. Even if we don't keep it, we'll still be the parents."

"Do you want to?" Alex rubbed the bump again.

"Keep it?" Zoey asked. "I'm not sure. I keep thinking about what happened to your aunt and uncle. I don't want to do that."

Alex's aunt and uncle hadn't been able to have a baby, but they were all set to adopt a baby. Then after the baby was born, the mom had changed her mind. His aunt and uncle went home to an empty nursery. It had destroyed them and they eventually divorced.

"So, you want to wait until you give birth to decide?" Alex asked.

"Possibly. I know we're young and everything, but people raise babies in high school. You know there's a daycare in the back of the school, don't you?"

"I didn't."

"What do you want to do?"

"Me?" Alex asked. "It's up to you."

"Not entirely. Even if I wanted to give it up, you could still decide you want to raise the baby."

He let out a slow breath. All of a sudden, thirteen felt so young. "We have lots of time to figure this out. Maybe by then, Macy will even be able to give us her opinion."

Zoey didn't look convinced. "Maybe."

Fire

MACY PACED HER room, sweating. She had on several layers of white clothes, not knowing how long they would be outside. It was sometime in January, but she didn't know when since the community didn't celebrate holidays or even keep the same calendar.

It had to be close to the end of January, because at the meeting that night Jonah had gone on and on about anointing Chester as a prophet. Chester was supposed to become a prophet before spring. All that was left was that he convert someone from the world, and they had apparently met someone with potential earlier that day when they were out in the world.

Chester would be pissed when Macy escaped. That would probably ruin his chances at becoming a prophet. Not only would she have run away, but part of their precious fence would be gone, allowing anyone to leave if they wanted.

At the meeting, Luke kept making eye contact with her. He was as ready as she was to get out of there. Possibly more, since he had been planning this since long before Macy ever became part of the community.

She put her ear to the door, making sure that no one was up. Rebekah and Chester had finished their nightly ritual nearly an hour before.

Macy looked out the window. Where was Luke? She was going to have to remove some of her layers soon.

What if something had gone wrong? Her heart dropped at the thought. What if he had been caught and was locked away somewhere? What if he would never be seen again? Then it would be all her fault. If he got hurt, it was on her. She would have to live with that for the rest of her life.

Even though he did want to escape, this hadn't been his plan. He was willing to wait decades if that was what it took. But it was easier for him. He was at least with his mom. Macy was with a psychopath who she hated more every moment of every day.

Something hit her window, startling her. She looked out the curtain, but didn't see anything. It was too dark. But it had to be Luke. Who else would it be? Unless he had been caught and this was a trick. Macy narrowed her eyes, still not seeing anything. A porch light would have been helpful, but she would have to take her chances.

If Luke had been caught, he wouldn't have ratted her out. She took a deep breath and then walked to her door. Her heart pounded in her ears. That was going to make it hard to hear if Chester was up. She pulled the door open and it didn't make a sound.

Macy held her breath and tip-toed down the hall. She peeked into the living room, half-expecting to see Chester sitting on the couch. It was empty. In fact, she could hear him snoring down the hall.

She walked through the room and stopped in front of the door. "Please open quietly." She turned the knob, almost expecting sirens to wail, even though she knew there was no electricity for miles.

Macy went outside and closed the door as slow as possible, in disbelief that she was actually outside on her own. She couldn't see anything, but followed the path by memory. When she got to the edge of the property, someone grabbed her arm.

"Luke?"

"Yes. Let's hurry. I haven't seen anyone, but that doesn't mean we won't. I know a path we can take that doesn't get used often." He moved his hand down her arm and caressed her palm. Then he slid his fingers through hers. "Come on."

Macy followed him as best she could, trying to keep up in the dark.

After a few minutes, he said, "Here's the path."

"How can you see anything?"

"I stood outside for a while until my eyes adjusted. It helps that I know this place well. We're going to go a bit further until we get to a spot that's far enough from any homes that no one will hear the fire until we have a chance to get away."

"Are we just going to run to the highway?"

"Better than that. I've got my mom's car keys. I hope it still runs after all these years. If it doesn't, then yeah, we'll run."

"Do you know how to drive?"

"No. Do you?"

"I'm only fifteen."

"Well, I've driven a tractor for Farmer Jeremiah. It can't be all that different."

"Let's hope. What about Dorcas? She didn't want to take part in it?"

"She's actually acting as our lookout while we start the fire."

"Is she going to go with us?"

"If she can. If not, she's going to cover for us and continue the plan to go out with the prophets one day. She said that either way, she's happy for us."

"Okay." Macy followed him in silence as they made their way through the path. She found that the moon and the stars were actually helpful in helping her eyes adjust. "How much further?"

"We're almost there."

Macy swallowed. Her throat was dry and her heart was steadily increasing speed. Was she really going to be free from Chester? It was almost too much to think about.

"There's the fence."

She narrowed her eyes, looking for it. She saw something in the distance, but wasn't sure if it was the fence or not. It had to have been, it was the only thing she could see that wasn't part of the path. They made their way through the path and ended up face to face with the tall structure, the wire at the top gleaming in the moonlight.

Luke dug through his pockets and pulled out box of matches. "It's the moment of truth. Are you ready?"

"More than you know."

"I'm sure you are, Macy." He gave her a sad smile. "Let's get you to your family."

"What about you? What are you going to do when get to civilization?"

"Don't worry about me. I'm almost eighteen and I have a lot of skills. I can get a job and possibly a formal education."

A branch snapped in the distance. Macy froze, staring at Luke. "What was that?"

"Probably just Dorcas. She's looking out for us, remember?"

"I haven't even seen her. Are you sure?"

"Yes. She knows the drill. If anyone approaches, she's going to blow a whistle. Then you and me, we run."

Macy took a deep breath. "Okay. Let's go. I just want to get out of here."

He nodded and then took a step closer to the fence. Looking around, he pulled a match from the box.

Another branch snapped. Macy wasn't so sure that it was Dorcas, but she was afraid to speak her doubts.

Luke held the match to the bottom of the fence.

Macy had imagined the match causing an instant, huge fire, but it wasn't catching at all. Another branch snapped and she jumped toward Luke, nearly crashing into him. He didn't seem to notice.

"Can you find some twigs?" he asked. "We'll need to light some of those first to get the fire going."

"Sure." She found some not too far away and handed them over. "Let me light some of those."

He passed her a match and then the box. She struck the match and gave him back the box. She held a twig up to the match and watched as it lit up. Luke stuck his lit up twig at the bottom of the fence and Macy followed suit. He gave her another match and then added more twigs to the bottom of the fence.

She watched, hoping that one of them would ignite the fence. The more time that passed, the more nervous she became. Beads of sweat broke out on her forehead despite being able to see her labored breath. If they got caught before they could escape, they were going to end up in all kinds of trouble—if not dead.

Luke blew on the twigs, so she bent down and did the same. One of his twigs' fire caught and a tiny part of the fence lit up. It was practical-ly nothing, but she gave him a high five.

He bent down and blew on another twig. "Let's get the rest of these lit up. This is taking too long."

Macy lowered herself to the frosty ground and blew on the twigs nearest her. One of them caught on the fence, the flame moving ever so slowly up the tall beam. She moved to the next one and before long, a length about five feet of the fence was engulfed in flames.

Another branch snapped. This time, right behind them.

Heart pounding, Macy turned around. Chester stood, staring at them. The small flame reflected in his glasses.

A choked sound escaped from Macy's throat. Luke turned around, fear covering his face.

"What are you doing?" Chester demanded.

Luke grabbed Macy's arm and ran, pulling her along with him. She ran, all too aware of Chester's footsteps behind them. How had he found them?

She looked back and saw that he wasn't far behind. Macy picked up her pace, her legs burning. She didn't care, she had to keep going. But how were they going to get away now? Were they going to have to kill him? Was that even possible?

Luke took an unexpected turn in between a couple of buildings. He pulled her along as they zigged and zagged through more buildings. They needed to lose Chester or neither of them would see the next day. Macy had no idea where they were or how to get away.

They continued darting in between different buildings and then ended up down another path and eventually headed into a field of corn. There were small, narrow paths and their shoulders brushed the corn stalks as they ran. Macy thought she heard Chester behind them, but she couldn't be sure. It was hard to hear over the stalks scraping against her clothes.

Her throat was even drier than it had been before. Her legs were on fire, burning all the way up and down and even making its way up to her chest. That too felt like as though engulfed in flames. She'd had no chance to exercise over the last couple months and it showed. She pushed through, forcing herself to keep up with Luke.

"I can hear you two!" Chester shouted. He sounded pretty close.

Luke stopped and Macy ran into him. He put his hand up to his lips and then he sat on the ground, pulling her down too. They sat and Macy gasped for air, trying to breathe without making a sound.

"If he can hear us," Luke whispered, tickling her ear, "we're better off staying put. He'll have a harder time finding us, plus you need to rest."

She nodded, afraid to speak. If Chester found them, he might kill them—if he still had his gun or knife. Had he been able to get them past the prophets when they moved in? If so, they were definitely dead. If he went for help, that would give them a small window of time to get away.

Macy didn't know where they were in relation to the fence. Obviously, being in the middle of a corn field, they had to be pretty far from it. She looked at Luke, who appeared to be deep in thought.

Chester yelled something, but Macy couldn't understand what he said. He must have moved further away from them.

"What are we going to do?" she whispered.

Luke looked at her. "Let's wait a minute. It sounds like he's moving away from us. We're going to have to go the other way, which will put us at a different part of the fence than we were, and we're going to have to start over with the fire."

"Do you think we're still going to be able to get away?"

"Yes. I have my doubts about getting to the parking lot, though. Will you be able to make it to the highway if we have to run?"

"I'll do whatever I have to do. I didn't even know that you were planning on taking a car."

Leaves rustled nearby. Macy froze.

Running

DORCAS APPEARED IN front of them. "You two are difficult to find." She sounded out of breath. "Sorry about Chester. He snuck around a way I didn't see."

"Where is he now?" Luke asked.

"He's gone that way." Dorcas pointed to the left.

"So we're definitely going to have to run for a different part of the fence," Luke said.

"What's going to happen if he catches us?" Dorcas' eyes were wide.

Luke grabbed Macy's hand and squeezed. "He's not."

"But what if he does, Luke?" Dorcas asked. "You guys have to plan for that."

"I'll fight him off and let you and Macy run."

"Macy?" Dorcas looked confused for a moment. "Oh, her real name. All you have is matches, right?"

"Don't worry. My street smarts have stuck with me, Dorcas. You need to get Macy away from him if I end up fighting him. He kidnapped her. Who knows what else he's capable of? She has to get away even if I don't."

Macy gasped. "No."

Luke pulled her closer, wrapping his arm around her. Despite the fear shooting through her, his embrace was comforting. He looked into her eyes. "I knew the risks when we made the plans."

The blood drained from Macy's face. "But I—"

He shook his head. "Don't worry about it. When I saw how desperate you were to get away this morning, I knew I needed to help you."

"I'm sorry. I'm so sorry. I didn't want to put you in danger."

Dorcas frowned. "It's not time for remorse. We're past that. You two are in deep; Chester hasn't seen me yet, but I promised to do what I can to protect you guys, and I will."

"Can you hear him?" asked Luke.

They all sat in silence. Macy couldn't hear anything above their breathing.

Dorcas looked at Luke. "Either he's too far away to hear or he's sitting still like we are, waiting for us to make a move."

Luke nodded. "Let's wait a little longer. If he's waiting for us to make a move, I want to disappoint him."

Macy leaned closer to Luke, feeling both comforted and energized in his arms. She noticed her shoulder moving along with his breathing; she was breathing in tune with him.

"What are we going to do?" Macy asked. "I feel like we're sitting ducks."

"Wait just a bit longer," Luke said. "We need to be patient. I want to be sure that he's not waiting close by for us." He pulled out the box of matches and took some out. Then he handed Macy the box.

Macy nodded and then leaned her head against his chest. Her breathing had almost returned to normal. The muscles in her legs still ached, but the burning had at least stopped—for the time being, anyway.

It felt like ten minutes passed as they sat together in silence. It could have been just a couple minutes, but it was too hard to tell. Time had a way of passing at different speeds since she had been kidnapped.

Luke sat up straight, causing Macy to also. "I think we need to make a run for it now. Or perhaps a walk for it. Walking would be a lot quieter. We don't need to alert him to our location." He looked at Dorcas. "We already know he's out there. You should go home. That way you'll be safe and no one will be any wiser."

She shook her head. "I need to know that you guys are safe, Luke."

He let go of Macy and put a hand on Dorcas' shoulder. "Dorcas, you're dear to me like a sister. Please, go home. I need to know that you're safe too. We'll be all right. I promise."

Dorcas looked conflicted. "Whatever you say, Luke. I wish you both the best." She stood up and walked off.

He turned to Macy. "I had to say that line about her being like my sister. It was the only way she would actually go home. She has feelings for me that I can't reciprocate."

"Oh?" Macy didn't dare say more.

Luke lifted her hand and kissed the back of it. "Now to get you safely out of here." He pulled her up before she could respond to the kiss. He looked at her, this time his face was serious. "Like I said, we need to walk. Be careful not to brush against the stalks. They're too noisy, but at least they're a great way to hide."

Macy nodded. Still holding her hand, he started walking, but their arms brushed against the corn, so he let go. It was for the better anyway because it was too difficult for Macy to focus when her hand was in his. They made their way through the corn mostly avoiding the stalks. Every once in a while, one of them would accidentally brush against one.

It looked like the fence was visible in the distance. "Are we almost out of here?" Macy whispered.

"Pretty close, but don't get too confident."

"That's right, Heather." Chester jumped out in front of them.

Unable to contain herself, Macy let out a blood-curdling scream.

Luke spread his arms out, acting as a shield between Macy and Chester. He looked back at Macy. "Run."

"Not without you."

He gave her an exasperated look. "Go! I'll catch up."

Chester gave an evil laugh. "No, he won't."

"Don't listen to him. Run, Macy!"

"Her name is Heather." Chester shoved Luke.

"No. Her name is Macy. That's the name her real parents gave her, you lawless heathen."

"Heathen? Who are you calling a heathen? I'm about to be anointed as a high prophet. If you repent, I might consider granting you forgiveness for your trespass, young man."

"You're the last person to be able to give me absolution." Luke turned to Macy again. "Run, will you?"

"Sorry, I won't leave your side, Luke."

Chester grabbed Luke's shirt and choked him. "I'm not going to offer this again. Go now and save yourself. I may even consider going easy on Heather if you run. Nobody else needs to know about this."

Macy smelled smoke. The fence must have finally been engulfed in flames. If they could just get away from Chester, they would be able to make their escape. "Luke, it's okay. Go. I don't want you getting hurt."

Chester pulled on Luke's collar again. "Listen to her. She knows what's good for you." He let go of Luke's shirt and shoved him back. "This is your last chance. Don't test me."

Luke fixed his collar. "Macy deserves to go back home to her family. You're not her family. Why do you need her? You and Rebekah can have your own kids."

Chester furrowed his eyebrows. "Not that it's any of your business, Son, but Heather is my daughter and I will not lose her again."

"You need to rethink that." Luke ran at Chester, ramming his shoulders into his chest. Chester gasped for air, stumbling back and looking surprised. He grabbed Luke's hair and shoved his face into a corn stalk.

Full of rage, Macy ran at Chester. She slammed into him, causing him to stumble slightly. Not even enough to let go of Luke. She dug her nails into his arm. He pushed his elbow out, but she wasn't going to let that stop her. She squeezed even harder. "Let go of him!"

"Macy, run! Get out of here," Luke begged.

"I wouldn't listen to him," Chester said. He let go of Luke and pried her off his arm. His eyes were full of anger, but she felt less intimidated with Luke at her side. The two of them could take him.

Luke jumped on Chester, knocking him down. Halfway through the air, Chester grabbed Macy's arm and pulled her down with him. Her face scraped along a stalk, burning as she went down. She landed with a thud and then rolled against Chester. Luke landed on his knees and punched Chester in the nose.

Chester shoved Macy off him and hit Luke in the jaw. Macy jumped up and grabbed his arm, trying to keep him from hitting Luke any more. Luke hit Chester in the cheek, barely missing his glasses.

Chester shoved Macy down. She stood back up and saw Chester and Luke were wrapped around each other, wrestling and punching on the dirt. She couldn't see a way to jump in without getting hit by either one of them.

She remembered the box of matches that Luke had given her. She pulled it out of her pocket and lit one. As soon as the flame came to life, she set it against the stalk of corn that had scratched her face. It took a moment, but it caught on fire, the flame simultaneously going up and down the stalk.

Macy put the match against another stalk and watched it light up as the match itself died. She looked over at Luke and Chester. They were on the ground, still fighting.

Chester's glasses gleamed in the light of the fire behind her. Now was her chance to break those big, ugly glasses. She went over and reached down, grabbing them off his face. He shouted something at her, but she wasn't listening.

Behind her, she could feel the heat from the growing fire. Not only that, but she could hear the crackling and whooshing sounds as it moved along. The smoke tickled her nose and throat.

Before dropping the glasses on the ground, Macy kicked Chester just because she could. Then she stomped on the glasses, breaking them. The frames bent and the lenses were both broken into several pieces. Rage built in her gut and she jumped up and down on them until they were unrecognizable.

Chester yelled something, but Macy was too focused on destroying the glasses even further. Once she and Luke got away, she would never have to worry about keeping Chester happy again. She stomped on what was left of the glasses one more time for good measure and then turned to him and yanked on what hair he had, pulling him away from Luke.

There was just enough space between them that Luke was able to get up. Chester looked around, patting the ground, obviously looking for his glasses. Macy ran over to Luke and grabbed his hand. "Let's get out of here."

"My leg is hurt. I'm not going to be able to run. You should run ahead of me."

"What? I'm not leaving you behind. Get up." She yanked his arm.

"I'm only going to slow you down."

"Who cares? We're leaving together."

"Even if we get out of the community, I'm never going to make it to the main road."

"Yes you will. Hurry up before he attacks again. If he doesn't get us, the fire will. We're going to be surrounded soon."

Luke sighed and then nodded. He took a step, limping. Pain covered his face.

Macy gasped. "What did he do to you? Lean on me."

He did, and they made their way down the narrow path with the raging fire chasing them on one side. It wouldn't be long before Chester was also chasing them. She knew that the lack of glasses would only slow him down, not stop him. The only thing that would stop him would be if she shoved him into the fire—and maybe that wouldn't even do it.

"Are you sure you want me slowing you down?"

"How could I not, Luke?"

"My real name—"

A shot rang through the air. Macy looked around, unable to tell where it came from. She knew it had be Chester, but where was he?

Corn nearby rustled and Dorcas appeared. "You guys have to leave now. He's got a gun. I found a place to escape near the feed stable. I told some of the kids who want to get out. They're already headed there. We have to go *now*."

"I thought you were going home," Luke said.

Dorcas shook her head. "Not a chance."

Luke shook his head. "I should have known. I think my leg is strong enough to run on."

"Are you sure?" Macy asked. "You were just limping a moment ago."

"It's not as bad as I thought." He took her hand. "Follow me."

Several more shots rang through the air, but that time, Macy could feel the breeze of a couple bullets. "Get down!" she shouted.

She threw herself to the ground, pulling Luke with her.

"Are you okay?" she asked.

He didn't respond, but she noticed his hand holding his arm.

Fear squeezed through Macy's entire body. She couldn't breathe or talk. When more shots were fired, she found her voice, but it didn't sound like her. "Are you okay?" she repeated, her voice several octaves higher than normal. Macy moved his hand and could easily see a dark red spot on his white shirt. A horrible sound escaped her throat.

Luke looked into her eyes. "I'll be fine." His voice sounded pained. "It only grazed me. Let's go."

Another shot sounded, this time louder.

Dorcas screamed, clutching her stomach. Macy saw a growing red spot on the middle of her clothes.

Luke ran to Dorcas and she fell into his arms. "You guys have to leave me here."

Tears filled Luke's eyes. "I won't, dear sister."

"You have to or this was all for nothing. Luke, you have to escape and get out of here."

"Not without you. I'll carry you."

Dorcas shook her head. "You need to escape." Her eyes closed.

"No!" Luke shook her. "Don't close your eyes. You can't give up— we have to get out of here."

Dorcas opened her eyes slowly, looking at Luke. "I *am* getting away. But it's going to have to be up to you to get yourself out."

"Please don't. You can't talk like this."

Dorcas closed her eyes and she went limp.

Luke shook his head, tears flying. He shook her again, but Dorcas didn't respond.

"Dorcas," he whispered. Her head turned and rested on his chest.

"We have to go," Macy said, reaching for his arm. "I'm sorry."

Luke nodded, wiping his tears. He set Dorcas on the ground with care. "I've got to get you out of here." He took her hand again, getting Dorcas' blood on Macy.

They rounded a corner and came face to face with Chester.

Reality

ALYSSA SAT UP in bed, gasping for air and drenched in sweat. Another nightmare. That one felt so real.

Chad sat up. "Are you okay, Lyss?"

She shook her head, clinging to the comforter. "I had a horrible dream."

He scooted closer to her. "Tell me about it."

"Macy—she," Alyssa's lips shook, "was trapped somewhere, screaming."

Chad pulled her into an embrace. "It was only a dream."

"It didn't *feel* like one." She was shaking. "It was so vivid."

"Your subconscious is working out your fears, that's all."

"There was a fire. I think she's in danger, Chad."

"Shh." He held her closer.

Alyssa pulled away. "I won't shush. I really think she's in trouble."

"I wasn't telling you to be quiet. I was helping to calm you, like when the kids were upset when they were younger." Though it was dark, he was pretty sure she glared at him. "What else did you see in the dream? Anything to identify where she was?"

"There was a blaze. She was outside. That's all I know. The longer I'm awake, the less I can remember."

"Do you want me to turn on the news and see if there are fires anywhere?"

"How would that help anything?"

"Let's say that somehow you two are communicating, it could help us find her. Think about it, Lyss. It's winter. There aren't likely many fires. It's not like in the summer, when there are a lot of wildfires. In the summertime, a dream like that wouldn't be helpful. But now, it could be."

"So you believe me?"

"Of course." Chad wasn't sure that he did, but he wanted her to know he was on her side. He helped her up and handed her a robe before putting on his. They went into the bonus room and he turned the TV on, scrolling for the news.

They sat there, watching the ticker at the bottom of the screen as the reporter talked about the stock market. There was nothing about any fires.

Alyssa frowned. "There goes that theory, and you probably think I'm an idiot, to boot."

"Not a chance. Just because it's not on there, doesn't mean it didn't happen. If it's a small fire in an obscure location, it might never make the news. You practically have to burn a house down while trying to kill a spider to get the media to pick it up." Chad pulled out his phone and opened the browser app to search for fires. "Nothing online either. Sorry, Lyss."

Alyssa frowned. "We should get back to bed. I'm sorry I woke you up and made you get out of bed."

He clicked the remote, turning the TV off. "Nothing to be sorry for."

When they settled back into bed, Alyssa turned to him. "Do you think we'll ever get her back? Or do you think that girl from Clearview...?" Tears filled her eyes.

"No. I don't think it's her. There's no other evidence of her being there. All of her stuff has been found locally."

"I hope you're right. But they haven't found anything else in a while. It—"

"Get some sleep, Lyss. We both need it. The DNA results will be back soon enough. I'm sure they'll find that it's not Macy."

"But it's such a small town and there aren't any missing girls in Clearview."

"Remember what Detective Fleshman said? There are a lot of missing girls, but most don't make the news. Girls who—"

"Know what? You're right. We should get some sleep. I don't want to think about this right now. No statistics. Sleep is what's going to help us. That and positive thinking."

"That's right. Send her positive thoughts. Macy will get them." He kissed her forehead and held her until her breathing deepened. Then he rolled onto his own pillow, unable to get back to sleep.

It was so hard to know what to think. He wished that real life was more like those shows—instant DNA results. Why had their dentist office have to catch on fire? And why hadn't they kept their records online? It wasn't like it was the nineties or they were living in some third world country.

On one hand, he really just wanted answers. Then they could all move on with their lives, one way or another. Of course the last thing he wanted was for Macy to be dead, but at the same time he hated living in limbo. If she was gone, they deserved to know the truth. She wouldn't have wanted them living like this.

Tears filled his eyes. He hated thinking about what Macy would or wouldn't have wanted. It was the last thing he should have to think about. No parent should outlive their child. From the moment she was born, he felt like his heart lived on the outside of his body, running around. It was now split in two. One half here at home, safe and sound, and the other out there somewhere—hopefully still alive.

How had his life spun out of control so fast? He had been on the fast track to the career of his dreams with his blog picking up popularity so fast. Had he done something wrong? Was he to blame for any of this?

Was he being punished for spending too much time working, ignoring his family? He thought he had been working hard for them, so they could have a better life once it took off. The plan had been to be able to quit his job, and then he would have had all that extra time to spend with them.

It was clear now—too late—that he should have spent more time with them. He didn't know nearly enough about either of his children. That much had been made clear since Macy disappeared.

Or was he being punished for his relationship with Lydia? He had cut that off even though she kept turning up whenever he went out. Chad had done everything he could to make that right—short of fessing up, and that wasn't going to happen. He told Lydia it was over and he was working on his marriage. Alyssa loved him again and he her.

All they need was to have Macy back and everything would be as good as it had been years earlier when they'd had the dream life. He hadn't appreciated it then, and now he was paying for it. He looked up toward the ceiling and promised anyone or anything that might be listening that he would never take his family for granted again.

Dark

LUKE YANKED MACY'S arm, pulling her away from Chester. Her feet stumbled underneath her, but she managed to get her footing and keep up with Luke. He ran so fast it was hard for her to keep up, but the adrenaline helped. Luke hadn't been kidding about his leg being okay. Either that or it was adrenaline, like Macy felt. Whatever it was, hopefully it would serve to keep them alive.

She heard Chester chasing them, but it sounded like he was having a hard time without his glasses. It sounded like he kept running into the corn stalks.

"Is your leg going to be okay?" Macy asked.

"Yeah, but we need to hurry."

"How far away is the feed thing Dorcas mentioned?" Macy asked.

"Not too far, but it won't be long until someone discovers the opening and blocks it. That's why we have to hurry."

They darted between corn stalks, turning down new rows constantly. Finally, they broke free. Luke stopped for a moment and looked around. He pointed right. "This way."

They ran toward some buildings that reminded Macy of the barn back at Chester's parents' farm. Her throat closed up even as she ran. If Chester planned to lock her up again, she would fight him until the death.

Luke led her past those and down a little path. "The fence isn't far off. Hopefully the opening is close."

They passed the barn-like buildings, this time around the back. Macy saw something unusual in the fence about twenty feet away, but even though her eyes had adjusted to the dark, it was hard to tell. They were far enough from the fire they'd started that she couldn't even see any sign of that, either.

"I think I see it," Luke said. He led her to the spot Macy had seen.

When they got there, it was a small opening, barely big enough for one person. "You go first. You're so tall, I'm worried you might not fit," she said.

"All the more reason for you to go first." He let go of her hand and extended his arm toward the opening. "Go."

"I want to make sure you'll fit first."

His eyes narrowed. "Go!" he shouted, looking angry. "If I have trouble you can help pull me through."

Macy jumped and then ran to the spot and squeezed through, scratching her hand and face in the process. When she was fully out she looked back in. "Come on."

"Sorry to speak harshly. It was the only way I could get you to go first."

"I don't care. Go through."

Luke looked away. "People are coming."

"Hurry!" Macy put her arm through and grabbed his hand. "We've got to go."

He slid his fingers through hers and slid about halfway through the hole.

"What are you waiting for?"

"I'm stuck."

"Are you serious?" Macy exclaimed. She let go of his hand and pulled on the fence. The wood wouldn't budge. "Hold your stomach in or something." She pulled harder on the plank and her hand slipped, bending a nail all the way back. She let out a cry of pain.

Worry covered Luke's face and he pushed against the wood. It buckled under his grip. He fell to the ground next to her, nearly knocking Macy over. She moved out of the way and grabbed his hands, helping him up.

Voices could be heard from the other side of the fence.

Luke put a finger up to his mouth and pointed to the right. He slid his fingers through hers and squeezed.

Macy held her breath as they tip-toed away. She could make out Jonah and Eve's voices yelling about the hole in the fence.

Luke and Macy continued walking quietly until the prophets' voices faded away.

He looked into Macy's eyes. "Now."

They both burst into a run.

"Listen for the others," Luke said. "I'm not sure who escaped, but we have a better chance at getting away with more people."

"What if we run into a prophet? Or someone else who wants to take us back?"

"We'll run from them obviously, but Dorcas said some of the kids got out. We have to find them."

Macy nodded and they ran in silence.

Something howled in the distance, sending chills down her spine. "Maybe we should just head for the highway."

Luke shook his head. "That's what they're going to expect. We need to go through the woods and find the world on the other side."

"Maybe." She didn't like the idea of going farther into the woods, but she wasn't going to leave Luke's side.

He squeezed her hand. "I'll keep you safe. I promise."

They ran in silence for a while and then Luke slowed down. "Do you hear that?"

Macy listened. All she heard were owls and the occasional coyote. She shook her head.

"I think I hear the others. This way."

They ran through the thick trees and bushes barely able to see. At least they were far enough away from the community that Macy couldn't hear the sounds of it any more.

"Where are the others?" Macy asked.

"Not far. Can you hear them now?"

"What am I supposed to listen for?"

"Conversation."

"I really don't know how you hear it."

"I used to stand guard at night for a while," Luke said. "I learned to listen for the smallest sounds."

Macy strained to hear something, but she couldn't hear anything beyond the running of their feet or the howling animals in the distance.

Luke slowed, forcing Macy to also. She could hear something—finally. She could barely hear hushed whispers. They crept toward the noise. There were some swishing noises and Macy found herself face to face with about half a dozen kids all wearing white. They were standing defensively, like they were ready to attack.

Macy held her breath. She didn't know how much more she could take.

One near the front relaxed. "It's just Luke and Heather."

The others changed their positions, each looking relieved.

"How did you get away?" asked the one in front. Macy couldn't remember his name. "The fire was all around the opening."

Luke pulled Macy close and wrapped his arm around her. "We found another way out. We were near the corn fields."

"Are they coming after us?"

"They're sure to," Luke said, "but for now, we appear to be in the clear."

"We need to set up camp somewhere."

"Do we have any supplies, David?" Luke asked. "I've got matches, but not much else."

David shook his head. "We weren't prepared to leave."

"Then we're better off moving," Luke said.

"Everyone's tired. We need to get some rest," David said.

Luke stood taller against Macy. "We're going to be a lot worse off than tired if the prophets find us. Who's with me?"

Most of the others behind David agreed with Luke.

"Good," said Luke. "The farther away we get, the better. Once we reach the world, we can speak with their authorities and get the help we need. For now, we just focus on getting there."

"Let's discuss a plan," David said.

"Yes, let's." Luke turned to Macy. "Sit down and rest. I'm not sure how long we're going go before we rest again."

"At least we're free. I can't believe I'm away from Chester." Macy looked around, never having felt more free.

Luke wrapped his arms around her and placed his lips on hers softly. "And I'll make sure you're not just away from him, but that you get back to your family."

OVER

Gone – Book Three

Stacy Claflin

http://www.stacyclaflin.com

To receive book updates from the author,
sign up here (http://bit.ly/1ONrfMw).

Alone

Heather squirmed against the tight restraints. The jacket wouldn't budge. She tried to readjust her right shoulder because the jacket pinned her in the most uncomfortable angle. Pain shot through her arm in all directions.

How had she come to this? She was a normal sixteen year old—or she had been until everything crumbled around her. Her dad had killed her mom. Why wouldn't anyone listen to her? He needed to be locked up, not her.

She stopped fighting the straight jacket and found that her arm didn't hurt so much. She needed a new plan. So far, nothing else had worked. That much was obvious. Heather looked up at the camera in the ceiling.

They were watching her, those sadistic nurses. How they were able to keep their jobs, she would never know. If she ever got out, she'd tell everyone what really went on. But she didn't know how she would ever get out. She had turned into the problem patient and they were intent on fixing her.

How long would they keep her in seclusion this time? Time moved slower than ever in there, so she never could tell. Didn't they know they were making her crazy? Or maybe her dad paid someone off to torment her so she appeared to go off the deep end.

Sure, attacking the head nurse hadn't been her best moment, but Heather hadn't seen any other options. No one would listen to her. She had tried convincing them of her mental health, tried to make them listen. But no, they had to keep pushing her. It should have been no surprise that she snapped.

Heather had already gone through enough with losing her mom, but then to be locked away like a criminal? They took her for observation, at least that's what they told her. The fact that her dad didn't visit her should have told them something, but it hadn't.

Where was that jerk, anyway? He must have been enjoying the time to himself. Or could he be on the run because of what he had done to her mom? Heather doubted that, because if anyone knew he had killed her, Heather wouldn't be locked up.

Instead, she suffered their torture while trying to deal with the fact that her mom was never coming back and her dad was responsible. Anger burned within the pit of her stomach. She wanted to scream and kick herself free. Not that it would get her the attention she wanted. She would only get more time in solitary.

She fought to free herself from the jacket again. More pain shot through her shoulder and arm. Tears ran down her face. They probably laughed at her from behind the camera.

They had sent her into the room to punish her, and now with her in tears it was icing on the cake. They won and she lost. She stared into the camera, imagining the icy-cold eyes of the head nurse.

Finally, the tears stopped and she looked away from the camera— her only link to humanity. How long had it been since she had had real contact with people? Not the people inside the building, but her friends at school. Did they miss her? If they did, why hadn't anyone come to see her?

More tears stung, but she blinked them away. What waited for her outside the walls? Anyone? Did anyone care that she languished inside a nut house, turning into someone who belonged there?

Maybe if someone would have bothered visiting her, she wouldn't have found herself going down this path. Or if any of the nurses bothered to be nice to her. That would have gone a long way. But no, they taunted her instead. Just like they were doing now.

If she could push her anger aside and ignore the injustices, would that help? If she pretended as though the cruel witches were actually human beings with feelings? Would that help?

The thought of being nice to them sent chills through her. It would be like admitting defeat, or worse, saying what they had done to her had been okay. On the other hand, if it was a step toward getting out, it might be worth it.

Heather took a deep breath and thought about her grandparents and their farm. It had been so long since she had been out there. She had missed going there for Christmas break. There was nothing like Christmas on the farm. She even had her own room there, even though it wasn't how she would have had it. She would give anything to see them.

She closed her eyes and imagined being in the kitchen with Grandma, making some soup. She loved to make it from scratch, and nothing else compared to it or anything she made. Her mouth watered as she actually smelled the soup. In the background, she heard Grandpa's old sitcoms. He probably knew each episode by heart, but that didn't stop him from watching them over and over.

It had been so nice to visit them, even though she knew it wasn't real. At least not yet. She would get back there. Heather had no other option. Next she pictured her home, but it sat empty. She tried to draw up images of Mom, but she was still gone. Tears escaped Heather's closed eyes. How would she get through the rest of her life without her mom? Especially since her dad had gone off the deep end?

She had to get out of the mental hospital. Even if it meant sucking up to the nurses. She knew she wasn't insane. Anyone living through what she had to endure would act up, too.

Heather took a deep breath, and prepared what she would say. She opened her eyes and stared into the camera. The words fought to stay inside. She didn't want to say them, but she had no other choice. "I'm sorry. I shouldn't have hit that nurse."

Waiting

THE WIND HOWLED, pushing on the light tent. Coyotes howled in response, not too far in the distance.

Macy Mercer wrapped a blanket around herself, shuddering. "They don't sound so far away this time."

Allie shook her head, pulling her own blanket tighter. "I hope the guys are okay."

"They are." Macy sounded a lot surer than she felt. She looked into Allie's scared, green eyes. "They know what they're doing, and when they come back, we'll have a nice meal too."

Another animal howled, but this time midway through it let out a high-pitched yelp. Barking followed.

Allie moved closer to Macy, who opened up and wrapped her blanket around the younger girl.

Tina sat up across the tent. She looked around. "What's going on?"

"The boys went to get food," Macy said. "They wanted us to have protein."

"That wind won't give up." Tina moved her long, light brown hair out of her face. "You think Jonah's looking for us in this weather?"

"Wouldn't surprise me," Allie said. She shook in Macy's arms.

Macy held her tighter. "We've barely stopped in the last two days. Even if they are looking, we have such a good head start I don't think it matters."

Tina pulled her hair into a ponytail. "Yeah, but they have vehicles. We don't."

"They can't get cars through these woods," Macy countered. "We've all got cuts from those thorn bushes."

"Horses. They have horses."

"You think they could get horses through some of those paths?" Macy ran her hand along a scab that went from almost her eye down to her lip. "There's no way."

Tina narrowed her eyes. "They have things to cut away shrubbery. Jonah's the most determined man I've ever met."

Allie sniffled, making crying noises.

"Maybe we should talk about something else," Macy said. "We're scaring Allie."

"She should be scared—we all should be. That's what's going to keep us going, and keep us alive."

"We should be aware, sure," Macy said. "Not scared, though. That's not going to help us. We've made it this far, with so little food and sleep. Then we found this abandoned camp site."

"All the more reason to be afraid."

Macy raised an eyebrow.

"Did you stop to think why all this stuff was abandoned?" Tina asked. "People don't generally leave a tent full of blankets unless something's wrong."

"Maybe one of them got hurt, and they didn't have time to pack up. They just left to get to a hospital."

Tina ran her hands through her ponytail. "Whatever you want to tell yourself. I'm going back to sleep." She tucked herself into the sleeping bag, covering her head.

"Do you think she's right?" Allie asked.

"I think she has the right idea of going back to sleep. We need our rest."

"Can I sleep in your bag with you?"

"Sure." Macy reached over and pulled Allie's pillow over and then unzipped her sleeping back and connected the two.

Before long, Macy listened to the sounds of both the other girls' heavy breathing along with the wind whipping the tent. Was Tina right? Would Jonah and the others use horses to catch up to them?

It didn't seem likely. They didn't know what direction the group of kids had gone, and they probably assumed they went to the highway.

Macy had wanted to go there, but Luke said that would be the first place they looked.

They had been on the run for more than two days. It would be difficult for them to find the group of kids. They were at the base of the mountains, so the woods went for miles in every direction. How would they know where to start looking?

No. Luke had meant it when he told Macy that he was going to help her get back home to her family—her real family. Not with Chester and Rebekah. If Chester got his hands on her again…Macy shuddered.

She would fight him to the death. He had kidnapped her once, but it wasn't going to happen again. She'd been stupid enough to get into his truck in the first place. Since then he'd starved her, beaten her, tied her up and left her imprisoned…but the worst part was being away from her family for so long. It nearly ripped her heart out. Macy had wanted independence for so long—but not like this.

The wind whipped the tent, lifting one side from the ground. Macy sat up a little, listening for the guys. She couldn't hear a thing beyond the wind and the occasional animal in the distance. They seemed to be moving farther away. Was that good or bad? If they were leaving because they sensed something bad was going to happen, then Macy needed to be prepared for whatever that was.

At least all of the camping gear belonged to someone else. If it was destroyed or they had to leave it behind, it wouldn't matter. No one had any attachments to it.

The longer the boys were away, the more Macy's stomach twisted. She couldn't push away images of bad things happening to Luke. The thought of Chester getting a hold of him…it was too much. Maybe he was strong enough to fight him off. Unless Chester had his gun on him, then it might not matter.

Macy hadn't heard any shots, so that had to be a good sign. She couldn't do anything about it, and what she really needed was more rest before they moved on. Despite her worries, she closed her eyes and tried to relax her mind. There were five guys out there. They'd be able to handle themselves.

As she listened to the wind and the sounds of the other two girls' breathing, Macy found herself drifting off. Part of her wanted to fight it, but she gave in.

Conversation awoke her. She felt rested; how long had she been sleeping? Sitting up, she noticed the wind had stopped. Tina wasn't in the tent, but Allie still slept next to her.

Macy slid herself out of the sleeping bag, trying not to wake the younger girl, but she stirred and rubbed her eyes. "Is it time to get up?"

"I think the boys are back. You can sleep if you want. We'll probably eat and keep going."

"No. I want to go with you." Allie sat up and stretched.

Macy tried to fix her hair, but gave up. They all looked ragged after being in the woods for a few days. Half of them had dirt caked on their arms or face, and everyone's white clothes were dirty.

The two girls grabbed their shoes and put them on before exiting the tent. Tina sat by the campfire with the guys. Relief washed over Macy when she saw Luke. He smiled when he saw her and Macy threw herself into his arms. He squeezed her.

"What took you guys so long?" she asked.

"The wind scared a lot of animals into hiding, but we did find that guy." He pointed to something roasting over the fire. It looked like it had been a fox. "I'm not sure that it'll fill us all, but at least it's more substantial than berries."

Macy's mouth watered. The irony didn't escape her, and she wondered if she would ever go back to being vegan.

"Did you get rest?" Luke kissed the top of her head.

"I did. Don't you need some?"

"What I need is something to eat. My stomach hasn't stopped rumbling."

"How much longer until it's ready?"

"It hasn't been cooking long. Want to go for a walk?"

She stared into his eyes. "Are you sure you don't want to sit and relax?"

He took her hand, sliding his fingers through hers. "What I want is to spend some time with you while we're not on the run." He turned to a couple of the others and told them they wouldn't be gone long. He led her into the woods where there was barely a path.

"How much longer do you think until we reach the end of the woods?" Macy asked.

"I wish I had an idea. Just as long as we get there."

"What are you going to do when we reach civilization?"

He squeezed her hand. "Help you get back to your family."

"After that?"

"I'll figure something out. We need to tell the authorities about the community. There are other kids in there against their will, taken from their families. Maybe my mom will leave and we can find a home together, but I'm not counting on that. She's really happy there."

They came to a boulder, and Luke sat. He indicated for her to sit too. She did and he wrapped his arm around her. "I'm almost eighteen, so I'll probably find myself a job. I'll manage."

"Without a real education? I mean, I know you've been in school, but I don't think the community lessons will count for anything."

"You worry too much."

"No I don't. You need—"

"We have to focus on getting out of the woods first. Then we can—"

"If you're under eighteen, you could get a foster family and then go to high school. You could catch up and even graduate."

He held her closer. "I'll do that. Okay?"

"You're just saying that."

"Maybe."

"So, what's your real name? You never did tell me. Everyone else is going by them except you."

"I've grown to like Luke."

"You were going to tell me in the corn fields. Remember?" Macy asked.

He was quiet for a moment. "I was, wasn't I? Lucas is actually my middle name, so even though I changed my name, I've still held onto a piece of myself."

"Did you go by that before the community?" asked Macy.

"If I tell you, will you keep calling me Luke?"

"Sure, but you have to tell me. Otherwise, I'm going to have to make up something." She turned to look at him. "You look like," she paused, "a Walter."

"Walter?" Luke laughed. "Really?"

"Yeah," Macy teased. "If you don't tell me your name, I'm going to call you Walter."

"I'm definitely not Walter. Looks like I need to tell you."

"You should…Walter."

Luke shook his head. "My first name is Raymond."

"Raymond? You don't look like a Raymond."

"You'll let me stick with Luke?"

"Luke it is."

He ran his fingertips underneath her chin and placed his lips on hers.

Macy's heart pounded against her chest, and before she had time to react, Luke pulled back. "We should rejoin the others."

Pursuit

LUKE AND MACY walked back to the camp hand in hand. Everyone was sitting around the campfire.

"What'd we miss?" Luke asked.

"We're just trying to figure out how much longer until we're out of here," Tina said.

"It's got to be a ways," Luke said. "There are no sounds of anything other than wildlife. We have to plan for the worst."

"What's the worst?" Allie asked. She shivered.

"A week, maybe more," Tina said.

"No." Macy shook her head. "The worst would be Jonah and Chester finding us."

The others all said their agreements.

"How's the fox look?" Luke asked.

Trent poked it with a stick, moving it around. "It actually looks pretty close."

"Good," said Luke. "We should look around the camp and see if there's anything we need to take with us."

Most everyone dispersed, going through the two tents and the other random stuff left behind by the previous inhabitants.

"Why do you think they left without their stuff?" Macy asked.

Trent poked the fox again. "Could be anything, but I've learned not to question a good thing."

"You don't think we need to worry?" Macy asked.

He shook his head. "If they were coming back, they would have already. Could have been a storm or wildlife that chased them off. Who knows?"

"Too bad they didn't leave us a car," Luke said.

Trent laughed. "That would've been helpful."

"I don't even see any tire tracks," Macy said.

"That's not surprising," Luke said. "It's been so windy. We were lucky to find the tents still standing."

Macy stood closer to the fire to warm up while Trent and Luke discussed the best options for getting out of the woods. She half-listened to them while letting her mind wander back to her family.

She'd been gone at least a couple months. Did they still hold hope for finding her alive? Had Chester sent them any more messages? He had posted her fake status saying she ran away and then he left her bloody clothes. Did they even think she was trying to get to them?

Tears filled her eyes. If they could just get back to civilization, she wouldn't have to wait much longer to find out. She thought about them for a little while longer until everyone else gathered back around the campfire.

Trent looked at the fox again. "Looks good enough to eat. Let's dig in. Anyone find a knife?"

Allie held up a rusty pocket knife. "It's kind of gross though."

Luke took it. "Thanks, Allie." He opened it up and held the blade into the flame. "This will kill any germs."

Before long, they were all cutting off pieces. Macy was surprised that everyone was so generous—making sure that others had some before digging in. They all had to be as hungry as her, but they probably weren't used it. Between Chester starving her and her self-starvation before that, she could handle the hunger—not that she was going to turn down the food.

Her mouth watered as she held the warm meat in her hands. Macy looked at it for a moment, holding onto the smell before finally digging in.

After everyone had some, Trent and Luke handed out seconds. The portions weren't as big, but the animal was down to the bones after that. Allie and Tina brought some berries they had collected and everyone passed those around.

Macy pulled closer to the fire as she finished the berries. It felt good to have food in her stomach again. That coupled with the sleep, she felt that she could go on until they got out of the woods.

"Should we stay another night or get going?" Trent asked.

"As much as I'd like to stay where we have a camp," Luke said, "I don't like staying in one place. Jonah isn't one to give up easily. We need to move on."

Trent looked disappointed, but nodded. "You're right."

"Why don't you take a nap?" Macy asked. "You guys were gone hunting for a long time. Get some rest."

"I think I will." Trent got up and went into the tent the guys had slept in.

Luke wrapped his arm around Macy. "Are you cold?"

"It feels like it's going to snow."

He sniffed. "Smells like it too."

Macy giggled. "You can smell snow coming?"

"You can't? It always has that smell right before."

Macy sniffed. "Yeah, I guess I can smell something different in the air."

"That's snow." Luke pulled her closer. "You know what I think?"

"What?"

"There's going to be—"

Loud rustling noises sounded not far away. Luke jumped up, grabbing the pocket knife from the side of the fire.

"What's that?" Macy whispered.

Luke put a finger to his mouth.

Macy stood up. Everyone looked around, wide-eyed and silent.

Another rustling sound.

Blood drained from Macy's face. She didn't know if she was more scared of a wild animal or Chester. Either way she could end up dead, but Chester knew how to torture. She scooted closer to Luke.

Trent came out of the tent. He grabbed a large stick and held it up.

More rustling noises. This time they were closer.

"Found them! Over here!"

Jonah.

The sounds of hooves and more rustling noises came from the same direction.

Kids around the camp screamed.

"Run!" yelled Trent.

They went in different directions. Luke grabbed Macy's hand and pulled her in the opposite direction as Jonah's voice. She fought to keep up. Her heart pounded in her ears and she had a hard time getting her feet to do what she wanted.

Luke led her through thick bushes where the leaves scratched her face as they ran. There was no path and they kept running into trees and other plants blocking their way.

Macy heard a high-pitched scream followed by Allie's voice screaming no.

A strange sound escaped from Macy's throat.

"We have to keep going," Luke said.

"What are they going to do to Allie?"

Luke held a pricker bush out of the way. "Hopefully just a public shaming. Come on."

"Shouldn't we try to help her?"

"I promised to get you back to your family. Let's go."

Macy moved around the pricker bush. "But she's so young."

Luke pulled on her hand and they ran through a tight path. "I know, but from the sounds of those hooves, there's too many of them. We wouldn't be able to fight off the prophets. Jonah probably has half the men from the community."

"I feel horrible about leaving them."

"Chester is undoubtedly after you. If anything, they're using the others as bait to draw you in. You don't want to fall into his trap, do you?"

Images of being locked under Chester's barn flooded her mind. "No. We have to go."

Luke squeezed her hand. "There's nothing we can do to help the ones the prophets catch, but I can protect you and get you back home."

Macy's throat closed up. All of this was her fault. If she hadn't gotten into Chester's truck in the first place, none of this would have ever happened. She wouldn't have been taken, he wouldn't have tortured her. Now all these other people were going to be hurt. She couldn't get Allie's face out of her mind. "I hope Allie's going to be okay."

"Her parents are assistant prophets. I'm sure she will." Luke's tone didn't sound as sure as his words.

"I hope so."

They ran in silence for a few minutes and then more screams could be heard from the direction of the camp site. Macy couldn't tell who it was, but it sounded like at least three. Were she and Luke the only ones to escape?

Luke turned and gave her a sympathetic look, but didn't slow down. They kept running, passing through tight paths, getting scratched along the way. Not that it was anything compared to whatever the other kids were going to go through.

He squeezed her hand. "Hurry up, Macy."

Before long she was gasping for air.

"Do you need to slow down?" asked Luke.

"I don't think we can, can we?"

"If you need to, we can stop."

Her lungs burned and her mouth was parched.

"Maybe just for a minute."

Luke stopped, also taking deep breaths. "We're probably okay for a few minutes, but we'd better run again as soon as we can."

In between gasps, Macy said, "It's getting dark."

Luke looked up. "We should have another hour of light."

"Then what?"

"We should keep going as long as we can."

Macy's stomach twisted in a tight knot. She felt like she was going to throw up, but she was determined to keep the food down. Who knew when she would be able to eat that much again?

"Are you ready?" Luke asked.

Tears filled her eyes.

Luke's expression softened. "Don't cry."

Her lips wavered. "I can't help it. I'm so tired of everything. I don't want to keep running."

He pulled her close. "You have to. We're close. I can feel it. It's always darkest before the dawn. Just keep going a little farther. Can you do that?"

Macy blinked and the tears fell to her face. "I have to. I can't go back to Chester."

Luke kissed her cheek. "Don't think of that. Think about getting back home. You probably have your own room. What do you have in there?"

"All my stuff. Everything."

"Think about that. Come on." He caressed her palm and then slid his fingers through hers. "Ready?"

Macy took a deep breath. "Guess I'm gonna have to be."

Luke looked into her eyes. "You are." He tugged on her hand and they were off and running again.

Tears flew through the air behind her. Macy couldn't help it. She was tired and didn't know if she had the energy to keep going until they hit civilization.

Found

"**W**E SHOULD TAKE a break," Luke said. It felt like they had been running for days, but it had only gotten dark a short while before. "Okay." The moon shone bright, helping them to see as they ran.

Luke smiled, slowing down. "Not going to argue?"

Macy shook her head. Her legs burned. "Is your leg okay? You hurt it in the corn field, and we haven't stopped except for last night."

"It hurts a bit, but I'm fine."

She squeezed his hand and then pulled away from his grip. Macy rubbed her hand. It ached from being in the same position the entire time they ran. "Are we going to sleep here?" She looked around, not seeing anything that looked appealing. Rocks and thorn bushes mostly.

"Do you have a better idea?"

"Not really. I wish we had a place to hide."

"If we sit by that rock we'll be somewhat hidden by the bush."

Macy squinted. "Probably."

Luke sat against the rock and held out his arm. She sat next to him and he wrapped his arm around her. "At least we can keep each other warm. That's not so bad is it?"

A smile tugged at Macy's mouth. "No. I can't complain about that."

"We should take turns staying awake. You get some sleep first."

"But I slept while you were hunting that fox."

"You're not going to sway me, pretty thing. Close your eyes and get some rest. You're going to need it."

"So are you."

"I'll wake you, and then it'll be my turn. Close those eyes."

"Yes, sir," Macy teased. She closed her eyes and leaned her head against his chest. She pushed her face against it, noticing his muscles.

She listened to his heartbeat as he told her a boring story in a soft, soothing tone. Before long, her eyes grew heavy, and she gave into sleep.

"Macy."

"Mph."

"Macy, wake up."

She sat up. "Is everything okay? Did they find us?"

"No," Luke said. "You mind sitting up while I sleep?"

"Of course. You need your sleep." She yawned.

"Here, take this." Luke handed her a thick stick. "I've been sharpening it with the knife. We can use it as a weapon if we have to."

"Okay. Do you want me to work on one while you sleep?"

"If you want. We can't have too much protection." Luke handed her the knife. "We can use that, too." He leaned his head against her shoulder.

She kissed his hair. "Get some rest."

He snored.

"I'll take that as a yes." She held up the knife and looked for another stick. There was one just out of reach. She used her feet to pull it to her, not wanting to disturb Luke's rest. She grabbed it and slid the knife along the edge, pointing away from her.

She worked on the stick until it had a sharp point. After finishing, she slid the three weapons in between her and the tree they sat against.

Macy listened to Luke's heavy breathing and felt sleepy herself. She couldn't allow herself to sleep.

Her eyelids grew heavier. She sang a song in her head, trying to distract herself. She had to stay awake.

A branch snapped nearby. Macy sat up, holding her breath. Her heart pounded in her ears, making it hard to hear. She tried to calm herself. If she wanted to survive, she needed to stay alert.

Another branch snapped. Macy looked around. A fat raccoon darted in front of her. She let out a sigh of relief.

Everything was quiet for a while, and to keep herself from falling back asleep she thought about what she would do when she got back home. First she would hug everyone and apologize profusely. She would swear never to sneak out again—and she would keep the promise. Then she would let Alex tease her all he wanted, and then when he ran out of things to say she would run down to Zoey's house and find out what she'd missed.

She found that she couldn't even think about her parents, beyond apologizing to them. She'd been gone so long. What must they be going through? She shook her head, a lump forming in her throat. No. She'd cried enough already. More than enough. Macy needed to be strong to get back home.

If they wanted to ground her for life, Macy would have no qualms. She just needed to get out of the woods.

The thought of that was enough to wake her and get rid of the sleepiness. She'd never have to be locked away under the barn again or stuck in a crazy cult, locked inside there too. Being grounded at home with people who loved her would be freedom compared to everything she'd been through recently.

A noise caught Macy's attention. It sounded pretty far away, and she couldn't tell what it might be. She sat a little taller, slowly sliding her hand behind her where she'd put the weapons. Her fingers wrapped around one of the sticks.

She heard another noise, this time closer. It sounded like rustling leaves. Could it be a breeze? She didn't feel anything, but there could be a wind somewhere else.

Another branch snapped. Could it be a raccoon again? Her skin crawled, starting from her back and moving down to her legs. She sat up taller, ready to wake Luke if she needed to. She didn't want to wake him over a forest animal.

More leaves rustled, this time closer and louder. It sounded larger than a critter. They needed to move on.

Macy couldn't find her voice, so she elbowed Luke. He moved his head, but didn't wake. She nudged him again, this time harder. He didn't respond.

She scanned the area, still not seeing anything. Her pulse was on fire. She'd have to find her voice if they were to get away. She heard another rustle.

"Luke," she whispered. "Wake up. Something's headed our way."

He sat up, looking around. "What? Where?"

"That way." Macy pointed. A branch snapped loudly as if to prove her point.

"Where's the knife?" Luke asked.

Macy pulled the knife and other stick out from behind her.

Luke took the knife, leaving her with both sticks. He stood up, pressing his back against the tree. Macy did the same.

"We need to go the direction we came," whispered Luke. "Follow me."

Macy nodded. Luke headed toward the tiny path they had taken, and she hurried to keep up. They made it a few yards before Macy stepped on a branch. It snapped with a loud crack. She cringed. "Sorry."

"We have to hurry." Luke grabbed her hand and pulled her though the path.

They darted between bushes, trees, and thorns. Macy's hair kept getting caught in the thorns.

"There you two are."

Macy's heart stopped.

Chester.

Luke pulled Macy. "Keep going."

She forced her feet to move faster, but she was all too aware of Chester behind them. She couldn't let him catch them. Macy held the two sticks in her hand tighter.

Macy felt a hand on her shoulder. She turned around and screamed, regretting it immediately. If the prophets were out there searching near Chester, she had just informed them of their location.

Luke tugged her arm again. Though Chester had touched her shoulder, he hadn't managed to grab her.

It wasn't over…it was just beginning. They were going to get away from him.

They had managed to lose him in the corn field, and they could do it out here. It would be easier, because they had wide open spaces. They weren't locked inside the community.

Macy tried to kick dirt behind her as she ran. It probably wouldn't do anything to slow down Chester, but she had to do something.

"Where are you going?" Chester called. "We need to talk, Heather."

"Her name's not Heather," Luke yelled without looking back.

Macy picked up her speed and got right behind Luke. She could feel the material of his shirt on her face.

"You're headed for a nest of mountain lions," Chester warned. "Turn around and live, Heather."

"What?" Macy exclaimed.

"He's lying," Luke said. "Keep going."

"No, I'm not," Chester said, sounding closer. "There's a whole group of them. Turn around."

"You turn around," Macy said. "We'll take care of ourselves. Go back to Rebekah."

"Not without you. We're a family."

Macy let go of Luke's hand. She stopped and turned around and stopped. "We aren't a family. We've never been a family. I'm not Heather, and you know it. You ripped me away from my real family."

Luke grabbed her hand and pulled her away. "Don't let him get to you."

Rage built up in the pit of Macy's stomach. "I can't help it. I've never been able to tell him how I feel."

"Write him a letter when he's in jail."

Macy felt Chester's hand on her shoulder again. This time, he squeezed and pulled her toward him.

Done

CHESTER HELD MACY, his glasses gleaming in the moonlight.

"How did you fix your glasses?" she asked.

"Fix them?" He laughed. "I keep a spare set because I need them so desperately. Now come with me, Heather. We have some matters to discuss."

Her blood ran cold. She wanted to look back at Luke, but didn't dare take her eyes off Chester. She tried pulling away from him. His hand slipped, and she ran in the opposite direction, feeling thorns scraping her on all sides.

She heard Chester muttering over the sounds of her and Luke's running. Each time she brushed against foliage, it made noise. Her senses were overwhelmed and she didn't even have time to process anything.

Chester wasn't far behind and he was yelling at her to slow down and give up, still calling her Heather. When would he give up that delusion?

Macy kept turning and running, trying to keep up with Luke. Her legs burned even worse than before, but she didn't let that stop her.

Eventually, she was sure that they had lost Chester.

Macy slowed down, breathing heavily. Even that burned, just like everything else. Luke turned and looked at her, appearing out of breath, too.

She stopped and put her hands on her legs, trying to catch her breath. Had they actually lost Chester? Even if they had, they needed to keep going.

She thought she heard something come her way, so she jumped up, grabbed Luke's hand and ran. She brushed past more thorns, beginning to wonder if they were only going in circles.

Leaves rustled behind them, and then she heard heavy breathing. Not only were they lost, but Chester had managed to find them again.

Macy put more energy into her run. When they got a fork in the path, she tried to remember which direction they came from, but everything looked the same. Luke tugged on her arm, going right.

They came to another fork and turned left. After about only five steps, she slammed into someone—it had to be Chester. Macy looked up and saw him, the moonlight gleaming against his lenses.

He reached out and grabbed her. "Finally, I got you, Heather. It's time to go home and discuss your punishment. For your sake, I hope the prophets don't want to get involved. I'll go a lot easier on you than them."

Macy squirmed, kicking at him. "Yeah, I bet you will."

Chester dug his fingers into her arms. "You know I will."

She turned her head and bit into his wrist as hard as she could. She could taste blood, but she continued to bite down even harder.

"Let go of her." Luke punched Chester across the face.

He ripped his arm from her mouth and then lunged for Luke, who moved out of the way causing Chester to land on the ground with a thud.

Macy spit the blood out, wiping it on her white shirt.

Luke grabbed onto her arm and she ran, stumbling over her feet. She caught herself before falling and ran as fast as she could. But she only got a couple yards before she felt a tugging on her shirt, which made her gag.

Chester pulled her so close she could smell the strong community soap on him. "Stop fighting me. I lost you once, and that's not going to happen again—ever." He pulled on the shirt again, choking her. She pushed against him, kicking. She was aiming for his crotch, but couldn't reach at the angle he held her.

Luke ran at them, but Chester pulled a gun out with his free hand and shoved it in Luke's face.

"No!" Macy begged.

She twisted her body and forced herself down at an angle that forced him to loosen his grip. She gasped for air and ran. Luke grabbed her arm and they ran together.

Chester was barely a few steps behind. He kept reaching for her. She could feel his fingers rub against her back, unable to grab onto her shirt.

Macy picked up her speed, ignoring the pain in her lungs. She still hadn't gotten her breath fully back after his choking her. She gasped for air, not really able to get any decent breaths.

The path ended right in front of her, so she couldn't turn anywhere. Not having time to process that, she slammed into a tree. Chester pinned her against it, wrapping his arms around her.

He forced the gun into her temple.

"Get out of here, Luke, or I'll kill her."

"You wouldn't."

"Would you like to find out?" Chester asked. Something on the gun clicked.

Macy let out a cry.

"Macy, I can't leave you," Luke said.

"Go," Macy begged. "Save yourself."

"No, save her," Chester said. "Get out of here or you'll be wearing her brains, kid."

"Find a way out and finish our plan," Macy said.

Chester moved the gun toward Luke. "I changed my mind. There's no reason for me to let you go."

"Don't!" screamed Macy. "Run, Luke. Please."

"Oh, aren't you two cute?" Chester asked. He shoved the gun against Macy's temple. "You'd better leave now, Luke. My finger's about to slip."

Fear covered Luke's face. "I'll be back for you." Luke held her eye contact for a moment and then ran out of sight.

Macy couldn't move her arms or upper body. She couldn't even reach down to bite him again. However, she could still kick, so that's what she did. She kicked him as hard as she could, screaming at the top of her lungs.

"Do you really think that's going to help anything, Heather? Like I said, you should hope the prophets don't get involved with your punishment."

Macy squirmed and twisted, barely able to move. She twisted and swayed, finally getting a little room. She elbowed him in the stomach, and he let out a gasp, momentarily loosening his grip. Macy ran away from him, but when she looked back, he was already running after her.

Turning her head back around, she picked up her speed. As soon as she felt a tug on her shirt again, she ran faster, but his grip made her stumble, and she found herself falling straight for the ground. She put her hands out to protect her face from the impending dirt.

Dirt flew into Macy's eyes as her face hit the ground. Chester landed next to her with a thud. She wiped at her eyes frantically, the dirt burning them.

Chester wrapped his arms around her so tightly she could barely breathe. She struggled against him while still trying to get the painful flecks out of her eyes. Unable to see, she shoved her hands in his face, hoping to throw off his glasses again.

"It's not much fun when you can't see, is it? Funny how fast karma acts at times."

Macy threw her weight against him, kicking and clawing at him, hating him all the more for that comment. Somehow the last piece of dirt finally flew from her eye, but she still couldn't see because her eyes watered so much.

"Oh, did I make you cry? Or do you actually have remorse for running away?"

"No!" She fought back harder, but he just laughed and then somehow managed to stand up and pull her up, too.

"It's over, Heather. You need to give up."

"I'm not Heather." She kicked, hit, and squirmed more. Her feet weren't touching the ground, making it all the more difficult.

"We're back to *that* again, are we? You know you're Heather. I don't know why you keep fighting me. You must have learned disobedience from your first mom." He stopped and stared into her eyes. "Do you want to know what that got her? She's dead. Heather, your mom isn't in Paris, living the high life with some guy named Jacques. That's what happens to people who refuse to obey me. Don't think you're immune, either. You'd do well to learn from your true mom."

"I knew it! I knew you killed Karla, too." She kneed him in the crotch and he let out a yell, loosening his grip.

Macy stumbled as her feet hit the ground. Anger flashed over his face, but she ran away from him while she had the chance. Her only hope was finding her way to Luke and then getting out of the woods.

Macy took a few turns, pretty sure that she was going the way she came, but it was hard to tell with the paths being worse than a maze. She went a while without running into any intersecting paths. Finally, she ran into another wall of trees, too thick to get through. She stopped, gasping for air and listening for Chester.

If she couldn't get away from Chester, would this be it for her? Was it really over?

Macy heard running. She froze. Where was Chester? She walked down the path until she reached another one and then she looked around. Chester was nowhere to be seen. She could still hear fast footsteps somewhere close, but she couldn't see anything. Macy knew she had to keep moving. If she didn't, he would definitely find her again.

Still breathing deeply, she walked down the path. She could still hear the running, but it sounded far enough away that she was safe, at least for the time being. She couldn't get out of the forest on her own. Hopefully Luke was close by.

The footsteps sounded closer. Did they belong to Luke or Chester? Macy stopped again. She couldn't even tell where they came from. She held her breath.

She couldn't hear anymore running. It was her only chance. Macy burst into a run, not giving herself the chance to over-think anything. Maybe her instincts would take her where she needed to go. She ran, not seeing anyone.

As she passed two intersecting paths, she saw Chester from the corner of her eyes. Her stomach twisted in knots, but before she even had the chance to pick up speed, he leaped toward her and grabbed at her again. She could feel his fingers brush against her side, but he didn't get her or her shirt.

Macy ran faster, but tripped over something. Stumbling, she regained her balance, but she could sense Chester behind her. He wasn't going to give up. She felt his fingers again. Then a tugging on her shirt. He had managed to grasp it again. Macy picked up speed, feeling the resistance.

She had layers. Let him rip the shirt off. At an intersection, she turned without warning. Macy could still feel his hold as she took another sharp turn.

Chester yanked on her shirt. Macy pulled the other way and somehow ended up landing on the ground again. She closed her eyes, not getting anything in them. She could feel the ground scrape against her face as she slid, stopping only inches from a large boulder.

He landed on top of Macy, knocking the wind out of her. He grabbed a chunk of her hair and yanked her head back. "You need to make a choice, and you need to make it now. Stop fighting me. It's your only choice, really. Unless you actually want to join Dorcas and your first mom."

Macy couldn't answer. She still couldn't get a decent breath. She felt the gun pressed against her head again.

"Silence is not an option, Heather. Either you're on my side or not."

Macy refused to speak. He couldn't make her.

"Do you need some convincing, Heather?"

Macy didn't say anything. She heard a horrible popping sound and then felt a searing pain in her leg.

"Want me to break the other one?" He moved off her.

This was her last chance. She got up and ran, but as soon as her sore leg hit the ground, she felt an even worse pain. Macy lost her balance and fell into a patch of pricker bushes.

Dark

MACY OPENED HER eyes, but still didn't see anything because of the darkness. She felt around. Softness surrounded her. She had to have been in a bed.

She couldn't still be in the community. It didn't feel like that hard, uncomfortable bed. That one had been stiff and the bedding smelled like that awful soap they used for everything. She pulled a blanket up to her face. It had a light, pleasant scent. She didn't recognize it, so she couldn't be back at the farm house or in her own bed, either.

Where *was* she?

Macy tried to move her legs, but only one would comply.

A fire came to mind, and then the escaping in the woods only to be found by Chester again. She couldn't remember anything after that. Had Chester caught her?

Macy looked around the room, hoping that her eyes would have adjusted, but she still couldn't see a thing. She sat up. She hadn't gone blind, had she?

She felt her eyes and they were fine. Macy breathed a sigh of relief. She felt her left leg. Something hard covered it. It had to have been a cast. Had she been in a hospital? She couldn't be in one, because she knew they never kept rooms pitch black.

Leaning back down, Macy decided not to worry about it. She appeared to be safe, at least for the time being. The bed smelled clean and was comfortable. Even more important, Chester didn't appear to be nearby.

Feeling sleepy, she closed her eyes. She thought of Luke. Had he been able to get out of the forest? He wouldn't have returned to the community, would he?

She felt tears gearing up. Why had she insisted on leaving the community that night? Dorcas would still be alive, and she would at least have been able to see Luke at school. And what had happened to the kids at campsite?

The light came on, assaulting her eyes. Macy covered them with her arm. She heard someone moving around in the room. Did they know she had woken?

Macy moved her arm away from her eyes, but the light was still too bright. She blinked several times. The light finally felt normal so she looked around.

Rebekah stood folding clothes with her back to Macy.

"Where am I?" Macy asked.

Rebekah turned around. She wore plain but colored clothes and had her hair down, making her look even prettier than she had with the white garb.

"Your dad said you might not recognize it here since it had been so long. This is your old room, Heather."

Macy looked around. They weren't at the farm house. It had to be the house that Heather had been in when her mom had gone missing. Could this be the room where she had written her diaries before being taken to a mental hospital?

She looked around at the furniture. The dresser was the one that had been in her room in the farm house. She had found one of Heather's diaries in there. Macy recognized the shelf full of books and DVDs where she had found another diary.

"What's going on?" she asked.

"I'm folding your clothes. You're supposed to rest." Rebekah sounded mad.

"Is my leg broken?"

Rebekah continued with the clothes. "I wouldn't know. We wrapped it up, but aren't taking you to the hospital. It'll have to heal on its own, whatever's wrong with it. Your knee swelled badly, so my guess is that it's sprained."

"Why are we here?"

She turned and stared at Macy. "Because of what you did."

"What?"

Anger covered her face. "I did everything I could to help you feel at home in the community. I even kept your friendship with Luke a secret, but I never would have if I had known what you two were plotting."

"Why aren't we back there?"

"Why? Because we got kicked out. All of us. Because of you."

"Even you? Couldn't you have—?"

"No, I couldn't. Marriage is forever. Where my husband goes, I follow. So, here we are. Back in the world. But you're staying in the house for a while. Even if you weren't stuck here because of that leg, he said you're to stay in the house. You're not going anywhere for a long time, Heather."

Disagree

C HAD PUBLISHED HIS latest post, this one a regular sports post. As much as it had killed him, a couple weeks before, he had to stop the daily postings about Macy. There were only so many ways he could spin the same thing, and it had been weeks since there was anything new to report. Not only that, but his page views were going down, which meant that people had either lost interest or given up on ever finding her.

He wasn't going to give up on her, but at the same time, he had to find a way to move on with his life until she returned. And part of that meant taking care of the rest of the family. Alyssa had become more distraught as time went by. It was nearly spring, and Macy had been gone since before Thanksgiving.

Chad checked for new comments and responded right away. His heart wasn't in it, but he wrote with his typical humor on the sports posts. The comments on his Macy posts had moved from sad condolences to theories and people sharing what clues they thought they had found. His response to the clues was telling people to contact the cops if they thought it was real.

Chad picked up his phone, looking for any missed calls or texts. Detective Fleshman was supposed to get back to him that morning. They still didn't have any results from the DNA of the young Jane Doe in the morgue. The first set had been compromised somehow and the next batch had come up inconclusive. Chad certainly didn't understand the medical mumbo-jumbo he and Alyssa had been told. All he knew was that they didn't have the answers they desperately needed.

Would they ever have the results? The body had to be decomposing, even though they probably had ways to slow the process.

The screen in front of him was blurry. It was time for a break. He got up and stretched before going upstairs.

Alex and Zoey sat at the kitchen table with text books, papers, and laptops spread all over the table.

"How's the studying?"

Alex scowled. "I hate history. How is it relevant? Math at least makes sense."

Chad patted Alex's head. "They say those who don't learn history are doomed to repeat it."

"Whatever." Alex went back to his work.

Zoey looked up. "Any word from the police?"

"Not yet."

Her face fell. "When are we going to know?"

Chad pulled some leftovers out from the fridge. "Wish I knew." He scooped some food onto a plate and put it in the microwave. "I keep checking my phone. They have to get some results this time. The third time's a charm, right?"

"I hope so. Or we'll have to wait even longer."

Alex got up and grabbed a pop. "Maybe by then she'll be back home and it won't matter. We all know that dead chick isn't Macy."

"We *hope* it's not her," Zoey said.

"It's not." Alex sat down, twisted the cap off and drank.

Zoey rubbed her stomach, looking sad.

Chad tried not to think about what was under her over-sized shirt—his grandchild. He was barely past forty and he had to think about being a grandparent. It was crazy, but nothing was harder to believe than his thirteen year old becoming a dad. He still couldn't wrap his mind around that one.

"When do your parents get in, Zoey?" asked Chad.

She made a face. "Don't remind me. I wish she'd just stay in Japan with him. Maybe they'll get into a big fight and he'll decide not to come here. Why do you ask? You trying to get rid of me?"

"What?" Chad asked. "No. You're always welcome here. Just like always." Why did he feel like he was digging himself into a hole? "Do you want anything while I'm up?"

"No, but thanks." Zoey went back to her studies. They were both doing an online homeschooling program because they couldn't deal with the social pressures and everything else.

The microwave beeped and Chad got his food and then escaped to the bonus room. He turned on the TV and the news came on. After about fifteen minutes, he realized that they hadn't once mentioned Macy. That made him almost as upset as when they wouldn't stop talking about her. He wasn't sure which was worse.

Alyssa walked by the doorway and then doubled back and sat down next to him. "Did you hear from Fleshman yet?"

He shook his head, his mouth full of beans.

"Me neither." Her lips curled down. "I wish they would at least tell us something. I hate waiting. It seems like that's all we do anymore."

Chad swallowed. "It's not their fault. The tests are being done in Seattle. Maybe even being sent out? The whole thing is confusing, and I can't keep it straight."

"It has to be her."

He nearly choked on broccoli. "What?"

"She's been missing for almost four months, Chad. There haven't been any new clues since, what, December?"

"So you think Macy's dead?"

Tears filled her eyes. "What else am I supposed to think?"

"That she's alive! We can't give up on her." He set his plate down on the coffee table a little too hard.

"What does it matter? We can't do anything about it. Whether she's alive or dead, she's not with us. I, for one, need to mourn. Living in limbo is killing me."

"Then we need to get out and form another search party. If we start one, there are plenty of people who will join us. I can print off more fliers."

"It's not going to *do* anything. Everyone around here already knows that she's missing. Her pictures have been plastered everywhere for months. I need closure."

"Closure? Are you serious?"

Alyssa narrowed her eyes. "Do I look like I'm kidding?"

"You can move on with your life without having closure. You don't need to believe that our daughter is dead. Get back to going to the gym—not that you need to, you look great. Join the book club again. You used to really enjoy that. But don't give up on Macy. Please."

Alyssa's eyes shone with tears. "We have to face reality, Chad. With every day that goes by, and there have been a lot of days, the chances go down of her coming home safely."

Chad took a deep breath. He needed to tread carefully or they would find themselves arguing again, like they had before Macy disappeared. The last thing he wanted was to lose what they'd gained.

He put his arm around Alyssa. "Whatever you do, I'm behind you."

"But you think I'm an idiot for thinking she's dead. I can see it in your eyes. You're living in a Pollyanna world, believing that everything will end up working out. How can it? One baby is gone and the other is going have a baby of his own."

Counting to ten silently, Chad took deep breaths. He spoke slowly. "I like to believe that I'm living in a place of reality, but we can agree to disagree on that. As far as the baby, we don't even know if Zoey is going to keep it."

"Seriously? She's going to make up her mind after holding the baby. There's no way she's going to give up her baby after *holding* it. She's going to fall in love immediately. That's how it works."

"Or she could take one look at the little face and realize she's not ready for the responsibility. She could love the baby enough to make the right decision to give it to a family who desperately wants one."

Alyssa shook her head. "You really do live in a fantasy world."

"Look, I'm trying my best to be patient, but if you keep saying things like that, I can't give you any guarantees. Let's agree to disagree. If we have to, we'll avoid the topic."

"Agree to disagree? We're not talking about wallpaper, Chad. These discussions can't be avoided."

Chad took another slow, deliberate breath. "All I'm saying is that we love each other. The world is falling apart around us and we need to stick together. Macy isn't here, and there's not a damn thing we can do about it. We've done everything we can, and now we just have to live with her absence. Our thirteen year old is going to make us grandparents and we can't change that, either. But we *can* hold onto each other."

She blinked and tears fell onto her face. "I wish I could believe that."

"What do you mean?"

"It's not that easy. Love isn't enough."

"I never said it would be easy. I said we need to stick together. For each other and our kids—regardless of how things end up." Chad begged her with his eyes. He needed her to keep hoping.

Alyssa took his hand. "I do love you. You and Alex are all I have."

"And Macy."

"Not any more." More tears fell.

Chad wanted to convince her that Macy was out there—that she needed them to not give up—but he knew it wouldn't get them anywhere. How could she give up? He scooted closer to her and wrapped his arms around her.

They sat in silence.

How would Chad get through this if she gave up?

After a while, he asked, "What's going on with Zoey?"

"What do you mean?"

"I asked her about her parents, and she got really upset."

"Don't you pay attention? She's hurt because her dad has never had any interest in being in her life. Now that she's pregnant and his career is over, he wants to be involved. Not only is it a slap in the face, but she has all those extra hormones to deal with. It's a double whammy. Teenage hormones and pregnancy. I can't imagine dealing with both at the same time."

"Oh, that explains it." He would never understand female hormones, but from what he had seen, they were very real. He remembered with Alyssa's pregnancies, he had to tread lightly. He would have to do double duty with Zoey.

Chad looked at his empty plate.

"Do you want me to make you something to eat and bring it up?"

"No. I can't eat. We need to start looking into funeral arrangements."

The room shrunk around him. "What?"

"She deserves a memorial service."

"Macy hasn't been pronounced dead. Can't you at least wait for that before you jump the gun?"

"You think I'm acting rash?"

"We haven't even gotten the DNA results back. We have no reason to believe the body is Macy. You can't do this. If she is alive somewhere, you'll just send her the message that we've given up."

"How can I get through to you, Chad? I need closure. I have to be able to say goodbye and move on with my life so I can focus on Alex. That poor kid needs us, and he's dealing with her loss, too. It's not fair. He deserves to have me taking care of him properly."

"He's actually doing pretty well if you hadn't noticed. His grades are higher than they've ever been. The teacher in charge of the online school says he may actually get through the eighth grade stuff before school gets out for the summer. He's not only caught up, but will probably get ahead."

Alyssa folded her arms. "He still needs me to be there for him fully. Not like I've been."

"You can do that without giving Macy a funeral, Lyss. We can act like a family again while still waiting for her to return."

"No, actually I can't. I'm not waiting for the mail, Chad. This is our daughter. I can't wait for her *and* continue on with my life. All I can think about is how she should be with us, but she's not."

They stared each other down. It was obvious that neither one was going to back down.

Arguing

C HAD CLOSED HIS laptop, his eyes heavy from responding to over a hundred comments. It had to be past midnight, but he didn't care to check the time. His stomach growled because he hadn't eaten since lunch. He didn't want to after that disagreement with Alyssa. How could she be so eager to plan Macy's funeral?

It didn't make sense to him, and he wasn't going to allow it. Macy wasn't dead, and he wasn't going let her have a funeral unless she was.

Why was Alyssa being so emotional—jumping to conclusions like this? She needed to keep a calm head. They all did. It was the only way they would make it through the ordeal until Macy did return.

Chad made his way up the stairs. The doors to both Macy's and Alex's rooms were closed with no light coming from underneath. Hopefully that meant Zoey and Alex were both sleeping in separate rooms, with Zoey staying in Macy's. Not that it mattered at that point where they slept.

The light was on in his and Alyssa's room, not that it surprised him. Alyssa was still sleeping at odd times. Sometimes she was too upset to sleep, other times, not being able to stay awake when she wanted to.

Chad stopped cold when he walked in. She had suitcases on their bed—his suitcases.

He steadied his voice. "What's going on, Lyss?"

"You need to move out for a little while."

"Excuse me?"

"We can't keep going on like this anymore."

"Like what?" he demanded.

"My point exactly."

"What's that supposed to mean?"

"You don't get it."

Anger ran through him. "There's nothing to *get*, Alyssa. Our daughter is missing and we don't agree on where she's at."

"Exactly. That's a major obstacle, and not one I'm willing to live with."

"So, basically you're going to threaten me with moving out if I don't agree with you? Nice. Really nice."

She narrowed her eyes. "It's not about choosing sides. It's about facing reality—and you refuse to do that. You're going to hang onto this forever. I can see it, twenty years from now, me begging to give our little girl a funeral and you putting your foot down, saying no, she's going to come back. Just wait. It's the beginning of March, Chad. I've done nothing but wait since the middle of November. When those test results finally come, you'll see who's right."

"Then wait for them to come in. Want me to call Fleshman right now? I can, and I'll probably wake him. You know what he'll tell us? He doesn't know. Don't you think if that body was Macy's, someone would be able to figure it out by now?"

"I bet if they would have let us look at it, we could have told them months ago," Alyssa said. "We could have moved on a long time ago."

"They don't want us dealing with the emotional trauma if it is her. The body is so messed up they couldn't identify her face or any markings."

"Yeah, and it has enough similarities to give reasonable doubt. Similar height, weight, and hair color. For whatever reason, they can't get those test results right. Why is that?" She stared him down.

"I don't know, but you need to put my clothes back on the hangers. I don't want them getting wrinkled."

"Hang them yourself when you get wherever you're going." Alyssa narrowed her eyes.

Chad went over to the bed and dumped out the closest luggage and then tossed the suitcase on the floor. "I'm not going anywhere."

"You're not staying here."

"Look. If you need space, that's fine. I'll sleep in the bonus room or even down in my office, but you're not kicking me out of my house. I've done nothing wrong."

"Not good enough." Alyssa folded her arms.

"You're right. I should have a bed. I'll take Macy's, because that's probably empty."

Alyssa glared at him. "I made sure they went to bed in the proper rooms."

"And I'm sure they stayed there, too," Chad said sarcastically. He dumped out the other suitcase. "Put those back on their hangers or I'm sending them all to the dry cleaner to get pressed. I'm not going to wear wrinkled clothes."

"Then don't dump them on the bed. I had them all nicely folded."

"Put them in the closet, then."

"Chad, I'm done arguing about your clothes. In fact, I'm done arguing, period."

"Good. Put my stuff away while I get ready for bed. You're going to have to deal with me snoring next to you, because I'm not going anywhere."

"Yes, you are."

He stepped closer to her. "I'm not going anywhere. I was willing to sleep in a different room, but now I'm not."

"You have to. I'm kicking you out."

Chad laughed bitterly. "Really? Out of my own house? The house that I paid for? Tell me, how are you going to pay for everything? Not just the house payment, but the utilities. Everything costs money, and you don't make anything. Not that you couldn't. You could make more than I could. But you don't. You like being a domestic engineer and I'm happy to provide that for you. But not if you try kicking me out of the house I've worked so hard for."

Her lips formed a straight line and her face reddened. "Have you heard of child support and alimony?"

"Don't threaten it unless you mean it. Do you hear me? Don't even go there unless you're prepared. And just to let you know, the state of Washington doesn't do alimony. You could get child support, but not spousal. And believe me, since I'm the one with the money, I could afford a much better attorney than you. Like I said, don't go there unless you're serious."

She looked shaken. Good. How dare she throw this at him? Attempting to kick him out and then throw divorce at him. What had gotten into her?

"How do you know so much about that?" she asked.

"I haven't looked into it, if that's what you're implying. Half the people we know are split. Men gossip in the office too, you know. So, have you changed your mind?"

"You won't go?" she asked.

"I think I've made myself clear. If you need to get away from me, take some time and visit your parents. I'll even pay for a first class plane ticket. Even when you're threatening me with divorce and alimony."

"You think going to my parents' house is going to help?"

Maybe they could talk some sense into her. "It would get you away from me, and since you obviously don't want to be anywhere near me it might help."

"Chad, this isn't a joke."

"I'm not kidding around, Lyss."

"Well, if we're going to make this work, we have to get on the same page," she said.

"Then we either have to agree to disagree or you're going to have to agree to wait for actual proof before planning a memorial service. And let me tell you something. Even if you leave me and keep planning it, I'm going to fight you every step of the way. No one should have a funeral unless they're actually dead. I won't let that happen to Macy."

She stepped closer to him. "And when someone is dead, they deserve a memorial."

"We have no proof. Wait until the results come in. Then we'll know who's right and what to do."

"Or we'll just find out that particular girl isn't her. Then we'll be back to knowing nothing. We may never find a body. Then what?"

"Why are you doing this? How can you give up?"

"Give up? You think I'm giving up?"

"What else would you call it?"

"You're impossible. Really, you won't just leave?"

"I'm not going anywhere."

"Only me."

"Only you what?"

"Anyone else kicks their husband out and they go. Not me."

"You know what I think? I think a good night's rest is in order. It's late and we're tired. Let's talk about this in the morning."

"If you won't go, then I will."

"Where are you going? Flights are much more expensive when you purchase them at the airport."

Alyssa's face flushed red. "My parents aren't the only people I know. Do you think I'm that much of a loser?"

"Of course not. Are you going to stay at a friend's house? How long?"

"I'm not your child! I don't have to tell you what I'm doing. In fact, I don't have to tell you anything."

Sadness ran through Chad, replacing the anger. "Are you sure you want to go, Lyss? Really, I'll sleep in another room and we can talk about this again in the morning. Or we can talk tomorrow night. I'll give you all the space you need."

She gave him an exasperated look. "You really don't get it."

"Clearly."

They stared at each other. Chad tried to express with his eyes where his mouth had failed. They needed each other more than ever. Separating, even for a short time, wasn't going to make anything better.

Finally he said, "I hope you won't go."

"Since you won't, you leave me no choice."

"Please, Alyssa. Think about all the tough times we've gone through. Being together is what helped us. We need each other now more than ever. You say you want to be here for Alex—do you really think that taking off is going to help him? His sister is missing and—"

"You don't need to explain what's going on in my son's life. He's old enough and smart enough to know this isn't about him."

"Let me brush my teeth and then you can have the bedroom." Chad let out a slow breath as he walked to their bathroom. Tears were threatening, but he had to hold it together. What had gotten into her? Was it the grief talking? Did she have her own hormonal issues? She was too young for the female life change, wasn't she?

He took his time brushing and going to the bathroom, hoping that a strike of brilliance would hit him. That way when he came out of the bathroom, he could say the right thing and she would change her mind so they could fall asleep in each other's arms.

By the time he was done, he had no such strike of luck. He looked around the empty bedroom. Had she gone to check on the kids? He went down the hall, finding it empty. He went through the rest of the house, still not finding her.

Heart sinking, he looked outside to where her car had been for the last couple of days.

It wasn't there. Knowing it wouldn't be in the garage, he looked anyway. His car sat there, looking lonely and dejected.

Or was that Chad?

Sorrows

ALYSSA PULLED INTO the same parking spot she had the last time she was at the bar. Drinking hadn't solved any problems then, but at least she had been able to forget her troubles for a little while. She looked around the parking lot, relieved to see Rusty's tow truck missing.

The last thing she needed was a lecture from him again. She wasn't going to drink and drive, so there was nothing to feel guilty about. She had packed a pillow and blankets so she would sleep in the back of her car. If Rusty did show up, insisting to tow her again, this time she had cash to pay him and for the hotel he would drop her off at.

She fixed her hat, making sure it covered her eyes. Her family was practically at celebrity status between being on the news for Macy's disappearance and Chad's blog. Over the last month, he had had them making videos and uploading them to the blog since the news hadn't been talking about the case as much.

Her face was everywhere and the last thing she wanted was to be recognized. She only wanted to drink as many fishbowls of alcohol as she could without passing out. Not that losing consciousness sounded so bad. Anything to take her away from her life and the constant reminders of what a failure she was. One kid missing and the other ready to become a parent. They would certainly skip over her when handing out the Mother of Year award.

Walking into the bar, she was glad to see it was busy. No one paid any attention to her.

There was only one available table way in the back. She couldn't have asked for anything more. She sat down and watched everyone while she waited for the waitress. There were several lively games of pool going on as well as plenty of TVs with different sports to choose from. There were also quite a few loud conversations, with people who had already had too much to drink. It was no wonder that Rusty came to this bar. He probably made a fine living towing drunks home.

The same waitress from months earlier made her way to Alyssa's table, again chewing a big wad of gum. She listed off the specials for the night, holding a pad of paper and a pen. Alyssa noticed her name tag said Sela.

"Do you still have the fishbowl drinks?"

"Yeah, but they're not on special. Have you tried—?"

"I'll take a fishbowl. I don't care what it costs."

"Fishbowl it is." She wrote on the paper. "Anything else?"

Alyssa remembered the nachos not going over so well. "Surprise me with your favorite appetizer."

The waitress smiled and nodding, writing. "Sure thing." She walked away.

Yawning, Alyssa hoped the food and drink would help to wake her up. It was late and she hadn't slept well since Macy disappeared. Hopefully tonight she could forget all about everything and finally get the sleep she needed. She watched the nearest game of pool, trying to convince herself it was interesting.

Sela brought over a fishbowl and set it on the table. "The food's still cooking."

"Thanks, Sela." She grabbed the straw and drank as fast as she could. Feeling warm, Alyssa took her coat off. She wanted to take the itchy hat off, but she didn't want anyone to recognize her. Especially Rusty. Maybe she would be lucky and he was driving drunks home from a different bar that night.

Just as she emptied the fishbowl, Sela came with a steaming plate. From Alyssa's angle, she couldn't see what was on it.

Sela's eyes widened. "Ready for another bowl already?"

Alyssa pushed it toward her, nodding.

"I'll get that for you right away." She set the food in front of Alyssa. It looked like a combo platter. It had cheese sticks, onion rings, tiny baked potatoes, egg rolls, quesadilla slices, and little chicken wings. It was enough for two or three, but Alyssa didn't care. Her mouth watered as she tried to decide what to eat first.

She looked up to say thank you, but Sela had already disappeared. Alyssa picked up an egg roll and bit down. It melted in her mouth. It was even better than the food at her favorite Chinese restaurant.

When she had a mouth full of a baked potato, Sela arrived with another fishbowl. Not wanting to be rude by not thanking her twice in a row, Alyssa gave her thumbs-up.

"No problem. Enjoy."

Alyssa planned to. She finished the potato and then went to work on the new fishbowl. Before long, she was eating, but not even aware of what was in her mouth. She had finished most of the platter, having left all of the cheese sticks. She was used to the kids eating all of those, so it was just habit.

"You again."

Looking up, Alyssa saw Rusty standing next to her. It took a moment to register because of her buzz. She wanted to groan, knowing a lecture was coming, but he was so gorgeous she couldn't. The way his curls fell around his face and ears was too much. "Hi, Rusty."

"Mind if I sit down?"

"Sure. Have some food. It's the least I can do since you paid my bill last time."

"Don't forget about the free ride home." He smiled.

Oh, heavens, that smile. What was he doing as tow truck driver? Alyssa knew she should have been embarrassed, but she couldn't take her eyes off his face.

Rusty picked up a cheese stick and took a bite. "I've always loved these. I haven't seen you around in a while. I had hoped you were doing okay."

He had thought about her? Alyssa started to smile, but then remembered her face was everywhere. How could he have not thought about her? She shrugged, not wanting to talk about her life. She had gone there to forget. Or had she actually wanted to see Rusty? There *were* plenty of bars between her house and this one.

It was hard to remember why she had come here, although she was more than aware of her fight with Chad. That jerk wouldn't leave the house like a normal husband.

"What brings you here?" Rusty picked up another cheese stick.

"Nothing I want to talk about."

He nodded. "What do you want to talk about?"

She looked at the platter. "These onion rings. Have you ever tasted anything like them? It's like food from heaven."

Rusty laughed, the skin around his eyes crinkling. He looked even more beautiful. "They are pretty good." He looked at the fishbowl. "How many have you had?"

"Only two."

"Looks like you'll need another ride home then."

"Oh, seriously."

He shook his head, his curls bouncing around.

She waved Sela over. "I'll take another fishbowl."

"Coming right up." She eyed Rusty and walked off, not giving him a chance to say no.

"You really think you need a third one?"

"I came here to forget about life. So, yeah, I do need another."

"Haven't you forgotten yet?"

Alyssa shook her head. "I only have a buzz. I need to get plastered."

"Plastered, huh? Well, I'd better stay here with you then. You mind the company?"

"Not at all. I could look at you all night." She could feel her face turn bright red. Why had she said that?

Rusty's face looked a little pink as well. "Okay, I suppose that works. You'll let me tow you home?"

"I'm just going to sleep in my car. You can tow someone else tonight."

"You're planning to spend the night in your car—in this neighborhood? Have you lost your mind?"

"That's pretty much why I came here. To lose it. You know what I mean. To forget everything. Now I'm not even making sense to myself."

"I can't let you sleep in your car."

"I told you I'm not going home."

He nodded and then took the last onion ring. "Manna from heaven."

Was he trying to distract her? She nodded, faking a smile. "You can drop me off at a hotel. Anywhere but home."

"We don't have to talk about it. What shows do you like to watch?"

Alyssa stopped. "I can't remember the last time I watched something."

"What did you used to watch?"

Sela dropped off the fishbowl and Rusty looked at her. "We'll get the check now. No more drinks."

"Sure thing, Rusty."

Why did Alyssa feel so bad at the mention of shows? Probably because it reminded her of the fact that she hadn't done anything normal in such a long time. Maybe that was part of the reason she felt like getting out of the house—that and the fact that Chad refused to leave.

She grabbed the bowl and took the longest sip she could manage. Alyssa didn't want to think about home or Chad or anything. Swallowing, she looked at Rusty, feeling a bit dizzy. "So what have you been up to?"

"Same old. Towing people home to keep them off the streets."

"Is that all you do? And you do it for free?"

"Not usually. A man does have to make a living." He grinned. Like a Greek god.

"Have you considered modeling?" Alyssa asked.

Rusty raised an eyebrow. "Modeling? No."

"You could rake in a lot more with that than driving a tow truck. You could always do that for your good deed of the day."

He shook his head, the beautiful curls jumping around again. "No interest in modeling." How was he still single?

Alyssa had never looked at another man other than Chad in all their years together, but there was something she really liked about Rusty. Her mind wasn't working clearly enough to figure out why.

She took another drink.

"Are you done with that?"

"It's half full."

"I'll pay for it if you stop now."

Alyssa held up her purse. "I brought plenty of money. I don't need a handout."

"Think of it as me paying you to stop."

"You already know I'm not climbing into my car. Not to drive it, anyway."

"And you're aware that you're going to ride in my truck while I tow your car. I don't want you spreading the manna all over my interior." Did his eyes twinkle, or was that her imagination?

She smiled. "My stomach feels fine."

Sela came by with the bill and Rusty took it.

Alyssa snatched it from him. "I told you I have the money."

He tapped the table. "If you leave the drink alone, you can pay. Otherwise, I will."

She raised an eyebrow. "Are you for real?"

"That's the deal."

Men. Why were they always trying to control her? First with Chad refusing to leave and now this. "Fine." She shoved the bowl as far away from her as possible. "Happy?"

"Satisfied."

Alyssa grabbed her purse and found the pocket with the cash. She pulled out enough for everything plus a tip and then set it on top of the receipt.

"You ready to go?" Rusty ran his hands through his hair, leaning back.

"Not really. Why don't we sit here and wait for the alcohol to make its way through me. Then you can leave without having to worry about the free tow."

"It's not really free. I write it off at tax time. I actually have an appointment with my accountant, so I could use another write-off."

"You know what I mean."

"This place is going to close before you're ready to drive safely."

"I told you I'm not driving."

"And I'm not letting you sleep in this neighborhood."

They stared at each other.

"You're impossible." Alyssa shook her head. Maybe it was a man thing.

Rusty leaned forward, raising an eyebrow. "Actually, you are."

"Me? You've lost your mind."

"Nope. It's perfectly sound." He grinned.

"What are we going to do? Tow me to a hotel?" She shrugged. "Or I could just sleep here."

"In the bar?"

"Yeah. Why not?"

"For starters, they don't allow it. Then we're back to the fact that I won't leave you in this neighborhood in your car."

"I hope you're able to come up with a good suggestion, because I'm done. I'm perfectly happy sleeping in the car."

Rusty sighed, looking worn out or perhaps frustrated. He was quiet for a minute before speaking again. "I have a spare room at my house. We actually used it as a guest room, but I haven't had anyone over since the accident."

She stared at him. "You want me to go back to your place?"

"It's not like that. I don't want to drop you off at a hotel. I'd feel a lot better if someone was there to watch out for you."

"I'm not a kid."

"No, you're not. But I want to make sure you're okay. Last time, you went home to your family. This time, you're refusing. You can even lock the guest room, if you'd feel better about staying there. And it's at the other end of the house from my room. It's either that or I'm taking you home."

Alyssa frowned. "Do you do this for everyone?"

His lips curled into a smile. "Never."

Guest

ALYSSA TRIPPED WALKING into Rusty's house. It was a lot nicer than she had expected from a bachelor pad. He must have left everything the way his wife had and then hired a cleaning service, because no guy she knew was that tidy. The front room practically sparkled.

She looked around, taking it all in. It was a sprawling rambler on a large lot. Even though it was dark, and the house too big to see the back yard, she pictured a large play structure where the kids had probably spent hours playing.

That was probably why he had taken a special interest in her. They had both lost children and that was something that most people couldn't understand. Alyssa sure wished that she didn't. Even with fishbowls full of alcohol, she couldn't truly forget.

"You have a really nice place."

Rusty closed and locked the front door. "Thanks. I left it the way Lani left it. She had a real eye for design."

Alyssa nodded, afraid the alcohol would make her say something stupid. For the first time since ordering, she regretted drinking so much. She didn't trust her mouth, but felt like she should say something nice about his wife. She just didn't dare yet.

"Are you tired? I can show you to the guest room or I can show you around. What do you feel like?"

Her stomach squeezed. "Actually, could you show me to the bathroom?"

"Uh, oh. Follow me." He led her down a hall to the right and pointed to a door. "There you go."

She nodded a thanks and ran in, closing the door. Alyssa flipped on the light switch and the fan. Hopefully the fan was loud enough that he wouldn't hear her retching. She got to the toilet just in time.

Ordering food when drinking that much was a waste of time and money.

When she was finally done throwing up, she splashed water on her face and then found some toothpaste and put some on her finger. She rubbed it on her teeth and then swished it around her mouth.

After rinsing, she went into the hall and didn't see him. That was a relief. Even though he probably knew she was losing her food—again— at least he had given her privacy. She went down the hall from where she came and saw the front room was empty. Where had he gone? She didn't even know where she was supposed to crash.

"Rusty?"

Silence.

Alyssa's heart rate picked up. What was going on? Maybe coming to his house had been a bad idea. "Are you awake?"

A noise from the left startled her. Rusty appeared and gave her his gorgeous smile. "Sorry. I decided to use the restroom too. Do you want the grand tour before I show you to your room?"

Relief flooded her and she smiled back. "That sounds great." It was strange to be alone in a house with a guy other than Chad, but she felt perfectly at ease with Rusty.

"This way." He went back down the hall and she followed, unable to avoid noticing that he was just as easy on the eyes from the back as the front. She took her gaze off him and looked at the pictures on the wall. It was a shrine to his beautiful family.

They entered a large, bright kitchen. It was modern and gorgeous. For a moment, Alyssa was jealous, but then she remembered that he was probably quite lonely in such a large kitchen that must have held so many memories.

Rusty leaned against the island, nearly bumping his head on one of the pots hanging from the ceiling. "Feel free to use the kitchen whenever you wish. If you're hungry, eat. Use whatever looks good." He winked.

"Maybe I will. I owe you for the tows and now for giving me place to stay."

"You don't owe me anything. But if you do feel you need to repay me, please consider dropping the alcohol. I told you what I went through after losing my family. Rehab sucks."

Alyssa held onto her stomach. "No. That's okay. I'm already thinking about finding a new way to deal with my grief."

"You want some toast or crackers?"

She shook her head.

"You're looking pretty green, Mrs. Mercer."

"Alyssa. Please call me Alyssa."

"Of course. Would you prefer toast or crackers? Your stomach needs something bland." He indicated for her to sit at the table.

He wasn't going to take no for an answer, was he? "Crackers are fine." She sat down at the nearest chair.

Rusty went into the pantry and came out with a white box and opened it, pouring square crackers onto a plate. He set it in front of her and then sat across from her. "Do you need to call anyone and let them know you won't be home tonight?"

"I made that clear before I left." She picked up a cracker and bit into it, spilling crumbs onto the table. "Sorry."

"No problem. Anything you want to talk about? I'm all ears."

She looked into his beautiful eyes. He looked like he actually wanted to listen.

"People often tell me their troubles as I tow them places. I'm good at keeping secrets." He gave her a reassuring nod.

Alyssa let out a slow, deliberate sigh. Did she dare open up? Maybe she should wait to make that decision until after the alcohol had left her system. "I really appreciate you opening your home to me, Rusty, but I'm suddenly exhausted. I hope you're not offended if I just go to bed?"

"Not at all." He stood up. "Let me show you to your room. It's just down the hall."

Still feeling the buzz, Alyssa held onto the table as she got up from the chair. She followed him down another hall and ended up facing several doors.

Rusty pointed to one on the left. "That's another bathroom and the laundry room. And that one," he pointed to the door at the end of the hall, "leads to the back yard. The one behind you is the guest room. Do you need anything? You didn't bring in a bag."

Alyssa shook her head. "It's in my car."

"Want me to fetch it for you?"

"I can get it."

"No, I'm steadier on my feet. I'll only be a minute."

"Can't argue with that." She dug her keys out of her purse and handed him the one that went to her car.

He took off, and Alyssa used the bathroom again. She really shouldn't have drunk that much. There had to be another way to deal with her life. She had been sneaking more of Chad's beers—and she didn't even like beer. He had to have noticed, but hadn't said anything.

Sighing she flushed the toilet. After washing her hands, she looked around the room. It was as Rusty had described. A full bathroom with a washer and dryer and shelving that held laundry items. She grabbed a washcloth and ran it under warm water and washed her face. Too bad she hadn't brought her creams, but she hadn't thought that far ahead.

When she got into the hall, she didn't see Rusty. Maybe she should have told him where the bag was. Her car was an embarrassing mess. She hadn't been taking care of it since Macy disappeared. That was something else that needed to change along with giving up alcohol. She had to get her life back, even though it would never be close to the same again. Living in limbo was done.

Alyssa went into the room that Rusty had said would be hers for the night. She found the light switch and turned it on. The first thing she saw was her bag sitting in the middle of a queen sized bed. Her keys were on top of the bag.

She closed the door behind her and stuck her keys in the purse and then dug her pajamas out from the bag. Soon she was in the middle of the ultra-soft bed all by herself. When was the last time she had gone to bed and not had to worry about anyone disturbing her? If one of the kids didn't need her, then Chad did.

Guilt stabbed at her for enjoying the peace. She shoved it away.

After everything she had done for everyone all those years, there was nothing wrong with taking some time to take care of herself. Even with all the stress and heartache of Macy being gone, she had still taken care of Alex, Chad, and even Zoey.

Not that she minded taking care of everyone. Even Chad, who could take care of himself. Sure, she had spent a lot of time sobbing by herself—especially in the beginning—but she had also made sure that everyone was taken care. She'd had to step it up when people stopped bringing over meals.

Alyssa had taken that as her first small sign that it was time to move on with life. Things needed to return to normal as much as possible. They were still alive, and she needed to get herself together enough to take care of her remaining child. Alex was who she had to focus on now. She needed this time to pull herself together without distraction.

Before she could focus on taking care of Alex properly, she needed to mourn Macy. She would allow herself to grieve while she had this bedroom all by herself, and then she would plan the funeral—even if it ruined her relationship with Chad. If he didn't love Alyssa enough to give her what she needed, then she didn't need him in her life anymore.

She stretched and then rolled over, spreading herself across the bed diagonally. Closing her eyes, she saw Alex's face in her mind.

Hopefully, he wouldn't be too upset over her being gone in the morning. Chad would let him know that she was safe, and with Zoey still there, he might not even notice her absence.

She would have to ask Rusty how he dealt with the loss. How on earth had he been able to move on? He seemed to be happy enough. In fact, she would have never guessed what he had been through if he hadn't told her.

Memories of Macy filled Alyssa's mind in the dark silence. Tears came. "Why did you go, Macy? Didn't you know how much losing you would kill the rest of us?" She buried her face into the pillow and sobbed. Once the tears stopped—even they had had their limit—she sat up, wrapping her arms around her knees.

It felt good to speak to Macy. If she had died like Alyssa believed, maybe Macy could even hear Alyssa speaking to her. "Macy, I hope you know how much we all love you. Did you know before you took off? Were you only planning on being gone that night? The only thing missing, aside from you, of course, was your favorite purse."

Alyssa sighed. "Was there anything we could have done differently? I would give anything to go back in time and stop you from going. Or let you go and have Zoey and Alex go with you so you wouldn't be alone for a second. Did you mean to leave us? I can't imagine that you did. I know you left that message online, but there's so much doubt around that. Most everyone thinks you were forced to write that. Were you? I hope not. More than anything, I hope not."

She squeezed her knees tighter. "It rips me apart to think about anything bad happening to you. I should have been there to protect you. I tried, I really did. I looked for you until my body hurt. I begged others to help. Your dad, he's been getting the word out on his blog nonstop. And we get along again. We're not fighting anymore, Macy. Well, not until tonight."

Fresh tears filled her eyes, thinking about her fight with Chad. "We can't agree on what to do about you. I don't know if that'll tear us apart or not. I need to give you the memorial service you deserve. What if we never find you? Are we going to never give you a proper service? That's not right. But no matter what happens, Dad and I both love you with all of our hearts. Even if we can't be together anymore." Tears dropped onto her arms.

"Though I think us not being together would hurt Alex more than you. Hopefully, you're in Heaven or someplace good. I can't imagine you going anywhere else. You're so sweet. Feisty, yes." Alyssa couldn't help smiling. "No one could ever doubt your spunk. I'll never forget how mad you got when Dad and I tried to keep you from going vegan. You weren't going to take no for an answer. And you didn't. When I saw you buying your own food, I finally caved. Remember that? I wanted to take you to the gym with me, but you were afraid you'd see kids from school there. You used Dad's weights in the garage."

Alyssa felt a wave of relief wash over her. It felt so good to talk *to* Macy. She really felt like her daughter could hear her. She leaned back and fell into a sleep deeper than she had experienced in a long time.

Stress

MACY LISTENED FOR noise outside the bedroom. Even with her ear pressed against the door, she couldn't hear anything. She would be expected up soon, but she didn't want to see either Chester or Rebekah before she had to.

She held her breath as she opened the door, careful to lift the door up slightly at the just the right spot so it wouldn't squeak. She had managed to open it without a sound yet again. Looking down the empty hall, she pretended she was a ninja as she made her way to the bathroom.

Her leg was fine, though she never did figure out if it had been broken or sprained. It had taken about six weeks to heal, and Rebekah had said she thought that was normal for a broken bone. Macy wasn't so sure, but she was just grateful that she had been walking around for a while.

Although as soon as she could get around, Chester and Rebekah had put her to work. She had to do all kinds of housework and for whatever reason, they still had her studying the community books.

When she was done in the bathroom, she listened to see if they were awake. She'd heard them late into the night. Even though they now lived in a house with every modern convenience, that didn't keep her from hearing their newlywed activities each night.

It disgusted her, but she did her best to keep perspective. It gave her more reason to work on her plan to get out of there. Chester had the house sealed tight. Most of the windows were nailed shut or otherwise made impossible to open. The loud, ear-piercing alarm was set at all times. He hadn't even told Rebekah the code to turn it off.

Looking around, she went into the living room. She walked to the window and peeked around the curtain and moved a blind up. It was light outside and she could see kids her age standing at a bus stop. Most of them were teasing each other and a couple others stood off to the side, looking tired and annoyed.

As much as she had hated school before being kidnapped, Macy would give anything to go back. She would even take the kids who had bullied her. Not only did Chester make them look like scared mice in comparison, but Macy had grown in her confidence. She had survived much more than she ever would have thought possible. She could stand up for herself against some insecure teens.

Macy watched the kids across the street. Had they been Heather's friends?

Heather was part of why Chester had gone so far as to keep their presence hidden from the neighbors. She was locked away at the local mental hospital because of everything Chester had put her through. If Macy was seen, people would know something was up. It was too risky.

Even Chester only went out at night, when he was certain no one would see him. His truck was hidden away in the garage, which had coverings over the windows. Rebekah never left the house either. She was mad about being ripped from the community, and wanted nothing to do with the world.

Macy also knew Rebekah had a warrant out for her arrest from her days in a band. She knew better than to ask Rebekah about it, but she couldn't help wondering if that played into her refusal to leave also.

A noise behind Macy startled her and she jumped back, putting the curtain back in place.

"Do you miss your friends, Heather?" Chester asked. He tied his bathrobe, looking nonplussed.

"Something like that." Pretending to be Heather had become a natural part of life. She no longer wanted to scream that she wasn't Heather.

"Maybe someday you can go outside again and see them," Chester said, referring to the kids outside. "But for now, we have chores. Your true mom is tired from the pregnancy, so you're going to have to do her chores today. Can you handle that?"

Macy held back a groan. "No problem." Doing the extra chores was a small price to pay if it meant keeping Chester's temper at bay.

Macy had expected him to be even angrier with her than he always was already about them being kicked out of the community, but he hadn't been any worse since being in the house. Rebekah was the one who had changed. She had been so kind to Macy before, but now the resentment was all over her face.

"Why don't you start with making breakfast?" Chester asked, his voice cheery. "Then you can take your mom hers in bed."

Macy went to the kitchen. In her real family, breakfast meant either cold cereal or something frozen stuck in the microwave, but living as Chester Woodran's fake daughter, it meant a huge production.

Macy would have to make waffles or pancakes from scratch and then make some kind of complicated egg dish—scrambled, which was easy, was not allowed. The whole thing would make a huge mess, taking her more than an hour to cook and then clean everything. Although she was glad to have electricity again. Living in *the world,* they weren't stuck with the community's insane rules.

The shower sounded as Macy gathered the ingredients. At least she would be left alone for a little bit. Even when Chester wasn't being a jerk, he talked nonstop. He never had anything interesting to say, but he had no shortage of things to rattle on about. Macy knew his thoughts on politics, farming, the news, how people treated him, what life had been like as a child, and a plethora of other topics.

She was sure he loved the sound of his voice so much he had to force others to listen to it also. It might not be so annoying if he wasn't so insistent his opinions were right and anyone who disagreed was wrong.

By the time Chester came into the kitchen again, Macy had everything on the table.

"That smells delicious, Heather. Why don't you grab a tray and take a plate in for your mom?"

Macy's chest tightened. She knew once she got into the bedroom, Rebekah's hate would be felt from across a room.

"Did you hear me?" Chester asked.

"Yes." Macy turned around and went through a couple cabinets until she found the tray he was talking about. She put a plate and silverware on and then filled everything.

She turned around and faced Chester, hoping he would take it into the room instead.

"What are you looking at me for? Take it in to your mom. Be sure to tell her you hope she feels better."

"Okay." Macy did her best to ignore the knots twisting in her stomach. She squeezed the tray and made her way back to Chester and Rebekah's room, dragging her feet. If he said anything about her speed, she would blame it on her leg. He couldn't say anything about that since he was the one who had injured her.

Macy steadied the tray and held her breath, bracing herself. She would go in and out as fast as possible. Maybe Rebekah would even be asleep or at least pretend to be asleep to avoid Macy.

Unfortunately, Rebekah was sitting up with the light on. She was reading what appeared to be a book from the community. Not that she had read anything else that Macy had ever seen.

Rebekah looked up from the large book and shot Macy a disgusted look.

"I've got some breakfast for you." Macy tried to smile, but it didn't quite work.

"Just set it on your dad's side. It won't fit over my belly any more."

Macy nodded, not making eye contact. She walked around to the other side of the bed and pushed the tray closer to her. "I hope you feel better."

"Sure you do."

The words stung. Macy looked at her. "You know, it wasn't my intention to get you kicked out of there. I'm sorry."

"It doesn't matter."

"Yes, it does," Macy said. "We used to get along and—"

"What I meant was that it won't get me back in there. Our entire family has been permanently banned. Jonah, Eve, and the other prophets made that abundantly clear."

"That's not the end of the world. The—"

"Please just go. You're stressing me out."

Macy shook her head and left the room. Why couldn't Rebekah see that the community was a cult? They would probably end up having some mass suicide at some point. She had read in school about that happening to other groups like that.

She went back to the kitchen to find Chester eating. "Is your mom resting?"

"Yes."

"Good. You'd better eat, because we have a lot of chores to do today."

Macy grabbed some food and ate. It should have bugged her that she was comfortable with everything, but it didn't. As much as she wanted to get back to her family, somehow life with Chester and Rebekah had settled into a form of normalcy, even though it sucked. But even when Chester was being nice, it was only so he could catch her off guard when he later snapped.

At first, Macy had been hopeful when he was being nice, but it hadn't taken her long to figure out that it was like the calm before the storm. His politeness made her more nervous than when he was stomping around, complaining.

He set his fork on the plate. The noise startled Macy.

Chester looked into her eyes through his big, ugly glasses. "Today we're going to deep clean. Forget about the laundry and all the other daily chores. Start with the kitchen and then do the bathrooms. By then it should be lunch and we can see how you've done. I'll be in my study."

Macy nodded, biting back a comment. It wasn't fair that she had to do all the work, but she knew better than to say anything. The last thing she needed was to find herself back in the barn or locked back up in Heather's room. Even though she didn't have much freedom, she could at least walk around the house.

She *was* going to get out. Even though Chester kept the alarm on at all times to keep her in, she had a much better chance of getting away here than she had anywhere else. Back at the farm, they were miles away from the nearest people—and that house had been tight with security as well. The community that had proven deadly to escape.

Chester slammed his hands on the table, scaring Macy. "Stop daydreaming and get to work."

Discovery

MACY FINISHED SCRUBBING the floor in the dining room and then took the supplies back to the laundry room. On her way back, she stopped in the hall, hearing Chester's voice. At first she thought he was talking to her, but then she realized he was on the phone in his study. He wouldn't talk to her in there—he wouldn't let her near the only room with a computer.

She looked up and down the hall, making sure Rebekah wasn't in sight. She pressed her ear against the door, trying to hear what he was saying. It was too muffled to make out more than a couple words in a row. He had to have been trying to speak low, because the way his voice traveled, she could usually hear him from across the house.

He sounded irritated, but that was nothing new. Macy couldn't help being curious. She hadn't heard him talking with anyone since they came to the house months ago. He'd been doing his best to recreate the community by keeping them all secluded from the outside. The only difference was they had electricity.

The only times he left the house were at night to buy *supplies* as he called them. Usually, only groceries, but the way he made such a deal about going out to get them, he had to call them supplies. Like he was a top level spy.

Something slammed in the study and Macy jumped. She ran down the hall on her tip-toes. If Chester was irritated, then she really didn't want him finding her eavesdropping. She went back to the dining room to check the floor for wet spots from mopping. There weren't any that she could see, but she needed to look busy if Chester came by. Her heart still raced and she forced herself to look natural.

A few minutes passed without him returning, and she relaxed. Macy stopped drying the already-dry floor and stood, looking around. There wasn't any noise. She didn't know where he was, but she needed to keep cleaning.

Macy went to the cabinets and dusted, taking down each piece of fine China with care. When she replaced the last one, she turned around and saw Chester watching her. She held her breath, not wanting to show him how startled she was.

He folded his arms and curled one side of his lip. He was giving her such a subtle smirk that it was worse than an outright one. "I have to go somewhere for a little bit."

"In the light?"

"Don't speak unless spoken to. Keep an eye on your mom. She's sleeping now, but she'll probably need something when she wakes. Also, I want you to clean the living room next."

Macy sighed, forcing herself to stay silent. She was exhausted. She'd been deep cleaning for hours and wanted a break. Her body ached, especially where her leg had been injured.

"Is there a problem?"

"No."

"Good. Get to work and don't forget to check on your true mom. And if I'm not home, do you know when to start dinner?"

"Yes."

"Okay. Get to work." He turned around and walked toward the front door. Macy could hear him punching in the code for the alarm. He was making a production of it to get the point across. They both knew the threat of the barn was as real as it always had been.

Macy looked over at the living room in disgust. How could he expect her to keep deep cleaning without a break? He had barely given her any time to scarf down the lunch she made everyone.

Sweat ran down her forehead and she wiped it with the back of her hand, finding it stuck to her hair. She probably looked horrible, not that it mattered. She grabbed the rags from around the room and took them to the laundry, starting another load.

She grabbed some more supplies and went into the hall. Something caught her eye. Macy stared down the hall, trying to figure out what was out of place.

Then she saw it. The door to Chester's study wasn't closed all the way. Was it a trap, or had he let his guard down? She went back to the dining room and looked around for him. He appeared to still be gone. She had heard his car leave the garage, and the fact that he had left while it was still light showed that something was wrong.

Maybe he had left the door open accidentally. Macy looked into their bedroom and saw Rebekah sleeping.

Macy appeared to be in the clear. She took a deep breath, dropping the rags onto the floor. Her heart felt like it was going to pound right out of her chest.

Who knew if she would find anything? But the way he kept it locked up all the time, there was no way she could just leave the room alone. If she walked in and found a camera pointed at her, she could later say that she had been making sure everything was okay since he always leaves the door closed.

She pushed the door open ever so slowly. It creaked slightly, but opened easily enough. Holding her breath, she walked in, not knowing what to expect. She half-expected to see pictures and graphs all over the walls, like she always saw on TV when murderers were stalking someone.

It just looked like a regular home office, though. There was a desk piled with papers. A laptop sat there, screen off. A floor-to-ceiling shelf held books and knick knacks. Papers were scattered on the floor underneath a window with drawn shades.

Macy scanned the room, looking for a hidden camera, but didn't see anything. She knew if there was anything recording her, if she took a step into the room, that would be all it would take for her to end up locked away somewhere. Maybe for good.

She walked over to the desk and looked at the piles of papers without touching anything. The laptop seemed to call her, but she was certain if she got online, he would know. But what if she just looked at some files? Would he know that?

It wasn't a risk Macy was willing to take. She could pick up some papers and he wouldn't know, but he probably had ways he was monitoring his computer.

A crashing noise startled her. Macy jumped and ran to the doorway, looking down the hall. She didn't see anything. Going down to Chester's bedroom, she checked on Rebekah and saw her lunch tray on the floor. She must have rolled over and knocked it down. How had it not woken her?

Macy went over and checked on her breathing and then picked up the mess from the floor. She brought the tray back out to the kitchen and then returned to Chester's study. She looked at the papers sitting on his desk, memorizing their placement. Then she picked up a few, looking through them.

They were all boring. Bills, from what she could tell. She was about to set them back into place when she froze. Now on top of the desk sat a paper with big words on the top: Shady Hills Mental Health Facility.

Was that where Heather had been taken? Was she still there? Heather had never returned to fill out any more of her diaries that Macy could find, so Macy knew nothing beyond the fact that Heather had been sent there.

Macy scanned the paper. The letter was addressed to Chester Woodran, the non-custodial father. So they *had* removed his parental rights. Macy had been right.

He had kidnapped her because he couldn't get his real daughter back.

Macy read it as fast as she could, knowing that she needed to get the living room clean before Chester returned. According to the letter, Heather had behavioral problems and didn't show any signs of being ready to be released.

If Chester had lost his parenting rights, why were they sending him updates? Did he still have some kind of right even though he didn't have custody?

Macy knew time was ticking by. She didn't know where Chester had gone, but she couldn't shake the feeling that she needed to hurry out of the study.

Heather wasn't crazy. She had read the girl's diary entries. Considering she had lived with a monster her entire life and had to deal with the murder of her mom who she'd been so close to, Heather was probably acting out because no one would listen to her. Obviously no one believed Chester to be a murderer if he was being sent updates about Heather.

Maybe together, she and Heather could get him thrown into jail. They definitely could get him for kidnapping. The murder charges would be more difficult if they didn't have a body, but at least they could get him in prison. Surely premeditated kidnapping would be a long sentence.

Macy put the papers back on the desk where they had been. She backed out of the room and looked at the door. It had been left slightly open, but Chester didn't know that. Or did he?

What if he asked if she went in? Her heart sped up. She would have to lie. Not only that, but she would have to practice it until he came back home. She would have to be convincing. Unless he really hadn't noticed.

It was strange that he would be so careless though. It had to be a setup. But she closed the door. Living with him was making her crazy. It was a door. A door. And that was all it took for her to have an argument with herself.

Macy went into the living room and cleaned as fast as she could. Chester wouldn't notice anything because it wasn't a trap. He wouldn't do that because of how protective he was over that room. He wouldn't give her access to it just to see what she would do.

Opportunity

MACY SAT UP in bed, gasping for air. Sweat dripped into her face, and she wiped it away. She'd had another dream about being locked up in the barn. She squeezed the soft comforter, breathing heavily.

It was just a dream. It wasn't real. Not this time anyway. She hadn't had a dream about going back there in a while. It had to have been the guilt—if that was the right word—about sneaking into Chester's office.

He hadn't said a word about it when he came home. In fact, he'd been distracted about something, not even bothering to criticize the way Macy had cleaned the living room. Usually, he enjoyed pointing out every small thing she hadn't cleaned perfectly.

Her throat was dry and she needed something to drink. The last thing Macy wanted to do was to leave the bedroom and risk running into either Chester or Rebekah. The alarm clock showed that it was just before three in the morning, so the chances of them being up were low, but not impossible.

Rebekah was sometimes up at strange times, especially since she spent most of the days in bed resting. Chester...well, he was Chester. He took pride in being unpredictable, so there was no telling where he would be or when.

Macy's eyes were heavy and it was tempting to go back to sleep, but her throat almost hurt it was so dry. She climbed out of bed, listening for any sound. If she heard anything, she would just deal with the dry throat. There was no way she was going to face either one of them if she didn't have to.

Once she got over the stress of the nightmare, the dryness would most likely go away. But if they were both sleeping, she would rather drink some water and be done with it.

Everything was quiet, so she sneaked into the kitchen and poured water into a cup without making any noise.

After she drank two full glasses of water, she headed back to the bedroom, but before she got there, she noticed a slight breeze before she got to the hall. Why would there be a breeze? Chester didn't open any windows—ever. Most of them were rigged so as to be impossible to open. They had either been bolted or painted shut, plus they were attached to the alarm system.

Macy walked toward the front door. That was where the breeze felt like it was coming from. She looked around and noticed the door to the garage was cracked open.

What was going on? Why was Chester being so careless all of a sudden? Did it have to do with whatever was distracting him? What *was* distracting him?

She pushed the door slightly, half-expecting the alarm to sound even though she knew it wouldn't since it was already open. She peeked in and saw that his truck was gone.

As far as Macy knew, he only left the house about once a week, but now twice in a day?

A noise outside startled her and she jumped. Macy heard the mechanical sounds of the garage door gearing up to open. She closed the door all the way and ran back to the bedroom. Her heart raced and her mouth was dry, despite having just had two glasses of water.

She closed the door and leaned against it, breathing hard, but trying to stay quiet. There was a thud. It sounded like the door to the garage slamming shut.

Macy put her ear to the door. Chester was always talking to himself so maybe he would say something that would tell Macy what was going on. It had to be something big if he was being so careless, leaving the doors open.

His footsteps went down the hall. Macy braced herself, ready to jump into bed and pretend to sleep. He walked past the door, talking to himself as usual. It wasn't anything that gave her any clues. He was only saying something about someone being a complete moron.

That could have referred to just about anyone. He thought every-body was stupid and often expressed his disdain for humanity in general.

Macy thought about his parents. They were so sweet, how could Chester have possibly come from them? His mom was always so nice to everyone. His dad was crotchety, sure, but in an endearing way. He was nothing like Chester.

Her eyes grew heavy again as her heart rate returned to normal. She was too curious to give in. Macy went to the wall that connected to Chester and Rebekah's walk-in closet. If the door was open, maybe she could hear something.

Pressing her ear to the wall, she could hear some muffled shuffling noises, but nothing else. He had to have stopped grumbling to keep from waking Rebekah. Was he trying to keep his middle-of-the-night excursion a secret from her, too?

She froze. Voices. They were speaking to each other. She could only hear two tones, no words. They were both talking, but what were they saying? There had to be a way to find out.

Macy cupped her hands and put them against the wall and listened. It was better, but not by much. She was able to pick up a few words here and there, but not enough to tell her anything. She tried harder, but wasn't able to hear anything.

She had to go to the bathroom. Probably from drinking all that water. That was the excuse she needed. She made her way back to the door and opened it.

Their voices traveled through the hall. If she went a little closer to their door, she might be able to hear what they were discussing. Her heart raced, making it harder to listen. She took several deep breaths as she made her way to their door.

She stood in front of the wall, just next to the door. Rebekah was talking and she sounded irritated. Macy could only make out a few words, but she couldn't make sense of them, so she inched closer.

Now Chester was speaking. "It's better than I thought."

"How can you be sure?" Rebekah asked. "You weren't gone long enough to be able to give a good enough examination. Not only that, but it's dark."

"What would you have me do? Take a day trip?"

"That would make a lot more sense, don't you think?"

"What would I tell Heather? We can't tell her about this yet."

Macy's eyes widened. They couldn't tell her what?

"You don't have to tell her where you're going, Chet. Just tell her you have an errand. You don't owe her an explanation. She's just a child. Tell her you need to take care of something and that I'm in charge. End of story."

"I suppose, but she's going to figure out that something's going on."

"Let her wonder. She'll find out soon enough."

Macy tip-toed closer.

"How are we going to keep her in line? We have to make sure she doesn't try anything."

"You could always lock her up like you've been talking about. But she wouldn't be able to take care of me while you're gone. I can't make my own food. I can barely stand up without getting sick."

"Are you sure I can't take you to a doctor?"

"Doctors are evil, Chet. You know that. The medicines they use, they use them to control people's minds. It's a rough pregnancy, that's all. I've seen it many times back home at the community. What we need is for you to go back to the land and really look at it—in the daylight. Otherwise, we won't really know if it's the right place to start our new community."

The blood drained from Macy's face. They were planning to start a new community?

She walked back to the bedroom and closed the door behind her.

Macy knew deep down in her gut if they entered a new community, she wasn't getting out. Chester would make sure of it, and it sounded as though Rebekah was behind him.

That also explained why she was still studying the community writings. Rebekah and Chester would be the new Jonah and Eve.

If he was going to be gone for an entire day and Rebekah could barely get out of bed, that would be her chance to get away. Chester wouldn't be able to do anything about it.

Macy wouldn't go back to another community. She just couldn't. Escape was her only option, and fast. Macy climbed back into bed, her mind racing but her body exhausted. Her eyes fought to close while every inch of her ached.

How would she get out? Simply go out the front door and let the alarm wail?

Macy pulled the covers up close to her face as the drowsiness took over. She sniffed them, smiling. They smelled so nice and fresh because she had washed all the linens earlier. If nothing else, being kidnapped had taught her to find joy in the little things.

Macy finally gave into her heavy eyelids and thought of ways to escape as she drifted off.

Resolve

C HAD LOOKED OUT the front window again. He expected Alyssa to walk through the door, but it was clear she was serious about going somewhere to get space.

As tempting as it was to call her friends one by one, Chad knew it was a bad idea. She wanted space and if he called, she would push him away even further.

He went upstairs to where Alex and Zoey were doing their studies as usual at the kitchen table.

"Is Mom still sleeping?" Alex asked.

How to answer that one? Chad would have to tell him some version of the truth, but he couldn't bear to give him all of it. Was it because he didn't think Alex could handle it…or because he didn't think he himself could?

Chad cleared his throat. "She's been having a hard time dealing with everything, so she's gone to a friend's house."

"For how long?" Alex asked.

"Until she's able to think clearly."

"Did you two get into a fight, Dad?"

"She just needs space to think. It was too much being here where there are so many memories of Macy. That's all."

Alex didn't look convinced. "If you say so."

"I do. Are you two going to be okay if I go out for a little while? I have to pick up some stuff from the store."

"Whatever." Alex went back his laptop.

Zoey gave Chad a sympathetic look.

"If you guys need anything, I'll keep my cell phone close."

"Okay." Alex didn't look up.

Chad frowned, but didn't say anything. The last thing he needed was for Alex to decide to move into Zoey's house. Not that he would let them stay there alone, but Valerie was due back with Zoey's dad soon and the tables could turn all too easily. Then he would be alone in the house.

He went down to his office and grabbed his cell phone and wallet. Who was he kidding? He didn't know what they needed from the store. Maybe he would get some takeout for lunch and then they could use the leftovers for dinner too. Or he could pick up some milk and eggs.

A lump formed in his throat. He wasn't cut out to do the single dad thing. He also didn't want to do anything to make things worse with the child who was still with him. Hopefully Alyssa would come around because they had been getting along so well before the argument.

He had been excited about the thought of Macy coming back home to find them getting along. He already knew that dream was a long shot, but with Alyssa now thinking that Macy was dead, the dream was nearly crushed.

Even though it did cause a fight between him and Alyssa, he wasn't going to change his stance. He would hold onto his belief until there was hard evidence. And when Macy did get back, she deserved to have a kitchen full of food.

That was it. He would go to the store and buy every vegan item he could find. He would even try some of it. That way, when she got back, they could eat that crazy stuff together, no matter what it tasted it like.

Chad shut off his laptop and went into the garage, on a mission. Maybe he would even grow to like the vegan foods. He knew he could stand to lose a few more pounds. Some weight had come off because he hadn't been eating as much, but there was still room for improvement.

Perhaps if he lost those last few pounds, it would be enough to convince Alyssa to stay home. She was always so fit and healthy, and even though he wasn't what anyone would call overweight, his love handles had to be a turn off for someone as beautiful as her.

He started the car and drove to the grocery store, but before he got there, he saw the natural grocery store that Macy liked so much. He smiled, remembering how she had chattered on about it when they were building it. Yes, that was where he would go.

Pulling into the parking lot, he felt more alive than he had in a long time. Chad was going to win back his wife and have something in common with his daughter when she got back. Since he was on a roll, he knew he would think of something brilliant to bring him closer to Alex also.

He walked through the automatic sliding doors and immediately he felt overwhelmed. This place looked nothing like the grocery stores he went to with Alyssa. To the left, there were enormous displays of fresh fruit, half of which he didn't recognize. To the right was a line of checkout stands. Everyone in line had their own cloth bags, and there wasn't a plastic bag in sight.

His nose tingled. It even smelled different in there. Not bad, just different. He didn't have a clue what the scent was, but he figured it was something natural. He scanned the store, trying to figure out where to begin.

"Hey, stranger."

Chad turned around to see Lydia standing next to him. "You shop here?"

"Of course. My body is a temple." She smiled, flipping her dark hair behind her shoulder. "What are you doing here?"

"Shopping for my family." He put the emphasis on the word family due to their past.

"I would have expected you to go to the discount grocery down the road."

"What's that supposed to mean?"

"Just that you're a pizza and beer kind of guy."

"Yeah, well, I'm trying to change that."

"They sell pizza and beer here too, you know. It's just not what you're used to."

"I'll have to pick some up. Well, I'll see you around."

"This place can be hard to navigate if you're not used to it. I can help you out, and it'll take half the time."

Chad was trying to fix his family. Having his ex-lover show him around the store wasn't the way to go about it. "I can figure it out myself, but thanks."

"If you're sure."

"I am."

"Okay. See you around." She walked away, headed for some kind of star-shaped fruit. He watched as she picked one up and gave it a squeeze and then set it down only to pick up and squeeze another. Lydia put that one in her basket.

She turned around and winked.

Chad turned away and walked toward a shelf full of creams and lotions. He picked one up and pretended that it was the most interesting thing he'd ever seen. Why had he been watching her? It had to have been because he wasn't even sure how to shop in this foreign store.

He put the lotion back on the shelf and went in the opposite direction of Lydia. He wandered the store, staring at brands he had never heard of, although some looked vaguely familiar. Had Macy bought some of those and he'd seen them at home?

Time passed and Chad still hadn't found even one item to place in his basket. How would he ever eat the same items that Macy did if he couldn't even decide what to get? He realized that he wasn't even sure qualified as vegan. He knew she wouldn't eat cheese—how would she eat pizza?—but he wasn't sure what else she didn't eat, aside from meat of course.

The items in front of Chad seemed to be taunting him. Would Macy eat them when she returned? It wasn't even clear, at least to him, what he was looking at. Even though the packaging was in English, it may as well have been Greek.

"You want some help now?"

Lydia. He didn't even need to turn around. "Just trying to decide."

"I can see that. Let me help."

He turned and looked at her for a moment. "Do you really shop here often, Lydia? Or do you follow me? We run into each other an awful lot. I know this isn't the biggest town, but I run into you more than anyone else."

"Great minds." She held up her basket, packed full of fruits, veggies, and an assortment of other things he didn't recognize. "But I really do love this place."

He eyed her basket and then looked at his nearly-empty one. "Oh, all right. But don't read into it, Lydia."

"Me?" She gave him an innocent look and then shook her head. "I'm only here to help a neighbor out."

Right. Chad knew he would have to keep his guard up. Why did he always have to run into her? Was it really just a coincidence? That was likely how they had hooked up in the first place. He couldn't remember for sure, but he wouldn't have gotten together with her if she hadn't kept showing up everywhere.

"So…what is it we're looking for?" she asked.

"Vegan food."

Lydia tilted her head. She had an expression that he couldn't read. She knew about Macy's veganism—Chad had ranted to her about it enough. Did she think he was pathetic since he was out buying food for his daughter who many thought wouldn't return?

She stood up straight. "We're in the wrong section for that. This stuff is full of butter, milk, and eggs. Follow me. I'll show you where they keep what you're looking for."

They went down several aisles and stopped in one that looked almost identical from the one they had started in. "Everything here is vegan. It either has some kind of dairy substitute or is simply made without it. Are you looking for anything in particular?"

He shook his head. "All of Macy's food expired long ago and I want to make sure she has plenty when she returns." If Lydia did feel sorry for him, thinking that he was hanging onto a dream, let her. He didn't need her approval.

"You'll find everything here. Do you want anything else?"

Chad scanned the packages, feeling as lost as before, but at least he knew he was looking at vegan foods. "No. I'm good."

"Glad to help. I'll see you around, Chad." She turned around and took a few steps.

Guilt stung at him for being so rude. "How are you doing, Lydia?"

She turned around and walked back over to him.

"Sorry I didn't ask about you. I was just…distracted. This store is like stepping into a foreign country."

Lydia laughed. "I remember feeling that way."

"How *are* you doing? Does Dean stay home any longer than before?"

"No. You know him. He's really married to his work. I'm not even the mistress."

Was that how Alyssa had felt when he had his job and was getting the blog started?

"Don't worry about me. I'm doing well—keeping busy. How are you holding up?"

Chad frowned. "Just hanging in there. We're waiting on the DNA results."

"Still?" She leaned against a shelf. "I figured the news had moved on and never bothered to update."

"They'll be all over it either way. I don't know if we'll ever get the results, though. It's taking forever."

"Want to talk about it? They have a deli and there are plenty of vegan options, but they also have a ton of meat and cheeses too."

His stomach rumbled loudly and then he looked away.

"Come on. My treat. You look like you have a lot on your mind." Lydia gave him a look that told him she wasn't going to take no for an answer.

Pouring

C HAD BIT INTO his sandwich, unsure what to think of it. He was figured it wouldn't be very filling with only veggies, seeds, and some vegan condiments. He was surprised at the taste. It wasn't bland and gross as he had expected, even though it was still nothing like what he was used to.

He thought of greasy pizza and spicy chicken wings. Would he really be able to give those up? If it would bring Macy back, he would give up anything for life.

"What do you think?" Lydia asked.

"It's good." He picked something out from his teeth. It might have been some kind of sprout, but he couldn't be sure. He wasn't sure that he had ever eaten those before. It looked like grass with a seed at the end. It actually tasted good with the green spread—avocados?

"See? I told you. It's one of my favorites. Sometimes I come here just to have one."

They sat in silence for a few minutes, eating their identical sandwiches. Chad looked around, trying to make sense of the store. Everyone else was bustling around, finding what they needed easily. It reminded him of his first day skiing when everyone else was zooming down the mountain, even preschoolers, and he couldn't get two feet down the bunny slope without biffing it.

"How are things with Alyssa?"

Chad looked at Lydia, startled. She had never asked about Alyssa before, at least not that he could recall.

"You said that you two were working things out. How's that going?"

"It's been going great." He wasn't about to admit the fight to Lydia. Alyssa would return home, refreshed from a girls' night or two and then they would pick up where they left off.

Lydia raised an eyebrow, probably picking up on the fact that he was leaving out details. They had spent hours upon hours talking. She knew him nearly as well as Alyssa did. "Well, that's good news," Lydia said. "I'm sure Alex is happy about that."

"Yeah, for the most part."

"How's he doing?"

"He's homeschooling right now. With Macy being gone, it was too much for him." Not only that, but also the fact that he was going to be a dad himself soon. What would Lydia think of Chad being a grandpa? He almost laughed. If he wanted to push her away, that might just do it.

"What's so funny?"

Chad looked at her surprised. Had he actually laughed out loud and not noticed?

"You're smiling about something."

"Life just never plays out how we expect, you know?"

"Oh, I know." Chad knew she was referring to the fact that her husband was nothing more than a checkbook and she was the kind of girl who wanted to be treated like a princess—adored and admired. "Anything you want to talk about?"

He shook his head. "Alex has made a bit of a mess of his life, but it'll all work out somehow."

Lydia gave him a knowing look. "He's a teenager now. It's his job to make stupid decisions."

Chad raked his fingers through his hair. "My kids, they take that to the extreme. My parents, when they were alive, used to tell me that one day I would be paid back for the hell I put them through. I didn't put them through anything like this."

Concern washed over her face. "What did Alex do? Kill someone?"

His eyes widened. "Not so loud! Everyone knows who I am, even though they're being nice and pretending not to notice me."

"Sorry. What did he do? I won't tell anyone."

504

"I really don't want to talk about it."

"You look like you need to."

"No. Really, I don't." He pulled out his phone and checked the time. "I should get back home."

"If you do want to talk, you know my number. We can still be friends. Unless you told Alyssa and…?"

"No!" Chad nearly choked on his sandwich. "Don't ever bring it up to her."

A slow smile spread across her face. "Trust me, that's not something I would ever do."

"I need to get back home. Alex might need some help with his schoolwork or something."

Lydia eyed his basket. "If you need your regular groceries, you should pick up some more food. I can show you—"

"I do need some, but after seeing the prices here, I'll stop off somewhere else to get those."

"Can't say that I blame you." She wrapped up her garbage and stood. "Although if you want your family eating healthier, this is the place to go."

Chad finished off his sparkling water. "If I tried that, I might starve my son. He's particular about his brands."

"I would never guess where he got that." Lydia grinned.

"What's that supposed to mean?"

Lydia laughed. "I saw the way you were eying the stuff here."

"That's because it's like a foreign country." He couldn't help smiling. Talking with her was so natural and fun—and that was a problem, especially with Alyssa already mad at him.

"If that's what you have to tell yourself. I'll see you around. If you ever need anything, don't hesitate to ask, okay? That's what neighbors are for. I mean it."

"Thanks. I'll let you know if I do." He picked up his basket and before he could reach for his trash, Lydia picked it up.

"I'll get that. Take care of yourself."

He nodded and then headed for the registers. He was in dangerous territory and well aware of it. With things as they were, it would be all too easy to pour everything out to Lydia. That had been the problem when they had started talking when he and Alyssa first hit their marital problems.

After checking out, and feeling like an idiot for not having brought his own bag, he decided to go home before stopping off for normal food. He needed to what he bought into the fridge before it went bad, and after eating lunch, the timeframe was growing smaller by the minute.

When he got home, Alex was at the kitchen table by himself. Hopefully he wasn't having trouble in paradise too. "Hey, son. How's it going?"

"Just bombed a quiz, so now I have extra work." He let a dramatic sigh. "I really wanted to be done."

"So take a break. Maybe you'll be able to think clearer when you come back."

"It's so hard to focus. Mom can't even do it. She can barely function, and now she's not even here. Where'd she go? Her phone keeps going straight to voice mail."

Chad's heart sank, but he fought to keep his face straight. "She must be having a good talk with some friends."

Alex scowled. "But she shouldn't turn off her phone. What if we have an emergency? If we need her? You don't even know where she went."

"She's an adult. We can't tell her what to do."

"But she also has a family. She can't forget about us."

"You know Mom. She wouldn't forget about you. This is as hard on us as it is on you. We all have to deal with it in our own ways."

"I know, I know. I'm never going to hear the end of this, am I?"

"Turning your young parents into grandparents? Don't count on that any time soon."

Alex cracked a smile. "Sorry. If it makes you feel any better, I would have made different decisions if I could go back in time."

"If you ever figure out time travel, let me in on it, okay? There are a few things I'd like to do differently myself."

"Like never let Macy go out that night."

"Definitely the first thing I'd take care of. Why don't you relax? Take a nap, maybe. You look like you really need a break."

"A nap? Really?"

"You look like you could use one."

"I'm not three."

"Neither am I, but I really want one." He pulled the first item out of the bag and put it in the fridge.

Alex gave him a funny look. "What's that? It looks like Macy's food."

"I decided to buy some so that when she comes back, she'll have something to eat. We can eat it too. Don't feel like you have to stay away. I bought plenty."

"Why? Are you going to start eating vegan food?"

"I might give it a try. I could stand to lose a few pounds."

"For an old dude, you're in good shape."

Chad looked at Alex for a moment, and he could see his son was worried that he had said something wrong. Normally, Chad would have been offended at being called old, but at that moment, he found it hilarious. A laugh fought to escape.

Alex's eyes widened, watching Chad. He scooted his chair back.

Finally, the laughter made its way out of Chad's throat. Alex jumped. That only made Chad roar all the more. He leaned against the counter, clutching his stomach. It had been so long since he'd laughed—really laughed—that it ached.

He looked over at Alex and saw that he was laughing too. They made eye contact and both went into a deeper fit. Chad's eyes filled with tears and soon ran down his face. He laughed until his gut hurt too much to keep going. He gasped for breath, wiping at his eyes.

When they had both calmed down, Alex gave him a funny look. "It really wasn't that funny."

"I know. We must've needed a good laugh."

"Yeah, I guess so. Sorry I was rude earlier."

"Don't worry about it." Chad wasn't even sure what Alex was referring to. "We're all under stress."

"I think I will take that nap." Alex yawned.

"Where's Zoey? Is everything okay?"

"She just went to her house to get some clothes and stuff."

"You didn't want to go with her?"

He frowned. "Not after failing that stupid quiz. I have to get on track before I fall behind. I have to retake it and pass by tomorrow morning."

"Want me to take it for you?" Chad joked.

"Funny. Not that it would work. They use the webcam to make sure the right person is doing the work."

Chad's sore stomach dropped. "They can't hear us talking, can they?"

Alex shook his head. "I have the mic turned off. They just care about the camera, but I'm surprised they don't want the mic turned on too. I guess they think they could tell if we were cheating."

"Probably. Get yourself that nap. I'm going to take one as well. Maybe by then, Mom will be ready to come back."

The front door opened and Chad looked down the stairs, hoping Alyssa was back already. It was Zoey, with a tear-streaked face.

Reality

THE LOOK ON his dad's face struck terror through Alex's body. He jumped up, expecting to see his mom at the door wrapped in bandages. Instead, Zoey stood there with red, puffy eyes and tear stains down her face. Her hair was messy.

Alex's stomach twisted in knots. "What's wrong?"

"My parents are coming in tonight. They want me to go back home tomorrow. Mom scheduled my next doctor's appointment and she's bringing my sperm donor."

"Your…? You mean your dad."

Anger flashed over her face. "Not my dad. Where's he been? In Japan playing baseball my whole life. He's not a dad. All he's ever done is supply half my genes and some money." She slammed the door. "I told her I'm going to stay here."

Alex's dad sighed behind him. Alex remembered Zoey's mom threatening them with kidnapping charges when Zoey said she would stay at their house instead of going home. His dad was probably worried about that. Probably even more so with his mom out who-knows-where and not even answering her phone.

"Isn't it good that he wants to be involved?" Alex asked.

Zoey shot him a death look and then kicked off her shoes. She stormed up the steps. "It's a little late for that. The stupid jerk never bothered to call me on any birthday or Christmas. Hasn't sent any presents or cards or anything. Apparently, I'm supposed to accept the fact that he sent some money, but you know what? That's a load of crap. Mom's the one who's been here my whole life. He's got another think coming if he wants to walk in and take over the role of a parent."

"Want to do something to get your mind off it?" Alex asked. "I was going to take a nap, but we could watch a movie or something."

"You think watching a movie is going to fix anything?" she demanded.

He backed up. "I didn't say it would fix anything."

"No, I don't want to watch anything. I want to…I don't know. I just…I'm so pissed!"

"What's going to help? You need to calm down. It's not good for the baby."

She narrowed her eyes and stepped closer to Alex. "Don't tell me to calm down. That just pisses me off even more."

"What did I do?" Alex asked.

Her lips formed a straight line and her nostrils flared. "You have to ask?"

Alex sighed. It felt like he was in the middle of one his parents' fights. "Do you want to talk about what happened over there?"

"No. I just want to break something." She stared at him.

"I hope not me."

"Ugh. Let's go watch a movie, but I want to see something in the theater. Something as violent and bloody as possible."

Alex's dad stepped forward. "It's your lucky day, Zoey. There's a gory war movie *and* I happen to be available to drive you guys."

"Sounds good to me." She turned around and put her shoes back on.

Dumbfounded, Alex gave his dad a look of confusion.

Chad shrugged his shoulders and mouthed, "Women."

Alex smiled. Maybe his dad was more relatable than he thought.

Before he knew it, they were across town buying a tub of popcorn as big as his torso, with nearly as much butter and salt. Zoey had gotten a big plate of nachos. Twice she told the guy to put more cheese on it. When they got into their seats, she ate chips with so much cheese on them, he thought they would break.

She caught him watching her. "Want one?"

He shook his head. Her tone told him that he had better not take her up on the offer. "Hopefully, the movie makes you feel better because I don't know how much more of this I can take," he muttered.

"What?" she asked.

"I said I wasn't hungry anyway," Alex said.

Zoey stared at him, as though trying to decide whether or not she believed him.

Luckily for Alex, the room went dark and loud music blared from the speakers on the walls. A screaming army general showed up on the screen and Alex settled into his seat, eating salty, butter-soaked popcorn.

When the movie ended, he looked over at Zoey. The empty nacho tray rested on her lap. Her eyes were closed and she was snoring. So much for not wanting a nap. He turned to his dad. "You wanna wake her?"

He shook his head. "Let's watch the credits. Maybe they have something funny at the end."

"After this movie?"

"You never know."

"Fine by me." He watched the names roll over the screen and realized they would have to agree on a name if they wanted to keep the baby. They had probably discussed it before, but it hadn't felt real until that moment. He looked at the names, hoping for inspiration. But they didn't even know if it was a boy or girl yet, although they would know soon enough.

His breathing felt constricted. What if she did want to keep it? He thought of crying and diapers while trying to do homework. Would they keep with the homeschooling? They would pretty much have to, wouldn't they? He didn't know how much daycare cost, but since neither of them had a job, they couldn't afford it.

Maybe his mom could babysit. She wasn't working either, and it would give her a distraction from thinking about Macy. What grandma didn't love her grandkids? His grandma was always saying that she never saw them enough.

Thinking about his mom as a grandma was weird—almost weirder than thinking of himself as a dad, which was crazy enough.

The credits and music stopped. Zoey sat up, looking around. She rubbed her eyes, knocking the nacho dish onto the floor. "I must have fallen asleep."

Alex bit back a comment about it being a good thing they didn't stay home for a nap. "You wanna go home? To my house, I mean. You can relax in my room or Macy's. Whatever you want to do." He picked up her tray from the floor and dropped in into the canyon that was his popcorn container.

She stretched. "Yeah, maybe we should. I didn't know I was so tired." She struggled to get out of the chair, so Alex held out his hand. Zoey tried again to get out, but finally took his hand. She mumbled a barely-audible thanks and they made their way out into the main lobby.

His dad stopped walking without warning and Alex bumped into him.

"What's going on, Dad?"

He didn't answer. He only stared across the lobby at a group of women.

Alex recognized some of them from the neighborhood. Alex looked over at Zoey. Was it his imagination or did she look irritated? She had been in a better mood after waking. Was she mad at him again? "Dad, let's go. I think we should get Zoey home. Maybe we could stop for ice cream or something." Hopefully that would give him bonus points, and she would stop being upset with him. He wasn't used to it, and he really didn't like it.

Both his dad and Zoey were staring at the women, not answering him. Maybe Zoey wasn't in the mood for ice cream?

One of the ladies broke away from the group and headed their way. She had made them dinner shortly after Macy disappeared. Her name was Laura or something.

She smiled at them as she got closer. "Hi Chad, Alex." She looked at Zoey. "What's your name again, dear?"

Zoey shot her a nasty look. "Zoey."

Alex felt bad for the lady. She hadn't done anything to deserve Zoey's wrath.

Laura smiled anyway. "That's right. Good to see you, Zoey. I'm Lydia."

Oh, Lydia. Alex knew it had started with an L.

His dad was fidgeting next to him. What was up? His dad was one of those people who talked easily with everyone he met. What had his mom always called it? Charisma.

Lydia looked at his dad. "Would you like me to stop by and make some dinner tonight? The HOA hasn't had any sign ups to bring you guys any meals for a long time. You guys seemed to enjoy the lasagna I made last time."

Alex's mouth watered. He remembered that meal. "Yeah. That was delicious. My mom's at a friend's house anyway. We'd probably just eat cereal for dinner tonight."

Both his dad and Zoey shot him a dirty look. What had he done?

Lydia smiled. "That sounds perfect. The girls and me," she indicated toward the other ladies she had been with, "we're going to see that new romantic comedy and then I can come over. You guys just relax and I'll take over the kitchen."

Zoey scowled.

Chad rubbed his hands together, looking nervous. "If you want to. I don't want to put you out."

Lydia twirled a strand of hair. "It's no trouble. Dean's always out of town. It'll be nice to not have dinner alone for a change. Well, it looks like everyone's heading for the movie. I'll see you guys in a few hours!"

The three of them walked to the car in silence. His dad looked deep in thought while Zoey continued to give him the evil eye.

What was so wrong with having her make their dinner? His mom obviously wasn't going to make anything, and Lydia would have been home alone, anyway. She may as well make them her lasagna. His stomach rumbled just thinking about it.

When they got home, his dad announced he was going to check his blog comments. He went downstairs and Alex followed Zoey upstairs. When they got to the bonus room, she stared at him. "How could you do that?"

"Do what?"

"Encourage her to make dinner over here."

"So we can have a delicious home-cooked meal. I don't remember if you ate her lasagna or not, but it was one of the best things I've ever eaten. And I'm not just saying that. Would you rather have frozen waffles?"

"Actually, yes." She sat down on the couch and turned on music videos.

Alex sat next to her. "Why?"

Zoey narrowed her eyes. "Are you really that blind?"

"Apparently I am. Want to fill me in?"

Zoey stared at him. "Have you noticed the way she looks at your dad?"

"What? She's married. He's married."

"Like people don't have affairs."

"Not my parents."

"She thinks your dad is hot and neither of their spouses are home tonight."

"Get your mind out of the gutter. There's no way she wants to be with my dad. That's just gross."

"I know you see him as just your dad, but one thing you need to realize is that he's hot."

"You think my dad's hot?" Alex's voice squeaked.

She rolled her eyes. "Look, he's practically like my own dad. He's more of a dad to me than that jerk of a sperm donor. I'm just stating the facts. For a guy his age, he's sexy. When Lydia's here, watch how she looks at him. She wants him like you want that lasagna."

Alex shook his head. "No, that's not possible. It's also disgusting. Besides, even if she does think he's hot, she knows they're both married. There's no way."

"You're so naive."

"Am not."

"Are too. She's looking for love. Her husband must never be home, because every time I've ever seen her, he's out of town. Your dad's an easy target. He's dealing with a missing daughter and if your mom is out of the house tonight...."

"Fine, let's not leave them alone tonight. Okay? We'll suffocate them until she goes back home, and then you'll see."

"Actually, you'll see," Zoey said.

Nerve

MACY SAT AT the kitchen table pretending to do her *community* studies. At least Chester was giving her a break from all the cleaning. It gave her a chance to think about her escape plan, which was essentially nothing at this point. She had fallen asleep as soon as she closed her eyes the night before.

"What's this?"

She looked up to see Chester standing where the dining room and hall met. He held up her—Heather's—bedding.

Macy tried to keep sarcasm out of her voice. "A bed spread."

"A bed spread?" Chester shouted.

Her heart sank. He was in a rage again.

Chester walked up to her, holding the covers close to her. "Just a bed spread?" His face was red and he had that scary look in his eyes again.

Macy nodded, her stomach twisting in knots. Was he going to lock her up because of some issue with the bedding, so they wouldn't worry about her trying to escape while he was gone?

"That's all you have? Really?"

"What do you want me to say?" Macy blinked back tears. She didn't want to be locked up somewhere. Had she been stupid to get her hopes up about getting away? She should have known he would have a plan other than keeping her in with Rebekah and an alarm system.

"Do you call this clean?"

"What?"

"Your covers, Heather. They're atrocious," Chester growled. He held them up to his face and gave her a disgusted look. "You were supposed to wash all the linens yesterday."

"I did."

"Did you? It doesn't smell like it to me. Does it to you?" He shoved them into her face. "Smell!"

Macy didn't have to. The stench hit her before the covers touched her face. They reeked of body odor. It smelled like an entire football team had rolled around on them after playing a game.

"Is that clean?"

She shook her head no. How had they gotten so gross? Macy had washed them. In fact, she remembered how fresh they had smelled the night before. Before going to sleep, she had even enjoyed the fresh, clean smell.

"That's right! They don't smell clean. Do you need a lesson in laundry?" he shouted. His spit landed on her face, but she knew better than to wipe it away. "How could you think these were clean? Tell me!"

"They were clean," Macy whispered.

"What did you say?"

"They *were* clean."

"You call this clean?"

She shook her head. "They didn't smell like that before."

"What are you trying to say?" He grabbed her shirt and pulled her out of the chair.

Macy looked away. "I don't know what happened, but when I washed them, they were clean. I smelled them last night, and they were fresh."

"Are you telling me that I don't know what I'm talking about?"

"No."

"Don't lie to me. Tell me you screwed up."

"But I didn't. When they—"

"I *said* tell me the truth." He shoved her into the table, jamming her side into the corner.

Macy gasped in pain. "I am. It was clean. I smelled it myself."

Chester shoved her farther into the side of the table. "Then how did it get like this?"

"I don't know."

"Are you not bathing properly? Did you make them smell like this?"

"No. No." She shook her head while tears blurred her vision.

"What is it then? Do you need lessons on showering or laundry? Which is it?"

Macy looked away, not answering. She didn't need instruction on any of that.

"Don't ignore me." He squeezed her shirt tighter, causing the collar to choke her. "What do you need a lesson on?"

He let go of her shirt, causing her to fall. She hit her shoulder and head against the table as she slid down to the floor, gasping for air.

"What do I need to give you lessons on?"

"Laundry."

"So you admit that you didn't wash the linens correctly?"

Looking away, she nodded.

"I can't hear you!"

"Yes," she said as loud as she could muster.

Chester grabbed her arm and yanked her up. "Why couldn't you have just admitted that in the first place?" He shoved the covers against her face. "Make sure they don't smell like that again. Do you understand?"

"Yes."

He dragged her to the laundry room and her feet stumbled, trying to keep up. He threw the bedding into the front loader and slammed it shut. "The first thing you have to do is make sure what you're washing is in the washing machine. Is that too complicated?"

"No."

"Good. Don't mess it up again." He picked up the bottle of laundry detergent and read the instructions verbatim. "Shall I show you?"

Macy nodded.

He pulled off the lid with dramatic flair and brought the bottle inches from her. "Watch as I measure." He poured the liquid to the second line and then poured it to the machine. "This is the correct setting for linens." He spun the dial around. "Next we make sure everything else is on the proper setting." He pushed the rest of the buttons, explaining the importance of each one as he went along.

"Do you think you can replicate that in the future?"

"Yes."

"Or would you rather I write down instructions?"

"No."

"Good. Now, get back to your studies. It's important you under-stand everything contained within the books."

"Okay." She turned around and went back into the dining room, blinking back tears. She had cleaned all of the bedding the right way. There was no way she would have been able to sleep in her bed if they had smelled that foul the night before. Whatever had happened to them, it wasn't her fault. Not that it mattered, because she was the one who was getting in trouble for it.

Chester walked by her without a word and got a drink of water from the kitchen. After he put the glass in the dishwasher, he walked to the table and stared at Macy. "I'm going to take a shower. When I get out, we're going to have a little quiz about your reading. Understand?"

Macy nodded, afraid to speak. She knew if she said a word, she would dissolve into tears.

"Good." He walked away, and as he did, Macy got a whiff of body odor.

Anger burned within her. He had to have rubbed her clean covers all over himself, making them stink. Then he turned around and yelled at her, making her feel like she had done something wrong. All along, he had known that it wasn't her fault.

He had to have been trying to break her down to make sure she wouldn't go anywhere while he was away.

Unfortunately for him, his plan had backfired. Macy now wanted to get back home even more than before. Determination ran through her. She would find a way of escape before Chester dragged her back to another community.

The sounds of the shower starting startled Macy. Was this her opportunity? Sure, he wasn't miles away, but he was in the shower. Macy would have the advantage. She was fully clothed and he wasn't. Surely he wouldn't run after in the nude. Or would he?

She got up and looked down the hall. The door was closed and she could hear him banging things around in the shower. Her heart pounded nearly out of her chest. This was it. It had to be. She was *done* dealing with his abuse.

Barely able to walk straight, she went to the line of shoes by the door and put hers on. They weren't the best running shoes, but they were better than nothing.

Macy looked down the hall again, this time shaking violently. She could barely see straight and her fingers and feet felt cold.

The shower was still going, but probably not for much longer. If she waited too long, she'd lose her chance. She took a deep breath and placed her hand on the knob of the front door. It was now or never.

She swallowed, her dry throat not allowing any movement. Her hand clung to the knob as she turned it. Macy pulled the door toward her. The alarm screamed and wailed, notifying everyone within a several block range of what she had done.

Her feet moved into motion before she had time to think. She pushed the screen door open and she was out in the sun. The air was chilly, but the sun itself felt good. When had the last time been when she was able to go outside?

Macy made her way across the yard and went left down the street. The alarm still screamed, and Chester was bound to be after her in a matter of moments. All he would have to do was get out of the shower and throw on some pants.

There was no way he could be surprised that she would escape after how he had just treated her. It was almost as though he was testing her.

She kept looking back, expecting to see him. It was only a matter of time. She turned down another street.

"Heather!" called someone from a yard.

Macy turned and saw a girl about her age waving.

"Stop, Heather! What are you doing home? When did you…?"

The voice trailed away as Macy picked up her pace. With that fool yelling Heather's name, Chester would know what direction she went. She looked for another street to go down, but came to a dead end.

She couldn't turn around. She would either have to hide or go through someone's yard to get to the street behind. She could still hear the sound of the house alarm wailing. If Chester had that hooked up, the police would be coming soon. That could be good or bad.

If they found her first, she could tell them that Chester had kidnapped her. Then maybe they would take her home. Although if they went to the house and talked with him or Rebekah first, they would probably say she had tried to run away. What if they forced her to go back? What if they wouldn't listen to her like they hadn't listened to Heather?

She ran through the yard in front of her and went around to the side of the house. There was a gate, but no latch. She reached around, scratching her arm on the fence. She found the latch and unhooked it.

A dog barked and ran past her for the street. There was no time to feel bad about the dog escaping. She ran into the yard and looked for a way over the fence. She saw a plastic climbing toy. It was just high enough, so she pushed it up to the fence and climbed on top. Then she grabbed the top of the fence and climbed up. She looked into another back yard.

Voices could be heard not far away from the street behind her. She should have closed the gate; everyone would know she ran into that yard. She braced herself for the jump, knowing that her leg was still weak. If she landed wrong she could reinjure it, but there was no time to worry.

She jumped, preparing to land on her good leg and then roll. Macy landed on a patch of grass and somehow managed to avoid hitting her bad leg. She rolled a few times and then jumped up and ran for the next gate. Her knee stung a little, most likely because she hadn't been outside to run or even walk much. The only 'exercise' she had gotten in a long time was housework.

Ignoring the pain, she got the gate open and made sure to close it. She wasn't going to leave a blatant path for Chester to follow.

Sirens blared in the distance over the sound of Chester's house alarm. Macy needed to get to them before Chester did. Otherwise, he would tell them that she was Heather and had run away. She could explain that she'd been kidnapped, but the police might not believe her.

Chester had pictures that looked just like her all over his house.

Macy ran to the edge of the house. She hid and also looked up and down the street. At least this road wasn't a dead end. She could go down the opposite way and get away from Chester and the sirens and alarm.

There wasn't anyone out on the street. Macy took a deep breath and made a run for it. She went down the street as fast as she could, keeping an eye out for another place to turn so that she could hopefully get out of the neighborhood. Once out, she would decide her next step.

The road curved up ahead, going toward Chester's house. Macy wanted to go the other way, but that meant going through more yards and she would rather take her chances with the open road. It might curve again or even cross another one, giving her a way out.

Perhaps going back to Chester's house wasn't such a bad idea. If the police weren't talking to him yet, she could tell them that he was a madman who had kidnapped her from her family.

Macy took a couple steps, but then heard yelling from behind her, and the sirens were getting louder and closer. They were going to be headed for Chester's house. He would undoubtedly tell them she was Heather and she was running away. He would probably even have some crazy story, making her sound dangerous.

She gasped for air. Why wasn't there a cross street? The road was probably going to loop around and leave her face to face with Chester.

"There you are!"

Macy looked over to see Chester heading her way.

Determined

MACY'S HEART STOPPED for a moment. Chester was about a block away. She turned around and ran faster. Her sore leg protested, but she didn't care. She would take care of it later.

He was yelling something at her. Macy turned her head back and saw that he was only wearing pants. She had been right in guessing he would throw some on and go after her.

"Stop, Heather! We need to talk about this."

Macy pushed herself to go faster. Her lungs and calves burned while her knee protested. It didn't matter. He would kill her if he brought her back to the house. Any injuries she incurred running would heal.

"Heather, wait!"

She looked back. He was getting closer. "No!"

Macy forced herself to run even faster. She passed the house that she had used to go through the back yard. Macy pushed forward. She would get away. There was no other option.

Fingers brushed against her back.

Macy screamed both from terror and in hopes to startle him enough to back off. She ran ahead, forcing her body to go faster. Letting him catch her was not an option. No matter what it took, he was not going to lock her up again. Chester was done controlling her and scaring her into submission.

He could do what he wanted to Rebekah. She had moved into the house willingly. She saw the way Chester treated Macy. She had been in a rock band at one point. Somewhere within her was the ability to see what was really going on.

She felt a tugging sensation on her shirt. Chester had her shirt.

Macy threw herself to the ground, forcing him to let go. She tumbled and then rolled over the hard pavement and a couple rocks that were definitely going to leave bruises.

Chester yelled out at her. She looked over at him as she stopped rolling. He was falling toward the ground—it looked like it was happening in slow motion—and he was headed for her. The last thing she needed was him crushing her.

Macy rolled one more time. As she did, he slid across the pavement. First his arm hit and then he rolled onto his chest, still sliding forward. Then his cheek hit the ground, sending his big, ugly glasses flying. He rolled onto his back, exposing his now-bloody bare torso.

He moaned and then sat up, patting the ground. "Where are my glasses?"

Macy jumped up and ran, but then she stopped. "You need your glasses, Chester?" She didn't wait for an answer. Macy went over to where they rested, picked them up, and then chucked them into the yard. "Go and find them. I could have crushed them, but you know what? I'm going to be nice, unlike you. If you were a nicer person, you wouldn't have to force people to act like they love you. Heather used to love you. Her mom, too."

Macy turned around and ran, unsuccessfully trying to ignore her knee. The pain was worse. At least Chester was behind her and would take a while to find his glasses.

The sirens grew louder, but they didn't sound like they were moving any more. The cops had to have already arrived at Chester's house. The road curved and she found herself looking at several cop cars parked in front of the Woodran residence.

Did all roads lead to that house? Panic rushed through her. If she turned around, she would have to face Chester. She saw Rebekah standing on the front porch talking to a couple officers.

Macy's only way out was to go past the house and the cops. If Rebekah saw her, it would be over. As far as she knew, Macy was Heather.

"Heather!" shouted someone from behind.

Without thinking, Macy turned around. A lady about her parents' age stood behind her. She was wearing what looked like nurses' scrubs.

They had cartoon puppies on them.

An officer came out of one of the cruisers. He looked back and forth between the nurse and Macy.

"Is this the runaway?"

The nurse looked confused. "Runaway? This is Heather Woodran. She's a patient over at Shady Hills where I'm a nurse. I'm Candice Roberts."

Macy's heart sank. She looked for a way to escape.

"I was told that she ran away from home," said the officer. "That's what set off the alarm."

Candice shook her head. "She had to have escaped Shady Hills. There's no way she was released. Heather has been…well, having issues. That's all I can say legally. Also, her dad lost custody and can only see her with supervision. I have no idea how she got here, officer, but I assure you she needs to get back to Shady Hills. You're going to want to look into how he got her out."

"But I'm—" Macy said.

"Heather, stay quiet if you know what's good for you," said Candice.

"I'm not—"

"How do you feel about going back into solitary? It won't just be for a couple days this time."

Macy's eyes widened. What had Heather been through? Macy would have to stay quiet for the time being. There would have to be a better time to explain who she really was.

The officer scribbled notes onto a tablet with a stylus. "If that's the case, I'll have to drive her back."

"I'm on my way to work now. I can take her. It's no problem." Candice wrapped a hand around Macy's arm and squeezed.

Why was freedom so fleeting? There was no way she could break away and outrun a nurse and a cop.

"Let me call down to Shady Hills and if what you say is true, I'll release her into your care." He pulled a smartphone out of his pocket. "You two stay right there." He walked over to his car, talking on the phone.

Candice squeezed Macy's arm tighter. "How did you get out? That place is sealed up tight."

Macy glared at her. "Maybe it's not as secure as you thought. Or maybe you underestimated me."

"You're going back into solitary for this."

Macy shook her head. "Trust me, after everything I've been through, you can't scare me."

"How dare—?"

The officer walked back to them. "The office at Shady Hills confirmed that Heather Woodran is a long-term patient and you're one of her overseeing nurses, Mrs. Roberts. I'll just need to see your identification, and then if you sign here, you're free to take her."

Candice gave Macy a dirty look. "Gladly." She pulled out her driver's license and then took the tablet and signed with the stylus, all without letting go of Macy. When she handed the tablet back to the officer, she yanked Macy's arm and pulled her across the street.

Chester came down the street with a limp of his own to go with his bloody torso. His glasses were also crooked. "Hey, Candice! What are you doing with Heather?"

"Taking her back to Shady Hills—where she belongs. Go get yourself cleaned up, Chet. What the hell happened to you, anyway?"

"None of your business. Hand her over. I'll take her."

Macy stood closer to Candice. No matter how mean she seemed, Macy would rather go with her than Chester.

"We all know you lost custody," Candice said. "I'm not going to jail over you. Pull your life together and get custody back, then you can have her."

Chester furrowed his eyebrows. "Hand her over now."

The look in his eyes shot terror throughout Macy. "He's not even my dad! He kidnapped me. Get him away!"

"Kidnapped you?" Candice gave her a bewildered look. "Have you forgotten that I've known you your whole life? Your mom was pregnant with you when we met. I brought your parents dinner the night they came home from the hospital. You really need to get your crap together, kid, or you're never going to leave Shady Hills."

Chester reached out for Macy.

"Officers!" Candice shouted.

"I'm going home." Chester narrowed his eyes. "Don't think you've heard last of me. Any of you."

Candice gave a bitter laugh. "I would never think that, Chet. Go get yourself cleaned up and take care of that pregnant girl on your steps. No wonder you've all been hiding away in there." She shook her head and dragged Macy into a little silver sports car. "Buckle up and don't try anything. There are three police cars right there. I won't hesitate to have them take you downtown, and trust me, you don't want to go there. It makes Shady Hills look like the Hilton."

Macy pulled her arm away from Candice's grip. She got in without a word. At least she was getting away from Chester, and hopefully for good. What would happen when they got there and realized there were two Heather Woodrans?

As they drove to the mental hospital, Macy looked all around for clues as to where they were. It was hard to focus because Candice kept lecturing her about her behavior.

Finally, Macy turned and looked at her while they were at a stop light. "What exactly do I have to look forward to? My mom is dead, not that anyone will listen to me about that. My dad doesn't have custody, not that I'd really want to stay with him anyway."

"You would either stay with extended family or go into foster care. There are a lot of really nice families. You'd even be able to go back to school, although at this point, you would be really far behind."

"Why won't anyone listen to me about my mom?"

"Because we know she's alive."

That was impossible. "How do you know that?"

"We've talked with her." Candice shook her head, looking irritated.

Everything seemed to shrink around Macy. "You did? When? Why haven't I talked to her?" Or had Heather actually talked with her? If so, what was she still doing in Shady Hills?

"Have you actually forgotten? You did, but you tried to convince us that it wasn't her."

"And you didn't believe me? I'm her daughter. I'd know a fake

Karla Woodran more than anyone."

"I spoke with her too, Heather. Don't forget how long I've known her."

Macy folded her arms. It was pointless to keep arguing with the woman. Chester had obviously found someone who sounded just like Heather's mom to talk with people over the phone. That explained how he was able to avoid jail. Poor Heather. Talking to someone who sounded like her mom had probably crushed her, and then having no one believe her that it wasn't her mom probably sent her over the edge. No wonder she was still there.

Heather was probably having a worse time than Macy. They'd both been ripped from their families, but she knew her mom was dead. Macy at least knew there was hope of seeing her family again.

"Did I finally render Heather Woodran speechless?" Candice asked, her tone full of snark.

Macy glared at her, but didn't say anything. Whatever she did say would just dig herself—and Heather—deeper. What she needed was to find a way to get the both of them out of the hospital. It wasn't going to be an easy task, but at least they would be able to put their heads together when Macy got to Shady Hills.

Candice pulled the car into a parking lot. The building was several stories tall and though it was clean and well-kept, it gave Macy the chills. They got out and Macy thought about taking another run for it, but she had a limp and her body ached from earlier. Besides, she needed to talk with Heather, and going in was her only way of doing that. They would find a way out together.

She followed Candice, keeping her gaze toward the ground. She had become accustomed to that from living in the community, since she wasn't supposed to look at any guys without their permission. But it worked here too, because she didn't want anyone figuring out that there were two Heathers.

They walked by a large registration desk. Clearly no one had any questions about Candice being with Heather. Then Candice pulled out a card and scanned it in front of a large, metal door. It opened slowly and they went inside, the door closing on its own behind them. They went through several more doors just like that one.

Macy started to doubt their escape. Unless Macy or Heather could sneak one of the cards from someone. There were two of them. One could stay in the room while the other sneaked out to get a card. Maybe they did have a chance.

Candice and Macy came to another desk, but this one was smaller and didn't have anyone sitting at it. Candice grabbed Macy's arm and led her down a hall. They went into a room marked 108.

Candice glared at her. "You stay in your room. Do you understand? I can lock it from the outside, and probably should. I don't know how you got out, but you're lucky that I'm the one who found you. I don't want you sent to the third floor. We'll just pretend this never happened. I don't think the police officer actually made any kind of report when he called in about you. He just asked if you were a resident and if I was a nurse. Next time, I won't be so lenient. Are we at an understanding?" Her eyes narrowed.

"Yeah."

"Not even a thanks? Why am I surprised? Look, Heather. Just get your street clothes off and stay in here. Do us both a favor."

Worried

Zoey frowned, sitting on Alex's bed. The dinner had gone seamlessly, and Lydia had been on her best behavior, not giving any indication that she had any feelings for Chad.

"See?" Alex asked. "There was nothing to worry about."

"Don't look at me like that," Zoey said. "Lydia only acted like that because we were so close. This won't be the last of her."

"If she does show up again, then I'll keep watch, okay? But she just acted like any other neighbor who came over with dinner when Macy disappeared. Remember? You were there."

"Yeah, but she's the only one who stayed to eat with us, right?"

"She's lonely. You heard her talk about her husband. She said he's home three nights a month if she's lucky. Remember?"

"Right. She's lonely and your dad's hot."

"Stop calling my dad hot. And Lydia's not available. She's married."

"You're not usually so naive. What gives?"

"Quit calling me that. Shouldn't we work on our homework?" Alex asked. He looked eager for a new topic of conversation.

Zoey could feel tears threatening. "Why can't you leave me alone? My life has been crumbling around me for months now, getting worse with each passing month."

"You think mine isn't?"

"Not like mine is!"

"How so? My *sister* has been gone without a trace. I'm thirteen and going to be a dad. Now my mom won't come home."

Rage ran through Zoey. "Your missing sister is my best friend! Yeah, you're going to be a dad, but you're not the one getting bigger every day. I'm going to have to buy new shoes. You know why? Because even my feet are fat. People don't look at you and automatically know you're going to be a parent. I'm a neon sign for teenage pregnancy."

"Yeah, but when you wear flowing shirts like that one, it's not that noticeable."

"You don't know anything!" She got up and stormed out of the room.

He followed her. "What do you mean?"

"It means you didn't notice anyone pointing at me when we were at the movies today. You didn't hear what people said, loud enough for me to hear." She blinked back tears. What she wouldn't have given for a cigarette.

"Nobody said anything. If anyone had, I would have gotten in their faces and if necessary, beaten the crap out of them."

"Well, you know what? They did, and you weren't my knight in shining armor."

"What did they say?"

"Forget it, Alex. It's pointless. People were calling me a whore right under your nose and you didn't even notice."

"Why didn't you say anything?"

"Because the only thing I wanted was to get away from them. They were on their way out as we were going in. Besides, we can't fight everyone. Are we going to fight every time we go into public?"

"If people are going to call you names, then yes."

"That's why we left school. The best thing is probably for me to stay away from places like the movies and the mall. It's only a matter of time until the news picks up on this. I'm surprised they haven't yet."

"It's because they don't care about Macy anymore."

"My point is that I don't want to go out. At least the news isn't hounding you guys. That's, like, the one good thing going on."

"What about me?" Alex looked hurt.

"You? What about you?"

"Aren't I a good thing?"

Zoey frowned. "Most of the time."

"So, I'm not now? Is that what you're saying?"

"If the shoe fits."

He opened his mouth and then shut it.

"If you have something to say, say it."

"Zoey, I don't want to fight."

"Say it!"

Alex looked frustrated. "I'm not trying to compare who's having a harder time, okay? I know you love Macy like a sister. I know the pregnancy is obviously harder on you. Probably in a lot more ways than I think. You're the one solid in my life with everything else falling apart. I really don't want to fight."

"It's a little late for that." Zoey stormed to Macy's room.

"Are you going to stay there tonight?" Alex asked.

"Yep." She slammed the door behind her. She locked it and threw herself onto the bed, finally allowing the tears to fall. It felt like the world was crushing her, and arguing with Alex only made things worse. How could he have not seen those jerks pointing at her and calling her names?

She sat up and looked around Macy's room which had almost become hers.

Scratching noises brought her attention to the ferret cage. The cute, little face stared up at her. Ducky begged for attention. Sighing, she opened the cage and he ran down the levels and into her lap. He jumped around, making Zoey laugh, despite everything else. She picked him up and carried him to the bed.

Ducky scampered across the bed, hopping around like a flea. The poor thing was attention-starved. She hadn't paid him much attention, and she doubted anyone else had, either, aside from cleaning the cage. He darted under the covers and she watched as he moved around, making the blankets go up and down in the process.

She peeked into his cage—the litter box had piled up and the food dish was empty. Zoey wasn't supposed to clean any litter boxes—doctor's orders—so she would have to tell Alex or Chad. But she had to feed the poor thing.

Keeping her attention on the bouncing covers to make sure he didn't escape, Zoey got up and grabbed the bag of food and filled the food dish.

When she sat back down, Ducky popped out of the covers. He climbed up her shirt onto her shoulder and went around the back of her neck to the other side, tickling her. He got caught in her hair, so she had to pull him out, untangling her hair in the process.

It was nice to have the distraction. Ducky was so cute, and the way he jumped around was hilarious. If her life didn't suck so much, she would have laughed at him. Once free of her hair, he jumped around on top of the covers for a while, a few times trying to run down the bed, but Zoey grabbed him each time. The last thing she wanted to do was to have to chase him around the room.

When Macy had first gotten him, he had gotten stuck—or just enjoyed hiding—inside of the dresser behind a drawer. The two of them had spent hours chasing after him, trying to get him out. He darted through the drawers, out onto the floor, around the room, and back into the dresser again.

That was why Zoey was so careful not to let him off the bed. It had been hard enough for two of them to catch him, she didn't want to do have to chase him through the room on her own. He seemed to have more energy than ever before, and that was saying a lot for a ferret. He slept most of the day, cram-packing all that energy into a few short hours.

She was about ready to put him back in the cage when he dawdled over to her and snuggled against her bulging belly. Zoey leaned back and stroked his little body while he snuggled against her.

"You miss her, too? How are we going to get her back?" Zoey sat there, petting him until he fell asleep. "What are we going to do about anything?" Zoey's eyes got heavy and she didn't want to fall asleep and have Ducky wake up and get lost, so she put him back in the smelly cage and then climbed into Macy's bed, too tired to care about the stink of the litter box.

When she woke up, it was dark and she had to go to the bathroom really bad. She remembered when that intruder had broken into the Mercer's house, knocking Zoey out and leaving her in their garage. She held her breath, not wanting to go out.

The doctor had warned her flashbacks could occur at any time, even if it had been a long time. It had been months and she had almost forgotten about it, but she was terrified to go into the hall. She had been going to the bathroom in the middle of the night for a while with no problems. She also knew the Mercer's had bought a top of the line security system and still had the police keeping an eye on the place. Even though they didn't park out front anymore, they made a point to drive by often enough, especially at night.

The pressure on her bladder urged her to get out of bed. She slid her swelling feet onto the floor and tip-toed to the door. She put her ear against it, listening. The only thing she could hear was the sound of her own labored breathing.

Zoey opened the door, half-expecting to see the man standing there with a knife. Yes, she had an active imagination, but there was good reason for it this time. The hall was empty and dark, only lit with a night light several feet away. It was enough to see she had nothing to worry about.

She went to the bathroom and then considered going to Alex's room. She was still ticked at him for being so dense. Even if he hadn't heard what those kids had said at the theater, he should have believed her. He had been acting like such a buffoon, but she still wanted to be with him.

Tip-toeing again, she went to his room and slid the door open. The room was dark and she could hear his heavy breathing, so she closed the door behind her—not that Chad would care that they were in there together. Alyssa would, but she wasn't there.

Sliding in next to him, she made herself comfortable under the covers. She remembered the Star Wars sheets he'd had to put on the bed when the laundry had piled up. Alex had been really embarrassed, but Zoey was more impressed that they had found them in the queen size.

Alex stirred next to her. "Zoey?"

"Yeah." She moved closer to him, feeling her anger melt away.

He wrapped an arm around her. "You're not mad at me?"

She shook her head, not actually answering.

"I love you," he whispered and then his breathing slipped back to what it had been. She listened to the rhythm for a few minutes before falling asleep herself.

Mirror

MACY STOOD AT the window of Heather's room in the hospital. It was late, but she couldn't sleep. Heather still hadn't come back to the room, although she did see another nurse, who came in looking surprised.

She had said, "Heather, what are you doing here? I thought you were still on the second floor."

Macy smiled. "Got off on good behavior."

The nurse's eyes widened. "Really? Well, that's certainly good news." Then she had brought Macy dinner, which wasn't very good, but was at least something in her stomach. And it was something that Macy hadn't had to cook herself.

That had been hours ago. Candice had checked on her a couple times, but said she was busy with other patients. Macy was anxious to meet Heather, the girl she had been pretending to be for months. The girl who no one questioned was her, not even her grandparents or her neighbor who had known her since she was a baby. Even Macy, when looking at Heather's pictures, had a hard time believing they weren't of her. She had seen twins who had looked less alike than Heather and her.

The door opened and Macy jumped. She ran to a corner and slid down to the floor. Someone was shoved into the room. "Stay there and be good. You don't want to go back to the second floor, Heather. I'm locking the door, but hopefully tomorrow we won't have to." The door slammed shut and Macy heard the lock go into place.

Her heart picked up speed. How was she going to introduce herself to Heather?

Heather swore and then turned on the light. She turned around and froze when she saw Macy. "Who the...? What? Is this some kind of trick? Are they trying to—?"

Macy stood up. "Heather, I—"

"Are they trying to mess with me? Who are you and why do you look exactly like me? Even your hair!" She picked up a book and held it as though it were a weapon. She stared at Macy. "You look *just* like me. What's going on?"

"Let me explain. Please."

Heather lowered the book slightly, giving Macy a suspicious look. "I guess I have nothing better to do. But first, who *are* you?"

Macy held her hands up slightly, showing her that she wasn't going to hurt her. She sat in a chair. "It's a long story. You might want to sit."

"This should be good." Heather sat on the bed, not taking her eyes off Macy.

"My name is Macy Mercer and your dad kidnapped me to replace you."

Heather's face appeared to soften. "What?"

Macy wrung her hands together. "He found me online and pretended to be someone else—a teenage boy—so I would meet him. When I did, he kidnapped me. He locked me up until I agreed to call him Dad." Macy went on to explain some of what Chester had put her through, describing him and her grandparents so Heather would know she wasn't lying. She even described the farm house and the house she had just left.

The book dropped from Heather's hands and hit the floor. "He replaced me?" Her eyes shone with tears. "What about Mom? Did he replace her, too?"

"Yeah, he replaced her too, with a younger model. I'm sorry."

Tears spilled down her cheeks. "How did you know I was here? How did you get in? Do the nurses finally believe me?"

"I got away from your dad and then your stupid neighbor brought me here."

"Candice."

Macy nodded. "But it actually worked out because I wanted to help get you out of here."

"How'd you know I was here? If Dad wanted you to be me, he wouldn't have told you I was here."

"I found your diaries."

"You read my private journals?" Heather's face flashed with anger. "How dare you?"

"How could I not? I didn't know what had happened to you or your mom. I knew nothing. You think Chester was going to tell me anything? Besides, I at least knew where to find you. That's why I didn't fight to get away from Candice. She was my ticket to get in here to help you get out."

Heather calmed down. "I probably would have done the same thing. Well, what about your family?"

"I need to get back to them after we get out of here. They have to be worried sick. I've been gone for months now."

"How are we going to get out? There are heavy, locked doors everywhere. You have to have a card to open them and the nurses don't leave those lying around. Trust me, I've looked."

"I have two ideas. Maybe together we can come up with more. But I thought we could either steal one of those cards to get out the doors or we can work to convince the nurses that you're cured."

Heather laughed. "Cured? There's nothing wrong with me. They're the jerks who won't listen to me. Dad has had everything covered, down to finding someone who sounds just like Mom to talk to everyone over the phone, pretending to be in Paris with her new love." She scowled. "I hate him so much. Anyway, that's why I'm so quick to believe that he replaced me with someone who looks exactly like me. Did you go to my school? Did my friends believe you?"

"He never let me out of the house. Can you think of another way to get us out?"

"It's going to take forever for them to believe that I've changed. I'm their trouble patient—and that's saying a lot around here. I just stopped caring. They wouldn't listen to me about Dad. He knows how to make people think what he wants."

"Do you think it's possible to sneak one of the key cards?"

"I've tried. They only ever keep those clipped onto the nurses' shirts."

"You don't think they have extras in that front desk somewhere?"

"They're not going to let us just walk up and go through the drawers."

"No, but they don't keep it manned all the time. When Candice brought me in, no one was there."

"Really? That's pretty rare. There must've been an incident. I've never seen it empty."

"What if we cause an incident? You act up and then I'll run to the desk when everyone is busy."

Heather looked like she was considering it. "The only problem with that is that if I act up, I'm going to solitary for a long, long time. What if they find both of us? Then they'd be forced to listen to us. I mean, really, if you've been kidnapped, they have to be able to find that out. They can pretend Mom's in Paris, but they can find out about you."

"Yeah, but then we're back to *you* being locked up here." Macy frowned.

"But you could tell them I'm not crazy. You've seen what Dad is capable of. If you tell them everything he did, they'll have no choice but to believe me and everything I've been saying all along. They'll know why I act out—because they won't listen to me. You'll get to go home, I'll get out of here, and Mom will finally get justice."

"Where will you go? Who will you stay with?"

"Either my grandparents or with my aunt and uncle. I guess it depends on who wants to take me. As long as I get out of here, I don't care."

"What do you think our best option is?" Macy asked.

"You know what? It would be fun to mess with the nurses and doctors here. After everything they've put me through, treating me worse than a criminal."

Macy groaned. "I just want to get home to my family. It's what, March? Your dad took me in November."

"Please help me mess with them. It's going to take us a while to get out of here anyway. We may as well have some fun."

"If we march out there together and tell them everything, they have to listen to us. The cops were just at your house this morning. Your dad is the one who needs to be taken care of—all of this is his fault. Everything he did to you and your mom, he needs to pay. He also needs to pay for kidnapping me. The staff here, they're nothing more than another one of his victims."

Heather snorted. "Trust me, girlfriend. They're not innocent. Come on, what's another day? We can screw with them and then tell them the truth after."

"And then have them pissed at us? They won't listen to us."

"You think they'll listen to us now? How long have you been here in my room posing as me? I was on the second floor all day. You know how to pretend to be me."

Macy put her face into her hands. Why was Heather being so difficult? She looked up and stared Heather in the eyes. "I've been pretending to be you for practically half a year. I just want to be me again and go home. I haven't seen my family in so long."

"At least you get to see yours." Tears shone in her eyes again. "My mom's dead and my dad's going to jail—not that I want to see him. I've had everything ripped from me, too, but when I leave here I'm not getting it back."

Macy's anger melted somewhat. "I'm sorry about that. I really am. But don't you want out of here? I want to *help* you get out. That's why I didn't fight Candice much when she tried to bring me here. I did try telling her I was kidnapped, but she wouldn't hear anything of it. She was convinced that I was you. Forget about getting back at them. Let's just try to get out of here. I know your grandparents would be more than happy to have you home with them. Think about them."

"How are they? I haven't seen them in, like, a year."

"Good. Ingrid taught me how to make some meals from scratch. She couldn't believe that you forgot."

A corner of Heather's mouth curled upward. "I'll bet. I've been cooking with her since I was little. Mom used to get so nervous with me so close to the stove. How's Grandpa?"

"Crotchety, but good."

"That sounds about right. Does he still bump heads with Dad all the time?"

"Yeah, they annoyed each other constantly."

"It would be good to see them." Heather ran her hands through her tangled hair. "I really would like to get back at the nurses, but you're right, it's not fair to you. You've had to deal with Dad all this time. So what are we going to do? Just walk out there together and say *listen to us*?"

Macy shrugged. "I've been trying to figure that out ever since I got here."

"I don't know if you noticed, but they locked us in. We either have to wait till morning or make a scene to get them in here. Then we have to hope they don't separate us."

"No one is going to check on you before morning?"

"Not unless I give them reason to."

"But it's a hospital. Aren't they supposed to check on you?"

Heather shook her head. "I'm locked inside with no way to get out. If I was on suicide watch or something, they'd have me in a room with a camera, but otherwise, nope. They just let us sleep and think."

Macy leaned her head against the wall. "I just want to get home."

"You may as well get comfortable. We can think up ideas before morning. Do you want the bed? I've slept in a padded room wearing a tight jacket. I can handle the floor."

"I've slept in the barn's cellar and in the back of your dad's truck. I can deal with the floor too."

Heather's eyes widened. "He put you in the storm cellar?"

"Until I agreed to call him Dad and answer to your name."

She looked like she was going to be sick. "I always wondered if he put Mom down there when she was missing. When she came back she kept saying the barn."

Macy remembered that from Heather's diaries, but wasn't going to say anything. "I did find a tube of lipstick down there."

Tears ran down Heather's face. "You know what? You're right. Screw the nurses. It's my dad we need to focus on." She got up and walked toward the door.

"Wait. What are you doing?"

"I'm going to pound on the door. With you here, they have to listen to me. They have to listen to *us*."

"Hold on." Macy's heart raced so much she started to have trouble breathing. "Are you sure they'll listen to us? The last thing I want is to end up a patient here, too. They wouldn't send us to solitary? I don't want to be locked up anymore."

"We're already locked up, in case you haven't noticed."

"Yeah, but at least we're not alone. Do you know how long it's been since I've had someone to talk to? To actually plan something out with someone else?" It had been Luke three months earlier. "We'd better think this through."

Heather narrowed her eyes. "Why are you changing your mind all of a sudden?"

"Last time I acted rashly trying to escape, someone died."

"What the hell? Who?"

Macy went over to the bed and sat. "You'd better get comfortable. This is so crazy. You're going to want to sit."

Would Heather even believe that Chester had taken her to a cult's compound and had nearly risen to one of their top leaders?

Talking

ALYSSA ROLLED OVER in bed, feeling more refreshed than she had in a long time. The alarm clock next to the bed showed it was 8:37. How could she feel so refreshed after so little sleep? She had probably gone to bed after three, and it was probably after four by the time she fell asleep.

She stretched and realized she had to go the bathroom really bad. It was so bad that she was afraid she wouldn't make it across the hall. Alyssa scrambled out of bed, holding her breath. She barely made it.

Once she was washing her hands, she looked at herself in the mirror. She looked better—not back to normal, but better than she had in a while. The circles under her eyes had faded. She really felt rested too. It didn't make any sense.

How could she feel and look so much better after only a few hours of sleep?

Alyssa touched her face. It was oily. In fact, her hair felt the same way. On the inside, she felt great, but on the outside, she was gross. She needed a shower, especially since Rusty was bound to check on her soon.

She poked her head out the door to make sure he wasn't in sight and then she ran to the bedroom and grabbed her bag. She locked the bathroom and then got her supplies out of the bag, getting ready for a much needed shower.

Once Alyssa was cleaned up, she stepped out of the bathroom and the smell of bacon, eggs, and coffee greeted her. Her stomach rumbled.

Alyssa smiled as she threw her bag on the bed. Rusty was making *her* breakfast? Maybe she felt so rested because she was still asleep. No one cooked for her unless it was someone bringing the family dinner.

"Good morning," she said, announcing her presence as she walked into the kitchen.

Rusty turned around, wearing a red apron and holding a spatula. He smiled. "Did you sleep well?"

"I did, actually. I can't believe it's so early."

He gave her a funny look.

"What?"

"You slept for more than a day. You missed yesterday completely." He turned back to the stove, stirring something in a pan.

"I—you mean I slept over twenty-four hours?"

"Obviously you needed it. Have a seat. What do you take in your coffee?"

She sat down in the same chair she had sat in the night before. No, two nights before. "Creamer or milk and sugar. Whatever you have is fine. Not that I really need any after such a long sleep. Breakfast smells great. Can I help?"

"Nope. Let me take care of it. I'm almost done. It's nice to have someone else to cook for again."

Again? He was gorgeous and a cook? Lani had been one lucky lady. "I'm not going to complain about that."

"Glad to hear it." He used the spatula again and then moved over to the coffee maker.

As she watched him, her stomach growled again, and it was loud. Her face warmed up, hoping he couldn't hear it over the sizzling bacon. If he did, he didn't respond.

After a few minutes, he set a cup of coffee and a plate full of food in front of her. Alyssa's mouth watered. "That looks delicious."

Rusty sat down across from her with his own food. "I try, but don't rave about until after you eat it. Dig in. You must be starving after sleeping so long."

Looking at the food, she felt overwhelmed by everything. Why had he gone out of his way to take care of her? He hadn't had to tow her twice for free, bring her home, or cook this delicious meal. Voice cracking, she said, "Thank you."

He winked. "Again, not until you've tried it. Staring doesn't count."

She blinked back some tears. "No, really. I mean for everything. You haven't had to do anything for me, but you've done so much."

"People have helped me out also when I needed it. You know what they've asked me to do? Pay it forward. You're better than the decisions you've been making, Alyssa. I can see that much. I've been there, drowning in despair."

"That's it exactly."

"So eat now, before it gets cold. I want you to try it while it's still hot."

She cut a piece of the veggie filled, cheesy omelet. It nearly melted in her mouth.

Rusty looked at her expectantly.

Alyssa swallowed. "It's divine."

He smiled. "Perfect. Eat as much as you want. I made plenty. We'll probably warm it up and turn it into burritos later."

Later? How long was he expecting her to stay? Was he just being hospitable or did actually want her there? Not wanting to offend him or let the food get cold, she dug back in.

"Want more?" he asked as soon as she emptied her plate.

She did, but was afraid of stuffing herself. "I'm going to let it settle a little first." She picked up the coffee and brought it to her mouth. "Mmm. This is really good, too."

He grinned, his gorgeous eyes shining. "I do cook a mean breakfast, don't I?"

"That you do." She turned in her chair, blocking the bright morning sun shining on her face. It was going to be a beautiful Northwest spring day once the frost melted.

"Glad you like it, because I don't make much else unless I break out the grill."

"Do you grill all year?"

"Otherwise I'd eat out too much."

"In that case, I'll have to pay you back with a nice dinner."

"Sounds good to me." Rusty put his hands behind his head and looked at Alyssa.

They sat in a comfortable silence, sipping their coffees. Squinting, Alyssa looked outside at the back yard. As expected, there was a big play structure full of slides, swings, and climbers. His kids must have enjoyed it—and they probably thought they would have had many more years to enjoy it.

Tears filling her eyes, she turned to look at him. "How do you do it? Get through every day, I mean." The hole inside of her felt like it had been ripped even wider, knowing what he had gone through.

"Some days, that's all it is—getting through it. I would give anything for another day with them. Just one more hug." His face clouded over. "There are times I can't stand to be here. Other times, I can't leave. The memories are all I have aside from the things they left behind."

Alyssa wiped tears away. "That's exactly how I feel. As much as it kills me, I have to move on. I can't keep living like I've been."

He nodded, looking at something behind her. She turned around to see several children's drawings and paintings hanging on the wall.

She turned around. "It's so unfair."

A tear ran down Rusty's face. "That it is. But on the other hand, I'm grateful for the time with them I did have. I wouldn't give that up for anything, even though the pain sometimes feels like it's going to kill me."

"It's never going to go away, is it?" asked Alyssa.

He wiped his cheek. "It gets better, but it also gets worse. I don't think it ever disappears. At least I hope not. I don't want to forget. Somehow the pain helps to keep the other emotions alive, too."

Alyssa raised an eyebrow.

"It does get easier to a degree, as I'm sure you've found. First, there's the initial horror followed by the stages of grief until we hit acceptance."

She nodded. "That's where I'm at. I think. But it gets worse?"

"I went through hell on the first anniversary of crash. I nearly went back to the booze, but the thought of going back to rehab was enough to keep me away. That and knowing none of them would want me to turn into a drunk. I nearly lost the house when I was in rehab—the very house where my kids lived their entire lives." Be blinked fast for a moment. "I used that as my anchor to keep everything together. That was when I decided to go into towing with the primary aim of keeping drunks off the road. I couldn't save my family, but maybe I could save someone else's."

Alyssa nodded, afraid of her voice. If she spoke, she might end up a sobbing mess.

"Then I joined a grief group. I'm not sure if it helped, but I couldn't keep going." His lips curled down. "There were too many people there who didn't want to move on. That wasn't what I wanted."

"The therapist didn't try to move the focus?"

"It was just a group. I think if it had a counselor of some kind, that would have helped. It was run by people who wanted to connect with other grieving people. That was probably part of the problem. That and the fact that the ones who were stuck tended to dominate things. I couldn't deal with it."

Taking another sip, Alyssa nodded. They sat quietly again for a while. She looked at the framed paintings on the walls and thought those—and everything else in the house—must be reminders of Lani and the boys. How did he do it?

She at least still had Chad and Alex. What would she have done if she had lost all three of them? There was no way she would have held it together as well as Rusty had. She cleared her throat. "Last night when I was lying in bed, I spoke to Macy. I felt a lot better. Actually, I think that's why I was able to sleep so well."

Rusty sniffled, giving her a sad look. "They still haven't found anything?"

Alyssa played with her hands under the table. "No. I don't know what the holdup is. I'm sick of it though. I just want answers. That's what Chad and I have been fighting about. I don't see how she can still be alive after all this time. It's time to move on and accept she's not coming back. Do you think I'm a horrible person? Do you think I'm giving up?"

"No, you're not horrible for giving up. I'm in no position to judge.

I never had to live with the unknown. Reality was forced upon me from the moment it happened."

"I don't *want* her be dead," Alyssa said, her voice high. "That's the last thing I want, but I don't see how there's another possible outcome. Even if that one girl isn't her, we still know nothing about Macy. She's gone and she's not coming back. I can't keep acting like she is." The tears came again and Alyssa knew she was going to lose control.

She put her forehead on the table and sobbed. She was vaguely aware of Rusty sitting next to her and putting his arm around her. He didn't say anything. After what felt like forever, she looked up at Rusty, knowing she looked like crap and also not caring. "I'm not a bad mother. I'm not. I just have to face the facts."

"You don't have to explain yourself to me. You've gotta do what you think is right."

Why couldn't Chad be this understanding? She crumpled, aware of the table coming at her face but not caring enough to do anything about it. She felt hands grasp her and found her head against Rusty's chest. He held onto her tightly.

"You're safe here. Just let it all out. Scream, cry or whatever you need to."

She closed her eyes, giving into the sobs once again. Screaming sounded nice, but she didn't have it in her then. She would have to do that another time. Alyssa felt drowsy, unable to open her eyes as she cried and shook. She really did feel safe.

Feelings

ALYSSA OPENED HER eyes trying to figure out where she was. It took a moment to realize she was in Rusty's guest room. How had she gotten there? The last thing she remembered was sobbing against his chest.

She smelled something cooking. Was that what had woken her up? She stretched and thought about what to do. Part of her wanted to stay in bed and never get up again, but that wouldn't solve anything. On the other hand, she wasn't sure how she felt about getting up to face Rusty after turning into an emotional mess like that.

Closing her eyes, she pretended that she was a careless teenager sleeping in a weekend. She had been able to out-sleep anyone back then.

The smell of food grew stronger and her stomach rumbled. She grabbed her bag and went into the bathroom. She looked as bad as she had suspected. She brushed her hair, but that didn't help, so she pulled it back into a simple ponytail before putting on some eye makeup and lip color. Nothing too fancy, but enough to look human again.

She got a flashback of teaching Macy how to put on makeup. At only twelve, she wanted to be grown up. Alyssa had been excited to show her how to put it on, even though she knew Chad would throw a fit—which he had, of course, since he didn't want Macy growing up.

Alyssa threw her eyeliner in the bag. Now he had his wish.

Not wanting to think about him any longer, she stormed into the guest room and threw her bag on the bed. Alyssa had to calm down before going into the kitchen. Rusty didn't deserve her anger, nor did she want to talk about Chad with him.

She made the bed and then paced the room, trying to calm herself. When she felt halfway normal, she decided to go to the kitchen. Maybe helping him with dinner would get her mind off everything. It smelled like he was making those omelet burritos he had mentioned earlier.

Tightening her fists, Alyssa took several deep breaths. She still felt anger burning toward Chad deep in her gut, but she would have to ignore that. At least she had someone to talk with who understood her.

She opened the door and went into the kitchen. Rusty had his back to her, cooking over the stove again. Alyssa walked over to him. "Do you want some help with that?"

He jumped. "You startled me. Did you get enough rest?"

"I suppose so. I can't remember going back to bed."

"You wouldn't. You fell asleep out here and I carried you back there."

"Sorry. Usually I'm not so lazy."

"You're not. Clearly your body needs rest. I have a feeling it's not something you've given yourself much of in a while."

"Not for lack of trying."

"Sometimes a new environment can make all the difference. I did the same thing when I went to rehab. If they would've let me, I would have slept for a week. Here, can you stir this?" He handed her a wooden spoon.

"Sure."

He grabbed some tortillas and salsa and somehow turned their breakfast into a respectable dinner.

"I thought you could only make breakfast and use a barbecue."

Rusty shrugged. "Maybe I exaggerated a little."

Alyssa actually smiled.

He pointed to a little pot at the back of the stove. "Can you stir those, please?"

She picked up another spoon and stirred, getting the refried beans unstuck from the bottom.

"Add some of this." He handed her a jar of sauce.

"What's this?" She looked at the blank jar.

"My special ingredient."

"Okay." She sprinkled a little on and stirred again.

"You'll need more of that."

She dumped a bunch in.

"Easy there. Not so much."

Alyssa smiled. "Make up your mind." She forgot about her problems as they finished making the burritos, even laughing and teasing each other. By the time they sat down to eat, she felt better than she had in a long time. Maybe a change of scenery—and people—was exactly what she needed.

When they were done eating, Rusty gathered the dishes and put them into the sink. He turned on the water and Alyssa stood up. "Don't even think about it. I'm going to clean those."

He moved aside. "Be my guest. I'll be right back."

She washed the dishes, ignoring the dishwasher. She scrubbed away her frustrations on the dishes, pots, and pans. When she was done, she went to the living and found Rusty putting on his coat.

"Grab your coat. We're going on a walk," he said.

"We are?"

"You need some fresh air. Hurry up. I'm not going to wait forever." The skin around his eyes wrinkled, indicating that he was holding back a smile.

"Yes, sir." She went back to the guest room and grabbed her coat, putting it on as she headed for the living room. The front door was open and Rusty was nowhere to be seen. Alyssa peeked outside and saw him standing on the porch, looking at the sky. The sun was going down and it was colored in pinks and oranges.

She stepped outside. "It's beautiful."

He nodded, still looking at it. "Nothing like sunsets around here." He closed and locked the door. "We'd better hurry before it gets dark."

"Are we going anywhere in particular?"

"There's a trail not too far away. It's peaceful and helps me to stay centered."

"Sounds nice." She followed him, trying to stay at his side. They walked in silence as she took in the beauty of the tall, dark green pine trees surrounding them with the sunset framing them. Soon they were walking along a dirt trail. Squirrels scampered along the ground, chattering at each other. She heard a stream somewhere and with it, the occasional frog calling out.

They came to a fork in the trail and they went left. The sound of the stream grew louder and he stopped in front of a row of benches. He sat down without a word and Alyssa sat on the same bench, but not too close. She looked around at the scenery, her eyes resting on the sky, its hues darker.

She breathed in the fresh air, noticing the spring scents of new life. Even the dirt smelled sweet. A flock of noisy geese flew overhead in a V-shape. She ran her hands through her ponytail, noticing that her body felt relaxed.

Then it hit her. Alyssa hadn't thought of Macy the entire walk. She hadn't once thought of her dead daughter. She was a horrible parent. Wasn't she supposed to take Macy with her wherever she went?

"Are you okay?" Rusty asked.

She turned to look at Rusty, unable to admit the truth. She just stared at him, finding it hard to focus on the details of his face because it was getting dark.

"Alyssa?"

Would he understand? Or would he think she was as horrible as she felt?

"What's the matter? Remember, I've been through this too."

"I forgot about her."

"You forgot...?"

"Macy. I didn't think about her the entire time we've been out here." Alyssa expected tears, but those were missing too.

Rusty nodded, probably having a knowing look on his face. "It's a normal part of moving on. I remember the first time I noticed that too. I felt terrible, but we can't hang onto them every moment. We didn't before. Even when they were with us, there were times we lived and didn't think about them."

"I don't know how I feel about this. I don't want to forget. I want to move on, but..."

"You're not forgetting her. Actually, you're in the acceptance stage.

That's part of it."

The tears finally came. "I don't want to accept it. It doesn't feel right. It…" She wiped the tears, feeling like a jumbled mess.

He scooted over and sat about an inch away. "It's okay to feel whatever you feel. Feelings simply are. They're not right or wrong. I've been through all of this."

She leaned her head against his shoulder. "I felt normal again. It was wonderful, but horrible at the same time."

"That's nothing to feel guilty about. We can't go through life mourning forever. We would end up depressed and eventually suicidal. Our families wouldn't want that, would they?"

"No. I remember times when I was upset, and Macy hated that. She always tried to cheer me up." More tears filled her eyes. Even though it was nearly dark, she tried to blink them away.

"See? She would want you having times like this—enjoying life."

Alyssa's throat made an awful noise as the tears fell onto her face. She gave into the sob, determined not to turn into a blubbering mess this time.

Rusty put his arm around her. She imagined Macy telling her to move on. As guilty as she felt, she knew that was what she had to do. It wasn't good for her and it wasn't any good for Alex, either. He needed her to be strong.

The air suddenly felt cold and she shivered, leaning closer to Rusty.

"Are you ready to get back?"

"Not really, but we probably should. Hopefully we can see the path."

Rusty pulled something out from his jacket. She heard a click and then saw a light. He was holding a huge flashlight. "This will make sure that we do." He stood and held his hand out.

Alyssa took it and stood.

He let go and started walking. "Let yourself relax and think about nothing. It's good for you."

"All right." Alyssa said a silent apology to Macy and then focused on what she could see in the light.

They walked the rest of the way back to his house in silence. The stars were bright and beautiful and the moon was off to the side, only a small sliver. There were a few clouds, but it was a mostly clear night.

When they reached the house, Alyssa found herself wanting to stay outside. There was a swing on his porch, so she sat.

"Do you want to sit by yourself or would like company?" asked Rusty.

"You can stay. Or if you have to get to work, you can go. I don't want to keep you from anything."

"No. I'll go out later." He sat down.

She looked at him, this time able to see him better thanks to the porch light. One curl hung right over his forehead. She wanted to brush it away.

He leaned back into the swing. "Even though it was hard, I'm glad you went for the walk. There's something about nature that helps bring us where we need to be. At least it works that way with me."

"Me, too. Thank you, Rusty."

"It's nothing."

"Nothing? It's everything. You can't imagine how much you've helped."

"I've just given you a chance to get away from everything. You can stay as long as you need to—I mean that. Consider the room yours. Even when you go back home and need to get away, please come here rather than the bar. I don't want to find you there again."

Swallowing, she looked into his eyes. Before she knew what was happening, she leaned over and placed her lips on top of his. He smelled of aftershave and dinner.

He pulled back. "I'm sorry if I gave you the wrong impression. I was only—"

"Oh my gosh. I can't believe I just did that." Her face heated up. Of course he wouldn't find her attractive. He was off the charts handsome and she was a hot mess—all the time. He had driven her home twice because she was drunk. Just like the person who had killed his family. "I'll go now." She ran for the door, but it was locked.

Rusty got up and moved her hands from the door, giving her a kind look. "Don't be embarrassed. You're beautiful, Alyssa, but you're also grieving. If I allowed anything to happen, I would be taking advantage of you. Not only that, but you're married."

"Just let me inside."

He put his hand on her shoulder. "Do you know what I would give for one more day with my wife? You have that opportunity with Chad. Take all the time you need to work through your feelings here. I'm your *friend,* but what I really want is to see you back with your family."

Alyssa sighed and leaned against the door.

Returning

ALYSSA TURNED THE lock on her front door, holding her breath. Would Chad and Alex be angry with her or happy to see her? She hadn't even told Alex she was going anywhere, and she had been gone a couple of days. She was only there to get some more clothes and talk with Alex. With any luck, she would be able to avoid Chad. If he was working on his blog, she might actually be able to stay off his radar.

She walked in and closed the door behind her.

Alex appeared at the top of the stairs. "Mom."

Alyssa couldn't tell if he was happy to see her or upset.

"Oh, baby. I'm sorry I took off like I did." She went up the stairs, trying to read his face. He didn't give her any clues. She wrapped her arms around him and he returned the hug, squeezing tight.

"I was worried, but Dad said you needed some time to think about everything."

Alyssa nodded, stepping back. "He's right. You were already asleep when I realized I needed some space to think." If Chad hadn't mentioned their fight, neither would she.

"Are you staying?" he asked.

She tousled his hair. "I'm going to stay with a friend for a little while. But if you need me, call."

"Why didn't you answer your phone? It kept going to voice mail."

"I didn't bring my charger with me, but this time I will. I'm really sorry, Alex. How have you been doing the last couple of days?"

He shrugged, looking annoyed. "Dad's been on his computer non-stop, and Zoey isn't feeling well."

"Is she okay?"

"I guess. Her back's hurting and she's tired a lot."

"Do you want to grab some ice cream? It would be nice to sit and talk."

"We don't have any."

"Let's go out and get some. It'll do you good to get out of the house. It's helped me a lot."

"Not enough to stay here. I'm getting ready for bed, actually. Zoey's appointment is in the morning and I'm going with her this time."

Alyssa gave him another hug. "Let's plan to do something. I miss you."

"Are you moving out?"

"Honestly, I don't know. I'm not looking that far ahead. I need some time."

"To get away from Dad? I thought you guys were getting along."

She bit her lip. "We just need to work things out."

"What's to work out? We need you here. Not at Sharon's house or wherever you've been. Why didn't you call? Is there no phone there?"

Alyssa should have known that he would be upset. "I slept all of yesterday, sweetie. As in, I didn't even wake up once. I'll call you tomorrow, I promise. I want to hear about the appointment. And then maybe we can get some lunch."

"Whatever. 'Night, Mom." He turned around, but before he could walk away, Alyssa grabbed him and gave him a big hug.

"I really have missed you, Alex."

He hugged her back. "I know. Me too, Mom." Alex went up the stairs and down the hall and toward his room. Alyssa could hear him close the door behind him.

The last thing she needed was to lose him, too. He was right there. If she messed things up with him, then she really was an awful mom. She would need to get herself together so she could come home soon.

What if Chad continued to insist that Macy was still alive out there? If he held onto that fantasy, insisting that Alyssa did too, there was no way she could stay at home.

As much as it had ripped her apart out in the woods, moving on was what she needed. She couldn't hold onto the hope of Macy's return. Even though she wanted nothing more, she knew her daughter wasn't going to be back. All she could cling to was the hope that Macy hadn't suffered.

She needed to get to the place where Rusty was—somehow able to feel blessed that he had had the time he did with his family. Realizing that she had been standing in the same spot for a few minutes, she went up the stairs and thought about what she was going to pack. Mostly just clothes; she had already packed the other stuff she needed.

When she walked into her room, Chad was sitting on the bed. His back was to her, but she could see the glow from his phone. It sounded like he was texting.

She cleared her throat.

He turned around and looked surprised, hopeful even. "Are you staying?" he asked.

She shook her head. "I need some more clothes."

"You look good. Have you gotten some sleep finally?"

"That's almost all I've done. I missed yesterday entirely, actually."

"That explains why we haven't heard from you."

She went into the closet and grabbed some clothes from their hangers.

Chad's arms wrapped around her shoulders, pulling her into him. Her entire body tensed. She held her clothes close to her stomach.

He took a deep breath. "You smell like the outdoors."

"I went for a walk before coming here."

"Won't you stay? I've missed you so much. So has Alex. He—"

"I've already talked with him."

"What can I do to convince you to stay?"

She turned around, staring him down. "We can't agree to disagree. That works for some things, Chad, but not this. We have to accept the facts and move on. I can't do that if you refuse. We're living in two different realities."

He frowned. "You really want to give her a funeral?"

"She deserves it."

"What will we tell her when she returns? That we gave up on her?"

Alyssa pursed her lips, anger burning. "I'm not giving up on my daughter. I'm accepting the facts. It's what she would have wanted us to do. She wouldn't have wanted us to live like this."

Chad took a long, deep breath. "What if we agree to wait for the DNA results?"

"That could be another three months. Maybe longer the way they move. I can't keep my life on hold. I may sound like a horrible person, but I need closure."

"Are you moving out?"

"I'm giving myself space to heal. If you would give that to me, we can discuss my staying here. I can't move on if you don't."

"I can't give up on her. But I don't want you to leave, either."

"Then it looks like we have a stalemate." She turned around and grabbed more clothes, not even paying attention to what she was taking. She just made sure not to take any summer dresses.

When her arms were full, she threw the clothes onto the bed and went back into the closet and found her largest suitcase.

"We can make this work, Lyss." Chad begged her with his eyes.

She threw the luggage onto the bed. "No, we can't." She piled the clothes in, not bothering to fold them. "I can't do this. Not anymore. We've been together our entire lives and I'm sorry that it's come down to this, but we're obviously not made for each other anymore."

"What will Macy think when she comes home to find you gone?"

"She's not coming home! Don't you get that? She's never going to be back." She slammed the suitcase shut and zipped it, fighting tears.

"Alex needs you. I need you."

"Don't pull a guilt trip on me. If you really want to make this work, you'll pull your head out of your butt and face reality. Until then, I can't be here." She lifted the baggage with grunt.

"Let me help you with that."

"Stop! Just leave me alone." She put it on the floor and wheeled it out of the room.

"Where are you staying?"

"With a friend. Don't worry, I'll bring my charger."

"How can you do this?"

Alyssa turned around. "How can I do this? If you have to ask, you really don't get it. I'll see you later." She stopped in front of Alex's door. "Honey, I'm leaving. I'll call you tomorrow."

"Okay," came Alex's voice from the other side of the door.

She waited a moment and realized with a stinging sensation that he wasn't going to come out. "Talk to you then. I love you."

He said something, but it was too muffled to understand.

"You won't stay even for him?" Chad asked, still behind her.

"Not if you're going to be here. I can't handle it. Getting away was the best thing I've done for myself. You can think I'm selfish if you want. I really don't care anymore. Like I've already said too many times, this isn't something we can agree to disagree about."

A pressing weight pushed against her on all sides. She needed to get out of the house even though it was probably going to be awkward around Rusty after having kissed him. Looking at Chad, she knew she should feel guilty about it, but she didn't need any more guilt in her life. If anything, he had pushed her away—right to Rusty.

Alyssa looked around the hall, everything reminding her of Macy. There was no way she could stay there and move on with so many memories. Maybe she could come back after she had a chance to heal— if that ever happened. Could she get to the place where Rusty was? He was functioning and living a productive life in the same house that his family had lived in.

Chad looked at her. "Are you thinking about staying?"

"No. Maybe if we were on the same page, but even then, I don't know. It would be a start, at least." She yanked on the suitcase and went down the stairs with it. Somehow she managed to get it in the car without any tears or arguments.

As she drove away, the suffocation released its hold. It let go all the more as she got farther away. By the time she pulled back into Rusty's driveway, she felt human again. The tow truck was gone, which meant that he wasn't there. After the earlier embarrassment, it was a relief.

She obviously needed some space from him to think about every-thing. Getting away to talk with Alex the next day would help also. Exhaustion hit her and she was glad to be able to go in and just sleep. She took the key out of the ignition and then checked for the key Rusty had given her.

When she got inside, she went straight for the guest room and barely took the time to get into her pajamas before climbing into bed. She had another conversation with Macy, explaining why she had to stay at Rusty's instead of at home. Macy would understand.

Then Alyssa remembered to plug in her phone. She turned it on and scrolled through the missed calls and texts. There were quite a few from Alex and Chad over the last couple of days.

She went over to the gallery of pictures and the one it opened up to—the last one she had taken—was Macy smiling at her. She was holding Ducky. It was shortly after Macy had gotten the little black and white ferret. Smiling, Alyssa scrolled through the pictures, stopping at each one of Macy.

Some of them she couldn't even remember taking. It was like seeing them for the first time. It was a gift from Macy just when she needed it most. Alyssa scrolled through the pictures until her vision was too blurry. She blinked away the tears, turned the phone on silent, and went to sleep.

Demands

CHAD WOKE WITH a start, having rolled onto Alyssa's empty side of the bed.

They had been getting along so well over the last few months, it was still a shock to have her gone, mad at him. As much as he wanted to her to stay, he wasn't going to give in and have a memorial service for their daughter who was still alive. He couldn't explain it, and that was part of the problem, but he had a feeling that Macy was alive out there somewhere.

It was a feeling that he had learned not to ignore. It was actually the same one that he had had when he met Alyssa back in high school. He knew she was the one. Even though he was young—about Macy's age, maybe a little older; it was hard to remember the little details over twenty years later—he knew without a doubt that Alyssa was the girl for him. He *knew* they were going to get married and have a family together.

He had been right about that, and he was right about this too. That meant that even though it upset Alyssa, he wasn't going to give in and admit defeat. If somehow the DNA results showed that the girl in the morgue was his daughter, then he would have to give in and face those facts, but he knew that wouldn't happen.

Why was it taking so long to get those results? After nearly four months, he would have expected something. With technology as it was, they should have been able to get what they needed.

Chad rolled to the other side of the bed and checked his phone. Alyssa hadn't called. Hopefully that meant she had spent the evening talking with Sharon and gotten some much-needed sleep.

He needed to get up and check the blog comments and write a new post, but he knew he wasn't in any state of mind to focus on that. It would be half-hearted at best and he couldn't do that. If he had to get a late start, so be it.

What he needed to do was go down to the police station—not just call—and pester them until he got answers that he could live with. He had been patient long enough. Now it was time to put pressure on them.

Maybe that was the problem. He had just done everything the cops told them to do. Now it was time to say no.

He took a quick shower before heading to the kitchen. It startled him to see Alex and Zoey sitting at the table. They were eating cold cereal and had their school work out.

"Up so early?"

"My appointment is today," Zoey said.

"Oh, right. It's hard to believe you'll already find out the sex. What do you guys think it'll be?"

Alex looked up, pale.

Zoey shrugged her shoulders, taking a bite of rainbow-colored food.

"No ideas? I thought the moms always had a feeling."

"Not me."

Chad stared at Alex. "You okay, son?"

Alex sat up. "I'm great, Dad. Couldn't be better."

"Hey, I need to show you something." He turned to Zoey. "Mind if I borrow him for a minute?"

"Sure. I gotta get this assignment turned in before we go anyway." She turned to her laptop.

"Perfect. Come on, Alex." Chad went upstairs to the bonus room and sat on the couch.

Alex sat next to him. "What do you need to show me in here?"

"Nothing. I just want to talk to you alone."

"What is it? I have homework to turn in too."

"I want to make sure you're okay."

"I told you down there. I'm fine."

Chad tilted his head and gave Alex a knowing look, the same look his own dad used to give him when he was alive.

Alex scowled. "Okay. I'm not fine. I feel like I'm going to puke. Happy?"

"Of course not. Is there anything I can do?"

"Like what?"

Good question. Alyssa was always the one who knew what to do when it came to the kids. "Do you want me to go with you to the appointment? I can skip my blog post today."

"You would do that for me?"

He put his hand on Alex's shoulder. "Of course."

Alex gave him a strange look. "Thanks, but I'm going with Zoey and her mom."

Chad sighed, relieved. Seeing an ultrasound was too much reality for him. Maybe that was giving Alex anxiety. "Are you worried about seeing the baby?"

Alex looked away. "I dunno."

"I'll never forget when I first saw your sister and you on the screen. It was amazing and terrifying at the same time."

"Really?" Alex turned to him, looking somewhat relieved himself. "You felt that way? Both times?"

Chad nodded.

"But weren't you ready for it the second time?"

"Nope. Both times, it freaked me out. I can't tell you how scared I was that I would be in charge of someone's life. I kept a calm face for your mom because she needed my support, but inside I was freaking out."

"How did you deal with it?"

"I went out with the guys and had some beer. Obviously, you can't do that, but we can have some guy time tonight. We could hit the arcade."

Alex looked like he was considering it. "If you'll buy me the unlimited pass."

That was expensive and he had always told Alex he could get the pass one day. "Sure. Today's the day I get it for you. We'll play until you don't want to see another video game again."

"Or until they close."

"Whichever comes first."

"Deal. Thanks, Dad." Alex gave him a hug, surprising Chad.

He hugged Alex back. "My pleasure. I've got some errands to take care of today, so if I'm not here when you get back, I won't be long."

"Okay." Alex left the room.

Chad couldn't help smiling. He had actually handled that pretty well. Alyssa would have been proud, even though she wouldn't have liked Alex playing arcade games for hours on end. The kid deserved it. Chad remembered the stress and reality that those sonograms brought. He couldn't begin to imagine dealing with it at thirteen.

Besides, Alyssa wasn't even there. If she wanted to be involved in these decisions, she shouldn't have run off to her friend's place.

His stomach rumbled and he went back downstairs. The kids were busy on their computers, so he didn't bother them. He grabbed some frozen pancakes and stuck them in the microwave. After eating, he said a quick goodbye and then got in the car, thinking about what he would say to the cops.

Their shifts varied, so he didn't even know if he would be able to talk to the ones he had been working with since Macy disappeared. Even if they were off duty, he would put some pressure on whoever was there.

Chad marched into the station like he belonged there. He ignored the people sitting in the waiting room and walked straight to the front desk.

"Is Detective Fleshman here?"

"He's off duty. Can I help you?"

"How about Officers Anderson or Reynolds?"

"I believe Officer Reynolds is still here. He had a bunch of paper-work after his last—wait a minute. You are?"

"Chad Mercer. They're working with me on the case of my missing daughter."

Recognition washed over his face. "Oh, right. They're still looking for her?"

Chad could hear hushed conversation behind him. "Yes, of course.

Will you tell Reynolds that I need to speak with him?"

"Have a seat."

"I'll just stand here." Chad stepped back, keeping watch on the desk.

"Whatever. I'll let him know you're here." The officer got up and disappeared behind a wall.

Chad pulled out his phone and scrolled through his apps, pretending to be involved in a texting conversation. He was all too aware of the stares and whispers. Unfortunately, it had become a regular part of life outside the house. Couldn't people understand he was just a regular guy who happened to have a missing daughter? He was normal, just like them, except for the fact that his heart had been ripped out of his chest and stomped on while the world watched.

"Reynolds will see you. You know where room six is?"

Chad put his phone in his pocket and nodded. He knew where the rooms were and he could find number six since they were all labeled. He went around the desk and down the hall. He would have been happy to have gone his whole life without ever seeing those walls.

He found door number six and went in. It was empty. He paced back and forth before walking around the table several times. He was more than aware of the *mirror* on the back wall. He was tempted to wave or make a face at whoever might be watching him. Didn't they have rooms without the two-way mirrors for non-criminals?

Tired of walking around, he pulled a chair out and sat down. After a few minutes, Officer Reynolds walked in, wearing his signature hat. "Hey, Chad. I hope you weren't waiting too long. Paperwork is my least favorite part of the job."

"What's going on with the DNA testing?"

"They've yet to get a viable sample." Reynolds sat across from Chad.

"I know that much. What is anyone doing to get one?"

"If the latest test yields nothing, they're going to send her out of state to a more sophisticated lab."

"I knew that, too. More needs to be done. Since they've had such a challenging time getting a good sample, why don't they take more? Run five at a time. Do something."

Reynolds set his hat on the table and looked into Chad's eyes. "We're doing all we can. There are other cases and they can't be ignored."

"Is Macy's case getting pushed back?"

"No. If it wasn't important, they would drop it. It's still a missing child case and that's why it's going outside of the state after this. Macy is still a priority."

"I just want to make sure."

"We haven't moved on."

Chad narrowed his eyes. "I still say more needs to be done."

Meeting

ZOEY PACED HER room, looking out the window every five seconds. Despite all of her protests, she was about to meet her dad—no, her sperm donor. That's all he was. Nothing more. She would take a look into his eyes and see where she got the majority of her looks. She did look like her mom, not that anyone ever noticed because of her coloring.

She looked out the window again. Where were they? Her mom had texted her that they were on their way. Maybe there was traffic. Hopefully they were arguing. That way her mom would make him stay somewhere else.

How dare she invite him to live with them? Neither one of them knew the man. Sure, she had slept with him for a while. Maybe she had even wanted to get pregnant. She always prided herself on being a strong single mom and she knew he was going back to Japan.

Maybe Zoey's anger had been misplaced. Her mom might have been the one who had decided that Zoey didn't need a dad. Who was she to decide that? Just because she didn't want to deal with a husband, and that was incredibly selfish.

She looked around the room and stopped when she saw a small jewelry box her mom had given her years ago. Zoey walked over to it and held it up to the light, looking at the intricate designs. Then she clutched it in her hand and threw it on the hardwood floor, watching it smash into dozens of pieces.

Instead of chewing the sperm donor out, she was going to let them both have it. They had both agreed to the stupid, selfish plan. Did either of them give even one thought to Zoey and what she would have wanted? It didn't look that way. One wanted to get halfway across the world to hit a ball and the other wanted to be the sole decision maker in Zoey's life.

She picked up the last birthday card her mom had given her and ripped into tiny pieces, letting them fall on the floor next to the jewelry box pieces.

Zoey was glad that she had been smoking before getting pregnant—it hit her mom where it hurt. Just like she deserved. Even though Zoey had been dealing with horribly painful headaches among other things since quitting, she was glad she told her mom about her smoking. The look on her face had been worth it.

She was even happier to have gotten pregnant. That hit them both where it hurt. She was sure that neither of them wanted to be grandparents at their age. It was too bad she couldn't do more to make them pay. Although having a pregnant fifteen year old daughter was a pretty good hit.

Zoey heard a car pull into the driveway. The moment of truth was about to arrive. She went to her window and looked down. Sure enough, there was her mom's car with someone in the passenger seat next to her. He even appeared to be wearing a baseball cap. How fitting. Too bad the jerk couldn't play anymore. Then Zoey wouldn't have to deal with him at all.

Should she go down and meet them, or should she make them come up to get her? Zoey looked at the mess on the floor and didn't want to deal with a lecture. Not that she cared if her mom saw what she had broken. Let her, so it would hurt.

Zoey stepped over the mess and made her way down the stairs as slowly as possible. She could hear something downstairs by the door.

"Is that you, Zo?" called her mom.

"No. It's a burglar."

Her mom muttered something, but Zoey was too far away to hear. "Hurry up. Your dad's excited to meet you."

Zoey bit her tongue. There was so much wrong with that sentence she didn't even know where to begin. "Coming." She didn't pick up her pace. She took her time making her way to them. Before she rounded the corner, she flattened her shirt so that her stomach stuck out as much as possible. Usually, she wore the loosest clothing possible, but not today. She wanted her *dad* to have a good view.

She turned down the hall and walked to the entry, trying not to look at him, but curiosity made her want to look. How much did she look like him? Zoey kept her focus on her mom. "Are we ready for the appointment?"

Valerie scowled. "You have time to meet your dad." She turned to him. "Zoey, this is your dad. Kenji, this is Zoey."

Zoey glanced at him and gave a slight nod of the head. "Hi." She turned back to her mom. "Are we ready? We need to get Alex."

"Would you stop being rude? Give him a proper greeting?"

A proper welcome? Zoey turned to him. She tried to look past him, not taking in his features. "Hi, Kenji. Thanks for not being in my life. It's been awesome."

He opened his mouth, but Valerie spoke up first.

"Zoey!" She turned to Kenji. "I'm so sorry. I knew she might be in a mood, but I didn't expect this."

"Then I guess you don't know me very well, do you? I'm going to get Alex."

"Alex? Wait, we talked about this."

"No, Mom. You talked about it, but you didn't listen to me. Alex is coming with me. He hasn't been to any of my appointments. He deserves to be at this one. You know, he's been involved this whole time."

Kenji made eye contact with Zoey. "I understand this is hard for you. It's going to take time. I should have been involved, but I thought it was best if I didn't. We both did." He looked at Valerie. "I do care about you and hope you'll give me a chance. If you don't want to for a while, I respect that."

"Kenji, don't. She needs to—"

"This is a big adjustment and she has every right to be angry." He turned to look her in the eyes. "If you feel the need to—what the expression?—tell me off, you're more than welcome. Anything you need to say to me is good. Then I hope we can move past it and get to know each other."

Zoey stared at him, feeling deflated. If he knew he deserved to be ripped into, it was going to take half the pleasure out of it. "Maybe I'll take you up on that. I'm going to get Alex. See you in the car."

"Why don't you help us unload the rest of his stuff?" Valerie asked.

"Nope. I'm going to get Alex."

Her mom looked like she was going to explode. Good.

"She's fine," Kenji said.

"No, she's not! Zoey, you better—"

"Zoey, go get your boyfriend. I'll take care of my luggage."

"See you in the car." Zoey walked past them and out the door. Once the door closed behind her, she found herself shaking. She tried to stop, but couldn't. Why not? He was just some guy from the other side of the planet. Nothing to get worked up over. He was just another random stranger. Nothing more.

She took a deep breath and then made her way over to Alex's house. The driveway was empty. Did that mean neither of his parents were home? Not that it mattered. There were enough parents at her house to make up for the whole street.

The front door opened before she even got there. Alex closed it behind him. "Are we ready?"

"Yeah. My mom and sperm donor arrived just in time. I don't know how my mom does it. She always knows how to plan everything perfectly."

"So, what's he like?"

"Who knows? I barely said hi to him before coming to get you."

"Really? I know you're pissed, but aren't you curious?"

"Not really. Let's go. I want to find out if the baby's a boy or a girl. I'm tired of everyone calling it *it*."

"Okay." He looked like he wanted to say more, but he took her hand. "I want to know what it is, too."

Alex took her hand they walked to her house in silence. Zoey stopped when they got to her mom's car.

"We're not going in the house?"

"I told them we'd meet them in the car."

"Okay." He opened the back door and waited for Zoey to go in first. They settled in. "Is he nice, at least?"

Zoey shrugged. "He said I could chew him out if I wanted."

"Are you going to?"

"Probably, though it takes half the fun out of it since he said that."

"Fun?"

"You know what I mean. Not like ha-ha fun, but it'll feel good to let him have it. But if he's nice and not a jerk, it won't be the same. I wanted him to be mean. He said he was wrong and seemed to believe it. Said he thought keeping his distance was for the best."

He bumped her. "You're not half-bad, so he can't be too bad."

Zoey gave him a light shove and glared at him.

Alex laughed and then the corners of Zoey's mouth twitched. "Don't try to make me feel better."

"I'm just sayin'. I like you."

"Really? I would have never guessed."

He feigned a hurt expression and they both laughed. "At least you're smiling now."

"We'll see how long that lasts."

Alex looked toward the front of the house.

"Are they coming?" Zoey asked.

"Yeah. I'm trying to get a good look at your dad."

"Sperm donor," Zoey corrected.

"He looks a lot like you. Like, it's obvious he's your dad."

Zoey rolled her eyes. "I'm supposed to care?"

"Maybe you should give him a chance."

"And maybe you should back off."

Zoey's *parents* came to the car and Kenji introduced himself to Alex. It looked like Alex was going to pee himself. Was he nervous about meeting her sperm donor?

"Hi, sir. It's nice to meet you." Alex held out his hand between the front seats.

"Good to meet you, too. Seems we have a lot in common."

Alex squirmed in his seat. "Yeah?"

Kenji winked. "We're both nervous about seeing our children for the first time today."

"Huh. That's true. You're nervous?"

"Of course. She has every right to hate me. Maybe you could put in a good word for me?"

"I'm right here," Zoey said.

Kenji didn't take his eyes off Alex. "She has her mom's spunk. Have you ever noticed that?"

A slow smile spread across Alex's face. "Yeah, that's true."

Zoey glared at Alex. Whose side was he on, anyway?

Valerie started the car. "At least someone's being respectful to you." She gave Zoey a disapproving look to which Zoey promptly returned one of her own. "Are we ready?"

Zoey's mouth went dry. What was going on? How could she be in the car with her dad on the way to find out if her child was a boy or a girl? She took Alex's hand and gave it a squeeze. He lifted her hand and gave it a light kiss. Then he gave her a look that told her everything would be okay.

Temptation

CHAD WAS TOO frustrated to go back home and face Alex and Zoey. Why couldn't the cops get answers? Either the body was Macy's or it wasn't. Was it really that difficult with all the technology available?

If they would have at least let him look at the body, he could have told them whether or not it was her. If he wasn't so sure, he wouldn't be arguing with Alyssa.

As much as he loved her, he wasn't going to give in and say he thought Macy was gone. He didn't believe it and he wasn't going to let anyone think he did. When she returned home, he wanted to be able to look her in the eyes and tell her he hadn't given up on her, not for a moment.

She was going to return. Each passing day only brought Macy's return closer. He was sure of it. He wasn't going to judge Alyssa for her stance, but he wasn't going to take it with her. Even if it meant damaging their marriage. She was the one who wouldn't agree to disagree. They could still live under the same roof and hold different beliefs.

The car was suffocating. He pulled into the parking lot of the closest park. He would walk around the trails to burn off some energy. He couldn't think straight. Between the cops and Alyssa, he'd had about all he could take.

That wasn't true. The lack of results and Alyssa's demands were the icing on the cake of his life. He'd already had all he could take between his two kids. Anyone else in his shoes would have lost their minds already. He was actually holding everything together pretty well.

He slammed his door shut and locked it with the remote. Aside from a few random joggers, the park was empty. He looked up at the sky with the menacing clouds. No wonder only the die hards were out. Chad didn't care if he ended up soaked. He had energy to burn. Even though he wasn't dressed for a run, he was taking one.

Lifting weights had been one way he used to clear his head, but he hadn't even looked at those in months. He broke into a run and passed everyone else jogging. His lungs burned, but he didn't care. It actually felt good.

By the time the trail circled around and he was back where he started, he was almost completely out of breath. He had given himself fully to the run. He hadn't paid any attention to the scenery around him or given himself the chance to think about anything. None of his problems crossed his mind as he ran through the length of the trail.

He stopped at a bench, leaning his arm against the back of it, gasping for air. Sweat ran down his face, neck and back. He wiped it out of his eyes, wishing he had thought to bring something to drink. His mouth was parched.

Chad was vaguely aware of footsteps behind him, but he didn't really care.

"Hey, Chad, I thought that was you. What are you doing running in slacks?"

He turned around to face Lydia. "Do you follow me everywhere I go?" he asked in between gasps for air.

"Maybe. What are you doing out here?"

"I needed some exercise."

"In those shoes?"

"What's wrong with my shoes?"

"They're not exactly running shoes. You're going to have some painful blisters."

"I don't really care." He sat down on the other side of the bench.

"Well, you should. If you're going take care of—"

"Don't lecture me."

Lydia sat next to Chad. "I'm not lecturing. I'm concerned. I know we're done, but I still love you."

"Don't say that."

"Chad, it's true."

He stared her in the eyes. "That doesn't mean you need to tell me."

"I can't just walk away when you're clearly in some kind of trouble."

"I'm not in trouble. I just needed some air." He looked away. The clouds were getting darker, just like his mood.

A hand rested on his shoulder. "Is it Macy?"

Chad pushed her hand away. "Damn it, Lydia. Would you keep your hands off?"

She looked hurt. "Where's Alyssa?"

He stood up. "Would you just leave me alone? I didn't ask you to come and check on me. Go away."

"If that's what you really want. Is it?"

"What I want is for everything to return to the way it was before my daughter went missing."

"That's when we were together."

"Before that. It was a mistake. I should have worked on my marriage instead of turning to you."

"I'm not trying to pull you away from your family, Chad. You looked distressed and because I care, I had to check on you. I don't want to leave you like this because it's obvious that something's going on. If you want to talk about something, tell me. No one else is around and I'm not going to tell anyone anything. You know that much. Your secrets are safe with me."

He stared into her dark eyes. She looked like she meant it, and he did know she could keep a secret. Lydia also had a way of making him feel better when the world seemed against him.

It was dangerous territory, but who else did he have to talk with? Most of his friends had stopped contacting him because no one knew what to say about Macy's disappearance. It wasn't like they were the kind of buddies he could pour his heart out to anyway. Over the last few years, he had pushed everyone away while he worked on the blog. He was a big man on the Internet, but what had it gotten him?

"My life is falling apart on every front."

"I'm listening."

"You swear to keep this to yourself?"

"Your secrets are always safe with me," Lydia repeated.

Chad paused, running his hands through his hair. He looked around to make sure no one else was close enough to hear. "Alex…he got a girl pregnant."

Lydia's eyes widened. "I'm so sorry."

"He's only thirteen and she's going through with everything. They might give it up for adoption, but they're not going to decide anything yet. I'm sure this is all because of Macy being gone, but it makes her disappearance that much harder to deal with."

"How's Alex handling it?"

Chad shook his head. "I don't think he understands the gravity of the situation. He keeps pushing me away, though, so I don't know. I can't figure out what he's thinking."

"Like you said, he's only thirteen. It's a difficult age. He's trying to figure out who he is."

"That's exactly why he doesn't need to be a dad! He's not even close to ready, no matter what he thinks." Tears filled his eyes and he brushed them away.

"Oh, Chad. Is there anything I can do? Do you guys need anything?"

"No. We just have to take it one day at a time. All I can do is hope that the kids make the right decision. I'm not raising it for them."

"What does Alyssa think?"

"She's not happy, but that's the least of our problems."

Lydia raised an eyebrow, but said nothing.

Chad wiped at new tears. "She's staying with a friend. Lyss thinks Macy is dead, and she's mad I don't." He broke down and cried into his hands. "What if she doesn't come back home?" He leaned forward, resting his elbows on his lap as he let out gut-wrenching sobs. His body shook, and he thought he felt Lydia wrap an arm around him, but he wasn't sure and didn't care enough to fight her.

His life was falling apart and there was nothing he could do about it. He couldn't hold it together anymore—that much was clear. Why else would he be crying in the middle of a park? He wiped his nose with his sleeve and seeing the disgusting mess, he hid it before Lydia could see it.

She pulled her purse into her lap and then handed him a small pack of tissues.

Chad took it and wiped his face and then tried to be discreet wiping his sleeve. He took another one and put it to his face, feeling another round of sobs coming. His chest tightened, and the lump in his throat felt like it was going to explode. He shook harder than before, foreign sounds escaping his throat as his crying intensified.

Lydia rubbed his back, telling him that it was okay to let it out.

He cried all the more. Chad thought about his wife and both of their kids—and the gigantic mess they all had. What had happened to the days when he had been able to fix most problems with a kiss? Kissing scrapes and bruises for the kids and some romance for Alyssa. None of that worked anymore. He was helpless to fix any of their problems or hurts. He couldn't even help himself. And now he was sobbing in public, being comforted by his former lover.

This was rock bottom. Things couldn't get any worse than this. No, that wasn't true. The DNA results could come in and prove that he would never get to see his daughter again. That would be rock bottom.

He continued to sob until there was nothing left. Not another tear would come. Chad pulled more tissues from the little pack and wiped his face and blew his nose several times. He looked over at Lydia and noticed it was raining.

Lightning flashed in the distance. "Should we get inside?"

"We don't have to. It's pretty far away."

"But it's raining."

Lydia shrugged. "It's up to you."

"I don't care about getting soaked. You probably do."

She shook her head. "I'm more worried about you. Are you going to be okay?"

Chad looked into her eyes. Her hair was soaked, dripping onto her coat. She looked beautiful, especially with the look on her face mixed with concern and love. It was nice to have someone who cared about him. Someone who wanted to be there for him without needing anything.

Lydia stared back into his eyes, not saying anything or moving. Her expression showed how much she cared about him.

Chad knew she didn't judge him for believing his daughter was alive. He moved his face closer to hers. He wanted to kiss her and forget about everything else in the world. She could make him forget his troubles, even if it was only for a short time. The world could be right again.

Eagerness filled her eyes as Chad moved at a snail's pace closer to her. He just wanted to make all of his problems disappear and she could do that for him. And she would too.

Chad stopped and pulled back, shaking his head. "I can't. I can't do this."

"You don't have to. I'm here for you, however you need me."

Regret washed over him. He wasn't even sure what for. Because of the mistakes he had made? For pushing his family away? For loving Lydia? For wanting her at that moment while his daughter was in trouble?

More tears filled his eyes and he broke into another crying fit. How much of this did he have in him? Chad had held himself together for so long and now everything was unraveling. As his tears fell, the rain drops landed on his shirt, soaking into his back. He didn't care. He could get pneumonia and die for all he cared. Everyone else would be better off with him gone anyway.

He looked up at Lydia. She had tears shining in her eyes.

"What's wrong?"

"I hate seeing you like this. It's killing me that you hurt so much."

Chad put his face back into his hands, allowing the sobs to take over. Why was it that Lydia cared so much about him and Alyssa seemed to despise him again? And for what? Because he wouldn't say Macy could have a funeral? He wasn't going to give his child a funeral unless she was dead, and he had no reason to believe that she was.

He shook, feeling as though he would collapse soon. At least he was with someone who actually cared about him, even if he couldn't allow himself to give into his own feelings for her. Despite the fact that Alyssa was staying with Sharon instead of him, he was going to remain faithful to her. It wasn't like she was staying with another man.

Hiding

MACY ROLLED OVER, bumping into something. She rubbed her eyes, trying to remember where she was. A blank wall faced her and she was squished. She looked over to see Heather sleeping next to her. Everything from the previous day came rushing back.

What were they going to do? After she had told Heather everything, they were both exhausted and decided to share the small bed.

The lock on the outside of the door made a jiggling noise. Heather sat up and stared at Macy. She jumped out of bed and ran to the far corner of the room.

Candice came in and looked at Macy. "I talked the other nurses into letting you sleep in today. How do you feel?"

Macy stretched. "I haven't slept that well in a long time." Candice had no idea just how true that was.

"I'm glad to hear it. My shift is over and I'll be off a few days. Please be good. We really just want you to get out of here. I want nothing more than to see you back on the street, hanging out with your friends. You've been here entirely too long. You should have just been here for a day or two of observation. Can you play nice for a couple days?"

Macy nodded.

"I'm serious, Heather. You need to get back to school and see your friends again. You were such a good girl before your mom took off. I wish she would come back and take responsibility. She has no idea what she's doing to you."

Macy looked over at Heather from the corner of her eyes. She looked furious. Macy looked back to Candice. "I'll do my best."

She didn't look convinced. "Just go along with the program, and you'll be out before you know it. Even if you don't like it, accept reality. That will be your first step toward healing and getting out of here."

"Okay," said Macy.

Candice raised an eyebrow. "Really? You're not going to fight me and try to convince me that your mom isn't in Paris?"

Macy shook her head. "First step toward healing. I have to accept the facts."

"Wow. I'm impressed, Heather. Maybe you actually will be out in time to enjoy your summer. Keep it up." She disappeared and closed the door. Macy could hear it lock.

Heather moved to the bed, still looking angry. "How could you agree with her like that? I thought you were on my side and believe my mom's dead."

"I am and I do, but it's not going to do either of us any good if we keep trying to convince them. They're not going to do anything about it, anyway. We need to get out of here, and then we'll go to the police. I think they have to listen. Let's just focus on one thing at a time. First, getting out of here. Next, getting your dad in jail for a long, long time. Hopefully a life sentence."

Heather took a deep breath and nodded. "It's a good thing she talked with you, because I can't put up a front like that. No way am I going to let anyone get away with saying that Mom is a home-wrecker. Not when she was a loving mom. Why won't anyone listen to me?"

Macy slid her feet to the ground. "Because your dad is the one convincing them otherwise. What he wants, he gets. But that's about to end."

The door opened again and Heather darted back to the corner. A new nurse looked at Macy. "Is it true? I hear that you might have a change of heart?"

"Maybe," said Macy.

"Let's see how well you handle time with some others. Can you be nice if we let you spend some time with other kids?"

Macy looked over at Heather, not sure what to do. Heather nodded and indicated for her to go with her.

"Of course I can," Macy said. She gave a convincing look.

"We can't risk another incident like last time. If you show even a sign of doing that again, I'll have no other choice except to bring you right back here. Or worse."

Macy looked back at Heather. She shrugged her shoulders and had a slight smile on her face.

"I won't act up."

"Glad to hear it. Come on."

Macy went with the nurse, not sure what to expect. Heather had dark circles under her eyes, so maybe she would get some more sleep. Macy had a feeling that she had gotten less sleep than Macy over the months. Hopefully, she would just sleep and not do anything to jeopardize them getting out.

The nurse led her to a small cafeteria. "There's a guard posted by the door. He knows to keep an eye on you. Got it?"

"Sure."

"Have a seat and someone will bring you a tray. Remember, the better behaved you are, the more likely you will be to get out of here."

"I know. I'm ready for change." Macy made her way to one of the tables. She sat away from the others. It was nice to be around kids again, but she didn't want to get close to anyone. What if someone figured out that she wasn't Heather?

Some of the kids whispered, but no one actually paid her any attention. At least she was used to being treated much worse at school. Being ignored was nice compared to being mooed at, like at her school cafeteria. That was why she had started eating lunch in the bathroom and then gave up lunch altogether. Even after she lost all that weight, the kids at school only saw Muffin Top Macy.

Her blood pressure went up and took some deep breaths. This wasn't the time to think about it. Heather's anger is what had kept her there for so long. In order for the both of them to get out, she needed to keep her cool.

Without a word, someone came in and set a tray of food in front of her. Although she was glad to not have to cook, the food didn't look at all appealing. Stiff-looking spaghetti sat on the middle of the plate with ground meat sauce sliding down. Applesauce was slopped next to it, reminding her of the pigs' feed at the farm. Burnt green beans were off to the side.

Regardless of how it looked, she needed to eat. She picked up the fork and started with the applesauce, because it looked the least offensive. It tasted okay, though it was a little dry. She could feel eyes on her as she ate.

Macy pictured her family. Getting back to them was the goal. She needed to act sweet and happy regardless of how anyone treated her. These people didn't matter, but getting back home did. What if she could be back that day? Her heart sped up.

She thought about Alex running around the bonus room, singing to his favorite songs. He loved creating his own "music videos," and she was usually the one who held his phone to record it. What she wouldn't give to do that again. She had complained countless times about it before, but now she'd gladly record him for hours.

Despite the level of nastiness of the food, she felt better. She'd had a decent night's sleep and now a meal. Macy was ready to get home. She looked around, not sure what to do. The room had emptied somewhat, leaving only a few more kids.

One of them got up and put his tray on a counter and left the room. Macy did the same and followed the sounds of conversation. She found herself in a large room full of kids. Some were watching TV, others were playing games or writing, and another girl sat by a window reading.

Macy walked in, nerves on edge. No one seemed to notice her. She sat down on a couch and watched everyone. Her eyes were drawn to the movie. It was a PG one she had seen when she was a kid, but it had been so long since she had watched TV, she wanted to watch anyway. She didn't have the best angle, but she didn't want to join the others. If Heather had freaked out on them, who knew how they would react to her?

When the movie ended, the nurse who had given Macy her food turned the TV off. The other kids watching groaned and complained before dispersing around the room.

The nurse came over to Macy. "How are you doing? I haven't heard a single complaint about you. That's really good news."

"Like I told the other nurse, I'm ready to go home. I'll do whatever it takes to get there."

"Given your history, it's going to take some time, but if you keep this up, you'll find yourself on the outside soon. Despite what you believe, we're all on your side. We want to see you go back home and to school where you belong."

Macy nodded. She felt bad for Heather. No one would listen to her about her mom—thanks to Chester—and it hadn't gone well. She was desperate for someone to believe her. Macy could understand that. She'd been desperate to get out of the community, and look what had happened. Tears stung her eyes. She was going to have to live with that guilt the rest of her life.

"Tears?" asked the nurse. "You must be telling the truth. I'm glad to see you letting your guard down, Heather. Do you think you're ready to talk with the doctor again? This time without throwing things around his office."

"Yeah." Her voice cracked. She suddenly felt overwhelmed. The tears spilled onto her face.

The nurse sat next to her. "Is there anything you want to talk about?"

"It's all my fault."

"What is?"

"Everything." She pulled her feet onto the couch and then rested her face on her knees. She cried, not caring how loud she was or who was looking. She continued to cry until she had nothing left. When she looked up, the nurse still watched her. She handed Macy a tissue and then asked, "Do you feel better?"

She didn't, but Macy nodded, not finding any words. She just wanted to go back home.

"I think the doctor would clear his schedule if you're ready to talk with him."

Macy wiped her face. "I am. Can we stop off at my room first?"

"What for?"

"Please."

"Sure. Let's go." She led Macy back to Heather's room. Macy looked around for Heather and found her hiding near the door again. She motioned for Heather to come out.

Heather looked at her like she was crazy. Macy motioned some more until Heather came out and stood next to her.

The nurse looked back and forth between Heather and Macy, wide eyed. "What...? How did...? What's going on?"

Macy looked her in the eyes. "The two of us, we want to speak to the doctor. We need to be heard."

Results

C HAD KICKED OFF his wet shoes and closed the door behind him. His clothes clung to him and he needed to get those off as well. Even though he was inside, rain water ran down from his hair into his face. He wiped it away.

"Is anyone home?"

The house was unusually quiet. Had Alex gone to Zoey's appointment already?

"Alex, are you here?"

Silence. He shivered as water slid down his back. He would have to dry out the inside of his car as well, but first he needed to get a shower. He felt empty inside after having sobbed and poured his heart out to Lydia.

He had been afraid she was going to take his outpouring of grief the wrong way, but she kept her word and acted like a friend. She had listened and consoled, not giving him a judging word or look once. His heart ached. Why wouldn't Alyssa treat him like that? Who was he kidding? He knew the answer to that. She was stuck in her own heartache.

Neither one of them was able to give what the other needed. Maybe this time apart *was* what they needed. Hopefully Sharon, or whoever she was staying with, was able to give her the same kind of friendship that Lydia had given him.

"Is anyone home? Final chance to speak up before I strip."

No one responded, so Chad pulled his shirt off, though it clung to him, fighting to stay on. He threw it on the tiled floor and then attempted to pull his pants off too. The drenched jeans fought even more than the shirt had. He had to sit on the stairs and play tug-of-war with them to finally get them off.

He grabbed the shirt and then threw the clothes in the laundry room on the way to his bedroom. He took a shower and put on dry clothes, and then he noticed his cell phone sitting on the bed. The light was blinking, so he picked it up to see what he had missed. Maybe it was Alyssa wanting to talk. His heart tightened at the hope of working things out with her.

Chad scrolled to the notifications and saw that he did have a missed call, but it wasn't from his wife. It was from Detective Fleshman. His heart exploded into a fit of beats. He couldn't explain it, but he could feel deep down that whatever Fleshman had to say was going to be a game changer.

There were no messages, so he called the detective back.

"Chad?"

"What's going on? I left my phone at home, so I missed your call."

"There's been a break in the case. Are you sitting down?"

The room shrunk around him. He sat on the bed, preparing for the worst. "I am now."

"We finally got the results."

Chad held his breath. "And?"

"It's not her. The DNA proves that the body isn't your daughter. The girl we found had connections to a cult commune we've been trying to find."

Chad fell back on the bed, having only heard that the body wasn't Macy. "I knew it wasn't her." Tears of gratitude filled his eyes. "What now?"

"Prepare for another media frenzy."

"Of course. But what about the case? What about Macy? We need to find her. Everything has been focused on that body for too long. She's out there somewhere—and she's alive. We have to find her."

"It's time to go through all of the clues with a fine tooth comb. We need to re-investigate clues that didn't get enough attention before. Word needs to get out again for people to keep an eye out for her. I've got someone working on doctoring her photos again to show what she would look like with different haircuts and colors."

"Thank you." Chad couldn't find the words to express his gratitude. His chest tightened, making it difficult to breathe.

Fleshman continued talking, now about the cult again, but Chad couldn't focus. Something about the mountains.

Chad interrupted him mid-sentence. "Can I call you back?"

"Of course. You've got my number."

"Thanks." Chad ended the call and pushed his phone away. He gave into another fit of sobs. He shook, cried, wailed, and even yelled. When he calmed down, he started to drift off to sleep when he heard something in the hall. "Is someone there?" He allowed himself the hope that it was actually Macy, not that she would be able to get in with the new locks and security codes.

"It's me." Alyssa appeared in the doorway.

Chad sat up, rubbing dried tears. His eyes felt puffy.

"Are you all right?" She looked concerned.

"Yeah. I just got off the phone with Fleshman."

She nodded. "I talked with him a little while ago."

"Is that why you're here?"

Alyssa nodded. She sat down next to him, looking deep in thought.

"Are you coming back home?" he asked.

Alyssa looked into his eyes and her face softened. "It kills me to see you so upset. Look at you." She ran the backs of her fingers along his face. "You're a mess."

"Our baby is alive. We have the proof now."

She stared at him, not saying anything.

"Don't you believe it now?"

Her fingers went down and traced his back. "We know that one girl isn't her."

"Macy's alive. She's coming back to us. Why can't you believe that?"

Tears shone in her eyes. "It's been so long, Chad. You know that. We've suffered through this for what feels like an eternity. April is almost here. Where would she be?"

"I don't know that I want to know, but one day she's going to tell us herself."

She rubbed his arm, staring into his eyes.

He cupped her chin in his palm. "Please come back home, Lyss. I can't lose you, too."

Alyssa's lips shook and tears spilled onto her cheeks. She nodded. "We'll see how it goes. You know, agreeing to disagree. If you're right, and I really wish you were, we'll see what happens with the new media campaign. Maybe something will come up proving me wrong. I've never hoped to be wrong more in my life."

"You still don't believe she's coming home." It wasn't a question— and it ripped his heart into pieces.

"I want to, but I can't lie."

They continued staring into each other's eyes. There was so much he wanted to say, but he was afraid of sending her running again. "I've missed you. Please stay home. I need you."

Something in her face changed. Her entire face twisted, and she leaned into his chest and sobbed. He wrapped his arms around her, pulling her close. She cried for a while and soon Chad found himself back in tears. He had never cried so much in his life, but it felt good.

He wasn't sure how much time passed; it seemed to stop completely except that the sky cleared and the room lit up.

Alyssa sat back. "I have something to confess."

Chad's heart skipped a beat. "What?"

She looked pained. "I...how do I say this?"

"Just tell me."

"I got the impression you think I've been staying with Sharon, but I haven't."

He couldn't speak. What did she mean? Where was she going with this? Chad knew if she was about to say she had been staying with some guy—who he would kill—he really had no room to judge. He couldn't blame her, not after his relationship with Lydia. But the other man, sure, he could murder him. There wasn't a jury around that would blame him.

Alyssa took a deep breath. "I've been staying with a guy named Rusty."

"Who the hell is Rusty?"

Her eyes widened, begging him to hear her out. "I've been staying in his guest room—alone. He lost his family, his entire family. That's how we started talking in the first place. But nothing happened. I swear."

"What do you mean nothing happened? You've been staying with some guy? Some random stranger? You can't tell me nothing happened." He knew he was being a hypocrite, but he didn't care. Anger burned within him at the thought of her being with another man.

She explained going to the bar and how he had told the waitress to stop bringing drinks and then refused to let her drive home.

"He could have towed you here. You realize that, don't you?"

"I know." She paused. "He did, the first time."

"What first time?"

"It was shortly after Macy disappeared. I couldn't take it and one night, I snuck out and ended up at the bar. I could barely speak, and he got me back home safely."

"When was that? I don't remember you going anywhere."

She frowned. "You slept through the whole thing."

Chad shook his head, the weight of what he had done with Lydia sinking in. If he felt this horrible just hearing about Alyssa staying at the house of some guy, how much worse would she feel knowing he'd had a relationship with Lydia before Macy disappeared?

"I swear, Chad, nothing happened. If you met him, you'd know right away that he's not over the loss of his family. Their pictures and their stuff is all over the house. It's like they just stepped out to go shopping or something."

"Why go to his house?"

"I was going to sleep in my car since I couldn't drive. He wanted to tow me home, but I needed space to think—and sleep apparently. I've never slept so much as I have the last few days. But anyway, since I wouldn't go home, he offered his guest room. I poured my heart out, and he listened. That's about it. If it makes you feel any better, it helped me to realize how much I wanted to get back and pour my heart out to you instead."

Chad nodded. "I had a similar experience."

Her eyes widened. "You did?"

"This morning I'd had all I could take. I ended up at a park, running around the trail." He pulled his feet up and rubbed his blisters. "I ran into Lydia Harris from the HOA and ended up sobbing in the park."

"Lydia? Isn't her husband always out of town?"

"Yeah."

"Don't get too close to her. She's lonely. I can see it in her eyes."

"I won't." Guilt stung at him for not telling Alyssa the entire story, but she didn't need to know everything. It was over. He wasn't going to see her, or anyone else for that matter, again. He was one hundred percent devoted to Alyssa as long as she would have him. If she knew about Lydia, it would crush her. He couldn't do that to her after everything that had already happened with Macy and Alex.

It would definitely be the end of their relationship—and he couldn't handle that. He regretted ever talking to Lydia with everything in him. He would never make that mistake again. He belonged to Alyssa wholly. They needed each other now more than ever. His guilt was punishment enough. There was no reason to break her heart. She didn't deserve it.

She ran her hand along his arm, giving him the chills. "We'll pour our souls out to each other only from now on. Right?"

"You've got it."

Alyssa leaned over and placed her soft lips on his. He pulled her closer, kissing her back.

Both of their phones rang.

They pulled back, giving each other confused looks.

Chad looked at his. "It's Fleshman."

"Reynolds. Something is going on." She slid her finger across the screen.

Chad did the same on his. "Fleshman? What's going on?"

Next to him, Alyssa talked to Reynolds, and he couldn't understand what either Fleshman or Alyssa were saying.

"Hold on, Detective." Chad went out into the hall. "I couldn't hear you. What were you saying?"

"We might not have to wait on the media. We already have a break in the case."

"Another one?"

"There's a girl several hours away claiming to be your daughter. There's a catch though."

The hall spun around Chad. He leaned against the wall. "What?"

"She's in a mental hospital, but the nurses are freaked out because they thought she was someone else. I'm more than a little confused, but we need to get over there and figure this out. They're not releasing her until they have proof that she is who she says."

His throat closed up.

"Chad? Are you still there?"

Somehow he managed to find his voice. "Text me the address. We'll be right there."

"Try not to get your hopes up. We—"

"Just text me the address." Chad ended the call. Could this really be it? Was he about to see Macy again? Or would this be yet another heartache?

He looked into the bedroom. Alyssa was on the phone with tears running down her face. He wanted to comfort her, but he needed to call Alex first. He would want to join them. He needed to know too.

Alex answered right away. "Dad, can you call me back later? We're about to find out if it's a boy or a girl. It took forever to get in."

"Okay. Your mom and I are going with the detective for a while. There have been some developments in the case. Check the news when you can."

"Wait. What?"

"The body isn't Macy, son. It looks like she's alive."

"She's alive?"

Chad could hear exclamations from Zoey and Valerie on the other end. "I'll call you in a few hours and we can exchange news."

Breakdown

W HEN THEY PULLED into the parking lot of the Shady Hills
Mental Health Facility, Alyssa saw Detective Fleshman and
Officer Anderson getting out of their police cruiser.

She didn't wait for Chad to fully stop the car before she jumped out
and ran to the police.

"What's going on? Where's my baby?"

"That's what we need to figure out," Anderson said, tipping his hat.
"There's a girl named Heather claiming to be Macy. She's been in there
longer that Macy's been missing, so we—"

"No, there's two girls they thought were Heather," Fleshman corrected.

"And the strange thing is that when the Mercers' house was broken
into, the intruder mentioned someone named Heather. Do you
remember that?" He flipped through his notepad. "See? Right here.
Zoey said he called Macy's room Heather's."

Alyssa looked at them like they had lost their minds. "What?"

Fleshman gave her an apologetic look. "It's complicated. We'll wait
for Chad and then get in there and figure out what's going on."

Chad ran up to them. "Is Macy in there?" He looked as desperate as
Alyssa felt. He took Alyssa's hand.

"That's what we're here to find out," said Anderson.

"Would you just take us to our daughter?" Alyssa blurted out. "I'm
sorry. I can't go another minute without seeing her."

"Sorry. Let's go."

Fleshman walked toward the building and Alyssa hurried to keep
up. Her heart raced. Would this be the end of the nightmare or merely

another dead end? She prayed Macy would be inside.

When they got inside, Anderson explained what was going on to the lady at the front desk. Alyssa had to bite her tongue. She wanted to scream for her to let them in.

The receptionist looked through some notes. "I see that they're expecting you. Have a seat and someone will come for you soon."

Alyssa squeezed Chad's hand. She looked at the big doors they would go through. She would rip them off their hinges if she had to. She would give them one minute to send someone before she started making demands.

Fleshman and Anderson both took seats, but Chad and Alyssa remained standing. Alyssa kept her attention on the big clock on the wall. As soon as one minute passed, she looked at Fleshman. "What's taking them so long?"

"Give them some time. This building is enormous. Even if they come for us right away, it could be five or ten minutes."

"Five or ten minutes? I can't wait that long."

The officers exchanged a look and then Anderson turned to Alyssa. "You've been patient all this time. Give it a few more minutes and then you might get to see your daughter. We don't know, but we really need you to remain calm. Can you do that?"

Chad squeezed her hand. "We will. You won't regret allowing us to come along with you."

Fleshman nodded. "Good to hear. We don't know that we'll see her right away. Maybe we will, maybe we won't. Just follow our lead and hopefully you'll have your daughter in your arms soon enough."

"They'll let her out, right?" Alyssa asked. "Why is she even in here?"

Anderson shook his head. "We don't have those answers yet."

"What answers *do* you have?"

"Not a lot," Fleshman said. "There's a girl here who's been giving the staff trouble since before Macy disappeared. Her parents are out of the picture and—"

"What does this have to do with my child?" Alyssa demanded.

Chad gave her hand a gentle squeeze. "Lyss, let him talk."

"I don't see how you can stay so calm."

"Because I don't want to be sent outside while they go in and see Macy."

Alyssa looked back to Fleshman, clenching her fists. "Continue."

"This other girl, Heather, she's been claiming that her dad killed her mom. She's in denial that her mom left them. The staff says it's a real sad case, but earlier today, there were two of her. Another girl appeared somehow, who looks just like her. The only way they can tell the difference is that the new one has shorter hair, but it's the same length as Heather's when she came in months ago."

"What's your point?" Alyssa asked.

"The second one is claiming that she's Macy. She says she was kidnapped by Heather's dad and she also believes that he killed Heather's mom."

Alyssa leaned against Chad. "I…I don't understand."

Chad held her tight. "You mean that the other dad, he took Macy to replace his daughter?"

"It's beginning to look that way," Anderson said. "The local authorities are said to be questioning him now. There are a lot of pieces to be put together. A big one is you two identifying whether or not the second girl is in fact Macy."

"Do you have a picture?" Alyssa asked. "Why won't they let us in there? What's taking them so long?" She pulled away from Chad and ran to the front desk, her vision more blurry by the moment. Blinking the tears onto her face, she stared down the receptionist. "Let us in there! My daughter has been missing since November! I *need* to see her."

"I'm sorry. We have strict protocol. You must have a staff member escort you in."

"You're staff!" Alyssa slammed her hand on the desk, causing the receptionist to jump. She looked at her name tag. "Look, Lynette. I don't know if you have children, but not knowing where your child is, that's the worst feeling in the world. It gets even harder the more time passes. When they're little and run out of your sight at the mall for a minute, sheer terror runs through you. Ever been there? If they hide somewhere, making that terror go for another five minutes, that's hell.

I've been there once when my son was little. Can you imagine those five minutes turning into almost half a year? There isn't a word to describe that!"

Lynette was visibly shaken. "I—I'm really sorry for everything you've been through. I don't have kids, but my niece, one time she ran off when I was taking care of her. I kind of understand what you're saying. I wish I could do something for you."

"Let me in! Take me to my daughter…please." More tears fell to her cheeks.

Alyssa felt hands on her shoulders. "Let's go wait with the officers, Lyss."

"Take me in there," Alyssa begged.

Lynette shook. "I'm really sorry. I don't have the key card to get in."

"Damn you people!" Alyssa shook her shoulder to get past Chad and ran to the big, metal door. She banged on it. "I'm coming, baby! I'll be there as soon as I can." Her fists hurt as she pounded, but she didn't care.

Hands pulled her away. They dragged her back to the waiting area. "Stop! I need to get to Macy." She pushed against Chad, who held her even tighter. "Let go of me."

Fleshman appeared in front of her. "Mrs. Mercer, you need to get control of yourself now. Do you understand me? We brought you with us because we thought you would be able to help us. If you keep acting like this, we're going to have no choice except to take you into custody."

She stopped struggling. "You would arrest me?"

"That's the last thing I want to do after everything you've been through. Your daughter may very well be on the other side of those doors, but we need your cooperation. It will be a lot easier if you stay calm. The big question is: do you want to be with your husband when he identifies the girl as either your daughter or not?"

"Of course I do."

"It won't be much longer. You've waited this long. Can you wait another few minutes until someone comes for us?"

"Fine." Alyssa pushed against Chad, who let go of her. She sat down on a chair near the window and stared out. How dare they think they could arrest her? After everything she'd been through? The two of them, they *knew*. They had been working closely with her and Chad. They had been in daily contact for a while.

Chad sat on the floor in front of her, resting his hands on her knees. "I know how you feel, Lyss. Really, I do. I want to scream and break things, but it won't do any good. For the first time since she disappeared, we have real hope—real reason to believe that she's alive and safe. It's killing me that she could be in this very building, but we still can't get to her."

"This is worse than torture. They have no clue what this is like."

He shook his head. "We're so close, yet so far. But we have to hold it together—for Macy. She's been through more than we can imagine. If what Fleshman said is true, she been with a kidnapper all this time. Not only that, but she's going to get home and find out that she's going to be an aunt. We're going to have to hold it together, no matter how much we feel like falling apart."

"I've been doing nothing other than holding myself together for all these long, terrifying months."

"But this time, we'll have Macy with us. I hope to God that's the case, anyway."

She nodded. "I'll be strong for her. That's what I've been doing all along."

Chad grabbed her hands and slid his fingers between hers. They sat in silence for what felt like an eternity. Alyssa looked out the window for a little while, and then she looked back to Chad, who had his chin rested on her lap. Tears shone in his eyes and the pained expression on his face broke her already-crushed heart.

"Oh, Chad."

He looked up at her and the tears spilled to his cheeks. She let go of his hand and wiped the tears away. He sat up and stared into her eyes, more tears falling. She leaned forward and kissed his tears. He put his hands on her face and kissed her lips.

Chad pulled back and stared at her. "Are we going to be okay, Lyss?

Will you come back home to me?"

"Yes."

"Would you even if Macy wasn't coming home?"

Alyssa paused. The pain on his face made her heart hurt. "I wouldn't go anywhere else. I need you."

He pulled her into another kiss. "And I need you. I've never been surer of that than at this moment."

Someone cleared their throat behind them. "They're ready for us."

Alyssa turned around to see Detective Fleshman and Officer Anderson standing with a man in a white lab coat. She stood, but her legs wouldn't support her weight. She fell toward the ground, but Chad caught her.

"Lean against me."

She put all her weight against him. He kept his arms around her and somehow she managed to walk. "Are we really about to see Macy?" Alyssa whispered.

"I hope so." Though he held her with strong arms, Alyssa could feel him shaking. He was just as scared as she was.

Alyssa didn't know what scared her more, finding out that the girl wasn't Macy or hearing about what her daughter had gone through all the time she was missing. Had she been abused? They said the abductor had been trying to replace his daughter. Was there a chance that he had treated her well?

The large, metal door opened slowly. Alyssa's heart sank as she saw another heavy door. How long would it take to get to Macy? What would she do if the girl wasn't Macy? What would she if the girl *was*?

Doors

CHAD'S THROAT CLOSED up as the final metal door shut behind them. He looked at the scene in front of him. It looked like a typical hospital with another reception area and doors with numbers.

The doctor—what had he said his name was?—stopped and said something to the receptionist. He turned back to them. "I sure hope you will be able to offer some insight. We're still trying to figure out how this happened. Sure, we get kids trying to sneak out, but never in. This is a first."

"Where is she?" Alyssa asked, her voice strained.

Chad gave her shoulders a squeeze.

"They're in Heather's room and they're both sticking to the same story since we discovered the two of them."

"Lead the way," Fleshman said.

Chad looked at the doctor's tag. Dr. Jones, that was right. He focused on the door numbers as they walked down the hall. He couldn't bear to think about seeing Macy, or worse, not seeing her. What if neither of those girls were her? Could this be the practical joke of a sick girl who belonged in a mental hospital?

Dr. Jones stopped in front of a door and used a key to open the door.

Chad held his breath and exchanged and worried, nervous look with Alyssa. Her skin looked pale. He was sure his was too. Were they about to finally see Macy?

The doctor held the door open and motioned for them to come in.

Chad took Alyssa's hand and walked in with her. His heart pounded and felt as though it would jump out of his throat. He looked around the room, and his gaze settled on two girls. They looked exactly the same, and neither had Macy's dark hair, but they both had her beautiful face. He looked back and forth between them.

The one on the right smiled. "Mom! Dad!" She ran into both of them, wrapping one arm around Chad and the other around Alyssa. She squeezed hard and then started sobbing.

Chad was in shock and had to force himself to wrap his free arm around her. It was her, it was actually her. He had hugged her so many times, he would know her anywhere. He held her tighter, vaguely aware of Alyssa's sobs over Macy's. She kept saying Macy's name over and over again.

It didn't feel real. He had believed she was alive somewhere, but now that she was there in his arms, he wasn't sure what was going on. It was like he was afraid to believe it was real.

He rested his face on top of her head. "Is it really you, Macy?" he whispered.

"Daddy, I'm so sorry for everything. I'll never sneak out again. I swear."

Tears filled his eyes and soaked her hair. "And there's so much I'm going to do differently, baby. So much. I'm sorry for not listening to you and not...." Chad couldn't find his voice. He kissed the top of her head.

"I hate to break up this reunion, but we need to discuss some matters."

Chad looked up at the officers and the doctor. "As long as we get to take her home, we can talk about whatever you want."

Dr. Jones nodded. "Let's take this to my office. There's room for everyone to sit."

They followed the doctor, neither Chad nor Alyssa letting go of Macy. He watched Alyssa stroke Macy's hair the whole way to the office. The three of them sat on a couch with Macy in the middle. She kept looking back and forth between them.

"Are you okay?" Chad asked. "What have you been through?"

"All I wanted was to get back to you guys." She pushed her face into Chad's chest. "I'm so sorry for everything."

Fresh tears filled Chad's eyes. "You have nothing to be sorry about." He wrapped his arms around her, never wanting to let go. Alyssa leaned her head against Macy's, and Chad wrapped an arm around her too.

They sat like that for a minute, before the doctor asked for their attention. Chad looked up and around the room.

Dr. Jones looked at Chad. "So this girl, she's your daughter?"

"You even have to ask?"

"Officially, yes."

"Yes, this is our Macy. I was there when she was born. I would know her anywhere."

"Have you ever seen Heather before?"

Chad looked over at the other girl. "No, but she looks so much like Macy. I don't understand."

Macy sat up. "Chester—her dad—he found me online. He was looking for someone who looked just like Heather and he pretended to be a boy so I would meet with him. He wanted me to replace her since he lost custody of her."

"He killed my mom," Heather said. "Do you believe me now? He's crazy enough to kidnap someone to replace me. He killed my mom." Tears fell down her face. "She's not in Paris. She's not."

Dr. Jones frowned. "Your story is more believable now, Heather. We need to look into it, because we've talked with your mom."

"He found someone to replace me. You think he couldn't have found someone to pretend to be Mom over the phone?"

"Like I said, we'll look into it. Right now, we need to focus on one thing at a time. Once we get Macy's situation squared away, we'll figure out what's going on with you. Like I told you before, your dad is being questioned right now."

"I hope they lock him up forever."

"Me too," Macy said.

Dr. Jones looked at Macy. "Once you identify him as your kidnapper, he'll be arrested. He should be put away for years for that alone. If it turns out that he also killed his wife, let's hope he'll be sentenced for life."

Chad looked over at Fleshman and Anderson, who were both furiously taking notes.

Fleshman looked at Macy. "I know this will be difficult, but we need you to tell us everything."

"Wh…where do you want me to start?"

"From the first time you came into contact with Chester Woodran."

Macy shook and Chad pulled her close. "Mom and I are here, baby. I promise you won't get into trouble for a single thing. Tell them everything."

Chad listened in disbelief as Macy told her entire story, starting from the boy who started chatting with her on social media, showing her attention that no one else had. His heart broke into more pieces than before as she described everything the madman had done to his daughter.

Finally, he couldn't take it anymore. He glared at Fleshman. "Are you going to arrest that dirt bag yet or what?"

"Chad, let her finish the story. We can't proceed until we've taken her full statement."

"Go on, honey." Chad kissed the top of her head again.

Macy continued her story, telling the story of being taken to a cult. Chad wanted to interrupt and ask questions, but he knew there would time for that later. He pulled her closer. How would he ever let her go again?

"Wait," Fleshman said. "A cult? Where's it located?"

"Yeah," Macy said. "It's in the mountains. I don't really know where."

"That's fine. We'll talk to you more about that later. Maybe the body and the kidnapping are related."

Macy stared at the officers. "There are other kidnapped kids there in the community. You guys have to get there and take them home, too." She went on to explain what life was like there and then she told the story of her escape attempt. Her eyes filled with tears as she talked about Luke and Dorcas. When she told of Chester shooting Dorcas, Macy dissolved into tears, pushing her face into Chad's chest once again. He held her tight as she soaked his shirt with tears.

Heather stood up. "See? Dad killed a girl—just a kid! He didn't even think twice about it. He just did it. Why wouldn't he kill Mom? She probably wanted a divorce and he did away with her. He killed her. Will you listen to me now? Please!"

Dr. Jones nodded. "Sit down, Heather. I'm sure that your dad is going to be locked away for a long, long time. We need to focus on one thing at a time."

"Make sure Mom's death is on his list of offenses." Heather sat, crossing her arms.

"Macy, can you tell us the rest of the story? From what you've described, that was around the new year. What happened since then?"

Sniffing, Macy sat up. She looked into Chad's eyes. The look on her face broke Chad. New tears fell from his own eyes.

"Daddy, it's my fault that Dorcas died. It's all my fault."

"No. No, baby. It's not your fault. Chester's the one who pulled the trigger."

"But if I hadn't snuck out of the house, we never would have gone there. If I hadn't insisted on getting out of the community that night, she'd still be alive. It's my fault." She fell against him again.

Alyssa leaned over, rubbing Macy's back. "You did nothing wrong, honey. You were just trying to get away."

Macy nodded, her face still against Chad.

Officer Anderson came over to them and put his face near Macy's. "Macy, dear, listen to me. I'm a police officer and from everything you've told me, you have nothing to feel guilty about. All of this is on Chester. He's the one who lured you, kidnapped you, took you there, and shot the girl. He did it all. You did the right thing by trying to get away."

Macy sat up. "But it's still my fault."

Anderson shook his head. "No, honey, it's not."

Dr. Jones looked at Chad. "You're going to have to get her into counseling when you get back home. She can't walk around with that false guilt."

"We know that," Alyssa said. She continued to run her hands through Macy's hair. "Can you tell us the rest of the story, baby? What happened next?"

"But first you guys have to find Luke. He's missing and he probably needs help. I'm sure of it. I hope he didn't go back to the community. They might have…." Macy's eyes filled with tears again.

Rage ran through Chad as Macy told them about Chester breaking her leg. If the police didn't arrest Chester and put him on death row, Chad would find a way to kill the bastard with his own two hands.

He held her even tighter as he listened to her tell the rest of the story of how she was forced to cook and clean for the psychos. It was all he could to stay silent. Macy held it together remarkably well. He didn't know how she did it.

When she was done talking, she collapsed against him. He kissed the top of her head again.

Alyssa spoke up. "Are you guys going to arrest that man now? You've just made Macy relive every horrible moment of her ordeal."

"Her testimony is going to make a huge difference. We need to hear what Heather has to say about him too," Fleshman said.

"You don't have enough on him from what Macy said? He kidnapped her and did all those awful things to her against her will. He nearly killed her, too!"

"We have plenty, but we need to know the whole story. Heather's been trying to tell her side for a long time. We need to give her some floor space as well."

Dr. Jones squirmed in his seat, looking uncomfortable.

Chad looked over at Heather, still unable to get over how much she looked like his daughter. She looked like she had been through a lot, too, forced to stay in this hospital for even longer than Macy had been missing.

"What about everything she's been through?" Chad asked. "She's been locked up in here with no one listening to her. That's not right." He glared at the doctor. "Who was looking out for her? Seems to me the hospital should have to answer for that. Maybe if they would have listened, Macy could have been spared what she went through—or at least some of it."

Anderson nodded. "It'll be investigated thoroughly, I assure you." He turned to Heather. "Tell us your story, please."

Light

MACY WALKED OUTSIDE with her parents, blinking fast in the bright light. She still couldn't believe that it was really happening. She was free. And Chester had been arrested.

One of the police men who had been taking notes asked her dad if he wanted them to drive their car home.

"No. I can do it. Thanks for everything, you guys." He shook both of their hands. "When everyone else wanted us to give up, you kept helping us. We can't possibly thank you enough."

Macy looked back inside the building where Heather stood with some other officers. They were supposed to take her to the farm to stay with Chester's parents. What would they think when they found out Macy hadn't been Heather?

Heather caught Macy's stare and gave a little wave. Macy waved back. They were both going to be okay. Macy more than her, since she was going back home to her parents and brother.

"Come on, honey," said her mom.

Macy looked at her parents and followed them to her dad's car. She felt a strange joy well up inside of her. Not only was the car familiar, but it was going to take her back home. She would be able to sleep in her own bed, wear her own clothes, and hopefully sleep a lot.

Her dad opened the back door for her. He smiled, but tears shone in his eyes. Macy wrapped him in a hug. "I'm so sorry for everything, Dad. I—"

"Shh. Just get in the car. We're glad to have you back. No more talk about the past. Not now." He kissed the top of her head.

"Okay." She climbed in and breathed deeply. It smelled just like home. She leaned her head against the back of the seat and closed her eyes. As soon as she relaxed, she expected to hear Chester's voice. She sat up gasping.

"Are you okay?" her mom asked, turning around.

"Yeah. Sorry." It would it take a while to get used to being back at home.

"Do you need anything?" her dad asked. "Are you hungry? We can stop somewhere and get you any vegan meal you want. I saw sub shop by the freeway."

Macy shrugged. Her nerves had her stomach twisting in knots. "Maybe later. I kinda just want to get home. How's Alex?"

Her parents exchanged one of their looks.

"What?" Macy asked.

"You wouldn't believe how much he's missed you." Her dad started the car. "I've never seen a brother who loves his sister more."

Alyssa turned around again. "He was the one who figured out that you were gone that first morning. He hasn't stopped worrying about you since. None of us have."

"What about Zoey? Have you seen her?"

Her mom had a funny look on her face. "Yeah. She's been spending a lot of time with us. She and Alex have gotten close."

"Yeah, they've always been like siblings, too."

They didn't say anything, so Macy looked out the window. "Can I talk to him?" she asked.

"To Alex?" her mom asked.

"Yeah."

She handed Macy her phone.

Macy stared at it, nervous. Her throat closed up and new tears stung at her eyes. "I can't." She handed the phone back, sniffing. "I'd better wait until I see him. How long will that be?"

"It's a few hours."

Macy didn't want to wait that long, but she would rather give him a big hug before saying anything. "Okay. Mind if I sleep? I know you probably want to catch up, but I'm exhausted."

Her mom smiled at her. "If you need rest, baby, get some sleep.

After everything you've been through, I wouldn't be surprised if you slept for days."

"Yeah, honey," her dad said. "Don't worry about anything other than taking care of yourself."

"Thanks." She grabbed a coat and turned it into a makeshift pillow. As she leaned against it, she smelled her dad's cologne. She took a deep breath and smiled. Everything was going to be okay. She would get back home and everything would go back to the way it had been. She drifted off to sleep thinking about everything in her house.

Her mom's voice woke her up. Macy sat up, groggy. "What?"

"We're getting close."

Macy stretched and looked out the window. She recognized everything. They were about five minutes from home.

"Alex and Zoey are thrilled to see you. They're over at Zoey's now, but I let them know we're almost home."

Macy couldn't find any words. They pulled into the neighborhood and before she knew it, they pulled into their driveway and then into the garage.

"We don't want the neighbors swarming you," her dad said. "Everyone has been looking for you." He pushed a button on the visor, closing the garage door.

"That was nice of them." Macy yawned and then got out of the car. She looked around the garage, never so happy to see it. Everything looked exactly as she remembered it. They went inside and Macy continued to take everything in. It was all comfortably familiar, yet felt new at the same time. The house had the same maple scent it always did. Her mom loved those air fresheners.

They made their way up the stairs and as she scanned the front room, she saw Alex standing in front of Zoey. Macy's feet took off from under her and she ran into Alex's arms, causing him to stumble. He wrapped his arms around her. He shook. Was he actually crying? Macy looked into his eyes, and sure enough, tears were spilling out.

"Look at you," Macy said, through her own tears. She backed up a little. "You've really gotten bigger. Look, you're taller than me now."

"You too. Well, taller than you were, I mean. And your hair. I like it." He threw his arms around her again.

She squeezed him tight. "I've missed you so much, Alex."

"Me too. I never thought I'd see you again. I never gave up on you, but it was so long and everything. I can't believe you're actually here. Don't ever leave again, okay? You have to promise."

Macy smiled. "I'll do my best. I won't be sneaking out again, that's for sure."

"You'd better not. You'll have to deal with me if you do."

She gave him another squeeze. "I need to give Zoey a hug." Macy let go of Alex, almost needing to push him away because he wouldn't let go. She stared at Zoey before running into her arms. She looked different. More round in the face. Had she put on weight? Then she noticed her stomach. "Zoey! What happened? Well, I mean, I guess I know *what* happened. But, who…when…?"

Zoey smiled wide. "Shut up and give me a hug."

Macy gave her a soft hug, not wanting to injure her middle.

"Oh, come on. A real hug. You're not going to break me." Zoey squeezed Macy so tight she nearly choked.

"Why don't we give them some time?" her dad asked her mom.

Her mom nodded, taking his hand.

Macy's eyes popped wide. They were holding hands?

"We'll get some dinner ready," Macy's mom said, leaning against her dad.

"Sure." Macy shook her head. That would take some getting used to. Her parents had barely been able to be in the same room before she left.

The landline rang. Her dad sighed. "Looks like we're going to be fielding calls again."

Her mom's cell phone rang. "At least we have good news this time." They went upstairs.

Macy turned to Zoey. "You've got to tell me everything. Do you have a boyfriend?"

Zoey bit her lip and looked away. "Yeah, kinda."

"Kind of?" Macy asked.

"You might wanna sit," Zoey said.

"I've been sitting for the last three hours. I'd rather not. Can we go up to my room, and you can tell me on the way? I'm dying to see my stuff."

"You've got to tell us everything," Alex said. "I've had all these images running through my head. I want the truth—I need to get rid of the fake stuff. Dad said you were kidnapped, but that's all we know. What happened?"

Macy headed for the stairs. "I'll tell you everything in my room."

They followed her up to the bedroom. Macy threw herself on the bed and looked over at Ducky, who ran to the side of the cage and looked her way.

Zoey closed the door, but Alex opened it and went out.

"Where's he going?" Zoey asked.

"Does anything make sense that he does?" Macy asked, smiling. She sat up. "You have no idea how good it is to be back home."

"And you have no idea how great it is to have you back."

"Looks like you kept yourself occupied, though."

"Well, I was stressed about you being gone."

"You don't have to explain yourself. I hardly expected anyone to stop their life just because I wasn't there."

Zoey's eyes narrowed. "Well, that's what happened. Everyone was crushed. There were times I could barely breathe. You should've seen your parents and Alex. You wouldn't believe how upset Alex was. He's been in counseling for the longest time. He could barely function."

"Really?"

"Your brother loves you. Never doubt that, no matter how big of dork he's being."

Alex came in. "Who's a dork?"

"You," Zoey said.

"That figures." He handed Macy her diaries. "I was looking for clues to find you. Hope you're not mad that I read them."

Macy shook her head. "How could I be? Though we might have to talk later about how you knew where they were."

Alex's cheeks turned red. "We don't have to."

"It's so good to be back." Macy leaned against her headboard. "I never thought I'd get back home." She looked at Zoey's stomach again. "Are you going to keep changing the subject or are you going to tell me who the guy is?"

"You're looking at him," Alex said.

Macy stared at her brother for a moment before the reality of what he said hit her. "You mean…?"

Alex nodded. His face was somewhat squished together, like he was nervous or something. "I guess we had a funny way of dealing with our grief."

"Sorry, Macy," Zoey said. She also looked worried. "I know he's your brother. I hope you're not mad. I never meant to drag him into this."

Alex shook his head. "You didn't drag me into anything. I—"

"So, are you two together-together or was it, like, a one-time thing?" Macy felt light-headed.

Zoey grabbed Alex's hand. "We're together. We're in love."

"Oh." Macy never would have guessed they would have liked each other like that. She watched as they both looked back and forth between her and each other. It would take some getting used to, but it would probably be cool.

"Are you okay with us?" Zoey asked.

"As long as I'm not the third wheel, I guess so. It's going to take some getting used to, but I can't complain. Not after everything I've been through. I'm alive and home with you guys. I couldn't ask for anything more."

"Third wheel?" Alex asked. "Not a chance." He gave her a huge hug, nearly knocking her off the bed.

"Yeah, no way," Zoey added. "We're never letting you out of our sight, so you'd better get used to us being around."

"I can handle that." Macy smiled.

"Now we just need to find a guy for you," Zoey said.

"Don't look for a thirteen year old. I'm not—"

"Hey!" Zoey laughed. "Are you making fun of me?"

"Maybe."

"Where should we look, then?"

"Oh, I'm in no hurry to get a boyfriend."

Zoey's face got serious again. "Because of what you've been through?"

"There's that, but I kind of have one. I just have to find him."

"What? You mean Jared?"

"No. Jared was a lie." Macy's eyes got misty. "I met someone while I was away, but it…we got separated."

"What do you mean?" Zoey tilted her head. It was obvious that she knew there was more to the story.

"Can I tell you about Luke later? I need to get used to being back home first."

Zoey took one of Macy's hands. "Anything you need. Just tell us, and it's yours. Got it? We'll do anything for you. At least, I will."

"Me too," Alex said. He pushed Zoey aside and gave Macy another hug.

Macy's throat felt like it was going to close up. Tears of happiness threatened.

Not only was she home, she was the luckiest girl alive.

Frenzy

ALEX WATCHED AS Macy walked to her window and looked outside. She turned to Alex. "Why are there so many vans outside?"

He took a deep breath, preparing himself to explain how the media had forced their way into their lives. He walked over and looked. "It the media circus."

The doorbell rang again, proving his point. It had been ringing for about a half an hour.

"What do you mean?" Macy looked out again. "But why are they here?"

"When you were first gone, they wouldn't leave us alone. There was always someone out there, ready to ask us questions if we went outside. For the longest time, a van was parked across the street just recording our house."

"Why?"

"You were the most exciting thing on the news for a long time. It drove Mom and Dad crazy. It was annoying, but I thought it was a little funny. I mean, we were like stars or something. Only it really sucked because you were missing."

"Well, at least Zoey went home before all of this. She never would have made it down to her house. When will they leave?"

"Hopefully soon. They did eventually leave us alone. I think it helped that Dad used his blog to post updates. People could get the answers they wanted without watching the news. Plus with all the click-throughs or whatever, he was able to stop working."

Macy leaned against the wall. "Things have really changed, haven't they?"

"Yeah, but everything will go back to normal."

"You think? You and Zo are going to have a baby. That feels weird to even say."

"When we were at the appointment, her parents were talking about raising her."

"Her? It's a girl?"

Alex's lips curled slightly and his heart rate picked up. "Yeah, we found out today. It's been a huge day. You came back and we found out the baby's a girl."

"So, now that Zoey's dad is here, her parents are getting back together?"

"Yep. It's weird. They haven't seen each other in fifteen years and now they want to be family. I think he feels guilty."

"Are Mom and Dad okay with them raising the baby?" asked Macy.

"Not that it's their decision, but they don't want to raise a baby, and they don't want me ruining my life to raise her either, so I'm sure they'll be happy. We can see her whenever we want. Zoey and me are together all the time anyway."

"I don't know if I'll ever get used to that. Are you guys still…? Ew."

Alex's face became warm. "It's not gross. It's—"

"I don't wanna hear about it. Sorry I asked. What did Mom and Dad say when they found out?"

"Do we have to talk about this?" Alex squirmed.

Macy smiled and poked him. "I thought guys liked to brag about doing it."

"Not me, and you're my sister. It's just weird, you know? What about that Luke guy? Did you guys…?"

Sadness covered her face, and he immediately regretted asking.

Macy shook her head. "No. He gave me a kiss, though." She explained about the community and their escape.

Alex's heart felt like it had been ripped out of his chest. He put his arm around her. "I'm sure they'll find him."

Macy turned to look Alex in the eyes. Tears fell from her eyes and she put her head on Alex's shoulders. "You think so?"

"Why not? He sounds strong and capable. Besides, I want to see the guy who won you over."

They stood there like that for a while. Time either stood still or rushed by; Alex couldn't tell. He was just glad to have Macy back.

The bedroom door opened and he turned to see his mom.

"Is everything okay?" she asked.

Alex shrugged. "We were just talking. Did she tell you about Luke?"

"Oh, baby. Don't think about him." She came over and wrapped her arms around both of them. "Focus on being home. We want you to relax and unwind."

"I can't forget about everything, Mom."

"Honey, I'm not asking you to forget. Hey, do you want to see your picture on TV? You're all over the news."

"I am?"

Alex wasn't surprised, but that might the distraction his sister needed. "Yeah. You're practically a celeb. Come and see."

Macy shrugged. "Okay."

They went into the bonus room, where the news was already on. A picture of Macy from their dad's blog flashed on the screen. The word *Found* flashed underneath. Alex watched Macy. He couldn't tell what she was thinking.

When a dog food commercial came on, he asked, "What do you think of that?"

"It's weird to watch the news again."

"You haven't watched any TV?"

"Well, I saw some ancient reruns at the farmhouse, but that was months ago. It was before the community. I saw part of a movie yesterday at the mental hospital."

Farmhouse? Mental hospital? Alex shook his head. "You'll have to tell me about that later."

The doorbell rang.

"When will it stop?" Macy asked.

"Probably when Dad gets mad enough to scream at them," Alex said.

"Where is Dad?" Macy asked.

"Probably updating the blog. Once he gives everyone what they want, hopefully they'll leave us alone. That's worked before."

His mom shook her head. "I'm not so sure that'll work this time around. They're going to want to see Macy for themselves. Everyone is going to want to interview her. I suspect this could be worse than before."

Alex groaned. "They need to leave her alone! Don't they know she needs to relax and stuff? I'll go out there and—"

"Let Dad deal with them, Alex."

"Fine, but if they don't give her the space she needs, I can't guarantee anything." He scowled.

Macy's picture flashed on the screen. The newscaster spoke about where she had been found and then Chester's face appeared in the opposite corner of Macy's.

Alex noticed Macy tense up.

"Is that the guy?" Alex asked.

"That's Chester."

"Did he ever say why he took you?"

"Alex," his mom said in a warning tone, "she doesn't want to talk about it now."

"I don't mind, Mom." She told him about Heather and her mom.

"What a sick jerk," Alex said. "They'd better lock him away for a long time. If they ever let him out, I'll—"

"Alex, he has a lot of charges against him," his mom said. "I wouldn't worry about him getting out."

"He'd better not." Alex clenched his fists and stared at the picture of his sister's abductor. "He doesn't look like someone who would do all that. He's a nerd. Look at those glasses and that hair. He looks like someone who gets beat up, not someone who kidnapped someone and killed two people."

Macy sighed. "That's just it. He was picked on his whole life. I guess he just snapped. That's what it sounds like, anyway."

"Maybe there was a reason people bullied him. He doesn't deserve to live," Alex said.

"Honey—"

"No, Mom. It's the truth. He's a waste of space. I hope he gets a death sentence."

"We'll let the jury decide that."

"Whatever." Alex looked back and forth between the TV and his sister. Even though he'd been talking with her, it still didn't feel real yet. He kept waiting to wake up—in his bed, alone.

Macy caught him looking at her. She gave him a slight smile and took his hand. "I really missed you."

His throat closed up and tears stung at his eyes. "Me, too. You have no idea."

She squeezed his hand, her eyes shining with tears.

"Oh, you guys," Alyssa gushed. She wrapped them both in a hug. She pulled back and stared at Macy. "I hope you know I'm never letting you out of my sight."

"That's fine by me," Macy said. "I don't want to go anywhere ever again."

"That's good," Alex said, "because people are going to be all over you when you do leave the house. The news didn't leave us alone for a long time after you disappeared."

"What about school?" Macy asked. "Don't we have to go to school?"

"Zoey and I have been homeschooling."

Macy's eyes widened. "Why?"

Alex shrugged. "I couldn't really focus, plus I had to deal with all the things those jerks said."

"What do you mean? People have always been nice to you."

Anger burned in his chest. "They were saying things like you were dead. Had it gone much longer, I would have been expelled for beating kids up."

"And Zoey? Because of the baby?"

"Honey," Alyssa said, "we've all been beside ourselves with grief and worry. Life never just picked up where it left off. Dad couldn't keep working either. Luckily he had the blog to fall back on."

"Wait!" Macy said, looking at the TV. "I want to see this."

Alex looked at the screen and saw police busting down a large wooden gate in what appeared to be a forest.

"They're going to get the other kidnapped kids," Macy said. Her hand tightened around Alex's. He had forgotten she still held onto his hand.

The fence finally fell to the ground and the officers rushed in. People in white ran around, looking scared. Women with tight buns grabbed children and ran into little buildings. Men jumped on horses and ran off.

"You were *there*?" Alex asked. "The dude who kidnapped you was Amish?"

Macy shook her head. "Shh."

The screen faded away and then showed several people handcuffed and being taken into the police cruisers.

"Did you know them?" Alex asked.

"Those are the leaders. I bet Jonah didn't see *that* in his visions," Macy said, her voice dripping with sarcasm.

"What?" asked Alyssa.

"Never mind. Look. They're taking some kids. I hope they get to go back to their families, too."

"Was it weird talking with other kids who had been abducted?" Alyssa asked.

Macy shrugged. "We didn't really get to talk like that. It was forbidden to talk about life outside the community. Everyone was even given new names."

Alyssa's eyes widened. "What was your name?"

"We weren't there long enough, so everyone knew me as Heather."

"Heather?" Alex asked. "Oh, right. That d-bag's daughter."

Macy still hadn't taken her eyes off the screen.

"Are you looking for Luke?" Alex asked.

"Yeah. I haven't seen him. I don't know if that's good or bad."

"I'm sure he's safe," Alex said.

"Wait," Macy exclaimed. "There he is. That's him and his mom talking to some cops by that car right there." Macy jumped up and pointed. "That's Luke." Tears shone in her eyes.

"The police will make sure he's taken care of," said her mom, wrapping an arm around Macy. She kissed her forehead.

Macy shook. "I need to talk with him. We have to find him."

"We will."

Macy stared at the TV screen which was no longer on Luke or his mom. "You think we'll be able to find them?"

"The policemen who were with us when we found you, they'll help us however they can."

"I hope so," Macy said. She shook, staring at the television.

Returned

MACY FELT SOMETHING brush against her cheek, and she rolled over covering her face with the blankets. Something pushed on her leg. She pulled it close and tucked it under her arms.

"Time to wake up, Heather."

Macy's eyes popped open. What was Chester's voice doing at home? Wasn't she home? Had it all been a too-realistic dream?

"Heather, don't ignore me."

Her heart pounded in her ears.

"Don't evade me, or there's going to be trouble. You know what that means, don't you?"

Macy sat up, ready to claw his face. "Get out of my room."

"You're going to pay for everything you've done. How dare you run away from me? Try to get me into trouble? They're looking for your mom and questioning me. We have to leave before they arrest me."

"I'll scream, Chester. My family's just down the hall. They'll come, and then you will go back to jail."

Chester shook his head slowly. "That's where you're wrong, dear Heather. We don't have to worry about them anymore. Remember what I told you would happen if you ever ran away?"

The blood drained from Macy's face. "You didn't."

He held up a bloody butcher knife. "Now we don't have to worry about them any more. None of them. Come on, your true family awaits."

Tears streamed down her face. "You're lying."

Chester held the knife close and smelled it. "There's nothing like the smell of fresh blood. You want to know what your family's blood smells like?"

Macy screamed.

"I wouldn't do that if I were you."

She screamed even louder.

"Heather…."

"If they can't hear you, then the neighbors will. There are cops across the street."

"I took care of them, too. We have nothing standing in our way now. It's time to go home and be a family forever. I've even convinced Jonah and the prophets to forgive everything. Of course, you'll have to be under strict watch, but we can go back, and everything will be the same as it was. As it's meant to be."

"No. I won't go with you. You'll have to kill me too."

"That would break my heart, Heather."

Macy thought about telling him the real Heather was out of the hospital, but she wouldn't be able to live with herself if Heather had to go back to him.

"You won't take me again."

He grabbed her arm, pulling her out of bed. "You're wrong again."

"I'll scream louder." Macy dug her nails into his skin. "Let go of me."

"Your yelling didn't help you a minute ago, did it?" He yanked her arm.

Macy pushed her nails in farther. His blood escaped, dripping onto her fingers. "You like blood so much, there you go."

He held the knife to her throat. "I'll kill you slowly and painfully like I did them. You should have heard your dad and brother. They both cried like sissies."

"Liar." Macy screamed again, taking all the energy she had.

"Macy." That was her mom's voice.

She looked around for her mom. "Mom, where are you?"

"You're hearing things," Chester said. "I killed her, too. Come with me."

"Macy, wake up." That was her brother.

"Alex!" she screamed. "Stay away from him, you guys!"

Someone shook her from behind. "Wake up, Macy! Wake up."

"I can't see you." Macy shook as Chester pressed the knife into her flesh. "Get away," she begged.

"You need to wake up, Macy," said her dad.

"Where are you guys? Are you ghosts?" Macy looked around.

"Of course they're ghosts," Chester said. "They're angry I won. We're going back to the community, and you'll never leave it again. You won't embarrass me, and you'll always do as I say."

Macy shook her head. "Never. Not again. You'll have to kill me first."

"You keep saying that like I would actually do it. You'd like that, wouldn't you? Then you could be with those people you keep calling family. Don't you get it? I'm your family. You, me, Rebekah, and the baby."

"Just kill me. Please."

"Macy, open your eyes."

"Where are you, Mom?" Macy asked, looking around.

Chester pressed the tip of the knife harder against her neck. Then he turned her chin toward him. "You need to forget about them. Like you said, they're ghosts. You can't come back here again. There's no one to come to. We need to get home. Some of the puritans are getting our house ready as we speak."

"Macy, you have to wake up," cried Alex.

"Alex, are you real?"

"Stop talking to ghosts, you stupid girl." Chester squeezed her cheeks, staring at her through those big, ugly glasses that Macy hated so much. "If you don't stop this nonsense, you're going to make me mad. I'll lose my temper. You don't want that, do you? We can stop by Grandma and Grandpa's farm. How does that sound?"

Macy screamed, and then she hit and kicked him. She didn't even care if he pushed the knife in and killed her. She wasn't going to go anywhere with him, much less back to the community.

Something cold and wet covered her face. She looked at Chester, but his hands were on her and the knife.

Even though her eyes were open, she opened them again. Macy

blinked and sat up in her bed. How had she gotten back in there? She looked around, gasping for air. Where was Chester?

Her mom, dad, and brother stood around the bed staring at her, looking as scared as she felt.

"I told you the cold washcloth would work," Alex said.

"Where did he go? Did he kill me? Am I a ghost now too?" Macy looked around. "We have to get away from him. He—"

Her dad wrapped his arms around her, holding her tight. "Shh, baby. You're safe. It was only a dream."

Macy shook her head. "No, it was real. He was here. Chester had a bloody knife. He said he killed you all, and I had to go back with him. It was—"

"It wasn't real, honey," her dad said. "You're home, and we're all here. No one's going to take you away from us again."

Macy struggled to catch her breath.

"Do you want to tell us about the dream?" her mom asked. "Anytime you want to talk about anything—anything at all—we're all here for you. Unlike before, we'll listen. We'll hear you out without interrupting."

Alex grabbed her hand. "You're not going anywhere, and neither are we. In fact, you're stuck with us. You couldn't get rid of us if you wanted."

"I hope so." Macy went limp in her dad's arms. She gasped for air until she was breathing normally. Then she sat up and looked at all of them. "Why don't you guys go back to bed? I don't want to keep you up."

Her mom shook her head. "We're not going anywhere. Sleep means nothing now that you're back. We're here for you anytime you need us."

Tears filled Macy's eyes. "I'm so sorry I ever snuck out. I'm so sorry."

"We're sorry we wouldn't listen to you," her dad said.

Alex squeezed her hand. "And I'm sorry I teased you and didn't beat up all those kids who bullied you. That's what I should have done. I was a horrible brother, but now things are different."

Macy shook her head. "You weren't a bad brother. I know you were just trying to cheer me up."

He frowned. "Well, I was stupid."

Her mom looked into her eyes. "Do you want to talk about your nightmare?"

"No. I just want to forget about everything I went through. I'm home now. I guess I just have to get used to that."

"Do you want to go back to sleep?" her dad asked.

Macy thought about it. Her dreams were the one place where Chester could still hunt her down. "No. I think I'll check my emails or something. I probably have a ton."

"I have a better idea," her mom said. "Why don't we have another family movie night? You and Alex pick something to watch while Dad and I get snacks? How does popcorn, ice cream, candy, and pop sound?"

"Like a dream come true," Macy said.

Her dad stood up and helped her out of bed. "A middle of the night movie it is. Let's get the snacks, Lyss." He took her hand and they looked into each other's eyes.

Warmness filled Macy as she watched them. She looked over at Alex and he smiled.

"You two better hurry," said their mom, "because if you don't have a movie picked out by the time we get there, we'll pick out something."

"And you probably won't like it," her dad teased.

Alex and Macy exchanged a look.

"Don't you dare," Alex said. He grabbed Macy's arm and they ran to the bonus room together.

Macy walked over to the shelf and saw several DVD's that still had the shrink wrap. She grabbed a comedy that she had wanted to see before she was kidnapped. It felt like she had picked that out years earlier. "You guys never watched any of these?"

"Are you kidding?" Alex asked.

Macy's shoulders drooped. "I'm so sorry. I never should have—"

"Let's make an agreement. No more saying sorry for anything that happened before. I think we all have lots to be sorry for, but we should just move on instead."

"Yeah. You're right. We should—"

"Snacks are here," said their mom. Both of their parents came into the room with their arms full.

Macy and Alex exchanged an excited look. Their parents never let them eat all that junk food.

Her dad handed Macy a small bowl of popcorn. "This one has no butter."

"I don't care about being vegan anymore." She gave the bowl of butterless popcorn to Alex and grabbed the big tub from her dad.

"You think you're going to eat all that?" Alex teased.

"I might think about sharing. Maybe." Macy smiled.

Alyssa put everything in her arms on the coffee table. "What movie are we watching?"

Macy picked up the comedy. "I hope this is okay."

"It's perfect."

Alex took it from Macy and ripped the plastic off and threw it on the floor. Macy looked over at her mom, waiting for her to tell Alex to throw it away. Her mom shrugged and then pulled Macy into a hug. "I can't tell you how good it is to have you back."

"And I can't tell you how happy I am to be back. I can't believe how much has changed. You and Dad look happy."

"We've had some stuff to work through, and it did get rough for a while, but in the end we pulled together for you."

Macy hugged her back.

"Where's the DVD remote?" Alex asked.

"Use the universal," Macy said.

"The batteries died months ago. We've just been using the main remote since we've only watched the news."

Alex found the remote and turned the TV on. Chester's face showed up on the screen.

Macy choked on popcorn. Her mom whacked her back until it came free.

"Turn that off," her dad told Alex.

"No. Listen," Alex said.

The picture of Chester shrunk, and the newscaster came into view in front of a prison. "To recap: Chester Woodran is now under investigation for the murder of his wife. After a search of his home, journals were found detailing the location of his missing wife and how he allegedly killed her. The diaries also further proved his intent to kidnap Macy Mercer. Authorities are at the scene of the alleged burial spot now. We haven't been given the location yet."

Macy's heart pounded in her chest as she stood staring at the screen. "I thought he was going to get away with that," she whispered.

"In those journals," continued the newscaster, "Was also evidence of the murder of a teen who had been part of this commune. Her body was said to have been left in Clearview, and was somehow connected to a fire in a building used by dentists and orthodontists. Authorities are looking into this also. New updates will be available as soon we learn more."

"It's over. It's really over," Alex said.

Macy's parents both put their arms around her.

"It really is," her mom said. "Now we can all focus on healing."

"And we can start with this movie," Alex said, switching over to the DVD player.

They sat down together on the couch, munching on sugary, buttery goodness as Macy's heart returned to normal. She looked around as the movie started. She was pretty sure she had never been happier in all her life.

Time

Zoey LAUGHED, WATCHING Alex and Macy chase each other with squirt guns. She wanted to join them, but she could barely walk—it was more of a waddle—so there was no way she could join them. Probably next year.

"Go, Macy!" she called.

"Hey," Alex said, giving her a mock upset look. It was obvious he was going easy on his sister.

Macy turned around and soaked him.

Alex looked back to Zoey. "Thanks for the distraction. Did you two have that planned?"

"You know it." Zoey picked up her glass of ice water and took a drink. Was it getting even hotter? She leaned back into the lawn chair and fanned herself. Her stomach tightened. The baby must be stretching out. There was no room in there, and her skin couldn't stretch any more.

Alyssa sat next to her. "How are you doing, Zoey?"

"It's too hot."

"I'm not even pregnant and I agree. Can I get you anything?"

"A new body?"

Alyssa patted Zoey's knee. "Soon enough. Think you'll make your due date?"

"The doctor says she can come anytime two weeks before or after the date and it's still on time."

"You're only a week away."

"I know." Zoey repositioned herself. Her legs were going numb. "Will my feet go back to normal?"

"Sure they will. My feet swelled too, but I always went back to wearing my old shoes."

"Man, I hope so. I can't believe I had to buy flip flops two sizes too big—and they fit." Zoey frowned, ignoring her stomach tightening again. The baby was sure being active. "Is it true first babies are usually late?"

"Each one is different. A first can be early and the second can be late. No matter what, they like to keep us on our toes."

Zoey nodded.

"Let me get you some more water. Or do you want to come inside? It's cooler in there."

Her entire body ached and nothing sounded better than a nap, but Zoey didn't want to move. She handed Alyssa her glass and closed her eyes. She listened to Macy and Alex shrieking at each other. It was good to have Macy back and have things returning to normal. It had taken a while for Macy to become herself again. At first, every time she heard a noise she would jump. Now, not so much.

Zoey's stomach tightened again. This time she held her breath. Maybe it wasn't the baby moving around. It was more of a squeezing sensation—like her body was getting ready to push. A contraction? It couldn't be. She'd been feeling the tightening for months, although not as intense as it was right then.

It stopped and she relaxed. She opened her eyes and saw Macy and Alex helping Chad put meat and veggie burgers on the grill. Alex looked over at her and smiled. Zoey waved back. Alex turned back to his dad and spread sauce over the grill contents. Her eyes grew heavy, and just as she was about to give into them, Alyssa handed her a full glass of ice water.

"Thanks." She drank most of it and set it on a tray next to her.

Alyssa went over to the grill and Zoey looked up into the sky and watched a few small clouds. There was a painful kick in her ribs—that was the baby. She grimaced, waiting for more, but it was the just the one. Then her stomach tightened so painfully that she sat up. She couldn't even get a sound out. Beads of sweat formed along her face.

When the pain finally stopped, she leaned back against the chair, catching her breath. Should she tell someone? The Mercers all looked so happy to be together. They were hungry and getting ready to eat. Zoey could let them enjoy their meal and then ask Alyssa if what she was feeling was contractions. Her water hadn't broke, so she had to be fine.

Alex came over. "Do you want ketchup on your…are you okay?"

Zoey nodded. "Fine."

He sat on the chair next to her. "Are you sure? You're sweating."

"It's hot and I've got two people's body heat."

"I know, but you look…not right."

"Just eat."

"Aren't you hungry?"

"There's hardly any room in my stomach." She closed her eyes.

She felt Alex's lips on her forehead. "If you need anything, let me know."

"All right." Zoey felt something similar to really bad cramps and then her stomach tightened again. Once that stopped, she felt nauseated along with severe lower back pain. She sat up in time to throw up on the lawn and not get anything on the chair.

Everyone ran over, asking if she was okay. Zoey stood up. "My back hurts so bad." A new wave of nausea swept over her, but she didn't throw up. A new wave hit and her stomach heaved. "I'm going to be sick again. Oh—" She turned away and threw up on her other pile.

Someone put their arms around her and guided her toward the house. Zoey stopped walking when her legs felt wet. She looked down saw the puddle around her feet on the deck. "I'm so sorry."

"Nothing to be sorry about," Alyssa said. She turned to Macy. "Call her parents."

Macy ran inside.

Alyssa turned to Alex. "Go inside and get some towels and clean clothes for Zoey."

He looked pale, but ran in also.

"Sorry to ruin your lunch," Zoey said.

Alyssa shook her head. "You have nothing to be sorry about. We'll get you cleaned up and then head to the hospital. Do you have a hospital bag packed?"

"Mom's got something in her car."

"Okay. One less thing to worry about. We'll just get you there. Do you feel like you have to throw up again?"

Zoey shook her head. Her stomach tightened again, and she grasped it.

"Where's Alex?" Alyssa asked.

Macy burst out the door. "Valerie says she'll meet us there unless we can't take her. She's leaving work now."

"We'll take her," Alyssa said. "It wouldn't make sense for her to come here. Get your brother. We need towels."

Macy gave Zoey a sympathetic look and ran back inside.

Zoey felt another gush of liquid. "How many times can water break?"

"Only once, but it doesn't always rush out at the same time. We'll have you sit on some towels in the car just in case."

"Okay." Zoey's head was spinning. The pain was horrendous—all of it—but it was actually nice to have the distraction. She was scared of giving birth.

Alex and Macy ran outside, both carrying towels. They wiped Zoey's legs and soon she was inside changing her clothes. After that everything was a blur. She was vaguely aware of being in the car on top of a pile of towels.

When they got to the hospital, her parents were already there, both looking nervous. They ran over as soon as they saw her, asking her more questions than she could focus on.

A nurse came out and led them to her room. She asked even more questions than Zoey's parents. She answered them the best she could. Being in the hospital made everything feel even more real. Soon the baby would be out, and hopefully the pain would stop.

Zoey went into the bathroom and put on a gown while the nurse spoke with her parents. Where were Alex and Macy?

She went back into the room and was led to the bed, where she was hooked up to all kinds of things. The nurse said she would get the doctor.

Her parents spoke over each other again.

"Can you guys get Macy and Alex? I want them here." Zoey looked around the room. "It's big enough for everyone."

Her mom took Zoey's hand. "Are you sure you want to give the baby up for us to raise? You can still change your mind, you know."

Zoey shook her head. "It's better for everyone. We'll still live in the same house, and I can keep going to school and everything. It's not like she's going anywhere. Besides, I always wanted a sister." She tried to smile. "I just never thought it would be like this."

A doctor came in. "Dr. Johnson is on her way, but in the meantime, I'm going to check you out, Zoey. Is that okay?"

Zoey nodded, and then her stomach tightened again. This time it was so painful, she couldn't help but yell out. Once it passed, the doctor asked her the same questions the nurse had already asked and logged into a tablet. Zoey answered them again and then he examined her.

"It looks like you're progressing fast." He rattled off something about centimeters and other stuff that meant nothing to Zoey.

She was waiting for the next wave of pain to hit. "Can I get some medicine?"

When he left, Zoey looked around and asked her dad, "Where's Mom?"

"She went to get Macy and Alex. Do you want me to leave? I understand if you do."

Zoey shrugged. "You're fine, Dad."

His face softened. She had never called him that before, and seeing the look on his face, she was glad she chose that moment.

He wrapped his arms around her. "Even though I haven't been around, I want you to know—"

Another round of pain struck and Zoey clutched her stomach, crying out in pain again. She was vaguely aware of him taking her hand. When the agony finally receded, Zoey opened her eyes.

Alex was next to her. He looked upset. "I'm so sorry, Zoey. I never meant to do this to you."

Family

MACY'S HEART POUNDED as she walked down the hospital hall with her parents and Zoey's parents. Even though she'd had some time to adjust to the thought of becoming an aunt, her heart continued to beat harder. That wasn't even the crazy part. Her baby brother was a dad now, even though he wasn't going to raise the baby.

The nurse opened a door on the left. "They're ready to see you. Go on inside."

Macy held her breath as she walked in. She let everyone else go in ahead of her. She was nervous, and she couldn't figure out why. Everyone in the room were the people she knew and loved most.

But it was different now. The baby changed everything. Her brother and best friend were parents. Her mom and dad were now grandparents. She looked at them, trying to grasp that. They definitely didn't look old enough.

The nurse moved aside a curtain. Macy saw Zoey in the bed with Alex next to her. She looked around her parents, wanting to see the baby. Everyone crowded around the bed, gasping about the baby.

Macy went around to the other side of the bed. Zoey held a tiny bundle with a little face poking out from the blanket. The eyes were closed, but she could tell the baby was beautiful.

She walked to Alex's side and gave him a hug. "How do you feel?"

"Too much. I'm proud and scared and overwhelmed. I'm glad that Zoey's parents are going to take care of her, because I would just mess her up."

Macy put her arm around him. "And you'll get to see her anytime you want."

He looked down at the baby. "I'm glad. Even though I know I'm too young to take care of her, I don't want her going far. I feel like I need to protect her."

Macy kissed his cheek, and then turned to Zoey. "How are you?"

"I just want to sleep for the next week, but I'm so sore. How are you, Auntie?"

"Better than you guys." Macy smiled.

Zoey handed her the bundle, and Macy sat down, afraid she'd do something to hurt the baby. "What's her name?"

"We're going to let Mom and Dad name her. They wanted to let me, but I think they should."

"Maybe you could pick the middle name."

"That's a great idea," Zoey's dad said. "What do you think, Zoey?"

"Alex and I could."

Macy got up and handed the baby to her mom and then stood near the bed, talking with Zoey and Alex. Zoey fell asleep mid-sentence and then Macy sat in a chair, tugging Alex to sit next to her.

They were quiet for a moment, listening to the adults talk. Zoey's parents assured hers they could all visit the baby anytime, and that they would honor them as the baby's grandparents. Macy's mom thanked them and said they would respect them as the parents.

Macy looked back over at Alex. He looked like he was going to fall asleep, too.

"Are you okay?" she asked him.

"I want to sleep for the next day too. Then you know what?"

"What?"

"I'm never having sex again."

Macy laughed. "Ever again?"

"Well, maybe not never. But it's going to be a long, long time."

"I'm sure Zoey feels the same way." Macy patted his hand.

"She was in so much pain, Macy."

Macy looked over at Zoey. "She's doing well now."

Alex ran his hands through his hair. "You didn't see her."

"She had a baby, Alex. It's not supposed to be easy."

"I don't ever want to do that to her again. Like I said, I'm never—"

"Don't make any rash decisions now. Besides, take another look at the baby. She's totally amazing."

"Yeah, I know. I can't explain how I felt when I first saw her."

"You guys made a whole new person, Alex. She wasn't here this morning and now she is. Don't feel too bad. Get some rest." Macy stood up, kissed the top of his head and went over to her dad who was holding the baby. "Can you believe how cute she is?"

Her dad smiled at her. "She looks a lot like you and Alex did as babies."

Macy looked at the little, sleeping face thinking back to her and Alex's baby pictures. She hadn't looked at them since before she was kidnapped, and that made it hard to remember. "I'll have to take your word on it, Dad. I was pretty young then."

She sat, listening to everyone talk for a while and grew drowsy.

Macy looked at Alex. "I'm going to get something with caffeine from a machine. Want to come with me?"

He shook his head. "I'm going to stay here with Zoey and the baby."

Macy kissed the top of his head, and then went out into the hall. She looked around trying to remember where she had seen the vending machines. Macy thought it had been to the left, so she went that way. Just as she was about to turn a corner, she heard a voice she would know anywhere. Rebekah.

She peeked around the corner, and sure enough Rebekah stood in the hall talking to some nurses. Her stomach was bigger than Zoey's had been, and she was talking with a nurse. An older man and woman were also with them.

"Are the babies okay?" asked the man. "We didn't know there were two. We couldn't even get her to come to a doctor until now."

The nurse looked at him. "They'll be fine. We just need to get her ready for the birth. It appears that we're going to need to break her water." The nurse looked at some papers. "I have here that she's not to be left alone because of psychological issues. What's the plan after being discharged from the hospital?"

"We're her parents, and she's staying at home with us. Between the two of us and her brother, she's never left alone. We're not letting her out of our sight until the psychologist gives us the okay."

The nurse scribbled notes on the paper. "I see something on her about an arrest warrant. We don't generally release—"

"As long as she stays under the care of her psychologist, she's able to avoid that. If she fully rehabilitates, they're going to remove that from her record," said Rebekah's dad. "The babies will be safe."

"Okay." The nurse scribbled more notes, and then they walked down the hall in the opposite direction as Macy.

She leaned against the wall, breathing heavily. As shocked as she was about having seen Rebekah, she was glad that she was at least getting counseling. Even though their relationship had ended strained, Macy would always be glad for the friendship Rebekah had shown her when Macy first moved into the community.

Surprise

MACY WAVED TO the receptionist at her counselor's office as she put her hand on the doorknob. "Bye, Shelley. See you next week."

"Have a good one, kiddo."

The sun was bright, so Macy dug into her purse and put on her sunglasses. "Good thing I parked in the shade," she muttered. She pulled out her cell phone and saw she had no missed calls or texts. "Looks like I have the afternoon to myself. The mall sounds like fun."

As Macy neared her car, she noticed someone leaning against her car. She groaned. The last thing she wanted was to deal with another reporter. She prepared herself to give a harsh answer—the only kind that would get rid of them—but she stopped cold when he turned around and looked at her.

His eyes shone brightly in the warm sun and the skin around his eyes crinkled as his lips formed a smile. "Hi, Macy."

"Luke, what are you doing here?" She ran into his arms, squeezing him tight.

He hugged her back. "I have the afternoon off. Thought I'd come by and see my favorite girlfriend."

"You mean your only girlfriend." Macy looked into his eyes, her lips forming a grin. "I'm so glad you did. Where's your car? I didn't see it anywhere, and it's not easy to miss."

Luke laughed. "No, she's not, is she? Mom took *The Beast* in for a tune up and dropped me off here. Hope you can give me a ride."

"I'll have to think about that." Macy paused, pretending to consider it.

"Or I can walk home. No big deal. See ya around." He turned around and took a couple steps.

"Get back here." She grabbed the back of his shirt.

"Yes, Ma'am." Luke spun around and placed his lips on top of hers. He smelled of aftershave. "Mind if we make a quick stop first? I have to drop something off for my mom."

"Sure." Macy unlocked the doors of her car with the remote and then climbed in. "Where to?"

"Near the corner of Third and Russell."

She started the car. "What's over there?"

Luke smiled, looking as gorgeous as possible. "Nothing exciting until you get there."

Macy's breath caught. She never got tired of looking at him. She pulled out of the parking spot. "Did you guys finally get the last of the boxes unpacked?"

"Yeah. It's great to be in our own place now. Renting that small room until we got on our feet was stressful."

"When do I get to come over and cook you guys a meal?"

"As soon as you want. I know my mom won't mind."

"Now that she's working full time finally, I'm sure she'd love the help."

"And I wouldn't mind the company." He elbowed her in the arm.

Macy nudged Luke back. "Watch out. I'll make you cook."

Luke laughed. "Don't make threats you don't intend to keep."

They continued to tease each other as Macy navigated the heavy afternoon traffic. It was summer, but this part of town always seemed congested.

"Okay," said Macy. "We're on Russell Street, and Third is coming up. Where do I turn?"

"There's supposed to be a turn right after we pass Third. Go right."

When she pulled into the parking lot, she looked at the nondescript little building. "What is this place?"

"Oh, some kind of hall or something. Want to come in with me?" He batted his eyelashes.

Her heart skipped a beat. Even though he was teasing, she couldn't help adoring him. "Anything for a little extra time with you."

They got out and Luke took her hand and they walked in the front door. It was dim inside and looked set up for a party.

"What's going on?" Macy asked.

Luke turned the light on and nearly fifty people jumped out and yelled, "Surprise!"

Macy stared at them for a moment and then looked at Luke. "What's going on?" Macy repeated.

Zoey and Alex ran up to her, wrapping her in a hug.

"We love you, Macy," Zoey said.

"Thanks, but what's this for? It's not my birthday."

"It's the anniversary of your return home," Alex said. "I thought we should celebrate. Zoey's the one who thought we should surprise you."

"It worked." Macy clutched her heart.

Other guests swarmed Macy, hugging her and expressing their gratitude for her safe return a year earlier. Macy teared up as people shared about how worried they had been for her, spending hours searching or handing out fliers. Some of the people she barely knew.

Luke's mom, Caroline, wrapped her arms around Macy. "I can't thank you enough for everything you and your family has done for us. We really wouldn't have been able to get back on our feet without you guys."

"And I never would have gotten away from Chester without Luke."

Caroline shook her head. "I don't know how I ever fell for everything Jonah and the community taught."

Luke hugged his mom. "You were trying to get us off the streets, and they offered you that and more."

Tears shone in her eyes. "Thanks, Luke. If I could go back in time, I would do so much differently."

Other people came up to Macy, wanting to talk. Caroline squeezed her hand. "We'll talk later."

When Macy finally had some space, she sat down at a table to breathe. Zoey brought over a plate full of cake and other sweets. Alex and Luke followed, carrying what looked like cups of punch.

"Did we surprise you?" Zoey asked, smiling.

"My heart hasn't returned to its normal speed yet."

Zoey grinned. "Good. That's what we were going for."

Valerie came to the table and handed little Ariana to Zoey, and then gave Macy a huge hug. "You've always been like a second daughter to me. I was so relieved when you were found safe and sound." She turned to Zoey. "Can you hold Ari for a few minutes?"

"Of course." Zoey snuggled Ariana.

A girl walked to the table. It took Macy a minute to realize who she was.

"Heather! What are you doing here?" Macy jumped out of the chair and gave her a hug. "How are you? I heard your grandparents adopted you."

Luke grabbed a chair from another table and motioned for Heather to sit.

"They did," Heather said. "It's so much nicer living with them."

"I bet," Macy said. "Are you guys staying at the farm?"

"You didn't hear?" asked Heather.

Macy shook her head.

"After they found out what Dad used the barn for, they were so disgusted that Grandpa sold the animals and burned it down. They thought they could live in the house, but they couldn't. Grandma nearly had a nervous breakdown every time she looked where the barn used to be. So they sold their home of forty-five years and moved into our old house."

Macy thought about that for a minute. A sense of relief swept through her as she thought about the barn burning up. "And you get to school with your friends?"

Heather nodded. "It's weird though, knowing that Dad was there with you and his new wife."

Macy gave her a hug. "I'm so sorry for everything he's put you through."

"And I you. You didn't do anything—you're not even related to him. You really didn't deserve any of it."

"You don't either. At least I got to come home to my entire family, and I brought a boyfriend with me."

"And you got a niece!" Zoey said, holding Ariana up. "Sorry. Couldn't help overhearing. So, how are you fitting back into society after being in that loony bin?"

"Zoey," Macy hissed.

Heather laughed. "No, it's fine. I call it the nut house. Luckily my grandparents have been so helpful. I've been talking to one of their church counselors, and I'm in martial arts. That's helping me release a lot of energy and regain some self-esteem. Plus my friends come over for sleepovers, like, all the time. I'm less jumpy now. Not quite normal, but I think I'm getting there."

"I know how you feel," Macy said. "If I didn't have these guys," she looked at Alex, Zoey, and Luke, "I don't know what I'd do. Home-schooling helps, even though a lot of the girls who bullied me have apologized. I really don't want to go back."

Luke wrapped an arm around her. "She's making a lot of progress. When we first met up after she came home, she didn't want to go anywhere alone. Now she's fine with it." He kissed the top of her head.

"Yeah," Zoey agreed. "She was having these anxiety attacks for a while, and it totally didn't help that whenever she went somewhere some idiot reporter would jump out from nowhere and ask her a million questions."

Heather shook her head. "I can't even imagine. Yeah, I was having panic attacks too. They suck."

Macy and Heather exchanged a knowing look.

"We really should keep in touch," Macy said. "Maybe even have some sleepovers. I'd love to spend some more time with George and Ingrid, too. You'd have fun with my friends."

"Oh, definitely," Zoey said. "I know how to throw a party."

Macy shook her head, smiling. She turned back to Heather. "Can I get you anything? Some punch or cake?"

"You're the guest of honor, you shouldn't—"

"You should be, too. Let me get you something."

"If you insist. Thanks."

Macy got up and headed for the refreshment table. She could hear Zoey and Alex talking with Heather. Before Macy got to the table, she saw George and Ingrid at the far end of the room. She decided to thank them for everything they had done, even though they hadn't realized that Macy wasn't Heather.

Had they not been at the farmhouse when they were, Macy might not have had the strength to keep fighting. It also meant the world to Macy that Ingrid had taught her to cook from scratch.

Before she reached the table, Macy noticed her dad off to the side talking with a pretty, younger dark-haired lady. She looked somewhat familiar. Maybe she was a neighbor or his coworker.

Macy was curious and took the long way to George and Ingrid, passing by her dad. Neither he nor the lady appeared to notice her.

The lady looked upset. "I just wanted to let you know, Chad."

"Are you sure you need to? Why not make sure—?"

"No. I'm leaving right after the party. I can't tell anyone where I'm going. If what I discovered is true, it's not safe for me at home anymore."

"Why don't you take the evidence to the authorities?"

"I can't. Dean's a dangerous man. I need to start over. I just wanted you to know before I disappeared."

Macy's dad saw her standing there. He waved her away. Obviously he didn't want her hearing the conversation. Macy shrugged and walked away.

She went to George and Ingrid and gave them hugs. "Thank you so much for being kind to me. I know you didn't know who I was…but it meant everything to me. I've even taught my mom how to cook a couple things from scratch."

Ingrid's face scrunched up like she was going to cry. "I wish I would have known. There's no way we would have let you stay there if we knew you were ripped from your family. Looking back, I felt that something was off, but Chester had convinced us that you were acting strange because your mom took off. I feel like such a fool."

Macy gave her another hug. "Don't. He had a lot of people tricked. How's Heather doing, really?"

"Good," said George. "Like you, she has a lot to recover from, but she's handling it like a champ."

Macy smiled. "I'm glad she has you guys."

"Oh," said Ingrid, pulling out her large handbag, "before I forget. Is this yours?" She pulled out Macy's teddy bear. The one that had gotten her through some rough nights—when Chester wasn't hiding it from her. It must have somehow made its way from the community to the farmhouse.

Macy's eyes lit up. "My bear."

Ingrid handed it to her. "It was in Chester's things, but Heather had never seen it before. I thought it might be yours."

Macy hugged the bear and then talked with them for a few more minutes before she headed back to the table. Her parents joined them, and Macy looked around at everyone there. She was overwhelmed with how good things were. Everything was going to be okay. It really was.

Letter

Dear Chester,

I didn't think I would have the courage to write or send this letter, but here I am. It's been a year since we last saw each other, and you still haunt my dreams, but even that is lessening.

There were so many things I wanted to say (and scream) while I was with you. Mostly things that you already knew, but wouldn't let me say. I'm not Heather, never have been, and never will be. You know that as well as I do. The real Heather and I have become friends, actually. You lost her, and now you pretty much lost everything.

With more than two life sentences, you'll have a really long time to think about all the things you did to hurt so many people.

The only good that really came from you kidnapping and torturing me is that I got to meet Heather and Luke. Your daughter is doing well, but that's all I'm going to say. If you want to hear more about her, you'll have to hope she decides to ever talk to you again. It doesn't sound promising right now.

My counselor wanted me to write this letter. She didn't say I had to mail it, but I want to. You don't have to read it, I honestly don't care. I'm just glad for the chance to say what I need to. For a long time I hated you. Really hated you. Especially when you kidnapped me. But then I learned that it only ate away at me. My hate did nothing to you. I don't want to hate, so I'm letting it go.

But first, I have some questions for you. What makes you think you have the right to take someone from their family? Why do you think you're so special that you get to decide whether someone lives or dies? There's nothing special about you. You're a sick, sick man. I don't get it. Your parents are wonderful people. You had a beautiful family. Yet you gave it all up to control everyone.

I don't understand what could drive you to do all the things you did when you had everything in the world. But you know what? I'm done asking myself why. It would drive me crazy if I tried to make sense of it. There is no logic when it comes to you.

Actually, if you want to know the truth (and I doubt you do, because you hate the truth) I feel sorry for you. I've spent more time thinking about you than I care to admit. Go ahead and smirk. Think you've won. You haven't. I pity you, you poor excuse for a man.

Anyone who acts like you do obviously thinks he has no value. People who know they're worth something treat others well. You clearly know what a jerk you are, but instead of making yourself better you tried to force people to love you. You can't force love, especially when you're as horrible as you are. At one point, people loved you. Karla chose to marry you. Heather used to love you.

With this letter, I am letting you go. Letting go of the hold you have on me. Letting go of every memory of you. I'm done. It's over. You had a hold on me for a while, but no longer.

So goodbye, Chester.
Macy Mercer

Did you enjoy this trilogy? *There will be more to come from some of the side characters.*

There will be a story coming in 2015 following Lydia as she runs from Dean's secret. Rusty will have a story of his own also. Readers have asked for Luke to have a story, too.

Sign up for new release updates to be notified when the books are published.

http://stacyclaflin.com/newsletter/

If you enjoyed the Gone trilogy, you may enjoy my Transformed series. You can read the first book for *free* at most online retailers.

About:

What if your whole life was a lie?

Alexis Ferguson thinks she has everything figured out, but has no idea how wrong she is. Set up on a blind date, she meets a gorgeous stranger and feels that she's known him her entire life, but she has never seen him before.

He awakens in her long-forgotten dark memories, and now she must face the one who ordered her death years ago. Will she learn to use her strange new powers in time to save herself? Will she let him help her? Should she trust him?

Other books by Stacy Claflin

Gone series

Gone

Held

Over

The Transformed series

Now Available

Deception (#1)

Betrayal (#2)

Forgotten (#3)

Silent Bite (#3.5)

Ascension (#4)

Duplicity (#5)

Fallen

Taken (Novella)

Hidden Intentions (novel)

A Long Time Coming (Short Story)

The Fielding (Short Story)

The Orders (Short Story)

Coming Soon:

Sacrifice #6

Visit StacyClaflin.com for details.

Sign up for new release updates (stacyclaflin.com/newsletter).

Want to hang out and talk about books? Join My Book Hangout (facebook.com/groups/stacyclaflinbooks) and participate in the discussions. There are also exclusive giveaways, sneak peeks and more. Sometimes the members offer opinions on book covers too. You never know what you'll find.

Author's Note

I greatly appreciate you reading this book! I hope you enjoyed it.

I've spent many hours writing, re-writing, and editing this work. I even put together a team who helped with the editing process. As it is impossible to find every single error, if you find any, please contact me through my website and let me know so that I can fix them for future editions.

If you liked this book, please tell your friends and consider leaving a review. Reviews are important to help other readers find books and are much appreciated.

Thank you for your support!

CPSIA information can be obtained
at www.ICGtesting.com
Printed in the USA
LVOW12s1350111216

516785LV00004B/686/P